D0122929

VICTORY

FORGE BOOKS EDITED
BY STEPHEN COONTS

COMBAT

VICTORY

VICTORY

EDITED AND INTRODUCED BY

STEPHEN COONTS

3 1336 06158 6922

A TOM DOHERTY ASSOCIATES BOOK  NEW YORK

This is a work of fiction. All the characters and events portrayed in these stories are either fictitious or used fictitiously.

A Forge Book
Published by Tom Doherty Associates, LLC
175 Fifth Avenue
New York, NY 10010

www.tor.com

Forge® is a registered trademark of Tom Doherty Associates, LLC.

Library of Congress Cataloging-in-Publication Data

Victory / edited and introduced by Stephen Coonts.—1st ed.
        p.   cm.
    "A Tom Doherty Associates book."
    Contents: The sea witch / Stephen Coonts—Breakthrough on Bloody Ridge / Harold Coyle—Wolf flight / Jim DeFelice—Blood bond / Harold Robbins—Hangar rat / Dean Ing—Flame at Tarawa / Barrett Tillman—Eyes of the cat / James Cobb—V5 / David Hagberg—The eagle and the cross / R. J. Pineiro—Honor / Ralph Peters.
    ISBN 0-312-87462-6 (regular edition)
    ISBN 0-765-30581-X (limited edition)
    1. World War, 1939–1945—Fiction.   2. War stories, American.   I. Coonts, Stephen.

PS648.W65V53   2003
813'..6080358—dc21

2002045490

First Edition: May 2003

Printed in the United States of America

0   9   8   7   6   5   4   3   2   1

To all the men and women who fought for Liberty during World War II

CONTENTS

INTRODUCTION

I was born in 1946 on the leading edge of the baby boomer generation, one of the sons and daughters of the men and women who fought and survived the greatest war the humans on this planet have yet experienced, World War II.

Early in the twentieth century Winston Churchill noted that the wars of the people were going to be worse than the wars of the kings—which was prophecy. There have been other wars since World War II, horrific wars such as Korea and Vietnam. And yet, terrible as they were, they did not become the defining experience for an entire generation, as did World War II, World War I, and the American Civil War. At the dawn of the twenty-first century our wars are fought by volunteers, professional soldiers, and not very many of them. There are those who say that this is progress. In any event, it insulates the vast bulk of the population from the rigors and emotions and risks that define war.

I don't think that the age of general warfare is over. The biblical admonition to be fruitful and multiply has been blindly obeyed by the world's poorest people. There are now over six billion people on this modest planet, one that must provide the wherewithal to support all the creatures that live upon it, including the humans.

Too many people and not enough land, food, and jobs has always been a prescription for disaster.

Today nations around the world are busy developing weapons of mass destruction, a handy term to describe nuclear, chemical, and biological weapons that kill indiscriminately. In the early months of 2002, India and Pakistan, two of the world's poorest, most populous nations, went to the brink of nuclear war and stared into the abyss before backing away. As I write this in the final month of 2002, United Nations' weapons inspectors are again searching for weapons of mass destruction in Iraq, an outlaw nation led by one of the worst despots on the planet. What will happen next in Iraq is anyone's guess.

If that weren't enough, one of the world's major religions, Islam, has grown a perverted branch that holds that murdering those who don't believe as you do is a holy duty. Worse, some of the clergy of this religion teach their acolytes that suicide while committing mass murder is martyrdom that earns the criminal a ticket to paradise. This isn't a new thing—Islam has gone through these paroxysms before. Mercifully, most of the other religions that demand human sacrifice are no longer practiced on this planet.

And finally, there is the planet itself. These six billion people have arrived on earth during what many climatologists feel is a rare period of unusual warmth. The only thing we can say for certain about climates is that they change. If the world cools or suffers an extended drought, the planet's ability to support its present population will be severely impaired. But we don't have to wait that long for disaster to strike: If a supervolcano (such as Yellowstone) blows, or major earthquakes inundate populated coastal regions, or a cosmological disaster (such as a meteor) strikes, our happy, peaceful, post–World War II age will come to an abrupt end. Man may survive, but not six billion of us.

And man may not survive. Despite our best efforts our species may well go the way of the dinosaur and the woolly mammoth. The tale has yet to be written. In any event, armed conflict will probably be a part of man's experience as long as there are men.

As I write this fifty-seven years after the Japanese surrender aboard USS *Missouri* in Tokyo Bay, World War II is fading from our collective memories. Currently about one thousand veterans of World War II pass on every day. All too soon World War II will be only museum exhibits, history books that are read only in colleges and universities, black-and-white footage of Nazi troops, and thundering *Victory at Sea* movies that run late at night on the cable channels. Some of us also have knickknacks that our parents kept to remind them of those days when they were young and the world was on fire, yet all too soon old medals and fading photographs become merely artifacts of a bygone age.

The sons and daughters of the veterans understand that they are losing something important when their fathers pass on. Many have approached me, asking if I know of anyone who would help them write down their father's memories while he is still able to voice them, capture them for the generations yet unborn. Alas, except for a few underfunded oral history programs, these personal memories usually go unrecorded. Diaries have long been out of fashion, and the elderly veterans and their children are usually not writers. Even those who could write down their memory of their experiences often get so caught up in the business of living through each day that they think no one cares about their past.

Perhaps it has always been so. From the Trojan War to date, personal accounts by warriors are few and far between. Other than the occasional memoir by a famous general (often one out to polish his military reputation), the task of preserving the past is usually left to historians who weren't there . . . and to writers of fiction.

Historians write of decisions of state, of fleets and armies and the strategy of generals and great battles that brought victory or defeat. Fiction writers work on a smaller scale—they write about individuals.

Only in fiction can the essence of the human experience of war be laid bare. Only from fiction can we learn what it might have been like to survive the crucible, or to die in it. Only through fiction can we come to grips with the ultimate human challenge—kill or be killed. Only through fiction can we prepare ourselves for the trial by fire, when our turn comes.

STEPHEN COONTS

THE *SEA WITCH*

STEPHEN COONTS

STEPHEN COONTS is the author of seven *New York Times* best-selling novels, the first of which was the classic flying tale *Flight of the Intruder*, which spent over six months on the *New York Times* bestseller list. He graduated from West Virginia University with a degree in political science, and immediately was commissioned as an Ensign in the Navy, where he began flight training in Pensacola, Florida, training on the A-6 Intruder aircraft. After two combat cruises in Vietnam aboard the aircraft carrier USS *Enterprise* and one tour as assistant catapult and arresting gear officer aboard the USS *Nimitz*, he left active duty in 1977 to pursue a law degree, which he received from the University of Colorado. His novels have been published around the world and have been translated into more than a dozen different languages. He was honored by the U.S. Naval Institute with its Author of the Year award in 1986. His latest novel is *Liberty*. He and his wife, Deborah, reside near Las Vegas, Nevada.

ONE

"I'm looking," the skipper said, flipping through my logbook, "but I can't find any seaplane time." The skipper was Commander Martin Jones. His face was greasy from perspiration and he looked exhausted.

"I've had four or five rides in a PBY," I told him, "but always as a passenger." In fact, a PBY had just brought me here from Guadalcanal. It departed after delivering me, some mail, and a couple of tons of spare parts.

The Old Man gave me The Look.

"You're a dive-bomber pilot. What in hell are you doing in a Black Cat squadron?"

"It's a long story." Boy, was that ever the truth!

"I haven't got time for a long story," Jones said as he tossed the logbook on the wardroom table and reached for my service record. "Gimme the punch line." Aboard this small seaplane tender, the wardroom doubled as the ship's office.

"They said I was crazy."

That comment hung in the air like a wet fart. I leaned against the edge of the table to steady myself.

Hanging on her anchor, the tender was rolling a bit in the swell coming up the river from Namoia Bay, on the southwestern tip of New Guinea where the Owen Stanley Mountains ran into the sea. The only human habitation within two hundred miles was a village, Samarai, across the bay on an island. The sailors on the tender never went over there, nor was there any reason they should. If Namoia Bay wasn't the end of the earth, believe me, you could see it from here.

The commander flipped through my service record, scanning the entries. "Are you crazy?"

"No more than most," I replied. Proclaiming your sanity was a bit like proclaiming your virtue—highly suspect.

"This tender can support three PBYs," Commander Jones said, not looking at me. "We launch them late in the afternoon, and they hunt Jap ships at night, return sometime after dawn. Three days ago one of our birds didn't come back." He looked up, straight into my eyes. "The crew is somewhere out there," he swept his hand from left to right, "dead or alive. We'll look for them, of course, but the South Pacific is a big place, and there is a war on."

"Yes, sir."

"Until we get another plane from Australia, we'll only have two birds to carry the load."

I nodded.

"One of our copilots is sick with malaria, too bad to fly. You will fly in his place unless you've really flipped out or something."

"I'm fine, sir."

"Why did they get rid of you?"

"The Japs shot three SBDs out from under me, killed two of my gunners. The skipper said he couldn't afford me. So here I am."

The Old Man lit a cigarette and blew the smoke out through his nose.

"Tell me about it."

So I told it. We launched off the carrier one morning on a routine search mission and found a Jap destroyer in the slot, running north at flank speed. When the lookouts spotted us the destroyer captain cranked the helm full over, threw that can into as tight a circle as it would turn while every gun let loose at us. There were four of us in SBDs; I was flying as number three. As I rolled into my dive I put out the dive brakes, as usual, and dropped the landing gear.

With the dive brakes out the Dauntless goes down in an eighty-degree dive at about 250 knots. Takes a couple thousand feet to pull out. With the dive brakes and gear out, prop in flat pitch, she goes down at 150, vibrating like a banjo string. Still, you have all day to dope the wind and sweeten your aim, and you can pickle the bomb at a thousand feet, put the damn thing right down the smokestack before you have to pull out. Of course, while you are coming down like the angel of doom the Japs are blazing away with everything they have, and when you pull out of the dive you have no speed, so you are something of a sitting duck. You also run the risk of overcooling the engine, which is liable to stall when you pour the coal to it. Still, when you really want a hit . . .

I got that destroyer—the other three guys in my flight missed. I put my thousand-pounder right between the smokestacks and blew that can clean in half. It was a hell of a fine sight. Only the Japs had holed my engine, and it quit on the pullout, stopped dead. Oil was blowing all over the windshield, and I couldn't see anything dead ahead. Didn't matter—all that was out there was ocean.

My gunner and I rode the plane into the water. He hit his head or something and didn't get out of the plane, which sank before I could get him unstrapped.

I floated in the water, watched the front half of the destroyer quickly sink and the ass end burn. None of the Japs came after me. I rode my little life raft for a couple days before a PBY landed in the open sea and dragged me in through a waist-gun blister. With all the swells I didn't think he could get airborne again, but he did, somehow.

A couple days later the ship sent a half dozen planes to Henderson Field to operate from there. I figured Henderson could not be tougher to land on than a carrier and was reasonably dry land, so I volunteered. About a week later I tangled with some Zeros at fifteen thousand feet during a raid. I got one and others got me. Killed my new gunner, too. I bailed out and landed in the water right off the beach.

Jones was reading a note in my record while I talked. "Your commanding officer said you shot down a Zero on your first pass," Jones commented, "then disobeyed standing orders and turned to reengage. Four Zeros shot your Dauntless to pieces."

"Yes, sir."

"He says you like combat, like it a lot."

I didn't say anything to that.

"He said you love it."

"That's bullshit."

"Bullshit, sir."

"Sir."

"He says he pulled you out of SBDs to save your sorry ass."

"I read it, sir."

"So tell me the rest of it."

I took a deep breath, then began. "Six days ago another Zero shot me down after I dive-bombed a little freighter near Bougainville. I got the Maru all right, but as I pulled out and sucked up the gear a Zero swarmed all over me and shot the hell out of the plane, punched a bunch of holes in the gas tanks. There wasn't much I could do about it at 150 knots. My gunner got him, finally, but about fifty miles from Henderson Field we used the last of our gas. I put it in the water and we floated for a day and a half before a PT boat found us."

"Leaking fuel like that, were you worried about catching fire?" Commander Jones asked, watching me to see how I answered that.

"Yes, sir. We were match-head close."

He dropped his eyes. "Go on," he said.

"Kenny Ross, the skipper, was pissed. Said if I couldn't dive-bomb like everyone else and get hits, he didn't want me.

"I told him everyone else was missing—I was getting the hits, and I'd do whatever it took to keep getting them, which I guess wasn't exactly the answer he wanted to hear. He canned me."

The Black Cat squadron commander stubbed out his cigarette and lit another.

He rubbed his eyes, sucked a bit on the weed, then said, "I don't have anyone else, so you're our new copilot. You'll fly with Lieutenant Modahl. He's probably working on his plane. He wanted to go out this morning and look for our missing crew, but I wouldn't let him go without a copilot." The skipper glanced at his watch. "Go find him and send him in to see me."

"Yes, sir."

"Around here everybody does it my way," he added pointedly, staring into my face. "If I don't like the cut of your jib, bucko, you'll be the permanent night anchor-watch officer aboard this tender until the war is over or you die of old age, whichever happens first. Got that?"

"Aye aye, sir."

"Welcome aboard."

The tender was about the size of a Panamanian banana boat, which it might have been at one time. It certainly wasn't new, and it wasn't a Navy design. It had a big crane amidships for hoisting planes from the water. That day they were using the crane to lower bombs onto a float.

A plane was moored alongside, covered with a swarm of men. They had portable work stands in place around each engine and tarps rigged underneath to keep tools and parts from falling in the water.

Five-hundred-pound bombs were being loaded on racks under the big Catalina's wings. Standing there watching, I was amazed at the size of the bird—darn near as big as the tender, it seemed. The wingspan, I knew, was 104 feet, longer than a B-17.

The plane was painted black; not a glossy, shiny, raven's-feather black, but a dull, flat, light-absorbing black. I had never seen anything uglier. On the nose was a white outline of a witch riding a broomstick, and under the art, the name *Sea Witch*.

The air reeked, a mixture of the aromas of the rotting vegetation and dead fish that were floating amid the roots of the mangrove trees growing almost on the water's edge. The fresh water coming down the river kept the mangroves going, apparently, although the fish had been unable to withstand the avgas, oil, and grease that were regularly spilled in the water.

At least there was a bit of a breeze to keep the bugs at bay. The place must be a hellhole when the wind didn't blow!

None of the sailors working on the Cat wore a shirt, and many had cut off the legs of their dungarees. They were brown as nuts.

One of the men standing on the float winching the bombs up was wearing a swimsuit and tennis shoes—nothing else. I figured he was the officer, and after a minute or so of watching I was sure. He was helping with the job, but he was also directing the others.

"Lieutenant Modahl?"

He turned to look at me.

"I'm your new copilot."

After he got the second bomb on that wing, he clambered up the rope net that was hung over the side of the ship. When he was on deck he shook my hand. I told him my name, where I was from.

He asked a few questions about my experience, and I told him I'd never flown seaplanes—been flying the SBD Dauntless.

Modahl was taller than me by a bunch, over six feet. He must have weighed at least two hundred, and none of it looked like fat. He about broke my hand shaking it. I thought maybe he had played college football. He had black eyes and black hair, filthy hands with ground-in grease and broken fingernails. Only after he shook my hand did it occur to him to wipe the grease off his hands, which he did with a rag that had been lying nearby on the deck. He didn't smile, not once.

I figured if he could fly and fight, it didn't matter whether he smiled or not. Anyone in the South Pacific who was making friends just then didn't understand the situation.

Modahl:

The ensign was the sorriest specimen I had laid eyes on in a long time. About five feet four inches tall, he had poorly cut, flaming red hair, freckles, jug ears, and buckteeth. He looked maybe sixteen. His khakis didn't fit, were sweat-stained and rumpled—hell, they were just plain dirty.

He mumbled his words, didn't have much to say, kept glancing at the Cat, didn't look me in the eyes.

Joe Snyder and his crew were missing, Harvey Deets was lying in his bunk shivering himself to death with malaria, and I wound up with this kid as a copilot, one who had never even *flown* a seaplane! Why didn't they just put one of the storekeepers in the right seat? Hell, why didn't we just leave the damn seat empty?

No wonder the goddamn Japs were kicking our butts all over the Pacific.

The kid mumbled something about Jones wanting to see me. If the Old Man thought I was going to wet-nurse this kid, he was going to find out different before he got very much older.

I told the kid where to put his gear, then headed for the wardroom to find Commander Jones.

After Modahl went below, I climbed down the net to look over the Black Cat. The high wing sported two engines. The wing was raised well over the fuselage by a pedestal, which had been the key innovation of the design. The mechanic or flight engineer, I knew, had his station in the pedestal. The Cat had side blisters with a fifty-caliber on a swivel-mount in each, a thirty-caliber which fired aft through a tunnel, and a flexible thirty in a nose turret.

This Cat, however, had something I had never seen before. Four blast tubes covered with condoms protruded from the nose under the bow turret. I entered the Cat through one of the open blisters and went forward for a look. The bunk compartment was where passengers always rode; I had never been forward of that.

I went through a small watertight hatch—open now, of course—into the mechanic's compartment. Three steps led up to the mechanic's seat on the wing support pylon. The mech had a bunch of levers and switches up there to control the engines and cowl flaps in flight.

Moving on forward, I passed through the compartment used by the radio operator and the navigator. The radio gear took up all the space on the starboard side of the compartment, while the navigator had a table with a large compass mounted on the aft end. He had boxes for stowage of charts and a light mounted right over the table. The rear bulkhead was covered with a power distribution panel.

On forward was the cockpit, with raised seats for the pilot and copilot. The yokes were joined together on a cross-cockpit boom, so when one moved, the other did also. On the yoke was a set of light switches that told the mechanic what the pilot wanted him to do. They were labeled with things like, "Raise floats" and "Lower floats," which meant the wingtip floats, and directions for controlling the fuel mixture to the engines. The throttle and prop controls were mounted on the overhead.

The cockpit had windows on both sides and in the roof, all of which were open, but still, it was stifling in there with the heat and stink of rotting fish. The Catalina was also rocking a bit in the swell, which didn't help either.

The door to the bow compartment was between the pilot and copilot, below the instrument panel. One of the sailors was there installing ammo in the bow gun feed trays. He explained the setup.

Four fifty-caliber machine guns were mounted as tightly as possible in the bow compartment—the bombsight had been removed to make room and the bombardier's window plated over with sheet metal. Most of the space the guns didn't occupy was taken up by ammo feed trays. The trigger for the guns was on the pilot's yoke. The remainder of the space, and there wasn't much, was for the bow gunner, who had to straddle the fifties to fire the flexible thirty-caliber in the bow turret. Burlap bags were laid over the fixed fifties to protect the gunner from burns.

The sailor showing me the installation was pretty proud of it. His name was Hoffman. He was the bow gunner and bombardier, he said, and had just finished loading ammo in the trays. Through the gaps in the trays I could see the gleam of brass. Hoffman straddled the guns and opened the hatch in the top of the turret to let in some air and light.

"That hatch is open when you make an attack?" I asked.

"Yes, sir. Little drafty, but the visibility is great."

The Cat bobbing against the float and the heat in that closed space made me about half-seasick. I figured I was good for about one more minute.

"How do they work?" I asked, patting the guns.

"They're the Cat's nuts, sir. They really pour out the lead. They'll cut a hole in a ship's side in seconds. I hose the thirty around to keep their heads down while Mr. Modahl guts 'em."

"He goes after the Japs, does he?"

"Yes, sir. He says we gotta do it or somebody else will have to. Now me, I'd rather be sitting in the drugstore at Pismo Beach drinking sodas with my girl while someone else does the heavy lifting, but it isn't working out that way."

"I guess not."

"In fact, when we dive for those Jap ships, and I'm sitting on those guns, I'd rather be somewhere else, anywhere at all. I haven't peed my pants yet, but it's been close."

"Uh-huh."

"Guess everybody feels that way."

"Hard to get used to."

"Are you going to be flying with us?"

"I'm flying copilot for a while. They told me Deets has malaria."

"You know Cats, huh?"

"I don't know a damn thing about flying boats. I figure I can learn, though."

Hoffman wasn't thrilled, I could see that. If I were him, I would have wanted experienced people in the cockpit, too.

Oh well, how tough could it be? It wasn't like we were going to have to land this thing on a carrier deck.

Hoffman:

This ensign wasn't just wet behind the ears—he was dripping all over the deck. Our new copilot? He looked like he just got out of the eighth grade. What in hell were the zeros thinking?

That wasn't me you heard laughin', not by a damn sight. It wasn't very funny. This ensign must be what's on the bottom of the barrel.

It was like we had already lost the war; we were risking
our butts with an idiot pilot who thought he could win the
war all by himself, and if it went bad, we had a copilot
who's never flown a seaplane—hell, a copilot who oughta
be in junior high—to get our sorry asses home.

I patted those fifties, then crawled aft, out of the bow compartment, before I embarrassed myself by losing my breakfast. There
seemed to be a tiny breeze through the cockpit, and that helped.
That and the sunlight and the feeling I wasn't closed up in a tight
place.

There were lots of discolored places on the left side of the fuselage. I asked Hoffman about that. He looked vaguely surprised.
"Patches, sir. Japs shot up the *Witch* pretty bad. Killed the radioman
and left waist gunner. Mr. Modahl got us home, but it was a close
thing."

Hoffman went aft to get out of the airplane, leaving me in the
cockpit. I climbed into the right seat and looked things over, fingered all the switches and levers, studied everything. The more I
could learn now, the easier the first flight would be.

Everything looked straightforward . . . no surprises, really. But it
was a big, complicated plane. The lighting and intercom panels
were on the bulkhead behind the pilots' seats. There were no landing gear or flap handles, of course. Constant speed props, throttles,
RPM and manifold pressure gauges . . . I thought I could handle it.
All I needed would be a little coaching on the takeoff and landing.

The button on the pilot's yoke that fired the fifties was an add-
on, merely clamped to the yoke. A wire from the button disappeared into the bow compartment.

I gingerly moved the controls, just a tad, while I kept my right
hand on the throttles. Yeah, I could handle it. She would be slow
and ponderous, nothing like a Dauntless, but hell, flying is flying.

I climbed out and stood on the float watching the guys finish
loading and fusing the bombs. Three men were also sitting on the
wing completing the fueling. I climbed up the net to the tender's
deck and leaned on the rail, looking her over.

Modahl came walking down the deck, saw me, and came over. He had sort of a funny look on his face. "Okay," he said, and didn't say anything else.

He leaned on the rail, too, stood surveying the airplane.

"Nice plane," I remarked, trying to be funny.

"Yeah. Commander Jones says we can leave as soon as we're ready. When the guys are finished fueling and arming the plane, I think I'll have them fed, then we'll go."

"Yes, sir. Where to?"

"Jones and I thought we might as well run up to Buka and Rabaul and see what's in the harbor. Moon's almost full tonight—be a shame to waste it. Intelligence thinks there are about a dozen Jap ships at Rabaul, which is fairly well defended. We ought to send at least two Cats. Would if we had them, but we don't."

"Buka?"

"No one knows. The harbor might contain a fleet, or it might be empty."

"Okay."

"Tomorrow morning we'll see if we can find Joe Snyder."

"Where was Snyder going the night he disappeared?"

"Buka and Rabaul," Modahl replied, and climbed down the net to check the fuses on the weapons.

TWO

While the other guys were doing all the work, I went to my state-room and threw my stuff in the top bunk. Another officer was there, stripped to his skivvies in the jungle heat. He was seated at the only desk writing a long letter—he already had four or five pages of dense handwriting lying in front of him.

"I'm the new guy," I told him, "going to be Modahl's copilot."

He looked me over like I was a steer he was going to bid upon. "I'm Modahl's navigator, Rufus Pottinger."

"We're flying together, I guess."

I couldn't think of a thing to say. I wondered if that letter was to a girl or his mother. I guessed his mother—Pottinger didn't strike me as the romantic type, but you can never tell. There is someone for everyone, they say.

That thought got me thinking about my family. I didn't have a solitary soul to write to. I guess I was jealous of Pottinger. I stripped to my skivvies and asked him where the head was.

He looked at his watch. "You're in luck. The water will be on in fifteen minutes. For fifteen minutes. The skipper of this scow is miserly with the water."

I took a cake of soap, a towel, and a toothbrush and went to to visit the facilities.

Pottinger:

I'd heard of this guy. They had thrown him out of SBDs, sent him to PBYs. I guess that was an indicator of where we stood on the naval aviation totem pole.

The scuttlebutt was this ensign was some kind of suicidal maniac. You'd never know it to look at him. With flaming red hair, splotchy skin, and buckteeth, he was the kind of guy nobody ever paid much attention to.

He also had an annoying habit of failing to meet your gaze when he spoke to you—I noticed that right off. Not a guy with a great future in the Navy. The man had no presence.

I threw my pen on the desk and stretched. I got to thinking about Modahl and couldn't go on with my letter, so I folded it and put in in the drawer.

Modahl was a warrior to his fingertips. He also took crazy chances. Sure, you gotta go for it—that's combat. Still, you must use good sense. Stay alive to fight again tomorrow. I tried to tell him that dead men don't win wars, and he just laughed.

Now the ensign had been added to the mix. I confess, I was worried. At least Harvey Deets had curbed some of Modahl's wilder instincts. This ensign was a screwball with no brains, according to the rumor, which came straight from the yeoman in the captain's office who saw the message traffic.

In truth I wasn't cut out for this life. I was certainly no warrior—not like Modahl, or even this crazy redheaded ensign. Didn't have the nerves for it.

I wasn't sleeping much those days, couldn't eat, couldn't stop my hands from shaking. It sounds crazy, but I knew there was a bullet out there waiting for me. I knew I wasn't going to survive the war. The Japs were going to kill me.

And I didn't know if they would do it tonight, or tomorrow night, or some night after. But they would do it. I felt like a man on death row, waiting for the warden to come for me.

I couldn't say that in my letters home, of course. Mom would worry herself silly. But Jesus, I didn't know if I could screw up the courage to keep on going.

I hoped I wouldn't crack, wouldn't lose my manhood in front of Modahl and the others.

I guess I'd rather be dead than humiliate myself that way.

Modahl knew how I felt. I think he sensed it when I tried to talk some sense into him.

Oh, God, be with us tonight.

I sat through the brief and kept my ensign's mouth firmly shut. The others asked questions, especially Modahl, while I sort of half listened and thought about that great big ocean out there.

The distances involved were enormous. Buka on the northern tip of Bougainville was about 400 nautical miles away, Rabaul on the eastern tip of New Britain, about 450. This was the first time I would be flying the ocean without my plotting board, which felt strange. No way around it though—Catalinas carried a navigator, who was supposed to get you there and back. Modahl apparently thought Pottinger could handle it—and I guess he had so far.

Standing on the tender's deck, I surveyed the sky. The usual noon shower had dissipated, and now there was only the late-afternoon cumulus building over the ocean.

Behind me I could hear the crew whispering—of course they weren't thrilled at having a copilot without experience, but I wasn't either. I would have given anything right then to be manning a Dauntless on the deck of *Enterprise* rather than climbing into this heaving, stinking, ugly flying boat moored in the mouth of this jungle river.

The *Sea Witch*! Gimme a break!

The evening was hot, humid, with only an occasional puff of wind. The tender had so little fresh water it came out of the tap in a trickle, hardly enough to wet a washrag. I had taken a sponge bath, which was a wasted effort. I was already sodden. At least in the plane we would be free of the bugs that swarmed over us in the muggy air.

I was wearing khakis; Modahl was togged out in a pair of Aussie shorts and a khaki shirt with the sleeves rolled up—the only reason he wore that shirt instead of a tee shirt was to have a pocket for pens and cigarettes. Both of us wore pistols on web belts around our waists.

As I went down the net I overheard the word "crazy." That steamed me, but there wasn't anything I could do about it.

If they wanted to think I was nuts, let 'em. As long as they did their jobs it really didn't matter what they thought. Even if it did piss me off.

I got strapped into the right seat without help, but I was of little use to Modahl. I shouldn't have worried. The copilot was merely there to flip switches the pilot couldn't reach, provide extra muscle on the unboosted controls, and talk to the pilot to keep him awake in the middle of the night. I didn't figure Modahl would leave the plane to me and the autopilot on this first flight. Tonight, the bunks where members of the crew normally took turns napping were covered with a dozen flares and a dozen hundred-pound bombs, to be dumped out the tunnel hole aft.

The mechanic helped start the engines, Pratt & Whitney 1830s of twelve hundred horsepower each. That sounded like a lot, but the Cat was a huge plane, carrying four five-hundred-pound bombs on the racks, the hundred-pounders on the bunks, several hundred pounds of flares, God knows how much machine gun ammo, and fifteen hundred gallons of gasoline, which weighed nine thousand pounds. The plane could have carried more gas, but this load was plenty, enough to keep us airborne for over twenty hours.

I had no idea what the Cat weighed with all this stuff, and I suspect Modahl didn't either. I said something to the mechanic,

Dutch Amme, as we stood on the float waiting our turn to board, and he said the weight didn't matter. "As long as the thing'll float, it'll fly."

With Amme ready to start the engines, Modahl yelled to Hoffman to release the bowlines. Hoffman was standing on the chine on the left side of the bow. He flipped the line off the cleat, crawled across the nose to the other chine, got rid of that line, then climbed into the nose turret through the open hatch.

A dozen or so of the tender sailors pushed us away from the float. As soon as the bow began to swing, Amme began cranking the engine closest to the tender. It caught and blew a cloud of white smoke, and kept the nose swinging. Modahl pushed the rudder full over and pulled the yoke back into his lap as Amme cranked the second engine.

In less time than it takes to tell, we were taxiing away from the tender.

"You guys did that well," I remarked.

"Practice," Modahl said.

Everyone checked in on the intercom, and there was a lot of chatter as they checked systems, all while we were taxiing toward the river's mouth.

Finally, Modahl used the rudder and starboard engine to initiate a turn to kill time while the engines came up to temperature. The mechanic talked about the engines—temps and so on; Modahl listened and said little.

After two complete turns, the pilot closed the window on his side and told me to do the same. He flipped the signal light to tell Amme to set the mixtures to Auto Rich. While I was trying to get my window to latch, he straightened the rudder and matched the throttles. Props full forward, he pulled the yoke back into his lap and began adding power.

The engines began to sing.

The *Witch* accelerated slowly as Modahl steadily advanced the throttles while the flight engineer called out the manifold pressures and RPMs. He had the throttles full forward when the nose of the big Cat rose, and she began planing the smooth water in the lee of

the point. Modahl centered the yoke with both hands to keep us
on the step.

I glanced at the airspeed from time to time. We were so heavy
I began to wonder if we could ever get off. We passed fifty miles
per hour still planing, worked slowly to fifty-five, then sixty, the
engines howling at full power.

It took almost a minute to get to sixty-five with that heavy load,
but when we did Modahl pulled the yoke back into his lap and the
Cat broke free of the water. He eased the yoke forward, held her
just a few feet over the water in ground effect as our airspeed increased. When we had eighty on the dial Modahl inched the yoke
back slightly, and the *Witch* swam upward in the warm air.

"When the water is a little rougher or there is a breeze, she'll
come off easier," he told me. He flipped the switch to tell Amme
to raise the wingtip floats.

He climbed all the way to a thousand feet before he lowered the
nose and pulled the throttles back to cruise manifold pressure, then
the props back to cruise RPM. Of course, he had to readjust the
throttles and sync the props. Finally he got the props perfectly in
snyc, and the engine noise became a smooth, loud hum.

After Modahl trimmed he hand-flew the *Witch* a while. We went
out past the point, where he turned and set a course for the tip of
the island that lay to the northeast.

"Landing this thing is a piece of cake. It's a power-on landing
into smooth water: Just set up the altitude and a bit of a sink rate
and ease her down and on. In the open sea we full-stall her in.
After you watch me do a few I'll let you try it. Maybe tomorrow
evening if we aren't going out again."

"Yeah," I said. The fact that Modahl was making plans for tomorrow was comforting somehow, as I'm sure it was to the rest of
the crew, who were listening on the intercom. As if we were a road
repair gang on the way to fill a pothole.

When we got to the island northeast of Samarai, we flew along
the water's edge for twenty minutes, looking for people or a crashed
airplane or a signal—anything—hoping our lost Catalina crew had
made it this far.

We had been in the air over an hour when Modahl turned north-east for Bougainville. He engaged the autopilot and sat for a while watching it fly the plane. We were indicating 115 miles per hour, about a hundred knots. The wind was out of the west. Pottinger, the navigator, was watching the surface of the sea to establish our drift before sunset.

"Keep your eyes peeled, gang, for Joe Snyder and his guys. Sing out if you see anything."

The land was out of sight behind and the sun was sinking into the sea haze when Modahl finally put his feet up on the instrument panel and lit a cigarette. The sun on our left stern quarter illuminated the clouds, which covered about half the sky. The cloud bases were at least a thousand feet above us, the tops several thousand feet above that. The visibility was about twenty miles, I thought, as I studied the sun-dappled surface of the sea with binoculars.

Standing in the space behind us, between the seats, the radioman also studied the sea's surface. His name was something Varitek . . . I hadn't caught his first name. Everyone called him Varitek, even the other sailors.

The noise level in the plane was high; the headsets made it tolerable. Barely. Still, the drone of the engines and the clouds flamed by the setting sun and the changing patterns on the sea were very pleasant. We had cracked our side windows so there was a decent breeze flowing into the plane.

One of the sailors brought us coffee, hot and black. As Modahl smoked cigarettes, one after another, we sat there watching the colors of the clouds change and the sea grow dark. A sliver of the sun was still above the horizon when I got my first glimpse of the moon, round and golden, climbing the sky.

The other members of the crew were disappointed that they didn't see any trace of Snyder's plane. I hadn't thought they would, nor, apparently, did Modahl. He said little, merely smoked in silence as the clouds above us lost their evening glow.

"Watch the moonpath," Modahl told me after a while. "Anything we see up this way is Japanese, and fair game." He adjusted the cockpit lighting for night flying and asked the radioman for more coffee.

Modahl:

I couldn't get Joe Snyder and his crew out of my mind. A fellow shouldn't go forth to slay dragons preoccupied with other things, but I liked Joe, liked him a lot. And whatever happened to him could happen to me and mine.

The Japs were staging ships and supplies through Buka and Rabaul as they tried to kick us off Guadalcanal. They were working up to taking Port Moresby, then invading Australia, when our invasion of Guadal threw a monkey wrench in their plans. Now they were trying to reinforce their forces on Guadalcanal. A steady stream of troop transports and cargo ships had been in and out of those harbors, not to mention destroyers and cruisers, enough to put the fear in everybody. Then there are Jap planes—they had a nice airfield on Rabaul and a little strip near Buka. The legs on the Zeros were so long you just never knew where or when you would encounter them, though they stayed on the ground at night.

If they could have flown at night, the Cats couldn't. The guns in the side blisters were poor defense against enemy fighters. When attacked, the best defense was to get as close to the sea as possible so the Zeros couldn't make shooting passes without the danger of flying into the water. If a Japanese pilot ever slowed down and lined up behind a Cat a few feet over the water, he'd be meat on the table for the blister gunners—the Japs had yet to make that mistake and probably never would.

I sat there listening to the engines, wondering what happened to Joe, if he were still alive, if he would ever be found.

Varitek:

If you didn't believe you had a good chance of living

through the flight, you would never get aboard the plane. Somebody said that to me once, and it was absolutely true. It took guts to sit through the brief and man up and ride through a takeoff, knowing how big this ocean was, knowing that your life was dependent on the continued function of this cunning contraption of steel and duraluminum. Knowing your continued existence depended on the skill of your pilot.

On Modahl.

Modahl. If he made one bad decision, we were all dead.

These other guys, I saw them fingering rosaries or moving their lips in prayer. I didn't buy any of that sweet-hereafter Living on a Cloud Playing a Harp bullshit.

This is it, baby. This life is all you get. When it's over, it's over. And you ain't coming back as a cow or a dog or a flea on an elephant's ass.

I tried not to think about it, but the truth was, I was scared. Yeah, I believed in Modahl. He was a good officer and a good pilot. Sort of a holier-than-thou human being, not a regular kind of guy you'd like to drink beer with, but I didn't care about that. None of these officers were going to be your buddy, and who would want them to? Modahl could fly that winged boat. He was good at that, and that was all that mattered. That and the fact that he could get us home.

He could do that. Modahl could. He could get this plane and his ass and the asses of all of us home again, back to the tender.

Yeah.

Hoffman:

These other guys were so calm that afternoon, but I wasn't. Tell you the truth, I was scared. Waiting, waiting, waiting . . . it was enough to make a guy puke. I tried to eat and managed to get something down, but I upchucked it before we manned up.

I knew the guys on the Snyder crew—went to boot camp with a couple of them and shipped out with them to the South Pacific. Yeah, they were good guys, *guys just like me*, and they were dead now. Or floating around in the ocean waiting to die. Or marooned on an island somewhere. The folks at home saw the pictures in *Life* and thought tropical paradise, but these islands were hellholes of jungle, bugs, and snakes, with green shit growing right down to the water's edge. Everything was alive, and everything would eat you.

And the South Pacific was crawling with Japs. The sons of Nippon didn't take prisoners, the guys said, just tortured you for information, then whacked off your head with one of those old swords. Gave me the shivers just thinking about it.

If they captured me . . . well, *Jesus!*

No wonder I was puking like a soldier on a two-week drunk.

I just prayed that Modahl would get us home. One more time.

Pottinger:

This evening the wind was only a few knots out of the west-southwest. Our ground speed was, I estimated, 102 knots. We were precisely here on the chart, at this spot I marked with a tiny x. If I had doped the wind right. Beside the x I noted the time.

Later, as we approach Bougainville, Modahl would climb above the clouds and let me shoot the stars for an accurate fix. Of course, once we found the island, I would use it to plot running fixes.

I liked the precision of navigation. The answers were real, clear, and unequivocal, and could be determined with finest mathematical exactness. On the other hand, flying was more like playing a musical instrument. I could determine Modahl's mood by the way he handled the plane. Most of the time he treated it with the utmost respect, working the plane in the wind and sea like a maestro directing a symphony. When he was preoccupied, like tonight, Modahl just pounded the keys, horsed it around, never got in sync with it.

He was thinking about Joe Snyder's crew, I figured, wondering, pondering life and death.

Death was out there tonight, on that wide sea or in those enemy harbors.

It was always there, always a possibility when we set out on one of those long flights into the unknown.

The torture was not combat, a few intense minutes of bullets and bombs; torture was the waiting. The hours of waiting. The days. The nights. Waiting, wondering . . .

Sometimes the bullets and bombs came as almost a relief after all that waiting.

The *Sea Witch* was Modahl's weapon. The rest of us were tiny cogs in his machine, living parts. We would live or die as the fates willed it, and whichever way it came out didn't matter as long as Modahl struck the blow.

But the men had faith he'll take them home. Afterward.

I *wanted* to believe that. The others also. But I knew it wasn't true. Death was out there—I could feel it.

Modahl was only a man.

A man who wondered about Joe Snyder and probably had little faith in himself.

Was Modahl crazy, or was it us, who believed?

Nothing in this life was as black as a night at sea. You can tell people that, and they would nod, but no one could know how mercilessly dark a night could be until he saw the night sea for himself.

After the twilight was completely gone that night there was only the occasional flicker of the moonpath through gaps in the clouds, and now and then a glimpse of the stars. And the red lights on the instrument panel. Nothing else. The universe was as dark as the grave.

Modahl eased his butt in his seat, readjusted his feet on the instrument panel, tried to find a comfortable position, and reached for his cigarettes. The pack was empty; he crumpled it in disgust.

"You married?" he asked me.

"No."

"I am," he said, and rooted around in his flight bag for another pack of Luckies. He got one out, fired it off, then rearranged himself, settling back in.

He checked the compass, tapped the altimeter, glanced at his watch, and said nothing.

"Can I walk around a little?" I asked.

"Sure."

I got unstrapped and left him there, smoking, his feet on the panel.

The beat of the engines made the ship a living thing. Everything you touched vibrated; even the air seemed to pulsate. The waist and tunnel gunners were watching out the blisters, scratching, smoking, whatever. Pottinger was working on his chart, the radioman and bombardier were playing with the radar, Amme the mechanic was in his tower making entries in his logbooks.

I took a leak, drank a half a cup of coffee while I watched the two guys working with the radar, and asked some questions. The presentation was merely a line on a cathode-ray tube—a ship, they said, would show up as a spike on the line. Maybe. Range was perhaps twenty miles, when the sea conditions were right.

"Have you ever seen a ship on that thing?" I asked.

"Oh, yeah," the radioman said, then realized I was an officer and added a "sir."

I finished the coffee, then climbed back into the copilot's seat.

When my headset was plugged in again, I asked Modahl, "Do you ever have trouble staying awake?"

He shook his head no.

A half hour later he got out of his seat, took off his headset, and shouted in my ear: "I'm going to get some coffee, walk around. If the autopilot craps out, I'll feel it. Just hold course and heading."

"Yes, sir."

He left, and there I was, all alone in the cockpit of a PBY Catalina over the South Pacific at night, hunting Jap ships.

Right.

I put my feet up on the panel like Modahl had and sat watching the instruments, just in case the autopilot did decide that it had done enough work tonight. The clouds were breaking up as we went north, so every few seconds I stole a glance down the moon-path, just in case. It was about seventy degrees to the right of our nose. I knew the guys were watching it from the starboard blister, but I looked anyway.

We had been airborne for a bit over four hours. We had lost time searching the coast of that island, so I figured we had another hour to fly before we reached Buka. Maybe Modahl was talking to Pottinger about that now.

If my old man could only see me in this cockpit. When he lost the farm about eight years ago, five years after Mom died, he took my sister and me to town and turned us over to the sheriff. Said he couldn't feed us.

He kissed us both, then walked out the door. That was the last time I ever saw him.

Life defeated him. Beat him down.

Maybe someday, when the war was over, I'll try to find him. My sister and I weren't really adopted, just farmed out as foster kids, so legally he was still my dad.

My sister was killed last year in a car wreck, so he was the only one I had left. I didn't even know if he or Mom had brothers or sisters.

I was sitting there thinking about those days when I heard one sharp, hard word in my ears.

"Contact."

That was the radioman on the intercom. "We have a contact, fifteen miles, ten degrees left."

In about ten seconds Modahl charged into the cockpit and threw himself into the left seat.

"I've got it," he said, and twisted the autopilot steering. We turned about fifty degrees left before he leveled the wings.

"We'll go west, look for them on the moonpath, figure out what we've got."

He reached behind him and twisted the volume knob on the intercom panel so everyone could clearly hear his voice. "Wake up, people. We have a contact. We're maneuvering to put it on the moonpath for a visual."

"What do you think it is?"

"May just be stray electrons—that radar isn't anything to bet money on. If it's a ship, though, it's Japanese."

THREE

"We've lost the contact," Varitek, the radioman, told Modahl. "It's too far starboard for the radar."

"Okay. We'll turn toward it after a bit, so let me know when you get it again."

He leaned over and shouted at me. "It's no stray electron. Ghost images tend to stay on the screen regardless of how we turn."

He was fidgety. He got out the binoculars, looked down the moonpath.

He was doing that when he said, "I've got it. Something, anyway." He turned the plane, banking steeply to put the contact ahead of us.

As we were in the turn, he said, "It's a submarine, I think."

As he leveled the wings the radioman shouted, "Contact."

Modahl looked with binoculars. "It's a sub conning tower. About six miles. Running southeast, I think. We're in his stern quarter."

He banked the plane steeply right, then disengaged the autopilot and lifted the nose and added power. "We'll climb," he said. "Make a diving attack down the moonpath."

"Going to drop a bomb?"

"One, I think. There may be nothing at Buka or Rabaul."

He explained what he wanted to the crew over the intercom. "We'll use the guns on the conning tower," he said, "then drop the bomb as we go over. You guys in the blisters and tunnel, hit 'em with all you got as we go by. They'll go under before we can make another run, so let's make this one count."

Everyone put on life vests, just in case.

"Your job," Modahl said to me, "is to watch the altimeter and keep me from flying into the water. I want an altitude callout every ten seconds or so. Not every hundred feet, but every ten seconds."

"Yessir."

He called Hoffman to the cockpit and talked to him. "One bomb, the call will be 'ready, ready, now.' I'll pickle it off, but to make sure it goes, I want you to push your pickle when I do."

"Aye aye, sir."

Modahl:

The theory was simple enough: We were climbing to about twenty-five hundred feet, if I could get that high under those patchy clouds, then we would fly down the moonpath toward that sub. We'd see him, but he couldn't see us. At two miles I'd chop the throttles and dive. If everything went right, we'd be doing almost 250 mph when we passed three hundred feet in altitude, about a thousand feet from the sub, and I opened fire with the nose fifties.

I planned to pull out right over the conning tower and release the bomb. If I judged it right and the bomb didn't hang up on the rack, maybe it would hit close enough to the sub to damage its hull.

On pullout the guys in the back would sting the sub with their fifties.

Getting it all together would be the trick.

Hoffman:

I opened the hatch on the bow turret and climbed astraddle of those fifties. I patted those babies. I'd cleaned and greased and loaded them—if they jammed when we needed them Modahl would be royally pissed. Dutch Amme, the crew chief, would sign me up for a strangulation. Modahl was a nice enough guy, for an officer, but he and Amme wouldn't tolerate a fuck-up at a time like this, which was okay by me. None of us came all this way to wave at the bastards as we flew by.

The guns *would* work—I *knew* they would.

Pottinger:

We know the Japanese sailors are there—they are blissfully unaware of us up here in the darkness. Right now they have their sub on the surface, recharging batteries and running southeast, probably headed for the area off Guadalcanal . . . to hunt for American ships. When they find one, they will torpedo it from ambush.

We call it war but it's really murder, isn't it? Us or them, whoever pulls the trigger, no matter. The object of the game is to assassinate the other guy before he can do it to you.

We're like Al Capone's enforcers, out to whack the enemy unawares. For the greater glory of our side.

Modahl climbed to the west, with the moon at his back. He got to twenty-four hundred feet before he tickled the bottom of a cloud, so he stayed there and got us back to cruising speed before he started his turn to the left. He turned about 160 degrees, let me fly the *Witch* while he used the binoculars.

"We've got it again," the radioman said. "Thirty degrees left, right at the limits of the gimbals."

"Range?"

"Twelve miles."

"Come left ten," Modahl told me.

I concentrated fiercely on the instruments, holding altitude and turning to the heading he wanted. The Catalina was heavy on the controls, but not outrageously so. I'd call it lots of stability.

The seconds crept by. All the tiredness that I had felt just minutes before was gone. I was ready.

"I've got it," he said flatly, staring through the binoculars. "Turn up the moonpath."

I did so.

"Okay, everybody. Range about eight miles. Three minutes, then we dive to attack."

I tried to look over the nose, which was difficult in a Catalina.

"Still heading southeast," Modahl murmured. "You'll have to turn slightly right to keep it in the moonpath."

The turn also moved the nose so it wouldn't obstruct Modahl's vision.

Maybe I shouldn't have, but I wondered about those guys on that sub. If we pulled this off, these were their last few minutes of life. I guess few of us ever know when the end is near. Which is good, I suppose, since we all have to die.

The final seconds ticked away, then Modahl laid down the binoculars and reached for the controls. He secured the autopilot, and told me, "I'm going to run the trim full nose down. As we come off target, your job is to start cranking the trim back or I'll never be able to hold the nose up as our speed drops."

"Okay."

He retarded the throttles, then pulled back the props so they wouldn't act as dive brakes. Still, nose down as we were, we began to accelerate. Modahl ran the trim wheel forward. I called altitudes.

"Two thousand . . . nineteen hundred . . . eighteen . . ."

Glancing up, I saw the conning tower of the sub and the wake it made. I must have expected it to look larger, because the fact that it was so tiny surprised me.

"Twelve . . . eleven . . ."

The airspeed needle crept past 200 mph. We were diving for a spot just short of the sub so Modahl could raise the nose slightly and hammer them, then pull up to avoid crashing.

I could see the tower plainly now in the reflection of the moonlight, which made a long white ribbon of the wake.

"Six hundred . . . five . . . four-twenty-five . . ."

We were up to almost 250 mph, and Modahl was flattening his

dive, from about twenty degrees nose down to fifteen or sixteen. He had the tower of that sub boresighted now.

"Three-fifty . . ."

"Three hundred . . ."

"Ready," Modahl said for Varitek's benefit. He shoved the prop levers forward, then the throttles.

"Two-fifty . . ."

Modahl jabbed the red button on the yoke with his right thumb. Even with the shielding the blast tubes provided, the muzzle flashes were so bright that I almost visually lost the sub. The engines at full power were stupendously loud, but the jackhammer pounding just inches from my feet made the cockpit floor tremble like a leaf in a gale.

Hoffman:

I could see the sub's tower, see how we were hurtling through the darkness toward that little metal thing amid the swells. When the guns beneath me suddenly began hammering, the noise almost deafened me. I was expecting it, and yet, I wasn't.

I had been pointing the thirty at the Jap, now I held the trigger down.

The noise and heat and gas from the cycling breechblocks made it almost impossible to breathe. This was the fourth time I had done this, and it wasn't getting any better. I could scarcely breathe, the noise was off the scale, my flesh and bones vibrated. The burlap under me insulated me from the worst of the heat, yet if Modahl kept the triggers down, he was going to fry me. I was sitting on hellfire.

And I was screaming with joy . . . Despite everything, the experience was sublime.

"One hundred." I shouted the altitude over the bedlam. Some fool was screaming on the intercom, the engines were roaring at full power, the guns in the nose were hammering in one long, continuous burst . . . I had assumed that Modahl would pull out at a hundred. He didn't.

"Readeee . . ."

"Fifty feet," I shouted over the din, trying to make myself heard. I reached for the yoke.

"*Now!*" Modahl roared, pushing the bomb release with his left thumb, releasing the gun trigger, and pulling the yoke back into his stomach all at the same time.

I began cranking madly on the trim.

We must have taken the lenses off the periscopes with our keel. I distinctly felt us hit something . . . and the nose was rising through the horizontal, up, up, five degrees, ten, as the guns in the blisters and tunnel got off long rolling bursts. When they fell silent our airspeed was bleeding off rapidly, so Modahl pushed forward on the yoke.

"Hoffman, you asshole, did the bomb go?"

"No, sir. It didn't release."

"You shit. You silly, silly shit."

"Mr. Modahl—"

"Get your miserable ass up here and talk to me, Hoffman."

He cranked the plane around as tightly as he could, but too late. When we got level, inbound, with the moon in front of us, the sub was no longer there. She had dived.

"You fly it," Modahl said disgustedly, and turned the plane over to me.

Hoffman climbed up to stand behind the pilots' seats while Modahl inspected the hung bomb with an Aldis lamp. I tried not to look at the bright light so as to maintain some night vision—the light got me anyway. When Modahl had inspected the offending bomb to his satisfaction and finally killed the light, I was half-blinded.

Hoffman said, "Maybe we got the sub with the guns."

Modahl's lip curled in a vicious sneer, and he turned in his seat, looked at Hoffman as if he were a piece of shit.

"Which side are you on, Hoffman? Your shipmates risked their lives to get that bomb on target, to no avail. If that bomb comes off the rack armed while we're landing, the Japs win and our happy little band of heroes will go to hell together. I don't care if you have to grease those racks with your own blood. When we make an attack they goddamn well better work."

Hoffman still had pimples. When Modahl killed the Aldis lamp I could see them, red and angry, in the glow of the cockpit lights.

"Are you fucking crazy?" Modahl asked without bothering to turn around.

"No, sir," Hoffman stammered.

"Screaming on the intercom during an attack. Jesus! I oughta court-martial your silly ass."

"I'm sorry, sir. It just slipped out. Everything was so loud and—"

Modahl made a gesture, as if he were shooing a fly. But that wasn't the end of it. "Chief Amme," Modahl said on the intercom. "When we get back, I expect you and Hoffman to run the racks through at least a dozen cycles on each bomb station. I want a written report signed by you and Hoffman that the racks work perfectly."

"*Yes, sir.*"

"Pottinger, bring your chart to the cockpit. Let's figure out where we are and where the hell we go from here."

I was still hand-flying the plane, so Modahl said to me, "Head northwest and climb to four thousand, just in case we are closer to Bougainville than I think we are. We'll circle around the northern tip of the island and approach the harbor up the moonpath."

Modahl took off his headset and leaned toward me. "Hoffman's getting his rocks off down there."

"Maybe he's crazy, too," I suggested.

"We all are," Modahl said flatly, and nodded once, sharply. His lips turned down in a frown.

I dropped the subject.

"When you get tired, we'll let Otto fly the *Witch*." Otto was the autopilot. After a few minutes I nodded, and he engaged it.

Modahl:

Of course Hoffman was crazy. We all were to be out here at night in a flying boat hunting Japs in the world's biggest ocean. Yeah, sure, the Navy sent us here, but every one of us had the wit to have wrangled a nice cushy job somewhere in the States while someone else did the sweating.

It's addictive, like booze and tobacco. I just worried that I'd love it too much. And it's probably a sin. Not that I know much about sin . . . but I can feel the wrongness of it, the evil. That's the attraction, I guess. I liked the adrenaline and the risk and the feeling of . . . power. Liked it too much.

It was two o'clock in the morning when we approached Buka harbor from the sea. Jungle-covered hills surrounded the harbor on two sides. A low spit formed the third side. On the end of the spit stood a small lighthouse. In the moonlight we could see that the harbor was empty. Not a single ship.

Pottinger was standing behind us. "How long up to Rabaul?" Modahl asked.

"An hour and forty-five minutes or so. Depends on how cute you want to be on the approach."

"You know me. I try to be cute enough to stay alive."

"Yeah."

"Before we go, let's wake up the Japs in Buka. Why should they get a good night's sleep if we can't?"

"Think the Japs are still here?"

"You can bet your soul on it."

Modahl pointed out where the town lay, on the inland side of the harbor. It was completely blacked out, of course.

We made a large, lazy circle while the guys in back readied the parafrags. We would drop them out the tunnel while we flew over the town . . . they fell for a bit, then the parachutes opened, and they drifted unpredictably. This was a nonprecision attack if there ever was one. It was better than throwing bricks, though not by much.

We flew toward the town at three thousand feet. We were still a mile or so away when antiaircraft tracers began rising out of the darkness around the harbor. The streams of shells went up through our altitude, all right, so they had plenty of gun. They just didn't know where in the darkness we were. The streams waved randomly as the Japs fired burst after burst.

It looked harmless enough, though it wasn't. A shell fired randomly can kill you just as dead as an aimed one if it hits you.

"One minute," Modahl told the guys in back. He directed his next comment at me: "I'm saving the five-hundred-pounders for Rabaul. Surely we'll find a ship there or someplace."

"Thirty seconds."

We were in the tracers now, which bore a slight resemblance to Fourth of July fireworks.

"Drop 'em."

One tracer stream ignited just ahead of us and rose toward us. Modahl turned to avoid it. As I watched the glowing tracers I was well aware of how truly large the Catalina was, a black duraluminum cloud. How could they not hit it?

"That's the last of them." The word from the guys in back came as we passed out of the last of the tracers. The last few bombs would probably land in the jungle. Oh well.

We turned for the open sea. We were well away from the city when the frags begin exploding. They marched along through the blackness, popping very nicely as every gun in town fell silent.

"Rabaul," Modahl said, and turned the plane over to me.

FOUR

Rabaul!

The place was a legend. Although reputedly not as tough a nut as Truk, the big Jap base in the Carolines, Rabaul was the major Japanese stronghold in the South Pacific. Intelligence said they had several hundred planes—bombers, fighters, float fighters, seaplanes—and from thirty to fifty warships. This concentration of military power was defended with an impressive array of antiaircraft weapons.

The Army Air Corps was bombing Rabaul by day with B-17s, and the Navy was harassing them at night with Catalinas. None of these punches were going to knock them out, but if each blow hurt them a little, drew a little blood, the effect would be cumulative. Or so said the staff experts in Washington and Pearl.

Regardless of whatever else they might be, the Japanese were good soldiers, competent, capable, and ruthless. They probably had bagged Joe Snyder and his crew last night, and tonight, with this moon, they surely knew the Americans were coming.

I wondered if Snyder had attacked Rabaul before he headed for Buka, or vice versa. Whichever, the Japs in Buka probably radioed the news of our 2 A.M. raid to Rabaul. The guys in Rabaul knew how far it was between the two ports, and they had watches. They could probably predict within five minutes when we were going to arrive for the party.

I didn't remark on any of this to Modahl as we flew over the empty moonlit sea; he knew the facts as well as I and could draw his own conclusions. At least the clouds were dissipating. The stars were awe-inspiring.

Pottinger came up to the cockpit with his chart and huddled over it with Modahl. I sat watching the moonpath and monitoring Otto. I figured if Modahl wanted to include me in the strategy session, he would say so. My watch said almost three in the morning. We couldn't get there before four, so we were going to strike within an hour of dawn.

Finally, Modahl held the chart where I could see it, and said, "Here's Rabaul, on the northern coast of New Britain. This peninsula sticking out into the channel forms the western side of the harbor, which is a fine one. There are serious mountains on New Britain and on New Ireland, the island to the north and east. The highest is over seventy-five hundred feet high, so we want to avoid those.

"Here is what I want to do. We'll motor up the channel between the islands until we get on the moonpath; at this hour of the morning that will make our run in heading a little south of west. Then we'll go in. As luck would have it, that course brings us in over the mouth of the harbor.

"They'll figure we want to do that, but that's the only way I know actually to see what's there. The radar will just show us a bunch of blips that could be anything. If we see a ship we like, we'll climb, then do a diving attack with the engines at idle. Bomb at masthead height. What do you think?"

"Think we'll catch 'em asleep?"

He glanced at me, then dropped his eyes. "No."

"It'll be risky."

"We'll hit the biggest ship in there, whatever that is."

"Five-hundred-pounders won't sink a cruiser."

"The tender was out of thousand-pounders. Snyder took the last one."

"Uh-huh."

"We can cripple 'em, put a cruiser out of the war for a while. Maybe they'll send it back to Japan for repairs. That'll do."

"How about a destroyer? Five hundred pounds of torpex will blow a Jap can in half."

"They got lots of destroyers. Not so many cruisers."

He thought like I did: If there was a cruiser in there, the Japs knew it was the prime target and they'd be ready; still, that's the one I'd hit. When you're looking for a fight, hit the biggest guy in the bar.

Modahl:

The kid was right, of course. There was no way we were going to sucker punch the Japs with a hundred-knot PBY. Yet I knew there would be targets in Rabaul so we had to check Buka first.

Snyder not coming back last night was the wild card. If the Japanese had radar at Rabaul, they could take the darkness away from us. Ditto night fighters with radar. Intelligence said they didn't have radar, and we had seen no indications that Intel was wrong, but still, Joe did what we plan to do, and he didn't come home.

Probably flak got him. God knows, in a heavily defended harbor, flying over a couple of dozen warships, the flak was probably thick enough to walk on.

Bombing at masthead height is our only realistic method for delivering the bombs. Hell, we don't even have a bomb-sight: We took it out when we put in the bow guns. The Catalina is an up-close and personal weapon. We'll stick it in their ear and pull the trigger, which will work, amazingly enough, if we can take advantage of the darkness to surprise them.

We'll pull it off or we won't. That's the truth of it.

Pottinger:

Talk about going along for the ride: These two go blithely about their bloody work without a thought for the rest of the crew. The have ice water in their veins. And neither asked if damaging a ship was worth the life of every man in this plane. Or anybody's life.

They're assassins, pure and simple, and they thought they were invulnerable.

Of course, the Japanese were assassins too.

All of these assholes were in it for the blood.

One hundred knots is glacially slow when you're going to a fire. I was so nervous that I had trouble sitting still. Despite my faith in Pottinger's expertise, I kept staring into the darkness, trying to see what was out there. I didn't want to fly into a mountain and these islands certainly had 'em. When Pottinger said we had reached the mouth of the channel between the two, we turned north. Blindly.

As we motored up the channel at two thousand feet, I wondered why I didn't want to put off the moment of truth, to tomorrow night, or next week, or next year. Or forever. I decided that a man needs a future if he is to stay on an even keel, and with Rabaul up ahead, the future was nothing but a coin flip. I wanted it to be over.

Pottinger and Varitek, the radioman, were on the radar; they reported lots of blips. We came up the moonpath and looked with binoculars: We counted twenty-three ships in the harbor, about half of them warships and the rest freighters and tankers. Lots of targets.

"I think the one in the center of the harbor is a cruiser," Modahl said, and passed the binoculars to me. As he turned the plane to the north, to seaward, I turned the focus wheel of the binoculars and studied it through his side window. With the vibration of the plane and the low light level—all we had was moonlight—it was hard to tell. She was big, all right, and long enough, easily the biggest warship in the harbor.

"Looks like a cruiser to me," I agreed. I lost the moon as I tried to focus on other ships. Modahl turned the *Witch* 180 degrees and motored back south. This time the harbor was on my side.

"See anything that looks like a carrier?" he asked.

"I'm looking." Destroyer, destroyer, maybe a small cruiser . . . more destroyers. A sub. No, two subs.

"Two subs, no carrier," I said, still scanning.

"I'd like to bomb a carrier before I die," Modahl muttered. Everyone on the circuit heard that, of course, and I thought he should watch his lip. No use getting the crew in a sweat. But it was his crew, so I let the remark go by.

"The biggest ship I see is the cruiser in the center," I said, and handed back the glasses.

"Surrounded by cans. When they hear us, everyone opens fire, and Vesuvius will erupt under our ass."

"We can always do a destroyer. We can send one or two to the bottom. They are excellent targets."

"I know."

We turned and motored north again. He waited until the moonlight reflected on the harbor and studied it again with the binoculars. Pottinger was standing behind us. He didn't say anything, kept bent over so he could look out at the harbor.

"The cruiser," Modahl said with finality. He told the crew, as if they didn't know, "We are off Rabaul harbor. The Japs have twenty-three ships there, one of which appears to be a cruiser. Radio, send off a contact report. When you're finished we'll attack."

"What do you want me to say, Mr. Modahl?"

"Just what I said. Twenty-three ships, et cetera."

"Yes, sir."

"Tell me when you have an acknowledgment."

The cruiser lay at a forty-five-degree angle to the moonpath, which had to be the direction of our approach since we were bombing visually. To maximize our chances of getting a hit, we should train off the four bombs, that is, drop them one at a time with a set interval between them—we were going to try to drop the bomb that had hung on the rack at Buka. On the other hand, we could do the most damage if we salvoed all four bombs right down the smokestack. The obvious compromise was to salvo them in pairs with an appropriate interval between pairs—that was Modahl's choice. He didn't ask anyone's opinion; he merely announced how we were going to do it.

Hoffman consulted the chart. If we managed to get up to 250 mph at weapons release, an interval of two-tenths of a second would give us seventy-five feet between salvos. Modahl knew the math cold and gave his approval. Hoffman set two-tenths of a second on the intervalometer.

"How low are you going to go?" Pottinger asked. The cockpit lights reflected in the sweat on his face.

"As low as possible."

"We're going to get caught in the bombs' blast."

"Every foot of altitude increases our chances of missing."

"And of getting home," Pottinger said flatly.

"Get back to your station," Modahl snapped. "The enemy is there, and I intend to hit him."

"I'm merely pointing out the obvious."

"Take it up with Commander Jones the next time you see him."

"*If* I see him."

"Goddamn it, Pottinger! That's *enough*! Get back to your station and shut the fuck up."

The crew heard this exchange, which was one reason Modahl was so infuriated. Right then I would have bet serious money that Modahl and Pottinger would never again fly together.

We flew inbound at three thousand feet. Modahl had climbed higher so he could dive with the engines at idle and still get plenty of airspeed. I was used to the speed of the Dauntless, so motoring inbound toward the proper dive point—waiting, waiting, waiting— was like having poison ivy and being unable to scratch.

"Now," he said, finally, and we both pushed forward on the yokes as he pulled the throttles and the prop levers back. The engines gurgled . . . and the airspeed began increasing. Modahl ran the trim forward. Down we swooped, accelerating ever so slowly.

The cruiser was dead ahead, anchored, without a single light showing. The black shapes on the silver water, the darkness of the land surrounding the bay, the moon and stars above . . . it was like something from a dream. Or a nightmare.

I called the altitudes. "Nineteen, eighteen, seventeen . . ."

He pushed harder on the yoke, ran the nose trim full down. Speed passing 180, 190 . . .

Every gun in the Jap fleet opened fire, all at once.

"Holy . . . !"

Fortunately, they were all firing straight up or randomly. Nothing aimed our way.

The tracers were so bright I would clearly see everything in the cockpit. The Japs had heard us—they just didn't know where we were. Why they didn't shoot away from the moon was a mystery to me.

"Eleven . . . ten . . . nine . . ."

Even the shore batteries were firing. The whole area was erupting with tracers. And searchlights. Four searchlights came on, began waving back and forth.

A stream of weaving tracers from one of the destroyers flicked our way . . . and I felt the blows as three or four shells hit us triphammer fast.

"Five . . . four . . ."

Modahl was flattening out now, pulling on the yoke with all his strength as the evil black shape of the Japanese cruiser rushed toward us. The airspeed indicator needle quivering on 255 . . .

"Three . . ."

"Help me!" he shouted, and lifted his feet to the instrument panel for more leverage.

I grabbed the yoke, braced myself, and pulled. The altimeter passed two hundred . . . I knew there was some lag in the instrument, so we had to be lower . . . The nose was coming up, passing one hundred . . .

We were going to crash into the cruiser! I pulled with all my strength.

"Now!" Modahl shouted, so loud Hoffman could have heard it without earphones.

I felt the bombs come off; two sharp jolts. Dark as it was, I glimpsed the mast of the cruiser as we shot over it, almost close enough to touch.

As that sight registered, the bombs exploded . . . right under us! The blast lifted us, pushed . . .

Modahl rammed the throttles and props forward to the stops.

The *Witch* wasn't responding properly to the elevators.

"The trim," Modahl said desperately, and I grabbed the wheel and turned it with all my strength. It was still connected, still stiff, so maybe we weren't dead yet.

Just then a searchlight latched on to us, and another. The ghastly glare lit the cockpit.

"Shoot 'em out," Modahl roared to the gunners in the blisters and the tail, who opened fire within a heartbeat.

I was rotating the stiff trim wheel when I felt Modahl push the yoke forward. His hand dropped to mine, stopping the rotation of the trim wheel. Then the fifties in the nose lit off. He had opened fire!

Up ahead . . . a destroyer, shooting in all directions—no, the gunners saw us pinned in the searchlights and swung their guns in our direction!

Modahl held the trigger down—the fifties vibrated like a living thing as we raced toward the destroyer, the engines roaring at full power. With the glare of the searchlight and tracers and all the noise, it looked like we had arrived in hell.

And I could feel shells tearing into us, little thumps that reached me through the seat.

We were rocketing toward the destroyer, which was shooting, shooting, shooting . . .

Another searchlight hit us from the port side, nearly blinding me. Something smashed into the cockpit, the instrument panel seemed to explode. Simultaneously, the bow fifties stopped, and the plane slewed.

Modahl slumped in his seat.

I fought for the yoke, leveled the wings, screamed at that idiot Hoffman to stop firing, because he had opened up with the thirty-caliber as soon as the fifties lit off and was still blazing away, shooting BBs at the elephant: Even though we were pinned like a butterfly in the lights, in some weird way I thought that the muzzle flashes of the little machine gun would give away our position.

My mind wasn't functioning very well. I could hear the fifties in the blisters going, but I shouted, *"Hit the lights, hit the lights"* anyway, praying that the gunners would knock them out before the Japs shot us out of the sky.

We were only a few feet over the black water: The destroyer was right there in front of us, filling the windscreen, strobing streams of lava-hot tracer. I cranked the trim wheel like a madman, trying to get the nose up.

The superstructure of the destroyer blotted out everything else. I turned the trim wheel savagely to raise the nose and felt something impact the plane as we shot over the enemy ship.

More shells tore at us, then the tracer was arcing over our wings. One by one the lights disappeared—I think our gunners got two of them—and, mercifully, we exited the flak.

The port engine was missing, I was standing on the rudder trying to keep the nose straight, and Modahl was bleeding to death.

He coughed black blood up his throat.

Thank God he was off the controls!

Blood ran down his chest. He reached for me, then went limp.

Three hundred feet, slowing . . . at least we were out of the flak.

The gyro was smashed, the compass frozen: The glass was broken. Both airspeed indicators were shot out, only one of the altimeters worked . . .

Everyone was babbling on the intercom. The cruiser was on fire, someone said, bomb blasts and flak had damaged the tail, one of the gunners was down, shot, and—

Modahl was really dead, covered with blood, his eyes staring at his right knee.

The port engine quit.

Fumbling, I feathered the prop on the port engine. If it didn't feather, we were going in the water. Now.

It must have, because the good engine held us in the sky.

We were flying straight at the black peninsula on the western side of the bay. We were only three hundred feet above the ocean. Ahead were hills, trees, rocks, more flak guns—I twisted the yoke and used the rudder to turn the plane to the east.

We'll go down the channel, I thought, then it will be a straight shot south to Namoia Bay. Some islands north of there—if we can't make it home, maybe we can put down near one.

The gunners lifted and pulled Modahl out of the pilot's seat while I fought to get the *Sea Witch* to a thousand feet.

Varitek had caught a piece of flak, which tore a huge gash in his leg and ripped out an artery. The other guys sprinkled it with sulfa powder and tried to stanch the bleeding . . . I could hear the back-and-forth on the intercom, but they didn't seem to think he had much of a chance.

Dutch Amme climbed into the empty pilot's seat. He surveyed the damage with an electric torch, put his fingers in the hole the shell had made that killed Modahl. There were other holes, five of them, behind the pilot's seat, on the port side. Amazingly, the destroyer hadn't gotten him—someone we had passed had raked us with something about twenty-millimeter size.

"Searchlights . . . That's why Joe Snyder didn't come back."

"Yeah," I said, refusing to break my fierce concentration on the business at hand. I had the Cat out into the channel now, with the dark shape of New Ireland on my left and the hulk of New Britain on the right. From the chart I had seen, that meant we had to be heading south. Only 450 nautical miles to go to safety.

"The hull's tore all to hell," Amme said wearily. "When we land we'll go to the bottom within a minute, I'd say. You'll have to set her down gentle, or we might even break in half on touchdown."

Right! Like I knew how to set her down gently.

Amme talked for a bit about fuel, but I didn't pay much attention. It took all my concentration to hold the plane in a slight bank into the dead engine and keep a steady fifty pounds or so of pressure on the rudder, a task made none the easier by the fact that my hands and feet were still shaking. I wiped my eyes on the rolled-up sleeve of my khaki shirt.

The clouds were gone, and I could use the stars as a heading reference, so at least we were making some kind of progress in the direction we wanted to go.

"Tell radio to send out a report," I told Amme. " 'Searchlights at Rabaul.' Have him put in everything else he can think of."

"Varitek is in no shape to send anything."

"Have Pottinger do it. Anybody who knows some Morse code can send it in plain English."

"You want to claim the cruiser?"

"Have him put in just what we saw. People saw fire. Leave it at that."

"With Mr. Modahl dead . . . it would look good if we claimed the cruiser for him."

"Do like I told you," I snapped. "A hundred cruisers won't help him now. Then come back and help me fly this pig."

Ten minutes later Amme was back. "Some flak hit the radio power supply. We can't transmit."

FIVE

When the sun rose Varitek was dead. The mountains of New Britain were sinking into the sea in our right rear quarter, and ahead were endless sun-speckled sea and open, empty sky. Right then I would have appreciated some clouds. When I next looked back, the mountains were lost in the haze.

Dutch Amme sat in the left seat and I in the right. Both of us exerted pressure on the rudder and worked to keep the *Witch* flying straight. We did that by reference to the sun, which had come up over the sea's rim more or less where we thought it should if we were flying south. As it climbed the sky, we tried to make allowances.

I also kept an eye on the set of the swells, which seemed to show a steady wind from the southeast, a head wind. I flew across the swells at an angle and hoped this course would take us home.

Our airspeed, Amme estimated, was about 80 mph. At this speed, with a little head wind, it would take nearly seven hours to reach Namoia Bay.

Fuel was a problem. I had Amme repeat everything he had told me as we flew down the strait, only this time I listened and asked questions. The left wing had some holes in it, and we had lost gasoline. We were pouring the stuff into the right engine to stay airborne. The upshot of all this was that he thought we could stay up for maybe six hours, maybe a bit less.

"So you're saying we can't make Namoia Bay?"

Amme thrust his jaw out, eyed me belligerently. This, I had learned, was the way he dealt with authority, the world, officers. "That's right, sir. We'll be swimming before we get there."

Of course, the distance and flying time to Namoia Bay were also estimates. Still, running the *Witch* out of gas and making a forced landing in the open sea was a surefire way to die young. I knew just enough about Catalinas to know that even if we survived an open-ocean landing in this swell and were spotted from the air, no sane person would risk a plane and his life attempting to rescue us. Cats weren't designed to operate in typical Pacific rollers in the open sea.

If we couldn't make Namoia Bay, we needed a sheltered stretch of water to land on, the lee of an island or a lagoon or bay.

There were islands ahead, some big, some small, all covered with inhospitable jungle.

Then there was Buna, on the northern shore of the New Guinea peninsula.

"What about Buna?" I asked Amme and Pottinger, who was standing behind the seats. "Can we make it?"

"The Japs are still in Buna," Amme said.

"I heard they left," Pottinger replied.

"I'd hate to get there and find out you heard wrong," Amme shot back.

So much for Buna.

I had Pottinger sit in the right seat while I took a break to use the head. The interior of the plane was drafty, and when I saw the hull, I knew why. Damage was extensive, apparently from flak and the bomb blasts. Gaping holes, bent plates and stringers . . . I could look through the holes and see the sun reflecting on the ocean. The air whistling up through the wounds made the hair on the back of my head stand up. When we landed, we'd be lucky if this thing stayed above water long enough for us to get out of it. Hell, we'd be lucky if it stayed in one piece when it hit the water.

As I stood there looking at the damage, feeling the slipstream coming through the holes, I couldn't help thinking that this adventure was going to cement my reputation as a Jonah with the dive-bomber guys. They were going to put me in the park for the pigeons. Which pissed me off a little, though there wasn't a damn thing I could do about it.

Varitek's and Modahl's corpses lay in the walkway in the center compartment. I had to walk gingerly to get around. Just seeing them hit me hard. The way it looked, this plane was going to be their coffin. Somehow that seemed appropriate. I had hopes the rest of us could do better, though I was pretty worried.

When I got back to the cockpit I stood behind Amme and Pottinger, who were doing as good a job of wrestling this flying pig southward as I had. Still, they wanted me to take over, so I climbed back in the right seat. Amme suggested the left, but I was used to using the prop and throttle controls with my left hand and the stick with my right, so figured I would be most comfortable with that arrangement.

Someone opened a box or two of C rations, and we ate ravenously. With two guys dead, you think we'd have lost our appetites, but no.

> Amme:
>
> We were in a heap of hurt. We were in a shot-up, crippled, hunk-of-junk airplane in the middle of the South Pacific, the most miserable real estate on the planet, and our pilot had never landed a seaplane in his life. Jesus! The other guys pretended that things were going to work out, but I had done the fuel figures, and I knew. We weren't going to make it, even if this ensign was God's other son.
>
> I tried to tell the ensign and Pottinger; those two didn't seem too worried. Officers! They must get a lobotomy with their commission.
>
> Lieutenant Modahl was the very worst. Goddamned idiot. The fucking guy thought he was bulletproof and lived

it that way . . . until the Japs got him. Crazy or brave, dead is dead.

The truth is we were all going to end up dead, even me, and I wasn't brave or crazy.

Pottinger:

The crackers in the C rations nauseated me. The only gleam of hope in this whole mess was the right engine, which ran like a champ. Not enough gas, this little red-headed fool ensign for a pilot, a damaged hull . . .

Funny how a man's life can lead to a mess like this. Just two years ago I was studying Italian art at Yale . . .

Searchlights! The Japs rigged up searchlights to kill Black Cats. They probably nailed Snyder with them, and miracle of miracles, here came another victim. Those Americans!

Modahl. A braver man never wore shoe leather. I tried not to look at his face as we laid him out in back and covered him with his flight jacket.

In a few hours or days we'd all be as dead as Modahl and Varitek. I knew that, and yet, my mind refused to accept the reality. Wasn't that odd?

Or was it merely human?

"We're going to have to ditch somewhere," I told everyone on the intercom. "Everyone put on a life vest now. Break out the emergency supplies and the raft, get everything ready so when we go in the water we can get it out of the plane ASAP."

They knew what to do, they just needed someone to tell them to do it. I could handle that. After Amme got his vest on, I put on mine and hooked up the straps.

I had Pottinger bring the chart. I wanted a sheltered stretch of water to put the plane in beside an island we could survive on. And the farther from the Japs the better.

One of the Trobriand Islands. Which one would depend upon our fuel.

We were flying at about a thousand feet. Without the altimeter all I could do was look at the swells and guess. The higher we climbed, the more we could see, but if a Japanese fighter found us, our best defense was to fly just above the water to prevent him from completing firing passes.

I looked at the sun. Another two hours, I decided, then we would climb so we could see the Trobriand Islands from as far away as possible.

As we flew along I found myself thinking about Oklahoma when I was a kid, when my dad and sister and I were still living together. I couldn't remember what my mother looked like; she died when I was very young. I remembered my sister's face, though. Maybe she resembled Mama.

The island first appeared as a shadow on the horizon, just a darkening of that junction of sea and sky. I turned the plane ten degrees right to hit it dead on.

The minutes ticked away as I stared at it, wondering. Finally I checked my watch. Five hours. We had attacked the harbor five hours earlier.

Ten minutes later I could definitely see that it was an island, a low green thing, little rise on the spine, which meant it wasn't coral.

Pottinger was in the left seat at that time, so I pointed it out to him. He merely stared, didn't say anything. About that time Dutch Amme came down from the flight engineer's station and announced that the temps were rising on the starboard engine.

"And we're running out of gas. An hour more, at the most."

I pointed out the island to him, and he had to grab the back of the seat to keep from falling.

In less than a minute we had everyone trooping up to the cockpit to take a look. Finally, I ran them all back to their stations.

That island looked like the promised land.

Pottinger:

A miracle, that was what it was. We were delivered. We were going to make it, going to live. Going to have some tomorrows.

I didn't know whether to laugh or cry. The island was there, yet it was so far away. We would reach it, land in the lee, swim ashore . . .

Please God, let us live. Let me and these others live to marry and have children and contribute something to the world.

Hear me. Let us do this.

Hoffman:

I was so happy I couldn't stand still. I wanted to pound everyone on the back. Sure, I had been fighting despair, telling myself we weren't going to die when I really figured we might. The hull was a sieve—when the ensign set the *Witch* in the water we were going to have to get out as it sank. I knew that, everyone did. And still, *now* we had a chance.

"Fighter!"

One of the guys in the blisters saw it first and called it.

"A float fighter."

I rolled the trim over a bit, got us drifting downward toward the water. The elevator control cables had been damaged in the bomb blast. The trim wheel was the only reason we were still alive.

"He hasn't seen us yet. Still high, crossing from starboard to port behind us, heading nearly east it looks like."

After a bit, "Okay, he's three miles or so out to the east, going away. Never saw us."

The Japanese put some of their Zeros on floats, which made a lot of sense since the Zero had such great range. The float fighters could be operated out of bays and lagoons where airfields didn't exist and do a nice job of patrolling vast expanses of ocean. The performance penalty they paid to carry the floats was too great to allow them to go toe-to-toe with land or carrier-based fighters. They could slice and dice a Catalina, though.

"Shit, it's coming back."

I kept the Cat descending. We were a couple hundred feet above the water, far too high. I wanted us right on the wavetops.

"He's coming in from the port stern quarter, curving, coming down, about a half mile . . ."

I could hear someone sobbing on the intercom.

"I don't know who's making that goddamn noise," I said, "but it had better stop."

We were about a hundred feet high, I thought, when the float fighter opened fire. I saw his shells hit the water in front of us and heard the fifty in the port blister open up with a short burst. And another, then a long rolling blast as the plane shuddered from the impact of cannon shells.

The fighter pulled out straight ahead, so he went over us and out to my right. He flew straight until he was well out of range of our gun in the starboard blister, then initiated a gentle turn to come around behind.

"Anybody hurt?" I asked.

"He ripped the port wing, which is empty," Dutch Amme said.

"Good shooting, since he had to break off early."

I was down on the water by then, very carefully working the trim. I didn't have much altitude control remaining—if we hit the water at speed our problems would be permanently over.

I thought about turning into this guy when he committed himself to one side or the other. The island dead ahead had me paralyzed though. There it was, a strip of green between sea and sky. Instinctively, I knew that it was our only hope, and I didn't want to waste a drop of gas in my haste to get there.

Perhaps I could skid the plane a little to try to throw off the Zero pilot's aim. I fed in some rudder, twisted the yoke to hold it level.

And the lousy crate began sinking. We bounced once on a swell and that damn near did it for us right there. We lost some speed and hung right on the ragged edge of a stall. Long seconds crept by before we accelerated enough for me to exhale. By then I had the rudder where it belonged, but it was a close thing. At least the plane didn't come apart when it kissed the swell.

Pottinger was hanging on for dear life. "Don't kill us," he pleaded.

On the next pass the Zero tried to score on the starboard engine, the only one keeping us aloft. I could feel the shells slamming into us, tearing at the area just behind the cockpit. Instinctively I ducked my head, trying to make myself as small as possible.

I could hear one of the waist fifties pounding.

"Are you gunners going to shoot this guy or let him fuck us?"

With us against the water, the Zero couldn't press home his attacks, but he was hammering us good before he had to break off.

"He holed the right tank," Amme shouted. "We're losing fuel."

Oh, baby!

"He's streaming fuel or something," Hoffman screamed. "You guys hit him that last pass."

They all started talking at once. I couldn't shut them up.

"If he's crippled, the next pass will be right on the water, from dead astern," I told Pottinger. "He'll pour it to us."

"Naw. He'll head for home."

"Like hell. He'll kill us or die trying. That's what I'd do if I were him."

Sure enough, the enemy fighter came in low so he could press the attack and break off without hitting the ocean. He was directly behind, dead astern, so both the blister gunners cut loose with their fifties. Short bursts, then longer as he closed the distance.

Someone was screaming on the intercom, shouting curses at the Jap, when the intercom went dead.

I could feel the cannon shells punching home—the cannons in Zeros had low cyclic rates; I swear every round this guy fired hit us. One fifty abruptly stopped firing. The other finished with a long buzz saw burst, then the Zero swept overhead so close I could hear the roar of his engine. At that point it was running better than ours, which was missing badly.

I glanced up in time to see that the enemy fighter was trailing fire. He went into a slight left turn and gently descended until he hit the ocean about a mile from us. Just a little splash, then he was gone.

Our right engine still ran, though fuel was pouring out of the wing. As if we had any to spare.

The island lay dead ahead, but oh, too far, too far.

Now the engine began missing.

We'd never make it. Never.

Coughing, sputtering, the engine wasn't developing enough power to hold us up.

I shouted at Pottinger to hang on, but he had already let go of the controls and braced himself against the instrument panel. As I rolled the trim nose up, I gently retarded the throttle.

Just before we kissed the first swell the engine quit dead. We skipped once, I rolled the trim all the way back, pulled the yoke back even though the damn cables were severed, and the *Sea Witch* pancaked. She must have stopped dead in about ten feet. I kept traveling forward until my head hit the instrument panel, then I went out.

Pottinger:

The ensign wasn't strapped in. In all the excitement he must have forgotten. The panel made a hell of a gash in his forehead, so he was out cold and bleeding profusely.

The airplane was settling fast. I opened the cockpit hatch and pulled him out of his seat. I couldn't have gotten him up through the hatch if Hoffman hadn't come up to the cockpit. The ensign weighed about 120, which was plenty, let me tell you. It was all Hoffman and I could do to get him through the hatch, then we hoisted ourselves through.

The top of the fuselage was just above water. It was a miracle that the Jap float fighter didn't set us on fire, and he probably would have if we had been carrying more fuel.

"What about the others?" I asked Hoffman.

"Huntington is dead. The Zero got him. So is Amme. I don't know about Tucker or Svenson."

We were about to step off the bow to stay away from the props when a wave swept us into the sea. I popped the cartridges to inflate my vest, then struggled with the ensign's. I also had to tighten the straps of his vest, then attend to mine—no one ever put those things on tightly enough. I was struggling to do all this and keep our heads above water when I felt something hit my foot.

The ensign was still bleeding, and these waters were full of sharks. A wave of panic swept over me, then my foot hit it again. Something solid. I put my foot down.

The bottom. I was standing on the bottom with just my nose out of the water.

"Hoffman! Stand up!"

We were inside the reef. A miracle. Delivered by a miracle. The ensign had gotten us just close enough.

The *Sea Witch* refused to go under, of course, because she was resting on the bottom. Her black starboard wingtip and vertical stabilizer both protruded prominently from the water.

When we realized the situation, Hoffman worked his way aft and checked on the others. He found three bodies.

We had to get ashore, so we set out across the lagoon toward the beach, walking on the bottom and pulling the ensign, who floated in his inflated life vest.

"He took a hell of a lick," I told Hoffman.

"Maybe he'll wake up," Hoffman said, leaving unspoken the other half of it, that maybe he wouldn't.

Hoffman:

The only thing that kept me sane was taking care of the ensign as we struggled over the reef.

Maybe he was already dead, or dying. I didn't know. I tried not to think about it. Just keep his head up.

Oh, man. I couldn't believe they were all dead—Lieutenant Modahl, Chief Amme, Swede Svenson, Tucker, Huntington, Varitek. I tried not to think about it and could think of nothing else. All those guys dead!

We were next. The three of us. There we were, castaways on a jungle island in the middle of the ocean and not another soul on earth knew. How long could a guy stay alive? We'd be ant food before anyone ever found us. If they did.

Of course, if the Japs found us before the Americans, we wouldn't have to worry about survival.

Pottinger:

Fighting the currents and swells washing over that uneven reef and through the lagoon while dragging the ensign was the toughest thing I ever had to do. The floor of the lagoon was uneven, with holes in it, and sometimes Hoffman and I went under and fought like hell to keep from drowning.

We must have struggled for an hour before we got to knee-deep water, and another half hour before we finally dragged the ensign and ourselves up on the beach. We lay there gasping, desperately thirsty, so exhausted we could scarcely move.

Hoffman got to his knees, finally, and looked around. The beach was a narrow strip of sand, no more than ten yards wide; the jungle began right at the high-water mark.

At his urging we crawled into the undergrowth out of sight. The ensign we dragged. He was still breathing, had a pulse, and thank God the bleeding had stopped, but he didn't look good.

The *Witch* was about a mile out on the reef. The tail stuck up prominently like an aluminum sail.

"I hope the Japs don't see that," Hoffman remarked.

"If we can't find water, it won't matter," I told him. "We'll be praying for the Japs to come along and put us out of our misery."

After some discussion, he went one way down the beach and I went the other. We were looking for fresh water, a stream running into the sea . . . something.

At some point I became aware that I was lying in sand . . . in shade . . . in wet clothes . . . with bugs and gnats and all manner of insects eating on me.

My head was splitting, so I didn't pay much attention to the bugs, though I knew they were there.

I managed to pry my eyes open . . . and could barely make out light and darkness. I thrashed around a while and dug at my eyes and rubbed at the bugs and passed out again.

The second time I woke up it was dark. My eyes were better, I thought, yet there was nothing to see. I could hear waves lapping nervously.

The thought that we had made it to the island hit me then. I lay there trying to remember. After a while most of the flight came back, the flak in the darkness, the Zero on floats, settling toward the water with one engine dead and the other dying . . .

I became aware that Pottinger was there beside me. He had a baby bottle in his survival vest, which he had filled with freshwater. He let me drink it. I have never tasted anything sweeter.

Then he went away, back for more I guess.

After a while I realized someone else was there. It took me several minutes to decide it was Hoffman.

"Are we the only ones alive?" I asked, finally.

"Yes," Hoffman said.

SIX

The next day, our first full day on the island, I was feeling human again, so Pottinger, Hoffman and I went exploring. Fortunately, my head wasn't bleeding, and the headache was just that, a headache. We had solid land—okay, sand—under our feet, and we had a chance. Not much of one, but a chance. I was still wearing a pistol, and all of us had knives.

We were also hungry enough to eat a shoe.

We worked our way east along the beach, taking our time. As we walked we discussed the situation. Hoffman was for going out to the plane and trying to salvage a survival kit; Pottinger was against it. There was a line of thunderstorms off to the east and south that seemed to be coming our way. Still hours away, the storms were agitating the swells. Long, tall rollers crashed on the reef, and smaller swells swept through the lagoon.

Watching the swells roll through the shallows, I thought the wreck of the *Sea Witch* too far away and the water too dangerous. Then we saw a group of shark fins cruising along, and the whole idea of going back to the plane sort of evaporated. We certainly needed the survival kits; we were just going to have to wait for a calmer day.

I had seen the island from the air, though at a low angle, and knew it wasn't small. Trying to recall, I estimated it was eight or nine miles long and a mile wide at the widest part. Probably volcanic in origin, the center of the thing reached up a couple hundred feet or so in elevation, if my memory was correct. I remembered the little hump that I flew toward when we were down low against the sea.

The creeks running down from that rocky spine contained good water, so we wouldn't die of thirst. There was food in the sea, if we could figure out a way to get it. There were things to eat—birds and snakes and such—in the jungle, if we could catch them. All in all, I figured we could make out.

If there weren't any Japs on this island.

That was our immediate concern, so we hiked along, taking our time, looking and listening.

On the eastern end of the island the jungle petered out into an area of low scrub and sand dunes. It was getting along toward the middle of the day, so we sat to rest. After all I had been through, I could feel my own weakness, and I was sure the others could also. But sitting wasn't getting us anyplace, so we dusted our fannies and walked on.

The squall line was almost upon us when we found the first skid mark on the top of a dune.

"Darn if that furrow doesn't look like it was made by the keel of a seaplane," Hoffman said.

I took a really good look, and I had to agree.

I took out my pistol and worked the action, jacked a shell into my hand. The gun was gritty, full of sand and sea salt.

"Going to rain soon," Pottinger said, looking at the sky.

"Let's see if we can find a dry place and sit it out," I said, looking around. I spotted a clump of brush under a small stand of palms, and headed for it. The others were in no hurry, although the gray wall of rain from the storm was nearly upon us.

"Maybe it's Joe Snyder's crew, where he went down in *Charity's Sake*."

"Maybe," I admitted.

"Let's go look." If Hoffman had had a tail, he would have wagged it.

"Later."

"Hell, no matter where we hide, we're going to get wet. If it's them, they've got food, survival gear, all of that."

"Could be Japs, you know."

He was sure the Japanese didn't leave a seaplane mark.

The first gust of rain splattered us.

"I'm going to sit this one out," I said, and turned back toward the brush I had picked out. Pottinger was right behind.

Hoffman ran up beside me. "Please, sir. Let me go on ahead for a look."

I looked at Pottinger. He was a lieutenant (junior grade), senior to me, but since I was the deputy plane commander, he hadn't attempted to exert an ounce of authority. Nor did I think he wanted to.

"No," I told Hoffman. "The risk is too great. The Japs won't want to feed us if they get their hands on us."

"They won't get me."

"No."

"You're just worried I'll tell 'em you're here."

"If they catch you, kid, it won't matter what you tell 'em. They'll come looking for us."

"Mr. Pottinger." Hoffman turned to face the jaygee. "I appeal to you. All our gear is out in the lagoon. You know the guys in *Charity's Sake* as well as I do."

Pottinger looked at me and he looked at Hoffman and he looked at the squall line racing toward us. He was tired and hungry and had never made a life-or-death decision in his life.

"Snyder could have made it this far," he said to me.

"There's a chance," I admitted.

He bit his lip and made his decision. "Yes," he told the kid. "But be careful, for Christ's sake."

Hoffman grinned at Pottinger and scampered away just as the rain hit. I jogged over to the brush I had seen and crawled in. It wasn't much shelter. Pottinger joined me.

"It's probably Snyder," he said, more to himself than to me.

"Could be anybody."

There was a little washout under the logs. We huddled there.

"Hoffman's right about one thing," I told Pottinger. "We won't be much drier here than if we had stayed out in it."

While it rained I field-stripped the Colt and cleaned the sand and grit out of it as best I could, then put it back together and reloaded it. It wasn't much of a weapon, but it was something. I had a feeling we were going to need everything we had.

After the squall had passed, the fresh wind felt good. We sat on a log and let the wind dry us out.

We were alive, and the others were dead. So the wind played with our hair as we looked at the sea and sky with living eyes.

For how long?

I had seem much of death these last few months, had killed a few men myself . . . and oh, it was ugly. Ugly!

Anyone who thinks war is glorious has never seen a fresh corpse.

Yet we kill each other, ruthlessly, mercilessly, without qualm or remorse, all for the greater glory of our side.

Insanity. And this has been the human experience since the dawn of time.

Musing thus, I kept an eye out for Hoffman. He didn't come back. After an hour I was worried.

Pottinger was worried, too. "This isn't good," he said.

We waited another hour, a long, slow hour as the rain squall moved on out over the lagoon, and the sun came boiling through the dissipating clouds. Extraordinary how hot the tropical sun can get on bare skin.

The minutes dragged. My head thumped and my stomach tied itself into a knot. I wanted water badly.

One thing was certain; we couldn't stay put much longer. We needed to get about the business of finding drinkable water and something to eat.

"I guess I fucked that up," Pottinger said.

"Let's follow the keel mark," I suggested.

We didn't walk, we sneaked along, all bent over, even crawled through one place where the green stuff was thin. Hoffman's tracks were still visible in places, only partially obliterated by the rain. And so were the scrapes of the flying boat's keel, deep cuts in the sand where it touched, skipped, then touched again. The plane had torn the waist-high brush out of the ground everywhere it touched. Still, there was enough of it standing that it limited our visibility. And the visibility of the Japs, if there were Japs.

The thought had finally occured to Pottinger that if we could follow Hoffman, someone else could backtrack him. He was biting his lip so tightly that blood was leaking down his chin. His face was paper white.

The pistol felt good in my hand.

We had gone maybe a quarter of a mile when we saw the reflection of the sun off shiny metal. We got behind some brush and lay on the ground.

"That's no black Catalina," I whispered to Pottinger, who nodded.

Screwing up our courage, we crawled a few more yards on our hands and knees. Finally we came to the place where we could clearly see the metal, which turned out to be the twin tails of a large airplane. Japanese. The rest of the airplane appeared to be behind some trees and brush, partially out of sight.

"A Kawanishi flying boat," Pottinger whispered into my ear. "A Mavis." He was as scared as I was.

"I'm sorry," he said, his voice quavering. "You were right, and I was wrong. Letting Hoffman go running off alone was a mistake."

"Don't beat yourself up over it," I told him. "There aren't many right or wrong decisions. You make the best choice you can because the military put you there and told you to decide, then we all get on with it."

"Yeah."

"You gotta remember that none of this matters very much."

"Ahh . . ."

"You stay here. I'll go see what Hoffman's gotten himself into."

I wasn't going to go crawling over to that plane. Hoffman had probably done that. His tracks seemed to go that way. I set off at a ninety-degree angle, crawling on my belly, the pistol in my right hand.

When I'd gone at least a hundred yards, I turned to parallel the Mavis's landing track. After another hundred yards I heard voices. I froze.

They were speaking Japanese.

I lay there a bit, trying to see. The voices were demanding, imperious.

Taking my time, staying on my stomach, I crawled closer.

I heard Hoffman pleading, begging. "Don't hit me again, for Christ's sake." And a chunk of something heavy hitting flesh.

Ooh boy!

When they were finished with Hoffman, they were going to come looking for Pottinger and me. If they weren't already looking.

I had to know how many of them there were.

I crawled closer, trying to see around the roots of the grass bunches that grew on the dunes.

The Mavis had four engines, one of which was blackened and scorched. Either it caught fire in the air, or someone shot it up.

Finally I got to a place where I could see the men standing in a circle.

There were four of them. They were questioning Hoffman in Japanese. A lot of good that would do. I never met an American sailor who understood a word of it.

The Japs were taking turns beating Hoffman with a club of some kind. Clearly, they were enjoying it.

The Mavis was pretty torn up. Lots of holes, maybe fifty-caliber. It looked to me like a Wildcat or Dauntless had had its way with it.

I kept looking around, trying to see if there were any more Japs. Try as I might, I could see only those four. Two of them had rifles though.

About then they whacked Hoffman so hard he passed out. One of them went for water, dumped it on him to bring him around. Another, decked out in an officer's uniform, went over to a little pile of stuff under a palm tree and pulled out a sword.

They were going to chop off the kid's head.

Shit!

I should never have let him go trooping off by himself.

The range was about forty yards. I steadied that pistol with a two-hand grip and aimed it at the Jap with the rifle who was facing me. I wanted him first.

I took my time. Just put that front sight on his belt buckle and squeezed 'er off like it was Tuesday morning at the range. I knocked him off his feet.

I didn't have the luxury of time with the second one. I hit him, all right, probably winged him. The other one with the rifle went to his belly and was looking around, trying to see where the shots were coming from. I only had his head and one arm to shoot at, so I took a deep breath, exhaled, and touched it off. And got him.

The officer with the sword had figured out where I was by that time and was banging at me with a pistol.

I rolled away. Got to my feet and ran, staying as low as possible, ran toward the tail of the Mavis while the officer popped off three in my direction.

"How many of them were there, Hoffman?" I roared, loud as I could shout.

"Four," he answered, then I heard another shot.

I ran the length of the flying boat's fuselage, sneaked a peek around the bow. Hoffman lay sprawled in the dirt, blood on his chest, staring fixedly at the sky.

The Jap bastard had shot him!

I sneaked back along the hull of the Mavis, thinking the guy might follow me around.

Finally, I wised up. I got down on my belly and crawled away from the Mavis.

I figured the Jap officer wanted one of those rifles as badly as I did, and that was where he'd end up. I went out about a hundred yards and got to my feet. Staying bent over as much as possible, I trotted around to where I could see the Japs I had shot.

The officer wasn't in sight. I figured he was close by anyway.

I lay down behind a clump of grass, thought about the situation, wondered what to do next.

I had just about made up my mind to crawl out of there and set up an ambush down the beach when something whacked me in the left side so hard I almost lost consciousness.

Then I heard the shot. A rifle.

With what was left of my strength, I pulled my right hand under me. Then I lay still.

I was hit damned bad. As I lay there the shock of the bullet began wearing off and the pain started way up inside me.

I tried not to breathe, not to move, not to do anything. It was easy. I could feel the legs going numb, feel the life leaking out.

For the longest time I lay there staring at the sand, trying not to blink.

I heard him, finally. Heard the footfall.

He nudged me once with the barrel of his rifle, then used his foot to turn me over.

A look of surprise registered on his face when I shot him.

Pottinger:

I heard the shots, little pops on the wind, then silence. After a while another shot, louder, then twenty minutes or so later, one more, muffled.

After that, nothing.

Of course I had no way of knowing how many Japanese there were, what had happened, if Hoffman or the ensign were still alive . . .

I wanted desperately to know, but I couldn't make myself move. If I just sat up, I could see the tail of the Mavis . . . and they might see me.

I huddled there frozen, waiting for Hoffman and the ensign to come back. I waited until darkness fell.

Finally, I slept.

The next morning nothing moved. I could hear nothing but the wind. After a couple of hours I knew I was going to have to take a chance. I had to have food. I tried to move and found I couldn't. Another hour passed. Then another. Ashamed of myself and nauseated with fear, I crawled.

I found them around the Japanese flying boat, all dead. The four Japanese and the two Americans. The Japanese officer was lying across the ensign.

There was food, so I ate it. The water I drank.

I put them in a row in the sand and got busy on a grave. I shouldn't have let Hoffman go exploring. I should be lying there dead instead of the ensign.

Digging helped me deal with it.

The trouble came when I had to drag them to the grave. I was crying pretty badly by then, and the ensign and Hoffman were just so much dead meat. And starting to swell up. I tried not to look at their faces . . . and didn't succeed.

I dragged the two Americans into the same hole and filled it in the best I could.

I was shaking by then, so I set to digging on a bigger hole for the Japanese. It was getting dark by the time I got the bodies in that hole and filled it and tamped it down.

The next day I inventoried the supplies in the Mavis. There was fishing gear, canned food, bottled water, pads to sleep on, blankets, an ax, matches.

After I'd been on the island about a week I decided to burn the Mavis. The fuel tanks were shot full of holes and empty, which was probably why the Mavis was lying on this godforsaken spit of sand in the endless sea.

It took two days of hard work to load the fuselage with driftwood. I felt good doing it, as if I were accomplishing something important. Looking back, I realize that I was probably half-crazy at that time, irrational. I ate the Japanese rations, worked on stuffing the Mavis with driftwood, watched the sky, and cried uncontrollably every now and then.

By the end of the second day I had the plane fairly full of driftwood. The next morning at dawn I built a fire in there with some Japanese matches and rice paper. The metal in the plane caught fire about an hour later and burned for most of the day. I got pretty worried that evening, afraid that I had lit an eternal flame to arouse Japanese curiosity. The fire died, finally, about midnight, though it smoldered for two more days and nights. Thank God I had been sane enough to wait for morning to light it.

With the fire finally out, I packed all the supplies I had salvaged from the Mavis and moved four miles along the south side of the island to a spot where a freshwater creek emptied into the sea. It took three trips to carry the loot.

I never did try to cross the lagoon to the wreck of the *Sea Witch*. On one of my exploratory hikes around the island a few weeks later I saw that she was gone, broken up by a storm or swept off the reef into deeper water.

I fell into a routine. Every morning I fished. I always had something by noon, usually before, so I built a fire and cooked it and ate on it the rest of the day. During the afternoon I explored and gathered driftwood, which I piled into a huge pile. My thought was that if and when I saw a U.S. ship or plane, I would light it off as a signal fire. I had a hell of pile collected but finally ran out of matches that would light. The rain and the humidity ruined them. After that I ate my fish raw.

And so my days passed, one by one. I lost count. There was nothing on the island but the jungle and birds, and wind and rain and surf. And me. Just me and my ghosts alone on that speck of sand and jungle lost in an endless universe of sea and sky.

Later I learned that five months passed before I was rescued by the crew of a U.S. Navy patrol boat searching for a lost aircrew. Not the crew of the *Witch* or *Charity's Sake*, but a B-24 crew that had also disappeared into the vastness of the great Pacific. The war was way north and west by then.

I must have been a sight when they found me, burned a deep brown by the sun and almost naked, with only a rag around my waist. My beard and hair were wild and tangled, and I babbled incoherently.

The Navy sent me back to the States. They kept me in a naval hospital for a while until I sort of got it glued back together. Then they gave me a medical discharge.

Cut off from human contact during those long nights and long, long days on that island, I could never get the ensign and Modahl and the other guys from the *Witch* out of my mind. They have been with me every day of my life since.

I have never figured out why they died and I lived.

To this day I still don't know. It wasn't because I was a better person or a better warrior. They were the warriors— they carried me. They had courage, I didn't. They had faith in each other and themselves, and I didn't. Why was it that they died and I was spared?

The old Vikings would have said that Modahl and the ensign were the lucky ones.

In the years that have passed since I flew in the *Sea Witch* the world has continued to turn, the seasons have come and gone, babies have been born and old people have passed away. The earth continues as before.

As I get older I have learned that the ensign spoke the truth: The fate of individuals matters very little. We are dust on the wind.

BREAKTHROUGH ON BLOODY RIDGE

HAROLD COYLE

HAROLD COYLE graduated from the Virginia Military Institute in 1974, with a B.A. in history and a commission as a second lieutenant in Armor. His first assignment was in Germany, where he served for five years as a tank platoon leader, a tank company executive officer, a tank battalion assistant operations officer, and as a tank company commander. Following that he attended the Infantry Officers Advanced Course at Fort Benning, Georgia, became a branch chief in the Armor School's Weapons Department at Fort Knox, Kentucky, worked with the National Guard in New England, spent a year in the Republic of Korea as an assistant operations officer, and went to Fort Hood, Texas, for a tour of duty as the G-3 training officer of the 1st Cavalry Division and the operations officer of Task Force 1-32 Armor, a combined arms maneuver task force.

His last assignment with the Army was at the Command and General Staff College at Fort Leavenworth, Kansas. In January 1991, he reported to the 3rd Army, with which he served during Desert Storm. Resigning his commission after returning from the Gulf in the spring of 1991, he continues to serve as a lieutenant colonel in the Army's Individual Ready Reserve. He writes full time and has produced the following novels: *Team Yankee, Sword Point, Bright Star, Trial by Fire, The Ten Thousand, Code of Honor, Look Away, Until the End, Savage Wilderness, God's Children, Against All Enemies*, and *More Than Courage*.

PROLOGUE

Augustus 1942

On August 7, 1942, men of the Fifth Marines climbed over the sides of their landing craft and dropped into the shallow surf. Before them lay a picture-postcard view of a tropical island. From a distance the sandy beach, the lush green jungle, and the prominent hill that was their first day's objective seemed more like paradise than a battlefield. Only slowly would this and so many other illusions entertained by soldiers and leaders of both sides die on an island that would become known as Starvation Island.

This event also set into motion an advance that would end three years and eight days later with the complete and utter defeat of the Japanese Empire. The young Marines making their first amphibious assault of the war that morning had no way of knowing that their efforts here would lead to such a victory. The cruel fact was that since the Japanese attack on Pearl Harbor on December 7, 1941, American ground forces had known nothing but defeat. The only success of note that the American Army and Marines had managed to achieve at a terrible price during those eight months was to delay the advance of Japanese forces in the Philippines and Wake Island.

While those feats demonstrated that the Americans could fight, no event to date provided any proof that during the course of a campaign American troops could prevail over Japanese soldiers, who had been raised since childhood to serve and die for their Emperor.

It is all too easy for historians tucked safely away in their studies or standing behind a podium in cool, clean classrooms to pontificate on how American military might have made victory in World War II a foregone conclusion. Nothing can be further from the truth. Anyone who has taken the time to study war realizes that it is the soldier, the man charged with closing with the enemy and destroying him by use of firepower, maneuver, and shock effect, that decides battles. Even the most lavishly equipped army is of no value if its soldiers and the men selected to lead them do not have the courage and will to go eye to eye with their foe. In World War II, battles were often won not because one side or the other had superior weaponry or greater numbers, but because the men on the firing line and those who commanded them refused to be beaten.

The battle for Guadalcanal is well worth studying in detail because it is one of those rare occasions in military history that the fate of nations rested squarely upon the shoulders of a few good men. Decisions by the leaders on both sides during this campaign were made under combat conditions that are all but impossible to image. More often than not they were based upon fragmentary and erroneous information. Sometimes a leader had little to go on but his gut instinct. The decisions they made had a bearing on more than the outcome of the battle in which they were engaged. Their efforts would determine the course of the war in the Pacific Theater, for the fight for Guadalcanal was a campaign that could have easily gone either way. American commanders would not be confident of eventual victory until mid-November, while the Japanese did not face up to failure until late December. During that time American Marines and soldiers grappled with Japanese soldiers in a tropical hell. It was a battle that was brutal and uncompromising. In numerous small encounters and the heat of massive attacks, soldiers of both sides were pushed beyond the limits of human endurance and asked time and time again to go further. One such encounter took place in mid-September, when a brigade-sized unit under the command of Major General Kiyotake Kawaguchi met two understrength battalions commanded by Lieutenant Colonel Merritt A. Edson on a barren spine of land that would forever be known as Bloody Ridge.

ONE

Shortly after 0430 hours, Lieutenant Francis J. Pearson gave up the relative safety of the ancient destroyer transport and started to make his way down into the Higgins Boat tied alongside. While he grappled with the thick knotted rope of the cargo net, Pearson could feel other Marine Raiders who belonged to the platoon he commanded struggling to find footing or a handhold. Like their platoon commander, they were doing their best to clear the way for those behind them while at the same time taking care that they did not miss the Higgins Boat which rose and fell with each passing wave. Even when he felt his left foot make contact with the gunwale of the landing craft, Pearson knew this first challenge of the day was not over. One had to be careful to make sure not to let go of the cargo net before he had both feet firmly planted. To misjudge would either send him pitching backwards into the small craft and on top of those already aboard it or down into the sea between the steel sides of the fast transport and the Higgins Boat. The former would be embarrassing, the latter fatal.

Once aboard, Pearson made for the front of the boat as best he could. As an officer, that was where he belonged. Farthest forward and first out. Only when he shared a boat with his company commander or a battalion staff officer did he find he needed to yield this "honor." Today he would have it all to himself. In a few minutes, when the shallow-bottomed craft nudged its prow into the sand of the distant shore, Pearson would spring up and over the side of the Higgins Boat like a jack-in-the-box and into the shallow surf, ready to lead his platoon into whatever hell the Japanese had waiting for them.

But that was still in the future. For the next few minutes there would be little for him to do. Both Pearson and his men would be in the hands of the landing craft's coxswain and at the mercy of the Fates who governed the destiny of mere morals such as they with a capriciousness that was as outrageous as it was frightful. Francis J. Pearson had seen those fickle goddesses at work on Tulagi. While hunkered on the ground next to one of his BAR gunners, pointing out a target he wanted the man to take out, Pearson noticed that the man was making no effort to bring his weapon to bear. Angered, the young officer turned to face the man. Only then did Pearson notice that the BAR gunner's head was slumped over to one side. Aside from the glassy-eyed stare that saw nothing, only a small bright red dimple square in the middle of the man's forehead betrayed his fate. Though he was to see many other men die that day, that one particular incident spooked Pearson. Whoever had fired the shot that killed the BAR gunner had taken his time and aimed well. Pearson could not but help thinking that the same Jap could just as easily have dispatched him. Though he tried to tell himself such were the fortunes of war, the young Marine officer could not but help feel that no matter how good he was or how hard he tried, when the Fates decided that a man's time was up, there was nothing he could do to stop it.

The run in to the beach seemed to take forever. No one in the Higgins boat spoke as the huddled Marines crammed into the craft that swayed to and fro. There were no mysteries to ponder this time, no great unknowns to overcome. All their curiosity as to what would happen once they landed had been put to rest on Tulagi. On this day the only question that remained to be answered was how bad would it be?

There had been little time to prepare for this raid. Some of Pearson's men had even found it necessary to abandon meals they had been preparing. For men who were surviving on meager rations drawn mainly from captured Japanese stocks, that was a great sacrifice. Few took comfort in the rumor that the enemy they were expecting to encounter were poorly armed, starving, and warweary. Such rumors could not make the hunger a man felt disappear or allay the fears that threatened to rob him of his senses.

A sudden lurch forward telegraphed the news to all in the landing craft that it had taken them as far as it could to the beach. As one, the men along the gunwales leaped up and over the side, into the surf. Pearson was among the first to get his feet wet. After pausing only long enough to be sure of his footing, adjust his gear, and bring his .45 caliber. Reising up to the ready, the young Marine platoon leader flipped the safety off and charged headlong for the first patch of cover he caught sight of.

In this endeavor he was not alone. To his left and right men who were a bit more fleet of foot and equally concerned about their vulnerability splashed past him as they madly dashed forward. Throughout the furious race to negotiate the surf and get clear of the open beach, not a word was uttered. Every man present had done this so many times before, back at Quantico, Virginia, and on Samoa during training, that nothing needed to be said. Yet even the seemingly routine manner with which his men deployed and the eerie absence of enemy fire could not disguise the fact that this was not a training exercise. To a man, the Marines around Pearson waited for the first shot to be fired. Everyone expected it. The young platoon commander even found himself praying for it. Only then, when there was a clearly identified enemy against whom he could lash out, would he be freed from the awful tension that gripped him so tightly that he feared he would choke on his own bile.

But there was no enemy fire to greet them. The only noise that disturbed the predawn darkness was the splash of hundreds of feet sloshing through the surf and a hoarse chorus of gasping men driven by fear and physical exertion to gulp down mouthfuls of air while running forward for all they were worth. He was still in the water when Pearson saw that the spot he had chosen to head for was already being occupied by members of his platoon who had managed to dash past him. Having made no plans beyond exiting the Higgins Boat and going for that one piece of cover, the platoon commander slowed his pace, then stopped as soon as he was out of the surf. Looking this way and that, he scanned the beach for someplace that afforded any sort of cover.

He was in the midst of his search for sanctuary when he saw the tracks. At first he didn't see them for what they were. Only when he spotted a line of backpacks neatly laid out in rows just beyond the high-tide line did it dawn upon Pearson that his men and the other Marine Raiders were not the first soldiers to cross this particular strip of beach that night. The realization that fresh Japanese reinforcements were close at hand sent a chill down his spine. In an instant, he abandoned all thought of finding a place where he could hunker down and wait until the entire company was assembled and turned instead to find his company commander.

Pearson found that his superior, Major Nickerson, had already stumbled upon the fresh enemy tracks and jettisoned field packs. Both men agreed on what this meant. What the major didn't know with any degree of certainty was what impact their discovery would have on the raid that they were supposed to mount against Tasimboko, a village that lay about four thousand yards or so to the west along the same strip of beach they were standing on. For that decision, they would have to wait for their commander, Colonel Merritt A. Edson, who was coming ashore with the second wave. Until then, all Pearson and the other Raiders belonging to Company B could do was sit tight, keep their eyes and ears open, and pray for all they were worth.

By the time he made his way back to where his platoon had deployed to cover the shallow beachhead, Pearson found that some of the more stalwart individuals in his command had managed to shed their preassault willies and allow their curiosity to get the better of them. Despite the specter of imminent combat, a few were already busy poking about, examining the contents of the discarded packs and looking over an antitank gun that had also been abandoned. Pearson himself found that he could not resist the temptation to join his men in this impromptu inspection of their most unusual find. The scene reminded the young officer of the manner in which the Raiders themselves set aside their field packs at a rifle range they had marched to for training. Even the small gun had the look of a piece that was ready for a parade ground inspection and not a weapon that had endured the ravages of combat and the miserable tropical humidity that turned any uncared-for metal to rust.

The appearance of their battalion commander put an end to the sight-seeing and redirected Pearson's full attention back to the tactical situation that confronted his platoon. The examination of the abandoned equipment was now taken up by the battalion's Intel section, which included one of the least likely Marines in the entire Corps. Wearing thick glasses and skinny as a rail, John Erskine was initially rejected by the Marines because of his height. It was said that even if he stood on his toes he didn't reach the minimum required. But the man had one thing that the Marines needed desperately in 1941, the ability to read and write Japanese and an intimate knowledge of their culture. In short order, the son of a missionary who had spent his first sixteen years living in Japan was able to ascertain that the packs that had been discarded on the beach belonged to the Second Artillery Regiment of the Sendai Division, a unit that wasn't even supposed to be on Guadalcanal.

Yet as bad as this bit of information was, the sudden appearance of warships and a pair of transports emerging from the early-morning gloom just off Taivu Point sent a wave of alarm through the entire command. At that moment there were but three hundred Raiders ashore. The APD transports had yet to return with Company C and the understrength Paramarine battalion. No one needed to explain to Pearson or his men what it would mean if those warships and transports turned out to be Japanese. "Well, sir," one of Pearson's more cynical squad leaders said as he looked first at the unidentified vessels, then peered off into the jungle, "now I know what they mean when they say between a rock and a hard place."

Luck, however, was running with the Raiders that morning. Not only had their timetable delivered them at Taivu Point after the Japanese flotilla had brought in the Japanese gunners and departed, but the unexpected appearance of an American cruiser and pair of destroyers escorting two transports convinced the Japanese troops in the area that they were facing a major invasion. Though he did not know it, Edson and his small band of Raiders had been given a period of grace and a powerful psychological edge. This was further reinforced by the APD destroyer transports that had delivered the Raiders. On their way back to pick up the rest of Edson's force, the commanders of the USS *Manley* and USS *McKean* shelled the village of Tasimboko with their three-inch guns. Though the damage was minimal, this action served to enhance the impression that the one-day raid was actually a full-scale invasion. For a moment some of the defenders even managed to set aside the bushido code under which all Japanese soldiers lived and seek safety farther inland. Some, but not all.

Not wanting to wait until he had his entire command ashore, Edson began his march on Tasimboko, the objective of the raid. Although his battalion was already split, with only three companies ashore and the rest in transit, the bold and resourceful commander of the First Marine Raiders further divided it for this movement forward. While Company C, under the command of Captain Bob Thomas, held the beach and awaited the arrived of the rest of the battalion and the Paramarines, Captain John Antonelli's Company A struck inland in an effort to get around the flank of any resistance the Japanese might offer. Company B remained within sight of the coast throughout their westward movement. The lead platoon of this company was commanded by John Sweeney, an officer who had recently been promoted to captain but remained with his platoon. Pearson and his men followed.

The advance of Company B was slow, but not because of the terrain the Marine Raiders encountered. Along the coast the ground was quite level and the vegetation far less imposing than that found little more than a few hundred yards farther inland. There was even an occasional clearing in the undergrowth, a rarity on Guadalcanal. Pearson figured the reason for such a cautious pace was due to their commanding officer's being as spooked by the abandoned equipment and tracks they had found on the beach as he was. As if to reinforce his supposition, every few yards additional caches of backpacks as well as hundreds of discarded life preservers were spotted. They even came upon another antitank gun sitting out in plain view, as if waiting for inspection. All of this added up to something, something that even the dullest man in Pearson's platoon could tell was not at all favorable to them. After pausing but a moment to study the assortment of first-rate equipment trailing off in the direction of Tasimboko like bread crumbs dropped by Hansel and Gretel, Pearson took in a deep breath, tightened his grip on his Reising submachine gun, and pressed on. With each step he found himself wishing for something to happen, a wish not at all uncommon at such times but seldom fulfilled in a manner that is desirable.

The shot that shattered the dreadful silence wasn't recognized at first for what it was. Pearson was facing toward the rear of the column, checking to make sure his men were maintaining their proper distance, when something shrieked past him, cutting through leaves and branches and scattering their fragments behind. Before he could turn to look, a sharp crack from somewhere up near the front of the column shattered the early-morning stillness. It was followed by a detonation someplace in the rear of the column. Utterly confused, Pearson continued to look this way then that, trying to sort out what, exactly, was going on.

Gunnery Sergeant Karl Jacobi, his platoon sergeant, didn't need anyone to tell him what was going on or what he needed to do. Even as he dived for cover, he bellowed in his best drill sergeant voice, *"Hit the deck!"*

Responding to the order rather than the actual danger that had motivated it, Pearson complied. He dropped to the ground with such force that he all but bounced up. From somewhere behind him one of his men put in words the same thought that he himself was entertaining. "What the hell was that?"

Again it was Jacobi, known to all as Gunny Jay, who supplied the answer. "A Jap field gun. Now keep your head down and listen up for the lew-tenant's orders."

The last part of Jacobi's response struck Pearson. What orders? What was he suppose to be ordering his men to do? Hesitantly, he lifted his head just in time to witness the explosion of a second round, which impacted near the front of the column among Sweeney's lead platoon. Not until he heard the familiar crack of '03 Springfields and the deep hammering of a BAR returning fire did Pearson finally lift himself up off the ground a few inches and gaze at the line of prone Marines, who were looking back at him. "Stay low, keep your eyes open, and listen up." What he wanted them to listen for was beyond him. But given the present circumstances, Pearson figured it was the best he could do until he received an order from the C.O. to do something that fit the situation as it developed or deteriorated a bit further.

The engagement was taking place not more than a hundred yards ahead, yet it was completely out of sight, making the entire experience quite nerve-racking. Pearson could hear every shot as Sweeney's men deployed and brought more fire to bear on the enemy gun emplacement. The spattering of small-arms fire was punctuated every few seconds by other rounds from the enemy field gun, some of which found their mark among Sweeney's platoon and others that flew overhead as they went hunting for a target farther back along the column.

Determined that he wasn't simply going to sit there and wait for those damned Fates to draw his name, Pearson continued to look about as his mind raced to find something useful that he and his platoon could do. The obvious choice was a flanking maneuver, either to the left or right and around Sweeney's platoon. Since the beach was but a few yards to the right and offered little cover or room in which to maneuver, Pearson looked to the left, an option that would take them farther inland. Any effort on his part, he decided, would best be made by going that way. But how far he should go and when were questions he had no answers for. He wasn't even sure if he should take the initiative at all or simply wait for orders.

The young officer's tactical dilemma was resolved for him by the actions of the platoon in contact. Relying on good old-fashioned marksmanship, one of Sweeney's men managed to make his way forward to a spot from which he was able to put the enemy gunners under direct fire. After the young Marine fired two shots, each of which found its mark, a third Japanese gunner opted to seek safety in flight rather than die for the Emperor.

In the aftermath of the encounter that pitted a Marine Raider armed with a rifle type classified in 1903 against a 75mm regimental gun adopted into service in 1908, the rest of the day was a relative snap. In all, two Marines were killed and six wounded in sweeping aside what little resistance the Japanese rear guard offered in their defense of Tasimboko. For their efforts the Raiders were rewarded with a treasure trove of food, munitions, weapons, medical supplies, antitank mines, rubber boats with motors, communications equipment, and reams of raw intelligence left behind in what the Japanese had assumed was a safe rear area. Those Marines who managed to slip away from their squads and platoons for a few minutes helped themselves to tins of sliced beef and crab, while organized parties went about methodically destroying everything that could not be carried away. Even Richard Tregaskis, a war correspondent who was accompanying the Raiders that day, joined in by gathering up Japanese documents in a blanket and carrying them back to the First Marine Division's D-2.

Not every challenge a young officer is faced with in a combat zone involves life-or-death decisions. As soon as the officers were able to restore a modicum of order, Lieutenant Francis Pearson found himself charged with overseeing the destruction of the rice that was stockpiled throughout the area. This they accomplished in the most expedient way available. The Marines tore open the sacks of rice with their bayonets and spilled the contents onto the ground, where the mud, rain, insects, and incessant tromping of boots of other Marines in search of booty would do the rest.

While supervising his detail, Pearson could not help but notice that a number of his men not busy despoiling rice and other food-stuffs seemed to be sneaking about and darting behind corners of the native huts every time he glanced their way. At first he paid no attention to their behavior. It wasn't until he saw Gunnery Sergeant Jacobi leading three of the platoon's most notorious individuals down to the designated debarkation point on the beach along a rather circumspect route that Pearson became suspicious. Each man, including Jacobi, carried a partially filled rice sack close to his chest. Doing his best to act nonchalant, Pearson called out to his senior NCO, "Gunny Jay. Could I have a word with you?"

Like thieves caught in the beam of a policeman's flashlight, the four men stopped short and did their best to assume what they thought to be innocent poses. After whispering to his compatriots and handing one of them his rice sack, the gunnery sergeant shooed them along their way before jogging over to where Pearson was waiting. "Yes, sir. What can I do for you, sir."

"Dare I ask, Gunny, what's in those sacks?"

Straight-faced and without blinking, the twelve-year Marine veteran replied crisply. "No sir. You dare not."

"I see. Well, in that case, I find I have no choice but to rely upon your good judgment and common sense in ensuring that upon our return to Henderson things won't get out of hand."

Realizing that he was going to be allowed to keep the three cases of beer and half-gallon flask of sake that he had managed to secure, Jacobi smiled. "Oh, sir. You can bet your bars on that."

"Let's hope," Pearson replied dryly, "that it doesn't come to that."

"No, sir. I'll see to that."

"Okay, Gunny. Carry on."

Taking care to hide his joy, Jacobi took off at a trot to rejoin his foraging party. By 2200 hours that night, the tired but well-fed Raiders belonging to Pearson were enjoying the fruits of the day's labor in the relative security of the Marine lodgment at Henderson Field.

TWO

Unable to believe what he was seeing, sublieutenant Yoshio Sawa paused and blinked his eyes in an effort to clear them of sweat. When he had managed to refocus on the obstacle before him, the young officer examined the gigantic tree root that lay athwart his path. Still not sure that he was not imagining things, he looked back past the file of exhausted soldiers struggling under the weight of their equipment to catch up to him. Sure enough, not more than twenty meters back, Sawa caught sight of a tree root just like the one before him. Were it not for the fact that he could see the one he had just passed over mere moments before, he would have sworn that they were going about in circles and stumbling over the same damned tree root over and over again. Like everything else about the tangled jungle they had been moving through for days, nothing seemed to change. Each step just took them a little farther along, a little deeper into a labyrinth made up of gigantic trees that blocked the sun and nurtured a tangled chaos of vines, brambles, and thornbushes along the ground that seemed to reach out and snag anyone foolish enough to pass their way.

The young officer did not bother wasting his time scrutinizing the men behind him in an effort to gauge their condition. He had no need to. He knew how he felt, both physically and mentally, and didn't imagine that they could have been much better off. Instead, he returned to his examination of the root that blocked the trail before him.

Why, he found himself wondering, hadn't those leading the column simply gone around this obstacle? Why had they insisted upon plowing straight ahead without any regard to what lay in their path? A quick inspection of the terrain to his left and right quickly provided Sawa with an answer to those questions. It would not have made a bit of difference how the guides had gone. No matter which way he turned, his eyes were greeted with the same unimaginable morass of vegetation, rot, and stagnant pools. If anything, Sawa appreciated the fact that if the guides had attempted to bypass each and every obstruction, like this root, they would simply have added to the misery of those who followed by making an already meandering trail longer.

Resigned to the fact that he had no choice but to take on the offending tree root Yoshio Sawa once more stared at the obstacle before him. In the process of mustering the strength the task would require, the young sublieutenant found himself unable to keep his mind from drifting off in other directions. Along with his physical strength, his ability to maintain a sharp focus on the matter at hand was oozing away like the sweat that drenched him from head to toe. It has been a strange and twisting trail, he found himself thinking, that had led him to this wretched place.

Less than two years before he had been facing other barriers of an entirely different nature. In the summer of 1940, when he should have been preparing for his last year of law school, Sawa had found that the world he had been expected to enter no longer existed. It was as if he and his classmates suddenly were shaken out of a deep sleep only to find that everything they knew and understood no longer applied. Up until then the war in China had been the concern of the militarists. That all changed in the twinkling of an eye. Suddenly it was everyone's war. Events in Europe that had seemed so far away and of no interest to a student of the law were having very real and unpredictable effects on each and every citizen of Japan. Even his chosen profession no longer seemed to be relevant, as the national emergency that Japan faced caused the government to rewrite the law and the manner in which it dealt with its own people.

As with the tree root before him, Sawa and his friends had tried to find a way around the new hurdles being thrown before them on an almost daily basis. Only when it became clear that it would be impossible to follow the path he had set out upon did he face up to the reality of his times. With great temerity, not at all like that which he now felt, Sawa set aside his law books and took up the sword of an officer. It was, given his options, the only wise thing to do.

Wisdom and sanity, like circumstances, tend to change as time passes and one's place in the world drifts away from the known path of civilized man and into the dark wastelands of war. The young officer was reflecting upon this philosophical issue when he became conscious of the another's presence. Pushing aside his deep and misplaced thoughts, Sawa turned to notice that one of his soldiers was standing next to him, staring at the great tree root in much the same way that he had when he first came across it. Because the man was so close, Sawa found it necessary to crane his head back in order to focus on the soldier. When he took note of his officer's actions the man misunderstood them and jumped back, coming to a rigid position of attention as he did so. In anticipation of the blow he believed his officer was about to deliver, the soldier closed his eyes and braced himself to be slapped for being so impertinent as to stand shoulder to shoulder with a superior.

Like so many of those in his platoon, the man standing before Sawa was a simple farmer. Just as Sawa had been uprooted from all he knew, the former peasant had been swept way by the tides of war that had carried them all away and to this wretched place. Sawa imagined that while he had been plowing through books that codified the laws of civilized man, this poor fellow had spent his days tending to his pigs, chickens, and crops, day in and day out.

Now the two of them stood in a place neither could have imagined in his worst nightmares, joined by the common goal of finding other young men like themselves and killing them.

Sawa's conscious mind turned upon itself, admonishing him for allowing such whimsical thoughts to keep him from his duty. *You must not think such thoughts.* With the same strident tone that his training officers and his company commander used, this ever-vigilant voice from within reminded the former student of law that he was an officer in the Imperial Army, bound by the code of bushido. He had no time to entertain such irrelevant thoughts. Duty and the will of the Emperor were his masters now. Everything else meant nothing. Everything else had to be set aside until victory had been achieved.

In an effort to regain a correct posture Sawa made a threatening gesture that caused the soldier before him to recoil. Sawa had no intention of striking the man. He simply needed to make the man think he was going to do so in order to maintain the strict discipline that his commanding officer expected. Having thus reasserted himself and put the private in his place, Sawa turned, preparing to continue on. Then, as quickly as his sudden burst of martial spirit had appeared, it evaporated. The tree root was still there. It still needed to be surmounted.

Resigning himself to this sorry fact, Sawa slowly lifted his left leg and threw it over the root. Not only did this simple task take far more energy than it should have, but the need to take care as to where he placed his hands, feet, and legs during the maneuver complicated the seemingly simple task. Already he had fallen victim to a centipede during a similar crossing. Like every other inhabitant of this green hell, the nasty little creatures left their mark on the unwary. In the case of the centipede, its particular signature was a series of tiny yet painful wounds where every one of its tiny legs came into contact with human flesh.

Once he was fairly sure that the surface he would be straddling was clear of bugs and such, Sawa pulled himself up and over, ever conscious that the eyes of his peasant soldiers behind him were fixed upon him. It was times like this that the old Army saw, "Duty is heavier than a mountain," rang true. Duty was indeed heavy. If that were so, Sawa thought as he eased himself down onto the ground on the other side of the root, was the second half of the saying also true? Was death lighter than a feather?

Not wanting to ponder this grim thought and anxious to close up the gap in the column that his tarrying had created before his commanding officer noticed, Sawa brushed aside his foolish ruminations and mustered enough strength to break out into a trot. Like a senior sergeant calling cadence, the young Imperial officer took up repeating his own personal cadence under his breath with each footfall, "Duty—is—heavy. Duty—is—heavy. Duty—is—heavy."

Yoshio Sawa was not the only officer in the long serpentine column agonizing over his current plight. Though he did his best to maintain a calm demeanor, Major General Kiyotake Kawaguchi was beginning to have doubts about his ability to meet his own timetable for launching his attack against the Marine toehold as planned. Already many key elements of the plan he had laid out four days prior had either gone awry or failed to unfold as he expected. As if the destruction of so much of his supplies and the loss of valuable field pieces at Tasimboko weren't enough, the scattering of one of the battalions that he had insisted be brought to this island by barge further weakened his force. That unexpected development had forced him to acquiesce to an offer of additional troops that he had once refused. The experience had been a humbling one, like the struggle his brigade was currently engaged in against the jungle they were pushing through. Humiliating and frustrating.

The man who commanded the brigade comprised of units from the Kurame Division had expected the going to be both slow and arduous. Lack of local air superiority dictated that Kawaguchi move his main force deep into the jungle in order to avoid detection and attack from the air. This meant that every round of ammunition that would be used in the attack, every piece of the mountain guns tasked to support it, and every mouthful of rice needed to sustain his soldiers until they reached their objective had to be carried on the backs of his men. Such demands were part of every soldier's life. Kawaguchi expected those he led to meet every challenge without complaint, without question, and go on until victory was achieved. It was their duty to endure all the hardships that came their way and overcome every obstacle placed before them. But of late, Kawaguchi found himself wondering if perhaps there were simply too many obstacles being tossed into his path. Perhaps there was a point when neither will nor courage would be enough.

While making his way along the narrow jungle track in silence, the man charged with defeating the American Marines on this miserable island had a great deal of time to reflect upon these foreboding thoughts. While in Rubal he had exuded confidence as casually as the staff of the Seventeenth Area Army had. Both they and Kawaguchi had good reason to be sure of victory. In Borneo, Kawaguchi had met with nothing but success.

But this was not Borneo, the general reminded himself as he trudged along through the mud and stifling heat. There he had enjoyed easy victories against a pathetic foe who lacked everything, including overwhelming air and naval support. While it was true that the Imperial Navy controlled the seas around Guadalcanal by night, without air cover the Navy, like his command, had no choice but to scurry for shelter every morning when the sun appeared on the eastern horizon.

This pathetic state of affairs would not be corrected until the Rising Sun fell upon an airfield that was once more controlled by the Emperor's troops. Only then would the fleet be free to make good the losses in matériel and supplies that had been sustained at Tasimboko. Even more importantly, once Japanese aircraft were operating off the landing strip that the Americans had completed at Lunga Point, the Seventeenth Area Army would be able to return to its primary mission of seizing Port Moresby, New Caledonia, Fiji, and Samoa. Until then, both he and his men would have to slither about in the primordial muck, much like the deadly snakes and vicious insects that seemed to lie under every log.

THREE

Frustrated with his efforts to dig deeper into the coral crust he had spent the last hour gnawing away at, Francis Pearson rose on his knees, straightened his back, and looked about. Setting the entrenching tool he had been using on the tip of its dulled blade, the young Marine officer cupped his hands one over the other on the end of the handle before setting his chin on top of them. Ignoring the sweat that ran down his brow and into his eye sockets, Pearson gazed off into the jungle below.

Except for a think blanket of razor-sharp Kunai grass, the hogback or ridge their battalion commander had brought them to was bare. While following the narrow trail that ran along its crest one was treated to something that was rare on Guadalcanal, a view. Ranging in width from as little as fifty yards but never more than three hundred, the coral spine, which was shaped like a lazy S, stretched a thousand yards from the edge of Henderson Field in the north to where Pearson's platoon was digging in along its southern edge. After a brief interlude in a coconut grove near Lunga Point on the tenth of the month, this dominant piece of ground had become the home for the combined Raider and Paramarine battalion.

Well, at least for most of the Raiders. Some, like those belonging to Thomas's Company C, were off to the right, stretched out along a line that cut through a particularly nasty patch of jungle that lay between the lagoon where Company B's right flank was anchored and the Lunga River. While those poor souls had a much easier time as far as digging was concerned, the dense vegetation blocked even the slightest hint of a breeze. Besides exacerbating the stifling heat, the jungle down there left them with virtually no fields of fire except those the Raiders could clear with a handful of machetes and their bayonets. Lifting his chin off the handle upon which he had propped it, Pearson stared up into the sky.

Of course, Pearson concluded as he continued to look back at the top of the ridge, this was no heaven on earth either. Twice since their arrival Japanese bombers had paid them a visit, giving the lie to Colonel Edson's claim that this was a rest area. Even his dullest rifleman could see that this was, militarily speaking, prime real estate. And if he and the members of his platoon could see it, Pearson had little doubt that the commanding officer of those unseen Japanese whose supplies they had destroyed back at Tasimboko had to see it, too.

While he was pondering these troubling matters, Pearson felt a hand on his shoulder. Looking about he saw PFC William Sterling, his platoon runner, standing over him. "If you need a break, Lieutenant, I'll take a turn on the E-tool for a bit."

Rocking back on his heels, then onto his feet, Pearson grasped the shovel and turned it over to Sterling. "Be my guest. Just don't dig it too deep."

Kicking at the solid coral with the toe of his boot, Sterling grinned. "I'll keep that in mind, sir."

With that the young Marine officer set off on a tour of his line. The left of his platoon was held by First Squad leader Sergeant Russell Smith, a man who was not much older than he. Whether it was their similarity in age or the fact that they were, relatively speaking, new to the Corps, Pearson felt closer to Smith than to any of his other NCOs. Like Gunny Jay, the sergeants who led Pearson's Second and Third Squads were career Marines, men who had been busy learning their trade in the jungles of Nicaragua while Pearson was in high school trying to capitalize on his recent discovery that boys and girls were different. Perhaps that was why he kept the First Squad close at hand and sent one of the others whenever he had the need to send a squad farther afield. Since Gunny Jay said nothing about this particular habit, Pearson assumed that he was doing right.

The First Squad's left ended at the trail that ran down the spine of the ridge. Over on the eastern side of the trail was Company A of the Paramarines commanded by Captain William McKennen. To the right of the First Squad, occupying a spot that was about as commanding as any on the ridge, was a machine gun section that belonged to the Raider's Company E led by Corporal Allen Malin. In addition to the air-cooled .30 caliber machine gun, the section leader who was damned with an unfortunate name combination had managed to arm one of his men with a .30 caliber BAR and another with a Reising M-50 .45 caliber submachine gun. This additional firepower, the young officer reasoned, helped make up for the thinness of his line.

The center of the platoon's territory was held by Perry Mitchal's Second Squad. He was the quietest NCO in the unit. Not only did the man keep his own counsel unless he had something important to say, but even when angered, he never spoke above a whisper. Just that morning Pearson had witnessed that apparent contradiction when one of Mitchal's men, flustered by his inability to carve out a decent foxhole in the coral, threw down his entrenching tool and screamed that he wasn't going to waste another second trying. Without batting an eye, Mitchal laid aside his own E-tool, calmly walked over to where the enraged Marine stood, and grabbed the man by the collar of his shirt. In one smooth, deliberate motion, Mitchal lifted the Marine off his feet and held the astonished man inches from his face for several long seconds before the crusty NCO whispered, "Dig." With that, Mitchal put the man back down, watched as the stunned Marine retrieved his shovel, and waited until the man was back in his hole digging for all he was worth before returning to his own labors. Mitchal was a rock. If anyone could hold the center against the storm that Pearson expected to break upon them, it was Mitchal.

Pearson's westernmost positions were manned by Staff Sergeant Ken Carroll's Third Squad. Carroll felt that it was his purpose in life to make up for Mitchal when it came to gabbing. In civilian life Kenny Carroll would had been a con man. In the Marines he was one of those colorful characters who had bounced back and forth between private and sergeant so many times that some of the old hands joked he should use zippers to attach his stripes instead of stitches. Yet in a fight Carroll had the reputation for being a real no-holds-barred brawler. It was this particular characteristic that caused the commander of the Third Squad so much grief over his career and had led Pearson to select him to secure the platoon's critical right flank.

It wasn't until he had reached Carroll's squad that Pearson ran into Gunny Jay. The platoon sergeant had just come back from coordinating with the next platoon over, something Pearson had intended to do himself. Gunny Jay greeted his platoon leader with a nod. "Well, by tonight, we're going to be as ready as we're going to be."

Pearson didn't reply at first. Instead, he looked down at the fox-hole belonging to two men in Carroll's squad. "I want the men to go deeper."

Jacobi didn't bother inspecting that hole or any of the others. He already knew how deep they were. "Lew-tenant, I would like nothing better myself. But we can't keep going without a break. Unless you want every man jack among us to fall asleep by midnight and let the Nips come walking through here like nobody's business, they need time to sleep."

After a moment of halfhearted reflection, Pearson nodded. "Pass the word down the line. Have the men settle in, eat something, then rotate. Half awake, half resting."

Making no effort to hide his own weariness, Jacobi slowly nodded. "Aye aye, sir." With that, the two parted.

———

Pacing like an impatient cat, General Kawaguchi waited to hear from the three battalions that had made the long, arduous trek from Taivu Point to their designated assembly areas south of a ridge his staff called the Centipede. With night fast approaching and none of them where they were supposed to be, the only solace Kawaguchi managed to find in the pathetic state of affairs was the fact that he had, against his own better judgment, stayed with his decision to attack on the night of September 13 and not the twelfth as he had originally intended.*

This had not been an easy thing for Kawaguchi to admit. When he had departed Rubal, he had been so confident of victory that he had turned down an offer by the staff of the Seventeenth Area Army of an additional battalion. Only after he had arrived on this forsaken island did he discover that he had taken his task far too lightly. One by one, problems and misjudgments made by him and by the staff on Rubal conspired against him. Nothing was as easy as it had been imagined. His entire command lacked proper maps. The frightening nature of the jungle was unlike anything he had ever encounted. Even the incessant rain that pelted his command during a time of year that was supposed to be the dry season came as something of a shook.

Yet it wasn't until they were already committed to his plan of operation that Kawaguchi realized just how badly he had miscalculated the time it would take his units to cover the distance from the coast to the point from which he wished to launch his attack. His decision on the sixth to delay the attack by twenty-four hours had been a difficult one to make at the time in light of his boasts back on Rubal. But it had been a correct one, even in the face of a September 7 report disclosing that a convoy of troop transports bearing Marines had arrived in Fiji.

Now, after having endured a trek that would have broken lesser men, Kawaguchi was certain that he had made the right choice. He was just as certain of this as he was that his plan would succeed. Already embarrassed by the scattering of a battalion that had tried to reach the island by barge, a mode of transportation he himself had insisted upon, as well as the destruction of his base at Tasimboko, Kawaguchi had to succeed. Having overcome so many obstacles, he would let nothing stand in his way. Not the jungle, not the enemy air force, not even the two thousand Marines holding the airfield would keep him from securing a complete and crushing victory.

Exhausted, hungry, and completely disheartened, Sublieutenant Yoshio Sawa was far less sanguine than Kawaguchi was about their prospects of inflicting a smashing defeat upon the American Marines. He and his men would do well, he began to find himself thinking, simply to survive in this hellish place. After endless days of struggling with the jungle, Sawa felt as if he was nearing the end of his tether. *How can they keep going on like this?* he found himself wondering. His men were tough, as stoic and determined as any man in the Imperial Army. Yet there was only so much that a man could endure. There was only so much, Sawa reasoned, that one could ask.

But no one was asking anymore. From their commanding general all the way down the chain of command, every officer and NCO was *demanding* that their men keep going. All Sawa heard now up and down the line were admonishments to keep pressing on, keep marching, keep moving. And they did, one step at a time. Across countless rivers, along trails that did not deserve that title, and through torrential downpours. Together with his men, Sawa marched ever deeper into the all-consuming jungle.

"Ignore the hunger," a staff officer advised his men every time he passed Sawa's struggling platoon. "We will feast upon the food we take from the Marines."

"You have no need to rest now," Sawa's company commander admonished. "We will have plenty of time to rest once we have broken out of this jungle and reached the sea once more." That many of those men that he worked so hard to encourage would not find any rest here on earth was left unsaid.

Where the officers tended to use exhortations and promises to keep the men moving, the NCOs within Sawa's company relied on their sharp tongues and well-placed blows to drive their charges forward. Their exhortations had become so pervasive that the parrots perched in the trees above began to mimic the bellowing human taskmasters below. "Hay! Private! Keep Moving!" echoed through the jungle on the ground and from above. While some thought it funny, no one laughed when the annoying birds screeched out another common phrase, *"Hikoki!"* "Enemy Planes!" It did not matter what the source, this fearful warning sent officer and enlisted alike diving for the nearest cover, a fact that only added to the misery of all concerned and further slowed their advance.

On this day not even darkness brought an end to their struggles. In the jungle, where light was a rarity, the moonless night of September 12 turned the horrific march into an absolute nightmare. Men no longer marched because they had to, they did so out of habit. Sawa's world slowly shrank until it was reduced to an area no greater than the length of his own arms. Sometimes he went for an hour or more unable to see the back of the man who was not more than a meter before him. Only the sound of that man's labored breathing and his struggle to push through the jungle kept Sawa on the path along which his battalion was traveling.

What thoughts the former law student entertained during those endless hours of unspeakable suffering were almost as dark as the jungle that engulfed him. How was it possible that he had come to such a pathetic end? What great force had upended the neat, orderly world that he had worked so hard to become a part of? Surely this wasn't the work of his own people? While there were hotheads who dreamed of conquest and empires, the Emperor would not, could not allow them to lead his people into a war such as this.

No, Sawa told himself. It had not been his people who had brought this war on. Then and there he decided it had been the Americans. Had they not been so unreasonable, war would not have come. Had they simply understood and accepted the role that Japan played in the affairs of China, both nations would still be at peace. It was the Americans. *They* were the ones who were determined to deny Japan its rightful place in the world by insisting that Japan's army withdraw from China. *They* had been the ones who had imposed the embargo on steel and oil when his nation's leaders had refused to bow to the Americans' unreasonable demands. *They* were the ones who had left their homes and crossed the Pacific to take this island away from the Emperor. *They* were responsible for all of this. So, *They* would have to pay. Sooner or later Sawa knew this trail of misery would lead him to this unreasonable and barbaric foe. Soon the marching would be over and the fighting would begin. When that time came, Sawa pledged as he clutched his sword, *They* would be the ones who would die.

FOUR

The quiet and uneventful passing of night was greeted with a mixture of joy and foreboding by Company B. The seemingly endless hours spent alternating between fighting bouts of fear that the night jungle inspires and shaking off an all-consuming exhaustion that eroded one's vigilance were over for now. The Japanese had not come. Though no man doubted that they were out there and that in their own good time they would come, for the moment the world the Marine Raiders lived in was at peace.

That this tranquil interlude would not last long was a given. Even before the sun had crested the eastern horizon, the privates and lance corporals had collectively seen and heard enough to know that this day would not pass quietly. "Something" was up. Knowing their battalion commander, they had no doubt that this "Something" meant only one thing—they were going after the Japs.

The Marine Raiders, both Edson's First Battalion and Carlson's Second, had been organized, equipped, and trained to be elite strike forces. President Roosevelt himself had envisioned them as nothing less than an American version of England's famed commando units that had played hell with the Germans during Britain's darkest hours. Members of the fledging Raider battalions were even dispatched to England to observe commando training. But the Raiders evolved into something that was uniquely American. In part this was due to the men who commanded the first two units, and in part their final form and use emerged as a result of the debate within the Corps over the necessity of having units such as the Raiders. Many within the Fleet Marine Force saw the Raiders as nothing more than a publicity stunt, an effort to boost civilian morale in much the same way that Doolittle had in April of '42. According to them, any properly trained Marine could execute the sort of raids and special recon missions the supporters of Raider concept were envisioning. The creation of special formations, armed with exotic weapons and manned with the pick of the litter, was seen as wasteful and out of step with the true, long-term goals of the Corps.

Merritt A. Edson, nicknamed Red Mike because of the color of a beard he had once sported during the Banana Wars, understood the politics of the issue. He was astute enough to know that he needed to be flexible while keeping faithful to his vision. A true member of the Old Breed and a Marine through and through, Edson insisted that his battalion maintain the strict protocol and smartness that were hallmarks of the Corps. He was also a team player. These qualities muted much of the criticism opponents leveled at the Raider concept. They also allowed him to wield more influence than he might otherwise have.

Intelligence the First Marine Division's D-2 had garnered from Tasimboko and reports from native scouts led Edson to the conclusion that the next Japanese effort would come from the interior of the island. That view was shared by Colonel Gerald Thomas, the operations officer or D-3. Unfortunately, Major General Vandergrift did not concur with this assessment. He saw a counterlanding by the Japanese at Lunga Point or a major thrust along the coast from the east or west against the Marine perimeter as posing the greatest threat to the American lodgement on Guadalcanal. Since Vandergrift was the commanding general in both name and habit, he had deployed five of his six infantry battalions on either side of Lunga Point and along the narrow coastal plain. The sixth unit, Second Battalion, Fifth Marines was held back as a divisional reserve.

That left only the First Engineer Battalion, First Amphibious Tractor Battalion, and the First Pioneer Battalion to cover the southern portion of the perimeter. Surprisingly, none of those units occupied the centipede-shaped ridge that rose out of the jungle and pointed due north like a dagger at the center of Henderson Field. When Edson and Thomas presented to Vandergrift their operational estimate as to where the Japanese would attack together with the recommendation that Edson move his combined Raider-Paramarine Battalion up onto the ridge, the commanding general grudgingly agreed. In this manner a terrain feature that would have served the Japanese as an unimpeded highway right into the heart of the Marine perimeter on the ninth of September became a strongpoint that they would need to storm on the thirteenth.

Placing his combined battalion in a position where it would do the most good was not enough for Edson. His command was organized and trained to carry the war to the enemy, not simply to hold ground. Therefore, on the evening of the twelfth he gathered his company commanders together and laid out his plan for a spoiling attack to the south, an attack whose aim was to find and strike the Japanese before they had a chance to do the same to him. In the parlance of the day it was a "gutsy move," especially when one considered that it would pit Edson's eight hundred Raiders and Paramarines against more than twenty-five hundred Imperial soldiers that Major General Kawaguchi had gathered just south of the centipede-shaped ridge.

At first Yoshio Sawa took the crack of scattered rifle fire to be nothing more than random jungle noises. Only when the rip of machine guns and the thud of grenades joined in did he realize that the enemy was close at hand. Scrambling to his feet, he trotted toward a gaggle of anxious soldiers who had been stirred from their sleep by the growing sounds of battle. Like him, they were milling about and peering north into the jungle in an effort to see beyond the dense vegetation.

"Are we attacking already?" a bold private mused in a tone he was sure his officer could hear as both he and Sawa continued to stare at the unyielding jungle.

"No," Sawa snapped without having to weigh the question. "We attack tonight. It must be an enemy patrol that has run afoul of one of our outposts."

The private thought for a moment before nodding. "Ah, yes. I see."

Of course, like his platoon leader he didn't really see. No one who was with Sawa could see a damned thing. He was just accepting his officer's opinion as he continued to watch, listen, and wait.

Neither Sawa nor the private had long to wait. When it became clear that the engagement that had stirred them all from their fitful rest was more than a patrol brushing up against an outpost, the former law student stepped back from the group of soldiers he had been standing with and wearily looked to his left, then his right, in search of his company commander, Captain Tetsuzan Oyama. Sawa both feared and respected the captain, a professional soldier who had first seen action in China. Oyama would know what to do. He always seemed to know.

As if the mere act of thinking about him was enough to conjure up his superior, Oyama appeared. Walking calmly through the brush, Sawa's commanding officer clutched the scabbard of his sword as he slowly moved among his men and peered intently in the direction of the gunfire. When he was within a meter of Sawa, Oyama turned his gaze upon his worried subordinate. "Form your men into line of battle," he ordered with a casualness that belied his concern. "Be prepared to move forward on order. If we go in, the First Platoon will be on your right, Second to the left."

Snapping to attention, Sawa bowed his head slightly. "Yes, sir."

With that, Oyama continued on, moving off to the left, where he would repeat his order to the lieutenant commanding the Second Platoon. He showed no interest in explaining what was going on, and Sawa made no effort to inquire. The former student of law had his orders and something to do, which was good enough for him.

At some point during their move forward, Pearson had expected to come into contact with enemy outposts. These small clusters of lightly armed soldiers were a universal feature in war, deployed forward of a main line of resistance or assembly area to provide early warning and fend off small enemy patrols. When faced with a superior force, the soldiers manning such outposts are normally charged with firing a few rounds in an effort to cause the approaching enemy to hit the dirt and deploy. Having achieved that, in most cases the intrepid occupants of the outpost were free to slip away and make their way back to rejoin their now alert and well-prepared comrades before their foe was able to recover from their surprise and overwhelm them with superior fire or numbers.

The Marines leading Russell Smith's First Squad didn't give the Japanese they stumbled upon that option. Seeing no need to wait for a BAR gunner to come forward, the pair drew a bead on their foe and dropped them before they had a chance to make good their escape. By the time Pearson was able to make his way up along his platoon's line of march to a point where he could assess the situation, the one-sided firefight was over.

It quickly became apparent to Pearson that not every platoon was enjoying the same sort of luck his had just experienced. At the same time his point element made contact, the unit to Pearson's right hit another Japanese outpost. From the sounds of the incessant firing, that one was not only better manned, but seemed to be supported by at least one, and perhaps two 6.5mm Nambu light machine guns. Rather than diminishing, the fire grew in both intensity and volume. Even more ominous to the young Marine platoon commander was the fact that it seemed to be spreading.

Unsure of what to do next, Pearson listened for several minutes. Every now and then a voice could be heard above the growing din of battle. Most of the shouts he was able to make out were orders, quick sharp commands barked out by officers and NCOs struggling to deploy their men as quickly as possible. Mixed in with the orders bellowed by anxious and excited commanders were shrill screams of pain and desperate pleas for help from the wounded. When Pearson began to hear commands being given in Japanese, he realized that it was time for him to join the chorus, shake out his platoon, and brace for the coming storm.

Leaving his First Squad where it was since it was already partially deployed, Pearson started back along his platoon's line of march, issuing orders to his squad leaders as he came across them. When he came upon his Second Squad, which had been next in the line of march, the young Marine officer ordered its squad leader, Staff Sergeant Perry Mitchal, to move his squad off to the right, where the fighting seemed to be the heaviest. Not knowing what exactly was going on over there, he warned Mitchal to refuse his right and have his men hold their fire unless they had a good target. After Mitchal took off to place his men, Pearson continued on down the line, ordering Corporal Malin to take his machine gun section up to join the First Squad, where he was to orient his gun in the direction of where the Japanese outpost had been. He had just reached Sergeant Ken Carroll, who was in the rear of the platoon column with Gunnery Sergeant Jacobi, when a spate of fire erupted at the head of the column. The distinctive crack of '03 Springfields accompanied by the quick, short bursts of BARs contrasted with the snap of the Japanese 6.5mm Arisaka rifles. Taking only a moment to point Carroll off to the left, Pearson turned and ran as quickly as he could back to where the First Squad was engaging the enemy. Never more than a few steps behind him all the way was Gunny Jay.

Just before he reached Smith's squad, Pearson stumbled upon one of Malin's men lying in the middle of the fresh trail that the movement of his platoon had created during their advance. At first the young officer thought the man at his feet had gone to ground rather than continuing forward. Angered by the apparent act of cowardliness, Pearson kicked him with his boot, and yelled, "On your feet, Marine!"

When the figure didn't respond to his prodding, the young officer drew back. Bending, Pearson reached out, grabbed the man by his shoulder, and rolled him over. The lifeless Marine's mouth hung open as if frozen in the middle of a scream. His unseeing eyes gazed up into Pearson's. Unhinged by this sight and his unkindness to the dead, Pearson pulled away, stood up, and stared down at the dead Marine for a second. Only when the spreading sound of gunfire became too much for him to ignore did Pearson step over the corpse and continue on.

By the time he caught sight of Mitchal's First Squad, the exchange of fire was steady. Doing his best to ignore the distinctive *zing* of near misses that sailed past his head or smacked into nearby trees, Pearson peered over one of his own men lying prone on the ground in an effort to catch sight of the enemy. After several seconds of searching without seeing anything that remotely resembled a Japanese soldier, the young officer dropped to the ground and made his way over to where Mitchal was busily working the bolt of his rifle. "What the hell are your people shooting at?"

Stunned by this question, the veteran Marine rolled over onto his side and looked at his platoon commander. "Japs!"

"Where?"

Flopping back down onto his stomach, Mitchel cradled his rifle in one hand and pointed at a clump of vegetation not more that thirty yards distant. "Watch."

At first Pearson saw nothing. Then, after taking the time to concentrate on the spot that his squad leader had indicated, he saw a rustling of leaves followed by a muzzle flash. While he had been watching this, Mitchal had brought his own rifle up, aimed it, and fired. Remaining motionless the squad leader tried to determine if he had hit anything. Only after he was sure that the Jap he had been firing at was either dead or had moved to another spot did Mitchal slap the bolt of his Springfield with the palm of his right, grasp it, and jerk it back, sending a spent cartridge case sailing through the air.

"It ain't like banging away at the targets on a range, but it's better than sitting here with our thumbs up our asses."

Looking down the staggered line of Marines under Mitchal's command Pearson saw that they were doing just as their squad leader was. Only Malin, hammering away with his machine gun, made little effort to seek out discrete targets. Instead, he was relying on the traverse and elevation mechanism to control a grazing fire with which he was sweeping the area to his front. With his right hand he grasped his M1919 Browning light machine gun and fired a series of short bursts. After each burst, Malin twisted the traverse knob a bit to the left with his other hand before squeezing the trigger again. When Malin reached the limit of his sector of fire, he began to turn the traverse knob to the right. In this manner he put out a steady stream of fire that never rose more than a foot off the ground and saturated the entire area to his front with .30 caliber slugs. Snuggled up next to his corporal was the assistant gunner, feeding the belted ammo into the gun. To either side of this pair were the ammo bearers, both armed with automatic weapons they used to augment their section leader's awesome firepower while waiting to pass another box of ammunition to the assistant gunner. Only the persistent zing of enemy fire flying overhead and the dead Marine back on the trail served to remind the young officer that this was real combat and not just another live-fire exercise.

He was still huddled up behind Mitchal when two figures coming from opposite directions dropped on the ground to either side of him. To his left was Gunny Jay, coming over from where he had just finished watching Carroll deploy his squad. On the right was Captain John Sweeney, the former platoon leader who had taken over Company B when Major Lloyd Nickerson proved to be too ill to carry on. Without preamble Sweeney asked Pearson for an update on his situation. Not having had an opportunity to make his way along the entire length of his line, Pearson did the best he could. "I've got all three squads up in line, with this being the center. So far enemy fire is light, but it seems to be along the entire line. This is either a really big outpost or their main line."

Sweeney nodded. "Yeah, it's more than an outpost. We're to hold here and keep them occupied while Bob Thomas and Company C find a flank."

The first sensation that Pearson felt when he heard his company commander's orders was a sense of relief. They would not have to rise from the relative safety of the ground and go forward into the enemy fire. All his platoon had to do was continue just as they were. That other Marines led by young officers like himself would have to expose themselves to enemy fire didn't matter at the moment. Guilt over harboring such selfish thoughts only comes later, after the firing has faded.

Forlorn and seemingly isolated in the midst of the growing storm over which he had no control, Major General Kawaguchi's response to the unexpected confrontation between the three battalions that made up his central attack force and a large force of Marines ranged from anger to utter frustration to downright despair. As a professional soldier, he knew that war was not easy, that often battle was little more than an affair of chance. But in all his years he had never experienced anything like this. At every turn during the campaign all of his plans and efforts had been frustrated. Despite his best efforts, every time it seemed as if he had finally managed to master the situation, something unexpected occurred that caused it to slip away from him. *And now this!*

After storming forward a few meters, Kawaguchi stopped and peered off in the direction of the firing, which had matured into a general engagement. That he had lost the element of surprise, a key component in his plan of attack, was quite obvious. That the enemy force that had slammed into his slumbering command was no mere patrol was equally clear. Aside from that, Kawaguchi knew nothing with any degree of certainty. Unable to contact his battalion commanders, he could only guess as to what his subordinates would do in response to this latest turn of events.

Turning sharply upon his heels, Kawaguchi stormed back to where his staff stood waiting for his orders. Like him, they were of little value at the moment. Only after the situation had resolved itself one way or the other would the general have an opportunity to sort out the mess and begin the process of salvaging what he could of his plan.

With a suddenness that startled even the crustiest of Pearson's NCOs, a wave of Japanese emerged from the jungle before them with bayonets leveled. Accompanied by the shrilled scream of *"Totsugeki!"* the irresistible mass swept forward, giving the thin line of Marines facing it little time to rise off the ground and meet it.

Fighting an urge to recoil from the surging wall of humanity, Pearson somehow managed to make it to his feet and hold his ground. Tucking his submachine gun into his side, he aimed his weapon by turning his body and cutting loose with a steady burst at a group of three Japanese soldiers who seemed to have singled him out as their target. Gunny Jay, who had remained with him after Captain Sweeney had moved on, fished a grenade from one of his pockets, jerked the pin, and tossed it into the middle of another group off to the left. Corporal Malin, still working his machine gun, disconnected the traverse and elevation mechanism. Using the sight of the weapon itself to lay it, he methodically turned it on successive groups of Japanese as they rushed into his line of fire. Throughout these first frenzied moments the machine gunner continued to exercise great restraint as he unleashed quick, well-measured killing bursts.

Yet despite the best efforts of Pearson, Gunny Jay, Corporal Malin, and every Marine on the firing line, the Japanese could not be stopped. They were simply too close and too numerous. Stepping over and on the bodies of those who had been cut down before their very eyes, the following waves of Imperial soldiers surged forward and closed with Pearson's platoon. This collision of determined men gave rise to new sounds. Along with the crack of rifle fire and eruption of grenades a cacophony of human screams, shrill cries, angry epithets, and desperate pleas, mixed with the chilling crunch of bone being smashed by rifle butts.

Pearson was no longer able to piece together a comprehensive picture of what was going on around him. The best he could manage was a series of quick, seemingly disjointed images to which he responded. To his right he caught sight of a Japanese soldier impaling one of his men. Pinned to the ground by the long bayonet, the Marine wrapped his hands about the front hand grips of his foe's rifle as he bellowed, kicked, and twitched about violently. Swinging the muzzle of his Reising about, Pearson cut loose with a burst that caught the Japanese soldier square in the chest, throwing him back and away from his rifle, which remained firmly implanted in the stricken Marine.

Before he could do anything to aid the wounded Marine he had just saved, something else caught Pearson's attention. Bracing himself for a threat that he had yet to clearly identify, the young Marine officer spun about, firing blindly as he did. That seemingly rash response saved Pearson from being hacked to death by an enraged Japanese officer who was closing with him at a dead run. The enemy officer was so committed to his attack and so determined to kill Pearson that the .45 caliber slugs that ripped into him had no apparent effect. As the Japanese officer grasped the hilt of his razor-sharp sword high above his head, his momentum propelled him into Pearson, bowling the Marine over.

The blow of the enemy officer colliding with him and their uncontrolled impact on the ground knocked Pearson's Reising from his hand. Though stunned and pinned beneath his assailant, the young Marine officer somehow managed to pull his .45 pistol from its holster, jam it into the stomach of the man on top of him, and fire three quick rounds. With each discharge Pearson could feel the midsection of the Japanese officer jerk up for a moment before flopping back down onto the muzzle of Pearson's pistol. Only when he was positive that his foe was no longer able to harm him did Pearson cease fire.

"Lew-tenant! Are you alright?"

The distinctive pronouncement of his title and the sudden image of Gunny Jay standing above him as the Marine NCO pulled the body of the dead Japanese officer away was the first proof Pearson had that he had somehow managed to survive. Reaching up, he grasped the hand Gunny Jay was offering him.

Even before he was on his feet, his senior NCO stepped back and looked Pearson over. "Jesus Christ, sir! Are you alright?"

Looking down Pearson saw that he was covered in blood. Still badly shaken by his struggle with the crazed Japanese officer, he nodded. "Yeah, I think so."

Then, realizing that he was standing upright, the startled Marine officer jerked his head to the right, then to his left, searching for whatever new threat that might be coming his way. It took him a second or two to realize that the Japanese were gone. Well, he reflected as he cast his eyes upon the tangle of bodies strewn about at his feet, at least those who had survived were gone.

Sensing that his platoon commander was a bit confused and shaken, Jacobi reached out, put his hand on Pearson's shoulder, and explained the situation as it stood. "I don't know how, but we threw them back. As suddenly as they appeared, they were gone. We're still sorting out our own dead and wounded and taking fire, but I don't think it was too bad."

From where he stood Pearson could see three Marines lying on the ground, unattended and not moving. Despite the precarious position his platoon was still in and the incessant zing of bullets whizzing by, the young officer found himself wondering just exactly what Gunny Jay meant by "too bad."

"The captain said we're to stand fast and cover the withdrawal of the rest of the company," Gunny Jay added. "We're going back to the ridge."

To this, Pearson said nothing. In comparison to their current plight, he now saw the precarious line of defenses they had worked two days preparing as a veritable sanctuary. He would be glad to go back there, he found himself thinking as he collected himself and prepared to reassume command of his platoon. *Anywhere*, he figured, *has to be better than this spot.*

FIVE

The events of the afternoon were still fresh as Yoshio Sawa led his platoon forward to their final attack position. The brief but violent confrontation with the American Marines earlier that day had cast a pall upon an enterprise that in retrospect seemed to have been doomed before it had begun. The former law student could not imagine how the tired, hungry men who followed him, armed with little more than rifles and their courage, would be able to overcome the brutal firepower that had thrown their attack back that morning. While it was true that the mad rush they had made at the Marines was poorly organized, it was equally true that the Marines had been unprepared to receive it. Yet they had thrown his men back. If the Americans could achieve that while out in the open, what chance would his men have against Marines who were dug in?

Once more shrouded by the moonless night, the depleted ranks of Sawa's platoon crept on, following the lead of their company guide, who had scouted the route to their attack position before the sunset. They would not spend much time in that position. It was meant only as a control measure, a place where the company commander could organize his platoons into a proper offensive position and they could wait under cover until their battalion commander gave the signal to attack.

Sawa, however, had no desire to stop and wait. The events of the past few days had worn upon him, physically and mentally. He found that he no longer cringed every time he heard equipment being carried by one of his men bang together. The Marines had to know they were coming. Sawa was positive of that. No one was that stupid. Surely, American staff officers had managed to pull together enough evidence that the large force of which he was a part was about to fall upon them. They had to know that their ill-advised seizure of the airfield would not be allowed to go unchallenged forever.

So the young Imperial officer found himself chafing at the idea of sneaking about, the prospect of holding at the attack position angered him. Now that they were committed to this offensive, now that they were finally going forward, Sawa didn't want to stop. He wanted to keep going. If that meant that he would die, so be it. That sad fate was part of his duty, a burden that all Imperial soldiers must be prepared to shoulder. If anything, death would come as a blessing, one that promised to bring an end to a miserable existence. Duty, after all, was heavier than a mountain. Death, lighter than a feather.

Young Yoshio would have been startled by how similar his thoughts were to those his commanding general was entertaining at that very moment. Like his humblest of platoon leaders, Kawaguchi was also anxious to get on with the enterprise. Rocked by one unforeseen incident after another, the general had no longer any desire to hold back. Everything, he felt, had come down to nothing more than a simple roll of the dice. All his careful planning, all his meticulous preparation, all his insistence that they maintain the strictest of secrecy had been for naught. When the Americans weren't doing their utmost to frustrate his efforts, nature itself had done all it could to thwart him. Even now, the very darkness which he had counted on to cover his attack worried Kawaguchi. Darkness was an advantage. The pitch-blackness that engulfed them was not. Cowed by so many disappointments over the past few days, the general began to wonder how many of his units would become lost en route to their final attack positions. That, he mused, would be the final insult.

Casting aside those grim thoughts, thoughts matched only by the darkness of the night, Kawaguchi turned his mind to his plan. Closing his eyes, he envisioned a map that outlined all of the objectives his scattered battalions would soon be rushing forward to seize. With him, facing the southern rim of the Marine lodgement, were three battalions that comprised the main force of his command. Arrayed from right to left, this central group was made up of the Third Battalion of the 124th Infantry Regiment, the Second Battalion of the Fourth Infantry Regiment, and the First Battalion of the 124th Infantry Regiment. At 2200 hours the Third of the 124th would push north, moving along the eastern slopes of the centipede ridge to secure an objective at the northeastern end of the airfield's runway, which he dubbed "NI." They would then continue to the beach midway between Lunga Point and the Ilu River. Second of the Fourth would assault the centipede head-on, sweeping up onto the ridge and using it for the axis of their advance onto the center of the runway and beyond to two objectives designed "HE" and "NU" before going on to the sea. First of the 124th would follow the Lunga River until it broke out of the dense jungle that lay west of the centipede and struck the southwestern end of the runway. After securing a piece of high ground known as 15 Meter Height and marked as Objective "R," the First of the 124th would continue its advance to 35 Meter Height. There another of Kawaguchi's battalions, attacking from the west, would link up with the Central group. A fifth battalion, known as the *Kuma* or Bear Battalion, would attack from the east at the same time as all the others to pin and then roll up the Marines defending along the Ilu River. By dawn, if all went as he expected it would, the airfield would be cleared and ready to receive aircraft flown down from bases at Rubal.

None of his plans allowed for a reserve force. Kawaguchi had five battalions, each with eight hundred men. All five would go forward at the same time. Even before he had tried to take the jungle head-on, Kawaguchi had concluded that his opportunity to commit a reserve force at the right time and place during a night attack would be all but nil. So he made no provisions for one. Nothing would be held back. Every man would go forward at once.

All of that, of course, was now out of his hands. The time for him to influence the battle that was about to erupt was over. Having made his final dispositions after shaking off the effects of that morning's brief but bloody run-in with the Marines, Kawaguchi was prepared to step aside and allow his battalion, company, and platoon officers to secure the victory he had worked so hard to achieve.

Not far from where Major General Kawaguchi awaited the appointed hour of attack, another major general was also keeping his own lonely vigil. Having become painfully aware of just how right both Edson and his own operations officer had been, Major General Alexander Vandergrift used every precious minute his opponent and daylight gave him to brace his command for the coming storm. Leaving Edson's combined Raider-Paramarine Battalion on the centipede ridge, he ordered his reserve battalion, Second of the Fifth Marines commanded by Colonel William J. Whaling, to take up blocking positions south of Henderson Field between the runway itself and the northern edge of the centipede. Their job would be to serve as a backstop should any Japanese forces make their way past Edson's positions and emerge to the north.

To support both Edson and the Second of the Fifth Marines, Colonel Pedro de Valle, commander of the Eleventh Marines, the divisional artillery unit for the First Marine Division, brought every gun he dared to bear. To direct their fire, forward observers were located with both Edson's command and the Second of the Fifth Marines.

One change that Vandergrift refused to make during the last frantic hours was the displacement of his headquarters. The divisional CP had originally been located near the airfield, a place where it was subjected to daily air attacks directed at the airfield. On the tenth of September, it had been shifted to a spot in the northeastern lee of the centipede ridge, a location selected because of its relative safety. It had been this move that had allowed Colonel Thomas and Edson to conspire and move the Raiders and Para-marines onto the centipede. Though he was now having second thoughts about the move, Vandergrift refused to back down now.

Not satisfied with these preparations, Thomas met with both Colonel Clifton Cates, the commanding officer of the First Marine Regiment, and Colonel Leroy P. Hunt, who had the Fifth Marines, to advise them of the situation. During his discussions with each of these men, Thomas asked that they be prepared to dispatch some of their units south to reinforce the Second of the Fifth Marines at the airfield if, as he said, "things don't go well tonight for Edson."

On the ridge itself Lieutenant Francis Pearson woke with a start. It took him a moment to orient himself and appreciate the fact that night had fallen. It took him a bit longer to realize that not only had he somehow managed to drift off to sleep, but his runner, who shared the foxhole with him, had as well. Reaching across the tight confines of their shallow defensive pit, Pearson shook Sterling.

In a flash the young PFC was wide-awake, gripping his weapon and leaning against the forward lip of the foxhole searching for targets. "Are they coming?" he whispered when he didn't see any-thing right off.

"No, not yet," Pearson replied in a low voice. "I was just waking you, that's all."

Sterling was the sort of Marine that didn't need to be yelled at. He was forever doing his utmost to please his superiors, doing things that needed to be done before having to be told to do so. That quality, together with his speed and agility, were what had recommended him to Pearson. Ashamed that he had been caught dozing off, Sterling bowed his head and sheepishly apologized. "I didn't mean to conk out like that, sir. I just sort of . . ."

"Don't sweat it, Sterling. So did I. Just make sure that neither one of us does it again, okay?"

Having settled that issue, Pearson hunkered down and resumed the vigil he had been keeping before it had been interrupted by his unplanned nap. He didn't have long to wait.

SIX

The drone of a single aircraft broke the eerie silence that had fallen over the Marine lodgement. The unmistakable chug of the plane's engine identified it as a Japanese float plane, the sort launched from cruisers and battleships for spotting and reconnaissance. To the Marines all such float planes were known collectively as "Louie the Louse." While its name was somewhat of a joke, the appearance of the float plane was not. Louie was the harbinger of death and destruction. As with so many other aspects of the struggle for Guadalcanal, the Marines could do little but endure Louie and the suffering that followed in its wake.

Traveling at a stately pace, the float plane made its way across the narrow strip of land controlled by the First Marine Division. As it approached the northern tip of the centipede ridge, it began to drop green parachute flares. Just offshore, gunnery officers aboard the light cruiser *Sendi* and destroyers *Shikinami*, *Fubukl*, and *Suzukaze* used the light thrown off by these illumination devices to lay the main batteries of their respective ships. At 2130 hours the command to fire was given, shattering the still night and initiating Kawaguchi's long-awaited counteroffensive.

During previous visits by the Imperial Navy, Henderson Field had been ground zero for these nocturnal bombardments. Tonight, however, the occupants of that contested strip of land were spared for the moment. Instead, the six-inch shells of the *Sendi* coursed their way to the ridge where Edson and his polyglot force of Raiders and Paramarines waited.

Unchallenged by American warships, the small Japanese flotilla brazenly paraded back and forth off Lunga Point, spewing out shells at a steady cadence. Aboard each ship sailors toiled belowdecks in powder magazines, manhandling projectiles onto mechanical elevators that hoisted them to the sweltering confines of the gun turrets. There, their shipmates rammed the shells home into the waiting maws of their ship's guns before bracing themselves for firing. On the ridge, Lieutenant Francis Pearson and his platoon were utterly powerless to stop them. Their only recourse was to seek what safety they could in the shallow holes they had scraped into the coral hide of the centipede. None of the Marines took much solace when any Japanese shell missed the ridge completely and sailed harmlessly overhead into the jungle, causing much grief to the Japanese infantry massing for attack.

All told, the naval bombardment lasted twenty minutes. This preliminary to Kawaguchi's ground attack was immediately followed by a second barrage from six 75mm howitzers that Kawaguchi's gunners had managed to haul forward from Taivu Point. In conjunction with this renewed shelling, a shower of smaller flares were launched skyward from the ground just south of the Marines' positions on the centipede-shaped ridge. Unlike those dropped by the float plane during the course of the naval shelling, these were signal flares sent aloft by battalion commanders to alert their subordinates that the time to go forward had come.

At first there was nothing resembling a coherent or overwhelming attack. Rather than coming forward en masse, the attack began with gibbering voices and shouts that pierced the darkness.

Some of these noisy assailants used broken English to hurl defiant oaths or challenges at the nervous Marines. Knowing full well that the purpose of these random and seemingly ill-advised outbursts was to draw fire and thereby give away their positions, the Raiders simply watched, listened, and waited.

From his foxhole, Pearson peered over the edge into the jungle below, straining his eyes in an effort to catch a glimpse of the enemy host that was by then close at hand. During this strange interlude, a spattering of small-arms fire broke out along the line of outposts each Marine company had sent forward. Sometimes the exchange was fitful, almost hesitant, as single rifle shots were traded back and forth. Other confrontations between the Marines manning the outposts and the Japanese soldiers easing their way forward erupted with a sudden and all-consuming violence. Eventually these little pitched battles faded as the Marines occupying the outpost line withdrew to the main line of resistance, hid in the dense undergrowth to avoid detection, or were overwhelmed and dispatched by their assailants.

Sensing that their moment was at hand, Pearson passed the word to his left and right. "Get ready. They're coming." Turning to the forward observer from the Eleventh Marines, who had scraped out a position just behind Pearson's, the Marine lieutenant ordered him to alert the 105mm howitzer batteries that he would soon have a target for them. "Don't wait for me to ask," Pearson told the FO. "Feel free to lay it on as thick as you please."

The young Marine officer had no sooner finished making this statement than a fresh volley of ground-launched flares lit the sky above his position. Unlike those which had preceded it, this shower of flares elicited an immediate and stunning response. From the jungle below and across the entire front of Pearson's platoon half a dozen voices rose up as one with the shrilled cry of *"Banzai!"* In response to this call to battle, hundreds of excited voices echoed the exhortation before stepping off into the attack at a dead run.

For a moment all Pearson could do was watch as he tried to shake off the shock that this ancient war cry evoked. Then, rising onto his knees and leaning out of his foxhole as far as he could, he leveled his Reising submachine gun and flipped off the safety while he bellowed out his own response. *"Open fire! Open fire!"*

There had been no need to repeat the command. His second "Open fire," was drowned out by a hail of fire all along Company B's front. The report of no individual weapon could be heard, not even the Reising he himself was firing. Detonations of grenades, both those tossed downhill by his men and the grenades launched by the Japanese in return, using their strange 50mm knee mortars, were masked by the pulsating din of battle. Only the whine of 105mm shells passing overhead cut through the cacophony. When he heard the shriek of friendly artillery overhead, Pearson held his fire so as to observe its effects. In awe, the young Marine officer watched the impacting shells light up the jungle below, silhouetting the waves of screaming Japanese soldiers surging forward toward his position. When he saw that the leading edge of the enemy formation closing on his platoon's positions had not been affected by this initial volley, Pearson spun about and yelled to the FO behind him. *"Drop one hundred! Fire for effect!"*

The Marine artillery spotter had also observed what Pearson had and understood what was happening. And while he would have made a less radical shift in fire for fear that it would hit some of Pearson's own men, the artilleryman passed on the command.

Having done all he needed there, Pearson turned his attention back to the front. The Japanese were closer now, alarmingly close, and coming on without any sign of letup or hesitation. Even in front of Malin's machine gun, where the soldiers of the second wave were stepping on the backs of those cut down before them, the Japanese were gaining ground. With his men already firing as fast as they could work the actions on their rifles or feed more rounds into their automatic weapons, Pearson had nothing to do other than keeping the trigger of his own gun down and feeding it fresh magazines as quickly as his fingers allowed. He had no interest in counting the number of men he cut down. Once they were down, the dead and dying were unimportant, no longer a threat. It was the ones who were still on their feet, still screaming like lunatics as they pressed forward brandishing bayonet-tipped rifles and howling incessantly all the way, who mattered. "Just keep firing," he shouted over and over again, not knowing if he was admonishing his men, talking to himself, or simply pleading with his submachine gun. "Just keep firing."

Then, in the twinkling of an eye, the entire landscape before him was torn apart in a sheet of flame that rocked both him and PFC Sterling back on their heels. Stunned by the effects of his own artillery, Pearson was tempted to dive for the bottom of his foxhole and safety. He didn't. Instead, he managed to turn once more to where the shocked FO was reeling from the effects of the 105mm rounds that had barely missed them. Reaching out of his own foxhole Pearson grabbed the man by the arm. "That's perfect! Repeat! I say again repeat! Tell them back there to keep marching it back and forth just like that!"

Within seconds of commencing their advance, Sawa's company was raked by a storm of enemy small-arms fire that carried away the man who had been standing right next to him. This calamity made no difference to the young officer. With sword held high above his head and waving madly about in the air, he repeated his commanding officer's cry of *Banzai* and threw himself forward without a second thought.

The immediate aim of Captain Oyama's company was to pierce the enemy defensive positions that lay in the low ground just east of the centipede ridge. Oyama instructed his lieutenants to use the high ground to their left as a guide. "If you keep the ridge in sight as you go forward, you will not get lost." Having spent endless days moving through the jungle without having any clear idea where he was, Sawa was pleased that they would have a landmark such as the centipede during the course of the attack. After all, he told himself, he would have far more important things to worry about when they went forward.

It wasn't until they were actually committed to the attack that Sawa discovered how quickly all of the worldly concerns and trepidation he had been harboring for days simply evaporated like the morning mist. There was nothing that he needed to do. All the decisions had been made for him. He had no need to direct his men or tell them where they were to go or what was expected. Just as he was following Captain Oyama, they were following him, screaming as loudly and lustily as he was. It was as simple as that.

It was also very deadly. Their forward movement unleashed a barrage of enemy fire that was devastating and continuous. Up ahead, beyond his commanding officer Sawa could see a line of flashes that lit up the enemy positions like a string of animated fireflies. Even in his excited state he could hear and almost feel the zing of enemy rounds as they whirled past his head. Somehow in the midst of everything going on around him, the distinctive thud that fast-moving lead bullets make when they slam into human flesh and bone managed to penetrate the deafening roar of battle.

On they went. Men all around him were hit by enemy fire and thrown back as if they had been punched by a great invisible fist. Perhaps Sawa found himself thinking he could be next. It did not matter, he told himself. He was doing his duty in a manner befitting a servant of the Emperor. If he were to die here and now, he would take an honored place among his ancestors. It was in the midst of this chaos that Sawa realized that the old saying was true. Death was lighter than a feather.

Up ahead, Captain Oyama continued to set the pace for his company. Turning his head without making any effort to slow his pace, Sawa's commanding officer lowered his sword and pointed it back at the mass of soldiers following him. Holding his arm straight out and at his side, he made a wide sweeping motion until he had brought his sword back around to his front. Pointing it at a gap where there seemed to be no enemy fire, he yelled to all who could hear to make for that point. While he was unable to hear Oyama's orders, Sawa understood the significance of his commanding officer's action. Repeating his captain's gesture, Sawa angled off in that direction and, taking care not to hit any of his men with his sword, he pointed for the point at which they were to penetrate the enemy positions. "Over there!" he yelled as loud as he could. "Follow me over there!"

In his excitement, Sawa took scant notice of the deafening explosions that tore through the ranks of the company following his. The screams of men being torn to shreds by tiny shards of steel shell fragments was drowned out by the thunderous crash of high explosives. Even Sawa's own words, *"Totsugeki!"* (*"Charge!"*) and *"Banzai!"* repeated again and again were swallowed up by the clamor and tumult of battle. From out of the green hell that had dominated his every waking hour since arriving on this godforsaken island, the former law student continued his unflinching advance into a man-made one.

From his forward command post just behind his Company A, Colonel Merritt Edson was able to monitor the flow of the battle. With great satisfaction he took John Sweeney's report that Company B had thrown back the first massive attack with heavy losses to the enemy. Company A of the Paramarines also was able to communicate that they were managing to keep the enemy at arm's length. Unfortunately, both the commander of that unit and that of Company C Paramarines deployed down in the jungle to the east of the ridge relayed their fear that large numbers of enemy soldiers were finding gaps between their platoons. Hammered by repeated attacks and fearing that his two companies holding the left of the line would be isolated by enemy troops who were pouring through those gaps, the commander of the Paramarines ordered both Company A and Company C back.

Successfully withdrawing under pressure at night is extremely difficult. Doing so while enemy troops are in the process of penetrating your lines makes it all but impossible. The second line of positions that Edson had established in the middle of the centipede ridge were there to keep the whole line from collapsing if the first line could not hold. In theory, the Marines from the forward-deployed units would pass through the units manning the second line. Once in the rear and out of the immediate line of fire, the officers and NCOs of the withdrawing units would rally their men, reorganize them as best they could, and stand by to go forward either as reinforcements or as part of a counterattack. That was what Torgerson intended to do with companies A and B.

No sooner was the American withdrawal getting under way than a Japanese soldier threw a smoke grenade among the Paramarines. Already teetering on the edge, some of the Paramarines were panicked by the sudden and inexplicable appearance of a dense cloud of smoke. When someone yelled "GAS!" a stampede of terrified men all but swept away Edson's entire left flank. Eventually Paramarine officers and the heroic efforts of Major Kenneth D. Bailey of the Raiders brought an end to the rout and restored order within the ranks of the Paramarines. Unfortunately, by the time they did, the damage had been done. For several precious moments, Lieutenant Colonel Kusukichi Watanabe's Third Battalion, 124th Infantry was left unchallenged and unchecked. Surging forward, they sideswiped Edson's second line and continued north toward their first objective of the night, the northeastern edge of the runway.

Nor was their breakthrough the only crisis facing Edson. Whereas his Company B on the ridge had comparatively good fields of fire, Company C of the Raiders, commanded by Captain Bob Thomas, had virtually none. Located on the extreme right of the line, Thomas's men were in the dense jungle that filled the area between the Lunga River and a small lagoon. The Japanese soldiers belonging to the First Battalion of the 124th Infantry were on top of Company C before the Marines were able to fire more than a few rounds. Though the fighting was vicious and heroic, the sheer number of attackers decided the issue. Three things kept the collapse of Company C from turning into a total disaster.

The first was the horrible price the Raiders extracted from their assailants for their success. Even when there was no longer a coherent front line, pockets of Raiders and individual Marines continued to fight where they stood. The cost of this stubbornness to the Japanese was counted in more than simple casualties. The First of the 124th began to lose its cohesion as companies, platoons, and small groups of soldiers ceased advancing and turned instead to eradicate pockets of resistance that lashed out at them.

The next obstacle the Japanese faced in the confined space between the Lunga River and the ridge was Marines belonging to Company D of the Raiders and the First Pioneer Battalion. In the

Corps every Marine is a rifleman. The men of the First Pioneer Battalion were no exception, and they proved it that night. Together with the thirty-five Raiders of Company D, the First Pioneers continued the frightful attrition that Company C had begun, as contributing to the total loss of whatever structure the First of the 124th had managed to maintain up to that point.

The final factor that kept the First of the 124th from achieving anything of significance was the jungle itself. Within the Marine lodgement there was perhaps no place where the jungle was thicker and less navigable than in the low ground between the Lunga River, the lagoon, and the ridge. Already scattered by the vicious fight in which they were engaged, the Japanese became hopelessly lost in the tangle of vegetation made even more frightful by fierce Marine resistance. Though some Japanese officers finally did manage to make their way through this hell, they had few soldiers with them and absolutely no overall command structure. The Marines belonging to the reserve battalion deployed south of the airfield had no trouble driving those pitifully small groups back into the jungle from which they had emerged, one by one.

The same, however, could not be said over on the eastern side of the ridge, or even on the ridge itself.

It took Sergeant Russell Smith several minutes to realize what was wrong. Japanese soldiers who had been throwing themselves against his squad's position suddenly stopped coming at them head-on. Instead, he began to notice that they were sliding off to his left. Only when his men ran out of targets to their immediate front and ceased fire did it dawn upon the leader of Pearson's First Squad that there was no firing coming from the Paramarines dug in on the other side of the trails despite the number of Japs who were going over there. Fighting the urge to jump up and run over to the left to check things out himself, Smith called down the line to the two men he had posted over there. "Hill, Mossier! What's going on over there? Are the Paras still in their holes?"

After several long seconds Mossier called back, keeping his voice as low as he could while still being heard. "There ain't no one over there, Serge. They're gone!"

Stunned, Smith didn't know whether he should redeploy his men to cover his open flank or report this hideous piece of news to his lieutenant first. "Hill, Mossier! Watch your left. Everyone else, odd man face to the rear." Having done the best he could within his own squad, Smith crawled up out of his hole and headed off to find Pearson.

Both Smith and Captain Sweeney descended upon the young Marine officer within seconds of each other. Deferring to the breathless company commander, Smith held back as Sweeney informed Pearson that Company C of the Raiders had been broken. "There's Japs all over the place down there," he stated, doing his best to remain calm. "I'm refusing the right and bringing it back up onto the ridge."

Unable to hold back, Smith blurted out his news. "The left is gone, too. The Paramarines have pulled out."

Stunned, both company commander and platoon commander looked at Smith. Appreciating their state of mind, Smith reinforced the urgency of the situation his squad faced. "There ain't no one over there but Japs, and there's nothing I can do to stop 'em."

In the midst of this crisis a voice was heard coming from the direction of where Edson had his forward command post. "John Wolf, do you hear me?"

John Wolf was the code name that Sweeney had been assigned for use when communicating via radio, and the voice belonged to PFC Walter Burak, who was part of the battalion's communications section. Sweeney yelled back that he could. Burak then relayed his commander's message in the only way he knew how under the circumstances. "Red Mike says it's okay to withdraw."

Relieved by this timely intervention, Sweeney turned to Pearson. "Hold here while I get everyone else to the right on the move. Then break contact and follow as best you can."

Though he didn't much like the last part of his orders, the part that went "as best you can," Pearson had no choice but to respond, "Will do," and wait for his turn.

SEVEN

Pressing on, Yoshio Sawa paid no attention to how many of his men were still with him. His only concern at the moment was finding his company commander. To do so he needed to keep going forward as quickly as his ebbing strength and the jungle he was pushing his way through would let him. The young platoon leader had lost track of Captain Oyama when they had literally stumbled upon a lone Marine who had resolved to fight to the death.

The one-sided skirmish had been quick but vicious. One minute Sawa was making his way forward, the next a Marine jumped up from out of nowhere right in the middle of Sawa's platoon, firing his submachine gun. The exclamations of surprise mingled with the cries of those who were being cut down. Startled and enraged, Sawa spun about and pushed those who had been following out of his way. When he came face-to-face with the Marine, the man had just finished discarding an empty magazine and was reaching for another. Seizing his opportunity, Sawa brought his sword up over his head and rushed forward. Using every ounce of strength he could muster, the former law student brought his sword down, catching the Marine where the neck and the shoulder meet.

With an ease that seemed unreal, Sawa's blade cleaved its way through bone and flesh, sending the stricken Marine to his knees. Drawing his sword back, Sawa raised it and repeated his blow again, and again, and again. Even when the dead Marine toppled over onto the ground, Sawa continued to hack away at the corpse, propelled by an anger that he had never felt before. Only when he felt a hand on his shoulder did Sawa snap out of his fit of rage. "He is dead, sir," a voice whispered.

Shaken by his exertions and the frenzied attack, Sawa stepped back, still holding his sword above his head, ready to strike again. He did not know who had stopped him. For the longest time he didn't take notice of what was going on around him. He simply stood there with his ancient weapon held aloft, looking down upon the mutilated body of a man he had just butchered. Only slowly was he able to regain his composure, relax his stance, and turn his attention back to the tactical situation at hand. By then his company commander was nowhere in sight. In the brief span of two minutes, maybe less, Sawa and those men who were still with him had lost contact with everyone else in their company. It was only when he came to appreciate this that Sawa turned away from the slaughtered Marine and continued his advance north.

During the course of his search for Captain Oyama, Sawa could hear the sounds of other units moving about through the dense jungle. Whether they were Japanese or Marines was impossible to tell. Every now and then there would be a sudden eruption of small-arms fire as one party of soldiers ran into the enemy, much as had happened to Sawa and his small band of followers. Not knowing where to direct his men or their fire, Sawa chose to avoid any skirmishes and continue toward his objective.

His advance was brought to an abrupt halt when he came across a group of Japanese soldiers standing about in a small clearing. None of them paid him any attention. Instead, they continued to pick through a stack of boxes that littered the clearing. "What are you doing,?" Sawa demanded in his best officer's voice.

Like children caught making mischief, the soldiers nearest Sawa stepped away from him before snapping to attention. It took one of the bolder among them to explain. "Food, sir. We found this enemy food and were . . . we were eating, sir."

Stepping forward, Sawa looked into one of the open boxes. Reaching in, he retrieved a tin. Turning it this way and that, he studied it for a minute. Then, before he knew what he was doing Sawa laid aside his bloody sword and began searching his pockets for a small pocketknife he always carried.

Taking their cue from the platoon leader, the dozen or so men who were still with Sawa rushed in among the others already standing around the stack of boxes and grabbed what they could.

The three hundred Raiders and Paramarines Edson managed to rally around the portion of the ridge known as Hill 123 were in desperate straits. Ammunition was low, morale was sagging, and reinforcement was, under the circumstances, all but impossible. The only thing that there seemed to be plenty of was Japanese. Not only were they now pouring down the ridge from the vacated positions along the southern tip, but small groups kept popping up out of the jungle that covered the western slopes of the ridge.

Still, the Raiders and Paramarines fought on, resorting to bayonets and rifle butts when all else failed. In the effort to hang on to the ridge, they were supported throughout the night by the guns of the Eleventh Marines. When Colonel de Valle's batteries were no longer able to receive clear fire missions from forward observers who were either dead or fighting for their lives with Edson's men, the fire direction centers responded to whatever appeal for help they received, no matter how vague. One battery spent an hour simply sweeping the crest of the ridge back and forth. Its guns shifted a little to the left, then a little to the right, laying down a curtain of steel just south of where the Raiders stood. Those Japanese who were foolish enough to brave that fire found that personal courage was no match for high explosives.

Shortly after midnight even that support was threatened. Though bloodied and badly disorganized, the soldiers of Watanabe's Third Battalion, 124th Infantry were still advancing just east of the ridge.

It wasn't long before scattered and determined clusters of Imperial soldiers began breaking free of the jungle. Often led by an officer, these ad hoc mobs fanned out, initiating a rampage that threw the rear areas behind Edson's embattled command into confusion. Gunners who had been diligently serving their howitzers one minute suddenly found themselves under assault from raging Japanese soldiers bent on revenge. Using anything they could lay their hands on, the men of the Eleventh Marines fought to save their guns as well as their own lives. Even the staff of the First Marine Division fell victim to a succession of marauding attackers. From the commanding general himself down to the most junior enlisted man present, members of the division headquarters left their posts, took up their weapons, and joined the fight. As noble and heroic as this may sound, when generals and colonels are forced to fight for their lives, they are no longer available to command or direct the battle. Nor are signal troops free to keep lines open or relay desperate pleas for help.

Having expended the last of the ammunition for his Reising, Lieutenant Francis Pearson policed up a Springfield. There were plenty of them scattered about, cast off by the wounded or still clutched tightly by lifeless hands. Finding a weapon wasn't a problem. Securing ammunition for it was. Everything was running out, including time and hope. When Captain John Sweeney grabbed Pearson by the arm and ordered him to pull his platoon out of the line facing south and shift it around to support the fight for the division headquarters, Pearson stared at his commander dumbfounded. "What platoon? There's me, Gunny Jay, and six men. That's it."

Not having taken the time to keep track of such things, Sweeney blinked twice as he considered what Pearson was saying. Then he repeated his order. "If that's all you have, then they'll have to do. Now move out."

By the time Pearson managed to back away and pull his men off the firing line, he had only himself, Gunny Jay, and five men. "Follow me. We're going to save the division headquarters."

Exhausted but still able to find a touch of dark humor in their plight, Gunny Jay chuckled. "You've been in the sun too long, Lewtenant. You're becoming delusional."

The best Pearson could manage was a weak smile. "I'm not delusional, Gunny. I'm a fucking Marine!"

Crouching low as they made their way to the rear, the Marines found progress arrested by a figure standing in the middle of the trail they had been following. "Where are you people going?"

From his knees, Pearson looked up at Colonel Merritt Edson himself. Edson had spent the entire night going from crisis to crisis, rounding up all the strays that he could find and dispatching them to where he thought they were needed the most while keeping the firing line supplied with ammunition as best he could. Realizing that this officer didn't know about his orders, Pearson told Edson what Sweeney had just finished telling him.

Edson shook his head. "They aren't there anymore. The general and what's left of his staff pulled out ten minutes ago, headed for Geiger's CP down at the airfield."

Given how confused things had become, Pearson wasn't the least bit surprised by this news. As in all battles, events often overtake the orders that are issued in an effort to control them. Looking back from where he had just come, Pearson wondered if he should simply backtrack or go elsewhere. Deciding that the former would only serve to confuse the men who had taken over their portion of the line, the young officer looked back up at Edson. "Where do you want us?"

While Pearson had been pondering what he should do, Edson had been considering the same thing. Looking around, the Marine colonel hesitated before he spoke. When he did, Pearson could tell how much his words pained him. "We can't hold here any longer. They're getting around us, and there's no way to resupply up here." Then, casting his weary eyes down into Pearson's, Edson placed his hand upon the young officer's shoulder. "Son, spread your men out on either side of this trail and hold it. I'm going to start pulling everyone who can make it back. If anyone asks, tell them we're reforming behind the Second of the Fifth back at the southern end of the runway. Understood?"

Understood? What in the hell, Pearson wondered, was he asking him to understand? The order to hold there, which seemed to have no clear limit on how long he was to hold? Or his instructions to tell people where they were to rally? Only when he realized that it was neither the time nor the place to ask his commanding officer for clarification did Pearson nod. "Aye aye, sir."

With that Merritt Edson made his way forward to begin the tedious process of withdrawing his command while under attack.

Reinvigorated by the food he had managed to gulp down, Yoshio Sawa gathered up his own men and those he had stumbled upon in the small opening. After organizing them as best he could, he led them in the direction of the airfield.

Throughout their brief interlude and during their renewed advance, the fighting around them had continued unabated. The vicious and pervasive din of explosions, rifle fire, and the rattle of machine guns was just as fierce as it had been when the attack had begun. Surely, Sawa found himself thinking, the Marines could not last much longer. How could they when there had only been two thousand of them on the entire island? Based upon what he had seen himself, the former law student reasoned, they had to be nearing collapse. Looking back at his pitifully small collection of men, Sawa repeated this last thought with greater emphasis. *They have to be.*

After so many hardships and so much frustration, Sawa was startled when he stepped out into the open and gazed upon the flat expanse before him. In an instant he realized that he was looking at the airfield. *They had made it!* They had reached their objective! Well, he corrected himself, they had almost reached their objective.

Spinning about, Sawa waved his sword once over his head and pointed its tip in the direction of the airfield. "There is our objective! There is our victory! *Banzai! Charge!*"

Without waiting to see if his men were following, Sawa began to make a headlong dash forward. In his excitement he failed to take into account that the airfield was a very large objective and his command was very, very small. Nor did he bother to inspect the ground that lay between where he had stood at the edge of the jungle and where the runway began. Even if he had, it is doubtful that he would have seen the hastily dug positions where the men of the Second of the Fifth Marines sat waiting. Not until those Marines opened fire did Lieutenant Yoshio Sawa realize that his trials were not yet at an end.

DAWN, SEPTEMBER, 14, 1942

Feeling like a man twice his age, Francis Pearson shuffled down the edge of the runway, ignoring the planes of the famous Cactus Air Force of Guadalcanal as they roared past him and leaped into the air. He was followed by all that remained of his platoon, some of whom had become lost during the night and had not found their way back to the fold until just before dawn. Together with this gaggle of ragged figures, Pearson trudged on toward a spot near the beach that Colonel Edson had picked as a place to collect his shattered command and rest them. When John Sweeney mentioned that they were headed for a rest area, Gunny Jay groaned. "Jesus, sir. Not another one! We can't take any more of the colonel's rest areas." Even Sweeney, shaken by the terrible cost that the previous night's fighting had taken on his company, couldn't help but laugh.

"A rest area," Pearson muttered as he looked about at the torn and battered landscape. "It'll be a cold day in hell before they find a rest area on this island."

That thought was still rattling about in his head when his eyes fell upon a curious sight. Stopping, Pearson gazed down at the lone body of a Japanese officer lying facedown in the mud at his feet. The man's arm, stretched out as far as it could, still clutched a sword whose tip touched the steel mats Marine engineers had used to reinforce the runway.

Coming up next to his platoon leader Gunnery Sergeant Jacobi looked down at the Japanese officer as well. "Gee," the Marine NCO mused, "some of the bastards actually did make it to the airfield."

"Yeah, Gunny, he made it." Pearson sighed. Then, without giving the body of Yoshio Sawa another thought, Lieutenant Francis Pearson continued on.

FACT AND FICTION

AUGUST, 2001

Despite numerous attempts, the Japanese never recaptured Henderson Field. This story is based upon what I considered their best opportunity to do so.

The two young lieutenants and everyone within their platoons are fictional characters. Captain Tetsuzan Oyama is fictional. All other characters mentioned by name are real. Most of the actions taken by these fictional characters are based upon actual events and incidents that occurred on Guadalcanal and within the ranks of the First Raider Battalion USMC, and the Japanese forces commanded by Major General Kiyotake Kawaguchi during the September campaign, including Edson's raid on Tasimboko.

I marked the place in the story where it takes its "What if" turn with an asterik. When Major General Kiyotake Kawaguchi left Rubal, he had intended to make his attack at 2200 hours on the evening of the twelfth. Upon arriving on Guadalcanal and assessing the reality of the situation, Kawaguchi postponed his attack until the thirteenth. When he received word of the troop convoy at Fiji, the Japanese general once more changed the date back to the original one, which he favored. With the destruction of his long-range transmitter by the Raiders during the September 8 raid, Kawaguchi lost all contact with Rubal, making any further changes impossible.

The dispositions of Marine forces to include the Raiders and Paramarines prior to the attack are based upon the defensive scheme of the twelfth. Changes were made during the thirteenth, but only in response to the aborted attack Kawaguchi launched on the night of the twelfth. Since that attack did not take place in this story, there is no reason to believe that Edson would have made any major shifts before the night of the thirteenth.

The reconnaissance in strength depicted in this story conducted by the Raiders on the thirteenth was planned by Edson. In fact, he had just finished issuing his orders to his company commanders for that foray when the Japanese bombardment began on the twelfth.

The naval bombardment and preliminaries described in the story are as they actually occurred. Kawaguchi's plan of attack, the axis of advance for each of his battalions, and their objectives are taken from the orders issued by Kawaguchi. When the Japanese tried to launch their attacks on the twelfth, they did so in a rather haphazard manner. Those units that managed to arrive in time went straight from the approach march into the assault. Without any reconnaissance of the Marine positions or routes forward, battalions and companies quickly lost their way. Most units never did attack that night. Things did not go much better on the thirteenth. The Japanese once more stumbled about and went in piecemeal while the Third Battalion, 124th Infantry failed to make any serious contribution to the effort. In the story I made the assumption that the battalions of Kawaguchi's central force adhered to Japanese tactical doctrine and, despite Edson's spoiling attack, made the necessary preparations for a proper night attack.

The results of that attack and the response of the defenders is a mix of what actually happened and what might have happened.

A FINAL WORD

In the story the Japanese fail, just as they did on the twelfth and thirteenth of September 1942. It is my considered opinion that even if things had gone exactly as Kawaguchi had planned and the Japanese had somehow managed to seize the airfield, they could not have held it. There were simply too many Marine infantry battalions on the island, and the Japanese losses, even under the best of circumstances, would have been too prohibitive for them to hold on. The Marine commanders of the First Marine Regiment and the Fifth Marine Regiment, after brushing aside the feeble attacks thrown against them, would have turned on those Japanese forces that had made it to the airfield and wiped them out. While I do admit things would have been a lot costlier for the Marines, and there might have been a disruption in air operations, neither Vandergrift nor the commander of the Marine and naval aviation units on the island, Brigadier General Geiger, would have admitted defeat. Somehow they would have managed to pull things together and carry on, just as Marines always have done, and hopefully always will.

WOLF FLIGHT

JIM DEFELICE

JIM DEFELICE is the author of several techno-thrillers. His latest, *Coyote Bird*, is now available in paperback from Leisure Books. He can be contacted at jdchester@aol.com

Memory changes everything. It adds color and tones, reshapes hues, arranges backgrounds. Much of this is trivial. Whether the sun shone a particular way last June matters to no one, least of all to the man who was there. But memory also undertakes acts of treachery. It confuses action with intent. It makes us into heroes, larger than the life it invents.

And yet, we must remember. Without memory we cannot place ourselves in the world, cannot see the distance we have traveled, nor the places we have left to go. We cannot know if we deserve God's mercy, or must be denied it. So we wrestle with memory, remembering, correcting, remembering again. The stories our memories tell are refined over and over, and so are our selves. If in the end we are left with truth—if it lies at the bottom of the grave like bones after the worms have made off with the flesh—then we will know what God Himself knows, our own souls.

I have struggled with my memory long enough to know I am not a hero, though I knew one once. But this knowledge, like all knowledge, has not been without cost.

As for the hero, memory has taken its toll there, too. I can close my eyes and see his face, but I am no longer sure that what I see is truly his face. I have gained certainty over the years—I believe that he really was a certain height, that his hair really was jet-black and his nose slightly misshapen. But I have learned that certainty is often an illusion, in my case a sweet bribe for growing old.

And so I admit, in my long-winded way, that bits of the story I tell may be wrong. But its bones are as true as my own.

We called them Butcher Birds. And that's what they were—swift, violent birds of prey that flashed from above without warning, singling out the weaker members of our flock. And we were all weaker members in their gunsights. In the late fall and early winter of 1941, the Germans unleashed a new fighter against the British, the Focke Wulf Fw 190. It had a radial engine and could easily outperform the Spitfire V, the most advanced plane in the RAF inventory at the time. In its first encounter with Spitfires, an outnumbered group of Butcher Birds took down three RAF planes without a single loss. The lopsided victories increased as the planes began pouring off the production lines, until by early spring 1942 they threatened to wrest control of the air completely from the RAF, even over southern England. In one typical encounter, a large flight of Fw 190s took on a wing of Spitfires, downing eight and sending five home with serious damage, to no losses of their own.

Mine was among the planes damaged in that encounter. I cannot describe the fear I felt when the first German plane dived on me, for it seems to me now that I wasn't afraid. It seems, as my memory tells it, that I held my position on my leader's tail, protecting him as he pursued a German fighter. Whether that is true or not, today I cannot say. What I do remember clearly, what I feel strongly, is the fear moments later when I was forced by a second Fw 190 to break from my position.

It is no less noble for a fighter pilot to run from an enemy when he is in his sights than it is for him to press home an attack when he is on his opponent's tail. In the swirling swarm of a mass dogfight, such situations constantly present themselves. I was trained to get away, and had done so many times before, dipping down and pulling into a sharp turn, zagging back, easing up on the stick and leveling off to take on another fighter.

Except that day, the bullets continued to cross my wings even after my maneuvers. I flailed left and right, then, with my panic building, I nosed downward into a dive. It was then that my opponent's machine-gun bullets finally struck me. My heart raced; I felt as if a pair of fists were pummeling my temples. I pulled back sharply, hoping that the enemy plane wouldn't be able to change direction quickly enough to destroy me.

It was not the best strategy, and by rights I probably should have had my tail shorn off by my pursuer. But instead the Focke Wulf broke off, and I was able to escape.

I don't know even now why he did that, and didn't then. I have guessed that someone else jumped him, or that he thought I was a goner and went to take someone else. I have guessed that he was caught by surprise. I have even guessed that he ran out of ammunition. But none of the answers is really satisfactory. I know only that he did break off, and that I was able to wrestle my plane back into level flight more or less on the original course.

Two or three hours later, I was in a pub not far from our air station. And it was there that I met Captain Clark Peterson.

"Hey, Yank," he said as I leaned in for a beer. It was not surprising that he knew me, or had a rough idea who I was. I was the only American in the wing, originally a volunteer who had joined the RAF with the help of Canada; strings had been pulled somewhere along the line to allow me to remain while giving me American lieutenant's bars, though I still wore the British uniform.

Peterson also had a reputation. I knew of him vaguely as a man who had been caught with the daughter of some local official, though how important the official or daughter was didn't register. He bought me my drink, then began plumbing for details of the 190. Memory tells me now that we didn't speak long and that what I did say was useless, but the important thing is that somehow we became friends that night.

Somehow.

I can tell you how, or at least why I wanted to be his friend. Peterson was everything I wanted to be. As a pilot, I don't believe he had a peer. He'd shot down more than three dozen planes. He had also lost at least one plane himself; for me and many others, the fact that he had survived the shootdown was in itself an accomplishment.

But it wasn't his skill as a flier that impressed me so much as his confidence and smoothness. And yes, the way he reveled so much in sin—women and booze, specifically. He reeked of both.

My father was a minister; I grew up in the shadow of a small-town church. Truly I believed strongly in God—then, and now as well. But sin, or at least such sins as Peterson seemed to embrace, had an attraction for me. Then, and now as well.

The exact sequence of events over the next few weeks are boring and even a little confusing when laid out, but exactly thirty-six days after my encounter with the Fw 190, I found myself in the hold of a Handley Page H.P. 57 Halifax, a boxy, four-engine bomber that at the time was the mainstay of British Bomber Command. Except that this plane had been detailed to RAF Special Duty Operations, an arm of the Special Operations Executive, to which Peterson and I had recently been attached. The plane carried no bombs; Peterson and I were its only payload. The seven-man crew were under strict orders not to speak to us, and they obeyed those orders perfectly.

The takeoff was routine. We were over the Channel in a matter of minutes. I persuaded myself that I wasn't nervous; I remember, or believe I remember, thinking to myself how incredibly strange it was to be so calm.

There were windows on the side of the fuselage, and as I looked through one I saw an AAA shell cut a triangular hole in the sky, stamping through the blackness to the white words of the universe. In the next moment the plane began to stumble as flak exploded all around us. I thought for sure that we were going in, and I was calm no more.

"They're shooting at us!" I yelled. I lost my balance as the plane shuddered. I grabbed desperately to try to steady myself as the crew door was opened nearby. Peterson grabbed me by the arm, all grins, and helped pull me forward to the door.

"They're shooting at us," I told him.

"Yes," he said. He added something, but it was lost in the roar of the engines and the wind. Then his smile broadened, and he stepped out of the plane.

We'd boarded the plane wearing our jump gear and packs, though when I think back now I remember myself in just my uniform. I see myself standing at the door. I have trouble breaking my grip on the frame; wind buffets my body the way a river pours on rocks at the foot of a massive waterfall. Shells burst outside. I take a step and my knee snaps tight, refusing to budge.

I think anger made me overcome that fear. I was angry at myself—maybe for volunteering, maybe for chickening out, maybe for both. Somehow, I managed to throw myself into the chaotic wind and the dark night.

I forgot what I was supposed to do, forgot to tuck in my legs and curl down my head, forgot even to reach for the ripcord. God reached down and did it for me, pushing my hand against the rimmed handle in the center of my soul. My shoulders flew upward, and as my head jerked back under the spreading canopy, I regained control of myself.

The moon was nearly full. I could see the stone fence of a farmer's field ahead, and for a while I thought I was going to land precisely on the stones. I kicked my legs, then saw a tree close by. Preferring the wall to the tree, I stopped kicking. In the next moment something kicked me hard in the back and I found myself rolling sideways, tangling in my lines.

It was a horrible landing, far worse than any of the dozen or more I'd practiced. My mouth was full of dirt, and I smelled the metallic taint of blood in my nose. But at least I was still alive.

Peterson, laughing, pulled me up.

"Been waiting for you, Yank," he said. "Good jump."

"I didn't jump, I dived. How did you find me?"

He laughed even louder. "Well, I was watching."

"Why were they shooting at us?" I asked. "We're in bloody England, aren't we?"

"I imagine no one told them we were coming," said Peterson. He probably smiled indulgently at my using English slang; he usually did. "Come now. Let's gather your parachute, then ring the commander, shall we?"

The phone we found was in a pub about a half mile up the road. Along the way, I realized that my knee hadn't locked out of fright; I'd banged it in the plane and gashed it somehow.

" 'Only joy, now here you are,' " said Peterson.

I shook my head, not getting the reference.

" 'Fit to hear and easy my care,/ Let my whispering voice obtain/ Sweet reward for sharpest pain.' " Peterson smiled. "Sidney. Sir Philip Sidney."

"Oh."

"Poetry, lad. You really ought to study it. The stout will fix that," he added, pointing at my knee. I nodded and took a sip of my beer.

"You Yanks don't study much at school, do you?"

"Poetry, no."

"The art of seduction," said Peterson. He took my drink and added a shot of Scotch from a flask as part of the prescription, and by the second gulp I had completely forgotten about the cut, my knee, and my momentary hesitation.

The room was empty, except for us. The bartender explained that a German aircraft had attacked nearby and been shot down. All able-bodied men were out searching for the crew.

"Good job, that," said Peterson, hoisting his beer as a salute to the absent pensioners.

Until that night's final orientation, designed to get us—me—used to parachuting in the dark, the mission Peterson had suggested and volunteered for had been—how can I put it? It was like listening to someone else's dream.

We were to steal a Focke Wulf from one of the airfields in France. On the day he met me in the pub, Fighter Command as well as SOE had approved the plan. All that was needed were arrangements with the French Resistance.

And a second man to tag along, a backup and assistant in case things went wrong. Air Chief Marshall Sir Sholto Douglas himself had insisted on it, Peterson told me.

" 'Two heads better than one,' though to my mind he just knows too much about me."

I'm not positive that Peterson knew Douglas, the head of Fighter Command, or vice versa. He could have, and in fact if I had to make a judgment I would say he did. Peterson seemed to know everyone.

Approving the mission had been controversial, but in the end the toll being taken by the Fw 190s made it obvious that something had to be done, even if it were a desperate shot. Selecting Peterson for the mission, on the other hand, made a great deal of sense. For one thing, he'd come up with the idea, and he volunteered. For another, he spoke excellent French and decent German; he'd spent a year in Hamburg as a young man studying classical literature. During the early days of the German blitzkrieg he'd had engine trouble and landed behind the lines in France. He'd managed to slip back to his unit with only a few small tears in his uniform for grief. He may also have had some sort of commando training—he hinted as much, but never said so specifically.

What my qualifications were, I'm not sure. I, too, volunteered, though it seems to me that there would have been no lack of volunteers, even though the mission seemed suicidal when explained by anyone other than Peterson. I'd like to think that my piloting skills had something to do with it, or at least my ability to adapt to different planes quickly—my record *was* good there, though probably a dozen chaps were just as flexible. I did speak, or thought I spoke, French. I had also taken two years of German in high school. Before volunteering to help the British, I had been in the Army and took some Ranger training, which probably looked more impressive in the dossier than it was in real life. I'd made a dozen parachute jumps, but none had been at night.

Peterson liked me, and that, too, probably counted for a lot. But in the end I think I was picked to go, or allowed to go, because no one really had much of a hold on me. As an American I was always

the tenth man on a nine-man team, an afterthought who had somehow managed to wander into the locker room and onto the playing
field after the sides were chosen. Losing me would matter less to
most commanders than losing someone else.

In fairness, the man in charge of the mission, a Colonel Maclean,
gave me a way to bow out gracefully the morning after Peterson
and I took our jump under fire. Maclean, part of a commando group
working with SOE, had his headquarters in an old school building
whose upstairs rooms looked as if they'd only just been abandoned
by the kiddies for the weekend. We met in one of those rooms that
morning to go over some details; our place had already been secured on a bomber due to leave the next night.

A large map of the world hung at the front of the room in place
of the blackboard. My eyes wandered to it constantly, searching
among the letters and lines for my hometown in northern Penn-
sylvania. Peterson sat on one of the desks nearby, arms folded, listening with a grin as Maclean talked about recognition codes and
the weather. The colonel spent an inordinate amount of time on
the weather, perhaps because someone had told him once that pilots liked to hear about it.

"Tomorrow evening, then," he said finally. "Pilot knows, but the
rest of the crew won't be informed until just before takeoff. Security. It's a Lancaster, part of a regular flight, not one of ours, so
keep it dark, right?"

Instead of answering, Peterson made a joke about receiving six
of the best in a room like this. "Six of the best" was a beating. The
grammar school teachers apparently used to break their rulers and
straps on the pupils' backs.

"Off with you now," Maclean told him. "Lieutenant. A word."

Peterson got to his feet, his manner somehow suggesting swagger
while expending a minimum of effort. He wagged a finger at me.

"Naughty, naughty, Preacher Boy," he said.

Maclean said nothing, waiting for Peterson to leave. The colonel
had a certain grim efficiency about him, but then a lot of the officers I met in England had the same quality. They said confidently

that they would beat Jerry—that was how they often put it—but privately they realized that things might not work out that way. Even if they did, most knew they might not survive the war. I suspect most had been utterly shocked by how quickly the Germans had brushed aside the French. Whatever contempt they held their onetime allies in, to see them so easily and utterly beaten couldn't help but weaken their own confidence.

Before Maclean began to speak he reached into his pocket and pulled out a lighter. He turned it over in his hand a few times, running his fingers along the smooth skin. Then he took a pack of cigarettes from his shirt pocket and offered me one.

"I don't smoke, sir."

"Yes. Quite." He lit the cigarette and took a long pull. He reminded me of a member of the lay council in charge of my father's church, waiting to examine the books.

"This mission has been authorized and approved by all the important men," he said at last.

"Of course," I said, nodding.

"It's a voluntary mission. Strictly voluntary."

He looked at me like he had something else to say. I waited, and when he didn't say anything else, I shrugged.

I think—but this is only looking back through the long telescope and fog of memory—that he did not believe in the mission and wanted to scuttle it if he could. Peterson would have been delayed if I backed out. But maybe the colonel had taken a liking to me and wanted to save me.

Or maybe not. Maybe he thought I was too skittish, or maybe he'd noticed that I'd done poorly in the small-arms trials. Maybe one of the crewmen in the bomber noted that I had frozen. In any event, he said nothing else for nearly a full minute. I glanced over at the door, then back at him, then at the door again. He continued smoking his cigarette. Then, finally, I said something inane like, "The weather will be good, I hope."

He answered with: "We don't order someone to go behind the lines."

"Of course," I said.

"You are liable to be shot if you're captured. You will definitely be shot."

I nodded. Maclean was the first person to say that specifically, though it was obvious enough. I would jump in a flight suit so that it would look as if I'd bailed out of a plane, but after that—and even then, frankly—I expected that any German who found me would kill me as a spy.

After torturing me, naturally. It wasn't exactly something I dwelled on.

"I want you to know, son, if you change your mind—if you have any reservations, there's no shame in it. There will be other opportunities."

"I won't change my mind."

Maclean narrowed his eyes into a squint, trying one last time to peer into my skull and see what sort of madman I truly was.

"Very well," he said finally. "Dismissed."

I spent the night—well, how would you spend the night?

Sometime the next morning I got up from the barracks—actually another part of the converted school—and went out to get my bike and satisfy a curiosity I'd had since coming to the village a week before. That was how I thought of it—a curiosity. There was a large stone church in the center of town, and I wanted to go inside it. Not, I told myself, to make peace with God or nurse my nostalgia for home; certainly not to make a fleeting connection with my father, whose life's work was so intimately connected with such places. I felt instead that I wanted to see the inside of a real English church, something I hadn't done in the nearly eighteen months since I'd been there. And so I nodded at the sergeants at the gate, and rode on into town.

The churches of my youth were predominantly small, plain affairs. Their interiors were washed by yellow and green hues, and while there were a few fine touches—I remember particularly a handsome rail of intricately carved wood—on the whole there was nothing in the interior to distract the mind from the business at hand.

This church, however, was an English church, Anglican, or Episcopalian on my side of the Atlantic. The Catholic heritage was obvious, at least to an outsider. Where the doors of my father's churches were light, this one was ponderously heavy, so slow to give way that at first I thought it must be locked. Inside, the cool dampness of the stones mixed with the lingering perfume of incense— or so it seems now in my memory. There were no lights on, but the morning sun streamed through the painted glass windows sufficiently to color the inside an orange-yellow. The apostles stood in all their glory and shame on the glass—Peter denying Christ, Thomas being pushed to touch his wounds.

I sat in the next-to-last pew, soaking it in. My head hurt a bit, despite the aspirin I'd taken, and my stomach had the metal hollowness one feels a few hours after it has been forcefully emptied. I thought of Maclean offering me a way out; I wondered if he had a cure for a hangover.

I also wondered if he knew that I was scared. I was afraid of being afraid then. I didn't have enough experience with it.

Until the year I'd left home my greatest fear was being caught doing something wrong by my father. He didn't beat me, and actually rarely punished me. His lectures were more collections of silences than tirades. And yet his disapproval weighed like iron on my back.

I began to think of him there as I sat in the church. It was not, by any means, the sort of church he would serve in, yet I saw him walking to the lectern with his worn red book, his favorite service book, carefully sliding the ribbon back and beginning to speak.

A noise from the front startled me. A light came on—I thought, honestly thought, that through the side door near the altar my father would appear. He did not, of course, only a priest in black garb who talked to himself as he went about his business, inspecting some lights near the side. As I watched him silently I realized he was about my age and build, a short man, not overly athletic, self-absorbed as I often was.

While his calling had perhaps prevented him from joining the military, I realized as I watched him move that there could have been another reason as well. He dragged his right leg slightly, and after he knelt for a short prayer had trouble rising.

He turned and started. His features were similar to mine and for a moment I felt as if I were looking in a mirror.

He nodded.

I nodded back.

"If you'd like something, my son—"

It is always amusing how putting on the collar makes a man instantly older. Many a twenty-year-old minister has called a grandparent "son" or "daughter."

"No," I said.

He smiled and walked toward me.

"Difficult times," he said. "You're an American."

I nodded. I was wearing my RAF uniform, but even one word could give me away, and it had.

"Would you pray with me?" asked the priest.

Why not, I thought. I told him I would and got down on the kneeler. He bowed his head and began the Lord's Prayer. Just as I joined in a car horn beeped outside the church. I knew instantly it was Peterson, and I rose in mid-sentence.

"I'm sorry," I told the priest. He looked up at me, possibly shocked that I would get up in the middle of a prayer. But when you have been praying all your life, one prayer or another is not particularly important, or so I felt at the time. In any event, I had to answer Peterson; it was not in my power to resist.

"I have to go right away. Sorry." I kept repeating the word "sorry" as I left. The bright light outside temporarily blinded me; when I focused, I saw Peterson pulled halfway out of his car through the window, waving at me. Inside his coupe were two women; I could smell their perfume from the church steps.

"Hello, Preacher, knew I'd find you at work. Come, we've got a good six or seven hours yet," he shouted.

We had less than four before we were supposed to report to the airfield, which was a good distance away.

"I have my bike," I said. "And a hangover."

"Leave the bike," he said. "You don't need it now. As for the hangover—"

He slid back into the car, implying that the cure lay inside. Shaking my head, I went to find out.

After we came over the Channel and made landfall, the sky lit with the sweeping arcs of searchlights. The crew had told us to expect this; they'd been on the raid to Lübeck just a few nights before, setting the medieval German city on fire with a bellyful of incendiary bombs. The city had been chosen because so much of it was made of wood. They claimed it was still burning, and if they had pointed to a spot in the distance and said that was it, I would have believed them. The defenses that night seemed far less ferocious, though they would still have a good distance to go after we left. They had told us of the Me 110s, which would "have a good go" at the Lancaster's unprotected belly if they could get into position. The two-engine night fighters, generally vectored to the intercept or making use of the searchlights to pick out targets, would rise up through a formation, attacking planes from below. There was little the Lancasters could do to stop them; unlike the American B-17s, they lacked belly turrets.

Our plane was a specially inviting target, as it was at the very rear and side of the formation, and dropped steadily back to deposit us. The gunners at the rear and top stations turned in their mounts nervously. The crewman helping us looked up from his stopwatch every time one of the turrets rattled.

"Sixty seconds," said the crewman finally, and the nearby door was opened. Wind flew around—in my memory it is a tornado, thundering through the aircraft. I am swirled forward toward the door. I see Peterson grinning in front of me. I hear his words, his laugh. "We're up, Yank!" He laughs. He takes a puff on his cigarette, then, with it still in his mouth, he goes out the door.

I follow. It's much easier than it was over England. It is so easy that I know it was ridiculous to be afraid before. The parachute inflates slowly and I feel no jerk, hardly a pull. I remember this time to look up at the canopy, to make sure that it is full. I descend toward France and think that the parachute feels a lot like a swing under an old oak tree that once stood in my best friend's backyard.

That, at least, is how it is shaped in my memory. I know that as I fell, I could make out a village at the crest of a hill to my right. I was closer to the village than we had intended, but seeing it confirmed that we had been dropped very close to our target area.

The dark shadow of the ground rose to meet me swiftly. I stepped forward with my right foot and rolled, pretty close to the way I had been taught. My small kit had hit first. I gathered it up quickly, even before undoing the parachute lines. Had there been a wind, my doing so would have been a great mistake—I probably would have been blown all the way to Germany. But there was no wind, and the thing I wanted most of all, my Browning, came quickly to my hand. Strapped to my leg was a Colt .32 revolver that the commandos had given me, but it was my Browning I wanted. The gun was big and heavy; it felt more capable of doing damage if I were attacked.

I undid the parachute harness and began folding up the line, telling myself several times to go slow. I was about twenty yards deep in a meadow, hopefully in one of the farms along the road we'd targeted. The Resistance had been watching for us, but I didn't think about them until I got my parachute stowed. I expected Peterson to come up behind me at any moment, just as he had two nights before in England. When he didn't I was glad in a way; it gave me a chance to turn the tables on him.

Since he had gone out first, I guessed he had fallen to the northwest. From our practices I knew he could be as much as a half mile away. I got out the compass and reckoned the direction.

It was at that point, perhaps ten minutes into the mission, that I had to make my first real decision. The plan was to meet up with the Resistance people along the road to the village of Bois Clerc. I thought I had seen the road as I landed and that it was only twenty yards away. If that wasn't the road, it would surely lead to it, as the area for the drop had been chosen partly because there weren't many other roads.

I decided to look for Peterson rather than going to the road. It was probably the wrong decision, but in retrospect I doubt it would have changed much.

Parachute hidden beneath some brush, I set out with my gun in one hand and the signal flashlight in the other. I walked for exactly fifteen minutes, rising over a hill then down to another. The fifteen minutes, I reckoned, took me roughly a mile, though of course it may have been much more or much less. In my memory I walk with measured strides; in reality I probably was close to running. There were woods to my right, and I crossed two streams.

At the end of fifteen minutes, I realized I had gone too far. I also realized that it was very likely Peterson had found the road already and was waiting for me. I started back.

An hour later, I hadn't reached the road or found the spot where I originally landed.

Sometime after that, I found a small rise and sat at the crest, scanning around. There was a farm lane nearby, and what looked to be the roof of a house. I imagined that I could go there and get help simply by knocking on the door. I believed, in fact, that the entire French civilian population hated the Nazis. Colonel Maclean had said as much. I started toward the house when I heard the noise of a car or a truck in the distance to my right, which by that time was to the south. I could see no headlights—it's possible they were blacked out—but at least now I had a direction.

A band of trees stood at the edge of the field and the road. I worked through them slowly, not because I expected the Germans, but because I thought Peterson might be somewhere nearby. I didn't want to be surprised by him.

He wasn't along the road, which though dirt was well packed and wide enough for two cars. I began walking northeast, which would be the direction of the village. About ten minutes after I started, I heard the noise of a truck coming up from behind me. I crouched behind some rocks—or maybe it was a tree trunk, or a low row of hedges—at the side of the road.

As the truck crested a low rise, the moonlight caught its hulk. It was a German transport.

My mouth probably hung open as it passed. I leaned forward, trying to see in the darkness if there were troops at the rear or if it was empty. Before I could quite focus, something slammed me hard from the side.

I believe the first thing the Frenchman said to me was, "You are a fool, Englishman."

It's not the words that I have questions about—or the sentiment. He might have been speaking for quite some time. The words were in English. The Frenchman called himself *"Loup"* or "Wolf"; later he told me his real name or what I took for his real name, Pierre or something, but it was *Loup* that stayed with me, the Wolf. He had been following me for at least ten minutes, certain that I was the man he was supposed to pick up, yet apparently hesitating because he thought the Germans were already trailing me. The Nazis had several patrols in the area; while these usually didn't amount to much—the Resistance had used this spot for drops several times before—there was always the chance that the raw troops charged with making the searches might get lucky. The troops quartered in Bois Clerc were absolute inferiors; there had never been veterans there, and any troops of any worth in the entire country had been shipped east to attack Russia months ago.

Loup told me all this as I rose to my feet, my head still scrambled by his punch.

So where was my companion, he wanted to know. I had to answer in French, *"Je ne sais pas"* (I don't know), several times before he understood. His accent seemed more British than French to my American ear; my American accent undoubtedly sounded even odder to him and made it difficult for him to understand me much of the time.

We made our way up the road. After we'd gone about a mile, he stopped suddenly, listened, then pushed me to the other side. A minute later, a woman came up driving a horse cart.

Her name was Oriel. It means bird, but the word doesn't begin to describe her any better than I can. To give you an idea of how beautiful she was I would have to cut out part of my brain, implant the cells that hold that vision of her in yours. Only then would you begin to feel what I felt—what I still feel, thinking of her.

There's no way I knew how pretty she was at that moment. From the side of the road I couldn't see her face, probably didn't even see her body. Yet I think of that moment now and I can feel her lips and the soft crush of her breast. I don't see them in my mind—I feel them against my body. I don't remember her, I know her, as if she has only just left the room.

She did something with her wrists that stopped the horses. Then, with barely a turn away, she reached and picked up a rifle, and said in French, "Out!"

"It's one of them," said Loup.

Oriel answered that of course she knew it, but that was no excuse. By that time I had emerged from the tree line at the edge of the roadway, my hands spread at my sides but not raised.

"Where is the other?" she asked.

Loup explained that he did not know. They began discussing what to do; at one point I worried that they were simply going to leave Peterson on his own. That frightened me not because I thought the Germans would find him, but because I thought he would get to the airfield without me.

"We have to look for him," I said.

Oriel turned, and perhaps it was then that I got my first real glimpse of her beauty. Her face was round, far rounder than her sleek body would suggest. Her hair was tied back and curled behind her neck.

I struggled to repeat what I had just said in French, thinking she didn't understand.

"We aren't abandoning your commander," she said in English. "Get in."

I climbed into the cart as they continued to discuss what to do. Finally, they decided to proceed up the road and look for the others who were out searching for us. Loup climbed up and sat next to her. I felt a pang of disappointment, like a high school kid who suddenly discovers the girl he worked up the nerve to talk to is going steady with someone else. But Loup didn't sit that close to her on the bench; they seemed no closer than fellow workers might be. Nor did either of the two men we picked up a short time later seem to have any romantic attachment to her.

They wanted to inspect a field they called black dirt; it apparently had been some sort of a swamp before being drained after the previous war. It lay on the other side of an intersection with a much wider road, and it seemed to me that we were quite a distance from where Peterson would have landed. I kept telling them that, gesturing and trying to sketch out a map in the air. They looked at me as if I were a crazy American, which I suppose wasn't that far wrong.

They tied the horse to a post near the entrance to the field, then sorted themselves into a search pattern to walk across. I stepped up to take a spot at the far right.

And so it was I who found Peterson's body facedown in the field. The moonlight had waned, and I nearly tripped over the back of his leg. I froze for a moment as I recognized the shape of a man. His parachute was still attached, but only to one side of his body.

I knelt near his feet. I should have been much more analytic and careful, but all I could think of was how impossible it was, that Peterson—*Peterson*—would die. I couldn't think of a more impossible thing than his dying.

I pushed at his side, hoping, I guess, that he had been merely knocked out. The body didn't move. I touched it. It must have been cold, but whether it was, whether it gave way or stayed stiff, I honestly don't know; all these memories have occurred to me from time to time, all seemingly real.

Did I turn him over? I think so, but perhaps not. Was he pale? What expression did he have? A smile at the end? A grimace of horror? I don't know for certain; it's possible I didn't know then, as that corner of the field was very dark.

Behind me there were shouts. I stood up, and bullets began flying near me. Instead of throwing myself to the ground or running back in the direction I had come, I began to walk, calmly and slowly, away from Peterson's body, toward the cart. It was a crazy, ridiculous thing, and only if you believe in God or at least predestination can you explain why none of the bullets hit me. At some point, one of the Frenchmen—it may have been Loup—pulled me to the ground with a curse.

"Peterson is dead," I told him.

And then we both got to our feet and began to run.

No matter what anyone ever tells you, the French Lebel was trash as a rifle. I was not an infantryman, of course, and I was hardly an expert shot, but I could tell as soon as I was given the gun in an onion barn the next morning that it was junk. A bolt-action rifle, to my eye it looked closer to the guns used during the American Civil War than a modern rifle such as the M1. But for the French Resistance fighters, it had the serious advantage of being available.

Loup gave me the gun the next day, telling me to be careful and make sure it was a German I was firing at before using it. Most of the people who lived in the area would not protect me from the Germans if I was discovered, he said, but neither would they turn me in. He went into no further detail, and I didn't ask for any.

I spent the day sleeping in the barn behind the horse stall. Built into a shallow hillside, the barn had three floors; I've learned since that it was an unusual arrangement for a French barn, but at the time I couldn't have cared less. Because it was built into a hillside, the bottom two floors opened out onto the ground, though at opposite sides.

The top floor was an open storage area. Whatever vegetables had been kept there were long gone, eaten over the winter as food became scarce. The bottom floor, which connected to the middle by a trapdoor, was a root cellar, with a wall of kegs used for storing apple cider. These, too, were empty. There had been a flood down there sometime before; the dank odor drifted up through the floorboards. The middle floor, where I spent most of my time, housed tools and the horse which had been hitched to the wagon the night before. He was a good sleeper; I swear he snored much of the day.

I sat against the wood of the stall, one foot propped on the wall. I had the rifle under my arm and a blanket over me. I fell in and out of sleep, but none of it was restful. I couldn't fathom how

Peterson had died. I could do the mission alone—I knew I could do the mission alone—but not having him there lighting his cigarette and laughing, reaching into his pocket for his flask—how could that possibly be? He was the whole reason I'd come. He was the person I'd wanted to be growing up. He was my vision of a hero, my idea of swagger and authority and courage. And he was gone.

I told myself I should have reached into his pocket and taken the flask when I found him. I told myself I would go back that night and do so. The Frenchmen probably would object—Loup said I should wait in the barn a few days before moving, to make sure that the Germans had stopped searching, before moving on. Neither Loup nor the others knew what my mission was. For their safety as well as mine, I was to tell them as little as was necessary to accomplish it.

Somewhere in the afternoon I began to dream. The dream was a dark jumble that mixed different places and people together. One part had a Sunday service in it—my father stood before the congregation, speaking informally. Peterson was watching from the side, nodding. That surprised me. My father and my friend would not have agreed on much, and I doubt very much that Peterson would have listened approvingly to a sermon. But in the dream he nodded.

I was far in the back, and even though it was a small church, I couldn't hear what my father was saying. I wanted desperately to hear his words, but couldn't. Probably my father wasn't saying anything—the point of the dream, if dreams have points, might have been that I simply wanted to hear my father talk. But I kept leaning forward, and finally I began to run toward the front. The rest of the church disappeared. The floorboards fell away, and I found myself back over France, falling in the moonlight.

She caught me. Oriel, I mean. Her hand—callused from farm work—brushed across my cheek, and I landed in her arms.

I opened my eyes, and she was there.

"Easy," she said in English. "You're okay. You've been sleeping."

"You scared me."

She patted my leg indulgently. "I've brought you better clothes. And some dinner. Come, get changed." She stood up. If Peterson had been there—if I'd been Peterson—a few words would undoubtedly have drawn her to my side. But I had none of his charm, only wished I did.

"There," she said, laughing and pointing as she paused at the doorway. A pair of pants, two sweaters, and some shoes were piled neatly beside the wall.

I changed awkwardly. The pants were a bit short, but the shoes fit perfectly. My automatic was easily hidden beneath the sweaters, and the .32 once again snuggled at my calf. I tied my clothes and boots into a bundle and took them out with me, rifle in hand.

"Don't shoot," she joked. She was standing next to the horse. She'd tossed a rope around its neck; to the rope was tied a kerchief and then another, and finally a sack. "Go leave the gun against the corner beneath the blanket where you slept," she said. "Can you ride?"

"A horse?"

"No, me," she said with a laugh. She led the horse outside.

I'd never ridden a horse before. This one was exceedingly gentle. Oriel threw a blanket over its back, then pulled herself up. She balled the fabric of her dress in such a way that she could move her legs; they were bare to midthigh, and if I hadn't already been beguiled, I surely would have succumbed then.

I climbed on behind her. My heart pounded so hard it must have bounced her back and forth as we started into the field behind the barn, crossing to a small lane that led to an orchard. I knew her leaning against me as we rode wasn't accidental, but I wasn't sure what to do.

I knew what I wanted to do. But desire thickened my throat to the point where I almost couldn't breathe, let alone talk. Even if I could have spoken, I wouldn't have known what to say. She was just too beautiful in that moment.

We stopped and she slid off the horse. I had lost my opportunity. I started down, swinging my leg over the animal's rear—then promptly fell as the horse jittered forward.

She pulled me up and kissed me. Exactly what happened then is lost to me completely. I think—I know—we made love. I know I held her breasts in my hands. I know I lined her hips with my fingers. I know these things in my soul, and no amount of time, no trick of memory, can take them from me or diminish their reality.

For how long? Forever maybe, and for only a moment.

One sharded vision, one moment of feeling comes to me when I think of that afternoon: Oriel, riding against my stomach, white cumulous clouds puffy in the sky above her, beautiful round breasts filling my hands. I close my eyes and see heaven itself, a black, endless space devoid of war and pain. She rides and I feel for a brief moment what God must have felt creating the world—I open my eyes and see whiteness piercing the black, then I see her face, smiling down at me.

I am certain of that; my memory cannot have changed it. And I am certain that at that moment, I loved her, and she loved me.

And yet it was she who betrayed me to the Germans.

Loup stood near the corner of the barn when we returned. He was frowning; I thought again he was Oriel's boyfriend. He said something to her I couldn't catch, and my muscles tensed, ready for a fight. Oriel slid down and began protesting. I jumped down behind her, but as I walked forward I realized they weren't talking about me or what she and I had done in the field.

Loup turned to me and said we had to leave. Now.

She didn't want to. She kept shrugging, and said this was a safe place. They traded the French word, *"sauf,"* back and forth.

And then there was a car coming into the farmyard.

Two cars.

Loup smacked her across the face. I reared back to punch him, but he ducked, and with his left hand pulled me to the ground. As I rolled up I saw him running and started to chase him.

There were shouts behind me. German words, perhaps some French thrown in. There was no cover in the field, and for the first twenty yards as I ran I knew I would be killed. A trail of dust appeared on my left, tiny puffs as if miniature volcanoes were erupting there. I pushed my body right and somehow found myself running amid the trees.

There was another field beyond. It rose for about twenty yards. When I reached the top I threw myself down, rolling through dirt and rocks into a small stream. I ran across the water and then along its side.

There were more woods ahead. I ran to them. I reached for the Browning in my belt about the same time I got to the trees. I got the pistol out and as I ran it flew from my fingers. I had to stop and pat down the leaves and brush on my hands and knees to find it.

Loup whistled behind me. I followed as he ran through the thicket, then found a path. We crossed another stream, and just as we heard voices in the distance, the Frenchman grabbed a small motorcycle from a camouflaged hiding place behind some rocks.

It took forever to start. I sat behind him as he jumped up and down against the kick-lever. My hands had begun to shake; I gripped my pants with my left hand, trying to stop it, and folded my right, which still held the Browning, against my chest.

Dogs—there are dogs in the woods.

Gunfire—probably a burst from a machine pistol. Twenty or thirty yards away, no more.

Thunder.

The engine caught. In the first burst of acceleration Loup nearly toppled us. We pitched back to the right, and my shoulder smacked hard against a tree, but somehow we managed to remain upright. How close the Germans were at that point—if they were Germans at all—I have no idea. My eyes were closed against the dust and dirt and smoke that flew everywhere, and against the likely disaster.

We rode on the motorcycle for maybe ten minutes. Loup drove into a village—I know it wasn't Bois Clerc because the church lacked a real steeple. He parked the bike at the back of a building, then started to run; I followed. There was a truck at the end of the lane, and he jumped into the driver's seat and started it. I'm not sure whether he stole it or it had been placed there for his use; I didn't ask and didn't speak for more than an hour as we drove south, away from my target of course, though I wasn't about to tell him.

All of a sudden he began to laugh. He ducked his head down and turned it toward me and laughed.

I laughed, too. We laughed for a solid five minutes. He nearly ran over a donkey cart blocking the road, jamming the brakes and skidding a hair's width away from the old man trying to push with his back against the wheel. We laughed again.

By nightfall we had abandoned the truck and, starving, stolen some food at gunpoint from a poor man's kitchen. I had some money taped to my stomach and more in my pants and should have left it, but I was selfish, worried that I might need it to get back home. A few francs probably wouldn't have made a difference to me—as it turned out, they would have made no difference at all. To the homeowner, however, they might have bought food for a week or more. It would have been an act of kindness I regret to this day not having made.

Loup told me his real name that night, and something of his past. He had been a captain in the French army and had sneaked back to the Bois Clerc area after briefly escaping to England so he could organize the Resistance. As I listened I thought that he was telling me this as a way of somehow sharing my vulnerability—if he were captured I would be totally dependent on his not giving me away, and now he was similarly tied to me.

I told him the airfield where I had to go, but not what I intended to do there. He grimaced but immediately afterward nodded, and the next afternoon we set out.

We walked the entire way. It took the better part of five days. We would start around two or three o'clock in the afternoon, go until a little past six or so, rest, eat whatever we could find, then set out again, walking until past midnight. Once we slept in a cave formed by large rocks and an old tree, but the rest of the time Loup found barns or abandoned buildings. What sort of relationship he had with the owners I couldn't tell, though I guessed that, unlike the man we had robbed the first night, he at least knew who they were

and could count on them not to turn us in. We saw a few patrols—
once a black Gestapo car passed us as we walked along the side of
the road—but for the most part we passed like ghosts across the
countryside. It seemed no more troubling than a vacation tour, or
at least seems so now. I can't remember the hunger that must have
bit at my stomach, or feel how tired I must have been. The aches
that probably came close to paralyzing my legs and the cold that
pressed against the sides of my face and made my ears ring—all
lost to me. I remember only walking and, as I walked, feeling not
only safe but almost invincible.

At times I thought about Peterson. I had a vague notion that I
must do things the way he would have. I didn't spend a lot of time
thinking about how ridiculous it was that he had died, how worth-
less that was. As a pilot you see a lot of useless deaths, even during
war.

Few deaths aren't useless, war or no war.

One afternoon we walked through a large field as a farmer was
struggling with a horse to plow it. Loup pretended not to notice
the farmer, and the farmer did the same for us. I thought he looked
particularly inept, stumbling quite a bit behind an old horse. I imagined he wasn't really a farmer, or hadn't been until the war. We
turned down a lane near the field, pausing as Loup grabbed a
satchel near the fence. Inside were some crusts of bread and a small
bottle of milk; we ate as we walked.

The lane turned right, but we went left, climbing over a small,
rusted metal fence. As we climbed, I heard the drone of airplanes
in the distance.

One of the things that made the early Fw 190 so formidable was
its engine. I could give you statistics—the two-row fourteen-
cylinder radial BMW developed sixteen hundred horsepower and
could pull the plane to somewhere near four hundred knots, depending on the load and altitude. Despite some early problems with
overheating, it was a solid, reliable motor that had the advantage,
like all radials, of being air-cooled, which meant there was no radiator to be nicked by ground fire or during a duel. Despite the
fact that the engine literally weighed a ton and had to be supported

by a comparatively heavy airframe, it made the Focke Wulf one of the fastest planes of its time.

But the statistics can't describe the sound the engine made, something that began like a whine and turned into a guttural, ground-shaking roar as the planes passed. If you can imagine a bulldozer in the sky hurtling at the speed of a bullet, its throttle buried at the firewall—that would be close to the sound.

I looked toward the sky, trying to make out the planes as they shot by to the northeast and began spiraling upward. Loup finally yelled at me to come away.

"I'm going to steal one of those planes," I told him as we walked through the woods. "I'll need a day or two to watch their routine. And then I'll take it."

Loup said nothing. Perhaps he had guessed what I was up to when I told him my destination, or perhaps he had already decided I was crazy. I kept talking; the sight of the planes had unlocked something in my brain—sense, maybe.

"Most likely, they'll keep one or two of the planes on the ground when the squadron takes off, as backup," I explained. "That will be the plane to take. Or I may just go in when the mechanics warm them up, sneak onto the field, overpower them, and take off. That was the original plan."

I thought of Peterson, and consciously tried to emulate his smile and shrug. "I'll take one of the buggers, no matter what."

Loup remained silent. We walked a short distance to a narrow dirt road, turned down it, and followed to the back of a small brick and tile factory. A highway lay on the other side. I waited in the woods while he went inside; a short time later he came out and led me around to a door at the back. Inside, I changed my clothes and went out into a large room with kilns all along the walls. Only one or two of them seemed to be working; a half dozen men went about their business without taking any notice of me.

The security I'd felt for the past few days left me. Every one of these men could betray me, I thought; every one might be a collaborator as Oriel had been. But I said nothing, keeping my eyes to the floor as I followed Loup to a staircase. We emerged on a balcony overlooking the main level; about halfway down we entered what turned out to be the manager's office. Loup told me I would spend the night there, pointed to the green leather couch in front of the walnut desk, then locked the door behind me with a key.

I didn't sleep. I paced back and forth, I checked and rechecked my guns, I listened to the noises in the factory. I realized how ridiculous and stupid the plan was. Steal a German aircraft? Parachute behind the lines and simply take it? What idiot had approved it?

What idiot had volunteered to do it?

That was the moment when I finally missed Peterson, truly. I didn't blame him for persuading me to come—I blamed him for dying. It was as if he'd abandoned me.

Somewhere during the night, I began to think of Oriel. I felt her body again—in my mind we made love.

Shouldn't I have thought of her as evil? She'd tried to have me killed. She was the worst sort of devil, a classic temptress.

But I thought only of her body. I am ashamed to say that I masturbated to the memory.

And still I couldn't sleep.

I nearly shot Loup with the .32 in the morning. He opened the door wearing a black German military uniform and smiled when he saw the gun in my hand.

The smile reminded me of Peterson.

"Here," he said, bringing in a large parcel from the hall. "Get dressed quickly, and we'll have breakfast."

I found Loup outside, standing in front of a German sedan with a large man who was holding forth on—from what I could tell—the great difficulties of making bricks during a time of war. People did not want even the most utilitarian of bricks, he said. As for his specialty, artistic bricks—*nein*.

He said the one word in German—the rest had been French—and then nearly doubled over laughing.

"The American," said Loup, gesturing toward me. He introduced his companion as Monsieur Renoir, like the painter. Renoir shook my hand, then opened the rear door for me to get in.

Maybe I looked too nervous or anxious—I hadn't slept so I must have looked both—but Loup changed his mind about having breakfast first and told Renoir to go directly to the airfield. Along the way, he explained our cover story. Loup was a major with the SS on special assignment to the Ministry of Information, which intended to put a radio station at the airfield. Renoir, in real life a contractor as well as a brick manufacturer, would look at likely plots of land and act as if sizing them up for construction. I was a French bureaucrat who would keep my mouth completely shut, while trying to get as good an idea of the general layout and location of the planes as possible. I could expect to be ridiculed as a fool by Loup, who called himself Major Rahn—a durable German surname that gave nothing away.

Loup's willingness to help me inspect the base went far beyond his brief, and I was immensely grateful. And yet, I was also fearful—I worried that his aim was not to help me but to betray me, and my heart began pounding wildly as we approached the gate.

But the Frenchman knew his business well. The first guards who met us at the gate seemed dubious until he mentioned Goebbels and produced a letter supposedly signed by the Reich Information Minister. From that moment there was no problem; if anything, the Germans were too cooperative, as two or three officers made it their business to offer to show him around soon after we drove through the gate. Loup deferred to Renoir as the expert on buildings. Renoir insisted he knew his business, but welcomed the men anyway, launching into a long soliloquy on the merits of bricks. We were soon left alone.

We got no closer than a quarter mile to the runway, and the aircraft were kept beyond that, but I was at least able to get a good notion of the general layout. Two things surprised me—one, that the fighters did not have any hangars at all, but instead were dispersed between trees at the edge of a wooded area, and two, while there were troops patrolling the fence, there were none that I could see near the planes themselves. Besides the thirty-odd Fw 190s, there were several Messerschmitt Me 110s on the field.

A small patrol group of two planes prepared and took off as we walked the field looking for a suitable building site. Only two dozen men were involved in getting the planes ready, not including the pilots, but there seemed to be plenty of others in the buildings on the other side of the strip and ramp area. More importantly, the Germans didn't bother preparing a backup plane in case one of the flight had trouble. They did, however, have the mechanics start the aircraft and warm up the engines before the pilots boarded them to fly.

I watched the two Fw 190s taxi across the open field to a cement apron, which they followed around a ramp to the end of the runway. The pilots paused at the end there, canopies open, apparently waiting for clearance before proceeding. It seemed to me that was their most vulnerable point. I could hide there on the ground until they came, then jump on a wing, rush the cockpit, shoot the pilot, toss him out, and take his place.

It was a ridiculous plan. So was the second I came up with, which I told the others as we drove away from the field for breakfast:

A dozen men would sneak in around midmorning when things were quiet, steal the petrol truck, fuel a plane, and take off.

"And then how do we escape?" Loup asked.

"We ram the fuel truck into the fence and set it on fire," I said.

Loup and Renoir laughed.

"You can tell he's an American," said Renoir.

I waited until they stopped laughing and asked Loup what he thought.

"I don't have a dozen men," he told me. "But I will help you as best I can."

"How many do you have?"

"Two or three," he said. It wasn't clear if he was counting himself and Renoir.

I hadn't formulated a better plan the next day, when Loup and I returned to the airfield with three men with surveying equipment. As they pretended to examine sites, I attempted to get a better feel for the operations at the field. They seemed to be timed around the usual approach of RAF patrols in the sector. (The U.S. Army's Eighth Air Force had not yet arrived in England.) At 1 P.M. sharp a crew began to prepare the planes; the mechanics wore black overalls and would swarm on one or two of the planes at a time, bringing them out of their parking area, checking them over, topping off fuel, and arming them. The planes were then started, rechecked, and turned over to the pilots, who lined them up at the edge of the strip to prepare for takeoff. They worked quickly; it was a little past two when the full complement of planes launched.

Soon afterward, Loup gestured that it was time to leave. I wanted to stay to see what happened when the planes came back, but he shook his head firmly. I watched the others pack up, then walked as slowly as I could to the sedan. As I did, a large aircraft made its way onto the runway. It was a three-engine Junkers, a general transport type. I ignored it, but Loup stared at it and waited for it to land and taxi; as a group of officers got out of the passenger area he pulled up a set of binoculars, a very dangerous thing to do.

"Problem?" I asked.

He shrugged and put the car in gear.

Watching the airfield had not inspired me with a new plan. If anything, I was beginning to think the task hopeless. But I couldn't admit that to Loup; instead, I told him I wanted to go back again and stay longer, so I could see whether the planes were refueled and relaunched after their first patrol. They might be more vulnerable then.

I was grasping at straws, but he agreed. This time, Renoir joined us, the idea being that he would suggest building auxiliary buildings for the fighters, which would allow us to get close to them. I wondered, quite frankly, if he didn't think he might be able to make a little money in compensation for the danger he was putting himself in.

I told myself that I wouldn't blame him if he did. He seemed to me the fat-cat type, though he wasn't particularly fat and, in fairness, was taking great risks.

He wore a pinkie ring. That was where the prejudice came from.

He owned a factory and wore a pinkie ring—he must be rich.

We took a truck as well as a car to the field. This day, the Nazis were in a bad mood. They did not want us near their aircraft, no matter who had ordered us to find a radio station. A foul-tempered lieutenant met us at the gate and barraged Loup with questions. Finally, he simply waved in the man's face and drove away. For a moment I worried that the man in the truck would be too scared to follow, or that the lieutenant would take out his gun and shoot them, but nothing happened.

Loup decided to push things even further. He drove past the spot we had been looking at yesterday, down the dirt track beyond the runway, and out to the field near the dispersement area. The Focke Wulfs were parked less than ten yards away, with not even a single guard between us and the planes.

Two men with submachine guns came over quickly and demanded we leave. They spoke roughly to Loup even though he was an officer. They did not care for the SS, they said frankly, and if the French shit-eaters did not pack up their equipment quickly, they would all be shot, the major included.

Renoir tried to offer them a bribe, subtly suggesting that they might be thirsty, but the men didn't budge. Fortunately, another officer—I think he was the lieutenant's commander, a captain or *hauptmann*—came over. Loup unloaded his vindictive on him, demanding to see the base commander. Eventually another officer appeared, and Loup and Renoir went with him in Renoir's car to the main buildings. Just as they did so, I saw the crews starting out to prep the airplanes for takeoff.

I would like to say that I realized this was the moment to take the planes, but that I held off because I knew that doing so would leave Loup and his men stranded. I would like to say that I saw how it could be done easily—my small revolver in the one guard's face, his MP38 in my hands, the other guard down, the mechanics sprayed dead in seconds.

But I neither thought of taking off nor talked myself out of it for Loup's sake. I didn't even think of Peterson, who surely would have plunged ahead. The two guards scowled at the workmen and me, pointing their guns and making very unsubtle hints that they would shoot us if given the slightest reason. I kept my hands in my pockets and my eyes generally pitched to the ground. One of the guards said something about us being cowardly pigs, and I felt my face burn red.

Renoir and Loup returned a short time later with the German captain. Renoir had a large cigar in his mouth and he and the German laughed like old friends. In contrast, Loup was clearly worried; his forehead had furled downward and out, so that he looked like one of those dinosaurs with ridged facial armor plates. The German commander, it seemed, had invited everyone to lunch—the crew to mess with the enlisted men, Renoir, Loup, and I with him.

"*Moi?*" I asked. Loup, playing the role of the disdainful German officer, gave a snort of contempt, then explained in slow French that yes, dignitaries did not eat with ordinary soldiers.

So we went along to the commander's quarters, which was a large house at the edge of the compound, closer to the perimeter fence than the runway. The parlor floorboards creaked and dipped as we came in, some part of their support obviously missing. Heavy, ornate furniture sat in the hallway; the thick cabinets and finely carved bookcases seemed to have no business there, as the house itself was rather small and modest. A butler—I believe he was French—met us as we came inside and ushered us toward a large, back room filled with upholstered chairs. Fine china lined the mantel, but the walls were badly in need of paint. There were several shadows where paintings had hung for years as the paint around them faded.

Renoir, Loup and I took seats, Renoir continuing his patter, Loup continuing his scowl. I stared at the floor as much as possible.

The base commander and one of his aides soon came down the steps. They strode confidently into the room, the commander snapping out a "Heil Hitler" which Loup returned with gusto. Renoir copied the salute—it seemed to me with a great deal of mockery—and I mumbled one myself. It soon became clear that, though I'd been invited to eat with them, I was a nonperson and would be ignored if I stayed more or less silent, which I did. Renoir expostulated on what could be done to the house if he were allowed a free hand. He then segued into the great difficulty of finding good architects and work crews, compared that to the trouble of locating good wine. He somehow got the German commander—I wasn't quite sure of his rank—into a discussion of how much one might pay for 1930s Burgundy or Medoc, should a case or two fall into his hands. The commander, now smoking one of Renoir's cigars, fell into the swing of things, ordering his butler to bring some cognac from one of the cabinets.

It was some time before I realized that Renoir was in effect telling the commander that he would be taken care of if the project went ahead. Their discussion of wine was actually a way of haggling over the size of the bribe.

I wondered again what Peterson would have done in my position. This would have been his milieu, surely. But I couldn't decide what persona he would have taken—Loup's role as the German SS major working for Goebbels, probably. If he had, he would have added a bon mot or two about vintages, not sat there frowning as Loup did.

I began to fantasize about Peterson's being there, the part he would play. Somewhere along the line he would mention that he was a pilot; he would admire the Fw 190. He would ask for a flight. He would wangle his way into a cockpit, if only to sit for a while.

And then he would be off.

I could do that. Surely, I could do that.

But how to go from the role of a toad to that Peterson would play—a confident, cocky man?

He would simply move ahead, fill the space in a certain way, just be there. I could not.

So how was it that he was the one to die, I thought. Why him and not me? Without him, the mission was hopeless—I might as well strike out for the coast immediately.

A dress rustled in the hall, stockings moving against a tight slip and skirt. I looked up and saw Oriel.

Not Oriel, not her at all.

But in the first glimpse of the silk dress as my eyes moved upward, that was whose body I saw. And when the face couldn't sustain the lie—when the face belonged to a blonde not a brunette—still I thought of Oriel. I see her now as I say this, feel her breasts folding against my chest.

The German commander introduced his wife, an elegant woman of thirty, ten or twelve years younger than her husband. She looked at us as if expecting adoration. Renoir promptly swept into a bow and kissed her hand. She glowed. I stared at her, then belatedly nodded.

We moved to the dining room. It seemed to me that the walls narrowed as we walked. I moved through the landscape of someone else's dream—someone's nightmare, perhaps, my fear growing. And yet I was perfectly safe, protected by the utter arrogance of my host. Some fliers were going to join us, he said—two men about my age, one a Captain Schmidt, the other a Lieutenant Weiss, came in as we took our places at a large circular dining table. They, too, were taken with the commander's wife, paying her homage with sharp heel clicks. I moved toward a chair the butler held out for me.

Three other men came to fill out the table. Two wore suits; the third, who came into the room last, was dressed in an *Oberstleutnant's* uniform.

It was Peterson.

I probably did not gag, though undoubtedly my face turned white.

I thought, what a genius he is, to have convinced them he is an officer, a lieutenant colonel.

"Arrest them," said Peterson. "They are spies."

In one of the outrageous versions of this scene that my imagination teases me with, I lunge at Schmidt, pulling him in front of me as I yank out my pistol. I fire two shots. One kills the commander, the other one of the men who came in with Peterson.

I extend my arm to fire at Peterson, but his expression freezes me.

There is firing outside the room, inside the room. A body flies face downward onto the table—Loup, shot by a soldier with a machine pistol.

I grab the commander's wife—Oriel with blond hair instead of brown. I force my way outside. The light blinds me, and something hot pushes into my side. She's cut me with a knife.

Of course, none of that happened, but I don't know exactly what did. Loup, I believe, wasn't shot until the next morning. I wasn't stabbed in the side. It is very likely, very probable, that I did nothing at all to get away. Perhaps I reached for the Browning beneath my shirt, or went to my leg for the revolver, and was struck on the head. It may also be that I simply bowed my head and marched with them to the basement room of a nearby barracks, where I was locked away.

The next morning, one of the men who had been with Peterson interrogated me. He wanted to know why I was there. I said nothing, of course. It was surprisingly easy. The man did not hit me, nor did he threaten me. He paced back and forth in front of me as I sat on a wooden chair in an otherwise empty room. I'd been taken under guard from the basement room where I'd slept and brought there; a guard stood behind me with his pistol unholstered but said absolutely nothing during the interrogation. There were no handcuffs or ropes binding me. After about a half hour of questions the man nodded, and I was taken back downstairs to the room where I'd spent the night. There I sat cross-legged on the floor against the wall. At times, I wondered how I would be killed. I imagined a firing squad, though I thought it might be possible I would be hanged.

Morning turned to afternoon, marked by a small plate of food left at the door by the guard who had brought me to the interrogation. As I stared at the wall I thought of Peterson, and I thought, inevitably, of Oriel.

While I knew that Peterson must be a double agent, part of me hoped that he was deep in disguise, that he had decided to give me up so he could complete the mission. I thought of what had happened in the commander's dining room. I'd done nothing to give

Peterson away, said nothing about him. I was convinced that, if anything, my behavior had enhanced his cover story. At best, I'd acted exactly like a spy who should be arrested; at worst, I'd acted like a coward. Either way, it would help him.

I'm not sure why I thought of myself as a coward. I still do. There seems in my mind to be only black-and-white choices—and a hero would have gone down in a blaze of glory, insisting to be shot. A coward went quietly.

As the afternoon went on I thought of Oriel. The fantasy quickly became elaborate. We rode in an open car along the roads Loup and I had walked to get here. Spring came. The war ended.

It seems odd that, raised by a minister, I didn't think of the Bible for comfort. I've heard of other prisoners reciting verses to themselves, passing time and keeping themselves from despair by recalling the Word. Perhaps if I had been kept longer I would have. Or perhaps in this, too, my memory is mistaken. But it seems to me that the thing I thought of almost entirely as time went on was Oriel.

Somewhere after eight o'clock—I'm guessing because it had turned dark outside—the door swung open and a pair of guards entered. These men were carrying rifles and wore full, heavy coats. They said something in German which I interpreted to mean I should come with them, and so I did.

Outside, there was a large transport-type truck, the kind that could carry a dozen or so men in the open back. The guards gestured for me to climb up; when I did so they followed.

We waited for about fifteen minutes for the driver. We left finally with a single motorcycle for an escort. Obviously, they weren't particularly afraid of me escaping.

As the truck passed the gate to the airfield, I felt relieved. Surely if Peterson was still playing his ruse, as improbable as that might be, my leaving took him out of danger. He could complete the mission. It was absurd, it was pathetic—and yet it was what I thought.

Squatting on my haunches against the low side of the truck, I thought I might be able to escape. The night was fairly dark; the motorcycle escorting us was in the front, not the rear. My hands and legs were still unbound. The German guards were alert, and I was very close to them, but surely the odds were good that I could get over the side before they could shoot.

A fifty-fifty chance to get down to the roadway, then perhaps a twenty percent chance to get to the woods, bad odds, but surely better than the one hundred percent chance of being shot or hanged wherever they were taking me.

I started looking for a chance. One of the German guards had his Gewehr 41 aimed directly at my chest. I stared at it, willing it away. I realized it was an automatic weapon because of the cartridge box below the stock. That meant he would have several quick cracks at me, but now that I had decided what to do I was determined to go on.

Then he moved his aim.

I locked my eyes on the gun. We slowed, then turned, and suddenly he swung the gun away.

I went over the side instantly. For some reason I had expected to hit the ground almost immediately and roll off to the shoulder of the road. But of course the truckbed was well off the pavement and it took forever to hit the ground. When I did it was with the elbow of my left arm, and the pain overwhelmed me. I heard gunfire and cringed and now maybe, maybe at that moment finally, I thought of a prayer—the Lord's Prayer, as the young minister back in England had urged on me.

Then something hot and wet warmed my back, and I realized the truck was on fire. I pushed off the road, dragging my hand and still on my belly. There were screams, and someone pulled me to my feet.

I thought it would be Loup, or one of the men from the brick factory. But instead it was Schmidt, one of the pilots who had been in the commander's dining room. I pulled my right hand back to punch him, when I heard a voice say no. Renoir came from the shadows across the road, waving his hand.

"Run," he said in French. His voice sounded like a flame shooting out an open window. Run, run, run.

And so we ran. There were several men running behind and alongside me, partisans who had engineered my escape. The motorcycle had been blown to pieces by a mine, the truck torched by small gasoline firebombs. A man with a bolt-action rifle appeared in front of me, pushing his arm to the right as if he were directing traffic at the main intersection of a city. I turned and crossed a stream, and on the other side found a clearing where the others were gathering.

Renoir was actually quite fast and beat me to the clearing. He gave orders to the others as I caught my breath. And then he turned to Schmidt and asked why he had come.

The German shrugged. They obviously knew each other; Renoir shook his head and turned to me.

"We can get you to the coast," Renoir told me in his thick English. "It will take time."

"Where's Loup?"

He shook his head. "The commander and others knew me, and since they were taken in by him as well, they believed it when I said I believed his story completely. Or perhaps they only wanted to believe me, since it was so worth their while. But now, I, too, will have to go on."

"I have to steal the plane," I told him.

"It's too dangerous," he said. "No."

Non, non, non. Ne sois pas bête.

No, no, no, it can't be done. Those were his words.

And then, *Allez vous en.*

Go away. Except he didn't put it precisely that way.

"I will help you," said Schmidt in English, his voice almost a whisper. "Come with me."

There are men whom you meet for the first time and within a few minutes' conversation, with only a glance really, you know you can trust with your life.

Schmidt was not one of those men. Even if I had not been betrayed by Oriel and Peterson, I would not have trusted him, surely not at first.

He did have answers for my questions, most importantly: *Why did he want to help me?*

Because he was a Jew.

I am ashamed to say that, when he told me, I felt some revulsion. I would not like to admit that I was anti-Semitic then, and yet I did feel something like disdain for him.

See how I qualify it? "Some" revulsion. "Something like" disdain.

Here a man offers to help me accomplish an impossible mission, and I think of him with stereotypical prejudice.

But at least I was wise enough to accept.

Renoir said he could have nothing more to do with me and let Schmidt take me in his car. We'd driven about a half mile when the German glanced casually in the mirror. He was letting me know we were being followed.

"Who?" I asked.

"Your friend, Renoir," he said in German. When I didn't say anything, he repeated it for me in English, and from then on we spoke entirely in my language.

"Why would be follow us?" I asked.

"He either wants to make sure I don't give him away, or he will have us killed because you're a fool."

"And you're not?" I laughed.

"I'm not a fool. Two days ago, one of my squadronmates accused me of being a Jew. It's just a matter of time for me. Jews in Germany—do you know what is happening to them?"

"No."

"They are being moved east. Soon, there will be no Jews in Germany. You don't like Jews," he added, catching me by surprise.

I couldn't answer.

"You don't like Jews. You're an American. A Protestant."

"My father is a minister." I folded my arms, once again suspicious. Perhaps this was part of a convoluted plan to find out whose side Peterson was really on. I thought of everything I had said since the truck had been blown up. What was the best course? To deny I knew him? To say as little as possible? To bolt from the car?

I thought briefly of grabbing Schmidt's pistol from him as he drove. But I hesitated, and soon we were driving down a winding road to a ramshackle farm building.

"Some of the black men use this cottage for trysts. You'll be safe during the day. At night, hide in the woods."

"Black men?"

Schmidt smiled. "The mechanics. They wear black overalls and we call them black men. They won't be interested in you, just the local whores. If you hear someone coming, hide in the woods back there, where you can see the path."

I got out of the car.

"I will be back tomorrow," said Schmidt.

The floor was dirt, and the place smelled of perfume and farm animals. I found a bed in the second room—there were only two—with some reasonably clean bedclothes. I wrapped the blanket around me and went outside. Though it was dark, I found a place not far from the house where I could watch the approach and not be seen, or at least not be easily seen.

How likely was it, I wondered, that Schmidt was a Jew? How likely was it that German mechanics needed to use a dilapidated farm building to screw?

Had the escape been staged? The gunfire and the explosions had certainly killed the guards. I'd seen the truck in flames.

But I'd touched Peterson as well. I had seen he was dead. I'd known he was dead until he appeared in the officer's room.

Had I touched his body?

Was it someone dressed to look like him?

It took more than an hour, but finally Oriel filled my thoughts. I remained cold and awake, propped up against a tree trunk, but gradually my fear if not my doubts subsided.

Schmidt did not return the next day. Around noon I began to get restless as well as hungry. I began to explore the area, very cautiously at first, gradually getting bolder. The woods directly behind the building seemed to go on for miles. I walked to the west, going about a quarter mile until I saw a freshly plowed field. I walked along the edge, but could find no house or any sort of building connected to it; I couldn't even see the road that a tractor or farm truck would take to reach it. It seemed bizarre, a field plowed into the middle of the woods.

My hunger had grown to the point where I actually considered stripping bark off some of the trees. Certainly if there had been leaves out, I would have sampled some. Instead I went back to the building where Schmidt had left me and looked inside it to see if there might be some food somewhere.

The first room had a door to a cellar on the right immediately past the main entrance. A third of the stairs were missing. I tripped over the next to last, falling into a shallow pool of water. The elbow that I had hurt the night before screamed with pain; I cursed out loud, and pounded my fist into the water, splashing myself with the muck.

I cursed again, then heard the car outside.

Schmidt?

I froze, unsure whether to go up the stairs or stay there. I heard voices—a woman's in French, a man's in German. It wasn't Schmidt.

They made love twice while I listened below, curled behind the steps. There were wide spaces beneath some of the floorboards in the second room, and light filtered through, light and shadows. The woman was a screamer, and she came several times while the German plodded away at her. Each time she screamed I moved a half step away from the stairs, deeper into the shadows.

I can think of no worse torture than having to listen to another man make love to a woman.

One worse—had the woman been Oriel. But then I wouldn't have listened. Then I would have rushed up the steps and killed him. I would have broken his neck with my bare hands, thrown him down into the muck where I'd kept myself hidden, then taken his place. I would have made love to her for hours and days, plunging again and again as she screamed, as she held my hair, as her teeth edged into my shoulder until they drew blood.

When they finally left, I was so exhausted and tired I went upstairs and collapsed on their bed. The smell of their sweat and juices nearly made me retch. Yet I fell asleep and dreamed I was back home, sitting in church, listening to my father preach.

Except that it wasn't my father, it was Peterson, whose lesson for the day was love thy neighbor.

A car on the gravel woke me. I got out of the house just barely in time to avoid being seen.

Schmidt returned the next morning. He got out of his car, whistled loudly three times, then walked into the house. It was no later than six. Stiff, I pulled myself up by clinging to the tree I'd slept next to. I walked into the building like a man with rusted metal legs.

"I have food for you," said Schmidt. "Eat it. And then I have news. News."

Now, I told myself, was the time to throw him down. I could kill him, take the car—and what?

Escape. Forget the plane. I had been briefed on the roads to take back to the coast; surely I could find my way. I could meet the boat sent to meet our collapsible canoe.

I wolfed down the two loaves of bread he brought without even pausing for a breath. Now, I thought, now I'll do it. But my legs and arms were still stiff.

"You look like a wolf," he said, laughing.

There was a bottle of water in the basket. I picked it up and began to chug it. I got about halfway through before I realized it wasn't water at all; it was wine.

"It was all I could find," he said.

I kept drinking.

"There is another plane coming this afternoon, an experimental plane. It will provide a diversion. We can take the fighters then," he said.

"We?"

"I'm coming with you to England. That's the arrangement."

"Whose arrangement?"

"My arrangement. You and I will steal the planes, one apiece. We'll fly to England."

The idea froze my brain, and I couldn't react. I barely moved for the next hour as he described the procedures the flight crews would take, told me how to time my approach so that the oil in the engine would be sufficiently warm for takeoff, but the pilots wouldn't have appeared yet. He was second-in-command of the squadron and would arrange everything. The leathers, helmet, and bright life vest were in the back of the car.

He told me I would have to be careful about getting onto the base since the commander and several of the officers would remember my face. And, of course, the guards would remember me. On the other hand, no one knew that I had been rescued; the truck and its escorts weren't due back for several more days from Paris.

A good thing, he said, that I was not considered an important enough prisoner to be taken to Germany. He laughed, as if that were the funniest joke in the world.

If I wore the pilot's gear and stayed away from the crewmen, I'd never be challenged, certainly not when everyone else was paying attention to the experimental plane. Two aircraft would be ready to fly as escorts. Schmidt would arrive, yell to me, and we would be off. A *Wort* would help me with my parachute.

A *Wort*?

A crewman, a black man, said Schmidt. He would make it seem as if I were a guest, part of the entourage that had accompanied the test plane to the base. It would be easy; all was arranged.

It sounded like a crazy plan. Obviously, he was setting me up.

"How do I get past the fence?" I asked.

"You'll have to kill one of the guards at the perimeter," he said. "It's the easiest way. Guards can scan the entire fence line, every other post has two men. But there are no telephones or radios. The small post at the northeast corner is one of six with only one man, and it's the most isolated of them all. So if you caught the man patrolling there, you could get in."

Ridiculous.

Schmidt began asking me questions about what I was supposed

to do over the Channel, where I was to land. I lied and said that there were no specific plans, that he should follow me once we were in the air. I simply didn't trust him.

He nodded.

"You'll find a road two miles due north through the woods," he said. "Take it to the east. In a mile or two it will intersect with the road that runs along the southern side of the field. You'll have to get your bearings once you're there."

He went to the car and came back with the pilot's gear and a leather briefcase. He opened the briefcase and pulled out a Luger.

"Not mine." He smiled, handing it over. "I will see you at the airfield at three. Remember, say no more than a word at a time. And the commander knows you, and the guards at the gate. And Peterson, of course."

Peterson. Of course.

Some people draw a sharp distinction between what happens to the body and what becomes of the soul. I have never believed that there is an absolute separation. It's my heritage, I suppose; you can't grow up listening to a Presbyterian minister practice his sermons day after day and not think that what happens to you on the way to the druggist isn't a direct result of God's desire.

I put on the clothes Schmidt had brought with a sense of inevitable doom and set out. At first I wasn't particularly careful about the noise I made or even my direction. But then I began thinking of the Focke Wulf, and what it would be like to fly it. The intelligence people had given us ideas about it—they were only guesses, of course, since the whole reason for our mission was the fact that the plane was essentially unknown. One compared it to the P-40 Curtiss. I'd flown a Warhawk twice, and knew from my encounter with the Fw 190s it was not a very apt comparison. The British had also given me several hours in a captured Bf 109, one of several that had been used to develop adversary tactics the year before. I knew this wasn't a particularly good parallel either, though I hoped the instrument layout would be somewhat similar. The 109 was a tight aircraft, even compared to the Spitfire, itself a bit of squeeze.

I imagined the 190 would be immense. I imagined it would jump off the runway. I imagined shooting over the Channel in mere seconds, met by a pair of Hurricanes, who would realize who I was and dip their wings. I'd land, and be a hero.

By the time I found the dirt road the sun had climbed almost directly overhead. I could hear airplanes in the distance, and every so often I thought I heard a truck or car coming. With the jacket, helmet, and vest tucked in my arm, I decided it was better simply to walk along the side of the road than scamper off to hide. No Frenchman would bother me, and I would just wave off any German who stopped. Whether it was a good idea or not was never tested, as the sounds I heard or thought I heard never materialized.

My anxiety returned as I reached the perimeter road. There was a shallow wash on the other side; at the top sat the fence to the airfield. Unsure exactly where I was, I walked first east, then west, a hundred or so paces. Still unsure, I walked a little farther in each direction, my heart pounding like the bit in a steam drill breaking through pavement. The day's heat seemed to build with every step. My arms and back were wet. Afraid someone would see me wandering on the road, I retreated back to the woods.

I'd just reached it when an airplane roared off the field. Its shadow came over the road about two hundred yards to the left of where I was. Finally, I could picture where I was. I mapped the base in my head, then started down the road again to my right, putting my hands in my pockets as if I were nonchalantly out for a Sunday stroll.

The guardpost sat above a slight bend in the road, giving it a decent view of both directions. It wasn't much of a post—there were a few sandbags for protection on the roadside, and just behind them a set of boards made a low-slung weather break. I could see a machine-gun mount, or at least something that looked like one, but there was no machine gun.

The guard stood a few feet behind the sandbags. His rifle was slung over his shoulder, and he was facing the airfield.

If it had been night, it would have been child's play to get past him, or close enough to kill him. But during the day anyone crossing the road or coming up the incline would be in full view. His post was directly behind the fence; there was another fence beyond him, though I couldn't see it from where I was. Beyond the fence were a few trees, and then an open field to the area where the planes were stationed.

So this was the problem: a hundred yards of open terrain, culminating in a rock-strewn slope that would be hard to climb silently. Get past that, and I'd have to climb the fence before I could reach the guard.

I realized I hadn't decided how to kill him. If I used the pistol, surely it would be heard. But I had no knife, and the idea of taking him on with my bare hands wasn't realistic.

I'm not sure how long I squatted there. In my memory, it's a long time filled with wild plans of turning sticks into sharp, javelin-like weapons. More than likely, though, I was only there for a few minutes, long enough to watch him begin to wander around. I realized that the slope to my left, just around the bend, would be out of his sight unless he went in front of the sandbags. He seemed too bored to do that. I waited for him to turn around and look toward the woods. Instead, he walked in the opposite direction, toward the airfield.

I took a breath, and from that point on I stopped considering things. I simply moved, running across the road, then throwing myself down against the slope. My shoulder hit a sharp rock, but I ignored it, edging up as quietly as I could, watching the post. I took the Luger out of my belt; it felt so oily in my hand at first that it almost slipped. Then I began sliding upward along the slope, moving slightly backward to keep the crest of the sandbags just barely in view.

About halfway up, I saw a hole under the fence just to my right. The dirt was well worn there. I could crawl underneath, then have a clear run at the sentry, as long as he stayed away from the side of the slope.

I would hit him at the back of the head with the pistol. Once he was down, I'd just keep hitting him until he was dead.

And if I didn't kill him—if I didn't kill him I wouldn't much worry about what came next.

My legs trembled as I rose. I took a step—and the German guard appeared in front of the hole, no more than four feet from me.

He had a smirk on his face. Eight 9mm parabellum slugs erased it.

It was only after I'd emptied the magazine that I realized I couldn't hear. An aircraft had chosen that moment to thunder off the runway. It wasn't an Fw 190. I'm not sure what it was. It sounded closer to a diesel locomotive than an aircraft. It sounded like God's angels sweeping out from hell after vanquishing Satan.

I leaped onto the fence and jumped over. A pair of Fw 190s were just leaving the runway, following whatever had made the thunderous noise. I paid no attention; I saw nothing except the guard whom I'd just shot.

He was shorter than I, but at least thirty pounds heavier. Blood soaked his uniform shirt and jacket, but it appeared that only three of my bullets had hit him. One had gone square in the chest, another near the lapel.

The last hit square at his throat, hollowing it out. I pulled the man's body to the sandbags, then turned his face toward the ground so I wouldn't see his tongue, hanging out.

As I rose, I heard a car coming on the road beyond the inner fence. I ran quickly to pick up the soldier's gun. The car kept coming; it was open, some sort of convertible, a staff car or something of that sort, dully gray.

I drew the gun up to fire, then I saw that the driver was Schmidt.

He had someone with him. A woman.

Oriel.

Oriel, the beautiful demon. So it really was a trap.

I shouldered the gun. As I lined up the rifle I realized it wasn't Oriel at all, but the squadron commander's wife.

Schmidt pulled alongside the fence. I put down the gun and waited as he jumped from the car and ran over.

"What?" I asked.

"A change in plans," he said. "I'm going to steal the Messerschmitt."

"There are plenty of 109s. The RAF has plenty," I told him.

"No. The jet. I'm going to fly it."

In my memory, the Messerschmitt chooses this precise moment to pass overhead. It looks gray, and with its long, curved, empty nose the fuselage looks more like a shark than an airplane. Two long, cut-off cigars hang down from its wings, which are thin, almost narrow. It moves with a loud rush across the sky.

I see it perfectly, but it seems to me too convenient, and, besides, I did not yet know what plane Schmidt was talking about.

"What about me?" I asked.

"Take the plane as planned. Choose your moment the way I said."

"But when?"

He'd already started back to the car. I waited until he had driven away before I put down the gun and climbed over the fence. When I got over, I realized the Luger was empty and that I'd left the rifle behind. But instead of going back I turned and began walking toward the dispersion area.

Two Focke Wulfs sat close to the concrete. Two men were working on one; another man sat on the wing of a second. They weren't paying any attention to me. There weren't any pilots, either. The planes seemed to have been refueled, but their engines for some reason were not running.

It must have been then that I actually saw the plane. The three men near the Focke Wulfs stopped and stared at it as it landed.

I know now that it was an Me 262, the Messerschmitt jet fighter. The plane would remain in development for two more years, undergoing various changes and improvements, but from what I saw on the field that afternoon it was already an impressive machine, far, far beyond anything we had in the air ourselves. I've heard in fact that the plane could have been operational later that year, except that Hitler decided it should be a bomber instead of the fighter it was built to be.

The fool.

You could tell from the sound of it that it was fast. It came onto the long runway at a very good clip, and I imagine the pilot had to stand on his brakes to bring himself to a stop. The runway there was extremely long, which may have been why it had come. Even so, it took most of the length to stop, the tail wavering before finally settling down.

I envied Schmidt. I wanted to fly it. I stood and watched as the mechanics and a group of spectators ran to it. Two Focke Wulfs that had been escorting it landed; the crewmen who had been on the other planes went and began prepping them, but otherwise all eyes were on the jet. A fuel truck backed gingerly toward the plane, flanked by ten or twelve men. Many others milled nearby, craning their necks and bending to get a good view.

They were obviously going to run it back up into the sky as soon as they could. Which meant I had to be ready as well.

"An odd horse," said someone in German. It was one of the ground crew who'd been working on the Fw 190s. I grunted back in reply.

"We'll be servicing them in London, soon," said the German.

I laughed.

He asked for a cigarette. I shrugged and shook my head apologetically. He moved on.

At that moment, I felt as if God were protecting me. God wanted me to succeed. Truly, there was no other answer for my being here, or for the man neglecting to question me. I was going to succeed.

Cars crisscrossed back and forth near the Messerschmitt. I noticed two troop trucks parked nearby, and German soldiers were lined in a tight picket on two sides facing the fence.

By contrast, the Focke Wulfs were completely open and unguarded. All I had to do was wait for the crewmen to start one, then jump them.

But I had no weapon.

There was a toolbox nearby. I walked to it, glanced to make sure no one was looking, then scooped down to open the kit. My head is racing and I barely hear the car coming up behind me.

———

I have a pistol in my hand when the car stops. I can see it very clearly. It's an odd little thing, a Mauser M712, which has a square box magazine in front of the trigger. It's twelve inches long, about three pounds. There is a small lever switch on the left side of the gun, that at first I mistake for the safety, sliding it forward. The barrel hangs down awkwardly from my hand, the gun pitching forward because of its design. Finally, I realize the safety is at the back; I can't quite get it off with just my thumb, though, and must use two hands.

Where did the gun come from? Most likely from the toolbox. But as often as I try, I can't see it there, or remember precisely how it came into my hand. I only remember that I heard the car coming up suddenly, and I shoved my hand into my pocket, trying to hide the gun. The thick magazine hung up, and I stood with my palm against the back of it, half–sticking out from my clothes.

One pilot was in the sedan, dressed in flight gear. I watched the car stop. I thought it would be Schmidt, come once more with a change of plans because there were too many people near the jet. I could feel my heart pounding even harder, ready.

But it wasn't Schmidt. It was Peterson. We stood about eight feet apart, looking at each other in shock for a minute.

Then Peterson broke into his grin.

"Well, are you ready?" he asked.

I didn't know what to say.

"Come on. You take the plane on the right. I'll take the left."

He started for the Focke Wulf.

He must have seen the gun—it was hanging halfway out of my pocket. But he didn't say anything to the ground crew; they seemed to be waiting for him, and stepped back and saluted.

Another car started across the field behind me. A truck, too.

I started to run. I took the pistol out, staring at the back of it to make sure the safety was off. One of the ground crew tried to tackle me from the side, but he was easy to duck. I ran ten yards to the second plane, where a mechanic was just turning on the wing. I pressed the trigger of the gun. The muzzle flew up as I fired, but the bullet struck the German at the left side of the chest and he spun slightly, rolling onto the wing. With a leap I was at the cockpit.

Peterson, Schmidt, the man on the wing—they seem to vanish somehow. I hit the starter twice, three times, yanking at the lever that spins the engine even though it's already running. The fact that it's running doesn't sink in.

There's a screech at the side of my head. The man I shot claws his way up over the front of the plane, trying to grab on to the frame of the canopy and pull himself in. The throttle jumps in my hand—I can't get the engine to rev properly, and the plane shudders crazily. Then something in the motor seems to catch, and wind rushes across my face. The German throws himself down on me. My first thought is to go on ignoring him. I move the throttle to full but at first the plane remains in place, its wheel chocked, and perhaps I've left the brakes on.

The German punches the side of my face. I fall to the side, and at the same time, the plane jerks forward. I flail back at him, punching with all my might though I can't get much leverage—the plane's cockpit is actually extremely narrow, much tighter than I expected. I see the German's face, hatred welling up. I take another swing, and instead of hitting him I smash my hand on the metal spar holding the cockpit glass. Blood spurts out—it looks as if it comes from the metal, not my hand.

We're already moving, bumping along almost sideways toward the trees. I grab the stick and jerk the plane in the direction of the runway. I can't see forward very well—it was about as bad as looking out the front of a Spitfire.

Trim for takeoff. Schmidt told me I needed fifteen degrees on the flap and to keep the control column back or I'd start swinging wildly. I move in slow motion. The man on the wing is still draped over me, trying to grab the gear. I can see the compass on the instrument panel, but that's all I can see. The plane suddenly stops bumping, and I push the stick hard right, trying to steer onto the runway but I'm too late. The plane starts twisting, and there's a sharp pain in my left ear, then another, then something at my neck. The German is biting me, and, finally, I take my hands off the stick and with everything I have I punch him. I'm tired and drained and wondering where God has gone, and I pound him, I pound him as hard as I've pounded anything in my life.

The pain in my neck crumbles, and I'm on the runway headed in the wrong direction. A soldier fires at me. A bullet smashes through the armored glass at the side—it looks more like a bee than a bullet, wiggling through a spider's web.

The engine has steadied. I'm on the runway now. I'm starting, and I still can't see but it's sweet, oh so very sweet, and now I'm in the sky, climbing steadily.

A crank mechanism at the side closed the canopy. I couldn't get it to work. I must have fumbled with it for a good five minutes, perhaps even more. I didn't trim the wheels or check the instruments or even properly set my course—I fumbled with the crank, trying to get the cockpit snugged.

When it finally closed, I leaned back against the seat. For the first time, I checked the sky to get my bearings and see if I was being pursued. The Fw 190 had a good, high position for the pilot, much better than any other aircraft I'd flown. There was nothing behind me.

Another airplane flew about three or four thousand feet above me about a half mile ahead.

Peterson?

I nudged my stick back, climbing and angling slightly to get into an offset trail. I began checking the instruments. I had a full load of fuel. I'd made it. I'd pulled off the impossible.

I warned myself that there was still a long way to go. The Channel was a good thirty minutes to the north.

I'd practiced a lot with the radio of a Bf 109. This one seemed almost exactly the same as the unit I'd worked in England, but there was one problem—I didn't have a headset.

Peterson would.

Peterson. Thank God he found me.

———

When I look back, it seems odd that I accepted him so easily. I wasn't mad at him for giving me and Loup away. I might have rationalized that he had done so to save the mission, not himself. But I didn't. I didn't think about it at all. I didn't think about Schmidt or the jet either. I was too busy flying the unfamiliar plane.

Peterson climbed to about fifteen thousand feet. I remained a little lower than he, trailing off his right wing. Soon he began tacking westward, roughly in the direction of Dieppe. As I started to follow I spotted a group of fighters directly on the new course, flying at about twenty thousand feet, a good distance away. I thought they were RAF fighters on a sweep, or maybe escorting a reconnaissance flight, but as I watched them coming on I realized the planes had to be Germans. There were a dozen of them, a full squadron or *Jagdstaffel*, all Bf 109s.

More than likely, they'd ignore us, I thought. But if they didn't? I checked the gun panel. I was ready to fire, if I had to.

Twelve on two, even in planes as disproportionately matched as these, were not very good odds. But they were survivable. Our best bet ultimately would be to blow right past, just run through the gamut and go for it—the Messerschmitts couldn't hope to keep up. I hoped Peterson was saying something to them, pretending to be German so they wouldn't bother us.

As soon as I saw the first plane at the far right begin to bank, I realized they were setting up an attack. I slammed my hand on the throttle and pulled the stick back—my aim was to take away some of the height advantage the first section of fighters would have, powering past the heads-on attack, then swerving as the other fighters came in from behind.

Peterson remained straight and level. Confused, I hesitated, then started to ease back on the stick so I wouldn't overfly him, sliding back into a wing position. As I reached to throttle back I saw the Messerschmitts breaking into what was clearly an attack mode— three elements, one on each flank, one head-on.

I held my wing position, wondering what Peterson was going to do. I had one hand on the throttle, ready to jump when he accelerated.

His left wing tipped and he dived toward the west. Of all the possible maneuvers, it was the one that made the least sense, or so it seemed to me—the Messerschmitts were still a good way off, and this would only give the squadron more time to flail at us. But I followed anyway, instinctually trusting my flight leader as I'd been trained. As I passed through ten thousand feet, the first pair of Messerschmitts began a front-quarter attack; they were at too great a distance and angle to pose a real danger, but the sight of their streaking noses rattled me. A little shock of fear grew in my throat; my shoulders felt heavy, and I started to yell at Peterson, demanding to know what the hell he was doing. As if in answer the gray rain of machine-gun fire from a Messerschmitt laced the air before me— a German had somehow managed to dive on my tail. I flailed right, but then came back quickly, Peterson now moving into the left quadrant of my cockpit glass. The gunfire was gone.

I craned my neck to find my pursuer, expecting him either to be behind me or, more likely, closing on Peterson. But he'd disappeared; I finally saw a plane recovering off to my right and figured it was probably the Messerschmitt.

Somewhere around here, I lose Peterson. I have a memory of him well off to my left, then he's gone. The sky around me is clear momentarily, then I have another Bf 109 in my face. Its wing guns are bright red, bullets flaring out in dark lines across the sky. I bring my nose up and for the first time fire my cannon.

If memory were something kind, I would see the plane blowing apart, exploded by the 20mm shells from my guns. But I remember clearly that my bullets missed. I can see them trailing downward and off to the left, far from the path of the oncoming fighter.

It takes me a few moments before I can reorient myself, before I can stop the compass from sliding south. Two more Messerschmitts take up the attack, this time on my tail. Their tracers bloom over my wings, and for a good twenty seconds I think I am doomed. Jittering to the right and left, I somehow duck the bullets. The

Focke Wulf's engine finally drives me beyond them, and I'm in the clear.

Peterson is gone. Pushing up in the seat, I scan backward and forward, trying to find him and orient myself. There are two separate groups of planes to the southeast; they're climbing, not attacking, and they're far enough away that they won't be able to catch me. But I can't find Peterson at all. As I climb through fifteen thousand feet, I realize there's a pair of Me 109s at twelve thousand feet flying ahead of me, roughly three miles away.

I gun my engine and move to attack.

I was not being overly foolish. For one thing, if I had kept on my course the Messerschmitts would inevitably have seen me and launched their own attack. Striking them first kept surprise on my side.

I didn't stop to reason it out, though. I simply fell into the attack. The Messerschmitt closest to me was about a thousand feet higher than the other, and not quite parallel. As I came on I raked his right wing; it seemed to bubble as he turned toward my path. I let go of the trigger and pushed the stick hard to the left, the whole plane angling on its axis as I tried to pull the second Messerschmitt into my sights. But the pilot, who'd probably been the element leader and therefore more experienced than his wingman, turned his nose into my direction and I lost the shot. The Fw 190 flailed as I started to turn with him, then realizing that would be a mistake broke hard in my original direction. The Focke Wulf, which had been so easy to fly until then, took my excitement very badly; the plane bucked and nearly pushed herself over into a spin.

My head jumbled, disconnected from my body. If the German fighters had been more powerful or better handled, they would have nailed me then. As it was the leader managed a pass from almost directly overhead, and probably the only thing that saved me was my utter confusion—I pushed the plane into a fierce dive with both hands. The Messerschmitt flew past without landing a shot.

Sweat pouring from my body, I recovered and found I was clear. My arms slumped. The muscles at the bottom of my neck and top of my shoulders stung.

But I could see water ahead. I wanted it to be the Channel so badly that I was afraid to decide it really was.

I had no idea where exactly I was anymore, but at that point I didn't care. There would be plenty of places to land, plenty of airfields from Manston over to Needs Oar. I was so anxious now that I let down the landing gear, one of the signs we'd agreed on to signal RAF interceptors that we were on their side.

As the gear trundled into place and my airspeed dropped, a typhoon exploded over my right wing. A black funnel whipped downward, and it was only the sudden deceleration of the plane that saved me from being hit as an Fw 190 crossed over my path. As it arced back I saw the fuselage markings and realized it was Peterson.

I rocked my wings as he banked, trying to get him to realize it was me, thinking for some reason that he thought I was a *real* German in a *real* plane, not his wingman trying to complete the mission. He came at me hard, guns blazing. As the cannons lit, I shoved my aircraft hard left, ducking into a lopsided roll that nearly tore the gear off before I managed to regain control.

How did I know it was Peterson?

I can't recall the markings on the plane. I doubt very much that I had seen them before taking off or later in the sky. Logically, we both would have been moving too fast for me to get a good glimpse of them when he opened fire.

One Focke Wulf to me would be the same as any other. But I know it was him. That I know. That I know.

I leveled off at four or five thousand feet and immediately tried pulling the landing gear back up. But it had locked into position and wouldn't budge.

When I think of this part of the flight, I remember myself sinking into the seat, pulled down by the weight of my despair. The plane grows around me, the instrument panel towering above me. Black diamonds appear, crisscrossing in front of my wing. Something taps the backplate of my seat, rapping against the thick armor there. A white shroud seems to hover above the gunsight mechanism.

And then the Fw 190 streaks over my wing and sails to the right. I stare at it, completely in awe, wondering why God has chosen to save me, and how.

In the corner of my eye, there is a gray blur. I turn the plane to the east, and as I do I see that Peterson is being attacked by a strange aircraft moving faster than any I've ever seen. Its shark nose closes in on the tail of the Focke Wulf. Peterson turns hard to the east, ducking his wing, but it is too late—the Messerschmitt 262 collides with his midsection and the entire sky becomes a brilliant red flame.

I'm sure Schmidt was the pilot. No one else would have deliberately flown the aircraft into an Fw 190, even if they thought it was escaping to the enemy. The Messerschmitt would have been too valuable.

And besides, few men are brave enough to kill themselves that way. I could never have done so.

For the next fifteen minutes, I flew directly north, reaching the water, making land. A pair of Hurricanes came out to meet me less than a half mile from the English shore. They acted immediately as if they knew who I was, though I found out later that in fact my mission had been for all intents and purposes forgotten. We put down at New Romney—I try to recall the landing, which cost me a broken arm, a sprained knee, and a smashed head, but I can't. The right landing gear collapsed, but whether I spun or slid or fell off the runway—it's just not in my head to remember. I was lifted from the cockpit and carried to a very cold room before falling into another void.

Days pass. My nurse is Oriel, whose body grows with my child. Her touch remains as warm and sensual, and my head floats above us as we make love.

Finally, one afternoon I see a woman in a white smock standing near me.

"Oriel," I say.

She turns. It's not Oriel. The woman is pregnant, seven or eight months at least.

"Madeline," she says. "Madeline."

"Yes, Madeline." And it is at that point my struggle with memory begins.

Colonel Maclean came by the next morning, with two men I hadn't met before. With a grim face, he congratulated me on my achievement.

"The plane is in excellent shape," he said. "You did remarkably well. Remarkably well."

They had taped my knee so severely that it was difficult to sit up in the bed. One of the men, a captain, helped prop the pillows and made a joke about how he only played nurse for heroes.

"I'm not a hero," I said.

They all laughed, then nodded solemnly.

"Do you want to know what happened?" I said.

"That's why we're here, son," said the other officer.

"Do you want to write it down?"

"We will," said Maclean. "We'll have a stenographer come around. For now, why don't you give us the highlights?"

So I told them the story, essentially as I've told it here. There may even have been more gaps. I forced the words out of my mouth as fast as I could, trying to bring back everything, as if saying it that first time would freeze it, preserve it in my head. I told them about Oriel, even the shame of masturbating in the factory. I told them of Peterson and Schmidt, the real hero. They listened with blank faces, standing all the while. Once or twice a nurse appeared at the door, but a glare from Maclean sent her away.

When I was done, Maclean shook his head. "You don't remember very well."

"I do. What I remember, I remember. There are parts missing, I know. Gaps, little details. But I'm pretty sure of what I said."

"You don't remember very well," he repeated.

I insisted I did.

"Peterson was a hero, chap," said the captain abruptly. "So are you."

"No," I said. "I did get the plane, but I was lucky."

"You're being too hard on yourself," insisted the captain. "Think of what you've been through, where you were. My God, man. If you're not a hero, who is?"

"I didn't save anyone's life," I said.

"The plane will," said Maclean. "It will, son. You are a hero."

"If it weren't for Schmidt, I never would have gotten on the airfield, or known what to do with the plane, or gotten away."

"Schmidt doesn't exist. He's been invented by your faulty memory," said Maclean.

I was so dumbfounded, I couldn't answer.

"We've made a careful check of the radar that day," explained the older officer. "Yours was the only plane that came over the Channel. The Germans don't have an aircraft such as you've described. They've been working on jet technology, but they're still far behind even the Italians."

My head had started to hurt about halfway through the story. Now it pounded at the top of my eyes, forcing them to narrow.

"I'm not a hero," I insisted.

They give me a medal anyway.

Were they right? Was it all an invention?

No. I'm sure it wasn't. After the war I read about the Me 262. That isn't proof, surely, but it fits, it fits. It has to be true. They were either wrong or protecting other secrets, or their choice of Peterson.

I know too well what memory does. Eighty-plus years have taught me that it can never be fully trusted. But it could not have invented the plane, not then, not now. It could not have invented Schmidt.

———

How could Peterson have deceived us so completely? He hadn't volunteered for a dangerous mission—he'd arranged to go back home.

It's not his betrayal that stings the worst. It's the fact that he thought so lightly of me. The airport hadn't even been alerted; he just assumed I wouldn't make it there on my own. Truth is, he was probably right.

If Schmidt had flown the plane straight on to England, he would have been the one with the medal. As it turned out, another Focke Wulf had been recovered a day or two before I landed, so my plane wasn't really that important in the grand scheme of the war. But imagine an Me 262 two years before it appeared over the skies of Germany. Imagine it reverse-engineered by the British or the Americans. How many lives would have been saved by such a plane?

When I had a choice, I followed Peterson, not Schmidt. I dismissed him entirely from my mind. How could anyone with such poor judgment be a hero?

And yet the Air Cross was awarded to me. And if I doubt my memory too much, if I give in to the temptation to believe this is all invention, I have only to open the bottom drawer of my desk and hold the medal and read the lie of the citation proclaiming me a hero.

I am old now, long removed from these events, at times estranged from my memory of them. It's been nearly a decade since I have given up my ministry, twelve years beyond the day my wife passed on.

I tell the story of what happened nearly every night, though only to myself. The main details remain steady, but small bits flash and glow and fade, falling away into the shadows. Sometimes they reemerge, shards of glass from a window shattered long ago.

For many years, I told no one. Colonel Maclean and the others who heard it in the hospital room were the only people who knew it for many years. No stenographer ever came. There were two reports I was asked to sign, which I did without bothering to read them.

Then one day perhaps thirty years ago, when I was already past fifty, I tried to work the account into a sermon. But I fell short on the moral. If God had indeed saved me, as any good Presbyterian would say, what role had Oriel played? How could making love to her tell me so much about God, when surely she was in league with the devil?

Yet I could not tell the story without her. And so I never told it to my wife, nor my sons.

At times, I'm convinced Maclean was right, that my mind was clouded by the crash. That I really don't remember anything; that the past is all a figment of my imagination built from things other people have suggested. At other times I think I'm another victim of some uncharted mind disease similar to Alzheimer's, which substitutes one reality for another.

And then sometimes when I'm certain of this, I chance to see a young woman in a store or passing on the street. She turns her head slowly toward me, and I see Oriel again. Her soft weight presses once more against me in the field, and I look up to heaven and see the bright word of God shining past the blackness.

I fight my memory to remember this, and feel flushed from the victory.

AUTHOR'S NOTE

Aficionados of World War II aircraft are no doubt familiar with the sensation made by the Fw 190 when it first appeared in combat against the RAF, and probably know about the plan by Captain Phillip Pinckney and Jeffrey Quill to steal a Focke Wulf in June of 1942. "Operation Airthief" was dropped after an Fw 190 pilot became confused and landed in Wales instead of France, perhaps one of the most fortuitous combat mistakes of all time. Some details of the planned mission (which was to have featured a seaborne insertion and the theft of only one plane) are included in Dr. Alfred Price's *Focke Wulf*, a definitive book on the Fw 190, which was one of the references consulted for this novella—though I must admit I hadn't known of "Operation Airthief" until after I'd outlined and started working on the story.

The first versions of the Messerschmitt Me 262 jet fighter were being fitted and tested with jet engines at roughly the same time. As documented in J. Richard Smith and Eddie J. Creek's *Me 262*, all of the tests took place in Germany, not France, but would have had sufficient range and capability to perform as described here. Had Hitler not interfered, a production version of the jet fighter could have entered service in 1943, causing even more trouble for the Allies than the Fw 190.

Among the many other sources on period aircraft and the Luftwaffe, readers interested in seeing what the Butcher Birds looked like might look for Morten Jessen's *Focke Wulf 190*, which contains many photographs of the plane and their crews. I also found inspiration in a visit to the Imperial War Museum in London with my four-year-old son, where an Fw 190 is on permanent display.

While the technical and overall historical information is as accurate as I could make it, I've taken some liberties in the interests of storytelling, most notably in constructing and locating the airfield. Its description is a rough composite of three actual bases, not all of which were used by Fw 190s in the spring of 1942.

BLOOD BOND

HAROLD ROBBINS

HAROLD ROBBINS (1916–1997) was one of America's bestselling authors, selling more than fifty million copies of his novels during his half-century career. His books were notable for their thinly veiled depictions of famous people, including Howard Hughes, Lana Turner, and Jimmy Hoffa. He blended fact, drama, action, and sex into bestselling novel after novel. He used elements of his own life growing up as an orphan on the streets of New York City, and in later books took on Hollywood, the televangelism industry, and unions. Several of his novels were made into films, including *A Stone for Danny Fisher*, which was shot as *Kid Creole* and starred Elvis Presley. His first novel, *Never Love a Stranger*, was filmed in 1958 and featured John Drew Barrymore and Steve McQueen.

ONE

Blut.kitt [German: blood + cement] The Nazi pact that evil acts
bind together members of the SS into a brotherhood
—DEUTSCH DICTIONARY

BAVARIA, GERMANY • JUNE 1, 1944

The Luftwaffe flight attendant on the Junkers Ju 86 had frontal
artillery that jutted out straighter than the barrel of the 7.92mm
machine gun in the bomber's nose. She was peaches and cream
with juicy red lips. Just before dawn, ten thousand feet over Munich, she'd cooed over my SS captain's uniform and run her fingers
through my golden locks. I had to admit that I looked good in the
black uniform of the Master Race. Wouldn't she have been surprised if I'd told her I was Jewish.

I kept asking myself, What's a nice Jewish boy from Jersey doing
riding in a Nazi plane? It started with the Japs bombing Pearl
Harbor and just kept getting worse until finally I was sent to Germany to kill some Nazi bastard who sorely deserved it. Back on
Saturday, December 6, 1941, the day before the Japs hit us, I had

pitched a two-hitter at a charity exhibition game at Ebbetts Field
beating the Chicago Cubs, three to one. I was the best left-handed
power pitcher on the Dodger roster. Arnold Berkowitz is my real
name, Arnie the Barber is what the boys in the press box called me
because of my reputation for shaving the chins of batters who
leaned in too close on my inside fastballs.

That Saturday night I'd gone out to celebrate the win with my
teammates. I awoke the next morning with a hangover, a naked
redhead, her naked brunette sister, and news that the Japs had
pulled some real shit in Honolulu harbor.

Everybody ran down on Monday morning and enlisted. Except
me. I figured the war could wait until I got another season or two
under my belt, but Wild Bill Donovan started a superspy outfit
called the OSS and jerked me in. He said it was because I was
raised in Germany by American parents until I was thirteen and
spoke the vernacular. That's what he said, but I think the guy just
liked to talk baseball, and I was a captive audience. I hated like hell
exchanging a baseball uniform that paid me twenty thousand a year
to an army one that paid about twenty bucks a month. It wasn't
that I was unpatriotic. I'm as rah-rah as the next guy. But a guy
could get his nuts shot off throwing pineapples at the krauts or
Tojo. Wasn't that what happened to one of those guys Hemingway
wrote about?

Not that there wasn't one good aspect of living in wartime Washington. The town had mushroomed with the war boom, and the
gold to be mined was women. All kinds of women, ready to wave
the flag for the country. There was so much action, I'd heard Good-
year was running short on rubber for jeep tires. I was batting a
thousand until my foot landed in my big mouth.

After a few too many one night in a DC bar, during an argument
about whether the Georgia Peach was a greater player than the
Babe, I told Wild Bill that Cobb couldn't carry the Babe's jockstrap.
I bumped up my expert opinion a notch by letting Wild Bill know
in front of a senator that he didn't know shit from shinola about
baseball.

Next thing I knew, a tailor was measuring me for a storm trooper uniform. Actually, it was a black SS uniform, which strictly speaking wasn't a storm trooper outfit—that was the old brown shirt SA designation—but that's what we called all those goose-stepping bastards.

Oh, yeah, it was also my perfect German. That was the important part, Wild Bill said. That and some bullshit about my blood type. The assignment had nothing to do with an argument over baseball. *Jawohl, Herr General!*

TWO

Looking out the window as we began the descent for the airfield outside Berchtesgaden, I could see the Obersalzberg, the sixteen-hundred-foot-high mountaintop above the town. The terrain below was all peaks and valleys, crowned by the Walzmann, the country's second highest mountain, and the Königssee, a dark, deep, and mysterious alpine lake that had an almost mythical essence to me as a child. In the distance off to the left, were the spires of Salzburg, Austria.

The Obersalzberg, which literally translated meant "top of the salt mountain," was just about the most important chunk of real estate in the Third Reich, the Nazi empire that had most of Europe under its goose steps. Back in medieval times, they called salt taken out of the mines "white gold" and fought wars over it. Now the Berghof, Adolf's favorite residence, was up there, along with his Eagle's Nest retreat and the summer houses of Goering, Bormann, Speer, and other Nazi bigwigs. So was an operations center for the OKW, the Oberkommando der Wehrmacht, the German High Command. Along with ten miles of fence and more SS Leibstandarte—der Führer's personal bodyguard—than you could shake a stick at.

I wasn't overly confident about keeping up the pretense of being an SS captain. I was relying on other people and didn't know how well they'd done their part. The real SS Captain-Doctor Erich Wolfhardt had been kidnapped and murdered when he left his parents' house in Hamburg around midnight to go to the airport. I was smuggled into Hamburg and boarded the plane in his stead without ever seeing him—dead or alive. But, if the German underground agents carrying out that part of the mission had failed to make Wolfhardt disappear, or any number of other things had gone south, I would be exposed as a fraud as soon as we landed.

My destination was to a hospital tucked up in the mountains near Lake Königssee. The OSS agents who briefed me on the mission told me the hospital was in a picture-pretty setting. That was great, but I wasn't there for the flora and fauna. My big mouth had gotten me into what could only be described as a suicide mission. I was going to kill Adolf, you see.

The plane began its descent, and the Fräulein with blower's lips and tits that stood at attention said farewell.

"Lebewohl, Herr Hauptmann."

"Hauptsturmfuhrer," I corrected her. A captain in the regular army was called a Hauptmann. We storm troopers were a private club with our own unique ranks. Translated in a straight line, my SS rank meant captain-storm-leader.

"Sorry, Herr Hauptsturmfuhrer." She touched the two lightning-strike SS-runes on my right collar. "You must be on a very important mission. The plane was diverted from a general's use to fly you. The rumor is that you are to see der Führer himself."

Her blue eyes were wide with admiration and her red lips moist and swollen. What do they say about lips? That they're a sex symbol because they resemble the lips between a woman's legs?

"I serve der Führer," I said. "Obedience unto death." That last bit was the initiation pledge of new SS members. I thought it was a nice touch, a little humility while facing death.

I squeezed her fleshy, succulent tush. There's something about a woman in uniform—it makes them horny for a man in uniform. I found that out in DC before I rerouted my fate by pissing off General Donovan. He *was* wrong. Cobb was a prick who didn't do a fraction for the game of baseball that Ruth did. Wasn't Yankee Stadium the House That Ruth Built? What fucking luck, to be hit by a beanball—and not even in a ballpark.

"Perhaps on your return trip . . ." Her fingers brushed my crotch.

At which moment the navigator yelled back for us to strap in, we were coming in for a landing.

I'd have given anything to stay on board and hit one out of the park with the Fräulein: The plane was perfect for it. The Junkers was comfortable, a light bomber that looked tough on the outside with its three 7.92mm MG15 gun mounts—nose, dorsal, and a drop-down belly gun called a "dustbin turret." But the Ju 86 was a notoriously poor combat performer, and this one had been turned into a luxury suite inside for Nazi brass.

It would have been nice to have stayed aboard, sipped champagne, and given her a thorough examination, relying on my medical training. Did I mention that I was a gynecologist? A *Frauenarst*, as the krauts put it. I had a day's training for the rank of an SS captain and five hours of gynecological training, all by the OSS. That left me with the ability to tell a private from a general and know where to put the clamp when a woman was on the stirrups.

"Auf Wiedersehen, Liebchen." I gave her plush tush another squeeze before I went through the hatch. I knew exactly what I would ask for as my last meal if there was a firing squad waiting for me as I stepped out.

I climbed down the ladder to the tarmac as a staff car drove up and parked nearby. I pulled up the collar of my trench coat and headed for the car, my knees going soft as I got closer. A Standartenfuhrer, SS colonel, stepped out of the back door and waited for me. His Walther P38 was holstered on his hip. He had one hand on it while he used his other hand to bang his swagger stick against the side of his leg. He looked like a man waiting for a dog to kick.

This was going to be my first test. The only person I'd had to fool up to now was the flight attendant.

"Hauptsturmfuhrer Wolfhardt, reporting, sir." I gave him my best German, a stiff-arm salute, a *Heil Hitler!* and clicked my heels.

Then I waited for him to take out his Pistole and shoot me between the eyes. I expected him to see through my act on sight.

The colonel, whose name was Vogler, returned my salute, didn't shoot me, and we climbed into the backseat of the staff car.

"What have you been told about your assignment?" Colonel Vogler asked. He had a Swabian peasant's square face, paunchy, unhealthy skin pallor with pox facial pits, fat purple lips, and teeth so yellow it looked like he brushed his teeth with a plug of tobacco. He stared at me with small restless eyes, the eyes of a nervous Doberman.

I would have guessed that all SS officers were spit-and-polish nuts, but Vogler wasn't. His black SS uniform was just a bit off kilter. Not wrinkled, not sloppy, just not perfect. It needed to be let out a little to reduce the stretch at the belly, the collar points on his shirt were browning from too much hot iron-on starch, his boots were highly polished but showed old scuffs at the toes. But maybe it was the shape of his body that made him look less than snappy. He bulged in the middle from wide hips, the look some older women get. Decked out in the all-black uniform with a red-and-white Nazi armband, he looked like an eight ball that had been knocked around too many pool tables.

I wasn't sure what military unit he belonged to. The designation on his uniform was the Totenkopf, the skull and crossbones of the Death's Head detachments. All us SS wore the Totenkopf on our caps, but Vogler also had it as a unit designation. During my OSS briefing I was told that the Totenkopf unit insignia was worn by panzer combat divisions and "special" units behind the lines that guarded prison camps, but I didn't see how that would fit into a hospital environment, which was, I was told by the OSS briefers, my destination.

I wasn't impressed with either his SS colonel's uniform or the threatening implications of a special Death's Head unit. Watching the American military establishment burst at the seams during the early part of the war, with unqualified officers skyrocketing in rank, I'd learned that when a tide comes in it carries a lot of garbage with it. Vogler struck me as someone who flowed in the current when der Führer and his Beer Hall Putsch pals got the keys to the Reichstag. I figured he was a waiter at some Nazi social club before the war, and was standing in the right line when SS officer uniforms were passed out.

"I was merely told to report to the airfield. What my destination was, what my duties were to be—"

"And you weren't even curious." It wasn't a question.

"Curious? Of course I was curious. But I obey orders."

"Why do you think you're here?"

"To serve der Führer," I said with conviction.

"Nonsense, that's not an answer, we all serve der Führer every moment of every day, that is a duty imposed by the uniform we wear. Why do you think you were suddenly ordered to report to this particular area?"

I hesitated. Sounding too stupid would raise as much suspicion as being too knowledgeable.

"I'm a medical doctor—"

"Newly licensed, and a Frau's Doktor at that." He waved aside my medical qualifications. "No one would let you operate on a *Schweinhund*."

"Then there is another matter—"

"Yes?" He leaned toward me. His eyes had the preternatural gaze of a Doberman with a smaller dog in its mouth. His uniform had a musty smell of beer yeast, an unpleasant accompaniment to a peppermint scent on his breath. The combination meant he was a drinker trying to cover his tracks.

"But I'm not permitted to disclose it."

"Ja!" He slapped my leg with the swagger stick. "Very good, Hauptsturmfuhrer, that is exactly the correct answer. Had you given any other, I would have my driver turn around and take you back to the plane, with orders for the Eastern Front."

Now that was a chilling thought. The Russians had been pushing the krauts back since they knocked out Hitler's Sixth Army at Stalingrad last year, taking revenge all along the way for the butchering of their people. The krauts had shot Russian prisoners of war rather than feed them. The Russians shot the krauts rather than feed them. And everybody was freezing his ass off. Wouldn't it be ironic if I fucked up and found myself shipped out to the Russian front, a place colder than polar bear shit and hotter than the hinges of hell.

"You are one of a select group wearing the uniform of the Schutzstaffel who have been chosen to give a blood transfusion to der Führer should it become necessary. You must suspect that your sudden reassignment had something to do with that."

"Herr Colonel, I've dreaded the thought that my service might be needed because it would mean something is wrong with der Führer—"

"No, no, der Führer will have a minor operation, nothing more. You will be told the details when we reach the hospital. But that is why you are here."

I leaned closer to give the colonel a confidential look. "You understand, Colonel, that should der Führer need my blood, I would gladly give every drop." I touched my arm where my "A" blood type had been tattooed in the SS manner. "Bearing the same blood type as our leader is a matter of honor for me, not a sacrifice."

"Hauptsturmfuhrer Wolfhardt, if der Führer needed *all* your blood, I personally would cut your throat, hang you by your heels, and bleed you white. But that's not the case. This time."

"I can't tell you how happy I am to hear that der Führer's condition is not serious." Jesus H. Christ, what if the man's a bleeder?

"Listen carefully, Hauptsturmfuhrer. Prior to being honored as a potential donor for der Führer, you passed the investigation of those charged with checking your background. You have the correct blood type, you have no current diseases or history of hereditary diseases, you are considered to possess some intelligence, your blond hair, blue eyes, and pale skin are Aryan traits, and genealogists have confirmed no Jewish ancestors going back at least two hundred years." He tapped my leg with his swagger stick. "But you have not passed my investigation yet."

"Which is?"

"I am in charge of security at the hospital. It is my duty to ensure that der Führer's stay will be a safe one. That means anyone who is at the facility must be checked and double-checked by me. I will be observing you, Wolfhardt. When you look over your back you will see me. I'll be under your bed when you rest your head at night. Raise my suspicions and . . ." He made a cutting motion across his throat with the swagger stick, then tapped me again on the leg with it. "Is that understood?"

"I am here to serve mein Führer, Colonel. Like you, I will do whatever is necessary to achieve that goal. If it means laying down my life, I will do so."

"Since your selection you have been ordered to maintain a strict vegetarian diet. Have you followed that mandate?"

"Of course."

"You have never seen combat, have you, Herr Hauptsturm-fuhrer?" As Vogler spoke, his chest expanded, pushing the combat medals on his chest out a bit farther.

I recognized an Iron Cross, second class, a silver wound badge—indicating he'd been wounded more than twice—and an infantry assault badge. There were a couple others, but I couldn't remember what they stood for. I had to admit that the combat medals belied the impression he gave as a putz, but from everything I'd heard about the SS, these guys awarded each other medals faster than Girl Scouts handed out cookies.

"I understand that before your training to look between a Frau's legs, you worked as a *librarian* at the Wewelsburg. Personally, I find the smell of a battlefield much more invigorating than that of a library. Or what you find between a woman's legs."

I got it. The colonel thought of himself as a grizzled combat veteran and me as a milquetoast. I murmured something inconsequential. I hadn't been told about Wolfhardt's librarian stint—like what I was told about the SS, all I got about Wolfhardt was a thumbnail sketch. But I had been briefed about Wewelsburg. It was Himmler's fantasy castle, a fairy-tale place like Mad Ludwig's Neuschwanstein, but one created by a darker vision.

Himmler thought of his black corps as a mystic order of knighthood, like the Teutonic legends of the past. To serve as the spiritual center of his knightly brotherhood, he chose Wewelsburg, a castle in Westphalia, and spent a bundle of marks making it into his own Neuschwanstein. I was told that the library at the castle was a center for "racial research," with twelve thousand volumes of Aryan lore and anti-Semitic propaganda. The genealogical tables of SS members were kept in the library, and Himmler pored over them like a horse breeder examining studbooks.

The OSS briefers told me there was even an Arthurian "Round Table" for Himmler and twelve of his closest hangers-on, commanders he'd awarded SS "knighthoods" and chivalric coats of arms.

Adolf and Himmler carried the knighthood crap into the whole SS, from the mystic lightning-strike runes that symbolized the SS, to the daggers with "My Honor Is Loyalty" inscribed on the blades and swords handed out by Himmler to new officers. The silver SS ring I wore not only had the Totenkopf skull and crossbones, but mystic runes around it and Himmler's signature on the inner side. To keep up the pagan image, they even created their own mystic "religion," with marriage, christening, and death rites different from the Christian traditions.

It was all designed to create a fighting force that was not just a brotherhood, but one totally dedicated to Adolf and his pets. The strutting, goose-stepping bastards looked comical to the rest of us— until they started spilling blood. The SS isn't just Adolf's personal bodyguard, it's also his personal murder squad. The world's known since the Night of the Long Knives in '34 that Adolf had hundreds of political opponents murdered in cold blood. There'd been stories coming out of Europe about the SS rough treatment of the Jews and Slavs, people rounded up, sent off to prison camps, or working as slave laborers in factories. At OSS headquarters, General Donovan hinted that there might even be worse things going on, but he hadn't elaborated.

I would have liked to have asked Herr Colonel Combat Veteran what he was going to do after we finished kicking his and Adolf's asses and took away their fancy uniform and toys. Tough guys when they're ganging up on some shopkeeper with his wife and kids looking on, but how do they stack up man to man?

The staff car turned off the main road and began winding up a narrow, one-lane graveled passage that carried us from the valley floor. Not in the direction of Obersalzberg.

"I had expected to go directly to the Obersalzberg and der Führer's headquarters," I said.

"We're not going to the Obersalzberg, though we won't be far away. There is a medical infirmary there, but it is inadequate for der Führer's current needs. The procedure will be done at another medical facility, the one I am attached to. It's called Grunberg. You've heard of it?"

It wasn't just a question—there was something in his voice that said it was another trap. Was I supposed to have heard of it? Was the "green mountain" hospital so famous any German doctor would know about it? I decided there was no reason for him to be suspicious of me. That meant there must be something secret about Grunberg, something I wasn't supposed to know about. "No, I haven't," I said.

He grunted. "I'm not surprised. Prior to the war, it was a small sanitarium, for wealthy patients with tuberculosis or some like condition. It is now an SS facility. You would not have heard about it because its existence is on a need-to-know basis." He leaned toward me again to speak confidentially. "What you learn at Grunberg must stay there. Like me, you wear the uniform of the Schutzstaffel. You know that the SS has duties that the ordinary German citizen would not understand the necessity of, duties specified by der Führer himself and delegated to Reichsfuhrer-SS Himmler to carry out. Those duties must be kept confidential until they are completed. Ja?"

"Of course, Herr Standartenfuhrer." Sure, I got the message. There was something weird going up at the green mountain sanitarium that der Führer and his Dobermans didn't want anyone to know about. But what the hell was it? And why was a Death's

Head combat colonel attached to a medical facility? The OSS briefers hadn't told me anything about the hospital, it hadn't even got
mentioned in the briefing. They had assumed the surgery would be
done at the Obersalzberg medical clinic. Was there something going
on at the hospital that's going to get me in deeper shit than I was
already in?

At times like this, I wished they'd shipped Wild Bill out to the
Pacific Theater before he got around to punishing me, shipped him
out to someplace like the beach at Guadalcanal at the time the
Nips were defending it.

"What exactly is the nature of the medical work done at Grunberg?" I asked.

"Experimental."

"Ah, yes, of course. What kind of experiments?"

He tapped my leg with the stick. I really hated that tapping bit.
I had a coach once who walked around with a bat in hand all the
time and would nudge players with it to get their attention. I let
the coach know where I was going to stick it if he continued to
nudge me, but I didn't think that was a good approach with an SS
colonel.

"Important experiments," he said, "perhaps the most important
medical procedures ever attempted. It makes me proud to be a part
of it." Another tap. "It is inevitable that you will learn a great deal
during your short stay at the facility. You understand the conse-
quences if you engage in loose talk once you leave."

"Loose lips sink ships," I chirped.

He stared at me, and I froze in place, too terrified to even wet
my pants. I realized immediately I had made a mistake. The expression, a War Department message to soldiers and sailors to button up their lips, was on posters from Jersey to Frisco. It was hardly
something a German would know.

"Loose . . . lips . . . sink . . . ships." He screwed his lips about and
repeated the words again. "Where did you hear that expression?"

"Nowhere, Herr Standartenfuhrer, it just came to mind."

He went back into a brown study for a moment, frowning at the back of the driver's head. I wondered if I should leap out of the car and throw myself off the mountainside, or stay in the car and wait to get shot.

"Interesting," he said. "As a high-ranking security officer, I know only too well how many of our troop movements end up in enemy hands because of loose talk by our soldiers in beer halls and the bedroom." He nudged me in the ribs with the butt end of his swagger stick. "You know what I mean, pillow talk sinks ships, ja?"

"Correct, Herr Standartenfuhrer, that is exactly right."

Vogler gave me an appraising look. "You know, Wolfhardt, this phrase about pillow talk sinking ships, it is exactly the sort of thing that Reich Minister of Propaganda Goebbels needs to educate our troops about the dangers of loose talk. The person who provides the phrase to Herr Goebbels will be on the receiving end of some considerable credit if the minister finds merit in the suggestion."

"The phrase belongs to you," I said. "After all, you were the one who saw the merit in it. Please leave my name entirely out of any communications with Reich Minister Goebbels."

"Ja, Hauptsturmfuhrer,"—the swagger stick banged my leg— "from the moment you stepped off the plane, I recognized you as an officer whom I could have confidence in." He leaned over and blew beer and peppermint in my face. "Too many of you young Schutzstaffel are sheep in wolves' clothing, ja!" He poked my stomach with the stick. "No guts. They wear the black shirt because of family connections. Not like us, eh, Wolfhardt. We know why we are Schutzstaffel. We are the broom carriers, and the Jews are the vermin we sweep away."

THREE

Grunberg was tucked away in a meadow above Lake Königssee. The main building had the look of a mountain chalet, and perhaps it was the hunting lodge of a nobleman of an era past. The outer buildings were of more recent vintage, military-looking Quonset-type huts. A guard shack and barbed-wire fencing gave it the look of a prison camp. Despite its picturesque setting in a stand of sub-alpine spruce, the place gave me the cold chills after Vogler's cryptic hints about things going bump in the night at the place.

I was staring at the limestone-and-dolomite cliffs that plunged into the dark waters of the lake when Vogler asked, "Have you seen Königssee before?"

"When I was a twelve," I said, truthfully. "I came with a youth group that took a boat ride on the lake." The ride took place in 1926, a year before we left Germany. Adolf had been at his Jew-baiting for years before the trip, and I ended up in a fistfight with older boys after they made remarks about the Jude kid. I got my ass whipped, but I had long arms and big fists for my age and got in some good punches before I went down with three of them on me.

As we pulled up to the entrance to the main building, a man

wearing a white smock and carrying a clipboard was returning from
an outer building. He greeted us after we got out of the car.

"Sieg Heil."

Vogler introduced me to the man, Dr. Dorsch, director of the
hospital. Dorsch was tall and slender, with a long, thin nose he
could have batted three hundred with. He was dressed as the well-
groomed SS officer should be—you could slice cake with the
creases of his trousers, his white smock was starched to the point
of standing at attention if he took it off and set it on the ground.
His SS rank, Obersturmbannfuhrer, lieutenant colonel, was sewn
on his medical smock.

Doctors, especially psychiatrists, have always struck me as people
with deep patience and listening ability. Dorsch broke that mold.
He was a machine, in his walk and talk. Leaving Vogler somewhere
along the way, he took charge of me to show me the facility. He
almost goose-stepped me down the polished wood floor of the hospital as he briefed me about the place.

"I cannot tell you how honored we are that der Führer will be
treated here. It will give me the opportunity to instruct him upon
the important research that is being conducted. Frankly, Dr. Wolfhardt, we work in absolute secrecy and without the honors showered upon us that would come if the world knew what we were
discovering within these walls."

"What is the nature of your work, Herr Direktor?"

Dorsch stopped and pulled me aside, out of the mainstream of
people using the corridor. He spoke in a low, confidential voice,
which struck me as odd because I assumed people walking by
would be staff members who knew what was going on at the hospital.

"The work of Grunberg is authorized by Reichsfuhrer-SS Himmler himself. It is an important step in the final solution of racial
purity."

There was that expression again, the *final solution*. As far as I was
concerned, the final solution would happen when we finished mopping up the krauts and started looking under garbage can lids in
Berlin and Hamburg for hiding Nazis.

Dorsch went on in a confidential tone. "I know that as an SS officer, you will appreciate our work more than the ordinary person. Even more important, as a doctor, perhaps you will even be motivated to join us. You will find the work more vital to the future of the Fatherland than serving at the front."

"It sounds interesting, but I really don't know exactly—"

"It is the most exciting and satisfying work I have been involved with in my twenty years of psychiatric work. You understand, of course, that everything you see and hear must be kept in absolute secrecy."

"Of course."

"One can understand der Führer's disappointment and impatience with our regular armed forces, the Wehrmacht. It has had great success in conquering territories, but has no ability to implement Lebensraum, ja? As der Führer has said many times, eighty million Germans being crowded into a small territory is ridiculous, of course. The lands to the east must be cleared to make room for our expansion, for the Germanic people to occupy the soil and territory to which we are entitled on this earth. The final solution to the Jews and dealing with the Slavs have become the prime duties of the SS. I am proud to say that we are making a major contribution here at Grunberg."

I smiled and nodded and tried to look intelligent, but I didn't know what he was talking about. Everyone knew the Nazis were anti-Semitic and had been abusing the Jews, confiscating property, and throwing them into prison camps by the thousands—and weren't treating the Slavs and other ethnic groups much better, but what did he mean by *the final solution?* Lebensraum, that was Adolf's dream that the Germans live like colonial masters over millions of people. I remember my father telling me about Adolf's crazy dream—people the Germans lorded over would live in pigpens while the goose-steppers would live in palaces and manor houses.

But I guess someone forgot to tell Stalin he'd have to move out of the Kremlin and live in a pigpen. Adolf said Stalin's boys fought like "swamp rats" at Stalingrad. Those same swamp rats and "General Winter" had kicked der Führer's ass up and down several thousand miles of Russian front. Don't these guys read the papers? Hadn't anyone told them they were losing this war? If they would just face reality, I could pack up and go back to Brooklyn.

"Before Reichsfuhrer-SS Himmler assigned me to head this project, I was attached to an Einsatzgruppen in Poland," Dr. Dorsch said. "Before that I had been attached to a Totenkopf unit that specialized in confining undesirables. Colonel Vogler was with the same unit."

He spoke proudly, like a kid bragging about a Boy Scout merit badge. The OSS officers were supposed to have briefed me on everything they knew about the SS, but they'd left out die Einsatzgruppen. Another item on the laundry list the OSS had ignored.

The SS, officially the Schutzstaffel, originally were Adolf's Praetorian Guard and, after the war commenced, encompassed entire divisions called Waffen-SS. Suffice it to say, the SS did not play by German law or Wehrmacht regulations. I knew the Totenkopf, Death's Head units, were special SS prison and combat units. Dorsch and Vogler appeared to be in some sort of prison unit; "die Einsatzgruppen," which meant something like "task force," was new to me.

Dr. Dorsch was brimming with excitement. "I cannot tell you what total research freedom has meant to me. Sometimes I feel like Galileo, peering into his telescope, seeing new worlds for the first time. That I am performing a great duty for mein Führer and the Party, gives me endless joy."

A door flew open down the hall and a soldier wearing an SS sergeant's uniform burst into the hallway.

"I can't!" he screamed. "I can't do it anymore! They're staring at me, I see them at night staring at me!"

Two orderlies grabbed him and pulled him back through the door and closed it behind them.

Dr. Dorsch grabbed my arm and pointed at the closed door. "You see, you see, weaklings, incompetents, this is exactly the defeatism that we must deal with. Our Führer says we can win the war and accomplish our mission only if we have a positive attitude.

Do you understand the necessity for the program now?"

"Ja," I said.

What the hell was he talking about? I was curious, but decided that whatever it was, I wanted no part of it. Things were already too complicated as it was.

He gave me an appraising look. "I like your attitude, Wolfhardt. You must consider requesting a transfer into our program. I have a bit of influence at headquarters and would be able to implement such a request."

"Thank you, I am privileged and delighted at the suggestion. Unfortunately, my expertise is that of Frauenarst. I'm sure a Frau Doktor will not—"

"Nein, nein, a Frau Doktor would—ah, here is Dr. Dietrich."

A woman wearing a white smock with medical insignia approached.

"Dr. Hildegarde Dietrich, this is Hauptsturmfuhrer Wolfhardt." Dorsch lowered his voice. "Wolfhardt will be providing blood for the procedure that will be taking place here in a few days."

Dietrich's eyes widened. "What an honor for you! To know that your blood will be in the veins, in the brain, of our Führer." She clasped her fists to her chest. "You will be immortalized!"

Yeah, if I wasn't hung by my heels first.

Hildegarde meant "battle maiden," and the phrase fit Dr. Dietrich perfectly. She was a big blond Mädchen, a Brunhild, the warrior queen from the *Nibelungenlied*, with wide shoulders, strong arms, and powerful legs, the kind of legs that could wrap around a man and squeeze tight when she's getting laid. With her high heels, she was as tall as my five-foot-ten. I weighed in at one-sixty, and I'm sure she tipped the scale at not much less than one-fifty. She looked more like material for the Deutsch shot-putting team than a doctor.

"Dr. Dietrich will be your guide for the rest of the tour of the facility," Dorsch said. "Don't let her lure you on one of her climbs unless you are accustomed to bouncing up mountains like a mountain goat."

Dorsch left and I began goose-stepping down the corridor with her. Like Dorsch, she walked like she had a Luger up her ass.

As we went by the closed door, I said, "A sergeant in some mental distress burst out of there a moment ago."

"Yes, that's Dr. Dorsch's program. What did he tell you about *my* program?"

"Nothing."

"You will find my program very interesting, more so than Dr. Dorsch's. I am sure you will be so fascinated by our work, you will want to join the project. The work we do is vital to the mission der Führer has given to the German people."

I shook my head regretfully. "As a Frau Doktor—"

"Perfect. I, too, am a Frauenarst. It is mandatory for our work."

Oh shit. If the woman started talking shop, expecting me to discuss female problems, she'd find that the only thing I knew about a woman's anatomy were the sexual orifices.

"In fact, I am in great need of an assistant," she said. "My last assistant was suddenly transferred to the Eastern Front when reinforcements were needed. I understand that most assignments today are to the east. I knitted a pair of wool socks and sent them to him. He will need them." She gave me a look of pity.

What if I got stuck in this Nazi monkey suit and was sent off to be butchered and eaten or whatever the hell the Russians did to captured SS? When—*if*—I got back, I was going to stick a howitzer right up Wild Bill's ass.

"Your first assignment will be delivering a baby."

"A—a what?" I felt the earth opening up under my feet.

She stopped and faced me. "You know, Herr Hauptsturmfuhrer, a baby, a thing about this size" (she spaced her hands about a loaf of bread apart) "that cries and wets its diapers just like the dolls they sell at Christmas." She laughed at her joke. "We have a woman in heavy labor. Your services will be needed at any moment. From the look on your face, perhaps they forgot to show you how to cut a cord in medical school. Or are you one of these Frau Doktors whose only expertise is sticking his head between a woman's legs while she's riding the stirrups."

She laughed and gave me a good-natured shove that sent me reeling.

Jesus H. Christ. This was not going as planned. I had two doctors competing for my help with whatever weird medical experiments were being conducted in this loony bin, while I was expected to practice medicine. Der Führer better show up before the baby, or my next assignment would be to ship out to the Eastern Front and let a Russian T34 tank run over my frostbitten toes.

"As you well know, Hauptsturmfuhrer, all SS members are commanded by der Führer to have at least four children. By the laws of birth averages, two would be boys. That would guarantee that each man would bequeath two more like himself to serve der Führer. This order is for all SS men to impregnate their wives and to assist unmarried childless women over thirty to conceive. Naturally, only women who qualify racially are to receive SS sperm. That way we can guarantee that we remain an Aryan society with pure Aryan looks."

I almost had the bad manners—*fatally* bad manners—to laugh and ask if those "Aryan looks" were the "blond" hair of der Führer, the tall stature of Little Josef Goebbels, the slender waistline of Goering the Blubber Ball, or that of Himmler, a pathetic putz.

"After I received my medical degree, I was an organizer of Lebensborn facilities, the life fountain maternity homes that care for genetically and racially valuable mothers." Brunhild stopped and faced me with her hands on her hips and a defiant expression on her face. "I hope, Herr Doktor Wolfhardt, you are not one of those who have derided these necessary facilities as little more than brothels for SS members. I can assure you—"

"No, no, Dr. Dietrich, of course not, the Lebensborn are a valuable weapon in der Führer's arsenal."

I followed her outside to one of the large military huts that looked newly constructed. At the hut, she pushed open swinging doors, walked past a seated guard, and stopped at a department store–size window.

Half a dozen women and half that number of men were in a room. They were dressed in comfortable, lightweight clothing, the sort of thing one wore around the house to relax. All were young. I'm sure the women were all under twenty and the men not much older. They were socializing with each other, laughing and talking, sitting together, interaction that struck me as bordering on intimacy. Brunhild's defensive statement that she hadn't run brothels struck me. I noticed the young people didn't have a "street" look about them, they looked more like farm and college kids, but I got a sense of intimacy from the expressions on their faces and their body language.

The next thing that struck me was what incredible physical specimens they were. All of them. They had those classic "Aryan" looks that der Führer, Himmler, Goering, Goebbels and the rest of the Nazi gang fawned upon but lacked.

"Who are these people?" I asked. "Why are they on display?"

"These are my subjects," Dr. Dietrich said. "Come with me."

She took me through a door and into a dark hallway. She stopped suddenly and faced me. "You understand, Herr Hauptsturmfuhrer, that what you are about to see is top secret. Your position as a Frau Doktor and an SS officer gives me trust in sharing with you this monumental program."

"I can assure you, Doktor, there would be no loose pillow talk on my part that would expose the secret."

"Ja, pillow talk, that is exactly what we must avoid." She seemed to find great amusement in the comment. "Pillow talk, so appropriate."

Proceeding down the hallway, we passed curtained windows on the right side. The windows were smaller than the large department store window out front.

She stopped in front of a window and paused to give me another inquiring look before she turned and pulled back a curtain.

I gaped.

A man and woman were engaging in the preliminaries of what my grandfather would have called "coitus."

The naked couple, uninhibited by our presence—or the window was one-way glass—were passionately kissing each other. Their bodies glistened, as if they had been oiled before they started making love. The woman's breasts were full, her erect nipples were dark red. The man cupped one breast with his hand. The hand holding her breast moved down her stomach. She sat up a little, spreading her legs, to let him massage her vulva, all the while gripping his throbbing member.

"Why are they doing it here?" I asked.

"They are participating in my project."

"Just what is the nature of your project?"

She stepped closer to me. I felt her heat and a surge of my own. She ran her finger over my lips and down to the breast of my uniform jacket.

She jerked the curtain shut and led me back out the way we had come.

"Mein Freund, der Führer has invaded east and west, conquering everything for hundreds of miles in each direction. He has ordered that space in these conquered territories be cleared so they can be populated by Germans."

Here we go again. These people had *Lebensraum* on the brain. Adolf must be some orator to have pumped these people up so high that they're still preparing to colonize the world. The last time I heard, the Germans were in retreat on the Eastern Front, the Allies had taken North Africa and were pushing up the Italian boot, and there were more rumors about an impending invasion of France by Eisenhower crossing the Channel than Carter had pills. One thing I was discovering about average Germans was that they had the political IQ of baboons. Sure, they knew how to follow, but they didn't know how to ask questions about *why* they were in line.

"But where are we to get the people to populate these areas?" she said. "Not just ordinary people, of course, but those with the racial and genetic qualities that der Führer decreed have a right to living space? As you have no doubt already guessed, it is the repopulation of these conquered territories that our project is concerned with."

No, I hadn't guessed. I thought she was running some sort of officially sanctioned whorehouse. What she said made me stop in my tracks and stare at her. "Do you mean those people in there are *making babies*?

Her laughter shook the Alps.

"How do you think babies are made?" she howled. "By planting a pea under a can in the garden?"

"Doktor—"

"No, I am sorry, Wolfhardt, but I wish I had a picture of your face when I told you about our experiments. The project is not making babies, as you put it, but sexual conduct. It has been pointed out that a hundred good German soldiers could easily impregnate a thousand German women and create five hundred future soldiers every nine months. Think of it, Wolfhardt, each German soldier reproducing himself five times over every nine months! Isn't it a marvelous plan? But we need to know what makes a man and a woman unite sexually in a way that furthers the chances of fertilization. This is especially important where a woman is concerned because women are less able to get aroused than men. We are also experimenting with why some children, even with the same biological parents, come out with different-colored hair or even different-colored eyes."

"Marvelous," I muttered. Jesus H. Christ. It was an experimental breeding farm. A sex study to see how fast boys and girls could pump out babies. Along with some junk science about how Aryan types are produced. But the plan was beginning to grow on me. It was a sex study, pure and simple. Hell, it was a big relief that something dark and dangerous wasn't going on at the hospital. Sex was harmless—and a lot of fun. There I was worried about having fallen into some house of horror, and instead I had landed in the Garden of Eden—after the snake wised up Adam and Eve. I thought the math was interesting, too. Assuming that there was usually one man to one woman ratio in this world, SS members would have to use the wives and girlfriends of other men to impregnate women at a ten-to-one rate. Himmler really knew how to take care of his bullyboys.

"A marvelous plan, Doktor. Your project deserves the highest accolades from der Führer. When I see him, I shall heap praise that would please Caesar upon you and your project."

"You do not know how pleased I am to hear that. To be truthful, my project occupies only a small part of the funding and facility here. Dr. Dorsch's project gets the lion's share. Perhaps if der Führer himself was informed—"

The door to the rear of the main building opened, and two aides came out with the agitated sergeant between them. He was foaming at the mouth and muttering something incoherent. The only word I caught was *Mord*.

Hildegarde Dietrich and I stared at each other.

"Dr. Dorsch's program—" I started.

"Is exactly the opposite of mine."

"What do you mean by that?"

"It must be explained to you by Dr. Dorsch." An emotion swept across her face, as if she was struggling to tell me something. But was afraid to. She stepped closer and straightened my collar. "I must go now. Perhaps later, Herr Hauptsturmfuhrer, we will discuss your participation in my project at greater length."

"Whenever you are ready."

She nodded at an orderly approaching. "Scharfuhrer Hans will show you to your quarters."

A Scharfuhrer was a staff sergeant. As I followed the orderly, the word that the distraught soldier kept uttering stayed with me. *Mord* was the German word for "murder."

Hans, the orderly, showed me to a cottage. "It is reserved for visiting party dignitaries who wish to visit the facility and vacation here. You are being given the cottage despite your low rank because of your assignment."

He had one arm and an Iron Cross, first class. I asked him in which battle he had earned the prestigious medal.

"The English took my arm at Ypres. It cost them dearly."

I hadn't heard of the battle and my face showed my ignorance.

"The First World War, not this one," he said.

He was gruff, with a sandpaper personality. He went around opening windows, then stood at attention in front of me. I noticed he wore the insignia of the Leibstandarte, Adolf's personal SS unit.

"I am not attached to the hospital," he said. "I am part of the Obersalzberg SS detail, an orderly in der Führer's quarters. Any commands, Herr Hauptsturmfuhrer?"

"Were there any messages for me?" I regretted the question the moment it slipped out. An "orderly" to der Führer might be a Gestapo agent sent to check me out. Obviously, he had been sent to look me over, not serve me. I asked about a message because I was told that a member of the German underground at the facility would contact me. No clues as to who it might be were given to me for obvious reasons—if I was captured and tortured, I'd reveal the name.

"No messages. Were you expecting a communication?"

"No, not really, I just thought my family may have been told my new assignment." I kicked myself again. I was sinking a whole fleet with my loose lips. Families weren't told about secret military assignments. "You are excused," I told him.

I shut the door behind him, leaned back against it, and sighed. Jesus H. Christ, how had I gotten myself into this damn spy stuff. I promised myself that if I got out of this thing alive, I would get down on my hands and knees and kiss Donovan's ass until the man forgave me for my transgressions—as long as he kept me at a desk in D.C.

I didn't belong in this spy game. I didn't belong in the war. I knew the krauts were pricks and hated Jews, but hey, I'm not David the Giant Killer. As soon as the war was over, it would be business as usual—for everybody but me. I would be too old and too far out of shape to go back to playing major league ball. Most of the players in sports managed to dodge the draft. All except for me, old wrong-place-wrong-time Arnie Berkowitz. The injustice of it all was giving me a headache.

I went into the bathroom to look for an aspirin. I found headache powder in the medicine cabinet, probably something for VIP hangovers. I stuck a glass under the sink faucet and started to turn on the water when I saw the message. It was scribbled in soap on the basin. *PLAY BALL.*

I quickly washed away the message. Those were the code words for the underground contact. But who the hell had left them? And when would I get my final instructions?

I was sacked out on the bed late that night, lying on top the covers, wearing only my pants, when I heard a discreet tapping on my door. My heart did a flip-flop. This was it—I was about to meet my underground contact. I swung my feet off the bed and hurried to the door. Restraining an impulse to jerk it open, I quietly opened it a crack and peered out.

"Guten Abend, Erich." Dr. Hildegarde Dietrich grinned lewdly at me. She had two bottles of champagne. "I have a medical problem, a female one, I need to consult you about. May I come in?"

I cleared my throat. "Of course." Christ, could this kraut broad be my contact? She didn't act the cloak-and-dagger type, but I didn't either.

Inside, she sat the champagne bottles on the table.

"What's bothering you, Fräulein?"

"Call me Hildegarde," she purred. She moved closer to me.

I could feel sexual heat radiating from her body. Her cheeks were flushed rosy red. She wasn't wearing the starched white uniform I had seen her in earlier, but had on a soft silk dress, fastened by a row of small buttons down the front. Her blond hair lay in long waves.

"I need you to examine me."

She unclasped the top of her dress in one swift move, exposing her firm breasts, free of a brassiere. It knocked my breath away. Brunhild was stacked like a brick shithouse. She had extraordinary breasts—the pearly round mounds perfect, her plum-colored nipples erect. Under the clothes she was a typical kraut Fräulein, robust, well nourished.

"I have a problem here," she said, huskily, touching her nipples.

"I'll check them," I croaked. I put my fingers on her nipples. "These are all right," I whispered.

She slipped her dress off, letting it fall to the floor. No panties. She stepped away from the dress and stood naked in front of me, wearing only her high heels. The bush between her legs was blond.

She ran her fingers down my bare chest, giving me goose bumps. She moved in closer, rubbing her breasts against my chest. I was usually the more aggressive partner with women, but Brunhild had her own agenda, and I let her play it out.

She pulled down both my pants and shorts, pushing her breasts against me again. "And here," she said, touching her mouth. Her full lips closed on mine. Her tongue licked my lips and moved down the side of my face, the side of my neck, down to my chest and suckled a tit. I nearly jumped out of my skin.

"Now you must examine me here," she said, guiding my hand to her bushy mound.

FOUR

I was in a deep sleep early the next morning when my door burst open. I jerked up in bed. It was Hans, the orderly.

"Wake up, Hauptsturmfuhrer, you are going on a hunt."

"A what?"

"A hunt. Colonel Vogler will explain. Get dressed, I will take you to the armory for a weapon. As an officer, you will be expected to be armed with a P38."

What kind of hunting can you do with a semiautomatic pistol?

The armory was an underground bunker away from the main building and huts. There was another building beyond it, in a grove of trees on a hillside. The building hadn't been explained to me during my tour. While the other buildings appeared to be made of inexpensive military materials, this one had a sturdier look to it. And a seven-foot electrified barb-wire fence surrounding it. A kraut guard with a German shepherd on a leash was patrolling inside it. I asked Hans what function the highly guarded building served.

He gave me a moment of silence. "I am just an orderly. I do not know all the tasks for der Führer that are being performed here at Grunberg."

His reply was stiff and formal. I gave the fenced building another glance. It looked more like a prison building than a hospital facility.

The underground armory was much bigger than it appeared on the outside. And filled with large quantities of high explosives. Much of it was canisters with timers. Enough to blow the lid off the mountain.

"For mountain passes and bridges in case of invasion," Hans said. "The Obersalzberg is not far. It's possible the enemy might drop parachute troops into the area. If that happens, we are under orders to destroy bridges and roads."

Hans escorted me to where Dr. Dorsch and Colonel Vogler were selecting high-powered rifles with scopes.

"Did you wish to arm yourself with something that has more firepower than a pistol?" Vogler asked me.

"A pistol will be fine, unless you tell me we are hunting lions or tigers. I wasn't aware that there was big game in these mountains."

Vogler chuckled humorlessly. "This is two-legged game." He exchanged looks with Dorsch. "I believe a pistol will be adequate for your first time out."

Two-legged game. What the hell was going on at this place?

Two half-track troop carriers, each with twelve men aboard, were waiting, along with a four-wheel-drive staff car. I sat in the backseat of the staff car with Dorsch, and Vogler rode up front with the driver. I was curious as hell as to what was coming down, but kept my face blank.

Dorsch said to Vogler, "What do you think, Herr Standartenfuhrer, should we tell our young friend here what we are hunting or surprise him?"

Vogler glanced back with his Doberman eyes. "Tell him."

The doctor leaned closer to me. "You are going to be let in on a secret, Herr Hauptsturmfuhrer. I noticed when I mentioned yesterday that I had been in an Einsatzgruppen unit, you did not appear to know what it was."

"I've heard the name—"

"No, no, it's not necessary for you to apologize for your ignorance. Had you served in the conquered territories, I would have
expected you to have some familiarity with the units. All top SS
commanders know of the units, but that information is available at
lower levels only on a need-to-know basis. There are some people,
especially officers of the Wehrmacht, who do not agree with the
program and criticize it. There have even been instances in which
their failure to cooperate resulted in missed opportunities."

Vogler cut in, "In order for you to understand the Einsatzgruppen
mission, you must go back to the premise of der Führer's mission
for Germany."

"To give the German people breathing space," I said. "To ensure
that the less advanced people of the conquered territories, the Slavs
and other non-Germanic races in eastern Europe and the Soviet
Republics, are obedient and serve us."

"Exactly. And in terms of our discussion, to cleanse the conquered territory of unfit life."

"Unfit life," I repeated.

"Which, as you well know, are the Jews, Gypsies, Asiatic inferiors, along with useless eaters such as the insane, retarded, and
physically deformed, all of whom der Fuhrer has decreed must not
be allowed to exist because they take up resources needed for our
own people. In the case of the Jews and Gypsies, they are also
subversives who must be eliminated to keep them from plotting
against the Reich. In addition, it was necessary to wipe out the
entire body of Polish intelligentsia, not just its military and political
leaders, but the people who could take their place once they were
eliminated. With that done, there would be no fear of a Polish
leader stirring the people against us."

A cold feeling gripped me. I knew these Nazis were nutcases;
hell, you just had to read some of the crap in Adolf's *Mein Kampf*
to know that. I hadn't actually read the book. I figured anything
that took me away from the pitching mound other than getting my
cock lubed was a waste of time. But I had friends who said the guy
needed electroconvulsive therapy. But what the hell was Dorsch
talking about? It was beginning to sound like something more than

harassing Jews or rounding some of them up and sticking them in prison camps was happening.

Dorsch went on. "Der Führer has analogized the Jewish presence in this world to a virus. In fact, I have medical colleagues who suspect there is an actual virus carried in Jewish blood and who are resolved to find it. But even if we think of the infestation as a social one, it must be eliminated because Jewish blood will poison our Aryan blood, weakening us when we fight our enemies. To eliminate the infestation from the conquered areas, der Führer empowered a special action force, the Einsatzgruppen, to deal with it.

"Himmler assigned the responsibility to General Heydrich, probably the finest SS general who ever lived. That was in 1941, as Russia was being invaded. As you know, General Heydrich was murdered by the Czech underground the following year."

Vogler turned in the front seat. "And we retaliated against the Czechs and the Jews a hundred thousand to one."

I recalled reading about the incident. The entire male population of a Czech town, Lidice, was massacred, the town burned, the ruins dynamited, and the ground leveled. Barbaric punishment worthy of the Khans.

"Anyway," Dorsch said, "four Einsatz units, several thousand strong, were sent in behind the Wehrmacht advancing to the east, into Poland, Czechoslovakia, the Baltic region, the Ukraine, and so forth. I pride myself, as Colonel Vogler also does, on being members of the officer corps of this momentous undertaking. It may surprise you to learn that the people entrusted to lead this historic task were not professional soldiers but doctors, lawyers, accountants, and even a minister of the faith. In fact, Colonel Vogler, prior to the war, was an accountant with Krupp."

The frumpy Doberman glanced back, and I muttered something that made it sound like I was duly impressed.

"Our task was to sanitize the conquered area, to remove the infection," Vogler said. "We were under orders from the Reichsfuhrer-SS to eliminate the unnecessary life as humanely as possible, along with carriers of the virus."

Creeping horror started at the soles of my feet and worked its way up as I listened to the accountant and doctor use businesslike language to explain how people were murdered.

"You would be amazed at how many of these people went to their deaths," Dorsch said. "Most of the virus carriers lived in urban areas. That made them easier to round up in large numbers. And in those cases where they have lived under the Soviets, they often welcomed us as liberators rather than an enemy. We were also surprised at how cooperative the non-Jews were in turning over their Jewish neighbors to be eliminated. Often we were able to organize extermination units from the local areas to supplement our own work. This was especially effective in Latvia and Lithuania. In the beginning we would round up the Jews and unfits, march them into the woods, have them dig trenches for graves, and shoot them."

"That proved highly inefficient," Vogler said. "Fortunately, we were able to institute what came to be called the 'sardine method.' After a deep trench was dug, the first line of unfits were stood at the edge and shot in the back of the head so they fell forward into the grave. Then the next set of unfits had to lie down on top of the bodies and were then shot. Another layer was ordered to lie on top of those bodies, then the next and so on."

"Sometimes we could get five or six layers," Dorsch said.

I had a blank look frozen on my face. It was all I could do not to scream and jump at their throats. Two men, one of them who had taken the Hippocratic Oath to save lives with his training, were talking about mass murder with far less emotion than they would discuss the last soccer scores. The driver did not even appear interested in the conversation.

"Ja, the sardining helped, but we had other problems," Dorsch said. "The first was that the traditional method of execution was to have three soldiers shoot the victim at the same time. This tradition arose to spare the feelings of the executors. But it was too inefficient, much too slow. As we became overwhelmed with necessary executions, we stopped the practice of having three men fire simultaneously and had a single shooter place a well-placed shot at the back of the head. As a medical man, I can say that one shot usually did the job as well and humanely as three."

"Three was unnecessary," Vogler agreed. "Especially with the women and children."

My hand had found the door handle. I had an urge to leap from the car. I felt suffocated. I was a trapped animal, a mute witness to the indescribable horror of two educated, professional men talking about murdering thousands of helpless people, men, women, children of all ages. All because of a crazed notion that they were superior to their victims.

When Dorsch started explaining how more efficient it was to herd people into a building and set it on fire than shooting, I broke in, and asked, "It's still going on?"

"Going on? You mean the cleansing? Of course, it is. However, a more efficient way has been found to deal with the problem. My understanding is only about a million were eliminated by our Einsatzgruppen units, is that correct, Colonel?"

"I have heard a slightly higher figure."

Over a million people. Human beings. *Shot by hand, individually by individuals.* Not "statistics" killed by bombs or in battles during the blind fury of war, but shot one by one by other human beings. People simply pulled out of their houses, off the streets, out of line at the bakery, and murdered. What kind of animals could do such a thing? I felt as if I had stepped out of my own world, straying into some other dimension where everything was backward, where evil was good. For a moment I wondered if the two were joking with me, that it was some sort of SS mind game played on new initiates, something like a fraternity party snipe hunt. Had either one of them shown the slightest emotion, I would have figured they were faking it and that it was a joke. But they discussed the situation with total scientific detachment—the kind of scary bullshit science the Nazis were consumed with.

"What is the more efficient way that was found?" I asked. I didn't want to know, but I felt drawn by the sheer horror of what I had heard to hear more.

"The camps, of course. The process was enormously sped up. What is the matter, Wolfhardt, you look ill?"

"The road, the winding road, I've always gotten sick on mountain roads. They say it's an inner ear problem." Something occurred to me, and I used it to distract them from their focus on me. "But the Einsatzgruppen troops, there have been problems, haven't there? The soldier in the hospital corridor yesterday . . ."

"Yes," Dorsch said, "that soldier is an example of the problems facing the project. We found an interesting phenomenon occurred among those SS assigned to do the killings. Some men were not able to continue long term, especially when it came to eliminating the women and children. Yet others not only operated efficiently, but seemed to enjoy it. Some men were able to pull the trigger after simply being told that it was their duty to der Führer. Others needed more persuasion, to be told that it was a moral thing to do, that they were exterminating an enemy, even if the person to be terminated was a small baby. We needed to know why different men had different reactions to the situation. So now, Wolfhardt, you have discovered what our Grunberg project is about."

I nodded. "You're examining men, testing them to see if they can take the killings. More to the point, you're figuring out what the best motivating factors are."

"Excellent, Herr Hauptsturmfuhrer. You see, Vogler, I told you he was a quick study."

"He looks green to me," Vogler said.

"The road," I said. "But if more efficient ways have been found, what is the necessity—oh, I see, someone always has to do it, correct? Even if it's assembly line, like that American, what was his name, Henry Ford, even if it's done efficiently, still someone has to do . . . it."

"Yes, there's always a need for individual action, but also for the individual units," Dorsch said. "It's true that the camps now take care of the mass exterminations, but the final solution still requires that we have SS units who can handle matters on a local level. Someone has to round up these vermin, and sometimes that requires hunting them down. This will become especially true when we occupy Britain and the American continent. Can you imagine how many Einsatzgruppen we will need to ferret out the virus carriers and unfits in an area the size of America? With all its forests and mountains?"

Vogler turned in his seat again to lecture me. "We have developed what we call 'poacher units.' They are the creation of der Führer and Himmler putting their heads together. At first people were simply rounded up. They were told they were being transported to another area, to a camp, or were simply told they would be questioned and released. A different type of unit was needed after word spread among our targets that everyone being arrested was being eliminated. Pockets of resistance arose, such as in Warsaw, and there are many instances of Jews and Gypsies fleeing into the forests to hide. For those hiding in the forests, der Führer realized that there are many men in our jails for poaching game."

"A successful poacher must be a good hunter, a good shot," Dorsch said. "Why should they be wasted in jail when they can go into the forests and hunt down the unfits who are hiding there? So der Führer ordered that these criminals be put to good use. But we have found that many of them are unfit for the task When word got around the prisons what the task was, there were many volunteers. Those volunteers, many of whom were incarcerated for violent acts, proved much more effective than the common poachers. We are studying a cross section of men at the hospital, some who adapted well to the work, others, like the man you witnessed, who are too weak to assist in the program."

"Trying to find out why some men enjoy the task and others feel like murderers," I said.

Something in my tone ticked off Vogler. "Not murderers," he said, "but executioners. Every society in history has had a need for executioners to ensure that the public is safe from antisocial types who would do harm. Der Führer has instructed us that the Jew spreads his disease by violating Aryans with his blood. He is a rapist who hides in the dark to attack our young girls, to spread his seed and disease. Those of us who have the strength and conviction to carry out der Führer's command take up the slack for the weaklings."

His tone didn't leave any doubt who he thought of as a weakling. "What's going on now," I said, "is we're a poaching unit, hunting down Jews?"

"Exactly." Dorsch rubbed his hands together. "This is an excellent opportunity to have the men track down and exterminate vermin in the actual conditions they experience in the field. Having the men perform under actual conditions is so much more valuable than what we are able to provide at the hospital."

I thought about the building surrounded by barbwire. Was it sturdier to make it soundproof? Is that what was going on inside it? Men were committing murders? Killing people in cold blood so that this sick bastard of a doctor beside me could see their reactions?

Now I knew what Hildegarde Dietrich meant when she said her project was exactly opposite to Dorsch's. He was studying more efficient ways to eliminate the populations in the conquered areas. She was figuring out how to populate them with people having blond hair, blue eyes, and shit for brains.

"We're here," Vogler said.

"Here" was a pleasant viewpoint meadow on a ridge that gave us sweeping views of the areas below. A gourmet picnic was set out for Dorsch, Vogler, and me. The men on the half-tracks, the poachers, spread out to do a sweep down the hillside. A radio operator stayed with us to relay messages from a reconnaissance plane that was spotting the prey. Dorsch and Vogler drank wine and ate bread, cheese, and sausages while they used binoculars to get close-ups of the action below. They sounded like two kids arguing over a game of marbles. I realized that there were two different units. Vogler and Dorsch had made opposing bets as to which unit would capture the most undesirables.

I stood around like a mechanized zombie. I smiled when I was supposed to smile, laughed when it was called for, agreed when it was necessary. But my mind had shut down, and I was operating purely off nervous energy. The thought occurred to me that the atrocities taking place, the mass murder apparently of millions, wasn't known to the Allies. If Roosevelt and Churchill knew it, they kept it under their hats. Wild Bill hadn't dropped a hint to me that I might encounter this kind of insanity. The fact that the Jews were brutally treated and imprisoned was common knowledge. And the Russians were always howling about how many of their people—and soldiers—had been killed by the Germans or were working as slave laborers in German war factories.

But it was all thought of as being in a combat context, even the civilian deaths. I didn't know what "efficient" mode of death was being used at the camps, but the concept that thousands of men were being trained to perform cold-blooded murder was enough to fry my brains.

The call came in that captures had been made. We rode part of the way down, then left the car and walked in thick forest. At first I was curious as to why the prisoners weren't just brought out to us, but the reason struck me as we walked—the people were to be killed, buried in the dense forest. I hoped to God it was over before we got there.

We found them in a clearing, a younger and older man, a woman and two children, boys about eight and ten, huddled together and surrounded by SS. From the explanation given to the two officers by the poacher noncom in charge, the older man was the father of the younger one and the woman. The children belonged to the woman. The woman's husband had been eliminated a year earlier in a poacher action.

I stood a little apart from the group. My hand kept going to the Walther P38 on my hip. But there weren't enough bullets in the clip to hit even half the SS present, even if I managed to get off more than two shots before I was mowed down.

I sensed someone beside me and flinched as a little girl came up next to me. She was about five, a pretty little thing with big brown eyes. She looked at me gravely and took my hand. Her mother screamed for her to run. She looked frightened as her mother was silenced by the threat of an SS. She took my hand.

I stared down at her, at the hand in mine. I was petrified. My breathing stopped, my heart stopped, the world stopped spinning.

Vogler was suddenly beside me. "Is your pistol loaded, Herr Hauptsturmfuhrer Wolfhardt?"

I stared at him.

"I asked if your pistol was loaded."

I don't know what I said. I'm not even sure it was German. Something dribbled out of my mouth, some nonsense, maybe they weren't even words.

"Shoot the child!" he snapped to the noncom.

I turned my back on him and walked away. He called after me, and I kept walking. I fought a terrible urge to turn and pull the pistol and fire and fire and—

I heard a shot. My knees gave out on me and I stumbled and dropped to the ground. More shots. Not the blast of machine gun fire, but individual shots. Six people. Six shots. Nothing wasted.

FIVE

I was sitting on the fender of the staff car smoking a cigarette when Dorsch and Vogler came out of the bushes. They were in high spirits, laughing and talking. Their jolly mood disappeared when they saw me.

We got into the car with a cold silence among us. We hadn't gone more than a hundred meters over the rough terrain when Vogler twisted in his seat.

"You know, of course, that your reluctance to do your duty will be reported. I suspect that it will affect your next assignment." He rolled down his window and spit out. "In our group, we had a Dirlewanger box. Men without the stomach to do their duty went into it. They came out of it either as killers . . . or dead."

Dorsch smiled with false sympathy. "I suggest you write home for heavy winter socks. You have not fulfilled your obligation of Blutkitt."

I was no longer mortified or petrified. "Herren, I was selected for the present assignment by Reichsfuhrer-SS Himmler and der Füh-rer. I will be having private conversations with both of them. I would hope that I will not have to explain that I am not physically up to giving blood because I was diverted from my duty to der Führer by being forced to participate in a mission for which I had received no training."

I couldn't have gotten a better reaction if I'd shoved Herr Colonel's swagger stick up their asses. One thing about bullies—they can always be bullied. By the time we reached the hospital, they had both adopted the intimate *du* in addressing me, as opposed to the formal *zie*.

We all laughed heartily at their jokes and sipped fine brandy from Vogler's silver flask. By the time we got back to the hospital, we were downright jovial.

Parting, I clicked my heels smartly and snapped an enthusiastic *Heil Hitler!* By the time I reached my quarters, I was more relaxed and mellowed out than I'd been since I got word that I was being jerked off the pitcher's mound and into an army uniform.

Isn't life funny? Full of twists and curves. It's like watching a movie—you see someone driving down a road, and something happens that sends them off on another road, one that they never would have driven. I guess that day I slid off the main road and onto a detour. When it happened, so many other things about life, love, and the pursuit of happiness, what make Arnie the Barber tick, all fell into place. I no longer resented being selected for this mission. I was no longer even pissed at Donovan. He was wrong about the Babe—like I said, the Babe did more for baseball than Cobb, and if you counted walks as singles, his on-base percentage dwarfed Cobb's, as did his slugging average.

For the first time in my life I was enveloped in a warm cocoon of peace and tranquillity. At peace with myself, instead of constantly driven, worrying about my next pitch, worrying about how to get out of the war and back onto the pitcher's mound.

Suddenly, like a strike of lightning, when I had gotten onto my feet in the forest and walked to the car and lit up a cigarette from a pack I'd found in the glove compartment, I knew exactly what I was going to do with the rest of my life.

I was going to kill those two mutherfuckers *and* their boss, Adolf.

If I got my hands on that prick Himmler, I was going to waste him,
too.

Having reached that decision, "the rest of my life" was a contradiction in terms.

SIX

That night, I sat in the cottage, and stared out the window, a bottle of German dark in one hand, a cigarette in the other. I liked cigarettes. Like good beer and good women, they're soothing to the soul. But I gave up weeds because in the days when I smoked regularly, I'd wake up in the mornings feeling like a herd of elephants had trampled my chest. I hated making love to women who smoked, too. It was like kissing an ashtray. But now that I was under a self-imposed death sentence, I figured that smoking—along with all the beer and women I could get—weren't unreasonable goals.

Four beers hadn't drowned out the scene in the forest and the little girl with big eyes. It would haunt me for the—*hey, don't worry about that*, I told myself, *I'm not going to live that long anyway*. When I got back to the cottage earlier, I'd gone in and thrown up, but the bad taste in my mouth wouldn't go away.

"How could they do it?"

"They're animals."

I almost jumped out of my skin. It was Hans the orderly. I'd spoken aloud, thinking I was alone. I hadn't heard him come in.

"What'd you say?"

"I told you they're animals."

It took a moment for the fact that we were speaking English to sink in. His was heavily accented with German.

"I spent some time in the States after the last war," he said, "staying with my daughter in Cleveland. I used to watch the Indians play, I was a big fan of amerikanisches Schlagballspiel."

"That's a mouthful just to say baseball."

"We Germans never make anything simple."

"I played for Brooklyn."

"I never saw you play, I left before your time, but I read about you. For years after I left, my daughter occasionally mailed me the sports page from the *Cleveland Plain Dealer*." He nodded at the gun. "Put it away. *I play ball.*"

I had the automatic pistol, pointed at his gut, without even realizing it.

"Do you know what I saw today?" I asked.

"Everybody at the hospital knows what happened today. To you, it was a life-shattering moment. To me, it is just another day in hell."

"How could they? What sort of human beings—no, don't tell me they're animals, I don't want to hear that. They're not animals, they're human beings raised in a civilized society. I don't have any problem with Hitler being a nutcase, it happens sometimes, a guy gets a fixation on something like Jews or Negroes or paying taxes and goes off the deep end. But what Dorsch and Vogler described today was something beyond individual insanity, something that the whole nation has to be involved in. Hans, I was raised in Germany until I was thirteen years old. The people I knew weren't any different than the ones I've known in America."

Hans shrugged. "I've thought about it, a thousand times, a thousand nights in which I wake up, trying to understand how a man can shoot a child in the head. And then another. And another."

"Stop it!" I opened another beer and took a long swig. I had a buzz in my head but I still felt numb.

Hans said, "I heard that there were problems between you and the two senior officers, but the three of you appeared to be comrades when I saw you earlier."

"They got on my ass because I wouldn't kill a child in cold blood, but I threw them a knuckleball, one that wobbled at their heads all the way to the plate. I told them I'd tell der Führer I wouldn't be able to give blood."

Hans chuckled. "Very good. That will hold them for a while. But the word is that you have violated the Bluttkitt. They will smile to your face, but will be making plans behind your back. There will be repercussions, but let's hope not until after the transfusion."

"What is this Bluttkitt thing? I'm not familiar with the word."

"The blood bond wasn't around when you lived in Germany, it came in with the Nazis, and it is only used among the SS. I've heard der Führer got the concept from a history of Genghis Khan that Himmler sent as a Christmas present. The concept is that blood spilled binds together all those involved. It started with the Night of the Long Knives, in which Himmler and others proved their loyalty by murdering Nazis who opposed Hitler, men with whom they had laughed and drunk and fought together. When the war started and Hitler began what he calls his 'cleansing' of blood-lines, it was no longer a small cadre of SS who were involved in murder, but many thousands. They began a crime of unprecedented scope in the history of the world, something that will haunt the world when its ugliness is revealed. To ensure that all are implicated in the mass murders, they demand that other SS participate in the crimes."

"They're scared, that's why they want others to participate."

"Yes, exactly, together they are a gang of violent bullies, but separate them from the pack, and they become rabbits."

"But how? How? How do normal people—"

"Normal? I don't know what that word means anymore. If you mean that before they put on uniforms and began murdering people, they were not institutionalized as criminally insane, yes, they were like the rest of us. Perhaps it is just a matter of statistics."

"What do you mean?"

"In a city of a hundred thousand people, do you think it's possible that there are a hundred bad people? I mean, really bad, people who kill, rape, rob, or commit other violent crimes?"

"A hundred violent criminals in a city of hundred thousand? Probably."

"There you have it. One out of a thousand has the potential to be a homicidal maniac. There are eighty million Germans. Statistically, that means there are eighty thousand potential murders in the country."

I shook my head. "No, it's not a matter of statistics, that's too easy to account for what's going on here. You don't kill on the scale they were talking about, millions of deaths, without millions of people being involved directly or indirectly and tens of millions more knowing about it and telling more tens of millions. That means most of the country has bloody hands. No, what happened here isn't about statistics, it's about evil. Your pal Adolf opened the Hell Gates, and demons flew out, like one of those viruses he's so frightened of, taking over the minds of all eighty million Germans. That means I should shoot you right now, because it doesn't look like any of you missed getting infected."

Hans sat down and took the cigarette and beer I offered. He said, "It fascinates you, doesn't it? Your rational mind rejects what you saw today. But you know your eyes didn't lie."

"It fascinates me only in the sense of standing at the reptile cage in a zoo and wondering what it would be like to stick my hand in. What I saw today, what you described as happening on a mass scale, is such an extreme side of human nature that it defies rational explanation. I can understand mob mentality, the lynch mobs of the American South, Kristallnacht when mobs all over Germany went after Jews. Mob chemistry creates in people the same sort of mindless violence that coon dogs experience when they're ripping apart a cornered raccoon. But that's not what's happening here; these aren't crimes of the moment, done during an adrenaline high. Cold-blooded mass exterminations are being performed on the same sort of systematic basis that they produce airplane engines. *By ordinary people.*

"There are two types, as Dorsch told me, the ones who enjoy it and the ones who have to be convinced that it's their duty and morally correct. I can see that they're afraid of the ones that enjoy it because they can't be controlled. They might turn on them next. It's the 'normal' ones that can be convinced to do evil that they want. That's what the program is all about, discovering what would make an otherwise ordinary person commit a heinous crime. I need to know that, too. Before I die, I need to know how you krauts get ordinary human beings to commit mass murder of innocent people. I need to know that. I can't go to my grave without knowing how an ordinary Joe can put a gun to a child's head and pull the trigger."

"You're drunk."

"I've only had a couple beers."

He nudged an empty schnapps bottle on the floor with his foot. It rolled toward four empty beer bottles.

"Yeah, those too."

"You have to keep yourself together. The Führer arrives tomorrow."

"Tomorrow? Dorsch said it might not be for a week."

"Dorsch doesn't know; probably even Vogler won't know until minutes before it happens. Even I can't tell you the exact time. The Führer's security people find that surprise is a good method of protection."

"How do you know he's arriving tomorrow?"

"One of my contacts pumps gas for the Obersalzberg vehicles. He heard two of the Führer's radio operators talking about having to get a relay antenna into place on the mountain above the hospital tonight. The Führer keeps in continuous radio contact with his generals. The radio operators are always one step ahead, getting the equipment set up."

"Okay, what's the plan? I was told that you people needed a type A, Aryan type, for your plan to kill the Führer."

"Did they tell you how it would be done?"

"No, but I can guess. You stick a bomb in a briefcase, I put it down near the Führer when I go in for the transfusion, I give blood, walk away, and Adolf gets blown to pieces."

"Your chances of getting near the Führer with a bomb in a briefcase are about as good as Brooklyn beating the Yankees in the next World Series. That's why your superiors were told that we would use polio."

"Polio? How am I to get polio into the—wait a minute, *you're going to infect me with polio so I can transmit it to Adolf*? Are you people fuckin' nuts? You know what that would do to me?"

"No immediate harm would come to you, that was understood. It takes a while for the disease to take effect. The moment the Führer showed any symptoms of disease, you would be taken prisoner by the Gestapo. It is assumed that before you permitted yourself to be taken by the Gestapo or experienced painful symptoms, you would have, ah, completed the last part of the mission—"

"This is a suicide mission? I infect Adolf and kill myself?"

"Of course, that has been understood from the beginning."

Boy, I must have really pissed off Wild Bill. Yesterday, had I known this, I would have packed my bags, hopped on my horse, and headed into the sunset. Even now, the idea of affecting myself with a loathsome disease sent quivers through my crotch. But as long as I can kill myself . . .

I waved my beer bottle at him. "You know what they say, Scharfuhrer—in for a penny, in for a pound."

"The polio plan has been terminated. Our contact was to steal it from an experimental medical laboratory where he worked. Allied bombers recently destroyed the lab—and our man."

"Okay, so what's the backup plan?"

"I am in the process of finalizing it. It is better that you be told exactly when you need to. That way . . ."

"Yeah, if the Gestapo cuts off my balls and sticks them in my mouth, I won't give it away."

"In the meantime, you need to get psychologically prepared to meet the Führer."

"Tell me about your leader. What makes the bastard tick?"

"Like all of us, he has his likes and dislikes, his prejudices and his real or imagined view of the world and how he fits into it. But to understand the man, you have to realize that the Führer's thinking is dominated by the concept of *blood*. He is obsessed with the notion of purity of blood, even his own blood. He has his blood drawn by leeches because he believes it helps keep it pure. And he has Dr. Morell store vials of his blood. He won't eat meat because it contains animal blood. He's a vegetarian, with contempt for meat eaters. He says the strongest animal in the world, the elephant, is also a vegetarian." Hans laughed. "Sometimes at the dinner table when his staff is eating wurst, he threatens to have blood sausage made from his blood for them to eat."

"Did they—"

"Not yet, but who knows when dealing with the Führer."

"That's his thing about the Jews, the blood thing?"

"He considers Jews a race, not a religion. The blood sin is a mixing of bloods between races, regardless of whether it's Jewish blood, Negroid, or any other type, but those mixtures get his biggest tirades. In his mind, the infection of German soldiers by syphilis in their blood during the prior Great War, and a conspiracy by Jews, defeated the old Reich."

"Syphilis? Was it that epidemic?"

"In his mind it was." Hans gave me a strange look, as if he suddenly wondered if he could trust me. "I have been in the Führer's confidence for over twenty years, at his side, opening his mail, seeing his most personal communicates, eavesdropping on the most secret conversations. Do you know why he's so obsessed with purity of blood?"

"Because he's a Jew?" It was a wild-ass guess.

Hans shook his head. "There is a fear in all Germans that Jewish blood may be found in our backgrounds. In Hitler's case, his father was born out of wedlock, the son of a housekeeper or maid in a wealthy household. There have been rumors that the man who impregnated her, the head of the household, was Jewish. Although there is no real proof, because of the Führer's position, even the whispers are dangerous. Rumors have flown since he had the village where the supposed union between his grandmother and the Jew took place destroyed." Hans shook his head. "He is concerned about the possibility of Jewish blood in his veins, but of even more significant import is that the Führer is probably syphilitic."

My jaw dropped.

Hans lowered his voice, as if he feared someone was listening at the keyhole.

"The source," Hans laughed, "of the accusation has become known as 'the blue manuscript.' It is the least talked about—and most feared—secret in the Third Reich. When he came to power, the Führer ordered the Gestapo to seize his medical records from every doctor and hospital he'd been treated by in his entire life. The files came to Himmler, including one from the hospital at Pasewalk where he was treated during the prior war. The blue manuscript is made up of medical records stating that soldier Adolf Hitler has syphilis, the type that affects the nervous system and slowly causes a degeneration of the body. When you see him, you will notice that his left hand shakes. And his walk—he no longer has the forceful strut of the old days. He has started to walk like an old man. And he is only fifty-five years old."

"My God, if that ever came out—"

"No one would believe it. But it is the source of his preoccupation with infection, syphilis, and blood taint in general, what the Jewish-Austrian physician Freud would perhaps have called a pathological obsession. The Führer even devoted a large section in his book, *Mein Kampf*, to the subject of syphilis, ranting about it over and over. One of his favorite tirades about your President Roosevelt is his claim that the man's confined to a wheelchair not by polio but syphilis."

"That's ridiculous. Does Hitler think the Jews gave him syphilis?"

Hans shrugged. "Who knows? If you make the suggestion, he will probably adopt it.'

"The guy needs a head doctor."

"Jewish astrology, that's what the Führer calls psychiatry. He rejects all theories based upon Jewish authorities. I ask you, my friend, when you take all the meat off of science and leave only the bones, what are you left with? If you told him Columbus was Jewish, German geography books would be changed to show the earth as flat. He is so pathological about blood and infection, he will

speak one moment of Jewish blood tainting the lifeblood of the
nation and the next of a 'Jewish virus' that pollutes the blood of
Aryans—as if Jewish blood is an actual virus."

I shook my head. It was mind-boggling. This fruitcake had been
halfway to being Master of the World.

"How does syphilis affect his sex life? Doesn't he pass it on to
his women friends?"

Hans gave me another strange look.

"He doesn't have sex," I offered. "Or he's queer."

"No, he's not homosexual. But he has . . . unusual sexual needs."

"What do you mean?"

Hans got up. "Enough talk for tonight."

"Sit down, it's not enough. If I'm going to die because of this
bastard, I want to know everything there is about him. Put it out
on the table, pal."

Hans lit a cigarette and took in a deep drag, slowly letting it out
through his nose. "The Führer sometimes says that he fears intimate
relationships with a woman because he fears infection. He has said
so many times around the lunch table. In truth, I believe he fears
infecting the women, perhaps out of respect for them, perhaps out
of fear that his syphilis will be disclosed. But there is another twist
to the story of the Führer's sex life. It comes from a man who was
once very close to the Führer—Otto Strasser. Do you know who
he is?"

"Not really. The name sounds familiar," I added, to temper my
ignorance.

"Strasser and his brother Gregor were early leaders in the Nazi
party, becoming members in 1920. Gregor became, in fact, the second most popular and powerful member of the party, after the
Führer himself. The brothers opposed Hitler's domination of the
party and were marked for termination in the Blood Purge of 1934.
Gregor was murdered in the purge, but Otto fled, finally settling
in Canada, I believe. I knew them both, of course, and while my
feelings for them were tempered by my loyalty to the Führer, I
found them both to be men of high principle, at least in the polit-

ical realm. They were leftist and opposed the Führer's alliance with big business and his anti-Semitism. However, Otto Strasser naturally hates the Führer.

"Last year Strasser made an accusation to your OSS about the Führer's sex life that was so bizarre, an OSS agent was sent over to ask me if I could verify it. The accusation was about Geli Raubal, Hitler's niece, who was twenty years old when she and her mother moved in with Hitler to keep house for him in 1929. At that time, as head of the party, he was a leading political force in the country but would not be chancellor for another four years. Two years after they moved in, Geli killed herself with Hitler's pistol. Shot herself in the chest. That Hitler was madly in love with her despite the age difference—he was twenty years older—is not disputed. He often has said that she was the only woman he would have ever considered marrying."

"Hitler killed her," I said. "He fucked his niece, incest, then murdered her when he found out she was fucking someone else."

Hans frowned at me. "You Americans have too much of a fondness for motion pictures. They infect your brains like the Führer's viruses. It's true, Hitler found out the niece was having an affair with his chauffeur and broke it up. However, the scenario is even worse than you imagine. Strasser told OSS agents that he had grown close to Geli because he felt sorry for the young woman. Perhaps his real motive was to find some scandal about the relationship between Geli and her uncle. What he learned was so bizarre, that he was never able to use it because he didn't think anyone would believe it.

"Geli told him that rather than having normal sex with her, her uncle would make her undress until she stood before him naked. He would then lie on his back on the floor and have her squat over him. He would examine her female parts at close range, getting excited as he did. When his excitement was reaching its peak, he insisted that she urinate on him."

"Excuse me?"

"Piss, Herr Hauptsturmfuhrer, he had the young girl piss in his face. While he masturbated."

Jesus H. Christ. And I remembered something else weird about the guy. The OSS psychologist who was part of the team that briefed me said they had information about a kinky night Adolf had with a German actress. The woman, Rene Mueller, spent an evening with the Führer. They both undressed and she expected to get into bed and have sex—instead, Adolf got down on the floor and begged her to kick him. She refused, and he pleaded with her for the punishment, groveling and condemning himself as unworthy to touch her. She finally kicked him.

Rene Mueller told her director about the incident. And committed suicide.

Adolf had an interesting track record with kinky sex and suicidal women. A cynic like me might suspect he was smothering potential scandal by having the witnesses to his perversions killed.

"I'm right," I told Hans.

Hans frowned at me. "Right about what?"

"He killed his niece. Or had her killed to shut her up."

"How do you conclude that from the situation?"

I leaned forward and locked eyes with him. "Hans, not many people commit suicide—*by shooting themselves in the chest.*"

SEVEN

JUNE 3

The hospital's air raid siren whined and we all turned out with brass shined and collars starched. As I waited for der Führer's motorcade, I had to admit the guy traveled in style. The road leading into the hospital was lined with flowers and Nazi flags. We stood like school-children waiting for him. Every woman had a bouquet of flowers to shower on him. The first vehicles to arrive were four truckloads of SS. They poured out of the back of the trucks and spread out. There were a hundred machine guns at the ready before motor-cycles and smaller vehicles loaded with SS came into view. When der Führer's open Mercedes rolled down the reception line, cheer-ing broke out, and women rushed the car to throw flowers.

The thing that would stay with me for the rest of my life—that phrase that kept jumping off my tongue—was the expression on the faces of the women. You would have thought Jesus H. Christ had just arrived, walking on water. These women were having a religious experience. From the looks of pure ecstasy, some of them were creaming their pants.

What caliber of man could cause this response? The guy who

climbed out of the Mercedes, wearing rather ridiculous horse-riding pants, didn't look like a god or even Charles Atlas material. He was more the stuff of Charlie Chaplin. Frankly, der Führer could have starred in silent movies. Funny ones. He would have made a great waiter in a long white apron who trips and dumps a tray of food in a diner's lap.

About five-eight or -nine and maybe one-fifty or one-sixty, he had dark hair parted on the right with a forelock thrown over to his left temple, that funny little sawed-off Charlie Chaplin paintbrush mustache above thin lips, a weak chin, narrow shoulders, a sunken chest, and long feet paddling on the end of short legs.

He looked more like an officious clerk in a government office than the man who wanted to be Master of the World.

What made this guy special? Okay, he sent his goose-steppers all over Europe. But Germany had a population much larger than any other European country. He whipped France because his army was bigger, better equipped, and better led—not to mention the krauts didn't play by the rules, invading neutral Belgium to make an end run around the Maginot Line. Except for Russia, all the other countries he invaded from Norway to Greece were a fraction the size of Germany. And he jumped on the Russians with a surprise attack after signing a peace treaty.

The guy loses the air and sea war with the British to the west, so he turns around and invades the Russkies? Opening a second front before he wins the first? When his boys grind to a halt on the Eastern Front, bogged down in subzero temperatures, he declares war on us, the mightiest industrial nation on earth, after his Nip pals hit us at Pearl? This is the work of a military genius? Stalin has been kicking his ass, Allied bombers have been turning his cities into rubble, we took North Africa and are coming up the Italian boot, and there's talk about *when*—not if—we'll wade ashore on the French coast.

So what makes this guy special? How come grown men weep with joy when they see him? Why do women cream their pants at the sight of him?

And what makes ordinary people put a gun to the head of a

small child and pull the trigger for him? Maybe I'll find out before I kill him.

Dr. Dorsch and Colonel Vogler were at the front of the reception line, with the entire staff lined up behind them. Hans was in the group escorting der Führer as soon as Adolf climbed out of the Mercedes. I placed myself near the end of the line so I could get a good look at the man. When Adolf was almost abreast with me, Hans whispered something to an SS officer, who in turn whispered to der Führer.

Suddenly I was facing the man who had conquered Europe. He stepped up to me and locked eyes. I was so startled I nearly stumbled backward. His eyes were shocking. Milky blue, the color of a late-summer sky, they were intense, burning. Curious and probing to the point of being impolite. His face was very pale, and that made his eyes even more startling.

"Mein Führer," I said. I was shaken so bad, it was the only thing that came out, and it sounded false to my ear. I raised my hand in a *Heil Hitler*. It seemed to break the spell. He took those invasive orbs off my face and stared curiously at my hands.

"Let me see your hands."

I was startled again. And confused.

"My hands?"

"Your hands," an adjutant snapped. "Show der Führer your hands."

I held out my hands. Adolf Hitler, chancellor of Germany, godhead of the Third Reich, stared at them.

Now I have to tell you that I have very special hands. They're big, with long fingers and baskets for palms, but my hands aren't bear paws. They're world-class, elegant hands, the kind a concert pianist would make a deal with the devil to get. My hands are what got me into the majors. I have power in my shoulders, but it's my hand and wrist that control the ball, that send it where it needs to go.

Der Führer smiled at me. Yeah, really smiled. And nodded. "Very good," he said, "very good."

What the fuck was very good? This guy have some sort of fetish about hands? Christ, is he going to make me take off my shoes to examine my feet next?

He moved on, Hans and his personal cadre moving with him.

EIGHT

I was in my room, smoking another coffin nail, a Turkish cigarette that tasted like dog shit, when Hans came in. As soon as he closed the door, he grinned and rubbed his hands together.

"Very good, very good."

"Why don't you clue me in on what's so good?"

He lit one of my cigarettes and sat down, stretching out his legs.

"The Führer has some personality quirks—"

"Yeah, he likes to kill people, mostly Jews."

"Besides that. One of his traits is that he makes up his mind instantly about a person. He either likes or dislikes the person on sight. And once he makes up his mind, he rarely changes it. When I lived in Cleveland, there was an expression about a 'steel-trap mind.' It seemed to imply that once the person made up his mind about something, he locked on it like the jaws of a trap on an animal's leg. The Führer has exactly that type of mind. If there is anything that frustrates those around him, especially the generals conducting his war, it's the fact it's so difficult, or impossible, to get him to change his mind once he decides upon a course of action."

"So I passed the on-sight test?"

"Yes, it's your hands. I hoped it would be your eyes; I never thought about your hands."

"Hands? Eyes?"

"His mother's eyes. He was very close to her. She's been dead for a long time, but he still worships at her shrine, you might say. Sometimes he meets a person with the same shade of eyes. It always affects him."

"Did she have big hands, too?"

"Some people judge others by the bumps on their head. The Fuhrer looks at their hands. His own hands are quite graceful, the hands of an artist, which he is. They say that what most impressed him about Albert Speer, the Minister of Armaments, is his hands. Speer was just an architect, but one whose hands greatly impressed the Fuhrer."

"Hey, no shit, that's great. Maybe instead of killing this asshole, I'll just hang around, flick my fingers, and get a big job. Maybe he'll put me in charge of making bullets to kill little kids with." I got up and walked around to bleed off some of my anger. I was crying in my beer and I knew it. "Sorry," I said, sitting back down. "I just dropped in on this nightmare; you must have been living it for a long time. How did you get involved with the OSS?"

"My son married a Jewess. I got them out of the country in '39, convincing them to move to Cleveland where my daughter had immigrated. But my grandson, a boy of twenty, slipped back into Germany because he was in love with a girl he had gone to university with. She was also Jewish. By then, it was not easy to come and go. The boy and his girl had false papers and were arrested trying to cross the border into Switzerland. I didn't learn about it for months because he was using a false name. By the time I was able to trace what happened to him, he was dead."

"Killed by the SS? Einsatzgruppen?"

"Gestapo. They believed he was a member of an underground group helping Jews escape. They killed him slowly to find out who his contacts were. Had he actually known any, he could have given up the names and died quickly. Unfortunately, he was telling the truth when he said that he knew nothing."

Hans was made of iron. He spoke as neutrally as if he was reading a report about the incident. But there was emotion in his eyes. Not hurt, the years had washed away the pain of loss. What I saw was anger. I changed the subject. "What's the plan, Hans? Do I use my lovely hands to strangle Adolf?"

"He's to be killed with a bomb."

"How?"

"The Führer's room is directly above a waiting room on the first floor of the hospital. That entire wing of the hospital has been evacuated to ensure the Führer's privacy. The waiting room isn't being used. There's a small washroom that's entered from the waiting room. The bomb will go in the washroom."

"How do we get a bomb? Steal it from the armory?"

"I already have it. New weapons are frequently sent to Obersalzberg to be demonstrated for the Führer and the military chiefs. I diverted one months ago while others like it were being demonstrated. I've had it hidden, waiting for an opportunity. I am attached to Berghof security, but the opportunity hasn't arisen to use the bomb because I'm not a member of his inner circle."

"Won't the Führer's guards find it in their search?"

"It isn't there yet. We have to hide it. It's an underwater charge, relatively small and with a simple timer. The toilet reservoir is high on the wall, nearly to the ceiling. The other side of the ceiling is the floor of the Führer's bedroom. We'll put the bomb in the reservoir, set it to go off at a time we know the Fuhrer will be sleeping. When it goes off . . . the chancellor of the Third Reich will be dead."

"What do we do after that?"

"There is little chance we will escape, if that is your question. Suspicion will focus on everyone at the hospital, even me. Every person will be arrested and questioned. It won't be long before they figure out you are not Hauptsturmfuhrer Wolfhardt. My advice to you is to shoot yourself immediately after the bomb goes off."

"Thanks, pal, but how about a dash for the Swiss border? It's probably no more than two or three hours by car."

"Do you think that you can simply drive away from here? You

couldn't do it before the explosion, less so afterward, not with the security that surrounds the Führer. And you don't want to let yourself be captured. Grand Inquisitor Torquemada himself could have learned lessons in torture from the Gestapo. I will quickly be in the same situation you are. Once they learn from the residue that it was a specialized marine bomb, everyone who had any access at all to the bomb at Obersalzberg will be arrested and tortured. Unlike you, I would be forced to give up the identities of other members of the underground—and I don't fool myself into believing I would withstand their methods of persuasion. It will be our duty to kill ourselves before we are captured."

I had resolved in my own mind that I would die on this mission, but I assumed that I would go down fighting. But Hans was right— if I was wounded instead of being killed, *I'd regret it the rest of my life*.

Strange, but rather than being uptight about the prospect of dying, killing myself at that, I only had a funny feeling in my dick. Like it was telling me something.

"We can't plant the bomb tonight," Hans said. "Security is too alert the first night in a new location. The operation is set for the day after tomorrow. We will play it by ear, as you Americans say. Our best chance will probably be tomorrow night, or in the morning after the operation."

A knock on the door caused both of us to freeze. It came again, not really a knock, but pounding by a fist. "Hauptsturmfuhrer Wolfhardt, open the door!"

Hans turned ashen. "Colonel Keitel, the Führer's security chief."

I opened the door and found a short, studious-appearing man with thick glasses. Like his bosses Himmler and Hitler, he looked more like a clerk than a colonel.

"Guten Abend, Herr Standartenfuhrer."

"Der Führer commands your presence."

NINE

My goddammn dick was pounding as I marched with the colonel to the the hospital. It itched like hell. And burned. What the hell? I wondered. Was this some sort of nervous reaction to the murder-suicide plot?

Keitel suddenly stopped and whipped around to face me. "There is a matter that disturbs me, Hauptsturmfuhrer. The fact that you have lied."

I nearly pissed my pants. "Ja?"

"About the woman."

"The woman?"

"We are aware of what took place."

"Ja." What the hell?

"Such actions do not please der Führer. You are on a special duty list for der Führer. You know the prohibitions, do you not?"

"Yes, of course, Herr Colonel. Ah, which one did I violate?"

He reddened with anger. "Do you play games with me, Wolf-hardt? You know that you are not allowed to have sex while you are on der Führer's blood list."

Hildegarde, they knew about me screwing her.

"I can explain—"

"*You cannot explain.* Marriage was expressly forbidden. Having intimate activities with any woman is expressly forbidden because of the possibility of contamination. Der Führer has been told. There was another blood donor on his way to act as backup should you be disqualified, but the man was severely injured in an accident. If der Führer decides not to go through with the operation for fear of contamination, you will be severely punished."

I was speechless. I didn't know what to say. Marriage? My confusion must have helped because Keitel's voice lost some of its lashing tone when he spoke again.

"You must understand, Herr Hauptsturmfuhrer, that it was your duty not to marry while you were on the donor list." He lowered his voice. "Der Führer has a terrible fear of contamination. He saw how his fellow soldiers were struck down by venereal disease in the previous Great War. He carries the entire Fatherland on his back. Without him, the war would be lost, the Reich would fall." Keitel tapped my on the chest with his finger. "You will not be the cause of our thousand-year Reich's fall."

"There was a blood test taken on my arrival. I am not contaminated—"

"If it were not for the results of that blood test, I can assure you, Herr Hauptsturmfuhrer, you would be a guest of the Gestapo already."

On the second floor of the hospital, Colonel Keitel knocked quietly on a door. It was answered by an orderly, who told me to enter. Adolf was sitting in a great armchair overlooking the only window in the room. He was reading papers by the light of a floor lamp standing next to the chair. He didn't look up from his reading to acknowledge my entrance. Standing with the orderly at my side, I had a peaceful moment to study Hitler. His short, brown hair, cut military fashion, fell sideways over his face. His eyebrows and trim-cut mustache were of a shade darker than the hair on his head. What most struck me about the man was a certain quality of sincerity . . . or perhaps one would call it sincerity and resolution. There was a certain air of firmness about his thin lips, and his indomitable chin exuded a convincing air of strength.

It struck me suddenly why the German people followed him, why so many had voted for his party that he was appointed chancellor. *Hitler cared.* He cared about the unfairness of the Versailles Treaty, the punishment that plunged Germany into a state of economic depression. He cared about Germany being treated as a second-rate nation when it was the greatest industrial power in Europe. He told the German people that they were great. Hell, that they deserved to be masters of the world. He told them they had a destiny to fulfill. He told them they were *winners.*

I realized that *Adolf was a great coach.* He gave his people the same kind of inspirational spiel that coaches like Connie Mack gave the Philly players that led them to nine pennants and five World Series. *Get out there and fight fight fight you can do it boys you can do it you're the best.*

Thinking about it, baseball teams aren't run much differently from how the krauts ran their country. Everything was organized, everyone followed orders, it was all a united team effort, there were no individuals—just team members, and there sure as hell wasn't any democratic action. And there was another thing that made great coaches like Mack and Little Napoleon McGraw—they were self-made martyrs. They let everyone around them know that they were sacrificing their lives for the sake of the players and the fans.

Adolf gave the papers to the orderly. He indicated a chair facing him, and said, "Please sit down, Herr Hauptsturmfuhrer."

I took a seat facing der Führer. The orderly disappeared into the shadows in a corner of the room while Adolf studied me again with those probing, watchful eyes.

"Tell me about your wife," he said. He spoke gravely.

What did I know about my wife? I couldn't make it up as I went along, either. This guy had secret police on every corner of the country. I wasn't going to be able to fake it. I had to try another tactic. Hans said the guy was real puritanical, like a priest, that sort of thing. Didn't tell dirty jokes, didn't like them told in his presence, wasn't the kind of guy to whom you pointed out the size of a woman's knockers. He came across as a prudish bastard—even if he did like having women piss in his face.

"I married her because she's a good woman. Unspoiled. I wanted to make sure she wasn't spoiled after I went off to war. I also wanted to remain pure for her. And for Mein Führer."

His face lit up and he clapped his hands together. "Jawohl, that's what I thought. I knew the moment I saw you that you were not the type to marry anyone but a good girl. There were reports about her, of course, but what can you tell from a report? When I found out she had my mother's name, I was very pleased."

"That's one of the reasons I was attracted to her." What the hell was his mother's name?

"I have to tell you, Herr Hauptsturmfuhrer, there are many things about you that please me. I find it amusing that I am to be given blood from a wolf."

"A wolf? Oh, Wolfhardt. Hard wolf."

"As you must know, Adolf is derived from the old German word for noble wolf."

"Of course."

"I will tell you a secret, Herr Wolfhardt. I have many times used the name 'Wolf' as a pseudonym. And do you know what I call you SS?"

"A wolf pack?"

"Excellent." He stood up. "Come, it's time for my evening walk. We can talk as we get exercise."

There was silence between us until we left the hospital, trailed by two SS, with two more in front. We walked along a path where the lawn reached the forest. I made out guards among the trees. Hans was right about me killing der Führer and making a break— it looked like there were more guards than trees.

"I cannot tell you how I envy you, Herr Hauptsturmfuhrer. As a young man, I fought on the battlefield for my country, willing to give my life for the Fatherland, but now destiny has given me another role, a mission I must live to fulfill. I wish I was a young man like you, able to serve the Reich on the front lines. Or perform the special duties that our country's destiny requires."

"Ja." It was the best I could muster as the face of a little girl flashed in my mind.

"You probably believe that I do not have fears like other people, but you are wrong. I have a great fear, one that dominates my entire life. It is the fear that I will die before I have left the Reich strong enough to resist its enemies. The fear that the blood sin that engulfs much of the world will not be eradicated before I take my last breath. You realize, do you not, how important the matter of blood is to me? That blood is the foundation of civilization? That it is the cement that binds the brotherhood of the Schutzstaffel?"

"Of course, mein Führer," I murmured. He was the kind of guy who talked a lot but never listened to others, the kind I'd like to tie to a railroad track to get his full attention. When the tracks started vibrating because a train was on its way, and he swore he was listening, I'd bend down and say, "About this blood thing, Adolf, you're no Thoroughbred—if you were a stallion, they'd put you to sleep rather than spending the money to feed you. You're life unfit to live."

"One creature drinks the blood of another."

We had been walking quietly, each captured by his own thoughts, when he suddenly uttered this odd statement.

"Mein Führer?"

"It is the way of the world. The Jew knows it well, he's a spider that sucked the people's blood out of its pores. But there is a way to cleanse blood. You kill the carrier of contaminated blood. War, that is what cleans blood. We lost the last war because we did not know our true enemy and let our blood become contaminated. The Kaiser did not understand that the war was lost because of the dilution of blood by intermarriage with non-Aryans. When the Aryan gave up his blood purity, he lost his power to win wars, to dominate, he lost his place in paradise."

He was silent for a moment. I realized he was not talking to me but to the world. Hans was right about the steel-trap mind. My presence had gotten him onto the subject of blood. Once he clamped his jaws on, it dominated his thoughts completely.

"If I save Germany, I have performed a great deed. And I can only save the Fatherland if I keep the bloodlines pure."

He stopped walking and faced me.

"Fire, that is the solution, a fire that consumes them all. Let them call us inhuman. Our duty is clear. We must build fires that destroy the two-legged animals that carry the virus."

His eyes were wide—on *fire*. His gaze was mesmerizing. His voice had lost its soft quality. It was powerful, a sound that came from deep within him and exploded out his mouth like a shot from a cannon.

He spun on his heel and went back toward the hospital, leaving me standing by myself as his personal escort rushed by.

I felt the chill of the night and pulled my coat collar up higher. I stuck a cigarette in my mouth but quickly removed it, wondering if it was on the list of prohibitions.

Hans was right—the man had magnetism. He was totally consumed with his passions. And his passions were loony tunes. In the horror of what this nutcase was doing to the rest of the world, I saw a kind of ironic pathos for the German people. They got screwed over after WWI, and things really went to hell when inflation got so insane, a loaf of bread cost a billion marks. Then along came the stock market crash in America and a worldwide depression. One thing about Adolf and his goose-steppers, they had something going for them that none of the politicians in power did—they really cared. The man and his wolf pack really cared about Germany and wanted to see the country great again. The only problem was they had a twisted vision of what made the country great. If someone had assassinated der Führer in '39, he would have gone down in history books as Adolf the Great.

Someplace along the line of life, he got his head screwed on backward. Obsessive-compulsive, like someone washing his hands all day long. Only his obsession was blood. I heard that there are people who are fascinated with their own shit, you know, like to feel it, smell it. And about a guy who drank his own piss. But what made Adolf so weird about blood?

Maybe the blue manuscript was the key. He got a dose of syphilis in the army. A guy like him would lie awake nights, imagining millions of infectious microbes marching in his veins, being carried around by his rivers of blood. And he'd look for a scapegoat for the infection. He couldn't hate himself, he was too narcissistic to blame himself. There had to be a defect in the world that caused German soldiers to get a dose of the big S. The Jews, that was it, they polluted the blood of good German soldiers, made them susceptible to VD. Caused them to lose the war. And created an economy where it took a wheelbarrow full of marks for a loaf of bread.

It was all quite logical. All you had to do with start off with a bizarre premise and keep building on it. Adolf has such a fanatical belief in his crazy ideas, he convinced millions of Germans who didn't bother to think for themselves.

Good work, Adolf. It's thinking like that that's turning your cities into rubble and will someday see guys like Ike and Monty turn Germany into one big grave. You've got the fucking virus, Adolf, and it's between your ears.

I was stomping so intensely to my cottage I almost ran into Hildegarde without seeing her as she stepped out of the bushes near the cottage.

"Guten Abend, Herr Hauptsturmfuhrer."

"No fucking tonight," I told her. "Orders from headquarters."

"Ja, ja. Ah, are you, uh, well. Have you been experiencing any difficulty?"

"What kind of difficulty do you mean?"

"Nothing, nothing. I just, well, I know you are a donor for der Führer. Out of my love for him, I just want to make sure that you are quite well. In my role as a doctor, of course."

"Hildegarde, I am as healthy as a horse. Is that satisfactory?"

Relief washed across her face. "Ja, ja, that is perfect. Well, you have a good night, Erich. You must get your rest so your blood is strong for der Führer."

I went inside the cottage and lit my cigarette. The ambush by Brunhild and the burning in my pants had settled one thing in my mind—the bitch had given me a dose of clap. She probably sat on every Aryan-looking cock that reported to her program and saluted her. It was inevitable that she'd get nailed with something. If her

Führer found out she'd passed on clap to his blood donor, we'd both be guests at the nearest Gestapo hotel.

I hit the sack, my head buzzing from my conversation with Hitler. A pack of wolves, that's what I was surrounded by. And I'd have to get by their snarling teeth to kill White Fang.

TEN

JUNE 4

Hans was standing over my bed when I awoke.

"It's time," he said.

"Time?"

"You have to report to the hospital to be examined by the Füh-rer's physicians prior to the operation. You have already had your blood test, so it will be a visual examination. This gives us the opportunity to deliver the bomb."

I dressed and found him in the living room, smoking one of my Turkish cigarettes.

"How do we get the bomb into the hospital?" I asked.

"It's already there. I hid it in the basement the day I arrived. The operation is set for this afternoon, but you are going in early for the examination. If we hurry, we can catch the Führer in bed."

"It's almost nine. Won't the Führer be up and out of bed?"

"He's rarely up before ten. He stays up late at night, sometimes all night, talking to his cronies or having Waeger, his half-witted aide, sit and listen to him drone on endlessly about the old days."

"Okay, let's play ball."

He looked me over. "Where's your pistol?"

"What do I need that for? There are fifty SS with machine guns hanging around that place. I wouldn't stand a chance in a shoot-out."

"You need it to kill yourself with after the bomb goes off."

"Oh."

"Give me the gun, it will be easier for me to carry it in. The guards are used to me and will not look twice." He tucked the gun in his waistband under his coat. He hesitated at the door and turned to me. "Are you prepared to die today?"

"Fuck no. When that bomb goes off, I'm going to grab a machine gun from one of your Führer's wolves and shoot my way out. I don't mind dying, but I hate the preliminaries."

Approaching the guards at the hospital entrance, I tried not to look like a man who's already had his last meal. It was hard not to look grim. I felt numb inside. And distant, as if my mind and body were separate entities, with my mind about to fly away at any time. I wasn't thinking about the fact I was going to die. What struck me was that I was going to kill a man who was no ordinary mortal—he was someone children prayed to.

I thought about the children he had killed, and it steadied my resolve.

Hans identified me, and we entered. There were more guards in the reception area inside. We went through swinging doors on our right and down an empty corridor.

"The whole hospital's been evacuated," Hans said.

We paused at an open entryway three-quarters of the way down the corridor. "The waiting room," he whispered. He indicated a door across the room. "The toilet room." He pointed at the ceiling above the waiting room.

I got the idea. Adolf's bedroom.

"Stay here." He turned from the door and went down a nearby stairway that led to the basement. He came back a moment later with a sack that hung across his chest from a strap around his neck. It said "Marine Bomb" on it and must have been heavy—Hans was sweaty and out of breath. For the first time he looked rattled.

"Am I doing the right thing?" he asked me.

"What?"

He grabbed my arm. "The right thing, Wolfhardt, tell me, is this the right thing?"

"A child held my hand yesterday, a little girl. Then they shot her in the head. These are animals, not people. Think about your grandson."

He took a deep breath and wiped his forehead. "You are right, I don't know what came over me. He—you understand, I have known him and served him. Personally, he is a good man, a good man."

"Yeah, that's why he lets everyone else do his killing. Let's get this over with."

I followed him across the waiting area and was behind him as he opened the door to the toilet room. He came to an abrupt halt with an exclamation.

Colonel Keitel was seated on the toilet—reading a copy of *The Black Corps*.

We froze and stared at each other. The colonel's pants were down below his knees. His small eyes darted to the right—his pistol belt was hanging from a hook. He went for the pistol as Hans fumbled with getting out the one he'd tucked under his coat.

I shot by Hans and body-blocked Keitel, sending him into the wall. It was like hitting a cannonball. I was several inches taller, but the colonel was built broad and solid. He banged against the wall and bounced back at me, hitting me with his shoulder, ramming my solar plexus. Stunned, I swung feebly at his head with my right, hitting air. He pounded me in the stomach with piston blows, burying his fists in my stomach. I hit the wall behind me, and my knees folded. I scooted down to the floor on my ass, the wind knocked out of me.

Blurry motion off to my left told me that Hans was getting knocked around by the colonel. I saw the pistol go flying. The colonel went for the gun, and Hans ran out of the room. The colonel grabbed the gun and raced after him.

By sheer willpower, I dragged myself through the toilet room door. I got myself half-standing as Hans disappeared down the basement stairwell. The colonel pointed the gun down the stairwell. I tried to tell him not to shoot, that Hans had a bomb strapped to him, but it came out as a gasp. Then an explosion blew me to hell.

ELEVEN

JUNE 5

Darkness and shadows, murmurs of ghost voices. I was dead. It wasn't the sort of feeling that I expected from being dead. I thought heaven and hell were both brighter. Dark shades of light slowly brightened, growing until it hurt my eyes. The light at the end of the tunnel.

But the light at the end of the tunnel became a lamp over an operating table. A face came into focus. Dr. Dorsch stared down at me.

"I'm in hell," I croaked.

"Just Bavaria," Dorsch said.

The next face was that of Colonel Vogler. He stared down at me. I flinched. For sure, he was going to shoot me between the eyes.

"Let's get him into the operating room," Dorsch said.

Jesus H. Christ. I'm not dead. Hans had warned me not to let them take me alive. They're going to operate on me, take slices off until I told them everything I knew. I really fucked up. I wished I *was* dead.

I gurgled something about kill me quickly.

Vogler's face appeared over me again. Peppermint breath blew in my face. "You're a hero, Wolfhardt."

I must be in hell, I thought. How could I be a hero of the Third Reich? I and one-armed Hans just tried to blow der Führer to pieces.

I started moving. At least, the cart under me did. Dorsch talked as the cart rolled into and down a corridor.

"You've been unconscious for hours. You only got minor injuries from the explosion, but it gave you a concussion. Really nothing to worry about."

"Hans—"

"Yes, we know, he's a traitor, tried to kill der Führer. Your bravery in killing Hans is realized. Colonel Keitel was killed, too."

How the hell could they figure I killed Hans? It didn't make any sense.

"Where am I?"

"You're on your way into the operating room. The surgical procedure on der Führer is about to be done. He decided to go through with it despite the attempt. It's a very minor procedure, and he needs to get it out of the way."

The cart I was on was brought into the surgery and docked next to another cart on which Adolf lay on his back. He turned his head and smiled at me.

"I knew my wolf would protect me. You will not find me or your country ungrateful. You are a hero of the Third Reich."

Jesus H. Christ.

TWELVE

JUNE 6: 10:00 A.M.

Albert Speer, Minister of Armaments and Munitions, stepped out of a staff car in front of the Berghof on the Obersalzberg. It was five minutes to ten in the morning. He was there to attend a strategy meeting.

A tall, slender man who was once der Führer's personal architect, at thirty-nine years old, he was the youngest of Hitler's top echelon. Some people believed that Speer, more than any other single person, kept the German war machine operating. He was also sometimes described as the closest thing that Hitler had to a friend. Der Führer loved to talk to Speer about architecture, about the grand monuments in the capital city called Germania he would someday build.

Officers representing the army, navy, air force, joint command, and SS were waiting in an anteroom where tea and pastries had been set out. General Merker, representing the OHK, the high command of the army, rushed to Speer as soon as the minister entered the room.

"Have you heard? The invasion has begun. The Allies have made a landing along the Normandy coast."

"When?"

"It began around midnight. Full-scale at dawn."

"What does der Führer say? What is our response?"

Merker avoided Speer's eyes for a moment, then pulled the armaments minister into a corner.

"Der Führer has not been notified."

"What?"

"His orderlies refuse to notify him until he awakens and has his breakfast."

"That's insane."

Merker did not reply, and Speer knew why. An Allied invasion of France was expected as inevitable. Rumors daily flew in and out the window about when and where it would occur. Der Führer was convinced that Eisenhower would first feign a landing to draw the German response, then make an actual landing at another location. No one wanted to give der Führer bad news if he believed an actual attack had occurred. Or be subjected to his anger if he believed the attack was a false report.

"What does the army think?" Speer asked.

"Rommel is convinced that it is a major offensive and not a diversionary action. He has begged der Führer for weeks to give him authority over armored divisions held in reserve to drive the enemy back into the sea. But der Führer has refused the request and insists that he alone will give the order for the tanks to advance and only when he is convinced that it is not a ploy. The field marshal has been calling all morning, trying to talk to der Führer. Rundstedt can't get through, either. No calls until he rises."

"He should be advised of the matter immediately," Speer said.

"Perhaps, Herr Minister, *you* would like to be the one who enters der Führer's private quarters to tell him to come to the strategy meeting."

Speer had not become possibly the second most important man in Germany by being a fool. Der Führer would have a mind-set

about the situation when the briefing began. To get him to change
his mind would be as hard as talking a dog off a meat wagon.

Speer was not a military man. He was a designer with a good
sense of organization. But even he realized that Rommel should not
be left dangling when it was possible there was an actual Allied
invasion. He found Waeger, der Führer's chief orderly, in the
kitchen inspecting the preparations for his master's breakfast.

"When will der Führer be notified of the *potential* for invasion."
Speer carefully chose his words.

"Soon," the orderly said, "very soon."

Waeger brushed by Speer and returned to Hitler's private area,
posting himself outside der Führer's bedroom door. He had served
Adolf Hitler for twelve years, but he was not allowed to enter without knocking and actually hearing der Führer's voice approving the
entry. Adolf Hitler was a very private person. He had seen the man
with his shirt off only once and had never seen him with his pants
off. To his knowledge, his master did not undress completely even
for medical doctors. His obsession with privacy started many rumors, including one that der Führer had only one testicle, but Waeger did not gossip or listen to rumors. His only life was serving der
Führer, and he did that as a faithful dog. He was told not to disturb
his master, and he would not disobey the order.

That was true in any case, but was especially true this morning.
Several times Waeger had heard disturbing noises coming out of
der Führer's bedroom. An hour earlier der Führer had opened the
door a crack to tell him to get his doctor, Morell, on the telephone.
He had made the connection to Dr. Morell, who was several hours
away in Berlin, before passing the call to der Führer.

Dr. Morell was in Berlin, and it would be hours before he would
arrive by plane. There was another doctor on call, Brandt, but der
Führer refused to let him see him. Waeger knew that when it came
to anything der Führer considered personal, he consulted only Morell. Frequently, der Führer's problems had to do with stomach pain
and stomach gases. This morning, Waeger had heard der Führer go
into his private bathroom several times.

Even stranger, before getting off the telephone, he had heard der
Führer say something about his penis being swollen.

THIRTEEN

The strategy conference did not begin until early afternoon. Speer noted that his prediction was correct—Hitler resisted the idea that an actual Allied landing was taking place on the Normandy coast. He was convinced that the necessary size of an invading force meant that the Allies had to strike at a major port. Based upon that presumption, the larger ports had reinforced with heavy fortifications—bunkers and pillboxes. If the landing took place at a beach rather than a fortified port, the Germans would have fallen into the same Maginot Line mentality that cost the French the war.

Speer noticed that Hitler seemed more distracted than usual, sometimes unable to focus on the problem, even when confronted with patent evidence that an actual invasion had taken place. He fidgeted in his chair as if he was in pain and abruptly left the room several times. Speer wondered if der Führer was having a medical problem that was causing him discomfort.

Hours into the discussion, der Führer finally capitulated after descriptions of the Allied landings at Arromanches and Omaha Beach brought home an undeniable fact: The Allies had brought their own "ports" with them.

General Merker was red in the face and sweating profusely by the time the meeting ended. Speer walked out with him to where their chauffeurs and staff cars were waiting.

"Congratulations," he told Merker. "You won der Führer over."

"We have lost the war."

"What?"

"We have lost the war."

"Lower your voice," Speer said. They continued to walk. "Why do you say we've lost the war? Der Führer released the armored divisions Rommel asked for."

"It's too late."

"Why? The reports are that the invasion forces are still securing the beach area. They can still be driven into the sea."

Merker whipped around, still red in the face. "You're not a military man, Herr Speer, and neither is der Führer. It's too late, not because of men on the beaches, *but those in the sky*. Because of the delay, by the time the armored units are ready to move out, they will still be on the road when daylight comes. They will have lost the protection of darkness. The American and British air forces will butcher them."

He stomped off to his car, but swung around before he reached it. He shouted back to Speer, "Do you remember the story about the horseshoe nail?"

Speer mulled over the comment as he got into his own car. He recalled something about a horseshoe nail, a poem or proverb from his boyhood. He didn't remember the exact words, but recalled that the loss of a nail in a horseshoe set off a chain reaction—the shoe was lost, the horse went down, the battle and the kingdom lost.

"All for the want of a horseshoe nail," he said, aloud.

"Herr Minister?" his driver asked.

"Nothing. Take me back to my house."

Dr. Morell arrived as Speer's car was pulling out. Speer saw Morell exit his car and hurry into the Berghof as if the hounds of hell were at his heels. Speer wondered again if der Führer was having a medical problem.

Der Führer had been later than usual for the strategy meeting and had been more than ordinarily preoccupied. At times he appeared to be in pain. Speer wondered what it was that caused his distress. He hoped the illness didn't turn out to be the horseshoe nail that loses the kingdom.

FOURTEEN

June 6: 2:00 p.m.

My dick still hurt like crazy from the clap as I sat in the back of the Mercedes with Dr. Dorsch and Vogler. I asked Dorsch for the German version of penicillin, telling him I was afraid of infection from the minor shrapnel wounds I got from the blast. He gave me enough to cure all the whores in Hanover. I could have asked to fuck his wife, and he would have spread her legs for me.

You don't say no to the guy who saved der Führer's ass.

It was the two dirtbag black shirts, Dr. Dumb Nuts and Colonel Blimp, whom I had to thank for making me a hero. It was Dorsch who noticed the bullet wound in the top of Hans's bald head after Vogler had body parts collected on a hospital cart. Colonel Keitel hadn't stopped when he was ahead—after shooting Hans in the head, his next shot hit the bomb.

Dorsch removed the slug and Vogler compared the rifling on it to the only pistol around—mine. And presto! I was a hero, the guy who shot one-armed Hans after he tried to blow up der Führer with a stolen bomb. Colonel Keitel was also getting honorable mention and an Iron Cross, after I described his heroic—but fruitless—attempt to subdue the assassin.

Both men were in a jolly mood as we drove toward the airfield. Vogler whistled an SS marching song through his teeth, and Dorsch beamed like the midday sun. Life was good. Adolf had been in a jolly mood following the attempt on his life. A firm believer in his own destiny, he had taken it as part of the Universal Plan that the assassination attempt had failed. He had complimented both Dorsch on his hospital and Vogler on his security measures.

Was I devastated because I didn't kill Adolf? That I didn't die trying? Yeah, I felt real bad about it.

Okay, that's not exactly the truth. Like der Führer, I also believed in what's meant to be is meant to be. I was willing to go the whole nine yards—Adolf's ass was grass and I was a lawn mower. But it wasn't my fault that Colonel Keitel decided to take a crap at that precise time and place—it was divine intervention for all I knew. At least until I could get away from these Nazi bastards for five minutes and do some thinking. Ever since I received hero status, Dorsch and Vogler had been sticking to me like shit on a stick.

Vogler stopped whistling through his teeth long enough to ask, "You understand, Herr Sturmbannfuhrer, no mention of this attempt on der Führer's life must ever be made."

"Absolutely. My lips are sealed." Oh, that "Herr Sturmbannfuhrer" bit—did I mention I was now a major?

"Pillow talk sinks ships!" Vogler said.

"What's that you say?" Dorsch asked.

Vogler smirked and winked at me. "Top secret, Doktor, not for your ears." He checked out the window. "We are getting close to the airport. I can tell you now that der Führer has arranged a surprise for you."

"Yes, I know. I am very appreciative. I will wear the medal with honor." I was getting an Iron Cross, First Class. I just couldn't tell anyone how I earned it.

Both men laughed.

Dorsch shook his finger at me. "Ha, nein, nein, you cannot wear this surprise. Although it will no doubt bring you some comfort."

Vogler giggled like a girl. "And it will keep you warm in the winter, eh Doktor?"

"Ja! Ja! You can even pet its fur."

The two howled with laughter again.

My good feelings about the world were quickly evaporating. The last thing I wanted was a surprise. But it sounded harmless enough. "Der Führer's giving me a dog?"

Dorsch laughed so hard he lost his breath.

"Nein! Nein! Not a dog," Vogler said. "A pussy, you are getting, a pussy!"

A coldness had started in my feet, worked up the back of my legs, into the small of my back, and was crawling up my spine, fanning the hair on the back of my neck. I couldn't imagine what sort of surprise Adolf had planned for me. But I began to suspect that I would regret it *for the rest of my life*.

Yeah, that phrase had worked itself back into my head. *They're going to kill me. That's the surprise*. The realization flashed in my mind like those neon signs in Times Square. Der Führer wanted to keep the assassination attempt on his life secret. I was an eyewitness. But why bring me to the airport? Why not kill me back at the hospital? Maybe they were going to take me a couple miles and toss me out without a parachute.

The car pulled to a stop near a plane that was putting down its boarding ladder.

"Get out, Wolfhardt, get out, your surprise is waiting."

I got out with a dry mouth and the hair on the back of my neck standing straighter than a *Heil Hitler*. Both men got out and stood by me. A woman stepped out of the plane and started climbing down the ladder.

Vogler slapped me on the back.

"You see! You see! Isn't der Führer wonderful?"

What the shit?

"He had Frau Wolfhardt brought to you. *Your bride is here!*"

Jesus H. Christ.

HANGAR RAT

DEAN ING

DEAN ING has been an interceptor crew chief, construction worker on high Sierra dams, solid rocket designer, builder/driver of sports racers—his prototype Magnum was a *Road & Track* feature—and after a doctorate from the University of Oregon, a professor. For years, as one of the cadre of survival writers, he built and tested backpack hardware on Sierra solos. His techno-thriller, *The Ransom of Black Stealth One*, was a *New York Times* bestseller, and he has been finalist for both Nebula and Hugo Awards. His more humorous works have been characterized as "fast, furious, and funny." Slower and heavier now with two hip replacements and titanium abutments in his jaw, he includes among his hobbies testing models of his fictional vehicles, fly fishing, ergonomic design, and container gardening. His daughters comprise a minister, a longhorn rancher, an Alaskan tour guide, and an architect. He and his wife, Geneva, a fund-raiser for the Eugene Symphony, live in Oregon where he is currently building a mountainside library/shop.

ONE

They claim it would be impossible to strap a teenage test pilot into America's hottest-climbing interceptor and get them both back intact. With the latest generation, they may be right. It was different in 1944, maybe because teenagers were different then, because their parents were; I reckon you had to be there. We learned a lot of things early, and some of them in strange ways.

For example, you wouldn't think Adolf Hitler could be explained by a stamp collection. My dad managed it, though. You also wouldn't figure that a guy raised on a peach orchard near San Antonio, and his father and grandfather raised on that same farm, would grow up fluent in German. Not unless you got to wondering where central Texas towns like Fredericksburg and Luckenbach got their names.

A lot of us, like the Rahms and the Mollers, fought Comanches to settle the region. Some kept up the lingo and correspondence with cousins in the old country. My school bud Fred Moller and I sometimes got ribbed for it, and by the time we were in junior high it could get mean.

That's why, one day when I still had the cast on my leg—that would make me twelve, so the year was 1938—I asked Dad about something so embarrassing to him that it was never mentioned at home. "If this guy Hitler is stampeding everybody out of Germany, why don't the people vote him out?"

He was torquing head bolts on a full-race Menasco in our shop, Rahm Rennsport near Luckenbach, at the moment, and he took his time answering. Nobody rushed my dad, not if they wanted testing and tweaking by Jurgen Rahm, the best flight-test mechanic in the air-racing business. But if you waited, you got the best. "Show you at home later," he said finally, then motioned toward a workbench, and I brought him the wiring harness. Even then, I had been his hangar rat so long we didn't always need words. I miss him still . . .

After supper, he had Mama bring a shoe box of letters from our Stuttgart kin to my room, and with a glance made it clear that she and my little sis, Elke, should leave us be. I cleared a half-built Comet contest model from my drafting table, and he began to sort through the box.

He didn't open any envelopes, but set one apart. "Nineteen twenty," he said, and tapped the stamp, an orange *zehn pfennig Luft-post*, the German equivalent of a ten-cent airmail. He chose another; tapped the stamps, one being an orange *dreissig mark*. "Two years later," he said.

"Wow, thirty bucks," I said. I figured that meant they were all getting rich over there.

"Wait," he said, and laid out another envelope. "Nineteen twenty-three," was his only comment. The stamp was green, labeled 400 marks—but overprinted 100 *tausend* marks. A hundred thousand bucks? I didn't quite believe it, until he showed me a pink five *millionen* and then a green fifty *millionen*. "I think they went up to *zehn milliard* or so eventually," he said. Ten—billion, with a 'b'— dollars to send a letter? I was flabbergasted. Those letters were a few years older than I was. Dad wasn't smiling as he carefully replaced the letters in the Keds box.

"They say longshoreman's wages in Hamburg were about twenty billion a day," he said slowly. "Men carried the cash home in wheelbarrows, and the government couldn't afford to pay its own printing office. Imagine that happening here, Kurt; the whole country in chaos. *Lieber Gott*, can you see why people were so desperate they'd vote for anybody who could lead them out of such a nightmare?"

"Did he? Mister Hitler, I mean."

Dad nodded. "His methods are vicious, but there's a recent *Deutsche Flugpost zehn mark* stamp somewhere in here. No more chaos in Germany today. No more freedom, either.

"They've exchanged nightmares. Too many people will forgive him anything for giving them confidence again in their money. And some of his top people are slick as Roscoe Turner, and just as good on the stick," he added. I got it. Turner was a fine race pilot, but mostly he knew how to hog friendly headlines. "*Und so*, now half the good people in Germany believe Hitler is the greatest genius in history in spite of all the Sturm und Drang. And the rest are scattering like pigeons at the green flag because Herr Hitler thinks he's Superman."

I had to smile. You could hide an air racer in a two-car garage, but they had bodacious engines, and when the green flag dropped and a half dozen Menascos, Rangers, and Wright Whirlwinds cranked on the horsepower for a race, you could hear their thunder ten miles away, and that's not just tall Texas talk.

And so I understood, vaguely, what was coming when air racing was shelved after 1939. My heroes were now designing and testing military planes, and new engines were designed for reliability. Dad didn't have much machining work for Mr. Moller. The golden era of air racers was dead.

Between '39 and '41 Dad and I built a Hansen Baby Bullet, a twitchy little bugger with responses quick as a wink, the nearest thing you could get to a race plane, from plans. We painted it my school colors, red and white. After I soloed in a Piper, he taught me to fly the Babe. And after that whenever Dad tweaked someone's two-holer—more than one seat—I got in some stick time with him.

Then he put away his tools and tried to work the farm's orchard with one gimpy teenager. My left leg never grew much after that

fall from a ladder, so the only letter I earned on the Fredericksburg
Billies was for the javelin. But I made Dad proud in school, flew
the Babe now and then, and got a stiff neck watching Army planes
from nearby San Antonio airfields. I was a happy kid. The war was
half a world away, and my dad was the best man I ever met.

And our time together was running out. Pearl Harbor changed
everything. Almost everyone in air racing put old contacts to use,
building or flying military aircraft. Fred Moller and I learned not to
use German words at school. Dad applied as a civilian, ferrying
lend-lease Bell P-39s to the Russians by the Alaska route, even before he realized how good the pay would be. The idea was, this
forty-year-old could do his part and still spend some time at home.

For several months it worked fine. But there was lots of bad
weather in Alaska's interior, and some very large rocks sticking up
into it, and very few long airstrips. One day they'll find which of
those rocks Dad's P-39 hit. The only reason I didn't go nuts then
was that, with Mama and Elke to think about, I couldn't afford the
luxury.

I graduated at sixteen, fully licensed with a flight log to prove I
could fly everything from the Babe to a staggerwing Beech with
retract gear. That was the capper, I reckon, me being familiar with
hot crates. The Army was desperate for ferry pilots, and one of
Dad's old barnstormer pals sponsored me to fly new AT-6s from
the factory to Merced Army Air Field in California.

Some cadets weren't much older than I was by then. The T-6
"Texan" was a challenge, with retract gear and an engine note that
told everybody in the county you were coming. Shoot, I'd have
done it free. I had a built-in grudge against Herr Hitler, and the
military didn't crave guys with a bum leg.

Mama signed her permission. I was the man, now, with more
cash than I'd ever expected to see. I was a tad short, so I learned
to talk down in my throat and stand tall and wear a durn tie with
my Stetson around Merced because, if they thought you were a
kid, folks took advantage. And yeah, after some *Scheisskopf* stood
me a few beers in Fresno one night, I got rolled. Once. Cost me
nearly a hundred bucks and a splitting headache. Fred claimed

learning to drink was a man's game, and set out to prove it after
his dad moved the machine shop to San Antonio and set up an
auto body shop, too.

People who made their living around high-performance airplanes
tended to have a thing for cars, and I was no exception. The big
thing in California then was hopped-up cars; foreign makes, engine
swaps, weird fuel mixes—stuff I knew about. I was itching to buy
this gorgeous Alfa Romeo thing until I found out it was Italian; the
enemy—sort of. Then some ferry pilot from Los Angeles had his
girl drive his Willys coupe to Merced, and it quit on him, and I
agreed to get it running. No wonder it wouldn't run: Somebody
had stuffed that poor little coupe full of hot-cam Ford V-8 with a
bad distributor.

I paid two hundred cash for the coupe, dropped in a good distributor, and nearly passed out when I lit it up. In Kentucky they'd
have called it a rumrunner. I drove back to Luckenbach pretending
I was flying the Pesco Special and baldied a brand-new set of rear
tires in the process. Ya-HOO, San-an-Tone!

The ferry contract was running out in May of '44 when some colonel at Wright Field chased me down by phone at the T-6 factory.
I had a cold, which dropped my voice even more. The colonel
seemed a bit flustered, like he was juggling three jobs, and asked
just the core questions. Was I the Rahm from Luckenbach who
could read German? How many aircraft types had I flown and
tuned? Did I know that the test pilot who broke the B-26 of its
man-killing ways and had sponsored me as a ferry pilot, had now
suggested me as engine man for a highly classified crash program?
Could I commit to a project that would keep me at Randolph Field,
if they paid me 250 dollars a month?

Randolph was seventy air miles from Luckenbach. Stifling an
urge to wet my pants I rattled off the dozen or so hotter crates I'd
flown, and said, "You must've been talking to Frank Merrill, he's
the one who tamed that flying coffin." That's what Dad had said,
anyway. "And if he's on this new project, that's good enough for
me. Who else do you have on it, and what *is* it?"

He couldn't say what, only that it was originally out of Larry Bell's design loft, code name Pancho. Whatever it was, I wasn't hiring on to fly Pancho, just to help modify it under the guidance of some educated civilian hotshot. There would be other specialists for hydraulics, electrics, sheet metal, and supply. A Georgia Tech grad aero designer named Ullmer was in charge of the whole corral, and if I showed up at the project hangar within three days, I could sign on.

I took a deep breath. The P-39 was a Bell design, and I'd heard rumors that Mr. Bell's outfit was working on something that flew, or might eventually fly, with a jet engine. I'd have worked for nothing to be involved with Frank "Bub" Merrill, who had flown crates I'd helped soup up; with luck I might even fly the Baby Bullet to Randolph to sign on, tie, Stetson and all. Was I gonna deliberately create slathers of confusion by even hinting to this overworked colonel that there had been two Rahms from Luckenbach, especially with Merrill there to endorse me when I showed up? Come onnn . . .

TWO

Landing the Babe at Randolph Field in May '44 wasn't like it had been when you could dip a wing and get a green light, before the air got full of cadets and radios. Even though I did radio for clearance, I was escorted off the taxiway in my civilian crate by MPs in an olive drab Plymouth with gun barrels poking out the windows. After a few phone calls from a shack out near the compass rose, they decided I rated a clip-on pass. I made a note to myself that it was edged with red tape, though in those days security was fairly primitive.

Then they led me a mile or two, pointed at a separated hangar-and-shop, and sped away, letting me set my own wheel chocks. Maybe I shouldn't have worn my old boots on a cross-country, but the heels were two-inchers, and this was Texas, and for my first time on the job I figured bigger was better.

The MPs were already calling Project Pancho's isolated little facility the wetback hangar, and its big sliding doors were closed. The civilian who answered my knock at the side door turned out to be the structures man, Roy Dee Ray, an old fella with watery blue eyes and a lip full of snuff. My pass spoke for itself, so he let me in. And I saw, over his shoulder, something to set the blood singing in my veins. It wasn't a jet, and I didn't care.

Designers put their signatures on planes with the lines they draw, and the solitary little beast getting a postflight inspection in one corner was a baby Bell, smaller brother to the P-39. But its nose was much too long, its engine cowl narrow as a knife blade, and its cockpit canopy bubble far back near the tail, exactly like the very last and hottest air-race specials. It reminded me of *Chambermaid*, the tiny screamer Russell Chambers had built in his garage a few years before, the one of which Art Chester said, "Ya forgot the wings, Russ." But this one had long-legged little wheels to clear an outsize prop, so I guessed the engine had to be a Ranger. I was instantly in love.

The wing was low and, as we used to say when no ladies were near, short as my *Schwantz*. I figured this crate should maneuver like a squirrel on tequila. And if that loosened cowling was like the rest of it, the durn thing was plywood.

Plywood? My head spun. Military crates were aluminum and steel. This gorgeous flying mite would be only one-third the weight of a P-51, maybe less, and should come off the line like a rodeo quarterhorse, with the slashing attack of a plywood wolf. If it held together, that is, just like the civilian racers, with a skin you could penetrate with a penknife. It was a sure-enough God-durn Army air racer from hell, is what it was. I bet Jimmy Doolittle felt the same way, first time he saw the mankilling R-2 Gee Bee racer.

I had goose pimples. My eyes were misting enough that I needed a few seconds to focus on the fellas who had come up behind me. The short young one in front, with hair he must've combed with an eggbeater that day, was built square as a nail keg, thick hairy forearms poking from rolled-up sleeves, jabbering in double time with a mud-thick Jawja accent. Something like, whothehail let that kid in, this is a gawdam classified project, one hangar rat in here's more'n enough, Hell's fahr, Roy Dee . . .

But the guy behind him, taking long lank strides in whipcord khakis tucked into tall lace-up boots, cut through all that. "Whoa, Ben," he said, "he's one of ours." Windburnt, early forties, Texas twang, broad smile: It was Frank Merrill, and I guess that B-26 Marauder program had aged him. More softly he went on to me, "How ya doin', stud? Outgrown your knickers, I see. You've shot up like a weed since I saw ya last," and stuck out a callused hand that felt like a mesquite stub. I had been sixteen, and tongue-tied, when Dad introduced me before. And I had purely hated those durn knickers.

"Much obliged, Mr. Merrill," I said, knowing he had put me in line for this, and we shook while the short guy stared.

"Aw, call me Bub now, you're entitled," said Merrill. "I hear you've been showin' those Merced cadets how it's done." He winked. Ferry pilots did shoot some hot landings. Who was going to wash us feather merchants out?

The short fella found his voice again. He made fists against his hips as he shook his head and squinted at my pass. "Rahm? This's Jurgen Rahm? Bub, if this is one of your Texas gags—"

"Kurt Rahm," I said. This time when I stuck out a hand, he shook it quickly like he didn't mean it. "Jurgen was my dad," I added. "I was his hangar rat from the git-go. Uh, and you'd be Mr. Ullmer, I guess."

He nodded. After a long silent moment, he said, more to Merrill than me, "Just won't do. I need seasoned men, not some kid I've gotta teach to read a print."

"I read blueprints in grammar school," I said softly, feeling like I was in knickers again.

"Bub, he'd be your power-plant man," Ullmer objected. "You gonna strap inta that thing over there with a full set of experimental mods this kid installed, and firewall it?"

"Did it when he was practically a tadpole; he never killed me but twice," Merrill drawled. I think he was starting to enjoy himself. "Larry Bell endorsed him, but shoot, what does he know?"

I had never met Mr. Bell. If he had done that, it had been at Merrill's urging. Ullmer growled, "This isn't funny, Merrill."

"Yes it is. It's the pot bad-mouthin' the kettle, and that's always good for a laugh. How old are you, Ben?" No answer. "If you're two dozen, I'm Mussolini."

"I've done graduate work, f'gawd's sake, that's why I'm here," said Ullmer.

Merrill grinned. "So has he, in the school of hard knocks, and his professor was one of the best. That's why he's here."

I looked for a crack in the cement to hide in as the two faced each other. While Ullmer puffed and glowered, Bub Merrill laid a gentle hand on the younger man's shoulder, and said, "Let's drag this argument out in the open where we can see it. There's a secret crash program behind ever' prickly pear in Texas, or Bell and the Army wouldn't have to drop youngsters like him, and you, into the same bucket and shake 'em. I'll tell you something you didn't know: I wasn't the test pilot Bell wanted first."

"No shit," said Ullmer.

"None. He would'a borrowed Herb Fisher from Curtiss to fly this little chippie, but Herb wouldn't fit in the cockpit. Herb just likes his taters and gravy too much, that's a fact." Fisher was even more famous as a test pilot than Merrill was. Merrill's tone was soft, but for a proud man the facts were hard. "Anyway, we have to dance with who brung us, and if I can stand it, I reckon you can, too. If something goes wrong, it won't be you that finds out about it at forty thousand feet, or maybe at sagebrush altitude. It'll be me."

The casual mention of forty thousand, eight miles up, just about stripped my head bolts. It was my first hint of what Pancho was really about, and I silently guessed the little Bell would be strictly for unarmed, fast photorecon. Wrong . . .

Looking betrayed, Ullmer let his expression talk for him, and Merrill went on: "If you said the Army's already dealt the top tried-and-true professionals out to bigger programs, and is scrapin' the bottom of the barrel for these new projects, I wouldn't like it, but I wouldn't kick your butt for sayin' it. I don't know about our souls, but these are the times that try men's *cojones*."

Ben Ullmer strained like he'd swallowed a june bug, and looked at me again, still talking to Merrill. "You think he can maintain an engine this tricky?"

"Check him out," said Merrill. "He's not in Timbuktu; he's right here."

When they both looked at me, I gazed at the sweet little wooden wolf in the corner of the hangar and thought out loud. "Not enough room in there for a big Allison or its heat exchangers," I said. "I figure it for a V-12 Ranger 770, air-cooled, blown for high altitude, prob'ly inverted. Cylinder fin ducting's a weird mess, but there's tricks to get around that. My hands are small." I held them up to him. "Replacing those plugs is a knuckle-biter, though, and if fuel metering's not perfect, we'll be swapping plugs every few hours of airtime."

Bub Merrill's mouth twitched. Ullmer stared at me until, "I'll be a dirty bastard," he said.

"Naw, just smudged a little," said Bub.

Something flickered behind Ullmer's eyes. "With little hands like those you oughta be a radio announcer," he told me. We stared at him. He continued, poker-faced: "You know, 'wee paws, for station identification'?"

"One more like that, and I'm callin' the MPs," said Bub, but they both were grinning by then, the tension broken, Ullmer nodding at me. "Well, I guess you'll do, and you're right about the spark plugs. It's clear you're more experienced than you look, kid. Let's try that handshake again—Kurt, is it? And I'm plain Ben except when the Army brass is on hand." He led off toward the dagger-nosed, wooden-hided little bird I had already fallen in love with. "Come on, let's show you what Pancho is all about."

The name Pancho was kind of a friendly insider's joke. Pancho Barnes was a woman race pilot in California, a familiar name to everyone in the fraternity. Close-coupled, well liked, so friendly to test pilots she'd give a man the shirt off her back, maybe before he asked—not to be too blunt about it. Point is, Pancho was unconventional and willing. Put in that light, the plane was well named.

While they watched me poke around in Pancho's innards, my bosses mostly filled me in about something else that scared me at

first, and terrified me at last: the Junkers Ju 488. Nobody said it
out loud, but the best Nazi aircraft outperformed ours. I couldn't
avoid feeling a little weird about that, like there was a little pride
stuck in me upside down. I could sure avoid talking about it,
though.

Allied intelligence learned the Nazis had canceled their long-
range bomber design work, a hint that they'd given up on mass
bombardment of the U.S. But the Ju 488 was said to be already in
development by then, a huge twin-tail, four-engine monster pres-
surized to fly at thirty-seven thousand feet. Some French mechanic
had risked his tail forwarding pictures to prove that a pair were
already being secretly built somewhere in France. Just two.

If its bomb load was light, the Junkers could reach New York
City or Washington at 350 miles an hour, faster than a lot of our
fighters at such heights. And another man had died to send the
news that it had recently been uprated to a crash program. Bub
reminded me that even with our Norden bombsight, dropping a
few ordinary bombs from a single plane, from that high up, wasn't
likely to hit anything with precision. The Nazis were nuts about
secret terror weapons. What in God's name did they intend to drop
on our cities that only needed one plane per city?

Our people thought they knew what, but, said Bub, they weren't
telling. I thought about a story I had just read in the March issue
of *Astounding* magazine, a small reading vice my bud Fred and I
kept private to avoid the usual ribbing. But if there had really been
anything like the uranium bomb in the story, surely a science-fiction
magazine couldn't print short stories about it. It seemed likely the
plane's load was like a bag of germs—cholera, plague, something
of the sort.

If the Nazis were working so feverishly on the thing, said Ben
Ullmer, folks in our new Pentagon building decided we'd have to
cobble up something to intercept it. We wouldn't know it was up
there until it was nearing our shores, which meant whatever we
scrambled to meet it would have to climb about eight thousand
feet a minute and maneuver at over four hundred miles an hour
after climbing eight miles high. We needed to build at least two

squadrons of these special interceptors, one to cover Boston and New York, the other protecting Washington and the Newport News shipyards.

In the entire arsenals of democracy, we had nothing that even came close.

I said, "Aren't we building jet planes that could do it? I heard rumors in California."

"If we are," Ullmer said, "nobody's talking to me about it. The rumor I heard was, our jet engines aren't up to it yet, especially at altitude. I'd be surprised if there's not another program like Pancho, though, somewhere."

Bub cussed the War Production Board because, he said, Lockheed had a P-38K that might have been modified to hurtle up that high, that fast. Some committee of fools had turned down the proposal. Meanwhile, there was this little screamer called the XP-77 at the Bell factory that had been designed to outclimb, outturn, and outrun the Misubishi Zero. It had been designed when we thought we'd have to skimp on duralumin, so Mr. Bell's boys used plywood, which worked perfectly on the British Mosquito bomber. Now, we had other planes that could whip a Zero. The XP-77 needed a new mission, and here was a mission that needed a wilder, woollier XP-77. And needed it yesterday.

Being a good guy, Bub urged me to climb into the cockpit, and I hopped in so fast you'd think I had two good legs. Pretty close quarters, for sure. The instrument panel had holes for extra gauges. I asked what they'd be for.

Turbocharger stuff, said Ben. I looked my next question at him. "Extra stuff," he said, and hesitated.

"He's gotta install it," Bub reminded him, and when Ben still didn't answer, the pilot said it for him. "Ben's waiting for some stainless tanks and lines, other stuff he's dreamed up. Ben purely hates that we're stealing tricks from the enemy. Pissed off that he didn't do it first."

"Awright, here it is," Ben said, as if someone were pulling each word out of him with a grappling hook. "Their new rocket bomb, and that tailless Messerschmitt rocket plane, use nearly pure hydrogen peroxide with permanganate catalyst to create gobs of steam. A little steam turbine can have more balls than a bowling alley. The rocket fuel turbopump alone puts out over five hundred horses for a couple of minutes."

I thought about the 3 percent peroxide that foams up when you pour it on a cut. Thirty times that strong would be comparing TNT to a firecracker. "Lordy! The whole Ranger engine doesn't develop much more than that. But you can't get to forty thousand feet in two minutes," I said.

"No, but we'll use a smaller rig and a bigger tank and hope we can stretch the peroxide to last fifteen minutes. That way we pick up an extra hundred ponies 'cause we don't have to rob the engine to run the blower."

"Boy howdy, that's a new wrinkle," I admitted. "So Pancho uses a chemistry set to run her supercharger. Sounds too good to be true."

"It's good news and bad—or could be," Bub cautioned.

I glanced from him back to Ben, who nodded. "The nice part is, the exhaust goes out a little belly nozzle near the center of gravity. Steam rocket boost. The drawings are locked up, but I'll show you later," he added, and I knew from the way he said it that this was Ben Ullmer's own idea.

"And the not so nice part," Bub put in lazily, "is that all that concentrated peroxide will be right ahead of my rudder pedals. In my lap, so to speak. And it has some nasty habits."

Suddenly it seemed like the hangar was stifling, and I didn't want to be sitting where I was sitting. As I climbed out I said, "If it all went foaming off at once, how much would there be?"

"Just about fill this hangar to the roof," Bub told me. "But it wouldn't be foam. Just shreds of wood and live steam." He chuckled out loud. "That'd give the MPs a mystery when it cooled off, find a shed fulla boiled guys covered with wet toothpicks."

I could feel the sweat on my forehead. To keep from thinking about that, I said, "You must've calculated the engine rating."

"Just over a thousand ponies," said Ben.

"I'll have more wild horses than Genghis Khan." Bub grinned.

"Twist the prop clean off this crate," I predicted. Wrong again . . .

"Naw. Props, plural," Ben said. "We're also waiting for a pair of contrarotating props, which cures what'd otherwise be God's own torque reaction, and first thing you'll do is help me install the gearbox. That is, if Major Wonderful ever gets here with it."

They took me to the shop then, and showed me the soda pop cooler where bottles of Coke and Hires root beer and RC Cola swam in slushy ice. And there I met the other fellas, all civilians. Hydraulics man, Howard Lacey, was shy and rawboned, pushing fifty, and wore farmer overalls his wife ironed like they were Sunday best. The electrician's glasses were thick as the bottom of my RC bottle, and like most of the radio and electrician tribe his nickname was Sparks, Sparks Fonseca. He was fitting some vacuum tube sockets into a metal chassis, and, at the moment, we didn't connect very strongly.

And perched on the electrician's workbench, spindly little legs dangling as he supplied Sparks with tools like a nurse beside a surgeon, was the cutest little guy I ever saw. Well, "funny-looking" is more like it, but I'll stand by "cute." Rail-thin, TexMex coloring, hair in tight curls the shiny blue-black of a starling's throat. His shirt was too big for him and below rolled-up jeans his ankles poked out like brown sticks, ending in worn tennies, probably hand-me-downs, no socks. He was the size of a seven-year-old but probably a good deal older. He glanced at me quickly, shot me a two-second grin full of good teeth, then handed Sparks the right screwdriver, and said, *"Hola!"* to me in a kid-sized voice.

I said hi, but Ben was talking. "I told you we already had a hangar rat," said Ben, and almost laid a hand on the little fella's shoulder, but not quite. It was the first time I'd seen Ben Ullmer with a fond smile. "His mama's one of the housekeeping staff in officer country, so we got him a pass, and from the day he showed up here I swear I don't know who adopted who. He earns his Cokes.

"Doesn't talk a lot, but his English is good as mine," Ben went on. I caught Bub in an eye roll and pretended I didn't. "They know him at the maintenance hangars, so when you need a few A.N. locknuts or whatever, just write the spec numbers on a scrap, and he'll scoot over and get 'em. His pass says Miguel Hernandez, but he didn't look like a 'Mike' to me. He looked like Mickey, and he's not big enough to be a rat. You figure it out," he added.

The little guy's ears weren't all that big, but I got it: Mickey Mouse. I wondered if the kid got it, too, and if he did, whether he enjoyed it. In the Southwest a lot of folks had their patronizing jokes about the TexMex citizens, and didn't extend friendliness to handshakes. I wasn't one of those folks, so I held out my hand, and said, "I'm Kurt Rahm, Mickey." To show Ben Ullmer I wasn't afraid of him, because I was, I added, "Us hangar rats may need to stick together."

"He's not much for contact," said Sparks quickly.

"Uh, he doesn't," Ben began, and then stopped as Mickey's scrawny little paw inched out to take mine the way a young raccoon would reach if you offered him a sugar cube. A quick, warm grasp without even meeting my gaze, and, "Much obliged," he said, with no accent I could detect. That's what you said to thank somebody for a favor, and I think that's just what Mickey meant for my treating him as an equal.

Then the moment was gone, except that Sparks gave a long quizzical glance to the kid, while Ben said, "Well, he doesn't, usually. Beats me."

They introduced me to my workbench, too, with a new skyhook, a tall, wheeled A-frame for jerking heavy stuff like engines up and trundling them around. I'd bring my own tools later, but it looked like a neat setup complete with a lockable cage the size of a bathroom for classified stuff. I expected to be wheeling that Ranger engine in there now and then, because no doubt it would soon be classified as secret.

It may seem weird, but I'll call it quaint: At the start of June '44, civilian help and their kids pretty much got the run of the place, so long as they didn't do something dumb like wandering onto a taxiway or getting in the way of marching cadets. About all you had to do was keep your pass clipped where folks could see it.

They told me parking was behind the hangar, but I said, "I'd play

the fool taxiing a Hansen Babe back there," which got a chuckle
'til Ben and Bub realized I wasn't ribbing them.

"How'd you get a Baby Bullet?" Ben asked, and I told him you
build it with your dad is how, so it was my turn to show everybody
my little red-and-white crate, which I did.

Roy Dee, who was more cabinetmaker than sheet-metal man,
complimented me on the woodwork, and I admitted that was
mostly my dad's doing.

Ben thumped the taut tail fabric and nodded. "Reminds me of
the kid in Georgia who comes runnin' to his mom, and says, 'We
kilt a bear! Paw shot it.' "

Bub let it pass with a look that said, you're on your own now,
stud. "Well," I said, "my dad shot the Sitka spruce, but on everything else, I pulled the triggers."

"We got a few sharp corners to sand down, don't we, but none
of 'em's on this airchine of yours," Ben said, grinning, and checked
the brand-new Breitling watch on his wrist. He asked where I was
staying, and I said it was just a puddle-jump to Luckenbach, and
I'd drive my car down the next morning with my tools, maybe find
a room with my bud, Fred Moller, whose family had moved to
SanTone.

As Roy Dee and Bub helped stow my chocks, a car came around
the perimeter road, so low you couldn't see the coachwork over
the weeds, trailing a python of dust that should have brought the
MPs. I know now why it didn't: They all knew that car from a mile
away, and had learned they were just cops and he was the governor.
Kind of.

The car had a rumble that got a man's attention, like an aero
engine. Then I saw the car, a low swoopy futurecar the color of
daffodils, and realized it *was* an aero engine. "Holy cats; what's
this?" I said. Sure, aircraft people like airplany cars, but not many
cars looked or sounded so much like airplanes.

"Judging from the container I'd say our gearbox has come," said
Ben. A man-sized wooden box jounced beside the man at the wheel
as he pulled up before the hangar with the multiple-horns whonk
of a Liberty ship.

"No, the car," I said.

"The man and the car," Bub put in, with an unreadable expression, and he was right. The man had wavy dark hair, a Gable mustache, and a great tan. Of course a good tan's not much of a trick when you drive around south Texas in an 812 supercharged Cord convertible roadster. I'd seen a couple on California highways, gobbling up the lesser wheeled animals at a hundred or more, but never up close. Lycoming aircraft-based V-8, chromed dinosaur-gut exhausts coiling out from the hood, which looked like a sun yellow steel coffin stretching ahead of the driver. It was to be a long time after the war before other American cars outran an 812 Cord. In California, they said, if you couldn't get a date in a Cord, try trolling with a roll of hundred-dollar bills.

"Ain't he your basic splendid vision," asked Bub, "and doesn't he know it? That's our supply officer, Major Dylan. His life story takes a while, and if you don't wanta hear it for the next two hours, stud, better prime your engine."

So Bub swung my prop over, and as I eased away light on the throttle to keep from blowing people's hats off, I waved. The tanned handsome specimen in the Cord waved back. That's how I met Major Athol Dylan, USAAF.

THREE

Mama wasn't happy 'til I convinced her that I wasn't joining the Air Corps and wasn't going to fly a warplane, which actually I was though I didn't know it yet. I decided against calling a girl I dated in town; there'd be time enough for that when I settled into the new project. We weren't going steady anyway.

I made a long-distance call to the Mollers, full of my news, but Fred wasn't home. No surprise there. He'd talked his dad into letting him have a secondhand Indian motorcycle to make deliveries for Moller Machining, and once ol' Fred got himself astride that thing he was, as he put it, as hard to find as an Austin virgin. In fact, I knew that's mostly what Fred hunted, though he always told his folks he was fooling around in Brackenridge Park in SanTone, because the University of Texas in Austin was just an hour away by Indian. Fred put a lot of miles on that velocipede.

Eugen Moller had moved his family about midway between Randolph and Kelly Fields, off Rigsby in South San Antonio. He didn't wait for me to ask about a place to stay. "I've been wanting a chance to meddle in that Willys hybrid of yours anyway," he said, having seen it once and heard me romp it. He knew there was something under that hood with lots more beans than a little four-banger.

Gene Moller made more money now in SanTone than he had working with Dad. He got piecework machining for the military but
specialized in making new parts for special cars that pilots brought
there to the cradle of aviation. In wartime, parts manufacturers
were otherwise occupied "for the duration," as the phrase went.

I knew Mama and Elke would try to change my mind, but it was
nearing dusk, and I wanted to wake up in SanTone, so I told Mr.
Moller he could expect me late that night.

After two hours and a few tears from the womenfolk I finished
packing, nested my set of micrometers and dial indicators in the
passenger's seat of my coupe, promised to be back home in two
shakes, and lit out for the city.

Like many people running around the country doing war work,
I had a "C" ration card, and gas was a dime a gallon. With a half-
dozen military bases, San Antonio was no longer the sleepy two-
culture reminder of Spanish America, and even late at night the
city traffic was as heavy as the blossom-scented air.

When I pulled up in the Mollers' driveway, Fred was just dis-
mounting from his Indian. In my headlights he seemed even taller
than before, with those long legs and slender butt girls always
seemed to favor. We would've hugged if young Texans had done
that, but instead, Fred punched my upper arm lightly and offered
me his hip flask. I took one sip. Gahh, gin.

The house was dark so we hung around a while in the backyard
under a chinaberry tree, catching up, idling in the glider swing in
air that felt satiny on my skin while locusts sizzled and lightning
bugs practiced Morse code in the still, humid night.

Fred lit up a new vice, a pencil-slim cigar that smelled of rum,
and wanted to know what I was doing at Randolph. Of course I
could only tell him it was A and E—aircraft and engine—work. He
was about half-bonked, cussing everything impartially because I
wouldn't share military secrets, he didn't know whether he'd be
drafted, didn't know whether he cared if he was, and didn't want
to keep living at home where everybody bitched about everything
a man did. He said he had plenty of cash in his jeans. I didn't
remind him that his mama's cooking would keep anybody home,

and that he was so flush because he was living rent-free with a salary paid by Moller Machining.

"Wish I had some sisters or brothers," he said, and drained his flask. "Give my old man somebody else to aim at. By the way, how's Elke doing?"

Fred could ride to Kerrville or Luckenbach just as easily as Austin. "Whatever she's doing, she's doing it sixteen years old. You stay away from that pasture," I said. Elke always turned quiet and shy around him, but I didn't really worry. Much. He liked 'em older. I was used to Fred's ways, with him half a head taller than me, and when meeting up with girls, Fred taking the pick of the litter like it was fated. He purely loved it.

He also loved telling about it, so I said, "How are all the other fillies in the corral doing?" It was just drugstore cowboy talk, the Texas way of being one of the crowd and young at heart. Older guys from Maine and Minnesota, new to the Southwest, picked the lingo up as soon as they could, like a joke everybody was in on and tried to improve.

So Fred told me his latest poontang story. I could discount about half of it, but I listened, and snickered in the right places. According to Fred, Austin had better cruising than SanTone, with fewer military bases and more college girls. He said you could just stroll across the tree-dotted green slopes flanking Barton Springs, Austin's biggest swimming resort, and beat 'em away with a switch; but you couldn't cut through the bushes without stepping on the bobbing butt of somebody who'd forgot his switch.

It sounded great, but it sounded a little trashy, too. When Fred offered to take me along next time, I said I'd pass on the Indian, a 1940 Sport Scout with the slick wheel valances. "I like some bodywork around me," I explained. And before he could suggest we go to Austin in the Willys, I added, "I'd like to drive, but with all those jury-rigged parts, I wouldn't trust my heap far from town." I don't know why I said that. What I mean is, I don't know why I was building an alibi to steer clear of doubling with my old boyhood bud.

Fred reminded me that his dad's shop took on problems like

mine all the time. "Just in the past month they've fixed a Morgan three-wheeler, a Delahaye, a pair of Duesies, and the piss-rippin'est yellow Cord roadster you never saw."

I never saw, huh? I dived into the day's memories so I could one-up my bud. "You mean Dylan's," I drawled, casual as Adolphe Menjou. "The major's a purty little thing, isn't he?"

Ol' Fred got some smoke down the wrong way and, after hacking at it like a cat with a hairball, husked, "Damn if you don't get around. How come you know that Yankee?"

I hadn't even heard Dylan's accent, but just for fun I claimed him; laid it on thick. "Aw, he's one of ours. I expect I'll be drivin' that poor thing of his from time to time. The major's just one of the guys on our project," I said, as if I were a gum-swapping bud of a guy who, so far, had only waved at me.

"Listen, that high-stepper's on ever' project there is," Fred assured me. "I deliver a lot of stuff: Brooks General Hospital, Randolph, Kelly, Fort Sam, you name it. And the poon waves at him first. That sumbitch gets more tail than a bullfighter."

I didn't doubt it. "I guess a major must draw man-sized wages," I said.

"I guess. But there's lots of majors around, and not many yellow Cords. Nope, he's just got world-champ ways with five-card stud. Shit, he says so himself."

"He one of your new buds in town?"

"I wish." Fred chuckled, and yawned, and got up from the swing, adding, "I'm workin' on it."

That figured, I thought as we tiptoed into the house. If I could've been anybody I liked, it'd be a cross between my dad and General Doolittle. For Fred it'd be Major Athol Dylan, USAAF, world champion poker stud.

I was up and gone by seven, after raiding the icebox for a glass of Mrs. Moller's famous homemade buttermilk. There was something more than flower and tortilla scents in the SanTone air as I showed my pass at Randolph, people standing in little groups, carrying portable radios, so I turned on the coupe's radio as I rumbled down the perimeter road.

Invasion in Normandy! Waves of excitement crawled up my arms to tickle my neck hairs as WOAI, San Antonio's clear-channel station, filled me in on the thing the world had been awaiting for so long, and now in the early hours of June 6 had become a fact while I slept. I parked behind the hangar and stayed put, listening.

The news confused me. Some of the early fighting must have broken out before the Nazis knew it was the sure-'nough kick-ass showdown at San Jacinto, while I sat with Fred in that glider swing. The British, in gliders of an entirely different kind, had landed troops at some bridge in Normandy—wasn't that France? But Americans were coming ashore by the thousands at beaches in Utah and Omaha, which was still in Nebraska unless they'd moved it, and the only big body of water I knew of in Utah was the Great Salt Lake, and I didn't think we were invading the Mormons, too.

I did what I always did in such cases: kept my mouth shut and my ears open. The Elgin on my wrist told me it was nearly eight, and I didn't want to be late on this day of all days, so when Sparks Fonseca parked his Studebaker and got out carrying a portable radio, I got my armload of precision tools and went with him. He'd picked up little Mickey somewhere on the base, and instead of talking we just traded okay signals and listened to Sparks's radio.

Another radio was already on inside, and nobody was talking much. Everybody was full of beans in the shop, coffee beans at that, to judge from the aroma. Ben greeted us with a two-fingered "V" for Victory, half a cigar in his teeth, reminding me of a much older short guy in England. I wondered if Churchill was Ben Ullmer's hero. That gearbox the major had brought was free of its crate, its casing unbolted on my workbench, and Bub Merrill sat on a stool with sunlight streaming through a window to help him read a spec manual for the gearbox.

A lot of test pilots didn't bother with such details in those days, depending on the A and E guys to do things right. So they didn't always know how everything was supposed to work. Some of those

pilots didn't live to Bub's age because, when something went belly-
up under the cowl later, they didn't have a clue what it might be
and didn't know whether to feather a prop, firewall the throttle, or
step outside for a short parachute ride. Part of their mystique; part
of the b.s. that was dwindling as our hardware got more complicated. I think Bub was still in one piece because back in the thirties
he left the b.s. to guys who wore their sunglasses and scarf in the
shower.

After I looked the gearbox over and set my feeler gauges out,
Bub turned the manual over to me. He even asked how I wanted
my coffee, and I sang out for cream and two sugars, and an hour
later I knew Mickey was a pearl among hangar rats because he'd
been listening and, without a word, brought me another cup fla-
vored just right.

We got the gears properly lashed by noon, and Mickey disappeared for a while with the coffeepot nickels, reappearing after
what must've been a long trot to the PX with cheeseburgers and a
pair of Three Musketeers candy bars for me. It happened that Three
Musketeers was my favorite, maybe because in those days it was
really three little bitty different-flavored bars side by side, connected under a blanket of chocolate. Somebody had noticed I'd
come in without a brown bag or a lunch pail.

Fonseca told me the little guy loved chocolate but didn't care for
the vanilla or cherry flavors, so I carefully broke off the chocolate
third of each candy bar and gave it to Mickey. He said, "Hot tamale," a local joke on "hot dog," and winked, and then we all listened to Bub and Roy Dee discuss the Normandy invasion through
bites of sandwich and swigs of Hires.

Roy Dee may have had a hard life, but he was worth listening
to. Bub was hopeful that the Allies would take the town of Caen
that day, but Roy Dee said they wouldn't if they didn't do it fast.
While we ate lunch in Texas it was nearing sundown over Normandy and at dusk, he said, the Wehrmacht could bring in reinforcements our aircraft couldn't see to attack. Bub thought it over
and agreed. I got the impression that, if Rommel's army got lucky,
our guys could still get shoved back into the sea.

Ben was full of optimism about our beach landings until Bub said, "What we're hearing sounds good, young buck, but you notice they're not talking about Omaha Beach anymore. It's what they quit talking about that worries me." By then I understood about the code names, and knew that Utah and Omaha Beaches were near Cherbourg in Normandy. Cherbourg was still enemy soil, but as of that day, for a time at least, those beaches were ours.

Toward late afternoon, Major Athol Dylan showed up again, bringing special lubricants he'd had to liberate from Kelly Field. That was what a good supply officer did, cutting through red tape to keep deliveries on time. The stuff he brought matched the specs in the manual, and Dylan preened at our thanks.

That guy was really something: a little under six feet, careless grin and fresh haircut, the faintest tang of aftershave, tailored uniform showing off good shoulders, with his cap stowed rakishly under one epaulet. His tie? Knitted, the right color but about as regulation as an ostrich plume. His shoes? Shiny loafers, but in the correct rich brown, and unless somebody polished his ankles, he wore silk socks. From fifty feet off he was in uniform, but close up he was an illustrated manual for thumbing your nose at regulations. I reflected that if a man did a crucial job well and wore oak leaves, he could scorn the regs and not get jerked up by his short hairs. Yep, Fred Moller would just love him to death.

Dylan seemed more buoyant than any of us over the news on WOAI. "A whole new ball game," he kept saying, chain-smoking Pall Malls as he mooched coffee, often checking his foreign chronometer. He didn't have pilot wings over his single row of ribbons. I bet he wanted to, but Major Dylan was a supply officer and a finagler, not a flier. Wearing those wings without authorization, I think, would've been one nose-thumb too many. I had to admit he took his work seriously, delivering rush orders in his personal chariot instead of ordering some noncom to do it in one of those big Dodge Army trucks.

Presently, some switch in the major's head snapped, and he left as suddenly as he'd come. "Appointment," was his only explanation.

I guessed his accent was New York, maybe Philadelphia, and I concentrated on my torque wrench.

Nobody quit at five, and we set up workstands around Pancho's
nose to prepare for the new installation. Most wood-covered planes
had steel tube skeletons, but the P-77 got most of its strength from
its skin, like a big plywood egg. I worried when measurements
showed we'd have to lengthen that skin a few inches up front, but
Roy Dee tore a hunk of butcher paper from a roll and started making patterns. I felt right at home again because that's the way small
outfits had to do it, in a pinch. Rough it out, trim it to fit, then
transfer everything to new official blueprints later. It looked sloppy,
but we could have Pancho in taxi tests while a big factory would've
still been waiting for drawings.

I also knew by now what Sparks was cobbling up: a new skinny
shape for Pancho's radio, so it'd fit back under the tail where Ben
said it must. You can't fly a crate that doesn't balance—and you'd
better not try—so extra weight up front meant relocating other
things to the back. Pancho's battery and radio both wound up
where they needed to be—near the tail—thanks to Ben's slide rule
calculations and the new assembly drawings he cranked out on his
drafting board.

By sundown, we had brought the prop gearbox into the hangar
and slung it in place, ready for mounting. In the shop, with Howard
Lacey helping because he still didn't have any fluid lines to install,
Roy Dee had the durnedest rig I'd ever seen, actually bolted together from a kid's Erector set he kept in his tool kit. It made sense
because it wouldn't stretch or shrink, and held a reinforced partial
cone of new plywood skin in shape while the resorcinol glue set.
He called it the dunce cap and nobody argued.

And on WOAI, they were mentioning Omaha Beach again,
which relieved Bub more than somewhat. When I left, Ben was
saying he wished now that they'd named Pancho the Screaming
Eagle, to honor the 101st Airborne Division. That was my first full
day on Project Pancho, and I went back to the Moller place and
talked some more about the invasion. Mr. Moller asked only how

I was liking my new job, and I told him it looked like a cinch. I suppose I took it for granted that my work would proceed like the Normandy beachhead, rushing from success to success. I had no idea so many things could go so wrong.

FOUR

Within a week after June 6, every man in the wetback hangar could draw a map of northern France from memory, because we had one in full color, the size of a daybed, pinned on the shop wall bristling with pins and festooned with masking tape bearing penciled notations. Major Dylan had liberated it, reminding us with that lopsided hero's grin of his that we didn't know where we got it. We followed the action in France the way I used to follow the play-by-play announcer when the Fredericksburg Billies played Tivy High and Fred Moller ran sweeps from the single wing.

But as the second week of the invasion progressed, Pancho didn't, much. The Allies had fought their way into Carentan, with, hot damn, a pounding by sixteen-inch shells from the USS *Texas*. There was no longer much doubt now that our guys were headed for Berlin and not another Dunkirk.

In the hangar, we had the gearbox mounted and ready for its pair of three-bladed props, which were overdue. Okay, they were special from Sensenich, but they'd been promised before this, and when Ben raised Cain over it, Major Dylan cussed a New York blue streak at the snafu in the delivery system. In desperation, Ben Ullmer finally started tracing the missing parts by telephone until, after two more days, the major dropped by with small packages.

"I hear you're shooting yourselves in the foot, Ullmer," the major said. "It's hard for civilians to learn the Army's motto, 'hurry up and wait,' but you've gotta stay in line. If you were a chicken colonel, you might get someone cranked up on minor parts delays."

Ben set up his conversational artillery and started firing away. "Propellers aren't minor parts. You can scrounge locknuts and safety wire, but next time you see an airchine take off, Major, look real hard at the front end. If it hasn't got a prop, it's bein' pulled by a towrope. And nobody's ever towed a glider as high as we're supposed to go."

"I sympathize, believe me, Ullmer. But this is the Army, and you have to go through the proper channels. When they take flak from a civilian, they can turn on you like an armadillo."

I was nearby with Roy Dee, helping measure Pancho's radio chassis mount for installation, and I turned my laugh into a cough, out of politeness. Dylan was trying to improvise his own Southwest lingo, but if he'd ever seen an armadillo he would know they were about as fierce as garter snakes, and lots cuter.

"You're saying they'd sabotage a crash program out of spite," Ben said.

"Hey, the Army doesn't want to hear that word, buddy." Dylan frowned, his voice with an edge now, standing a little too close to Ben for good manners. "I never said it, and I don't wanna hear it. But they're only human. If they're flogging a dozen crash programs, they might pay closer attention to a big one than a small one. A word to the wise, okay?" And presently, he left. Lacey, who was also waiting for some fluid lines, stayed busy helping out at the maintenance shops, but the rest of us had been an unwilling audience to their exchange. Nobody spoke, so the silence deepened. And then Mickey farted, and we had the chuckle we needed to go on with our day.

And we waited several more days for the props. Then one day Bub Merrill didn't show up 'til the afternoon, which was no problem because he wasn't scheduled for any tests that day. When he did come in, he called Ben off in a corner.

Ben's mood improved a lot in short order. It got even better when, a couple of hours later, he got a phone call and listened for a minute. Then, "Sergeant," I heard him say, "I hope you're beautiful 'cause if you're here with 'em by tomorrow, I intend to kiss ya." Then he muttered something to Bub, slapped him on the back, and returned to his drafting board, chewing that awful ruin of a cigar and humming.

Bub kept quiet but, "That's got to be the props," I said to Sparks.

"If it's not, don't let ol' Ben get you alone in the john," Sparks said. Mickey smiled because I did.

The rest of the joke arrived next morning, when a group of soldiers showed up in a truck with crated props. If they'd been the wrong ones I reckon Ben would've had himself a hissy fit. Three privates unloaded the big paddles as Ben supervised, fussing like a mother hen because one little ding on a prop blade meant waiting for a replacement. The driver, a corporal, waved a set of papers at me. "Sarge says to get these signed. And to duck if some feather merchant named Ullmer gets too close." He was grinning like someone had told him what Ben had said.

So Ben signed, and we uncrated the props, and for the rest of the day whenever Ben came near somebody would yell, "Duck!"

We worked late to get those props mounted with the right spacers, Roy Dee getting in the way as he trimmed and adjusted the dunce cap so it wouldn't disrupt airflow in such a crucial area.

The morning after that, I happened to be early, and it was me who gave Mickey his ride to the hangar. He had cut across an open stretch near the compass rose, where they were about to release what we called a radiosonde. Once every day in early morning, the base meteorology guys would inflate a bright orange rubber balloon the size of a one-car garage, and release it into the open. Carried beneath it like a limp bedsheet with a cage full of clocks was a set of instruments and a multiband radio transmitter. The size of the balloon was because of its heavy set of batteries.

The weather guys tracked the balloon until it burst, many miles up, and when it popped, the radiosonde package floated back down to a gentle landing. People recovered about half of the instrument packages for the reward. The others, for all I know, might have ended up in the Gulf of Mexico.

While this goofy rig floated up and away on the breeze, and later while parachuting down, it constantly radioed back the information pilots needed: temperature and air pressure mostly.

When Sparks Fonseca came in ten minutes later, I told him I had picked Mickey up near the compass rose. He said those big orange balloons were a spectator sport for Mickey, who often hiked out to watch the radiosonde crew before the daily launch.

In midmorning the major showed up again, looking smug. "I found out how those parts went astray," he told Ben, while we were swarming over the airplane. "They were about to go into storage across town at Kelly Field. That's what happens when you have more than one airfield in town and some yardbird can't read a bill of lading. By the way, I need the copies you signed. Army files, you know."

Ben was busy like the rest of us, but little Mickey was sitting on a wingtip, out of the way, where he could watch us in hopes of being useful. He piped up, "I know where they are," and quick as scat he was off and running, the plane so gossamer it bobbed on its gear like a live thing when his weight was removed.

He came back with several sheets, pink and yellow, and after a brief look Dylan folded them into his jacket. Nobody had much time to talk invasion news with him, and I didn't know he'd gone until I heard the dwindling thrumm of the Cord's Lycoming.

With Mickey back on his perch, his head was about the height of a man, and next time I passed by him I thought I smelled booze. Now I don't give a durn if it was Jimmy Wedell—who was already dead by then, but he'd been proof you could fly a race plane drunk as a congressman—nobody, not even a kid who'd found a half-empty bottle, was going to drink around a project of mine. I went about my business and came back a few minutes later. "Mickey," I said, very softly but inches away from him, "if you've found some liquor someplace, you better ditch it. In any case, don't ever show up around here after you've been drinking it. Okay?"

"Okay," he said, "if I do, I will, and don't worry, I won't, but I haven't."

Which made me blink and then laugh out loud, and when Mickey snickered, too, I recognized the odor. Not alcohol; acetone. Great for cleaning stuff up, but not a potion people drank. "And you wanta be careful tasting anything else just because it smells good," I said. "Hyraulic fluid is poison, and acetone isn't much better for you. You understand me, Mickey?"

He nodded, his big dark eyes serious. Acetone was one of those highly flammable solvents found in every hangar, also used as a paint thinner. But there was something else about it, something to do with having it on your breath. I let my memory work on it and went on with my job. We still didn't have Ben's tricky steam turbine stuff, but now we could try out the props with the new gearbox.

When a Ranger engine first starts up, its exhaust is rich with unburnt avgas, and when you run it up you can fill a hangar in no time with choking fumes that take a while to disperse. That's why we pushed Pancho outside facing away from the hangar and chocked her for Bub Merrill's tests.

Everybody, even Lacey, was on hand. While the rasp of an air-cooled V-12 was an old song to me, it excited me to hear an extra unfamiliar whir in its music thanks to a pair of props, one right behind the other, geared to turn in opposite directions. Ben Ullmer rubbed his forearms—goose pimples, I bet—and grinned like a hound dog chewing a caramel. We weren't using two-way radios so we could only watch Bub in the cockpit, splitting his time among the controls, his instruments, and a clipboard. He kept us in mind, too, giving us the okay after each notation he made.

Finally, he let the Ranger idle and motioned for Ben and me to approach, his canopy bubble yawning open. We crowded up behind the wing root, our heads almost even with Bub's. "Checkoff list is complete, but, pard, I get a feeling she wants to taxi," he called out.

Ben took a big breath. "Not scheduled 'til tomorrow," he shouted. "You know that."

"Yeah, yeah; plan the flight, then fly the plan," he quoted the test pilot's mantra with a flyswatting wave of one gloved hand. "But the original schedule was for last week, so we're behind the plan. Still, you're the boss."

And while Ben looked at me as if I had an answer—so I did, with a thumbs-up—Bub sang out to this much younger man, "Come on, Daddy, I'm only goin' down to the corner," and gave the throttle a momentary nudge like a kid in a jalopy.

That blast of propwash must've done the trick. Ben slapped the plywood skin, and warned, "If that nosewheel clears the tarmac, no dessert for a week." He backed away, unable to see me giving another big okay from behind his shoulder, then we pulled the wooden chocks from the wheels as Bub sealed the canopy.

That nosewheel almost jumped off the instant Bub gunned the Ranger, but he throttled back, and we cheered as Pancho headed away from us, her nose nodding on the uneven tarmac. Bub made her swerve along, testing her brakes, then picked up his pace and briefly firewalled it. He must have been three hundred yards off, doing fifty or so in a moment before he braked and turned her around. He did it with the rudder, which needs fast airflow before it can turn the plane. When he brought her back I guided him with hand signals and waited for the props to fully stop before chocking his nosewheel. It was Mickey who huffed up dragging a little workstand, almost more than he could manage, for the pilot to step down on. Ben could've done it with one hand if he'd thought of it. That little hangar rat never missed a detail.

Bub didn't say much in front of the others, but after we pushed Pancho back in the hangar he had a little confab with me and Ben. The checklist showed no power plant squawks, but, "She's not pullin' like she oughta," he said. "Power's not down a lot, but I swear it's down. I can feel it here." He slapped his butt.

"Supercharger's not in the loop," I said.

"I factor that in," he said, frowning, then glanced at Ben Ullmer. "What? Why are you lookin' at me like that?"

Our designer was shaking his head in a "pity the poor morons" way. "You also factor in the gearbox losses?" Bub and I both dropped our chins; we had forgotten a small facet of the very thing we were testing. "The XP-77 wasn't built for contrarotation gearing. That engine's now running a whole 'nother subsystem without a blower to boost it. Gearbox friction, gents. We should be a little down on thrust, and we are. When we get a chemically driven blower crammed into this airchine we should be *way* up again. Next problem?"

There weren't any other problems we could see. It was what we couldn't see that would bedevil us.

Sparks Fonseca stayed late with Ben but the rest of us left on time that day, earlier than usual. I felt so good I called Moller Machining and told Mr. Moller I wouldn't be home for supper. Fred was there, so I offered to treat him to a movie that night, celebrate a bit, though I couldn't tell him why. He said celebrations oughta begin at the Buckhorn, and I said okay.

Without his usual ride, little Mickey had set off afoot, and I overtook him in the Willys. "Much obliged," he chirped, his pipe-stem legs too short to reach the floorboards. He didn't have much to say, as usual, pointing off toward some old but well-kept buildings not far from the Randolph tower.

I said, "Your mama work there?" He nodded happily. "That's a ways for you to walk, little guy," I admitted. "I don't reckon you have a bike, huh?"

"No. It's okay," he said, but I thought he sounded wistful. Of course a little TexMex kid whose mother mopped floors wouldn't see much spare cash for bikes and such.

Then I had an idea; actually, two ideas. The first one didn't exactly tickle my little friend. "Mickey, would it be all right if I talked to your mama?" From the sudden shift of his features I backpedaled fast. "Nothing bad, just a couple of things mamas like to know." This wasn't strictly true because I had remembered about an uncle in Bandera years before who'd smelled of acetone. Turns out he had diabetes.

After a moment's deep thought: "It would scare her."

"How do you know?"

More delay. Then, "It's what I think. Sparks knows; she doesn't like to talk much."

That, I thought I understood. In those days, Latin adults who didn't speak much English sometimes avoided us gringos to avoid embarrassment. What I mentioned next was the other idea. "You think it would scare her if you had a bike?"

"Why would it?"

"I dunno, buddy, that's why I asked. Some folks don't want their kids to get out on the range past the bobwire."

He said, "I could ask."

"Do that," I said, then we got too near little groups of guys trying to march in the streets of Randolph Field, and I let Mickey out and headed for downtown SanTone.

There were three places in town where you couldn't help but find someone you were meeting: the Aztec Theater, the Alamo, and the Buckhorn Saloon, all three downtown. The Aztec looked like Hollywood's idea of a heathen temple inside. The famous Alamo looked like a pile of whitewashed limestone after target practice, which is exactly what it was; those were places where you met your girl.

But if you were meeting a bud, you did it at the Buckhorn. I wanted something on my stomach before I stepped up to that mile-long Buckhorn bar with Fred, and had plenty of time. Being cheap as a nickel haircut, I wasn't about to spend most of a dollar on my favorite weakness, a pair of cheeseburgers. I stopped near an old Mexican with a pushcart, one of hundreds on the streets of San Antonio all looking alike, and bought three of the only things he carried: sweaty, fat little beef tamales wrapped in corn shucks. The aroma near drowned me in my own saliva. I never knew what all was in them and was afraid to ask. Spicy as a scandalous joke, hot as the girls it featured, and at a dime apiece, twice as dear as what a street tamale had cost in 1942. By the time I walked into the Buckhorn my tongue was begging for a beer; one burp from me would've set fire to your curtains.

Any Yankee who thought Texas talk was *all* b.s. needed a wallop
of bourbon after stepping inside the Buckhorn. The place had more
homegrown stuffed animals than a pie-eating contest—big critters.
In addition to a pair of stags with their antlers hopelessly locked up
in the combat that had starved them, there was an entire longhorn
steer, not just the horns. Oh yes: The horns spanned nearly nine
feet, God's truth. And over the bar, among a jillion other trophies,
including Russian boar some idiot had turned loose near Kerrville,
was the mounted head of a mule deer. With seventy-eight tines.
Okay, that ol' buck was a freak, but he was our freak. It's probably
all still there today.

Fred and I punched shoulders, and after I breathed on him he
accused me of munching a senorita, and two beers later he talked
me into cruising Brackenridge Park. We took the Willys, parked it
in tree shadows, and then walked.

Not too far off, some exotic animal cry reminded me of the
sprawling zoo nearby. I flat refused to say exactly what I was celebrating as we strolled the broken sidewalks under a canopy of
pecan, between spiky-leaved hedges of what we called algerita. For
once, Fred wasn't his cocky self and didn't pay his usual bird-dog
attention to the girls passing in fluffy peasant blouses. I complained
that he celebrated in funny ways.

He looked like he wanted to hit me. "Easy for you to say, Kurt.
Look at you, happy as a two-peckered billy goat, war work that
you like, good pay for the duration . . ." He broke it off and flopped
onto a park bench with a sigh, long legs stretched out so his scruffy
boot tops showed. He studied me in the dusk, lit one of those nasty
little cigars, took a drag. "You're goin' places. Sometimes you're
almost too much to take."

My jaw dropped. Big, outgoing, two good legs, both parents
alive, a devil with the girls; the guy I'd admired all my life. "You're
browned off because something good happened to us at work?"

"Naw," he said, and after thinking it over, "well, in a way, yeah.
Not just today. It's your got-damn' life. You fly planes by yourself.
You understand the math. You have a trade you love so much you
druther do it than drink, might plan your life around it if you're a

mind to. I would in your place." He waited for me to answer, but he saw I was too dumbfounded, so he went on. "You simple shit, you mean you don't know how much I envy you? And always did? I'd swap with you in a jiffy, bubba, leg and all," he finished in a near whisper, like a prayer.

I don't know what he expected from me. What he got was Dutch-uncle talk. If he wanted to learn a trade, he might spend more time looking over his dad's shoulder in the machine shop or the specialty auto shop, and I said so. But he didn't want to sweat over a lathe, he said, or bang his knuckles on other guys' cars either. I made several suggestions, but the trouble was, they all amounted to getting good at something he liked.

It came out in a roundabout way, but the upshot was, Fred liked what that hotshot major did. Not the scrounging supplies, or keeping records. No, he liked cruising around in a yellow Cord roadster and stuffing his pockets with poker winnings.

"Join the Army before it joins you. Go to officers' training," I said. "It's a start."

What he said next was something that had never occurred to me in all the years I'd known him. "Kurt, you know I got out of school after you did, but do you know *how* I got through? I'll tell you how: Because I romped and stomped in football and baseball and track. They didn't dare flunk me out if they wanted winning seasons. But you can't play high-school fuckaraound when you're nineteen, it's illegal. They just graduated me out of thanks, I reckon. I can't understand half the crap I read in *Astounding*, I do it because you do. But I got a stack of Planet Comics that'd choke a horse. It's not that I can't read. It's that I can't understand. Kurt, little bud, I know for a fact I couldn't make it through college or officer's training."

We chewed on that a while. One thing I knew he was good at was leadership, and the Army needed officers for that, too. But the Fred kind of leader would risk getting his butt shot off, and I didn't want to suggest it.

He did that himself, though, and perked up when I mentioned the Navy or Coast Guard. "I do swim pretty good," he said, and gave me a piece of the old grin. "But it doesn't sound much like yellow Cord country." While I was laughing at that, he mused, "You know, I wonder if guys with cars like that just don't like each other."

"Why not? Seems like they'd have things in common."

"You'd think so. But if you'd seen what I saw in Dad's auto shop today, you might think again." And he said while the major's Cord was inside the shop for some tinkering with its supercharger manifold, that slinky blue Delahaye coupe pulled up outside. "I've seen it when I was making deliveries at Kelly Field. Driver's an older guy, long sideburns, snappy dresser. He starts into the body shop, then notices the Cord, and jerks his head like he was snakebit and spots Major Dylan talking to Dad. Dylan looks at the Delahaye guy and looks back at Dad. Mr. Delahaye spins around like he had wheels on his feet and chirps his tires on his way to hellandgone." Fred mulled it over, then went on, "Maybe they'd done some street racing, and Mr. Delahaye lost. You think?"

I shrugged. "They didn't nod or wave or say howdy?"

"Nope, I got the idea they didn't want hide nor hair of each other."

"It's a puzzler," I agreed. "One thing sure, the old guy's name isn't really Delahaye. Or is it?"

Fred's turn to shrug. "I could find out. Dad keeps records of what he does on those specialty jobs. You know that guy, too?"

I said I didn't think so, without a name to tag him, then Fred stretched and yawned and punched my shoulder again and said he was in a mood for a movie. We went to *Hail The Conquering Hero* since Eddie Bracken was always good for a smile.

And after he collected his Indian and led me home for buttermilk, I asked him to keep a sharp eye out for an armadillo. In what condition, he asked. In all four wheels churnin' condition, I said, I had no use for something he scraped off the highway. That might be tougher, he said, and what in the world for? I just winked and told him it was a military secret. I was sure it would be if Major Athol Dylan had anything to say about it.

FIVE

Seems like you can never find an armadillo when you really need one. Worse still, our schedule slipped again during the next week for lack of special parts. Meanwhile, Ben Ullmer got some rare photocopies direct from Wright Field where somebody rode herd on projects like Pancho, and they kept me busy. They were taken from Luftwaffe manuals, the negatives recently smuggled out through Switzerland. Now I saw why it was important that I could read German, though I just about read all the print off a dictionary translating some of it. When you come across *Luftschraubenregelgetriebe* you wish they'd just learn English like sensible folks. No wonder they were mad at everybody. I should be immune, but some of those jawbreakers made me a little testy myself.

For once, Ben was *my* student, and after seeing those photocopies he paid me more respect. That steam turbine, built to Ben's drawings, was overdue, and the major swore he was tracking the delay, but Ben wasn't so worried about his hardware. He was nervous about the hazards of the chemicals that would run it, and the real experts were in Germany. Luftwaffe mechanics had to learn the handling dangers, which could take a man's finger off at the shoulder from what I read. Since practically anything including spit would make peroxide boil, everything that it touched had to be stainless steel with nary a blemish or rust spot. Roy Dee built some expensive stainless versions of ordinary stuff like funnels so we wouldn't have to order them and then listen to Major Dylan's excuses for a month.

The day we lugged three hundred more pounds of crate out of the Cord was another occasion for applause. The major was all smiles, maybe the kind of smile you strain through your teeth, until Bub Merrill came over to check the papers. Nobody else was beside them, and I was studying a photocopy while Ben and Lacey tore into the crates on a workbench. The major said something I didn't catch.

"Had to be done," Bub replied calmly.

A little louder now: "How many times are you going to aggravate people up the channel, Merrill?"

"Many as it takes," said Bub in the same monotone, like he was commenting on the weather.

"They tell me you've called in just about all the IOUs you had in the system," said the major.

Bub never raised his voice, but, "I suppose 'they' have names, Major," he said. "And if it's names like Larry Bell or Colonel Kearby I'm interested. Otherwise . . ." He smiled, shrugged, and turned his back on our military supply officer.

The major glanced around, and I tried to look like I hadn't been listening, but I think he caught me. Under his tan he was pale, little muscles in that handsome chiseled face twitching, and the look he gave me made me glad I wasn't wearing a uniform. I hoped he didn't have a dog because if he did, it was due for a few swift kicks. Before he brought his hands to his sides I saw his fingers had little tremors, like a fishing bobber when a perch tests your bait. And that made me curious, and gave me an idea for a harmless little experiment.

When the Cord charged off a few minutes later, Bub watched its dust wake from the window, hands on his hips, shaking his head ever so slightly. Then he heard Ben exclaim with pleasure over the contents of a box and strode across the shop with, "Listen to you;

I swear it must be Christmas morning." I sloped over and looked past Howard Lacey's shoulder while they oohed and ahhed at what looked like brushed steel spaghetti, only thicker and twisted into shapes Ben had called for. Lacey could fudge 'em a bit if need be, but Ben had every curve memorized, and if he was happy, I figured they were right on the money.

It took us two days to find out, and yes, we had to reroute wiring bundles away from new pipes that, when carrying live steam, would be hotter than Terlingua chili. It all fitted inside Pancho, though, boosting my respect for Ben's design work.

Superchargers can scatter. That's a nice word for "explode," when a stray bit of hardware gets gulped by vanes whirling at several thousand rpm. Bub Merrill appreciated the shroud of armor plate Ben designed to keep scattered debris from shooting back through the thin firewall like a grenade into the cockpit.

"If this puts us overweight," Ben told the pilot, tapping the hardened steel shroud to get a "whonnnng" like a padded gong, "I can always haul it back out." He cut a sly glance at Bub.

"No you won't," Bub countered. "If we need to drop ten pounds, I'll just get circumcised." More Texas talk; seemed like Ben would never get used to it.

About that time we found that the new peroxide tank had been partially slosh-coated inside. Special coatings are sometimes sprayed on metal surfaces in processing, but this was no place for it. We had to take the tank back out for an acid flush and steam-cleaning. It was Roy Dee whose inspection spotted that coating after we'd installed the tank.

"Well, we'd have found out the second we ran a smidgin of peroxide in there," Ben said.

"I doubt it," said the sheet-metal man. "The coating is only near the top. Good thing I have an inspection mirror."

Ben paused, gnawed his lip, and nodded. "I'd put it stronger. You're saying we wouldn't get a chemical reaction 'til the tank was pretty much full. Right?"

"Most likely," said Roy Dee, then realized what that meant. "Oh, shit, shaw, Shinola," he added, meeting Ben's gaze. "Well, that tank

won't jump back outa there by itself. I got work to do, Ben." And
he went after his toolbox.

And Ben made some calls to the company that furnished the
tank, because his drawings specified that the tank be flushed of any
such remnants of processing. They claimed they'd flushed it. Ben
told them to do it better next time. No, he didn't have time to
send it back, and he couldn't explain the problem for security reasons.

Later, when he came back from the military maintenance hangars
with the cleaned tank, Ben swore next time he'd add a new spec
to the list on the drawing. Military specifications get letters and
numbers. Ben said, "I'll add MIL-TFP-41. That should do it."

MIL normally stood for "military," but I didn't recognize the rest.
"I don't know that one," I said.

"Make—it—like—the—fuckin'—print—for once," he explained
in a growl. Designers had their own lingo, I guess.

That evening at the Mollers', I pecked out a note on Mrs.
Moller's typewriter. I said everybody liked Miguel so much we
hoped he was healthy, and we thought it was just possible that he
might have a touch of sugar diabetes. If she needed someone to
pay a doctor to find out, we would be glad to pay the bill. By "we,"
I meant me. I also asked if it was okay if we gave him a bike or
candy, and asked Sra. Hernandez if she would write me an answer;
Spanish would be okay, I said, figuring I could get it translated. I
sealed the note in an envelope for Mickey and gave it to him the
next day. I knew he'd give her the note because I told him no more
Three Musketeers for him until she wrote me an answer.

On our hangar battle map, pins labeled "General Patton's tanks"
advanced toward a town called St. Lo. The fighting was said to be
fierce, with our infantry slugging it out in hedgerows against the
troops of Field Marshal von Runstedt, with our P-47 fighter-
bombers racing along at hedgehop altitude, mowing down enemy
tanks and troops like deadly lawn mowers with their small bombs,
rockets, and eight machine guns each. Our P-51 Mustangs were
used to escort our bombers. Slower than jets, they had some luck
in air-to-air combat but wouldn't have lasted long hedgehopping,

with every soldier in the Wehrmacht trying to hit them. With the P-47 Thunderbolt it didn't seem to matter what hit it; the durn thing was a flying tank. Bub said a rumor had started up: If you want to send a picture to your girl, get into a sleek, gorgeous P-51 Mustang. If you want to come back in one piece, get into a fat, ugly Thunderbolt.

Rumors had it that our heavy bombers over Germany were sitting ducks for little Nazi jets, which made me worry more about whatever those Nazi long-distance Ju-488 bombers, Pancho's special enemy, might be carrying. We owned the air low over western France, but at high altitude over Germany it was another story. Our own Pancho had been dreamed up to help remedy that. Like the Nazis, we had to get our interceptors up fast and high near our own cities, but unlike them, we didn't yet have jet-propelled interceptors in production. According to Bub, Pancho might be almost as good, and in limited production lots sooner.

A year before, we'd have had a map of the Pacific on the wall, but the news from there was almost all good now, and in the wetback hangar we felt like our special enemy was in Europe. We cheered when WOAI announced our B-29s had started bombing Japan, and again when a U.S. task force caught half the Jap navy in the Philippine Sea and whaled the tar out of them.

Pancho's steam turbine, linked up to the supercharger, gave me fits when I installed it. In spite of our joking, my hands weren't small enough to get locknuts started on some of the bolts. Ben didn't want me to use Mickey's little fingers until Roy Dee reminded him they were using midgets in our aircraft factories for that very thing. Besides, I could do the rest and test Mickey's work myself. So little Mickey got to do some of the essentials on Pancho in small ways. And in a very, very big way.

When Mickey brought my envelope back, I read the reply and told him now we could pay him for the work he did. Sra. Hernandez had printed, in good English, that with many thanks, she did not want Miguel to see another doctor. There was no need for it. She made sure Miguel got his medicine, and we could give him whatever we liked, and repeated that candy was okay.

I drove home that weekend, flew the Babe one more time, then trundled it into our barn and pickled it for long-term storage. Then I oiled up my first old Schwinn, the Mickey-sized one built low with dinky wheels, and crammed it into the Willys's trunk. I spent all Sunday evening with Mama and Elke and, because I couldn't talk about the project, I told them about the funny little TexMex kid who was our own factory midget. Early Monday morning I got on the outside of too many of Mama's potato pancakes, then made tracks for Randolph Field, full as a tick.

In a season of special days, that was one I'll never forget. First thing I did at the hangar was unload the old Schwinn, a scraped-up victim of many a spill I took when I was Mickey's size. The little guy acted like he'd been loaned a Cord roadster until I told him it wasn't a loan but his own property now, and then he was plain speechless. It was comically clear he'd never ridden a bike before. It took Mickey half the morning before he could get off it when he wanted to, instead of when it wanted him to, but the wiry little cuss never lost a patch of hide in his two-wheel rodeo. Ben finally told Sparks and me if we wanted to watch Looney Tunes, do it at a movie, though he was fighting a smile, too.

An Army olive Ford sedan drove up at morning coffee-break time, leading a truck at about ten miles an hour, and I was surprised to see Major Dylan get out of the Ford. It wasn't his place to say, but he told Mickey to stay away from the hangar.

Then someone said, "He did it. Remember, the major did it." I couldn't tell who had said it, but sure enough, he had finally done something on his own.

While Mickey pedaled away far enough that he didn't have to hear any more orders from headquarters, Major Dylan told us what was in the truck, which I thought explained why he wasn't risking his big yellow boy toy. I gave him a point for having the nerve to escort that load. He got his papers signed and drove off a ways to park and watch.

The truck held several shiny tanks, each nested in a sponge-lined, wheeled wagon and carrying about ten gallons of peroxide. I wondered if the guys in fatigues got hazard pay; they unloaded those little wagons like they knew they weren't off-loading kegs of near beer. They didn't hang around when they were done, either.

The major came back after we wheeled the peroxide tanks to a hazmat shed near the hangar, and his hair was plastered to his forehead with dried sweat. It was then that I remembered my idea and came up to the major, tossed a couple of big ol' washers up, and caught them. They weren't A.N. parts, but common iron fender washers as wide as a tennis ball. Not many outlanders knew it, but the washer-toss was Luckenbach's version of horseshoes, and even Fred Moller had learned not to play against me for money. "Major, they tell me you're a gamblin' man," I said, and handed him the washers.

"So this is what passes for money in Texas," he said. "Funny, but they never anted up any of these when I cleaned out those guys in the Seybold Hotel."

"Nah, it's what *makes* money in Texas," I said. The Seybold, in Fort Worth, was the site of an ongoing poker game where cattlemen won and lost entire ranches on poker hands. "You dig a cup-sized hole, stand back a ways, and try to get your washer in it. I could show you how, if you had a dollar."

"I do believe I've been challenged," he said, hefting the washers, studying them as if there was a catch to it.

There is. The catch is, you've got to be good and steady at it, and I was. The worst that could happen was, I might lose a couple of bucks. Ben gave me the fish eye—this was work time—but he didn't say so, and he and the others came out to the parking area, where I dug a cup in that hard caliche dirt, then paced off the distance and drew a line.

I'll cut it short: I sandbagged a bit in practice and found that the major had good coordination, enough not to embarrass himself, and then we wagered an RC Cola. Because I skunked him we double-or-nothinged until he owed me a buck sixty, and when he wanted to double up again I asked if he had the cash on him. He pulled out a roll of bills that looked like a short snorter managing to look bored and determined and insulted all at once, and pulled off a

fiver. I allowed as how I was satisfied, and then I missed the cup a
mile—okay, a foot. I didn't feel like making an enemy of him but
more important, for the first time he had a chance to break even.
It was suck-it-up time. That was the point.

The major stood at the line, took a stance, and it was so quiet
you could hear a meadowlark off somewhere in the distance. He
finally took his shot, and beat me by an inch, and I pocketed the
washers and shook hands with him and said now he was an honorary plainsman.

So Major Athol Dylan marched away from there with his head
high and all his cash and his imagined honor intact. And the way
his sideburns had begun to leak, and the way his hand had been
shaking, if Major Athol Dylan ever won a poker hand at the Seybold Hotel it was with a bunch of blind tenderfeet who couldn't
smell flop sweat. While the major might have been a lot of things,
a poker stud wasn't on the list. He would take a risk, all right, but
playing cards for money he'd telegraph more signals than Western
Union. I pondered the notion of telling Fred about it; should I tell
him his hero was all hat and no cattle? Maybe not.

Ben Ullmer knew a dozen reasons why we shouldn't rush a
ground test of that peroxide turbine and only one reason why we
should: The suspense was killing us. Not a man broke for lunch;
we were too busy getting Pancho rolled outside with all her upper
cowl panels off, surrounded by workstands. We learned that with
our rig, gravity feed was the safest way to transfer peroxide. It was
nearly four when we wheeled the workstands away from Pancho,
Mickey again dragging that little stand up for Bub to use, and this
time I shooed our hangar rat away to a safer distance even though
we had put in only a gallon of peroxide.

Bub proceeded by clipboard as usual. He fired the Ranger up
with me standing fire-extinguisher duty. It reached steady temperature quickly, also as usual. We had landing gear and wing tie-downs
tight, which wasn't so usual, and it was a good thing we did. There
was nothing ordinary about the canvas-rip screech of those props
when Bub cranked on the supercharger, Pancho lunging against her
tie-downs like a plow mule, landing gear skidding a few inches de-

spite brakes, tie-downs, and all. That little beauty wanted to scat. I thought maybe Ben's thousand-horse guess was a little low. It was goose-pimple time.

But within ten seconds the duct temperatures were up to where they'd stay, and if you're going to have a steam leak, that's when you don't want it, so that's when we got one. Everyone else was looking below the plane where the steam exhaust rocketed out with a hoarse roar, but I saw a thin clear jet of something that became a steam plume between the turbine and the engine. If Pancho's plywood skin panels had been on, that clear live steam under pressure would've cut them clean through. I gave Bub the throat-cut signal: *Kill it, now.*

He did, and valved off the blower outlet so he could use up the remaining peroxide, because Ben had decreed that no peroxide would enter the wetback hangar. We stayed late to seal that steam leak, and it must have been eight in the evening before I headed for the Mollers', wishing I could tell Fred what a heck of a day I'd enjoyed.

What I couldn't know was, my day wasn't over by a bunch, and I could have told Fred anything I liked because he was in no shape to hear me.

SIX

I whistled my way up the Moller front steps, noting that since the Indian wasn't parked out front where everybody could see it, Fred couldn't be home. Sure enough he wasn't, and I didn't smell the kitchen magic that said Mrs. Moller was trying to make us bust our belts. It was never completely quiet at the Mollers'; not until now. Humid summer days like that, people kept windows open hoping to catch a breeze.

I called a cheery "hi" inside, then did it again louder. "Out here," Gene Moller called from the backyard. He wasn't a talker, and said nothing more, sitting alone in the glider swing, watching as I trotted outside. He made his guess by the smile on my face. "You haven't heard, then," he said, and it was a croak.

He sounded a hundred years old, and my face fell. First thing I thought was, that durn Indian had landed Fred behind bars, but I'd never say that to his dad. I shook my head and sat down. I said I'd driven from Luckenbach straight to work and had a long day. Then I waited.

As a man of few words, Fred's dad made every one count. "My boy's not expected to live," he said. His eyes were dry, but they hadn't been for long.

Clapping my hands at my temples, I couldn't even start a proper sentence. What, I said, and then how, and then when, and then I held my hands out, begging.

It took ten minutes to get enough details for me to deal with it. Saturday night, Fred was supposed to be in Brackenridge Park. He wasn't; around midnight, some farmer on his way home from marketday called the police in New Braunfels, midway on the Austin highway. Heading north, the farmer had rounded a curve to see a ball of blackness surrounded by a big ring of sparks coming his way, and a pair of headlights next to it coming head-on at high speed. In his lane.

What he was seeing was Fred's Indian, flipping over and over on its way into the dry brush near the highway. The car he saw only as blinding headlights swerved back into its own lane and zoomed past without slowing. The farmer stopped with his lights on. At the end of a settling dust trail lay what was left of the Indian but even when the wreckage began to burn, the farmer couldn't find its rider. He got the cycle's license plate number and drove on to the nearest phone at New Braunfels.

And it was nearly three hours before they found my bud out in the brush with his skull stove in, compound fractures of both legs, and other stuff Mr. Moller said that I don't even remember. They thought Fred was dead at first. He was found 130 feet from the first highway scrapes. The ambulance brought him back to San Antonio.

Mrs. Moller hadn't left the hospital since they got the call at dawn on Sunday. Mr. Moller had come home for changes of clothes but was too shaky to drive back. "Must be after six," he said.

Way after, but I let it ride. "I'll drive you—if that's okay," I said. He nodded. I had to help him up.

I'd never seen Gene Moller scared of anything, but he was afraid of what he'd find at the hospital. On the way, he said, "Fred found you something Saturday morning. It's in that ol' varmint cage near the back steps."

I knew what it had to be. If I'd told Fred why I wanted it, he wouldn't have done it. "Armadillo?"

"Little fella, size of a cantaloupe," Mr. Moller said. "I put in a few table scraps."

"He'll eat it," I said. Whatever it is, and the bugs that it draws, it's all the same to an armadillo.

It was twilight when we reached the hospital. Mrs. Moller's news was good: Tough as a longhorn, Fred was holding his own. But he still wasn't conscious. "They worked on him some more. His head's the right shape again," she said, shaky-voiced.

About ten, a doctor came in. He said the signs were good but that we ought to go home until morning. He promised they'd call if there was any change, and I drove the Mollers home. I hadn't even seen my bud yet, and it drove me nuts that there was nothing I could do. Hours later, I decided there might be something, then I managed to fall asleep.

Tuesday was another big day. Mrs. Moller promised to call me at the number I gave her if she had news, good or bad, and I lugged The Major to work, cage and all.

At least it helped take my mind off my bud. Nobody had to ask why I named our little beady-eyed critter The Major. Mickey took its food and water as his mission, though at first it rolled up in its patented armor plate whenever we went near. In time, I knew, it would get used to us. Ben heaved a sigh deep as a well when he saw that we weren't going to let it go right away. As Bub Merrill told him, "Resistance is futile. Shoot, I'll adopt him myself."

We did two more run-ups on Pancho that day, the second a long one to make sure we'd cured the steam leak. Mickey stuck pretty close to me all day, helping to the point of getting in my way; somehow he knew I had trouble on my mind. Every time Ben's phone rang I crossed my fingers, but it was never for me. I'd told him a close pal was hurt, and after work I used the phone.

Mrs. Moller said there had been no change. I said I'd eat out and be home late, but I didn't want to say more. Actually, I didn't eat at all. I needed three calls to find where the wreckage of the Indian was, and saying I was Fred's little brother, got close directions to where it, and Fred, had been found off the highway. They wanted to know why I needed to know. I said Fred had been carrying a set of keys the family needed. Okay, I lied.

I couldn't actually get to the wreckage in the locked New Braunfels impound yard, but I could see through the cyclone fence that any paint scrapes from a car to the Indian would've been burnt to cinders. No help there, so I scooted the Willys up and down the highway 'til I spotted some recently burnt brush. From that point, the highway scrapes and caliche scars were easy to find.

And just off the highway shoulder I found a few little flakes of paint, gleaming in the late sun, and the color of the sun. I gathered them up, along with pieces of cylinder fin and other bits that had broken off before the Indian caught fire. Then I sat in the Willys and shook, thinking about it.

The pieces of the Indian had no paint on them, so I couldn't prove what I was thinking. I wasn't even certain those paint flakes were the same shade of yellow as a certain Cord roadster. Watching shadows stretch through the brush, I tried to make sense of my suspicion; why I'd had this gut feeling I hadn't admitted to myself until I found bits of paint; why my bud might be racing his got-damn' hero; why Major Dylan might be on that stretch of highway at that time of night. I also wondered if telling anybody might, in some way, sabotage Project Pancho whether I was right or not.

I drove back to the hospital in twilight, and though they wouldn't let me see Fred, Gene Moller came out of his room with big tears rolling silently down his cheeks, and he was smiling. "He knows me," he said. "My boy's coming back." I pushed my dark thoughts away and let myself cry.

We didn't celebrate the Fourth much, as I recall. After years of salivating at fireworks stands I could barely see over, wishing for the day when I had the money for all the whistling red devils I could carry, now that day had come, and I had more important stuff on my mind. Made me wonder if life was really fair. For the first time in my memory I ignored the dozens of fireworks stands where you could buy Chinese crackers a nickel a pack, or a pack of baby giants for half a buck, or a rocket on a guide stick as high as your breastbone for forty cents. To look into the night sky that Fourth of July you'd have thought the war was being fought over SanTone. I didn't even stay up to watch.

Days later, they told us Fred was definitely improving. Not only that, but Pancho flew. Bub's flight card scheduled nothing beyond simple maneuvers in what we called a swing around the patch, but it was a long swing that would take him south over the scrub toward Beeville and Goliad. The transmitter was tuned for Ben's unit, and though Ben wanted something called a wire recorder to let him record Bub's transmissions, I guess those gadgets were too new for us to get one. We did the next best thing. Much as they hated to, Ben and Sparks both stayed in the shop with pencils and paper to take down everything Bub reported on the radio.

Pancho's takeoff wasn't any more wild and woolly than the last of the air racers until it was a few hundred yards down the runway, away from some cadet waiting his turn in a trainer. Mickey stood beside me at the mouth of the hangar. You couldn't pick out Pancho's engine note until a second after we saw a white trail erupt from below the fuselage. That meant Bub had cranked her up to METO, maximum-emergency takeoff power. And that meant a steam exhaust rocket assist by a turbosupercharger fueled from hell.

Now we heard it, a twin-engine note on the breeze, urgent as a hornet in heat, and Pancho leaped off the runway like I flat don't know what. I'm glad I didn't jerk when Mickey grabbed my hand in his and squeezed so hard it actually hurt. By now I was used to the fact that he always seemed to have a fever.

The guys had talked it over, and couldn't decide whether it would be less noticeable to stay low and get away from the field sooner, or climb like the devil and give anyone beyond the field less time to identify Pancho. Its weight and balance hadn't shifted from known P-77 habits, so Bub didn't have to feel it out so gently. The steam exhaust forced the decision. Ben didn't want anyone beyond the field perimeter to look up and see a tiny aircraft with a billowing white exhaust on its underbelly, without one of those new ten-second rocket bottles. So Bub Merrill stayed low only long enough to fully retract Pancho's gear, then, near the perimeter fence, turned her nose toward heaven.

And oh, Lord, Lord, how she climbed! I shouted for joy as she dwindled to a dot and became only a fleeting wisp of white, veering south.

While Roy Dee cheered, Mickey said, "Why are you laughing?"

I told him I had just remembered the one about the guy who had five cats and five entry holes cut in his back door. Why more than one hole? 'When I holler scat,' the guy says, 'I *mean* scat!' " I added, "Mickey, Pancho's for the guy who knows what scat means."

"You laugh at strange things," he said, and let go of my hand as if he were guilty.

We hurried back inside the shop, and, while listening to Bub, I took some notes in case the others needed them. Bub's gauges were all nominal as he leveled off at twelve thousand. Since we hadn't installed a new oxygen tank yet, he didn't risk climbing higher. Bub said his altimeter was reading ninety-five hundred after only sixty seconds off the runway. As far as I know, that was a record for props. Airspeed, once he leveled off, soon pushed past four hundred, and that was all the day's flight card called for.

"There's more on tap, Mother," Bub said, his voice made scratchy by vibration, "but if we adjust the exhaust nozzle, we might convert some of that into better climb."

"Roger, Wetback," Ben said. "How's the handling?"

"We're about to find out. Aileron roll to port in ten seconds."

Rolling Pancho with a tank half-full of hydrogen peroxide wasn't a maneuver I liked to think about. After an endless few seconds when no one breathed, we heard Bub's calm, "Sweet and steady. Aileron roll to starboard in ten seconds."

More silence, and Mickey's hot little hand crept into mine again. "This is a scary part, Kurt?"

"It is if there's even a speck of stuff to shake loose in the peroxide lines," I said, drawing a look from Ben that said, "Will you kindly take that kind of talk outside?" I shut up.

Finally, after a couple of shallow dives, Bub announced he'd flown the plan and was headed for the barn, and his only complaint was vibration. We wanted to start celebrating, but, as they'd said of the trickiest Gee Bee racer, even after you touch down you could wind up in a sack. I had to explain to Mickey that, yeah, maybe we were a little superstitious about celebrating too soon.

Lacey made a quick trip to the maintenance hangars for hydraulic fluid, knowing it'd be a half hour before Bub came whirring up our taxiway. They both arrived back at the hangar at the same time, and we had our little soda-pop celebration. Then, while I was helping Lacey unload his fluid cans, he said, "Guess who I saw parked, watching Merrill in the landing pattern."

"Everybody," I said, still pumped up over our success.

"Yeah," Lacey chuckled, "and our supply officer was part of everybody. You reckon he's allergic to celebrations?"

As casual as I could make it, I said, "Could be. You notice if his roadster was looking spiffy as usual?"

"Didn't see it. He was off by himself, standing next to an Army-issue Ford," Lacey said. That would figure, I thought, if the Cord had body damage. I had been watching for the Cord without success. And of all the body shops in San Antonio, I was pretty sure which one would be least likely to repair that damage.

That evening I got to see my best bud take food through a straw. One eye was under bandages and both of his legs were hung up like trapped animals, but Mr. Moller said to ignore the colors of Fred's face because he was on the mend. The Mollers took my arrival as their chance to get something new to them: a genuine hospital supper. For a minute after they left us alone, I just stood there. I decided it was time for some questions. I said, "You tell the police what happened yet?"

The pain medicine kept him woozy, but his one good eye tracked me okay, and his voice was clear enough. "Nah. What would I say? Rat-racin' some yahoo in a pickup truck and sideswiped him? Hey, I just cut it too close, little bud. Like you always said I would."

I stood there some more and swapped long looks with Fred, and as I did, a kind of cold fever began to build in me. "So you do remember," I said, keeping it mild.

"Sure."

"Then you must remember the pickup's color."

"Black; maybe dark blue," he said.

"Yeah, or maybe a roadster, in fact. Yellow," I said. "The color of the stripe down a man's back when he runs you off the road and won't stop while your damn' Indian burns."

Fred swallowed and closed his eye. "Shit. He tell you, then?"

"In a way," I said, realizing Fred had just turned my suspicion into certainty. It wasn't fair to Fred, but I took advantage of the moment. "What I don't get is, how you two connected up where you were."

A long silence. Then, "We connected earlier in the evening." Fred was tiring now. "Austin, at Barton Springs. Spotted the Cord. Went over to say hi. Him and the Delahaye guy."

"You sure it was him?"

"Delahaye coupe's hard to miss," Fred said.

"You ever get his name?"

"Uh-unh."

Well, that was one thing I could maybe find out myself. "So you egged him into a race home," I sighed.

"Not exactly. Major says, drop by later, we'll convoy to SanTone." Longer silence. "So I did. Kurt, we were just havin' fun. He didn't mean to, he must'a swerved around a chuckhole."

Swerved. Right. While they were blasting along at high speed. Well, whoever was at fault, you don't hit-and-run. "And you're afraid this would get him in trouble," I said.

The eye flicked open. "It would," he said. "Sure as hell."

"Sure as hell," I agreed. My bud looked like he'd talked himself to exhaustion, with my help. "Get some sleep. You look like the last rose of summer before last," I said.

"Whup your ass any day," he said. "Oh, you get my present?"

"Armadillo? Yep. Brung him to work. Thinking of training him for rodeos."

"Don't make me laugh; it hurts. What'd you name it?"

I pondered my answer because Fred wouldn't like the truth. "We call it Fred," I said, and left him shaking and cussing.

I linked up with the Mollers at their house. She was cooking a real meal, both of them still outraged at the uneatable suppers they'd walked away from at the hospital. "Take a seat," said Gene Moller. "Next time I spend a dollar thirty-five for a hospital meal, just wheel me straight to the loony ward."

I had the gut-rumbles anyhow, so I sat. Funny how hard it is to get around to asking a question you don't want the other guy to think too much about. Finally, without using its name, I asked him about that swoopy block-long foreign coupe I'd seen at the Moller shop.

"Delahaye," he said. "Looks like it could fly, doesn't it?" I nodded. Before I could phrase my follow-up, he went on: "But what else would we expect from a fella who owns the country's top aircraft factory?"

I thought, Boeing, North American, Bell? Oh God, *Bell?* The very idea made my stomach flop. Dry-mouthed, I said, "Which factory?"

"I forget," said Gene Moller. "It's not one of the big ones, just the best, according to him. Signs his checks Kevin Ireland, Esquire."

I nodded like it wasn't important, and watched Mrs. Moller serve up a real supper.

SEVEN

That vibration in Pancho's innards turned out to be a problem of prop-blade adjustment, which had to be reset and then monkeyed with on the ground. Mama used to say "Monkey isn't a verb." Dad would say, "It is when you work on race planes." Ben flew a consultant in to help, and I didn't get a chance to ask Bub Merrill about Mr. Kevin Ireland, Esquire, until later. I might've even asked Major Dylan, if I'd seen him around.

After I did ask Bub: "Funny you should bring up that name," he said, like he wanted me to explain.

"Why funny? He has work done on this terrific foreign car of his in town, is all."

"That's not all, but there's something called need to know. Ben needs to know more'n I do about these things, but I'm not sure he'd talk about it."

"What things, Bub? I say something wrong?"

"Naw. Let's just say Ben and Wolverine are competing."

That meant all of us were competing with Wolverine. But I didn't know what Wolverine was, and I said so.

"Well, they're kinda new. Wolverine Aero," said Bub. "A Michigan engineering outfit that reinvented itself after the founder went

West," he said, using vintage pilot's jargon for "died." "They rein-
corporated a year before Pearl Harbor." He brightened suddenly,
happy to be able to tell me something, I guess. "It's not a secret
that old man Ireland left his middle-aged son Kevin a pisspot full
of bucks and a bright design staff. Or that Kevin Ireland converted
the business into his hobby, which is trying to build his firm a name
in aircraft development. Only thing Ireland Junior was known for
was, he threw the wettest parties for a favored few of the race
pilots."

"Funny my dad never mentioned him," I said.

Bub laughed. "Favored few, I said. If Jurgen Rahm had been a
high roller who won the Collier Trophy instead of a guy who made
such things happen, he'd know Kevin Ireland, all right."

The way he said it I already didn't like Mr. Ireland. I also realized
that I was hatching up some uncomfortable ideas about powerful
men. "So what's he doing down here piloting a Delahaye coupe,"
I asked.

"I didn't hear the question," said Bub, and gave me a horsewink.
"And if you shouted, I still wouldn't. I'm not supposed to know
either," he added in a stage whisper.

I chewed that over for a moment. "So Mr. Ireland's down here
in the aero business. We aren't talkin' civil air stuff, I suppose."

"You suppose right." Bub wasn't a guy to volunteer criticisms,
and I got the idea he'd just as soon drop the subject.

But he wasn't a mealymouth either. I said, "So Ireland runs Wolverine Aero. Does he test-fly his own projects like, um, Howard
Hughes?"

"Nope. But he hovers over his people like an autogiro, maybe on
the theory that some expertise will rub off on him. And he wants
to be Hughes or Larry Bell so bad he can taste it."

"You think he'll make it?"

Bub sighed, pushed his hat back off his forehead, and said, "All
right, here it is, young stud: Howard Hughes has bags of money, a
rage to succeed, a mind like a slide rule, and world-class talent.
Take away the slide rule and the talent and you have Kevin Ireland.
If you want him. Can we leave it at that?"

"Sure. Sorry, Bub." I looked apologetic for him, and he grinned to show it was okay. I spent a good part of the afternoon mulling it over while Mickey hung around me and let The Major out of his cage, tempting him with lunch scraps. Until then I hadn't tried to think like a detective, but it was past time I did. About the time I decided I should have already checked out the other body shops around San Antonio, I told Mickey to look out for The Major's sharp little digging claws.

"You're pretty smart," Mickey said. I winked at him and forgot about it for a while.

I didn't want to be overheard, and I didn't want to make Mr. Moller suspicious, so I asked to take off a little early to go to the hospital. Ben figured he understood.

A little after four, with a handful of nickels and a notepad, I used a hospital pay phone before seeing Fred. I'd never checked the Yellow Pages for body shops, but we used to say driving in SanTone was a dodge'em marathon. No wonder I used up nearly all my nickels. Without finding anybody who had a repair order for any 812 Cord of any color.

Down the hall, my big bud was feeling better even if his face was in Technicolor. I told him he looked like all the scenes in *Fantasia* shown at once, and he said I oughta see his shins, and I shuddered. Mrs. Moller sat in a corner with her knitting, so I tried to be sly. "Promise me something, Fred."

"What?"

"Trust me; you have to promise in advance."

"You're nuts, but okay," he said.

"Some of your hotshot buddies might be heavy on practical jokes. If any of 'em come around here, promise you won't see 'em unless one of us is in the room," I said.

He thought that over, while in the corner, needles clicked. Then he grinned, which looked just awful with his missing teeth. "Only one so far," he said, "is one I happened to run into recently."

"Here in this room?"

"Came after hours, but he talked his way in. Almost didn't rec-

ognize him. And durn if he didn't forget to leave the candy he
brung me."

"He have much to say for himself?"

"Naw. Worried about me, of course. I told him what I told you:
My own fault broadsidin' a ol' pickup truck."

"Just as well he didn't leave you any candy, Fred. Too much
sweets might not be good for you," I said, my gaze burning a hole
in his.

"Well, he hasn't been back. Like I said, you're nuts, little bud,"
he joked, then changed the subject. But when I reminded him of
his promise, he nodded, and I left it at that.

I spent some solo time that evening in the backyard glider, wiping
sweat from my neck as locusts revved their engines in the mesquite,
wishing for a breeze with half my mind while Fibber McGee ca-
vorted on the Moller radio inside. With the other half of my mind
I was thinking how lucky Fred was that, one, he had told Major
Dylan he was sticking to his big lie about a pickup truck, and two,
that the major hadn't left his candy. If Fred had barely recognized
that scutter, he was probably wearing civvies using a fake name or
something. And why would he do that, and him so proud of his
almost uniform? I knew mighty got-damn' well why he might, but
without a record of repairs to his car I couldn't tie it down to what
cops call a motive. And my bud was too flat-ass bonehead dumb
and loyal to say what needed saying. Probably call me a liar if it
came to that.

We got Pancho's prop blades correctly reset on a Thursday, and on
Friday, Bub let me do the engine run-up, leaning into the cockpit
to talk in my ear as he stood on the workstand Mickey saw as his
personal job. It pissed Ben Ullmer off, I think, to see me at the
controls, but as Bub put it, a test pilot needs his crew chief to be
at home in the business office. That's how I became Pancho's crew
chief, signing off for notations in the flight log.

Bub went inside the hangar for some tape to mark a gauge.
Mickey hopped up on the stand, and we grinned at each other like
kids playing hooky. I nudged the throttle a tad just for fun, the

propwash nearly blowing Mickey off his perch, and I made a big slow circle in the air with my finger like I intended to do a swing around the patch. Mickey laughed out loud, then gave me a funny look. He shouted, "Going to Austin?"

I shook my head, and shouted, "They'd shoot me down," seeing Bub on his way back out to us, and motioned for Mickey to hop down. And then I thought, *Why not?* I didn't mean fly there in an airplane I was scared to death to sit in, but if Major Dylan and Mr. Ireland were linking up there an hour away, Austin might be a place to check body shops. Tomorrow was Saturday, and since Ben was scheduled for a fast plane to Wright Field, we'd have all weekend off.

For the second time Mickey said, "You're pretty smart," and it gave me the willies not being sure exactly what he meant. He nodded to me, no longer grinning, then Bub was on the stand, slicing little bits of tape to put on the manifold pressure gauge. Bub's pocketknife was like mine, scalpel-sharp; most pilots kept them honed in the days before quick-release chute harness.

I intended to have a talk with our hangar rat, but by the time we shut down Pancho's engine and shoved her back in the hangar, Mickey had left. Sparks told me my little bud had zoomed off like he was late for supper, on the bike I gave him. I think Sparks was peevish because Mickey had sorta adopted me, but he never said anything, and they still worked together.

Now and then when the weather changed, like that afternoon with a curtain of harmless high cirrus clouds giving way to cadet-killer cumulonimbus thunderheads sweeping in off the Gulf, the meteorology guys would try and get off an extra radiosonde balloon during the day before the wind made it iffy. I drove off watching little stick figures wrestle their big orange pear shape against fits of breeze. I think I saw Mickey there with his bike, but I figured there'd be other times, and I had other fish to fry.

First thing I did after crossing Austin's Congress Avenue Bridge to the middle of town was to find a parking place near the Driskill Hotel. Not only did they have no rooms, they said good luck finding

one anyplace in town. I decided I was going to cuss out loud the
next time someone gave me a sarcastic look, and said, "Don't you
know there's a war on?" I knew, all right; I just didn't know who-
all was fighting it. Yet.

It was already 5 P.M., and, from one of the hotel's pay phones,
I managed to find four auto body shops still open. They weren't
much help, and the other listings didn't answer. I thought ahead,
tore out the Yellow Pages I needed, then had a brainstorm and tore
out the page for paint stores. Luckenbach was a little closer than
SanTone, and while I used my 'C' card to fill up with Esso Extra
on South Congress, I got me a free Esso map of Austin. I was home
in Luckenbach giving Mama a big hug before dark, and she didn't
even complain when I said I'd have to be off again before breakfast.

I nearly had me a fit when Mama said Elke was on a date. A
date? My little kid sister? And her only sixteen . . .

I called the Mollers to say where I was, fixed the back screen
door and a leaky faucet, and gave Mama more money than she said
she needed. Then I got on the outside of some of her leftover has-
senpfeffer while I was doping out my next moves, circling locations
of body shops and paint stores on the Austin map. Most of my
circles were grouped near Congress and out East Sixth, with one
on the Bastrop highway. I had just folded everything up when a
Studebaker President pulled into the yard. I waited for what I
thought was too long before strolling out on the porch—Mama said
it was maybe ten seconds—to gape and stretch and pretend I wasn't
trying to see into the car.

Well, Elke didn't even act guilty. The driver scrambled out and
rushed up to pump my hand, and called me "Mr. Rahm," gabbing
a mile a minute, and durn if he didn't act like I was visiting royalty.
He had to get his daddy's car back by eleven, so Elke and I had a
little time together. The way my little sis was filling out her clothes
gave me prickly heat on my neck, but when I told her that blouse
showed more Elke than somewhat, she told me off more than
somewhat, and Mama settled us down with homemade peach ice
cream. We made up, but I resolved to get home more often. Maybe

buy Elke a blouse you couldn't stuff into the matchbox with my paint chips.

Those thunderheads had brought a sprinkle of early rain to the region, then moved on, the sun drying the highway as I drove. I was back in Austin before the body shops opened, dressed as flashy as I could manage, like a guy used to paying for his whims. In midmorning I changed tactics away from body shops because I figured stores that carried auto paint wouldn't be so hurried, and would want to sell me their stuff. At the third of my four listings, the salesman eyeballed the paint flakes in my matchbox and said he'd recently matched a special yellow chip like mine but didn't know what for. I paid him a buck to look up the record. It had been sold to the shop out Bastrop way. He warned me that they were a pretty pricey outfit, and that I could probably get just as good a job done in town. I thanked him and sauntered out.

A half hour later I parked the Willys again, jazzed its V-8 to get attention, and strolled into the shop with what I hoped was a devil-may-care grin. And a lie, since I didn't see the Cord anywhere.

I was tired of the Willys's color, I said. How much to paint it like my friend's supercharged Cord? The shop manager looked my coupe over while I tried to look patient. What color, he said. I took a chance: same color as the Cord you just painted, I said.

"Special job like that's gonna run ya a hunnerd-fifty. They'd sure see ya comin'," he said. "Though I'm playin' with a sorta orangy red you might like better than buttercup yella."

"Buttercup? You sure that was for Athol Dylan?"

"We don't need to match many special paints for 812 Cords, pal," he said. "But let me check." I bought me a red peanut pattie to give me something to bite while he thumbed over some bills. He finally frowned over one. "Nah. Fella's a Kevin Ireland, says here. Some other guy drove it here. Took it away yesterday."

"Tall guy, Yankee accent, looks like a movie star?"

"And perty proud of hisself," said the manager, nodding. "That's him. But the check was Ireland's."

"That ol' scutter," I said, like "Boys will be boys. The check clear?"

"Course it cleared."

"Well, they don't always. I'm gonna have some fun with this," I said, without the least idea what I was talking about but smiling my smile. "I'll give you a buck—no, two bucks, for that receipt."

I don't know what he thought I was doing, but he held up the receipt and smiled back. "Sawbuck and it's yours," he said.

And that's how I drove back to SanTone with proof of a left front panel repair and a buttercup yellow paint job to a Cord with Michigan plates. And for the five bucks, I got to stir around in the scrap pile where I found some metal Cord trim with paint smears that could've come from Fred's Indian.

Portrait studios in SanTone would've made me wait a week, but one lady said maybe I could get quick service from a place that did IDs and birth certificates, which I should've thought of to begin with. Cost me another five to get a pair of glossy prints of that receipt.

At the Moller place I bummed a big envelope and sealed the receipt and one copy inside with a note I made in my best drafts-man's printing. I gave it to Mr. Moller for him and only him to open, and only if something ever happened to me. I also told him what I knew he suspected already: that in all innocence Fred might have made friends with some wrong folks. And something else Mr. Moller probably hadn't suspected: If Fred had seen something he wasn't intended to see, the accident might've been an on-purpose, and they might try again, but that Fred would never believe it 'til he woke up dead one morning.

Then I hightailed it back to Luckenbach and took my womenfolk shopping in Fredericksburg. No point in doing it in Luckenbach, unless you could wear a blouse made in the blacksmith shop. Which, come to think of it, might've been a middlin' good idea . . .

For the next day and a half, it was almost like old times, only better and worse. Better because I was fool enough to think I had a handle on what would happen in the next few days; worse after Elke admitted she didn't care about high-school boys as long as tall, handsome, romantic, poor, wounded Fred Moller was still single. Lordy, Lordy . . .

I spent all Sunday, July 16, just hanging around the farm. Seemed like everybody in town had to drop by to see if I was still real. Near as I can figure, I was burping Sunday supper's dessert about the time when, six thousand miles away, other people were turning Project Pancho on its head. After giving a lick and a promise to chores around the farm I felt pretty good about myself, thinking of all the power I had in my pocket. It wasn't much preparation for Monday, a day that would put old times behind me forever.

EIGHT

Expecting Ben Ullmer to be back already by fast military flight, I was up with the chickens Monday morning so I could get to work an hour early. On my way I heard on WOAI that Marines were mopping up on the Pacific island of Saipan while, in France, our troops were fighting their way into St. Lo. It was easy to feel I was taking some small part in this global buttwhomp. Everybody on Project Pancho felt sure that, after Ben made his report, they'd have to clear us for those all-important flight trials to forty thousand feet. Maybe that very day!

That's why everybody but Mickey—and Ben, of course—showed up at the wetback hangar early. We all rolled Pancho outside, though a pair of us could've done it alone, and took extra care filling the peroxide tank. Bub, wearing his high lace-up boots with his gloves stuffed into his old flight jacket, helped me preflight Pancho.

Mickey leaned his bike against the hangar wall a little before nine and came inside wearing an expression I couldn't translate. When Bub asked me to fire Pancho up and get the oil properly warmed, I just about busted my buttons with pride, and Mickey hauled his little stand out for me. In the cockpit I ran up the Ranger little by little and fiddled with the controls, pretending I was Bub shooting down a stratospheric bomber—but I shut her down when the gauges told me to and strolled into the shop, where Bub was checking his chute harness.

That's where we were when the phone rang and as acting project leader, Bub answered. You could see the set of his shoulders droop as he talked. Nobody else breathed.

It was Ullmer, calling from Ohio, and while he had to talk carefully on the phone, his news was not good. Listening to Bub, I gathered that Sunday afternoon they'd told Ben to proceed with the next phase, which we knew would be the stratosphere runs. Then Sunday night, before the flight back, the Pentagon sent a classified bulletin of some kind, and everything changed. They pulled Ben off the Wright Field flight line, all excited and secretive. Something happened just now, they said; hold everything.

Ben waited in a Wright Field ready room with a team he recognized as technical guys from Wolverine Aero, though they didn't mingle. A lot of coffee got drunk up, everybody tense.

Sometime after dawn they got hauled off again to different meetings. The upshot was, Pancho's next phase got canceled. Not delayed; *canceled*. Ben guessed from the gloomy looks that Wolverine's team got the same treatment. Bub listened a while longer, and didn't say much more, but meanwhile he took off his flight jacket.

When Bub Merrill put down that receiver he looked like he wanted to cry. "Gents," he said softly, "we've got the day off. Ben won't be back 'til tomorrow, but he says he's never worked with a better team. I won't tell you what that means, but you can guess."

Roy Dee spoke first, always thinking a step ahead. "We'll have to drain that hellbrew outa Pancho," he said.

Bub thought it over. "No, I'll use it up on some taxi runs and lock up the hangar, if Kurt will stay a while and help. That's still on the current phase of testing if I say so. You boys go have a few bottles of Pearl, if that's your poison."

I hadn't been on any previous military programs, so I wasn't sure how serious this was until I saw Sparks and Howard packing up

the stuff at their workstations, quiet but reserved. It looked like
they didn't expect to be working there anymore. Mickey kept tossing quick looks at me and Bub, without saying anything. But after
the other mechanics left, the little guy said, "I'll leave your bike
outside for you."

"It's yours, Mickey," I said. "Nothing's changed that."

"I think I'll have to go soon," he said, in what I'd later recognize
as the understatement of the century.

"I think we all will, but that bike is yours, little bud," I said.

After some sad handshakes, though we expected to see the other
guys the next day, the shop emptied, leaving Bub and me with
Mickey. As we waved Roy Dee off outside, I saw an orange dot
disappearing into the sky, climbing fast, sliding westward on the
wind. The meteorology crew was already driving away from their
radiosonde shack. I had a sudden overpowering sense that we were
the only people left in the world.

Not for long, though. Lost in my own thoughts, I began to pack
some of my personal tools. I hadn't been back in the shop five
minutes before I heard someone near say, "He doesn't know. Tell
him."

I said, "Who doesn't know what," and looked around. Bub was
away in the hangar, and through the window I could see Mickey
outside playing with The Major, which was pretty tame now. Who
the heck? Goose pimples again.

Then I saw the brilliant yellow flash of Major Dylan's Cord as it
turned toward the hangar, and I forgot that voice, a stranger's but
somehow familiar, that I'd heard before. I felt in my pocket. The
photocopy was there.

Bub came into the shop from the hangar as Major Dylan entered
from the outside door. "Boy, it's always something, isn't it," the
officer said with a glum shake of his head. "Those damn' radio tubes
have been held up."

Pancho's radio was on the fritz. I think it was frequency crystals,
not tubes, we needed. Mickey came sidling in holding our tame
armadillo like a kitten.

Bub took it all in. Generally the most decent guy you'd want to meet, he was already peevish. "Mickey, why don't you let The Major go, or take him with you wherever you're headed," he said.

Dylan frowned. "Let me go? What the hell are you talking about?"

"The armadillo," I said quickly. "That's his name: The Major."

Dylan peered closely at the critter Mickey held. "I thought they were dangerous," he said. Mickey backed out of the shop.

"They are," I said. "They're useless as tits on a boar hog. They make a whole career just scratchin' around lookin' busy. But you know how you see 'em squashed on the highway? They'll run alongside and sideswipe you at night, run you plumb off the road, leave you for dead. Sometimes they misjudge, though. That's why we call this one The Major, even if we didn't paint him yellow."

Dylan didn't move a muscle for long seconds. Bub blinked at me as if I'd starting spouting Swahili. Then Dylan smiled at Bub. "The kid's gone fucking crazy," he said, giving me the squint eye.

Bub's glance was still full of wonderment but, "Makes perfect sense to me," he said.

"I just dropped by to tell you, and I told you," Dylan said, turning. "You wanta watch your mouth, kid," he told me. I believe he actually thought he could bluff this one out.

"And you want to watch who you hit-and-run," I said, wishing my voice didn't shake. "I didn't want to do anything that might goof up the project, but that's all over, I reckon." As Dylan stopped, I added to Bub, "Somebody saw this son of a buck and Mister Kevin Ireland, Esquire, with their heads together in Austin, and he got sideswiped on the highway for it. Those two try real hard not to be seen together, and if you do, they'll try and smear you."

Bub cocked his head at Dylan, but just said, "That so?"

Dylan said, "I'll put that down to childish notions. Does my Cord look like it's been in a car smashup?" Then as he saw me pull the folded photo out, he sneered, "What's that, a homemade subpoena?"

Whatever that was. "You'll wish it wasn't what it is," I said, handed it to him, and turned to Bub. "It's proof he's just had that yella dog of his repaired and repainted in Austin after hitting an Indian motorcycle. I've got more proofs, too."

"Well, I be damn," Bub marveled. Without any hurry, he reached for his jacket and pulled his gloves from it. He was putting them on as Dylan, starting to sweat, folded the photo up and began tearing it in pieces. "And all for nothing," said Bub. "Guess you haven't heard our project got canceled early this morning. Don't figure on going anywhere, Major. Kurt, you want to hand me the phone?"

Major Dylan's hand took me in the gizzard like the end of a four-by-four as he grabbed the telephone by its vertical stalk and ripped it away from the desk, wires and all. "This what you wanted," he said, and threw it at Bub. I leaned against the wall doubled over and tried to draw breath, but I couldn't.

Our pilot ducked, but didn't advance. I guess he was more interested in clearing up details. "What I wanted was to believe you were just useless and not a saboteur," he said. "I couldn't figure where you got all the cash you throw around. You're no cardsharp. But Ireland has one skill: He knows how to spend other people's money. How much did he spend getting you to delay a war project competing with his, Major Ath-hole Dylan?"

"That's Ayth-ull, you Texas redneck," Dylan flared.

"I know an ath-hole when I thee one," Bub went on, savoring his lisp, and took a step forward.

Dylan licked his lips and tried once more. "Look, it's not sabotage. Anyway, I'm a patriot. I didn't even agree to talk to Ireland 'til I could see the invasion was a success. I'm not stupid. At worst, I may have screwed off a little." He put his hand in his pocket.

"Maybe attempted murder a little," Bub reminded him. "Your trouble is, you were just smart enough to get yourself shot after all this gets cleared up. Nobody can kid himself like a smart guy, Major. In wartime they have firing squads for this." And he took another step.

"Goddamn feather merchants," Dylan gritted, and I give him credit for the guts to meet an older man halfway. Still out of breath, I grabbed a scungy old coffee cup, but it flew past Dylan's head.

For a man in his forties Bub got in a couple of good licks, but Dylan's right hand was full of something shiny now and my friend went down hard under a clubbing overhand right. I managed to grab an oak chair and stepped forward, swinging it around and over. It fetched up against Dylan's shoulder as he stamped on Bub's gloved hand while trying for his head, which just about made me crazy, and the impact swung Dylan half-around and the chair came apart, leaving me holding only its back and two legs so I was able to swing it around again and I reckon the son of a bitch figured half an oak chair beat what he held because he ducked away panicked and was out the door in a second, and he missed me with the set of brass knuckles he flung my way.

Papers and broken cups and a coffeepot and pieces of chair were underfoot, so I was late limping outside, still armed with what looked like a short oak ladder in my hands. Instead of jumping straight to his car, Dylan made for poor skinny little Mickey Hernandez, grabbing him up under one arm like a big doll. "I'll do him if you come after me," he snarled at me, dropping into the driver's seat and reaching toward his glove compartment, and then he made the ugliest sound I ever heard, like he was gagging.

He tried to leap up from his seat with our tiny hangar rat draped across his shoulder, and I knew Mickey's little monkey paws were strong, but what I saw was beyond belief. While one little brown hand gripped Dylan's hair, the other clamped into his throat; *way* into it. Dylan made another sound, half gurgle, half sigh, and his face started turning red and instead of hitting at Mickey he tried to pull the little guy's hands loose.

Mickey let himself be flung away across the roadster's sloping turtleback and scrambled down backward unhurt, his eyes round and fixed on this big scutter who had roughed him up. "Can you help him," was all he said when he was on his feet.

I didn't answer and I wasn't about to get too close while a guy who didn't like me, twice my size, was having himself a wild conniption. Dylan managed to stand, clawing at his throat, then flopped forward draped over his windshield and rolled onto his back. His neck was bleeding heavily from his own fingernails, his face an unlikely shade of maroon, and it was clear that he wasn't getting any air. His arms lost their strength, then his legs, and finally he slid down onto the doorframe faceup, his eyes open and blinking. It smelled like he'd soiled his pants.

"I can't do that. It's a crime," said the horrified Mickey.

"No it's not, you were just protecting yourself," I said, dropping the chairback to step near the major, who only twitched.

"Yes it is, no matter what. You don't understand our ethics," said Mickey in despair. I knew the word, but it wasn't one I'd ever expected out of a little kid.

I reached over and felt Dylan's chest. Then I wiped my hand on my pants. "Heart's beating," I said. "Mickey, how did you do that?" As I watched, the bleeding from Dylan's throat stopped.

"Scared." That wasn't what I meant, and it didn't seem like much of an answer to how you crush a man's throat. "He intended to kill us anyway. I knew in the night I'd have to go today, but I really have to go now," he added. "His heart stopped."

How could he know what the major intended? And if Mickey could know his heart had stopped pumping without being able to see Dylan's throat from where he stood, he was stranger than any little kid had a right to be. A whole slew of scary suspicions hit me at once that I wouldn't have had if I didn't read the magazines I did. "They'd ask me questions," he said, shaking his head, backing away. He turned and ran for the bike. "They'd bring doctors. No," he said.

But this last, he didn't say with his mouth. "You're not some little kid living with his mama," I accused.

"I volunteered for a project," he said. "We want to prevent a terrible mistake." His reply didn't sound like it was in my head, but it was. Mickey grabbed up his bike like it was a tumbleweed, easier than Fred Moller could've lifted it, and leaped on it. I swear his rear tire chirped from the power he applied.

I didn't want to touch Dylan again. I'm not sure why my eyes teared up then, maybe it was just seeing such a big good-looking healthy horse of a guy like him staring sightless up at the hot summer sky. Then I saw Bub Merrill lean into the doorway, holding one hand with the other, and I ran to him.

I wanted to drive Bub to get help for his broken fingers but he said he could manage. Besides, he reminded me, that would have left a secret project abandoned with Pancho sitting on the taxiway. As Bub drove away one-handed, I thought again of the way Mickey could talk to me. "Don't run, Mickey," I called, though he was nowhere in sight. "Can you hear me?"

His reply was faint but clear. "Not from very far. If you tell, no one will believe you."

Boy, that was no lie! I worried about what he might do if he got panicky again, and I was suddenly filled with questions. "What were you really doing here?"

Very faint now: "Watching, reporting. Helping when I—" Then nothing, and I realized there was a limit to his range, like a little Army walkie-talkie. I went into the shop and tried to fix the telephone cord to call somebody, anybody, but the receiver was broken, too. Surely Bub Merrill would tell somebody to come out to our remote hangar, though that might take a while.

My bandanna had seen better days, but I put it over the major's face to keep dust out of his eyes and mouth, I don't know why. And yep, in the Cord's glove compartment I saw a little automatic pistol, smaller than Army issue. I started pondering how Mickey usually seemed to know what folks around him were thinking. That was one of the things I'd be smart not to talk about. If my body temperature had been as feverish as his all the time, I wouldn't have wanted people to touch me much either—another don't-say-it.

And that acetone on his breath? That usually meant one thing, but in Mickey's case it could've meant another. Acetone—chocolate too, once I thought about it—might be as good an energy source as alcohol or gasoline, and the hangar had plenty of it. Did he drink the stuff? If he didn't have a mama nearby, he must've answered my note himself. No wonder his note had said not to put him in

front of a doctor—a human doctor, that is. I leaned against the Cord
and hoped the MPs would show up soon, wondering what I'd say
when they did. Mickey had been gone nearly an hour while I fiddled with the phone and waited.

And then I saw the radiosonde balloons. Not one, but three in
a tight cluster, drifting across overhead several hundred feet up and
rising like somebody was chasing them. I've always had twenty-
twelve vision, like my dad, and I could see the frame of a bike
without wheels slung under those balloons. I don't need to say who
was perched on the seat, holding on, and it explained why Mickey
might have hung around the meteorology shack on early mornings.

"Mickey," I shouted, "listen to me. Those balloons will take you
so high you'll pass out. Do you hear me? You'll fall."

"No I will not," was the reply, as sure of himself as if he were
standing beside me. "Don't worry, Kurt Rahm. I will go away as
soon as I have enough distance from your airfield. And you do not
need to shout," he added, as if I'd said something funny.

"I know better than to tell about this," I said. "Where did you
come from?"

"Far off."

"I have a million questions."

"I hear them. No, no one can know who will win, and we must not
fight directly. But if you do not win your war soon, we fear—" His
voice growing faint as before, then I heard only the breeze.

I shouted anyway. "Mickey! When those balloons get high
enough, it won't matter whether you let go. They pop. Mickey,
got-dammit, they pop!" What he'd been saying scared me. What
could his people fear? And if he fell from eight or ten miles high,
someone might find his body in the wreckage. He might not have
thought about that. Had he counted on a water landing? The prevailing wind wasn't taking him toward the Gulf of Mexico. To the
northwest, the direction he was going, there wasn't any water for
a thousand miles bigger than a rancher's stock tank.

I had two perfect reasons for trying to save him, one for his sake
and one for ours. A handgun like Dylan's wasn't any good beyond
a hundred feet, though if I'd had a rifle I might possibly have been

able to deflate one balloon so that he'd drift down slowly under the others. Tough as he was, that might save him. Maybe he'd thought of deflating one. Maybe not. He had already shown me that he didn't always do exactly the right thing when push came to shove. After all, he was only human. Well, almost.

It came to me then that, without a rifle, there was one and only one possible way I could still pop one of those balloons and save our gutsy little hangar rat. I could even wait until he was beyond San Antonio before I did it. And maybe get a question answered that was so important, it was worth ruining my career in aeronautics.

If I did it now, I might not be able to find him in that huge cloud-spotted Texas sky anyway. If I didn't, I flat-ass sure couldn't help him; not ever. And I thought—and still think to this day—he saved my bacon when Dylan was reaching for his pistol. That was all the goad I needed.

I was out of breath when I kicked the chocks away from Pancho's wheels and pulled the control locks off the ailerons. There was no time to go back and try to adjust Bub's chute harness to fit me. I had no radio either, but I had the hottest-climbing aircraft ever built in America. If I could take off from the taxiway, and locate that cluster of oranges again, and get close enough, my prop tips could rip through a balloon like it was a spiderweb.

I might even get Pancho back in one piece.

My run-up was brief because the oil was still half-warm, and also because I saw the dust devil of an Army jeep headed hell for leather toward the hangar. I sealed the canopy while taxiing and managed to cinch my straps, trying to recall the tidbits Bub had mentioned in casual debriefings.

Like any race plane with wings like afterthoughts, Pancho needed a lot of speed to take off and had tires too small to do it in comfort. I kept craning my neck to spot Mickey until I felt the rudder begin to work, giving me some control in what would have to be a slight crosswind takeoff. And as I eased the throttle farther forward, the props became less than a blur, acceleration pressing my head back against the headrest, and when I firewalled Pancho that Godhelpus peroxide turbine kicked in, and the shriek of contrarotating props met a hissing thunder from the belly's steam rocket boost and the airspeed indicator needle jumped like *I'd scared it*. That crosswind? I never noticed it.

In seconds I was so far beyond Bub's recommended takeoff speed I had only to ease back on the stick for Pancho to leap off the taxiway, and I needed a moment to find the gear-up toggle because I had never thought about using it. I got three thumps and green lights, spent a moment checking the sky, and nearly passed out from shock when I saw the needle sweeping past 250 knots. Randolph's perimeter fence was a thread far below, and I was headed in the wrong direction without clearance from the tower with who knew how many cadets piddling around in my way. Pancho's rearview mirror was mounted near the forward canopy lip left of center. It showed no hint of orange.

Scanning above and to my right I saw only one plane, a Vultee trainer, and I banked sharply intending to do it gently. With that much power, things happened a lot faster. Pancho carried me up and around so far, so fast, the altimeter seemed to be lagging, and from this day on skyrockets would be kid stuff. Ya-HOO, San-An-Tone and Luckenbach!

Soon I thought I'd be nearing Mickey's altitude, which I judged might be eight thousand by now, maybe ten, and the northwest edge of San Antonio slid below as my airspeed climbed to 350. This was completely out of my experience, but I had no time to be scared about that. What scared me now was, I saw no sign of Mickey, and with my speed still rising, I horsed back on the stick and traded airspeed for altitude.

Not until the altimeter showed fifteen thousand did I realize I was starting to breathe faster, too fast. I throttled back with the stick between my knees and fumbled for the rubber oxy mask Bub had folded into the map pocket near my right leg, its corrugated tubing hanging loose. By the time I got it connected to the oxygen supply I had spots of black dancing in my vision, and I must have spent more time than I thought getting the mask straps adjusted.

Maybe it didn't help to shout, but I did, and it sounded strange to me with the mask over my nose and mouth. "Mickey, I'm coming to help. Come in, Mickey!" I kept saying it, banking clockwise again, scanning between the fluffy little cotton-tops of cloud three miles up that could hide him, or another plane, until too late. I'll say this: If Pancho couldn't dodge in time, nothing could.

With my right wing dipped I could see the thread of a highway passing through a small town northwest of the city; it had to be Boerne. No longer worried about oxygen starvation, I kicked Pancho's pants again and sent her howling up to twenty-five thousand, spiraling to keep from leaving the region. Logic told me Mickey was a slave to the wind, and it could not have taken him this far away in such a short time.

So I knew I had overshot him, maybe in altitude as well as range. It was then that I had the sense to know I'd have a better chance of seeing that orange cluster against hard blue than against the differing hues of ranchland. I banked again toward the distant clutter of rectangles that was San Antonio, pushed the stick forward, and bulleted earthward until Pancho began to shudder. My airspeed was past redline, over five hundred knots, when I eased back and the shudder lessened to nothing and now I was below fifteen thousand feet, scanning up at the blue and patchy white with the city limits not far off. I resumed with, "Come in, Mickey," throttling back like a sane person and repeating it with less hope every moment.

Until, ". . . kill yourself, dear fool. Go away. How can I leave with you near? Yes, keep going. Land that amazing toy and—"

And nothing. He'd been near for a few seconds; maybe he could see me. I tightened my bank, throttled back, and used cloudlets to orient me back to a volume of airspace I had just left, climbing slightly. Pancho didn't like to fly any way but hot, like they said of a Gee Bee. I didn't know how, or if, I could handle her if I got into a spin. Good Idea Number One, my first in a while: Don't get into a spin.

It was then I spotted the orange tint on dirty white, a reflection on a piece of cloud, and thanked God and Mr. Bell for a winged bullet that could maneuver as tightly as Pancho. With my airspeed down around two hundred, in a very shallow climb while banking,

I put myself in a corkscrew orbit around the balloons I saw emerging between small clouds, now standing out against the blue. "Gotcha," I said. We watched each other as I circled. He had something like a knapsack, only smaller, hanging at his side from his neck.

His shirt was torn all to tatters. Because his skinny little chest was swollen as big as Fred Moller's. "Yes, I adapt to altitude," he said. "You were not to see this."

"Shut up, Mickey, and listen. If I can fly by and pop one balloon, you'll come down gently out in the country. Or sooner or later all the balloons will pop. That's what I was trying to—"

"Shut up yourself, Kurt Rahm. When I say I will leave, I mean suddenly in a way I chose weeks ago, and safely. But anything nearby will not be safe, and the sound wave—You do not want to be anywhere near, Kurt Rahm. And I do not want another man's life, yours above all. Please."

I had a sudden surge of hope. "Is that a chute of some kind you're carrying?"

"No, but it is what I need. Do not ask."

"Okay. But you owe me this one. It's why I came."

"No it is not. You would lie to me, Kurt Rahm? But your question worries you. It worries us, too."

"Then tell me," I begged. A peek at my altimeter said we were at twenty thousand feet, gradually moving back toward Boerne.

"Last night, with one of us, brave men destroyed the bombers your enemy hoped to send with a terrible weapon. No more bombers; no more need for Pancho. I may be sent to help somewhere else because if you win soon, your people may cancel a program that is terribly expensive and a huge mistake. We cannot see the future. We can only try to help you create a good one."

"What mistake? You have to tell me!"

"I must not. If men are lucky, you may never know. It is the same weapon your enemy hoped for. It promises, and lies. In other places it has destroyed entire peoples, sooner or later." His words held the earnestness of a revival preacher.

To tell the truth, it sort of pissed me off. "You know about it, but you expect us to drop it?"

"It is not too late. We were lucky. We first developed other, safer advanced ways to use energy. Ways that helped us explore but did not let a few of us endanger us all. Now please go away. Please!"

"I will," I said, "if you'll tell me a safer way."

With a return of something like humor, he said, "You will hold yourself hostage? You are surely one of your people. Very well: Study amplified light and radio waves. And now I am in very serious trouble. Go; *please!*"

"A deal's a deal," I said, and did an aileron roll because—well, because I could. "I hope you know what you're doing. Take it easy, Mickey."

Faintly, as I continued my climb, I heard: "Good-bye, little bud. We love you. But go!"

I recall grinning as I firewalled the throttle into another rocketing climb because Mickey had called *me* "little bud," when he was no bigger than a Packard's hood ornament. I straightened Pancho out to keep that blob of orange in my rearview as it dwindled to a dot, maybe a mile behind, when it was, instantly,

gone

I blinked and looked again. Still gone, and so was a segment of cloud near his location, a concave missing segment as if some invisible ball the size of a dirigible hangar had shouldered the cloud aside, and as I watched the remains of the cloud shattered, then rushed streaming back into the void, and another bit of cloud nearer behind me tore into confetti, which meant something I couldn't see was gaining on my race plane.

When the shock wave passed, it jolted Pancho so hard I got a whiplash, and I've heard thunder that loud but only once when I was a kid and the lightning bolt hit so near it created a warning sound like an artillery shell.

Bub Merrill had intended to do some more tests, and originally it included a climb to forty thousand feet. As long as I expected to be sent to Huntsville Prison, I figured on making it worth our while and the peroxide-tank gauge showed a third full. I didn't dare risk a bad landing with any of it still on board.

It turns out I had spent so much of the stuff chasing Mickey the tank went empty when Pancho was at thirty-eight thousand, the cockpit so cold that frost was collecting inside the canopy. So I never knew whether Project Pancho could actually put a prop-driven interceptor at forty thousand. But there was no question of it in my mind.

Getting that little bugger safely on the ground was mostly a problem in tactics because, with the stubby wing below and ahead of me, any landing would be part mystery and part Braille. I asked for clearance the way we did at airports without towers: flying around, waggling my wings, and waiting for a green light. After I got the green at Randolph I knew they'd warn other air traffic by radio, and I had upwards of two miles of real runway to land on. I almost did it with wheels up, but that's what warning horns are for, and with my fanny chewing washers out of the seat cushion I came in hot just above the perimeter fence and then let her settle. It was the worst landing I ever made, three bounces, but the great thing about the wetback hangar was, it was off near the end of the runway.

I was plumb out of spit by then. They tell me I shut Pancho down and climbed out alone before anyone got to me. I wouldn't know.

NINE

With all the medical teams stationed at Randolph Field to meet casualties airlifted from France, Bub Merrill found help right away. That's how come he was driving back to help me straighten out the mess with the major when he saw me taxiing toward the hangar. "Took me only an hour to figure out it wasn't me in there," he told me later, with Dutch-uncle sarcasm, after they found me near the plane sitting glassy-eyed on Mickey's little workstand.

He got some MPs to guard Pancho, and if he talked much to me while he walked me to the hangar with a bandaged hand over my shoulder, I don't remember it. I remember slopping RC Cola over my shirt as Bub helped me drink it from a coffee cup in the hangar. The Army officers around us didn't seem all that peeved at me. I understood why when I got my trembles under control and heard Bub say, "Were you afraid Major Dylan's friends would sabotage the plane if you didn't save it?" He was giving me an excuse, if I'd take it.

Coward that I was, I took it, nodding. Since all three officers were military cops and not pilots, and I was a licensed civilian pilot, they zeroed in on questions about the major. Bub stood by, trying to look friendly though I could see he wanted to punt me over the

perimeter fence. When I told about Dylan tearing up the photocopy, a captain said he'd found it on the floor and pieced it together.
Bub had already given his version of that, and a team was en route
to check on the Cord repair job paid for by Kevin Ireland.

I told the captain he might send another guy to Mr. Eugen
Moller's shop to get the rest of the story, since they probably
wouldn't get much from the crash victim. A lieutenant asked me
if the chairback near the Cord was what I used to crush Dylan's
throat, and I said it might be, but I wasn't sure. "It all happened
pretty fast. He was gonna shoot us, I think," I said, and I guess they
thought by "us" I meant me and Bub. They'd found the pistol, too,
and another lieutenant was taking notes. It wasn't long before they
told us not to worry and took off, one of them driving the Cord,
which I never saw again, or cared to.

Bub opened a Hires and sat on the edge of a desk and speared
me with a firm look. "You are one lucky son of a buck," he said. I
nodded. "How could I ever trust you again?" I shook my head.
"Why? What in creation were you thinking?"

Tell him the truth? Not in a jillion years. "It was an accident," I
began, trying to build a story that he'd accept. "You'd said you were
gonna do some taxi runs to use up the peroxide, but when you left
I thought MPs might take me away later; you know how those guys
are. I didn't trust anybody else to fiddle with Pancho. Blow himself
to smithereens."

"So you were gonna taxi up and down like a hot-rodder?"

If he'd buy that, I'd let him. Now and then a pilot does take off
before he intends to, and I claimed that's what happened to me. I
cranked my b.s. spigot on full force and sprayed poor Bub all over
with it, saying I was scared to risk landing hard on a taxiway with
that deadly tankful of stuff sloshing around, and once I was flying,
all I had to do was keep boring holes in the sky until the tank was
empty.

"Well, it worked," he said at last, "but don't—you—*ever,*—oh,
hell, never mind. Far as I'm concerned, it never happened." He
looked around. "Where's our hangar rat? Not that I'm too keen on
having folks know he was underfoot so much."

"After the way the major treated him? I'll be surprised if he comes back for a while. He took off," I said. "On my bike." There was my understatement for the season.

I helped pickle Pancho for storage after Ben Ullmer got back, and Ben's recommendation got me another project at Kelly Field. I learned that during the night of July 16, French saboteurs got into the Latecoere factory in Toulouse and blew those prototype Nazi bombers to shreds, exactly as Mickey had told me. How he kept abreast of all that is beyond me. I don't even know where he slept, or *if* he slept.

And I didn't know for over a year about the weapon project near Alamogordo in New Mexico, the most expensive weapon of the war and the one the Nazis were hoping to build. But I saved every cent I could and in September of '45, after Elke got married, I hightailed it to Cal Poly for a degree in aero engineering.

Mr. Kevin Ireland was never convicted of anything, but Wolverine Aero never got another contract either. Last I heard, he was in bankruptcy proceedings.

Fred Moller wouldn't believe what anybody said about his hero, and quit talking to me. I wrote him a few times from school. He never answered.

I met Ben Ullmer a few times over the years at seminars. He stuck with aero research and development, projects he couldn't talk about. Always gliding along the cutting edge, he collected the papers I wrote on laser propulsion. Last time we met he told me Bub Merrill had gone West after retiring to Kerrville, not far from San Antonio.

Forget Mickey's last tip? Not likely. At Cal Poly I ran across scientific work on amplifying light and radiation, including one by Einstein back in 1917. I switched to physics at CalTech in the fifties, married an architect, did some work with Hughes, and managed to contribute when maser energy developed into lasers. The longer I live, the clearer it seems that Mickey was right about safer ways to use great whopping gobs of energy.

Before I retired I concluded that we can reach the stars propelled by amplified light—high-energy lasers—and with better fortune we might have done it without nuclear energy. It was just bad luck that the war lasted long enough that we took the nuclear energy option. I live outside Alpine now, in west Texas. I'm sure some of us will escape the mistake Mickey was so afraid we'll make, sooner or later.

| FLAME AT TARAWA |

BARRETT TILLMAN

BARRETT TILLMAN is the author of four novels, including *Hell-cats*, which was nominated for the Military Novel of the Year in 1996, twenty nonfiction historical and biographical books, and more than 400 military and aviation articles in American, European, and Pacific Rim publications. He received his bachelor's degree in journalism from the University of Oregon in 1971 and spent the next decade writing freelance articles. He later worked with the Champlain Museum Press and as the managing editor of *The Hook* magazine. In 1989 he returned to freelance writing and has been at it ever since. His military nonfiction has been critically lauded and garnered him several awards, including the U.S. Air Force's Historical Foundation Award, the Nautical & Oceanographic Society's Outstanding Biography Award, and the Arthur Radford Award for Naval History and Achievement. He is also an honorary member of the Navy fighter squadrons VF-111 and VA-35. He lives and works in Mesa, Arizona.

ONE

I knew I was alive because I hurt so much. My nose and mouth held a horrible contagion of smell and taste that would have been unimaginable anywhere else on earth. Dimly, with effort, I sought to recall anything comparable in my twenty years. Nothing came close.

Through the throbbing in my brain I absorbed the absolute misery of my situation. Somehow—it wasn't at all clear—I had awoken to the wretched realization of my predicament before. Maybe more than once. Evidently I couldn't deal with it for more than several minutes at a time.

My stomach turned over again; I tried to vomit up whatever churned inside me, but nothing came. Only the dry heaves. The previous contents of my stomach were already strewn on my dungaree jacket or crusted on my mouth and chin. I gagged and choked out a small amount of saliva, but by now I had none to spare. If I'd been able to think more clearly, I'd have recognized the early stages of dehydration.

I groped around for something useful. My 782 gear—web belt with pistol, magazines, and canteens—was gone, evidently ditched during the past day or so. We flamethrower operators didn't carry packs because the sixty-pound M1A1 was all we could manage.

God in heaven, I need water. Just a little water . . .

I couldn't control my legs, but they twitched involuntarily in another spasm. I heard the splash of my spatted feet. Then the irony occurred to me: I was lying in water, about three inches deep. It was foul, putrid, awful. I lacked the ability or strength to move out of it.

At least I was out of the sun—the damnable equatorial sun, which made the coral sand so hot that you couldn't tolerate lying on it. But you had to, if you were on any of the four landing beaches of Betio Island in Tarawa Atoll during the third week of November in the Year of Our Lord Nineteen Hundred and Forty-three. If you stood up, you got nailed by a Jap sniper or stitched by a Jap machine gunner. If you stayed down, you still could get killed by a shell or grenade. Like Gunny Crouch said: If the direct fire don't kill you, the indirect fire will.

Okay, I was out of the sun. But that meant I was confined within the walls of some . . . place. What? Where was I? It was fairly dark, the only open spot visible to me being the large, irregular hole in the roof of—what? *Well, don't matter much. It's obviously a well-built place 'cause there's rebar sticking out of the cement, with coconut logs and sand or coral on top. Must be nearly impossible to see from the air. But the thick walls trap the heat. God a'mighty, it's hot, almost can't breathe.* I opened my mouth more and tried to suck in some oxygen. A futile effort—I inhaled the horrible smell again. *What the hell is it?*

Lying on my back, I squirmed in the polluted water, trying to find drier ground. I bumped into something spongy soft, lodged against my shoulders. With my heels braced in the muddy pool, I shoved backward on my elbows. I was so damn weak that I lacked the will to turn my head and identify the obstruction. Something flopped beside my left shoulder. In the dim light I thought I recognized a hand, minus two fingers.

God, I'm hallucinating. I closed my eyes, shook my head a little, trying to focus. When I looked again the mutilated hand was still there. It was attached to an arm that was mostly attached to a torso.

Gradually it dawned on me: I was up against a dead Jap, one of the naval infantrymen defending Betio against the Second Marine Division. He was what I was smelling—he and his pal. About ten feet away was the corpse of another *rikusentai*, wearing a shredded light green uniform. Even in semidarkness his face was a ghoulish Halloween mask. Both bodies were bloated in the extreme heat. Given much longer, they'd burst the confines of their remaining clothes.

I passed out again.

TWO

I only joined the Corps to impress my old man. By today's terms he was dysfunctional: a boozer who couldn't or wouldn't hold a full-time job. Heaven knows it was hard enough finding regular work during the Depression, but he seldom tried. The rest of us— my mother, two sisters, and I—did what we could to take up the slack, and somehow we scraped by. So did our entire generation— the one that somebody called the Greatest. Hell, we weren't the greatest. We just did what we had to do.

I didn't have to go to Tarawa.

In fact, I didn't have to be in the Corps. As an only son I could've remained exempt, especially since I was my mom's main bread-winner. Karen was married to a decent enough guy, but they had a baby of their own; Suzie was still in bobby sox and pigtails. Later I realized she had to be an "oops" since she was six years younger than me. Anyway, my mother understood me. When I told her I wanted to enlist she didn't try very hard to talk me out of it. She just asked why. I think that I looked over her shoulder—I was a good-sized kid for eighteen—and said something about doing the right thing. She knew what I meant. Besides, with a deferred entry I wouldn't be drafted by the damn Army.

Dad had been in the Army in the "First War," before we had so many that we started numbering them. In retrospect, I think he was embarrassed about his military service because after he died, I finally saw his discharge papers. He'd been gilding the lily for a lot of years with talk about France and Kaiser Bill. He'd been in a railroad supply outfit that arrived about a month before the armistice was signed in 1918. I was born five years later, two years after Karen. Anyway, he had an album with some clippings that included Floyd Gibbons's reports from Belleau Wood with the Fifth and Sixth Marines, which won a fighting reputation there. My old man was impressed; so was I.

After Pearl Harbor I was all pumped up to join the Marines—"first to fight." We knew about Wake Island, and we saw the movie with Brian Donlevy and William Bendix: "Send us more Japs." Man, that was for me—lemme at 'em. Suzie insisted I only joined because of the dress blues, and I don't mind saying that I was a pretty good-looking youngster with my cover set at a killing angle and a breezy confidence that I didn't really feel. Besides, a big brother wants to look good for his kid sister.

Boot camp was not like anything I'd experienced before. Yes, life was tough in the 1930s, but being part of a family made a big difference. At MCRD San Diego my family was a platoon full of fellow recruits and a couple of sadists with stripes: Sergeant Connelly and Corporal Unger. Their first job was to make us terrified of them; they succeeded. Next they began teaching us, as Connelly said, "The easy way or the hard way, but you *will* learn the Marine Corps way." Hands-on instruction was normal, expected. You couldn't get away with it today.

A few years ago I read about "stress cards" so recruits can take a time-out like misbehaving kindergarten kids. You want to know about stress? Tarawa was stress. DIs might still yell at recruits today, but can't swear at them, let alone manhandle them. Wouldn't I like to hear what Connelly and Unger would say about *that*! I didn't like them much—Unger left bruises on my upper arms when I was snapping in with the M1 rifle—but after Tarawa I damn sure appreciated them.

Somebody—maybe a Roman—said, "The more you sweat in peace, the less you bleed in war." He must have been a Marine.

The key to understanding newly minted Marines is that they want to be regulation, squared away, salty. Of course, the only way to become salty is to log sea miles. Some would even dunk their covers (hats to civilians) in salt water so the green cloth and the metal adornments took on a nautical cast.

The Corps took about six hundred thousand people during the war, and I heard that about 97 percent went overseas. Almost exclusively, that meant the Pacific. (General Marshall, the Army chief of staff, would not permit a Marine in Europe. Like most Army officers of the Great War, he resented the hell out of us.) Some Marines were drafted, but the huge majority volunteered, for a variety of reasons both sacred and profane. Patriotism was a big part of it, but hell—anybody in uniform was considered patriotic. Most of the Army troops were drafted, and the Department of Veterans Affairs says the average age was twenty-six. Marines, on the other hand, were younger, leaner, meaner. More motivated, I guess.

I knew a few guys who joined because of the uniform. Dress blues were *the* sexiest outfit going—at least that's what some recruiters said. Maybe it was the choker collar—harkening back to the neck protectors in the War of 1812, hence "leathernecks"—or the red stripe on the trousers. (I'm sure that some recruits were disappointed to learn that only officers and NCOs got the red stripe.) However, in later years I preferred the Dress Blue Bravo option with "tropical long" khaki shirt, dress trousers, and white hat. DIs sometimes wore the same uniform with campaign hat. Man, that was *sharp*, with or without a field scarf. (That's a tie to you, Mister.) There's no mistaking it—that uniform belongs to a military man. But I remember in the 1990s when the Air Force used sleeve stripes like the navy—a three-striper was a major rather than a commander. Honestly, the first time I saw a USAF officer in that getup, I didn't know what he was. My first impression was an airline pilot. My second impression was a much-decorated bus driver. Finally, the blue-suiters had the good sense to be embarrassed and reverted to the previous system.

Most generals have far too much time on their hands, anyway.

I guess every Marine thinks that he was part of the Old Corps, when it was rough, brother, rough. My cousin's boy was an airborne trooper in Vietnam, and some of what he told me sounded familiar; I could relate to it. Today—forget it. They talk the same talk, but no way do they walk the same walk. In the 1980s when I heard that that the Commandant had approved camouflage *maternity* fatigues, I took off my gold eagle, globe, and anchor lapel pin. I was embarrassed; wouldn't wear it until 10 November the next year. In my era, camouflage was special; it set you apart as a member of an elite, even if it was the *Waffen* SS. Yet today pregnant females wear "cammies."

Recently I read that everybody in the Army now wears a beret because all soldiers are "elite." I'm still waiting for somebody to explain *that* to me. For one thing, a beret is an absurd garment. I'm sorry, in this PC era, but I never saw one that didn't look queer. Beyond that, how in the name of Chesty Puller can *everybody* be elite? If everybody is special, then nobody is.

Every 15 April I still grind my teeth at the thought that *my* tax dollars buy faggoty hats and maternity cammies. The day the Marine Corps issues berets is the day I take off my gold lapel pin. For good.

Until then, Semper Fi.

THREE

I can't tell what I thought and what I think I thought. But lying in that squalid space, lapsing in and out of consciousness, it's certain that I spent some time trying to think pleasant thoughts. Nothing was more pleasant than New Zealand. Nothing before; nothing since.

New Zealand was wonderful. The New Zealanders were even better. Especially Bonnie. Bonnie McKenzie, "A wee bonnie lass," her father insisted. I agreed. Trouble was, he didn't much like me. Well, maybe that's too harsh. I think that Andrew McKenzie did like me in his own way. He just didn't think that a Yank private was good enough for his daughter—not by half.

Bonnie was nineteen, a year younger than I. She had raven hair, blue eyes, and a fair complexion with freckles. We told each other that we were in love, and maybe we were. Several hundred guys in the Second MarDiv married Kiwi girls, and most of the relationships I knew of seemed to take, including those that lasted " 'til death us do part."

The Second Division was based in and around Wellington, mainly at Queen Elizabeth Park. My engineer battalion of the Eighteenth Marines pitched camp at Paikakarika, which I could hardly pronounce. Fortunately, I never had to remember how to write it because our location was classified during those eight months. My family only knew that I was "somewhere in the South Pacific."

I quickly learned that the division was full of experience and talent. We had officers and NCOs from the Old Corps who'd fought bandits in the banana wars, served in China, and a goodly number who'd fought in this war, on Guadalcanal. Our training was entirely practical, blissfully absent of the chicken stuff so common in the military, even in the Corps. Our commanding general, Julian C. Smith, was as fine a leader as the Marines ever produced. He genuinely cared about us, and he was frequently present on maneuvers, standing in his gray raincoat, watching his boys through rain-flecked spectacles.

Other than basic equipment and squad, platoon, and company tactics, we concentrated on two things: physical conditioning and marksmanship. There was a competition among the battalions and within the division generally as to who could hike the farthest the fastest with fewest dropouts. It was a real stigma if you didn't finish a hike—the corpsmen kept busy treating blisters.

We got a lot of trigger time in New Zealand—even built a couple of extra ranges ourselves. Marksmanship was a fetish in the Old Corps, something akin to mysticism. But it was hardly surprising, considering the backgrounds of our leaders. The CO of the Second Battalion, Eighth Marines, Major "Jim" Crowe, had been a warrant officer before the war, a noted rifle coach and match shot. Major General Smith and his chief of staff, Colonel "Red Mike" Edson, also held Distinguished Rifleman ratings. In fact, Edson later was executive director of the NRA. His letter to the mothers of America probably wouldn't get printed today: Basically he said, "Mom, if you want your son to have the best chance of coming home alive, make sure he learns to shoot as a boy."

We engineers didn't shoot as much as the line infantrymen, though if we had, maybe I wouldn't have ended up humping a damned flamethrower. I had qualified as a high Marksman, which still put me in the lower tier of shooters. But if things went right (and of course they never did), we weren't supposed to use rifles very much. Our primary weapons were explosives and bridging equipment. We were expected to blow up obstacles blocking access to landing beaches, demolish enemy strongpoints, and erect crossings of rivers and canyons. All while under enemy fire.

After all, we weren't "the damned engineers" for nothing. The "damned" was less an insult than a curse; we were "damned" because we worked under very tough conditions. But regiment and division expected us to cope with the challenge, and we expected it of ourselves.

A couple of days after I sewed on my first stripe, I was so proud that I insisted on taking the McKenzies to dinner. It just about broke me, but it was worth it. Rationing had been in effect almost four years, but one thing about New Zealand—it has a lot of sheep. I never ever acquired a taste for mutton, but at least I could take Mr. and Mrs. McKenzie and Bonnie to a fairly nice place. My chevron definitely looked better than the previous "slick sleeve" appearance of my uniform blouse, but Andrew McKenzie had little concept of "private first class." He'd been in the home guard for a while, and understood "lance corporal," which sounded better, so I figured it was close enough. Ironically, the Corps adopted the lance corporal (E-3) rank in 1958.

I met Bonnie at a serviceman's club where she worked part-time as a volunteer hostess. Maybe it's the Scots-Irish influence, but it seemed that all the New Zealand girls were pretty, and many were downright beautiful. Naturally, I wasn't the only American she knew or dated, but we hit it off right away, mainly because she really liked to jitterbug. If I say so myself, I knew my way around a dance floor in those days—certainly more than most of the guys, who were issued two left feet. Bonnie and a couple of her galfriends admitted that their own feet took a beating most weekends, so anybody who could shuffle his boondockers in time with the music was ahead of the game.

Looking back, I thought that Bonnie and I had a torrid affair, but it was pretty tame by current standards. We didn't do much more than indulge in occasional (well, okay, frequent) heavy breathing, but she said I was the only one, and I believed her. When the division embarked for Tarawa it was "an understood thing" that we'd resume our romance when I returned. As things turned out, it wasn't possible.

I still think of her now and then.

FOUR

They told us that the Marine Corps didn't have many flamethrowers in late 1943, and the Second Division almost none. Therefore, we got sixty for Tarawa, all from Army stocks in Hawaiian warehouses. Since then I've seen different figures, but evidently no more than a couple of dozen made it ashore. At any rate, our combat engineer battalion assumed the flamethrower mission in addition to everything else: construction, demolition, and the like.

"Flame projectors" were highly useful for "reducing" enemy fortifications such as bunkers and pillboxes. Trouble was, we got them too late in our training cycle to integrate them into the twelve-man rifle squads. Later on, most infantry landing craft "boat teams" had a well-balanced platoon of riflemen, machine gunners, BAR men, explosives crew, and flame team, but that was in the future.

Marines and sailors don't always get along—they're like oil and water. To each other they're "jarheads" and "squids" because while Marines make their living running into machine-gun fire, sailors usually have it easy aboard ship, sleeping on clean sheets and eating hot meals. But there are exceptions, I'll tell you, brother: Seabees are mighty fine people, I learned that on Betio. To watch a bulldozer driver lower his blade and push a ton of coral and sand on top of a Jap bunker, with machine-gun rounds spanging off his cat, fills a leatherneck with admiration.

Then there's corpsmen—what the army calls medics. For some reason I never understood, the Marine Corps doesn't have its own medical personnel. They're all from the Navy, but you couldn't tell us apart on Betio or Saipan or Okinawa. They wear the same uniform, eat the same cold chow, sleep in the same mud, and get killed by the same ordnance. I never once saw a corpsman refuse to advance into fire to treat a wounded Marine. Hell, I don't think I even heard of it. If I ever got a slug of booze on any of those frigging islands, a corpsman could have half of my ration.

Because our flamethrowers were so late in arriving, we had no time to train properly. In fact, I didn't play with one until we sailed from New Zealand, bound for an en route rehearsal at Efate. When Platoon Sergeant Healey informed me of my new status (I was not consulted) I was pretty damn unhappy, not that it mattered. He said that because I only shot Marksman in boot camp, I was less useful as a combat rifleman, so it made good military sense to give me the flame gun. The Sharpshooters and exalted Experts got M1 Garands and BARs instead of flamethrowers, mortar tubes, or Browning heavy machine guns.

As a PFC I was designated a "flame gunner" with an assistant who carried a five-gallon jerry can of extra fuel, nitrogen propellant tank, and tools, plus his basic load with an M1 carbine. With my shoulders protesting beneath the weight of my burden I made damn sure that Private Dean, my A-gunner, also humped my shelter half, K-rats, and other gear. He wasn't very happy, not that it mattered.

The M1A1 weighed sixty pounds all-up, with two tanks of thickened fuel and the nitrogen propellant tank. Maximum range was fifty yards; we had at most ten seconds' firing time from five gallons of fuel.

Later in the war, as an NCO instructor, I learned the history of the weapon. The original model, the "mark one, mod oh," had serious problems, especially since the fuel often burned itself up on flight to target. A more viscous mixture was needed, one that burned slower and delivered more fire on target. Tests with fuel thickeners such as soap, rubber, and crankcase oil were unsat.

Standard Oil developed a rubber-based thickener, but it had poor shelf life. However, in late 1941 the National Research Council blended the fatty soaps of aluminum naphthanate and palmitate into a gelatinous substance that could be shipped in sealed containers. When mixed with gasoline the naphthetic and palmitic salts coagulated, lowering the flash point of the fuel. The new mixture, resembling applesauce, was called napalm.

However, the basic M1 flamethrower wasn't powerful enough to project the thicker fuel far enough. Changes to the fuel valve and pressure regulator solved the main problems, and the M1A1 had twice the range of the M1—about fifty yards. The "A1" was what we took to Tarawa Atoll.

We were told that the M1A1 often had unreliable ignition in the tropics owing to the battery spark system. The battery was supposed to ignite the small nitrogen supply in the wand, which in turn lit off the fuel. However, if the thickened fuel didn't flare, the gunner sometimes sprayed fuel on the target, which was ignited with tracers or phosphorous grenades.

Once acquainted with the theory of the damn thing, we set about learning how to use it. Mainly it was by guess and by God; standing on the fantail of the attack transport en route to our destination. The process was simple enough: Turn on the hydrogen and fuel tanks, check for adequate pressure, aim, then press the igniter switch and the flame handle. Gunnery Sergeant Crouch demonstrated for our benefit. When he spoke, we listened. He was an old guy—probably thirty-one to thirty-three—and we reckoned he'd had more women and booze than the rest of us combined. It was certainly true in my case: I was still two months from voting age. I could die a painful, violent death, but I couldn't buy a beer.

"The force of the propellant can push you backward," Gunny explained, "so you need to plant your feet and lean into it, like an automatic weapon." He took an exaggerated posture, bending at the knees and inclining his torso forward. When he lit off the device, a low *whooshing* sound emerged from the wand, followed by a long spurt of flame with thick, black smoke. He played the stream of fire back and forth, allowing the napalm to settle in the wake of our ship. It was damned impressive to notice how long the fire burned on top of the water.

"Another thing," Gunny said. "Don't any of you sons a'bitches let fly with this thing at too high an angle. If you do, and you're not braced, you can get pushed backward, or downhill, and the flame will rise and fall on top of you." He glared at us as only a Marine Corps gunnery sergeant can do. "You're s'posed to burn Japs, not Marines."

As far as tactics, they were rudimentary. Basically, a squad would approach a target pillbox or bunker and shoot at the firing slits, keeping the gunners' heads down. That was supposed to allow the flamethrower man to get close enough to douse the place with hell jelly, which would drive the Japs from their guns. (Nobody will continue fighting with his face on fire!) Then the demolitions men would toss in satchel charges or, failing that, riflemen would pitch in some grenades. The theory was that we'd regroup and advance to the next obstacle.

On Betio, though, it didn't work that way. The Japs had devised a very tough defense in depth, with interlocking fields of fire. Almost every strongpoint was covered by rifles or MGs from two more positions, so even if we suppressed the fire from one place and advanced to destroy it, we were exposed to the Japs on the flanks.

We spent the rest of that day and most of the next two taking turns, learning how to operate and maintain the wretched new weapon. Eventually there was a lot of prestige with being a flame gunner—they were very popular guys on the islands we visited. But even discounting the high casualty rate (66 percent on Betio alone), I'd have gladly dropped the honor. The damn thing scared me: bucking the force of the hydrogen propellant, feeling the searing heat on my face, watching what it did to structures and people. Lieutenant Anthony, our platoon leader, must have sensed my attitude because at one point he patted my shoulder, and said, "Just remember, Bertram, it's far better to give than receive."

FIVE

"Gentlemen, we are headed for the Gilbert Islands." Our operations officer, Major Harry Pelt, stood on the ship's deck, with an easel holding a large map of the Central Pacific. The *Arthur Middleton* was a 10,800-ton Coast Guard transport taking our Marine Corps landing team toward the equator. She and fifteen other attack cargo and transport ships comprised the Southern Task Force under Rear Admiral Harry Hill.

"Specifically," Pelt continued, "we are going to seize an atoll there, called Tarawa." He was careful to pronounce it correctly: *ta-ra-wa*. The Second Marine Division's destination had been kept semisecret since departing New Zealand.

"The Gilberts straddle the equator, running about a hundred miles north and south," Pelt added. He traced the archipelago, from Makin Atoll in the northwest to Arorae in the southeast. "Many of these islands were uninhabited, and Tarawa is like most atolls in this part of the world—a large lagoon surrounded by a coral reef. The place that interests us is this island." He tapped the map. "Betio." The spelling confounded the pronunciation, *bay*-shio.

"It looks like a pork chop," muttered a BAR man in the third row. Somebody laughed unconvincingly.

Pelt decided to ignore the wisecrack. "Actually, it looks more like a rifle," he said. "The stock is the west end, narrowing to the drooping barrel here on the east with the lock on the north. But it's very small: about two miles long by six hundred yards at the widest point. Betio covers less than three hundred acres, and apparently the highest elevation is only ten feet."

A squad leader raised his hand. "Sir, what's worth taking on such a small place?"

"I'm just coming to that," Pelt replied. "The Japanese have an airfield on Betio, about four thousand feet long. The brass says we can't allow them a bomber base to interfere with our shipping between the Gilberts and the Marshalls up here to the north. So we're going to take it and put our own planes in there."

Pelt paused for effect. He had no doubt that the Eighth Marine Regiment, with the rest of the Second Division, would seize Tarawa. The only uncertainty was what it would cost.

"Our flyboys have photographed Betio yard by yard." He did not mention that originally Rear Admiral Hill's staff relied on a century-old British map of the island. "We know pretty much what's there, and it's a tough nut. The Japs have about forty-seven hundred men, including construction troops. The others are mostly naval infantry. Jap marines."

A murmur skittered through the green-clad audience. American and Japanese marines had rarely clashed in the nearly two years since Pearl Harbor—the most notable exception being at Wake Island in December '41. The riflemen, machine gunners, flamethrowers, and corpsmen in the audience realized that they faced a serious enemy.

"Our force will enter the lagoon through this gap in the west side of the reef," Pelt continued. "On D day we'll embark in LCVPs and amtracks and assault the island, on these beaches." Again he tapped the map, ticking off the landing zones: Green Beach on the blunt west end; Red One, Two, and Three on the north.

"Most of the island is covered with palm trees, except for a section at the west end of the airstrip. There are pillboxes and bunkers all over the place, with preregistered fields of fire. Offshore there are obstacles—some with mines—intended to funnel our landing craft into artillery zones. We expect naval gunfire to eliminate much of those.

"Once you're ashore you'll find a three-to-five-foot seawall, probably coconut logs stacked up to prevent tracked vehicles from getting inland. Our engineers will handle those.

"Weapons include light and heavy machine guns, defiladed tanks with 37mm guns, antiaircraft weapons, and heavy coastal batteries up to 75mm or more. It's also reported that they have some 5.5- and 8-inch guns.

"Now then. Remember that at most the island is only about six hundred yards wide, which means you're never more than three hundred yards from the waterline. Defense in depth is just not possible for an invader, so expect determined counterattacks, especially after dark. The Japs aren't stupid: They know that the best way to defeat a landing is to overrun the beachhead. That's where supplies come from.

"Another thing: This is the first coral atoll we've tackled. There are lots of others like it in the Pacific, so this operation will be studied closely. It's important that we get it right."

Pelt spoke for another ten minutes, outlining the complex evolution of an opposed amphibious landing: assault units, ship-to-shore movement, phase lines, communications, naval gunfire, and air support. The Marine Corps had taught and preached the amphibious gospel since the end of the Great War; graduates of the Basic School at Quantico became evangelists. They knew the 1915 British disaster at Gallipoli inside out.

"You'll get equipment checks on D minus one and on D day morning but briefly, check your weapons and ammo. No loaded weapons or fixed bayonets at any time unless you're ordered. You should carry three days' worth of rations. And another thing: Carry your gas masks. We know from previous landings that they're the first thing troops discard, but you need to keep them handy. We know a lot about Tarawa but not everything."

Finally, Pelt looked around. "Now, I know you fellows must have a lot of questions, probably some I can't answer. But I'll try." He nodded at a platoon leader in the front row.

"Sir, if Betio is so small with no civilians, why don't we use gas?"

The ops officer almost flinched. He had asked the same question of his regimental commander and was rudely rebuffed. Consequently, Pelt passed on the sentiment: "Earlier this year the president said the United States will not use poison gas in this war."

Somewhere in the dungaree-clad audience a Republican mortarman voiced a heartfelt sentiment. "Screw Roosevelt."

There was some nervous laughter, and it occurred to me that there didn't seem to be many Democrats in the Marine Corps. FDR's son James was exec of a Raider battalion, but I heard he later became a Republican. Anyway, it didn't matter very much. A lot of us weren't old enough to vote.

SIX

They blew reveille at a quarter 'til midnight—the unholiest wake-up call I ever had. Everybody including our platoon leader, Lieutenant Alexander, was peeved. "The damn moon isn't even up yet," he groused.

The swabbies fed us well, though: steak and eggs with plenty of coffee. There was the usual gallows humor about condemned men and hearty meals, though it didn't seem to be a major concern. We'd been hearing for several days how the Navy was going to obliterate Betio Island and the Jap defenders. There were three old battleships in the fire support group—*Maryland*, *Tennessee*, and *Colorado*—plus four cruisers and a bunch of destroyers. That didn't even include four carriers, though we learned that the fly-fly boys promised a whole lot more than they could deliver. Later on the airedales learned to do a fine job for the infantry, but it took a while for their performance to match the brochure.

Before reporting to our boat stations each squad or platoon ran an equipment check. Our NCOs were good—several of them had been at Guadalcanal—and they knew what was important. As a flame gunner my loadout was unusual, even for so specialized a bunch as the engineers, but Sergeant Healey gave me the once-over just the same. "You got two full canteens?" he rasped.

"Yes, Sergeant."

I don't know why he asked because he hefted each canteen on my web belt just to be sure. He grinned like a wolf, and muttered, "When it comes to slaughter, you'll do your work on water, an' lick the bloomin' boots of them that's got it." I had no idea what he was talking about—I'd hardly heard of Kipling in '43—and I was astonished that Sergeant Healey had ever read poetry. But we had some odd birds in the Corps. He noted my .45 pistol, magazine pouch, and sheath knife, then asked, "Where's your ruck?"

I nodded to my A-gunner. "Dean has it."

Healey turned to Dean, who got to carry my gear plus his own. Fortunately, he was a big, strapping Dakota farm kid who could manage the burden: two shelter halves, both our allotments of K-rations, his own clean clothes plus a change of socks and skivvies for me, extra napalm fuel and hydrogen gas canister plus tools, not to mention his M1 carbine and ammo plus a couple of grenades. The riflemen all carried at least four Mk 2 "pineapples" with three-second fuzes.

The theory was that we could sustain ourselves for three days before we needed serious reinforcement or supply. That was the theory. In truth, the logistics people really screwed up, and what we needed most—M3 and especially M4 tanks—were loaded early aboard the ships rather than late. Consequently, the Navy had to move mountains of supplies to get at the Stuarts and Shermans rather than putting them ashore right away. The same applied to other essentials, including ammo, water, and medical supplies. Oddly enough, food wasn't a big problem for the first couple of days. Everybody ashore was too busy, too scared, or too dead to care much about eating. We lived on nervous energy.

Finally, we were herded to the ship's rail and went over the side, climbing down the cargo nets to the waiting Higgins Boats. Everybody was overloaded, but the flamethrower was bulky as well as heavy. I needed a couple of helping hands getting into the boat. From there we were delivered to the LSTs (Landing Ship, Tank, but "Large Slow Targets" the sailors called them) for reboarding in the LVTs (Landing Vehicle Tracked) that comprised the first three waves.

The LVT was a lot like the LCVP (Landing Craft, Vehicle and Personnel), better known as the Higgins Boat, in that it was designed by a civilian who foresaw the need before the Navy did. What Andrew Jackson Higgins of New Orleans was to wooden landing craft, Donald Roebling of Clearwater, Florida, was to the tracked variety. He devised his amphibious vehicle as the "Swamp Gator" in the wake of severe hurricanes in the early 1930s. At that time there was no purpose-built rescue vehicle for such contingencies, but the Marine Corps noted its potential for combat, and had it built by the Food Machinery Corporation. However, Mr. Roebling had to finance the military prototype himself, "betting on the come" that he'd be reimbursed. The Corps had no contingency funds for such things in 1940.

Militarily, LVTs were thought most useful for taking supplies to a hostile shore, but it wasn't long before their versatility included troop carrier duty and even combat support with integral howitzers and flamethrowers.

Anyway, we spent almost six frigging hours in various landing craft, finally with eighteen men crowded into an LVT-2. As far as I know, it was the first time that tracked vehicles had been used for an actual assault. But Tarawa was different from everything that happened before. As an atoll, it had a large reef that blocked the Higgins Boats unless there was at least five feet of water over the coral barrier, but our Water Buffalos and the earlier LVT-1 Alligators could cross the reef without much difficulty. However, they weren't optimized for combat assault: no armor and no ramp to allow fast unloading.

The Second Division did some fast modifications. Enough suitable armor plate was found in New Zealand to protect the fronts of the Alligators already on hand. The more capable Buffalos were shipped by LST from the West Coast and barely made the embarkation in time. Their armor was next to useless—rifle and machine-gun fire could penetrate it at a couple hundred yards or more—but it was better than nothing. Suitability tests confirmed that both types of amtracks maintained seakeeping quality with the extra weight, and off we went.

From the engineers' perspective, the LVT-1s and -2s still left something to be desired. Troops could disembark by jumping over the side or stern, but heavy weapons and other gear had to be lowered pretty carefully—a real problem on a defended beach. Mortar tubes and base plates, flamethrowers, fuel cans, and the like, were serious impedimenta. A lot of that hardware went to the bottom of the sea because it was just too heavy or took too long to off-load amid incoming gunfire. A ramp in the stern of the tractor would've made things a lot easier and reduced casualties. That modification didn't arrive until the "dash three" model, called the Bushmaster. However, I hardly saw one until sometime before we hit Okinawa well over a year later.

We were hoisting ourselves and our gear into the amtracks when the LST skipper hailed all hands over the loudspeaker. He said the chaplain had some words of comfort for us: "This will be a great page in Marine Corps history," he intoned. "Wherever you are, stop and give a prayer . . . God bless you."

I don't remember how most of the fellows responded to that. I think I just cursed some more at the damnable weight of my flame-thrower. I didn't really get religion until a couple of days later.

Our amtrack had just left the LST's bow, when somebody said, "Hey, lookit." He was pointing southeasterly, toward the island. I craned my neck, glancing over the gunwale, and saw a red light arcing into the dark sky maybe five miles off. It was a star shell fired from Betio. We didn't know it at the time, but it was a warning from the Jap naval infantry. They'd finally spotted us.

The "tracks" then churned away from the LSTs, arrived at the assembly points, and waited until each wave was organized behind its guide boat. I was in the second wave for Red Beach Three. We had a rough ride owing to a westerly chop, which hit us from astern during the transit to the lagoon, then broad on the starboard beam during the final approach. The LVTs rode fairly low, as they were basically smallcraft that pitched and rolled. Everybody was wet; several guys got seasick and puked over the side. A couple of demolition men just up and heaved without thought to the wind. They got their breakfasts back in their faces—and so did some others with stronger stomachs. Gunny Crouch's utilities were flecked with what looked like scrambled eggs; I thought he'd pull his KA-BAR and skin the private alive. Instead, the old-timer just flicked the mess off with one finger. I guess he knew that far worse was awaiting us.

Entering the channel through the west side of the reef, we assumed an east–west line of bearing prior to our turn toward the beach. My engineer company was attached to Major "Jim" Crowe's Landing Team Three, assigned to occupy Red Beach Three. That was the easternmost beach on Betio's north shore, on the left flank of Landing Team Two in the middle.

Just inside the lagoon we passed the yellow buoy markers designating the line of departure. From there we made a ninety-degree starboard turn and began our run to shore.

Our run to Red Three began six thousand yards from shore. That's three nautical miles, and it took almost an hour. There was no opposition that we could tell, and not much to see. The island was hidden beneath a cloud of smoke and dust, which looked impressive to amphibians like me, who'd never been exposed to combat. "Looks damn good," chirped Dean. "Maybe the swabbos got it right."

Gunny Crouch just pulled his helmet low over his eyes, pretending to appear bored. "Don't bet on it," was all he said.

Our amtracks reached the reef at low tide, which caused some adverse comment from the platoon leader and senior NCOs. They saw more of the big picture than we privates and PFCs, knowing what it meant. The Higgins Boats in the fourth, fifth, and sixth waves wouldn't have the clearance they needed over the accumulated coral. There would be no choice but to off-load the troops for a long, long walk to the beach in waist- or chest-high water. As it was, our track crawled over the five-hundred-yard-wide reef without difficulty other than a lumpy ride, the 200-hp Continental engine groaning along.

I remember thinking as we lurched across the reef and churned toward shore that I'd made it. *Now I'm really a Marine*, I thought. I was making an amphibious landing on an opposed beach, where I assumed I'd fight and suffer—and survive.

Some guys will do anything for their self-image. Nations and military recruiters rely on it, but of course I didn't figure that out until years later.

Once across the reef, churning toward shore, things were surprisingly quiet. I remember seeing red-and-white pilings at frequent intervals in the lagoon, and wondering what they were. "Maybe they're building a seawall," somebody speculated. We were still dumb boots in some ways. They weren't pilings; they were range markers. The Japs had us boresighted, and we didn't even know it. The reason so many of the first wave LVTs got ashore was that the Japs expected us to land on the south coast, and it took them a while to shift troops to the other side. God knows, the northern approach was bad enough with some obstacles, a lot of barbed wire, and more bunkers than we could count.

At that point the riflemen were told, "Lock and load!" They had already applied the safeties on their Garands, so they locked the breeches open, thumbed in a clip of eight .30-06 cartridges, and nudged the operating rod handles forward. They were set to go. Same with the BAR men. The rest of us—especially us flame-throwers—couldn't do anything until we disembarked. By then I was getting itchy to be away from the LVT, with its stomach-churning motion and gasoline fumes.

Landing Team Three was supposed to disembark along the two-hundred-yard stretch of Red Three, east of the long pier bordering Red Two. However, because of the obstacles, our seventeen tracks mostly rolled ashore on the western half of the beach, a couple of hundred yards from the northern taxiway of the airfield. We got some MG fire as our Water Buffalos crunched out of the surf, and you could hear the high-pitched *pings* and more solid *whacks* as 6.5 and 7.7mm rounds impacted the armor plate.

Our second wave was ashore on Red Three, and the next wave of LVTs mostly got through. We thought things were going tolerably well, but didn't know what had happened six hundred or seven hundred yards offshore. Out there, the erratic tide that the planners were so worried about did in fact turn against them. LCVPs were unable to cross the reef, so coxswains dropped the ramps and unloaded the troops right there. The Marines in the fourth, fifth, and sixth waves had no choice but to wade hundreds of yards through waist- or chest-deep water while Jap gunners looked through their sights, noted the range markers, and opened fire.

Whenever Tarawa is discussed, there's always mention of the tides. It's odd how something like that takes on a life of its own—an historical conventional wisdom. The CW on Tarawa is that the "dodging" tide caught us by surprise, leading to so many casualties. But that's not so. The planners, and even some at the company level, knew that the information was risky, based on incomplete data. They realized that there was perhaps a fifty-fifty chance that we'd find the reef exposed, preventing the Higgins Boats from getting across.

Many years later I read that high tide was calculated for 1115 hours at five feet over the reef. The next best period was expected more than two weeks later, on 5 December. No other usable tide was forecast until January, which was out of the question.

It turned out that H hour and D day occurred on one of two days in 1943 with the lowest tides at Tarawa Atoll. That was the result of the moon's effect on the low (neap) tides; I don't pretend to understand the astrophysics, meteorology, and hydrodynamics of the situation. It's enough to know that the planners took a guess, and they guessed wrong. The average water level on 20 November was barely three feet—two feet less than the LCVPs needed to clear the reef.

In turn, that meant a gruesome walk through water for nearly half a mile in some places, under direct and indirect fire every step of the way. I was personally spared that nightmare because my engineer team rode an LVT. Thank you, Mr. Roebling. You probably saved this Marine's hide.

The only thing I can say in compensation is: It could have been much worse. But that's not much help to a thousand dead Americans.

SEVEN

As a kid I saw Lew Ayres in *All Quiet on the Western Front*. I never read the German novel; didn't much care for fiction unless it had guns and horses. But the movie made an impression on me, as it was meant to. Like most viewers, I thought the most memorable scene was the muddy shell hole where Paul Baumer kills the French *poilu*, using a boot knife. Ayres, who became a conscientious objector in the Next War—my war—portrayed the extreme ambivalence of the frontline soldier caught up in the frenzy of killing for survival with the grief of taking life. Now, trapped in my filthy, choking, waterlogged bunker, I thought about Paul Baumer.

I didn't feel anything like him.

Instead of a muddy, intact French corpse, I shared my hole with two filthy, putrefying Japanese cadavers. From what I could see of them, neither was very much like the erstwhile typesetter that Baumer grieved over. It didn't even occur to me to wonder what they'd done in civilian life. I didn't care how old they were, if they had families, or anything else about them. They were dead Japs—the best kind. Except they stank something awful.

I wasn't sure what killed them, but apparently not the large-caliber shell that penetrated the bunker. For all I knew there might be more of their kind buried in the water and rubble. Naval gunfire was one of the big failures at Tarawa, along with air support. The battlewagons like *Maryland* were too close to shore, so most of their sixteen-inch shells arrived in a shallow trajectory. Some men had seen them skip off of bunkers and splash into the lagoon on the south side. A couple of destroyers came in close enough for almost direct fire support, though. If I ever meet one of those tin-can sailors, I'll buy him a drink.

There were two holes: a small one in the front wall and a larger one overhead. Judging by the partial hole in the concrete, it was a 37 from one of the M3 light tanks that got ashore. We badly needed more M4 Shermans with their 75s because the Stuarts' guns hardly made a dent. Additionally, because the water level on Betio is barely eight feet, the larger explosion (undoubtedly from naval gunfire) had churned up enough coral to flood most of the floor. I wondered if the water was rising. If so, unless I regained some mobility, I was in danger of drowning.

The bunker seemed to be a machine-gun position, with firing slits on three sides and a door at the rear. I guessed it was large enough for three or four men—Japs, anyway. Somebody said the average Japanese male was about five-foot-two or -three; little guys with buckteeth and thick glasses who bowed and smiled a lot. A treacherous bunch of bastards who cut off prisoners' heads for sport and staked pregnant women to the ground. But even after what we knew of Nanking and Pearl and Bataan, and the stories our own guys had from the Canal, I don't think that I really hated the Japanese. I just wanted to kill my share of them as fast as possible and get the damned war over with. At age twenty I didn't have a plan, other than survival. I'd worry about a job, much less a career, back in civvy street. No way was I staying in the Corps, waiting for the War after the Next War. What would that be? World War Three or Four?

Of course, that was before the GI Bill, college, and the offer of extended service in the Reserves. After all, a Marine can change his mind, right?

God, it was miserable in there. I'd have sold my soul for a decent drink. I remember wondering if I'd go crazy enough to drink the foul water I lay in, with rotting, stinking flesh and guts strewn about. My head was clearing somewhat at that point, and I groped around, seeking some kind of weapon. That's when I must have begun thinking I'd rather kill myself than sink far enough to ingest that filth. Maybe I laughed at that point—a thin, choking laugh of two or three syllables. The Japs were supposed to be the suicidal ones, the *Banzai* boys who sought death before dishonor. Marines didn't work that way. Did they?

How had I gotten here?

I couldn't understand how I became semiparalyzed in the murky, stinking bunker. The smaller hole was in the wall before me, somewhat toward the top where the tank gunner had boresighted a firing slit. Okay, but how did that explain things? The entrance behind me seemed to remain closed, so evidently I didn't come in that way. Besides, why would I?

I tried to concentrate. What was I doing when I came here? Just when was that? This morning? The day before? Obviously I'd been without my flamethrower; apparently I had no gear with me at all unless I'd lost . . .

The carbine.

Dean's carbine. I had it with me when—what? When what happened? My head throbbed, my throat strained, and my stomach churned once more. I gagged and choked and heaved again. Maybe I messed my pants. I couldn't tell.

I didn't care.

Thinking back from the perspective of nearly sixty years, I guess I can be perfectly honest. Or at least try to be. I wouldn't want my children or grandchildren to know it, but I wanted just one of two things, lying in that wretched situation. I wanted out, or I wanted to die. Ha! I was a twentieth-century Patrick Henry: *Give me liberty or give me death!* But I was no longer living, just existing in a putrid, miserable purgatory with no point to staying alive. If I'd had my pistol I would have shot myself to end the misery, and that's a fact. Death would have been preferable to one more hour in that damned reeking place.

The odd thing was, I finally found a weapon after groping around. At first I just felt the metal at the edge of my fingertips. By stretching farther—so far it hurt—I dragged it a little closer. It was heavy, a Japanese Type 92 7.7mm machine gun, based on an old French Hotchkiss design. It fed from stripper clips laid on a tray. The barrel was bent about thirty degrees, though, and I probably couldn't have used it for suicide anyway—too cumbersome. What I needed was a Nambu pistol or even one of the light MGs. Weird thing, you know? It struck me there and then how odd the Japs were. Their infantry weapons were nowhere as good as ours, except their LMGs. If anything, they were better because the Type 96s were lighter and more portable than our air-cooled Brownings. The Nambus also were better than our beloved BAR; the Jap guns had thirty-round magazines versus twenty, and a quick-change barrel to boot. But the Japs didn't really understand firearms. They issued three-foot bayonets, and their officers carried swords. What can you say about people who put bayonet mounts on their light machine guns?

After a few moments I stopped thinking about weapon design. I just wanted something to end my existence.

How bad was it? Okay, I'll tell you. If my wonderful mother could have been there to hold my hand and plead for me to hang on just a while longer, for the sake of her unborn grandchildren, I'd have asked her to get me a gun or a knife. That's how far gone I was—awash in fouled water, bloated corpses, and self-pity.

Don't ever let anyone tell you that Marines don't cry.

EIGHT

During the last 150 yards or so, the amtrack gunners opened fire on the beach. It was comforting to hear the two pedestal-mounted Browning .50s *chug-chug* along, spewing hot brass into the troop compartment.

Later—much later—I read that only 53 of the 125 amtracks in the first three waves reached shore. The hard thing was to ignore the casualties in the water. Our briefing was adamant on that point—don't stop to pick up the wounded. The longer our landing craft were in the lagoon, the more time the Jap gunners had to zero in on them. It was the ultimate brutality of war, but still some of us groused about the order. Marines are trained to look out for each other, to work together. In fact, that's what *gung ho* means in Chinese. But the logic was inescapable: You could lose thirty men trying to rescue one, and we needed every single man on the island.

Betio's beaches averaged thirty to fifty yards wide, rising only five or six feet above the tide mark. On shore, the seawall was only twenty feet from the water. However, once we were ashore things quickly became too crowded. Men were lying shoulder to shoulder— a ragged green carpet on the white beach. Units got intermingled, command structures broke down, confusion reigned. It was a squad

leader's fight with platoon leaders deciding strategy, when the lieutenants survived. Our company and battalion commanders were
generally high-quality officers, but they had little radio communication because our gear wasn't properly waterproofed. The commanders were reduced to sending runners back and forth. Those
guys took horrible losses; I heard that a dozen or so were shot down
near Colonel Shoup's CP on Red Two.

Red Three covered the north shore from east of the long pier to
the end of the four-thousand-foot runway. Approximately in the
middle was the short Burns-Philip wharf, which was only accessible
at high tide. The coconut log seawall was not complete along Red
Three's right (westerly) flank, which permitted a couple of our
tracks to move inland. But as soon as my team disembarked, many
of us were pinned down near the seawall. People scattered, looking
for cover.

I popped up behind the coconut logs for a quick look at the
nearest bunker. I gauged it at forty yards—probably beyond effective range. Ducking behind cover again, I wormed my way several
yards to the left, grunting from the physical exertion. The rest of
the squad followed. Maybe five or six men—half the outfit. The
senior NCOs were nowhere in sight; the confusion was incredible.

"All right," I wheezed. The riflemen stopped; Dean, Hardy, and
Jaworski crayfishing to join me. I inhaled, trying to fill my lungs
with air rather than smoke, sand, and a growing stench—a combination of dead flesh, burning things, and fear.

I looked around, constrained by the M1A1 on my back. "We
gotta get closer to the bunker. Can't cross open ground, though."

"We need smoke," Hardy said. "Anybody got smoke grenades?"

Nobody answered. Looking around, I realized with a sudden chill
that I was in charge. But we couldn't do much on our own. We
needed more shooters and demolition men. I looked into Jaworski's
wide eyes. *He's even more scared than I am. Give him something to
do.* I said, "Jerry, scout around. See if you can find an NCO and
tell him we have a chance here."

With visible reluctance Private Jaworski crawled backward, his
spatted feet in the tide. Making the motion of a nesting crab, he

edged rearward until his dungaree pants were darkened with water, then turned about and raced on hands and knees back where he'd come. The boy dragged his rifle in the sand and sea—a mortal sin at Parris Island, a misdemeanor on Betio Island.

Time crept past, every tick of the second hand with a separate beginning, middle, and end. The narrow beach became more crowded as additional amtracks arrived. I led my bobtailed squad farther along the beach, making room for the new men and staying well away from the amphibious tractors, which inevitably drew heavy fire. The noise—at first almost overpowering—by then seemed normal.

It's hard to remember everything in that much confusion, especially after so long. I do know I pulled myself up close behind the coconut logs, closed my eyes, and tried to blot out the appalling sights and sounds around me. *Think*, I willed myself. *Think about something good. Something from home.* Nothing came to mind.

Several minutes after leaving, Jaworski was back with reinforcements. Sergeant Healey was with him, and I've never been so glad to see anybody. Healey was wounded, with a bandage on one arm and pockmarks on his face, but he was still in the fight.

"Also got these . . ." Jaworski gasped.

Hardy reached out, scooped up two smoke grenades. "Where'd you get 'em?" he asked.

Jaworski inhaled, a loud gasp in the cloying air. He started to speak, then shook his head. He rolled on his back, trying to breathe again.

I pulled the wrench kit from my pocket; the tools had gouged a hole in my thigh. I nodded backward to Dean, indicating that we should withdraw down the shallow incline. "Need more room," was all I could say. God, it was hard to breathe.

At the waterline I gave the tool kit to Dean, and he turned valves and twisted handles, trying to stay low. A grenade launcher round detonating thirty yards away tossed water onto us, but finally he tapped my helmet. We crawled back to Healey.

"Okay, here's what we do," Healey said. "Copping, take your BAR about ten–fifteen yards to the right. Rest of you guys, between here and there. Shoot at the gun slits, keep 'em down. Jaworski will throw the smoke." He looked at me. "Then Bertram will . . ." He paused, realizing what he was about to say. I swallowed hard. ". . . do it." He glanced around. "Somebody go with him to cover his approach."

"I better come with you, Bert." It was Hardy. I looked into his eyes. They were hazel. *Never noticed that before. Bunked with the sumbitch eight months; never knew it.* No words came; words were inadequate to describe what I felt.

"Let's do it."

The BAR man and the other shooters opened up. Chips and dust flew from the two bunkers facing us. With a lunge of my legs that required every bit of muscle and energy I possessed, I willed myself over that log seawall into the beaten zone of two or three machine guns. My boondockers didn't seem to touch the ground; my mouth was wide-open, sucking in all the humid oxygen I could ingest. I was aware of my heart. It never never felt so stressed. I was sweating buckets; salty drops fell from my helmet band and eyebrows. A Jap machine gun threw up spouts of sand and coral around us.

We made it. Hardy and I flopped down about fifteen paces from the gun slit of the closest bunker. He rolled over into an uncomfortable prone position, guarding my right side. He hollered something that sounded like "Clear!"

The guys behind the log wall were still shooting, but the volume was noticeably lower. It occurred to me that they'd all opened up at once, which meant the Garands began running empty within a few seconds of each other. *Gotta talk about that*, I thought. *Need more fire discipline.* Only the BAR was still firing regularly, that 550-rpm *chug-chug-chug* tapping out two- and three-round bursts. He was a good man, that BAR guy. He must've had the fastest reload in the battalion.

Suddenly the high, fast chatter of a Nambu 96 erupted almost close enough to touch. The Japs were back in action after ducking the original fusillade of covering fire. I could feel the muzzle blast, but the Jap gunner didn't know I was there. I was just outside his field of view.

Hardy was shooting now, bad sign. He called something more, probably *What th' hell you waitin' for?* I reared up on one knee, braced myself, and aimed the tube at the firing slit. I distinctly remember thinking, *Boy is he gonna be surprised.* Then I pressed the handle.

The low, rushing sound of ignited gas merged with the rest of the sounds on Red Three. The squad behind the logs; the Jap MGs; Hardy's Garand. I heard *blam, blam, blam-blam,* then the unmistakable *piing!* of his ejected clip.

I seared the Japs without ever seeing them, just the muzzle of one 6.5 Nambu. The gunfire stopped immediately inside the bunker as the gunners fled from the embrasure.

Almost immediately the demolition guys were beside me. One of them, a kid named Janek, pulled the handles on his satchel charge, counted one-potato, two-potato, and tossed it through the port. Then he rolled himself into a ball behind me.

I thought I'd better get out of the way.

With the package on my back I couldn't roll over, so I just flopped forward like a beached flounder. I pulled my helmet down over my ears, turned my face away from the bunker, and opened my mouth to relieve some of the pressure.

The satchel charge exploded on the sixth potato with a loud, piercing *ka-BOOM*. God, I love Composition C. Dust, wood, palm leaves, and other debris erupted into the air.

Before the dust began to settle, the rest of the squad was there. A couple of them fired full clips through the gunport just to be sure, but it was wasted ammo. The BAR man risked a look inside. "Can't see much," he panted. "Two, maybe three guns in there."

That was Step One. The procedure was: Repeat as necessary.

NINE

Getting across the beach wasn't as hard for us as it was for most others. But our initial success was misleading. We cleared Red Three fairly quickly with relatively few losses and headed inland. When we crossed an open space among the blasted-out palm trees, somebody hollered, "Hit the deck!"

Without thinking, I dropped prone, even with sixty pounds of flame gear strapped on. That's what training does for you. I didn't know why the warning was shouted until a carrier plane rolled in on us. I still remember the blunt wingtips—a Hellcat, I thought. But it was an Avenger, a carrier-based bomber. I still remember seeing the white belly and that cavernous bomb bay with the doors opened. The pilot nosed down, and I remember thinking it odd that we didn't hear his engine, but there was a lot of other noise. Small-arms fire was snapping and barking all around.

We only saw the plane for a few seconds because of the tall trees. It's odd how your mind works at times like that. I thought, *I've got about five gallons of jellied gasoline on my back, and that bastard up there is gonna start shooting at me.* For no good reason, I rolled onto my side and looked up. It was contrary to what we learned about air attack because a white face shows up against most earth backgrounds. But I felt I needed to put something between those airborne guns and my napalm, even if it was *me*.

Then I heard that big radial engine. The Grumman was probably over a thousand feet up when it pulled out, but the low, steady rumble of the engine came to me amid the gunfire on the ground.

The pilot dropped a couple of bombs—probably 250-pounders— and most of us cursed the flyboys, their mothers, and anyone else remotely associated with them. The Japs were bad enough—we damn sure didn't need our own planes trying to kill us. However, the bombs didn't seem to do any harm because the pilot dropped "long." Maybe he wasn't even aiming at us. Anyway, the explosions erupted in some trees about seventy yards away, but what cohesion our landing team had up to then was mostly lost. Guys scrambled every direction to get out from under.

About thirty of us got to the eastern taxiway of the airfield and started to settle in. But we couldn't stay long; we were exposed, out in the open with no secure flanks. At that point we didn't have the numbers to hold an extended perimeter.

That was when we began to respect the Japs' ability to infiltrate. We made an orderly withdrawal past MG nests and bunkers that we'd overrun just several minutes before, then were fired upon from those same places. We didn't see many Japs above ground— they were like gophers.

Another thing: I'd always heard that most Japs couldn't shoot straight. If so, they put every one of their marksmen on Betio. They were everywhere—in bunkers, trenches, trees—even in the wrecked ship off Red One. Those naval infantrymen could hit almost anything they could see, with everything from Arisaka rifles to three-inch coastal guns. They blew LVTs and LCVPs out of the water more than five hundred yards offshore. And they seemed to have all the ammo in Japan.

Shortly after reaching the taxiway I heard a squeaking, clanking sound. I think some of us assumed it was one of our tanks or even a bulldozer, but that was just skylarking—the kind of optimism you overhear at the slop chute. Several of us were facing in the direction of the noise when a Jap light tank rolled into our position. We were

stunned—we didn't expect naval infantry to have tanks though evidently division intelligence had some evidence. Reportedly there
were seven or more on Betio, but this was the only one that actually
attacked. Others were found dug into revetments, hull down so
only the turret showed.

Some riflemen scrambled on top of the Type 95, which seemed
almost comical. It was small and awkward-looking. It had a light
cannon—a 37mm—and a machine gun. But there were no sup-
porting infantrymen. Everybody knows that armor needs infantry
to operate effectively. Maybe these Japs hadn't read the manual.

Anyway, our guys were trying to toss grenades inside the tank.
But the Japs were buttoned up, and the Marines were badly exposed. A BAR man and one or two others were shot off the damned
little thing. We didn't have many antitank weapons on Betio—just
towed 37mm guns that arrived too late. Toward the end of the
three days there were some self-propelled 75s, and they were useful
against bunkers, but what we needed were bazookas. There weren't
any; I don't think any of us had ever seen one.

A captain ordered us to prepare to pull back, and that was a
disappointment. We had just started making progress when we
were told to withdraw. It was just as well, though. We were ordered
back to the beach and set up a perimeter maybe 150 yards deep.
Some guys griped about being run off by one little tin can, but as
I said, our flanks were exposed, and we'd have had to pull back
even without the tank showing up.

Carrier planes had already bombed us on the advance southward.
Then they strafed us on the withdrawal northward, maybe thinking
we were Japs making a counterattack. This time the planes were
Hellcats. We weren't very impressed.

Nevertheless, the bombing and strafing really upset us, in more
ways than one. I don't think that anybody who's never been under
air attack can appreciate how it feels. The emotion is one of complete vulnerability, like a field mouse under a hawk. Repeatedly in
memoirs, soldiers speak of feeling naked, unprotected. When I read
of the panzers trying to reach the Normandy beachhead, I understood what those Germans must have felt. Actually, their ordeal

was far, far worse than ours. They were under direct attack by fighter-bombers for hours, even days. On Betio I experienced a couple of incidents, then it was over.

For a long time I seemed to be the only flame gunner around—at least the only live one. The Japs recognized the danger we represented to their fixed defenses, and they made us combat engineers priority targets.

Man, I was frustrated, confused, angry—all at once. There was a lot of shooting, most of it inbound, and I wasn't doing any of it with my flamethrower. Finally, though, Sergeant Healey pulled me along with him. I grabbed Dean by the stacking swivel and took him in tow.

We scrunched into an abandoned MG nest, by the look of it. Sandbags were piled about four high and several deep. There were a lot of 6.5mm brass and some scraps of Jap gear. Healey pointed between two bullet-riddled bags leaking sand. "There," he said. "Burn it out."

I risked a glimpse. At first I didn't see anything worth igniting— just the usual debris, mostly shattered tree trunks and fallen palm fronds. Then I saw a muzzle flash. The Japs were tremendous at camouflage. A low-lying coconut bunker on a slight elevation had a good view of our sector. It was mostly covered with sand and foliage; amid the smoke and dust it was even harder to see.

Ducking back under cover, I called to Dean and had him turn on my fuel and hydrogen tanks. He fumbled a bit, then tapped my helmet. Then I turned to Sergeant Healey. "We'll all open up on that bunker," he said in a loud voice. He leaned close to me so I could hear him over the gunfire and other racket. "When they stop shooting, rush 'em and give 'em the hotfoot."

I said something that must have sounded like "Okay" (I thought I said "Shit!") because without another word the noncom shouted to his bobtailed squad. They all opened fire with Garands and carbines. Wood splinters and sand spouts erupted around the firing slit, but it was impossible to tell if the Nambu light MG had stopped shooting. Nothing to do but trust to luck.

I lowered my head like a fullback charging the Crimson Tide line and bolted from cover. It was one hell of a long way—about thirty-five, forty yards. I slumped behind a shot-off palm tree, leaned around the side, and pressed the firing lever with my right hand while activating the igniter with my left. *Ka-whoom!* The thing lit off with a low, rumbling roar and rocked me back. In my excitement and fear I'd forgotten Gunny Crouch's first lesson—I hadn't braced myself. The nozzle lifted, spreading the thickened fuel higher than I intended, but there was a residual benefit because it sent the flame stream across the top of the bunker and onto the far side. I adjusted aim, braced myself, and fired again. This time the stream went into the horizontal firing port. I held the lever down for a good three or four seconds.

From the corner of my eye there was movement: The sergeant and his team dashed forward, assault firing as they ran. One of them slid to a stop at the edge of the bunker, pulled the pin on a grenade, let the spoon go, and did a quick two count. Then he tossed the pineapple inside and rolled away. The thing went off with a hollow *bang.*

Healey and a couple of others were on top of the bunker immediately, watching the far side. I ran up beside them, not really sure what I'd do. What happened then is something I will never, never forget.

The door flung open and a Jap ran out. He was on fire. His clothes were burning on his back. So was his hair. It was so unexpected that none of us moved for a couple of seconds. Then everybody shot at once. The Jap pitched forward, facedown in the sand. "Damn," said one Marine.

I couldn't think of anything to say.

TEN

Finally, I thought I knew.

It was on toward nightfall, which would be a relief to the leathernecks still in the fight. Along the equator, evening fell quickly, and often it brought a breeze. Not much of one, but anything—absolutely anything—was a relief on that bitch of an island. Inside my bunker, though, I couldn't feel it.

What did I know? I thought: *Have to remember.*

Oh, yeah. Dean got it, and I went for fuel. But when?

Late on D plus one, before we left cover, I wanted to be sure that my A-gunner was nearby. I'd need a refill before long. Just as I turned to Dean, an explosion blew sand, coral, and debris over both of us. He was between me and the blast; I thought it was a mortar round. As it turned out, the Japs didn't have mortars on Betio, but they had plenty of grenade launchers. At first I didn't think much of it because it was a fairly small explosion, but Dean reeled, slumped to his knees, and dropped on one side.

I reached him after a hard, short crawl. He was breathing noisily, bleeding from the nose and mouth. He said something that I couldn't understand—a low gurgle. He repeated it a couple of times. I was scared and angry. With the flame rig strapped on, I couldn't do much for him. Somebody called for a corpsman—that went on for three days—but there were none near us. One of the other Marines rolled him over and pulled up his dungaree top. Dean had taken several splinters in his right side, apparently reaching the lung. A couple of other men dragged him to cover and did what they could, which wasn't much. Sulfa powder, bandages, direct pressure. Combat first aid.

I had one or two others pick up his spare tank, his carbine, and some magazines. We left him with another wounded man; I only saw him once again. At a reunion in the 1960s I learned he'd never fully recovered and died about 1955.

Each time I regained consciousness I seemed to think of something else. That is, other than my predicament and the fundamental need for water. For the longest time I tried to figure how the Japs had survived a direct shell hit on their bunker. They should have been shredded by a Sherman's 75mm gun, let alone a five- or eight-inch naval shell.

Then it occurred to me, something the company commander said in our briefing. "The Japs are masters at infiltration," he had said. He knew—he'd been on Guadal. "They train for it like nobody else, and they're about as good in daylight as at night."

The two corpses in "my" bunker had probably been a light machine gun crew, skittering through the wreckage and debris that was Betio to reoccupy the bunker after it was first shelled. Probably on D plus one. Maybe they found some of their friends spread across the overhead and bulkheads, maybe not. It didn't matter. Their position was now in the Marine rear, permitting them to back-shoot any unwary Americans advancing through the "secure" area.

I had no way of knowing how many Marines they ambushed that way, but finally somebody had tumbled to their game. Judging by the condition of the corpses, maybe they were killed by grenades. Certainly they had not burned, though I sort of wished they had.

How do you get people to do that? I wondered. I damn sure wouldn't have done it, and I don't think I knew anybody who would. Not for my buddies, not for the Corps, not for America.

Damn sure not for Roosevelt. For one thing, it was a death warrant, without a ghost of a fighting chance. Trapped in a position of their own choosing, behind the deepening American perimeter, they had to know they were going to die there. But they stuck to their post. I'm here to tell you: Those Japs were absolute bastards as human beings, but they were the kind of troops every commander dreams of. "Run over to that bush, take two steps left, and get shot." *Hai! Banzai!*

No wonder we had to nuke them twice.

ELEVEN

The Japs began killing themselves on the second day.

It was late that afternoon, I think, when the Word filtered down. That was the thing about the Corps: somebody always had the Word: the poop, the scuttlebutt, the hot dope. Usually it was wrong, of course, but it filled a lot of slack time. In this instance, it was correct.

Very few of us can choose how we die, but many of the Sasebo Seventh Special Naval Landing Force exercised their options. Some Japs who'd been surrounded and unable to sneak away had committed suicide. A company runner who passed through our lines had seen a couple of corpses: They blew themselves up with grenades. Others took off those peculiar two-toed shoes, put their rifle muzzles beneath their chins, and pressed (or, actually, pushed) the trigger with their big toes. Hey, whatever floats your boat.

The odd thing was, if individual Jap marines had decided to die, why not die fighting? Why not take another one or two or six Americans with them? It made no sense, personally or militarily. At least, not to us. Evidently it made a lot of sense to those Japs, and every one of us was glad of it. The others who fought it out were plenty bad enough.

Anyway, by evening of D plus one we had finally crossed the island, with elements of two battalions of the Second Regiment pushing south from Red Two. At least that's how it looked on the neatly drawn maps produced for the operational analysts and the history books. On my part of the perimeter, still inland from the Burns-Philip wharf, we only heard occasional snatches of info, but it was good to know that Marines now owned part of the south shore, called Black Beach. A battalion of the Sixth Marines was ashore on Green Beach at the west end, holding for the reserve battalion to land the next day and advance toward us.

We had spent most of the day trying to expand our perimeter southward and a little eastward. The whole area was full of bunkers, MG pits, and spider holes. You couldn't take anything for granted, and the battalion gunfire spotter had his hands full. I heard him talking to the destroyers offshore, and felt better for it. Our communications were erratic at best, but the lieutenant was able to call for naval gunfire in target grid 235, inside the eastern taxiway. For some reason I still remember the way he spoke—he was a Southern boy, and he had absorbed the careful enunciation they taught at artillery school. "Fahr mishun on gree-ud tu-oo, tha-ree, fahve. Ovah."

The first round impacted near the runway and the spotter called a correction, adding, "Fahr fur e-fay-ect." After the five-inchers pounded the area, he called to check fire, and we jumped off, taking advantage of the brief shock following a bombardment. But the Japs were resilient. That night they counterattacked.

My situation began when we tackled another batch of bunkers and rifle pits. I was getting low on fuel and propellant, and knew I'd be out of business shortly because we had no more refills. However, I thought there was enough firing time left to make it worthwhile for another effort, so I offered my team to a platoon from another company. The platoon leader—a first sergeant—had doped out the overlapping fields of fire and pointed to a well-camouflaged position to our left front, east of the taxiway. It appeared to be composed of coconut logs covered with palm fronds and sand. I poked my head over the fallen tree trunk for a quick look. There was no apparent shooting.

"You sure it's occupied?" I asked.

The NCO was an old-timer of about twenty-six. "Shit no, I'm not sure of anything on this frigging island." He spat out the words with grains of sand from his lips. Obviously, he'd been kissing the ground with the rest of us that day, which might have explained his candor. Ordinarily Marine Corps noncoms were dead-nuts certain about *everything*. Even when they were wrong.

"Well, I'm about out of juice," I replied. "Wouldn't want to waste it on an empty position."

The platoon leader regarded me for a long two count. Without turning his head, he barked an order. Something like, "Jones, draw fire."

Though Marine Corps discipline is different from Army discipline and damn sure different than the Navy variety, I didn't really expect Private Jones to jump up long enough for some Jap to boresight him. But damned if that's not what he did. He staggered to his feet, clamped his helmet down on his brain housing unit with his port hand, grasped his M1 with the starboard, and sprinted about twelve paces. Then he flopped down, his boondockers flailing above him as if he was still trying to run nose first.

Nobody shot at him. At least, not specifically.

I was about to comment to the sergeant upon my tactical sense when he bawled another order. "Able, Baker, Charles! Draw fire!"

It would've been comical in other circumstances. Two of the riflemen cautiously arose to comply with the order when the third, obviously more committed, piled into them from behind. All three went down in a tangle. They thrashed around, bawling and cursing, while the NCO slowly shook his head like a mother hen disgusted with her brood. Finally, he hollered, "Shake the lead out!" They did so, scampering in different directions, zigzagging all the while.

A machine gun opened up from the position about sixty yards away. We all ducked as wood chips flew from our protective tree trunk. The MG chattered away at Larry, Curly, and Moe, cycling at about six hundred rounds per minute. Mostly the gunner zigged when they zagged, but in those few seconds shooter and target zigged simultaneously. One of the decoys went down with a grazing wound to one leg.

I looked at the platoon leader again, probably wide-eyed in surprise, admiration, or astonishment. He spat out more sand. "Some Japs got more fire discipline than others. You gotta remember that one man can be a waste of ammo, or shooting at him might give away a position. Two can be marginal. But at this distance, three's a worthwhile target."

We were out of satchel charges, so this bunker was going to be taken on the cheap. As before, the riflemen opened up a hot masking fire while I worked my way into position, hoping all the time that there wasn't some sniper tracking me from above. A lot of trees still had foliage that could conceal a Jap.

This NCO knew his business. He staggered the firing rate of his Marines so at least two or three were shooting all the time while others reloaded. Again, Hardy and I wormed our way close to the side of the bunker, which had a firing slit on that end. Amid the noise I glimpsed empty brass piling up inside. No time to lose. I went into a crouch, aimed the flame gun, and opened up. The heat and flames roiled inside the bunker.

I depressed the initiator trigger again—nothing. "I'm empty!" I dropped the wand and began shrugging out of the bulky harness. A strap caught on my web belt; I felt impotent. "Help me dammit!" Hardy slung his M1 and stepped behind me, lifting some of the weight off my shoulders. In seconds I was free, and Hardy set down the weapon with an audible *thunk*.

Meanwhile, another Marine dashed several feet to my left, covering the rear exit to the position, but nobody emerged. I realized that our covering fire had stopped, and sort of recall hearing high-pitched noises from somewhere. I didn't need to hear it, though. The smell was confirmation enough.

TWELVE

Damm it, something's wrong.

The thought just wouldn't go away. Without quite knowing why, I felt that my recent memories were all wrapped around each other, getting in one another's way.

Maybe I was hallucinating—I just don't know. But for some weird reason I couldn't remember when I'd left Dean or when I'd finally run out of fuel and hunkered down in our perimeter on D plus one.

I knew that we began consolidating our lines early that afternoon, but there wasn't much for me to do. I hauled my empty flame-thrower to a convenient spot behind the main line of resistance, used the last of the water in my second canteen, and wondered about something to eat. With Dean gone, I'd lost my beast of burden and didn't feel like begging chow from the others.

Even if I'd had a refill, the M1A1 wasn't much use in a defensive situation, so I became a fifth wheel. Finally, I settled in with a light machine gun crew; three Marines setting up their air-cooled Browning. With nothing else to do, I offered to haul ammo or fill sandbags—anything to keep busy. I watched the gunner run a field headspace check, the quick and dirty way without resorting to a guage. He opened the breech, pulled back the charging handle a minuscule amount, and saw the bolt move incrementally. "Good to go," he said. If it moved too much or too little, he could get a malfunction at a most inopportune moment. The A-gunner fed him a cloth belt with 248 rounds while the third man set a spare ammo box and some grenades within reach.

We had been damned lucky that the Japs didn't attack during the first night. If they had, I seriously doubt we could have held the shallow perimeter on Red Two and Three. Much later it was learned that the generally disappointing naval gunfire had done some good: It destroyed a lot of the phone lines buried in Betio's shallow soil; and it probably killed Admiral Shibasaki with most of his staff. He knew his business—the defenses proved that beyond any doubt—and if he'd been alive to coordinate the counterattack, we'd have been in severe trouble.

Analysts later said that Tarawa was the only landing the Japs had a chance of defeating. After all, we only outnumbered them less than two to one, and every military textbook says the attacker needs three to one. If anything, an amphibious operation needs better odds than that.

I still get the galloping willies thinking what it would've been like, trying to get *off* that frigging island. Getting ashore was damn near impossible as it was.

So when *did* I run out of fuel?

I definitely went dry that afternoon, taking down the bunker with the first sergeant, but no way could one load have lasted me two days. And what about Dean's carbine? I didn't have it with me when I joined the Browning crew—just my pistol. Yet I was carrying it when I fell through the top of this miserable stinking bunker. Whenever *that* was. But was it before or after Dean was hit? It had to be after—just had to be.

It was much easier to close my eyes and visualize Bonnie McKenzie than to continue dwelling on my recent miserable history. But somehow it was important that I get things straight. After a while it dawned on me: I'd assumed that I made one trip back to the beach to reload, but there were two. I must have cadged a refill from one of the supply LVTs on one trek and maybe picked up a partial load from a casualty. Certainly there were lots of unused M1A1s on Betio Island. Losses among flame gunners were running about two out of every three.

It stood to reason, you know. If *you* were assigned to a last-stand bunker with a bunch of homicidal Marines headed toward you, which one would you shoot first? The one with the most terrifying weapon—right? Right. That was me: the Terror of Tarawa.

Where was I?

Oh. Yeah. How'd I get Dean's carbine again? He'd given it to me after he was wounded. Then I made those trips to the beach, but the first time I didn't have his piece because I think I refilled the bottles on my own pack. Next time I did have the carbine, apparently because I was looking for refills of fuel and propellant. After all, why lug the whole kit when a jerrican and a gas bottle will do? Okay, that makes sense. I could carry Dean's weapon and the refills at the same time.

But what did I do with the carbine in between? Give it to somebody else? Hardly makes sense—who'd want to carry two weapons?

Why in hell did it matter so much?

I remember wishing I had a pencil and some paper. Maybe I thought I'd write a Last Will and Testament or something—maybe just a note to my mom and sisters so they'd know I was thinking of them when I . . .

Belay that, boot! Sergeant Connelly was inside my head again, leaning close, bawling that rapid-fire stream of abuse that only Marine DIs seem able to deliver. *You don't frigging breathe unless I give you permission, yardbird! You people—it was always "you people"— live and die on my command! And I have not given you permission to die! Do you heeeear me?*

"SIR, YES SIR!"

Fifteen months later I still heard him.

I also heard other things, the oddest things. Like Sunday school. So help me, I started thinking of Sunday school. No damn reason whatsoever. Mainly I recalled the songs we practiced, and considering my appalling situation, the thought was either comforting or ironic. I remembered one in particular:

If you're happy and you know it, clap your hands (clap-clap).
If you're happy and you know it, clap your hands (clap-clap).
If your're happy and you know it, and you really want to show it,
  if you're happy and you know it, clap your hands (clap-clap).

I have no idea how long I thought, whispered, or gurgled those lyrics. Maybe for hours. But I was too weak and too damaged to clap my hands.

Another one was more appropriate:

Jesus loves me, this I know
  for the Bible tells me so.
Little ones to him belong;
  they are weak but He is strong.
Yes, Jesus loves me.
  Yes, Jesus loves me.
Yes, Jesus loves me.
  The Bible tells me so.

God's honest truth: I didn't know if Jesus loved me anymore, but I damn sure *hoped* that He did. The way it turned out, I guess that He really did, after all.

There was a story—it may be true—that the Marines found some Catholic nuns on an island where they'd hidden from the Japs for a couple of years. The sisters were French, and didn't speak much English. But within a matter of hours they'd learned basic American Marine English: "Can-dy ees dan-dy but liquor ees queek-er."

I hope it's true.

THIRTEEN

By evening of D plus one we had a damn good idea of what we were up against. Our combat veterans noticed a difference between the Tarawa Japs and the Guadalcanal variety. On the Canal we fought the Imperial Army almost exclusively, and it was a tough opponent. Its soldiers were extremely aggressive in an attack and tenacious in defense—very few surrendered. But according to some of our officers and senior NCOs, the Jap army was often sloppy and frequently overconfident. One of the elite units sent to Guadalcanal had cut its teeth in China, where it gained a fearsome reputation. But fighting half-trained, poorly led Chinese factions in no way prepared Colonel Ichiki's men for the U.S. Marine Corps. Basically, the battalion was destroyed in one night of combat; the survivors slowly starved to death.

However, the Japanese naval infantry was another breed of cat. That's what we encountered at Tarawa. Judging by their equipment and the handful of prisoners, they were neat, orderly, and efficient. In our terms, they were squared away.

Of course, it's probably not fair to compare a six-month meat grinder like Guadalcanal with a three-day fight like Betio. But unquestionably the land-fighting sailors were more flexible in combat.

They had nearly identical weapons to the army—just less variety—but used them more skillfully. Their combat philosophy was more sophisticated than the army's, as proven by the layered defenses we found on Betio. Just because we took out one bunker or position didn't mean the next one folded up. Not a bit: The Sasebo Landing Force knew the value of infiltration and fluid defense.

We knew what was coming, and began making preparations. After a while I was detached from my impromptu machine-gun crew. Somebody figured that with the losses among flamethrower operators, I was semispecial and should be held in reserve for the next day. Consequently, I was pulled back to the second line, so I hefted the carbine with a fifteen-round magazine inserted and a couple of spares nearby. Later, there were thirty-round "banana clips," but I never heard of those until Korea. Anyway, we knew the Japs wouldn't attack until after dark, so I placed the mags within easy reach, where I could find them by feel. I even closed my eyes and practiced grabbing them a couple of times.

Foolish boy.

One thing I did sort of wonder about was whether Dean and I shot the same zero. The Corps was big on basic marksmanship, of course, and we learned in boot camp that when a rifle is sighted for one man, the next guy to pick it up may shoot high or low, left or right. Eyes are just different, and that didn't begin to account for variations in technique such as shoulder mount or cheek weld. As it turned out, such things didn't matter on Betio. The shooting that night was usually within pistol distance.

The one thing I did right was having that big Colt fully loaded: a seven-round magazine and one in the chamber. Against all regulations my .45 was cocked and locked in the holster. I had two extra mags for that, too, in my belt pouch.

They hit us at 2300, an hour before midnight.

I had heard that some *banzai* attacks were little more than drunken mobs of crazed Japs stewed on sake or even dope. They'd come howling out of the dark, tossing grenades and waving bayoneted rifles and bamboo spears. They'd scream "Maline you die!" (just like the movies) or curse Roosevelt (hell, some of us did that) and throw themselves on our lines, where the gunnery sergeants had laid overlapping fields of fire. Let me tell you: Whoever brings a spear to a machine gun fight is going to lose. Big-time.

But the *rikusentai* were a cut or two above that. They began with infiltrators sneaking up to our lines, and even through the lines in some places. There were scattered fights beginning that evening, with combat on both sides and even behind us, which made me *very* nervous. What was really spooky, but we didn't realize it just then, was that some of the fighting was with knives and bayonets. Good fire discipline in those platoons—shooting gave away our positions, which is what the Japs wanted. Eventually the infiltrators—somebody said a few dozen—were killed or driven off. The Japs were actually scouts, sent to probe our lines and find the seams of our unit boundaries. The survivors scurried back to their leaders with the information.

They didn't waste much time.

Shortly after the initial wave, the Japs sent out a larger group, trying to overrun some of our advanced positions. It was dark by then—dark as only the tropics can be, with that sudden loss of daylight—and visibility suffered. However, by that time we had artillery on Betio as well as Bairiki islet two miles east. The Tenth Marines had assembled enough 105mm pack howitzers to be really useful, and combined with naval gunfire, the first attack was blown to rags and tatters. Our artillery spotters were really good—they called fire within fifty yards of our MLR, and the Japs got little to show for their losses.

Around 2400 another attack developed, and this one more or less conformed to the movie script. Lots of yelling and indiscriminate shooting, but it didn't cause us any harm that I could determine. Other than to keep us wide-eyed alert.

While all the foregoing was under way, Hardy and I huddled with our new partners and realized nobody was likely to get any sleep that night. The usual drill was one man awake in each hole, but even without the shelling I don't think any of us would have slept. We were living on adrenaline, round the clock.

But a long, tense lull set in after that attack. Maybe four hours ticked away, and some of us actually did dope off for a while. I'm not sure if I did or not, but I sort of remember a twitch or nudge when the real deal exploded.

Somewhere around 0300 things really popped. A battalion or more of Jap marines launched themselves at our line, and these boys were dead-nuts serious. They began with machine-gun fire from concealed and exposed positions, obviously hoping to pin us down. Then the attack was fully developed: howling, shooting, throwing grenades, and hollering the full Hollywood script: "Japanese drink 'melican blood!" It would've been like kid stuff if it weren't so damned determined.

Nothing stopped those Japs—not even mortars or artillery. They were piled up by the score along the line but just kept coming. They simply did not care if they lived or died as long as they took some Marines with them. My hole was about fifty yards behind the MLR, and it was apparent pretty damn soon that they were coming straight for us.

I'm not going to say the scene was hellish—that's too trite. It was too complex, too violent, too beautiful for any one word. Star shells, orange-white explosions, red tracers, frenzied movements, screams, curses, and unrelenting gunfire.

A group of Japs surged past the MLR and came straight at us. Hardy emptied two clips from his Garand so fast that somebody said it didn't sound like he reloaded. Half-kneeling, I shouldered the carbine and opened fire. They were surprisingly difficult targets—bandy-legged little men racing through the dark, dodging and weaving. I probably shot five or six rounds without hitting anything before I told myself, *Front sight*. One Jap in particular seemed determined to skewer me with his bayonet. I put the front bead on his second button and triggered several more rounds. He just kept coming. I could not believe it; I *knew* I was hitting him, but he hardly slowed. He was within eight or ten feet of my hole when he sagged to his knees. I shot him in the face, and he pitched forward.

Another Jap emerged behind him. I shot him a couple of times, then nothing. The bolt locked back on an empty mag. *Reload*, I screamed to myself. I groped in the dark for my carefully positioned magazines—and could not find them. Later I found one in the bottom of my hole. Apparently a Jap had kicked it in there while dying.

I was probably well into psychic trauma by then. My main weapon had failed to kill a determined enemy, and now I was empty. I reversed Dean's carbine, thinking to use it as a club, when I remembered the pistol. I dropped the damn carbine, pulled my Colt, and took solace in its weight.

I was aware of the physiological traits of distress: my elevated pulse, the pounding in my chest, the sudden leaden weight of my arms. My mouth was wide-open, sucking in the humid tropic air, eyes wide, but ears probably useless from all the shooting and shelling.

More Japs surged around us. Three came at us again, one shooting his bolt-action Arisaka from the hip—a waste of ammo. I pointed the Colt more than aimed it, one-handed as we were taught back then, and pulled the trigger. The .45 bucked in recoil, but I couldn't tell if I hit the Jap or not. He kept coming. I pulled the trigger again, this time aware that I had flinched badly—low and left like all right-handers. The Jap staggered, struck in the right leg. That big 230-grain bullet, propelled at eight hundred feet per second, took him down. I shot him again through the top of the head. Distance maybe eight feet. I shot at a couple more Japs. They went down. Maybe Hardy killed them.

Suddenly it was quiet. I was aware of something wet on my arm—blood. Not a lot but enough to notice. I didn't know what happened until I saw the greenish uniform of the dead Jap with his bayonet in our hole, partly on top of Hardy.

My trembling left hand fumbled its way to my mag pouch, found a reload, and seated it in the pistol. I looked at Hardy. He looked at me.

He was dead.

About daylight I went toward the beach, looking for a refill of fuel and more propellant. We'd be moving again, but without an A-gunner, and no refills, I was just another rifleman unless I got more napalm and hydrogen; maybe nitrogen, too, for the igniter. That was it! I remembered! I got permission from the squad leader—he was from another platoon—to go back to the grounded amtracks. They were meant as supply vehicles, anyway. One of our engineer "tracks" should have refills. *That's* what I was doing.

I picked my way back to Red Three, thinking I'd find somebody who could get me a refill. It wasn't far—maybe 150 yards—but tough going. The ground was incredibly tangled with palm fronds, tree trunks, shell holes, and debris. It was hard to make ten normal steps in a straight line.

Less than halfway along my route I detoured to the left to avoid a clump of splintered trees. The ground seemed to rise a couple of feet, but I went that way, seeking the easiest path. Abruptly I noticed a hollowed-out depression, obviously man-made, just to my left. It was an entrance of some sort. *Spider hole*, I thought, a position for a sniper or light Nambu. I flicked off the safety and turned almost 180 degrees, backing away from the possible threat.

Then I was falling.

I don't remember hitting bottom. Evidently I lost my helmet in the fall because I took a nasty thump on the back of my head. Poor discipline, leaving my chin straps unbuckled. I recalled feeling the footing giving way beneath me, a low crackling sound of something collapsing, and then falling backward. I tried to keep a grip on Dean's carbine.

When I came around, I was wet and smelly and mostly in darkness. *Carbine*, I thought. I felt with both hands but found nothing solid within reach. Just lots of water and spongy, filthy stuff. My head ached; I thought maybe my scalp was bleeding.

I remembered looking up. Jagged coconut logs and palm fronds silhouetted themselves against the brightening tropic sky.

The sky—I could see that and not much else.

Then I reasoned it out: I'd backed into the blasted opening of a dugout or bunker. Palm leaves from the ruined trees had fallen on top of the shell hole, looking like the rest of the vegetation I'd walked upon. *Wham*. I fell straight through, landing on my back and left shoulder, hitting my skull on something. My back and shoulder hurt in a persistent, throbbing sensation. I could move my extremities but didn't want to—normal motion caused too much pain. The one time I tried to sit up, a burning, stabbing sensation pierced my back. I passed out again.

FOURTEEN

They found me on D plus three, a couple of hours past daylight. Later the medic said I kept mumbling something nonsensical— "Clap your hands; clap your hands."

It was odd, you know? November was midsummer on Tarawa, and the equatorial heat built rapidly. I thought about that for a little while. Back home on 20 November there was probably snow on the ground. But that was clear across half the Pacific Ocean and most of the North American continent. There I guess it was only the nineteenth. Or was it the twenty-first? I never could keep things straight with the International Date Line. Hell, I don't know why I bothered—it didn't matter in my predicament. One day was just as awful as the next.

I don't remember a lot about the Marines discovering me; mainly American voices, distinct accents. There was somebody with a drawl, evidently the one in charge, and the inevitable New Yorker, all flippant and cynical. Odd thing about New Yorkers—they have a deserved reputation for rudeness, but many of them naturally address a stranger as "buddy." It turned out to be the Navy corpsman. That explained it.

I couldn't see well by then; evidently some fuel in the bunker had *got* in my eyes. Additionally, my pupils reacted to the harsh sunlight after about fifteen hours in relative darkness.

Somebody coughed repeatedly, and it dawned on me that he was reacting to *me*. Actually, "coughed" is too polite a term. The Marine choked and gagged. Only then did I realize that I could no longer smell anything. My nose had shut down, almost permanently. The last thing I smelled in this life for about eleven years was the horrid stench of those rotting Jap corpses in that tight, confined space.

A couple of men lifted me out of the shattered bunker, and the corpsman went to work. He swabbed my eyes with something that burned, but after a while I could see form and color. I croaked something unrecognizable to me or to my saviors, but they knew intuitively. Someone poured water on a handkerchief and pressed it to my lips. They were caked with sand and filth, but I sucked every drop from the cloth and begged for more. "Don't give him too much yet," the corpsman said. "It might kill him."

Somebody came up beside me with a carbine. He said "I got your weapon, Mac. It looks okay."

I turned to look at the carbine, curious as to where it had been. Without quite knowing why, I raised a hand, and the Marine pushed it toward me, holding the foregrip. I ran my fingers along the stock and felt something odd. Peering closely, I saw two notches carved in the wood. They were pretty fresh.

It wasn't Dean's carbine. He hadn't shot anybody.

I fingered the kill marks a little more, and the Marine said, "I see you got a couple there."

So *that* was it! I was getting my memory back. When I left the MG crew to get more fuel, one of the ammo bearers had loaned me *his* carbine. I'd shucked my 782 gear including the web belt with the trusty Colt, figuring that I'd travel light and maybe carry more of a useful load. What became of Dean's weapon I couldn't recall.

The odd thing was why I took a carbine at all, since I'd been disappointed in its stopping power. I don't know—maybe I was getting rock happy by then. The failure of the carbine to stop a Jap with five or six center-of-mass hits at twenty feet or so really unnerved me. Later it was determined that the cartridge, though .30 caliber, was too anemic to knock down a determined adversary unless he was struck in the brain or spine. But the reliable old warhorse, the M1911 pistol, seemed to do the job. Believe me, I'm a huge fan of the late John Moses Browning. I guess I just didn't want to pack the web belt with the heavy pistol, ammo, canteens, knife, and whatnot. By that night I was tired, scared, and dopey—a bad combination when your life is at stake.

They placed me on a litter, and four men I never saw before or after took me to the aid station. Along the way I heard gagging, retching sounds that could only be the thick, liquid emptying of someone's stomach. Fervent curses, earnest blasphemy, followed. Then silence. They were reacting to *me*.

At the aid station a doctor, a navy lieutenant, looked me over more thoroughly. He ordered someone to remove my dungarees; the orderly had to use scissors. I'd long since passed the point that I was aware of myself. The Japanese blood had clotted and stiffened my camouflage jacket and half the trousers. Some of it stuck to my skin. I didn't care.

Long story short, when I fell through the hole in that bunker I landed on something hard, resulting in a compression fracture of my spine. That's why I was partially paralyzed for all those miserable hours. The guys in sick bay said I was semidelirious the first couple of days, lapsing in and out of sleep or consciousness. I was disoriented, too: couldn't put things in order. I wondered if I'd spent one night or two in that stinking bunker, but it had to be one, the night of D plus two.

However, after several days I regained full sensation and partial mobility (though not all my short-term memory) so I wasn't sent Stateside. I recuperated in a couple of different hospitals, including one in Hawaii, which was tolerable. *Her* name was Helen, and she became my wife of fifty-one years.

Talk about silver linings . . .

FIFTEEN

I've had nearly sixty years to think about war and combat. People often confuse the two, but in modern war the "tooth to tail" ratio constantly gets less. Even in World War II, presumably the greatest of all time, for every trigger puller there were eight, ten, twenty other uniformed men and women stretching all the way back to the States. Clerks, bakers, instructors, doctors, truck drivers, mechanics; you name it. For the large majority, WWII was exasperating, inconvenient, and boring.

For others, of course, it was ugly, violent, and short.

There's only one way into this life, but there are so many ways to leave it. Wartime, of course, accelerates the process and adds an enormous variety of exits. You can be shot, bombed, shelled, stabbed, torpedoed, burned, or suffocated. You could as easily be killed by accident as by intention. I knew guys who drowned in training and in combat; I saw a man crippled by a crate that fell on him in New Zealand. We camped near a heavy weapons company that lost a lieutenant a few days before embarking. He was checking a water-cooled Browning that had some sort of problem while the other gun in the section was being cleaned. Somehow, a round had been left in the chamber of the number two gun and it fired when a cleaning rod was pushed through the muzzle. The rod went clean through the lieutenant, and he bled to death before the ambulance arrived.

The thing that struck me was how capricious it all was. My pal Ben Youngblood was in the LVT next to me; it took a shell hit and started burning. The mortarman standing next to Ben was torn apart by the explosion, leaving brains and blood on Ben's fatigues. Ben sustained some hearing loss—that was all.

Dedicated riflemen felt that their skill with an M1 was the best life insurance possible, and for some it was. Others, who regularly shot Expert and treated their Garands like babies, never made it to the beach.

Rear Admiral Keiji Shibasaki knew that his island would be attacked, and reportedly he boasted that a million men could not take Betio in a hundred years. But 18,309 Marines and sailors did it in seventy-six hours. Every square meter of the place was preregistered by carefully sited artillery, grenade launchers, and automatic weapons. The same applied to the reef and the lagoon, with its viciously unpredictable tides.

In all, 1,009 Americans were killed on Betio plus 2,101 wounded. The Japanese fought almost literally to the last man: Seventeen naval infantry survived with 129 Korean laborers. The stench was appalling: about 5,000 rotting corpses over 291 acres.

Try to imagine how that smelled.

I've been asked many times if I was scared on Betio. The truth is, there was little time for fear. The worst periods were those two nights, waiting for the *banzai* charge that finally came early on D plus two. But while moving and shooting, making plans with squad leaders, most of us could function. That was due to our training and our leadership.

So was I scared? Well, I'll say this: For three days I was pretty damn *concerned*.

Sometimes people learn that I was a World War II Marine—a Tarawa Marine—and they ask how I feel about the Japanese. So I tell them.

They were Japs to me; they'll frigging *always* be Japs. But that was then; this is now. Far as I'm concerned, we didn't bomb them enough or hang nearly enough of them for their war crimes. Mac-Arthur just plain let the emperor off the hook because of the post-war "big picture." Years ago I read that some bastard who had eaten the liver of an American POW was released from prison and elected to the Jap parliament. Well, that's way above my pay grade, but a Marine Reserve noncom has a right to his opinion, and you've just heard mine.

The *rikusentai*, the Jap marines, were doing pretty much what we were doing—serving our country. The fact that their side started the whole damned mess tended to get lost in the gut-level confrontations with rifles, satchel charges, and flamethrowers. Don't get me wrong: I don't admire the little bastards, but I still respect them as soldiers. They were incredibly tough, disciplined, and—contrary to what we expected—they could shoot.

I've met several Japanese people over the years, and in fact my Rotary Club has a sister organization in Yokosuka. We exchange visits once in a while. I've never been to Japan—don't ever plan to go there—but it's just not in me to hate anymore. I'm not sure that I ever did hate anybody, even on Tarawa.

Well, that's not strictly true. I hated Lyndon Baines Johnson and Robert Strange McNamara for the way they squandered my oldest boy's life in Vietnam, and *that's* a sentiment that will never die. The fact that Brian died in a stupid forklift accident at a place called Bien Hoa doesn't matter—the effect was the same as if a Viet Cong had shot him. He and fifty-eight thousand other Americans died for nothing. As the grunts said: He was "wasted."

But hate the Japs? No, not really. Not anymore. Hell, some of my VFW buddies won't even drive a Honda or a Subaru, but my daughter's Nissan was built in Tennessee. How can you hate anybody from Smyrna, Tennessee?

If I have any lasting regrets about the war, I suppose it's the fact that so little is known or remembered about the Pacific Theater. Kids today, if they know anything, talk about Pearl Harbor or Hiroshima—nothing in between. Tarawa was just about smack-dab in the middle, chronologically and geographically.

At some point I'm sure most of us on that miserable little island wondered if it was worth the death and suffering. After the war General "Howlin' Mad" Smith, the V Corps commander, said flat out that Tarawa wasn't worth it. He said we should have bypassed it like we did so many other places. However, Major General Julian Smith, who led the Second Division, and most others, like Admiral Spruance, insisted it was worth the price, in lessons learned if nothing else. I guess that's true: Someplace had to be the first atoll, and Tarawa was small enough that we could make our mistakes there rather than in a much bigger operation, like Kwajalein or Saipan.

The strategists said we had to have the Gilberts in order to take the Marshalls. Again, maybe that's true—I just don't know. But one thing is certain. Nearing the end of my life, I've had plenty of time to think about what matters most: family, friends, and self-respect. We inherit our families and choose our friends, but we have to earn respect, including the way we see ourselves.

I'm eighty now, in declining health, but still able to enjoy life. I root for the Packers and sip some bourbon and spoil my grandchildren, which somebody said is the best revenge, even when they're college students. I still love my late wife; I cherish my family, and I value my friends, though I don't hear from many of my WWII buddies anymore—we're pretty thin on the ground these days.

But once in a while, I find myself thinking back to November of '43. It doesn't take much: a whiff of gasoline at the service station; a really hot, muggy day; a green uniform; even a bus driver's trousers. In those moments I relive horrific events on a miserable little island in a world that—amazingly—in some ways was better than now. Maybe there's even a little spring left in my step when I recall with a fierce, quiet pride: I was a seagoing Marine. More than that, I was a flame gunner at Tarawa.

Semper Fi, Mac.

EYES OF THE CAT

JAMES COBB

JAMES COBB has lived his entire life within a thirty-mile radius of a major Army post, an Air Force base, and a Navy shipyard. He comments, "Accordingly, it seemed natural to become a kind of cut-rate Rudyard Kipling, trying to tell the stories of America's service people." Currently, he's writing the Amanda Garrett techno-thriller series, with four books, *Chooser of the Slain, Seastrike, Seafighter,* and *Target Lock* published. He's also doing the Kevin Pulaski suspense thrillers for St. Martin's Press. He lives in the Pacific Northwest and, when he's not writing, he indulges in travel, the classic American hot rod, and collecting historic firearms.

She would never be called a beautiful airplane.

Her broad, twin-engined wing was pylon-mounted, set well above a flattened, boatlike fuselage well studded with a variety of bulges, turrets, and blisters. Likewise, her horizontal stabilizers rode high on her upswept tail.

As a fighting machine she also left something to be desired. Her designed defensive armament was light and her bomb load comparatively small. She was lumberingly slow and could be a cranky and notional flier at times, demanding that her pilots pay attention to their work and to her idiosyncrasies.

But she had her advantages as well.

She was versatile. In both her seaplane and amphibian incarnations, any body of water deep enough for her to float in could serve as an airport. If water wasn't available, swamp mud or snow could do. She also had range. She could span oceans or loiter in a single patch of sky for an entire day.

Lastly, she was tough. She had that uncanny ruggedness and survivability that American aviation designers have the knack of building into their creations. She could absorb battle damage that would kill any number of prettier aircraft and still, somehow, drag herself home again.

Her crews could forgive her much for that.

She was old for a warbird when her hour came. Her replacements were already on the drawing board. But when the world burst into flames in the fall of 1939, she was what was available. She was what was ready to fly and to fight and to meet the crisis at hand.

She was legion in the service of the Allies; the Americans, the British and Commonwealth Powers, the Dutch, the Russians, the Free French, they all knew and respected her, and she ranged over every sea reach of the Second World War.

She was never formally christened with a dramatic combatant's title like "Avenger" or "Dauntless." The United States Navy simply called her the PBY. (Patrol Bomber, with the "Y" standing as the government designation of the Consolidated Aircraft Corporation, her builder.) The British dubbed her the Catalina, after the island lying off her Los Angeles birthplace.

But in the night skies above the South Pacific, certain of her breed earned themselves another name, a name that would become intertwined with a legend.

They called them the Black Cats.

Lieutenant Meredith Leeland-Rhys, of His Majesty's Royal Navy Volunteer Reserve, was certain he was going to perish, and the close proximity of the enemy had nothing to do with it.

After four years spent in wartime England, he was quite accustomed to the potential of a sudden, violent death. This climate was another matter entirely. He had left an early British spring to arrive in a late Solomon Islands summer, and the intervening ninety-four hours had not been near time enough for adaptation.

His tropic whites, the sole set he'd been able to borrow before enplaning, were sodden, both with sweat and with the blood-warm spray whipping back over the bow of the battered US Navy whaleboat. The spray served also to encrust his glasses and long-jawed features with sticky, half-dried salt. The smothering tropic humidity and pitching seas engaged in a conspiracy of nausea and dizziness, while the acetylene flame sun burned through both the crown of his uniform cap and his prematurely thinning hair. In the distance, beyond the body of water the whaleboat's coxswain had laconically called "Iron Bottom Bay," the mountainous outline of Guadalcanal Island shimmered, threatening to disappear in the heat haze.

Stripped to the waist, the mahogany-tanned boatswain's mate manning the launch's tiller seemed impervious to the environment. The Marine sentry assigned to Leeland-Rhys looked upon it merely as a good excuse for a nap, stretching out comfortably atop the equipment cases he was intended to guard.

Adding to Leeland-Rhys's discomfort, if such were possible, was the package he carried on his knees. The boat pool dispatcher had tossed it down into the launch just as they were casting off from the pier at Lungga Point. "Mind taking that across with you, Lieutenant? Commander Case has been bitching about this shipment all week, and they finally came in."

Leeland-Rhys had no objection to doing the favor. He only wished that the parcel had not been quite so prominently marked.

MEDICAL STORES / US NAVY
CONDOMS / PROPHYLACTIC/ FIVE HUNDRED

Beyond the indelicacy of it also came the question of what his prospective hosts intended to do with them all.

Back aft at the whaleboat's tiller, the coxswain straightened and pointed. "There you go, Lieutenant. Tulagi Seadrome, dead ahead."

"We say *leftenant*," Leeland-Rhys murmured halfheartedly over the rumble of the engine. He twisted around on the hard thwart seat to look ahead.

The whaleboat had nosed into a sheltered cove in the flank of one of the smaller islands on the northern side of Iron Bottom Bay. A single vessel lay at anchor there, the glassy waters of the cove lapping lightly at its rust-streaked flanks.

Formerly a World War I vintage "four piper" destroyer, the little ship had undergone an APV conversion. Now reincarnated as a fast seaplane tender, most of its armament and two of its distinctive, slender funnels had been exchanged for the enlarged deckhouses needed for a suite of aviation service equipment and personnel.

Spotted around the tender were a number of seaplane-mooring buoys, half a dozen of which were in use by a flotilla of PBY-5A Catalina amphibians. Three of the aircraft were in the standard blue-and-gray livery of US naval aviation, their white star insignia prominent on their sides.

The other three seemed to bear no insignia at all and were painted a dull, sooty black that absorbed the beating glare of the tropic sun.

As the whaleboat came opposite the APV's gangway, the coxswain popped the propeller into neutral. "Yo," he bellowed over the whine of the engine clutch, "got a load for the CO of Detachment Three! Whereaway?"

"Buoy Foxtrot!" The faint reply came. "The Black Cat straight off the stern!"

"Gotcha!" The coxswain got the launch under way again.

Leeland-Rhys was somewhat acquainted with the Catalina amphibians used by the Royal Navy. He'd assisted in the development of a number of systems for use aboard them. But the shadow-colored monster they now approached bore little resemblance to the airplane with which he was familiar.

There was a mottled effect to its dark paint that the Englishman had first attributed to some form of camouflaging. But as they drew closer, he realized that the mottling stemmed from a pattern of patches and dents on the combat-battered airframe.

A great many patches and dents.

The plane had been retrofitted with one of the new "Eyeball" nose turrets mounting a pair of thirty-caliber Brownings. Immediately below the turret, however, a metal plate had been bolted over the angled bomb-aimers window, a second and decidedly nonregulation cluster of heavy machine-gun muzzles protruding through it.

Reassuringly familiar was the set of antlerlike Yagi antennas that extended out from under the leading edges of the wings, the fittings for an ASV (Air-to-Surface-Vessel) radar. Those, at least, Leeland-

Rhys could understand. The Catalina had been one of the first air-craft in the world to be outfitted with such a detection system.

The cowling had been stripped from one of the plane's massive Pratt & Whitney radial engines. A pair of mechanics tinkered with the exposed mechanism suspended over the water on a flimsy workstand draped over the engine nacelle. Other aircrewmen am-bled over the top of the big plane's wings and fuselage, performing maintenance tasks with a monkeylike surety. Given the extremely casual and fragmentary state of their uniforms, it was impossible to tell officer from enlisted man.

One individual stood on a small work float tied off alongside the Catalina's bow. Dark-haired, of medium height and displaying the usual South Pacific Theater tan, he wore ragged, oil-stained khakis and a baseball cap, and apparently was of an artistic bent.

At the moment he was deeply engrossed in touching up the pic-ture painted below the cockpit of the Catalina, a most striking and detailed rendering of an attractive and well-endowed blond bobby-soxer. Clad in nothing but saddle shoes and hair ribbon, the young lady sat astride a torpedo, her head thrown back and a look of ecstasy on her features, the name "Zazz Girl" slashed beneath her in scarlet.

On a more serious note, a double row of rising sun flags and bomb symbols had also been stenciled beneath the cockpit window.

With a satisfied nod, the artist turned away from his work and looked to the approaching whaleboat.

Wondering if he should be yelling "ahoy" or something else ap-propriately nautical, Leeland-Rhys called out. "Excuse me, but I'm looking for Commander Case."

"You found him. You the radar guy?"

"Yes, sir. Leftenant Leeland-Rhys at your service, sir. I have some equipment with me."

"Great! Come alongside at the starboard waist blister. I'll meet you there." The aviator swung up the side of the Catalina to vanish through an overhead hatch into the cockpit.

True to his word he reappeared in the open waist blister just as the whaleboat nuzzled alongside. "Watch that throttle, swabby!" he roared at the coxswain. "Don't scratch the chrome!"

Case tied the launch's painter around the base of the blister's gun mount "Careful with the footwork coming across, Lieutenant," he said, as Leeland-Rhys gingerly prepared to transfer to the aircraft. "You don't want to step on Fido."

"That's *leftenant*, sir," Leeland-Rhys said apologetically. "And Fido?"

Case pointed down between the boat and the seaplane.

Below, in the azure waters, something moved.

"Bloody hell!"

Six striped feet of disturbed tiger shark flowed out from under the Catalina, reversed lithely, and disappeared back into the hull shadow.

"We used to shoot 'em," Case commented conversationally, "but the blood in the water attracts the big ones."

At close range, the dominant features for Lieutenant Commander Evan Randall Case were a pair of piercing green eyes and a focused intensity of word and action. "Right," he said, leaning in toward Leeland-Rhys. "How much of the dope did they feed you on the way in?"

The Englishman had to pause for a moment to translate before replying. "Uh, not much at all really. I was simply informed that there was a problem involving the location of a possible Japanese radar facility. I was dispatched with what we hope is the appropriate equipment to deal with the problem."

Said equipment was now being cursed into the waist compartment by the plane's crew chief and the Marine guard and coxswain from the launch. Case had summoned the *Zazz Girl*'s other officers to a conference with Leeland-Rhys in the amidships crew's quarters. The cramped space had a set of metal-framed, double-decked bunks on either side of a narrow walkway, the upper bunk being latched upright to provide a degree of headroom for those seated on the lower.

"There's the bitch, mate," Case's copilot commented. "Nobody can call if there's a Christless radar station or not." Flight Officer

Cyril Bates was an exchange officer from the Royal Australian Air Force, tall, lean, and intensely Aussie. Clad in boots, baggy shorts, and a wispy blond beard, he'd engulfed Leeland-Rhy's hand in a bone-crushing grip, introducing himself as, "the native guide for the bleedin' Yanks."

"One thing we can say," Ensign Phil Tibbs added. "If there is a radar, the Japs have it damn well hidden." The *Zazz Girl's* third officer was a striking differentiation from her two pilots. Morose and prematurely balding, he was heavyset to the verge of fleshiness, burning red rather than tanned. His fellow aviators introduced him as Phillip-the-Navigator, spoken as a single word. "AIRSOLS has gone over every island in that area with a fine-tooth comb. They haven't found a thing."

"AIRSOLS?" Leeland-Rhys queried, something he sensed he was going to be doing a great deal of.

"Air Solomons Command," Case replied, "our lords and masters over at Henderson Field. The army fly-fly boys doing our photo recon claim we're just seeing things up the Slot. I'm saying they're *not* seeing something. That's why you're here, Lieutenant. You're going to prove which of us has a screw loose."

"It's *left*" . . . Leeland-Rhys caught himself and sighed. "Oh, bugger it! I suppose it really doesn't matter that much. You see, gentleman, I'm not actually a naval officer, professionally speaking that is. In truth, I'm an associate professor of physics at Cambridge, electromagnetic propagation and related phenomena. The military rank is a . . . convenience."

Tibbs chuckled dryly. "Don't let it worry you, Professor. I'm really an insurance salesman."

"Too right," Bates added. "My dad and me run a hotel in Rockhampton." A detached and dreamy smile crossed the Australian's lean features. "We have a public bar, a private bar, and a lounge, and all three of them serve beer, endless quantities of wonderful, beautiful, cold, beer."

Case snorted. "Oh, quit bellyaching, Cyril. If anyone has a bitch around here, it's me. Before the war it was LA to Reno three times a week for Western Airlines and all the divorcées I could seduce.

Anyway, Prof, welcome to the great South Pacific Amateur Hour."

Leeland-Rhys found himself smiling. This wasn't what he'd been expecting at all . . . fortunately. "Thank you, gentlemen. I hope I can prove of assistance. Oh, and by the way, I have a parcel here," He awkwardly presented the carton of prophylactics. "They indicated over at the port that it was rather important."

Case brightened. "Damn square it is, Prof, at least to one of my guys."

"One of them?"

"Yeah. HEY, GUNS! WE GOT YOUR RUBBERS IN!"

The watertight hatch in the forward bulkhead swung open, and a bearded face under a blue-dyed navy Dixecup hat appeared. "Thank God for small favors, skipper." The sailor grinned. "My last set's totally shot. I didn't know what I was going to do for tonight."

Case tossed the package to the aviation hand. "Use them in good health, me son. And while you're at it, send the second Sparks back. I need words with him."

"Sure thing, skipper."

As the hatch closed Leeland-Rhys gathered himself to ask the question that had been nagging at him ever since he'd had the box of prophylactics tossed into his lap. Before he could speak, however, the hatch swung open once more.

"You wanted to see me, sir?"

"Yeah, Richie," Case replied, "I want you to give a briefing to the professor here on your scope ghosts. Prof, here's the guy who's really responsible for calling you out here, Radioman Second Class Richie Anjellico. He's our expert on, what'dyacall it, 'electromagnetic propagation and related phenomena.' "

Leeland-Rhys knew that all hands must be at least eighteen years of age to serve in the American Navy. The dark-haired youth in the sun-faded dungarees must simply look younger.

"It's like this, sir," Anjellico said, hunkering down on the duckboards that floored the compartment. "There's one sector out there where I keep getting abnormalities on my A scope . . . 'scope ghosts' the skipper calls them. To me, they looked like secondary spikes from another radar transmitter, like I get from the ASVs on the other Cats. But I've picked them up when the other planes haven't been around. I've even detected them when we've been the only PBY airborne over the Slot."

Leeland-Rhys frowned. "Possibly a secondary reflection of your own wave. Off an island or even a dense cloud mass."

The Englishman ran an annoyed hand back through his sweat-slick hair. Was this what all the fuss was about? Radar technology was still in its infancy, a tricky proposition at best for the most skilled of available operators. And the militaries were cranking out thousands of these . . . for lack of a better term, "children," with a bare minimum of training.

Anjellico shook his head emphatically. "No, sir! I know my set and how to use it. I performed all of the tests for false returns. I shifted frequencies and power settings, and I had Commander Case perform bearing changes. This was another active radar set cutting across my band. I'm sure of it."

"Have any of the other aircraft in your flight detected this phenomenon?"

"Not at first, sir, but I think I've got that figured out. I had the *Girl*'s ASV tweaked to work a skootch lower in the frequency range than standard. I seem to get a better surface return definition that way. That's when I started lifting the secondary spikes on my scope. When the operators on the *Hep Gee* and *Lazy Mae* pulled the same tweak, they started picking 'em up too."

Leeland-Rhys sighed . . . heavily. *God save us from the tinkering amateur!* Obviously it was a feedback effect of some nature, probably off the rectifiers. They should seal the bloody units when they leave the factory. He started to speak, then caught his arch comment before it could escape.

There were three other men present in the compartment. Three veteran combat aviators the Englishman reminded himself. And obviously they seemed to think the boy knew what he was talking about.

Case must have read his mind. "My guys all know their stuff, Professor." He stated slowly. "That includes Richie here. If he says something's cooking on his scope, then there is. If you don't believe me, there's a couple of hundred dead Japs who can give you references."

Leeland-Rhys decided that maybe things might not be quite so obvious after all.

"Is there any particular area where these phenomena occur?" He probed.

"Yes, sir," Anjellico answered promptly. "It only happens in one specific area. Right up in the guts of the Slot."

"Excuse me once more, but, 'the Slot'?"

"Yeah," Case interjected. "The Slot. Phil, you got that theater chart? Let's give the Prof a little orientation."

"It would be appreciated," Leeland-Rhys agreed.

Phillip-the-Navigator produced a well-worn map, unfolding it across the knees of the seated men.

"Here," Case indicated. "You see these three narrow islands up in the Bismarck Sea in a kind of a wishbone pattern? New Britain, New Ireland, and Bougainville, they belong to the Japs."

Case's finger whispered across the chart paper. "About 340 miles east-southeast as the Zero flies, you got this group of islands: Guadalcanal, Florida and Tulagi, Malaita, San Cristobal. They belong to us.

"In between, kind of connecting these two groups, are these two smaller island chains on either side of a strait formally christened New Georgia Sound. However, we who are on intimate terms with the place call it 'the Slot.' Choiseul and Santa Isabel make up the northern chain, Vella Lavella, Kolombangara, and New Georgia, along with a few odds and ends, make up the southern. These are the Central Solomons and exactly who they belong to is currently under discussion.

"The Japs have some little Podunk garrisons and outposts on some of the islands, and the Australians have coastwatchers and native guerrillas on some of the others. We aren't quite ready to move in and take over, and the Japs aren't quite ready to stop us. Whoever gets ready first, wins. Get the picture?"

Leeland-Rhys nodded, peering down at the chart through his salt-speckled glasses.

"During the day, AIRSOLS aircraft operating out of Henderson Field on Guadal dominate the Slot. We can sink any ship the Japs send in, so they can't resupply and reinforce their garrisons conventionally. They have to rely on *daihatsus* and the Tokyo Express."

"Pardon?" Leeland-Rhys said, looking up.

"A *daihatsu* is a Japanese army landing barge," Case elaborated. "They're about fifty feet long, are made out of wood, and are powered by a small gas or diesel engine. Sort of like a Higgins Boat. The Jap barge yards crank 'em out by the hundreds. They use them to run a supply shuttle between their main bases at Rabaul and Bougainville and their Central Solomon garrisons. These *daihatsu* convoys move by night, hugging the island coastlines. By day they lie low under camouflage in little inlets and creek mouths, avoiding our regular air patrols."

" 'At's where we come in." Bates tapped himself on the chest with a thick-nailed thumb.

"Right," Case agreed. "Thanks to our radar, we can spot the little bastards, even in the dark. We bomb 'em, strafe 'em, and sic our PT boats on 'em. Killing *daihatsus* is our primary job around here. That and scouting the Tokyo Express."

"And what's the Tokyo Express?" Leeland-Rhys inquired, becoming steadily more intrigued.

"The other way the Japs have of moving personnel and equipment into the Central Solomons. They'll assemble a task group of fast warships, destroyers mostly, with sometimes a cruiser or two thrown in, at their big fleet base at Rabaul on New Britain. There, they'll load 'em up with a big deck cargo of stores, food, medicine, ammo, whatever. The task group will sortie and move right up to the edge of AIRSOLS daytime strike coverage. Then, come sunset, zoom! They head down the Slot, going flank speed and balls to the wall all the way to one of the Jap garrisons.

"Their cargo has mostly been loaded into watertight steel drums that have been ballasted to float, so when they reach their destination, the stuff can just be heaved over the side to be collected by small craft. Any personnel to be transferred get pretty much heaved over the side, too. Then the Express turns around and beats it back up the Slot, getting out of range before our strike aircraft can launch at first light."

"And your squadron has to, ah, derail this Express as well?"

"Oh, we take a shot at 'em now and again." Case grinned. "Mostly, though, we scout and shadow and leave the shooting to the big boys. Whenever we spot an Express assembling, we move one of our own cruiser-destroyer forces into position here at our end of the Slot. When the Japs come down, our guys go up. When they meet, things can get pretty interesting."

Leeland-Rhys arched an eyebrow. He suspected he was hearing a considerable understatement. "Back to the radar abnormalities. Where exactly do they occur?"

"Always right here, sir," Anjellico replied promptly, sketching on the chart with a fingertip "Kind of in a triangular area that runs from the northern coast of New Georgia to the southeastern tip of Choiseul to the northeastern tip of Santa Isabel."

A large gray cat rolled over in Leeland-Rhys's belly. "Just there and nowhere else?"

"No, sir, just there."

"Gentlemen," Leeland-Rhys said slowly, "I hope you will forgive me for coming into this matter with a somewhat dubious attitude. Especially you, Mr. Anjellico. But that is exactly the location one would cover with a search radar if one wished to control the Central Solomon Islands. And furthermore, that's the exact propagation pattern such a Japanese search radar would produce."

"Ha!" Case reached forward and swiped the grinning Anjellico's cap lower over his eyes, Bates, the copilot, adding a bruising slap on the boy's shoulder.

"Furthermore," Leeland-Rhys continued, "the Japanese do possess a surface search radar called the Type 22 that operates on the ninety-megacycle band. Conceivably it could interact with an ASV in the way you have described. We even have a working model of one in our hands. It was captured by your lads right over on Guadalcanal, so we know they are using them in this theater. But there is a problem."

"What's that, Prof?" Case demanded.

"You say that an air search has been made for a radar installation in this area?" Leeland-Rhys gestured to the chart.

"Yeah, both by photo recon and Mark 1 eyeball."

"Then something should have been spotted. You see, the Japanese do have radar, but their systems are comparatively crude compared to ours. Crude and large. To date they've got nothing like our airborne ASV sets. They haven't perfected the cavity magnetron yet, don't you see . . . Uh, you didn't hear that word, by the way. This Japanese Type 22 system I mentioned would require a large fixed-mast array rather like a British Chain Home station . . . You chaps would call it a bedspring antenna . . . and it would have to be located with clear direct view of the . . . ah . . . Slot.

"In fact, I'll go one better. To produce that conic propagation pattern, it would have to be located very prominently at one of the three node points mentioned by Mr. Anjellico here. The northernmost point on the coast of New Georgia . . . the southeastern tip of Choiseul or one of its smaller satellite islands, or the northeastern tip of Santa Isabel."

Case scowled and shoved his baseball cap to the back of his head. "One problem, Prof. There's nothing at any of those three points. Our blip jockeys figured out that propagation deal, too. Only no antenna. No installations of any kind anywhere where there should be one."

It was Leeland-Rhys's turn to scowl. "Nothing at all?"

"I can take you to the intelligence office aboard the tender and show you the aerial photography. I'll give 'em credit, the army F-5s went in so low you can count the land crabs."

The Englishman felt himself deflate even further. Again he found himself wondering just what he was supposed to be doing out here. Only now he found himself viewing the problem from the point of his own inferiority.

"That's why they sent for you, Prof," Case went on, unaware he was rubbing salt in the wounds. "Our people are stumped. Either we're dead wrong about this, or the Japs have something new up their sleeve. You Brits are the whiz kids when it comes to radar. You invented the stuff. We figure you're our best shot at getting this sorted out."

Leeland-Rhys took a deep breath of humidity-dank air and let it puff from his lips.

"I certainly hope I can live up to your confidence, Commander. Firstly, I suppose we should see if we are dealing with an actual signal from a radar set. I've got something in my bag of tricks that might be able to resolve that question. It's called a passive intercept receiver, and it's designed to detect output on any of the known radar frequencies and verify that it is indeed an active radar sweep."

"How long will it take you to set it up?"

"Well, with the assistance of my associate"—Leeland-Rhys gave a nod toward Anjellico—"I believe I could have the unit installed and functional aboard your aircraft by this evening."

"That suits, Prof, because the Black Cats fly tonight."

Their takeoff run was long, far longer than for a land plane, the big twin radials thundering. The spank and jolt of the waves against the hull bottom shortened and sharpened as they slowly accelerated to flight speed. The wingtip floats lifted and, with a deliberate rock of the PBY's wings, Case broke the *Zazz Girl*'s keel loose from the suction of the water, and they climbed free.

The two other Black Cats of Detachment 3 followed in their wake. Cranking up their tip floats, the three night hunters closed into a loose vee formation. Circling once above Iron Bottom Bay, they lined out to the northwest, climbing slowly into the flaming sunset.

Leeland-Rhys had come forward to crouch between the two pilots' seats, and the airblast pouring in through the open cockpit side windows felt decidedly odd. It took him a moment to realize why. It was almost cool.

"Lord, but that feels good!" he exclaimed.

"Too right, Prof," Cyril Bates yelled back over the roar of air and engine. "That's one of the few benefits to this rum job. The luxury of not having to sweat for a bit. Wouldn't trade it for dollars!"

"How's your gizmo working?" Case inquired from the left-hand seat.

"Seems to be functional. I extended the antenna after takeoff and tested the receiver against the Guadalcanal defense radar. The trace came through quite clearly."

"Great. After the detachment disperses we'll set up a patrol area between New Georgia and Choiseul. The other guys will work farther north up Bougainville way so their ASVs won't screw up your readings."

"Excellent." Leeland-Rhys hesitated for a moment, finding it difficult to be delicate while yelling at the top of his lungs. "Commander Case, excuse me, but I simply have to ask. Those . . . medical stores . . . I brought with me this afternoon . . ."

Case threw his head back, and his laughter rang over the rumble of the engines. "It's okay, Prof. Eddie Dwarshnik, my ordnance hand, uses 'em on the Lahodney mount."

"Lahodney mount? I don't believe I know about that."

"No reason anyone not flying with the Cats should. It's something a buddy of mine, Lieutenant Bill Lahodney, cooked up. Bill's a Cat driver over New Guinea way, and he likes coming up with new ways to be mean to the Japs."

Case pointed under the control panel and down the access tunnel that led into the bow compartment. "You rip the bombsight out of the nose and replace it with a battery of four fifty-caliber machine guns fixed to fire forward."

Case then indicated a set of crosshairs and range scales painted on the windscreen in front of him. "The sights are done in luminous paint, and I have a trigger switch on the control yoke. It's great stuff for strafing, but you got to be careful of a few things. Like before takeoff, Dwarshnik tapes a condom over each gun muzzle so we don't get a slug of water down a barrel while we're taxiing."

Leeland-Rhys brightened. "I see. Most clever."

"Yeah, Dwarshnik is real religious about it. You see, he's also my bow turret gunner." The pilot pointed forward to where the head and shoulders of the ordnance man protruded into the Plexiglas dome of the thirty-caliber twin mount. "The only place he has to sit is astride the fifty-caliber tubes of the Lahodney on a burlap heat pad. Under those conditions you take barrel explosions real personal."

Leeland-Rhys could only agree. "Most understandable. But tell me, if you put machine guns in your bomb aimer's station, where did you put your bombsight?"

"On the bottom of the Pacific somewhere between here and New Caledonia. We heaved the damn thing over the side."

Case laughed again at Leeland-Rhys's nonplussed expression. "Let me clue you in on one of the great military secrets of the Second World War. The Norden bombsight's a piece of shit, at least for our kind of war."

"What do you use in its place?"

"We use what we call the TLAR, Prof," Bates interjected.

"The TLAR bombsight? I've never heard of it?"

"It's the best bombsight in the world, Prof."

The two Black Cat pilots grinned at each other in an ancient, shared joke. Extending their right fists ahead, they squinted one-eyed over an upraised thumb. "T . . . L . . . A . . . R . . . That Looks About Right."

Leeland-Rhys shook his head and retreated to the sanity of the radio/navigators compartment.

On the two-hour outbound flight to the patrol zone Leeland-Rhys prowled around the aircraft, taking the opportunity to reacquaint himself with the peculiarities of a Catalina's interior. Beyond fixing the location of the escape hatches and life raft in his mind, he peered up into the cramped confines of the flight engineer's station in the wing pylon. He crouched beside the observer-gunners in the waist blisters, and he peered down at the sea through the narrow confines of the tunnel gunner's hatch under the tail.

He most fancied the incredible view one had from the waist blisters. It was developing into a truly beautiful night at the war.

With the end of the dayfighter threat, the other two Black Cats had sheered off about their occasions, leaving the *Zazz Girl* to fly alone through the settling darkness.

To the north and south respectively, the distant shadow mountains of Santa Isabel and New Georgia scrolled past, jagged against a ten-million-star horizon. Below, New Georgia Sound, the Slot, Leeland-Rhys corrected himself, shimmered in the light of a quarter moon, the coastal skirts of the islands like black velvet cutouts against the rippled pewter of the sea.

Leeland-Rhys sat perched on the ammunition bin for the waist guns, battered by the slipstream pouring through the open Plexiglas bubbles and totally entranced. He was rather sorry when Radioman Anjellico came aft to fetch him.

"We're coming in on the patrol zone, sir," the younger man yelled over the drumbeat of the engines.

It was time to get to work.

It was marginally quieter in the radio/navigators compartment. Likewise, much hotter from the tube banks of the radio and radar equipment and considerably ranker from the cigar puffed by the PBY's senior radio operator, the "First Radio," seated at the big GO-9 long-range transceiver.

Anjellico, the *Zazz Girl*'s Second Radio, sank onto the low stool positioned in front of the ASV radar. Donning an interphone headset, he passed a second pair of earphones to Leeland-Rhys.

The ASV was already operating. It lacked one of the new PPI screens with the 360-degree rotating sweep. Instead, it covered a fixed 90-degree wedge directly in front of the aircraft. A single horizontal line glowed across the bottom third of its display, the A scope. A vertical cone-shaped spike would appear in the center of the screen when the aircraft came within range of a surface target, the height of the spike indicating the range. A dial above the A scope indicated the exact bearing of the target within the sweep of the radar.

Even as Leeland-Rhys looked on, the scope spiked decisively.

Anjellico grinned as the Englishman leaned forward.

"That's okay, sir. That's just a wreck piled up on a reef off Wilson Point on New Georgia. It's a Jap AK that got bombed and run ashore when we first landed on Guadal. We use it for a radar navigation checkpoint."

Anjellico adjusted the bearing dial. "We're coming up on it to port in . . . ten . . . five . . . now."

Leeland-Rhys peered out of the narrow lozenge-shaped porthole on the left side of the compartment. Below, the gaunt and distorted silhouette of the wrecked attack transport swept past under the wing, the surf boiling around the broken-keeled hull in the shimmering moonglow.

Leeland-Rhys looked back at the radarman and issued a thumbs-up. The lad did know his business.

The Englishman deployed his own equipment. Once more unreeling the long trailing antenna through a transfer gland in the hull, he switched on the oscillator of the passive detection receiver. Laying a pencil and notebook ready at hand, he began to dial up and down the electromagnetic spectrum.

Hours crawled past like the sweat beneath his shirt.

Zazz Girl flew a deliberate triangular course. Wilson Point on New Georgia to Rob Roy Island off Choiseul, across to Kokopani Point on Santa Isabel and back to Wilson Point once more, outlining the parameters of the search zone.

Once, twice, a third time . . .

The Japanese wreck became an old friend.

Shortly after midnight, Phillip-the-Navigator retired to the hot plate in the mechanic's compartment and produced a hot meal for all hands. A powdered egg and cubed Spam omelet, canned bread with bitter Australian marmalade, and powdered coffee. Leeland-Rhys found it surprisingly tolerable but was wise enough not to say so aloud.

The hunt continued. Cigarette packs emptied. Muscles cramped. Mouths soured. Twice Leeland-Rhys jerked to alert as a wave pattern flashed across the screen of the detector. Once it was a random touch of a distant RSV from one of the other distant Black Cats. The second occasion was a taste of the surface radar off a prowling American PT boat.

Anjellico proved to be a worthwhile relief from the tedium. Diffidently at first, but with growing enthusiasm, the youth pumped Leeland-Rhys with a steady stream of questions, not merely about radar operations but about physics as a whole. Strikingly astute questions.

A teacher as well as a scientist, Leeland-Rhys found himself responding with an enthusiasm of his own. It had been a long time since he had taught a class, even a class of one.

During a pause, he made a few inquiries of his own.

Anjellico shrugged, silhouetted in the green scope glow. "I dunno. I want to stay in electronics after the war. I figure it's going to be a pretty big thing. They're talking about maybe giving vets college funding after the war. Maybe . . ."

"Maybe what?" Leeland-Rhys prodded.

"Maybe get into research. Become a real scientist like you, sir. That's what I'd really like to do. It's kind of a screwy idea, I guess."

"I don't necessarily think so, Mr. Anjellico," Leeland-Rhys mused. "This war we are fighting seems to be changing how we go about a great many things. Already I find myself involved in events that only a short time ago I would have thought very 'screwy' indeed.

"Very possibly we are entering a time when what one is willing to strive for is becoming more important than the conventional wisdom of what one may achieve. One can hope so at any rate."

"I guess one can, sir." The radarman's grin flashed in the dimness, then faded abruptly. A jagged spike lanced upward abruptly on the A scope.

"Radar to pilot!" Anjellico yelled into his interphone headset. "Surface contact! Bearing five degrees of port bow. Medium signal strength. Multiple targets. Range five thousand yards."

The Zazz Girl's decks swayed with a course adjustment, the big patrol bomber nosing down slightly. "All hands! Man battle stations!" Commander Case's voice roared over the headsets. "Richie, make with the range and bearing!"

"Bearing now zero off the bow, range four thousand and closing!" Anjellico twisted around, looking back over his shoulder for an instant. "Mr. Rhys, get your antenna in right now!"

Leeland-Rhys didn't consider for an instant the incongruity of an enlisted radioman giving a commissioned officer of the Royal Navy an order. He just pounced on the reel of the detector set's trailing antenna, frantically cranking it back inside the aircraft.

Over his own headset he heard Anjellico calling out the distance to target to Case. "Range three thousand . . . Range two thousand, bearing still zero off the bow . . . range one thousand . . ."

"Stand by!" Case yelled back. "Targets in sight! FLARE! FLARE! FLARE!"

Something, presumably the cycling flare racks, thumped back under the tail section.

The night's darkness blinked out of existence, replaced by a dazzling flood of blue-white light pouring through the compartment windows.

Leeland-Rhys couldn't restrain himself. Abandoning the reel, he scrambled to one of the ports and peered out.

The piercing metallic glare from the magnesium parachute flares converted the sea into a rippling sheet of mercury crumpled by the wakes that trailed behind a trio of dark angular objects that swept past below the aircraft.

"We got *daihatsus*, guys," Case announced almost casually. "Prepare to engage . . . rolling in now."

Leeland-Rhys failed to note that everyone else in the compartment had taken a death grip on any solid handhold within reach.

Up to that point the flight of the *Zazz Girl* had been a placid, even a plodding experience. Now, however, the PBY's decks tilted to starboard almost a full ninety degrees. As the broad wing elevated, it lost lift, and the big amphibian fell out of the sky in a wild sideslip.

Leeland-Rhys skidded back across the cramped compartment, almost sliding under the equipment panels, before being caught by Anjellico and the radio operator. The airflow through the ventilators rose to a moan as the *Zazz Girl* reversed her course, diving under the dome of her flarelight and lining up on her revealed prey.

"Get a good hold, sir," Anjellico yelled. "We're going after these guys!"

Leeland-Rhys groped for words. "Is this going to be . . . difficult?"

"Depends, sir. *Daihatsus* always mount machine guns. But some times they'll fix one up with a pom-pom and a load of ammo and use it for an antiaircraft escort. It depends on if we have one of those gunboats down there."

Beyond the compartment windows, meteor-like streaks of light began to blaze past. Tracers, small ones, then much larger ones.

"We got a gunboat." Anjellico concluded.

Abruptly the quad fifty-caliber battery in the Catalina's nose cut loose with a stammering roar that shook the entire airframe, the stench of hot oil and gunpowder streaming back through the cockpit door in a lung-burning concentration. The bow turret was firing as well, the stuttering yap of its smaller rifle-caliber guns almost trifling when commingled with the deep-throated rage of the Lahodney mount.

Clinging to the electronics racks, Leeland-Rhys felt the gravity pull as the *Zazz Girl* bottomed out of her shallow dive. At that instant, up in the cockpit, Cyril Bates screamed "Bombs gone!"

The Black Cat lurched delicately, and something flickered past the compartment windows, five-hundred-pound bombs falling free of the wing racks.

Zazz Girl lifted her nose and soared, converting accumulated speed into altitude. The hammer of the nose guns ceased, the clamor leaping aft as the waist and tunnel mounts engaged, ripping off short bursts as they overflew the enemy.

Thud! Thud!

Two heavy surges of pressure shoved hard against the aircraft. She skewed for a moment, then banked onto her starboard wingtip, coming around to the attack once more.

Leeland-Rhys caught a glimpse out of the starboard window. Formerly there had been three Japanese barges crawling across the sea beneath the flarelight. Now there were but two and a large spreading circle of debris and turbulence.

The TLAR bombsight was indeed quite effective.

The Black Cat aligned to dive once more, wheeling in like the vast bird of prey she was.

Damn it all! He had to see!

Leeland-Rhys found himself crawling forward to the cockpit door. Pulling himself up onto his knees between the pilots seats, he peered forward.

Case and Bates were each flying one-handed, Case with his left on the control yoke and his right on the throttles and propeller controls overhead. Bates flew with his right, the fingers of his left curled around the T-grip bomb release in the central cockpit.

There was an eerie commonality of action between the two aviators. They moved as if they were a single four-armed entity, mastering the controls without the need of orders and reply. Their faces were almost . . . placid in the harsh light that flickered beyond the windscreen. Tradesmen, going about a comfortably familiar task.

"The gunboat?" Bates queried.

"Yeah," Case agreed. "Give him the last two eggs. We can gun the other guy."

"Righto."

The surviving pair of barges had turned in toward the coast of Choiseul Island, a meager half mile distant, churning furiously toward the refuge of the beach. But the PBY was once more thundering in upon them like an aluminum storm front.

Almost washed out by the flareblaze, sparks of light danced near the low deckhouses of the *daihatsus*, machine guns flaming defiance at their attacker. Amidships on one of the barges were the heavier, more deliberate muzzle flashes of a 25mm antiaircraft twin mount. Writhing tracer tentacles reached out for the *Zazz Girl*, closing around her, striving to crush out her life.

Leeland-Rhys heard a sound like nails being driven through tin sheeting and felt a series of faint, sharp taps radiating through the airframe of the Black Cat. It took him an instant to realize they were bullet impacts. Behind him in the radio/navigators compartment there was a burst of light like a photographer's flashbulb going off and a sharp and angry crack over the sound of the engines. Someone swore savagely.

Leeland-Rhys couldn't bring himself to look around.

Case's thumb shifted on the control yoke, brushing a spring-loaded switch.

The Lahodney quad mount crashed and yammered once more, ejected shell casings spraying back through the bow compartment tunnel. The hot metal seared at Leeland-Rhys's legs, but he didn't feel it as he stared on awestruck.

The tracers from the multiple fifty-calibers didn't disperse, instead they cut a single tight tunnel of flame down through the night to the sea, the wave crests exploding at their touch.

With infinite deftness, Case rocked back on the control yoke, marching the boiling firestream up to the side of the gun barge.

The *daihatsu* vanished inside a cloud of spray intercut with a myriad of small, flickering explosions. Then, abruptly, from out of the heart of the mist cloud, a geyser of flame spewed into the sky as the barge disintegrated amidships.

"Dead one! Shifting target!" Case slammed the PBY's rudder bar hard over, skidding the *Zazz Girl* in midair, lining up on the last barge. From a slow, almost dreamlike deliberation, events suddenly accelerated madly, the barge and the surface of the sea leaping up toward the windscreen.

"Take him! Take him now!" Case yelled.

Bates hauled back on the bomb release. "Bombs gone!"

The PBY shuddered as the last pair of five-hundred-pounders fell free. Case and Bates both hauled back hard on the control yokes, hogging the plane's nose into the sky. Leeland-Rhys caught a last fragmentary impression of the targeted *daihatsu*, as the *Zazz Girl's* bow swept over it, the barge's cargo bay crowded with Japanese soldiers firing their rifles at the Black Cat.

Thud! Thud!

This time she was closer to her own spilled venom, the patrol bomber staggering under the hammerblow shock waves of her own detonating ordnance.

The guns went silent, and the darkness returned as the parachute flares burned out. The pilots rolled the controls forward, leveling the aircraft, and Case pulled the throttles back to cruise power.

"Pilot to tunnel gunner," he said into his headset mike. "How'd we do on that last run?"

"Clean drop, skipper. We had Japs flying higher than we were on that one. The only thing still afloat is the gun barge, and I can see him burning real good. He's a goner."

"Okay that's a wrap then. All stations check for battle damage and report." Case glanced across at his copilot. "Sorry I threw that curve at you, Cyril. I shifted targets when I saw the gun barge blow. No sense wasting bombs on the guy after he torched."

"Right enough," the Australian replied. "Likewise, no sense coming around again for no reason. The silly bastards must have had one of the petrol power plants."

"Yeah, that or they were loaded with gas drums. Very obliging of them."

Bates noted Leeland-Rhys still frozen in the hatchway. "Oh hello, Prof. You had a seat in the boxes right enough. Quite the show, what?"

Leeland-Rhys didn't answer. He had lived with war for four years. He had fought it in laboratories and on the testing ranges. He had experienced it in the bomb shelters of the Battle of Britain and the Blitz, and he had lived amid its smoldering aftermath.

But he had never actually seen "war" before.

"Prof . . . hey, Prof?" It was Commander Case looking back at him now. "You okay?"

Leeland-Rhys mentally slapped himself in the face. "Yes, yes quite."

"We've gone through our bomb load and most of our strafing ammo. Unless you want for us to hang around out here a while longer, we're ready to head for the barn."

"Yes, I'm quite ready to 'head for the barn' as well. I don't think we're going to learn anything more out here tonight."

"I'd doubt it, too. We just had good kills, and the PTs are reporting some action down off Santa Isabel. Richie's scope ghosts never seem to show up on the nights we get the trade out here."

The random comment struck a chord through the numbness in the Leeland-Rhys mind. "Naturally. If you can see them. They can see you. They can warn their barges to seek for shelter . . . But they didn't tonight . . . not tonight."

Hands gripped Leeland-Rhys by the shoulders, moving him

aside. "We heading for home, skipper?" Philip-the-Navigator inquired, squeezing past the Englishman.

"Yeah, Phil, studying on it."

"You better plan on a field landing at Henderson then." Outlined in the instrument glow, the navigation officer paused to pluck an inch-long splinter out of his hairy forearm. "We'll need a patch job before we can go back to the tender." Leeland-Rhys felt an odd draft tug at his shirttail and turned back into the radio/navigators compartment. Richie Anjellico was bandaging the scoured shoulder of the cursing First Radio by the light of a battle lantern.

In front of the detector set, at the approximate location where Leeland-Rhys had positioned his stool, a hole the size of a man's head had been blown through the hull and duckboard decking.

In the week that followed Lieutenant/Professor Meredith Leeland-Rhys learned a great many things.

He learned to despise powdered eggs and Spam as a diet. He learned that the state of not-sweating was indeed a luxury beyond price and that inflamed prickly heat was one of the tortures of the damned.

He learned to live . . . intimately . . . with fly and mosquito swarms and that Atabrine did turn a man's skin yellow. He learned that Fido was indeed not a "big one." He learned the ringing verbal satisfaction of "God damn son of a bitch!"

He learned that in a combat zone anything that one either wanted or needed was either difficult to get, out of inventory and on back order, or totally unheard of. He learned that mechanisms that operated flawlessly on an English laboratory test bench malfunctioned with a sullen vindictiveness in an equatorial environment.

He learned to drink powdered coffee not as a replacement for tea but because that was all there was and better than nothing.

He learned that Commander Evan Case was a skilled jazz trumpeter who had played professionally in a swing band before becoming an aviator. He learned that Richie Anjellico's girl back home was an American "cheerleader" still in high school, and that he wrote to her on a near-daily basis, and that Phillip-the-Navigator studied the biographies of the British kings as a hobby.

Leeland-Rhys learned that military discipline does not necessarily require shining insignia and regulation books, and that spotless uniforms and crisp salutes are not always the mark of an elite fighting unit.

Leeland-Rhys learned how to be "crew" and that there were far worse things in the world to be than "the Prof."

What he didn't learn was what he had come for.

For a full week, the *Zazz Girl* had launched every evening. Returning to the critical triangle of water up-Slot, they had electronically trolled for the phantom radar installation.

Leeland-Rhys combined his laboratory theorems with Richie Anjellico's field experience, the scientist and the teenage sailor becoming a team within a team. For long hours through the night they stared at the shimmering lines that bisected their cathode tubes, waiting to pounce on the first irregularity, the first hint of a radar sweep from an unknown source.

It did not come.

Another attack was conducted on another barge formation, with two *daihatsus* sunk in exchange for a hole the size of a football being blown through one wing. Half of one night's search was aborted in a hunt for a Japanese I-Boat reported prowling south of the Russell Islands. Another night's diversion occurred when a coastwatcher, desperately ill with dengue fever, had to be airlifted out of an isolated cove on a place with the unlikely name of Vonavona.

Beyond that, futility.

It was midafternoon on the eighth day and far too hot for any kind of sleep. The crews of the Detachment 3 Black Cats sweltered on the decks of their seaplane tender. Beneath the shelter of its grimy sunshades, they sipped lukewarm Coca-Cola, cursing the Solomon Islands, savoring few scraps of fetid breeze, and longing for the escape of nightfall and flight.

Evan Case emerged from the deckhouse and made his way to

where the *Zazz Girl*'s crew sprawled. "Well, Prof," he said, dropping to the deck with his back to the gray-painted bulkhead, "I'm sure you will be pleased to know that you will shortly be leaving our august little group. It's been decided that we were seeing things and that you are too valuable an asset to waste on wild-goose chasing. You can expect your transfer orders back to England within the next day or so." To say that Leeland-Rhys had fallen in love with the South Pacific would be a massive inexactitude, yet there was a decided letdown at the pronouncement. In his own academician's way, he did not accept defeat easily.

"Damn!" He spat out the single oath.

Case comprehended. "Hell, Prof, it's not your fault. If the damn radar was there, you'd have found it, but apparently it's not."

"But that's just the point, Commander. There is a radar. I'm certain of it. All the evidence points to the Japanese having a powerful surface search installation in place to cover the Central Solomons. I've gone over your ASV from antenna to power source, and it's in perfect working order. I've also had plenty of opportunity to study the propagation environments, and there is nothing that could have produced a false return then that we wouldn't still be detecting now. If Mr. Anjellico says he saw an alternate trace on his set, then he did."

"But not lately, sir," the young radarman commented from his patch of deck. "We haven't picked up a single scope ghost since you've been here."

"Could be the Japs saw you coming, Prof," Phillip-the-Navigator commented wryly.

Flight Officer Bates sat up straighter on the ammunition can he was using for a seat. "Hang on! Might there be something to that? Are the Japs wise to this radar detecting bumph you've been about?"

Leeland-Rhys shrugged. "No reason they shouldn't be. As Mr. Anjellico has demonstrated, if you have a functioning radar set, you have, to a degree, a radar detector. Building a dedicated detector wouldn't be that much of a trick given you know the principles involved. We suspect the Germans are building them for their

U-boats, and we know Germany and Japan exchange a certain amount of technological information."

"So, might be the Japs have just turned the bloody thing off so we can't find it," Bates countered.

Leeland-Rhys shook his head. "Doesn't make sense. The entire idea behind a radar is to use it to gain a military advantage. As you all have pointed out more than once, when the Japanese have their set operational, your kill ratios drop off. The Japanese can track your forces as they come up the Slot, permitting them to warn their *daihatsu* convoys of your presence and position."

"That only makes sense," Phillip-the-Navigator commented.

"What doesn't make sense is why we're not seeing it in use now," Leeland-Rhys continued. "Obviously, they have gone to some extraordinary effort to build and conceal this radar installation. Obviously, it's effective in protecting their logistic efforts. Obviously, it is of great value to their war effort in this theater. So why are they returning the advantage to you by not using it?"

"Could be their set just busted down on them," Richie Anjellico spoke up.

"For an installation of this importance one would assume they would have prepared for such an eventuality."

"What if they're saving it."

Case's words were a pronouncement, not a question. With eyes shadowed by the bill of his baseball cap, he was staring down at the decking as if a message of great importance were etched in its grimy steel.

"Prof," he continued, "call me if I'm wrong, but a big, fancy search radar like we're talking about can't just be plugged in and switched on like a table lamp. It has to be tuned up or something before it works right, right?"

Leeland-Rhys replied, "Quite so. An installation like a Japanese Type 22 might require several weeks of ranging tests before it's fully operational."

"That's it then." Case looked up. "Let's say the Japs have some kind of plan that involves using this radar, something big, beyond routine operations. They bring their set in, they set it up, and they start tinkering with it. As they're doing this ranging test stuff, they're tracking our operations in the Slot and they're using the plot they gain to warn their people off. Waste not, want not, right? This testing caused the scope ghosts we originally detected on our ASV."

"Yes," Leeland-Rhys said slowly. "But once they get their radar fully functional, they shut the system down, holding it in reserve for the day when they can use it against us as an aspect of this larger plan. A plan that must be of such a scale as to make the losses they are taking within their logistics pipeline acceptable in exchange for protecting the existence of the radar."

Phillip-the-Navigator scowled. "I wish to God that didn't make so much sense."

Case stood up abruptly. "Prof, you come with me. Let's go have some words with theater intelligence."

As with all of the other aviation facilities aboard the converted four piper, the air group intelligence office was a chronically undersized jackleg affair located in an off corner near the radio room. In the face of the feeble efforts of the ventilation system it was also steambath torrid to the point of the paint peeling off the bulkheads. A blackout curtain drawn across the center of the space concealed a clicking decoding machine and its sweltering operator and a hot and harried lieutenant commander crouched at a child-sized desk wedged between a set of lockable filing cabinets. He looked up annoyed as Case and Leeland-Rhys appeared in the narrow doorway.

"Yes?"

"Just fine, Ed, how's the world treating you." Case leaned against the doorframe as there was no room inside the office for an extra person. "I got a question."

"I hope it's important, Ev."

"It might be. It has to do with the radar problem the prof and I have been working on. Do the Japs have anything big showing on the boards? Any kind of a major operation?"

The expression on the intelligence man's face changed abruptly from annoyance to puzzlement. "How did you know? We only got the word down here a couple of hours ago. I'm working on your advisory briefing now."

Case and Leeland-Rhys lifted eyebrows at each other. "We're good guessers," Case continued. "What have you got?"

"An army B-24 out of Cooktown got a look inside Rabaul Harbor last evening. There's a Tokyo Express forming up."

The intel removed a wire photograph from a file on his desk, passing it up to Case.

The photograph was in black and white and taken from a low angle across a mountain-girdled bay. Its focus was a group of ships dispersed across the anchorage.

There were five in total, four of them with the distinctive raked stacks and twin-turret-aft configuration of the Japanese Fleet destroyer. The fifth and most distant warship appeared larger and of an older design, with three stumpy funnels set amidships on a low-riding hull.

"It looks like a standard Japanese destroyer squadron configuration," the intelligence man commented. "Four tin cans with a light cruiser serving as the squadron leader. About average for an Express run."

"The cans all look like early mark Fubukis," Case commented, studying the photo intently. "Do you have a make on the CL?"

"We think it's a Kuma class, but we're not sure. There's something funny about the silhouette."

Case brought the photo closer to his face, squinting. "Yeah, I see what you mean. Can I borrow a glass, Ed?"

The intelligence man handed up a powerful magnifying glass. Case put it to use with a Sherlock Holmesian intensity.

"You know," he said after a few moments, "I bet I know what this thing is. It's a Jap torpedo cruiser."

The intel officer scowled skeptically. "What in the hell would a torpedo cruiser be doing down here in Rabaul leading a destroyer squadron?"

"I've one better," Leeland-Rhys interjected. "What in the hell is a torpedo cruiser?"

"The surface torpedo attack is at the core of all Imperial Navy fleet combat doctrine, Prof," Case replied, lowering the photograph and the glass. "They consider the torpedo to be the decisive factor in any surface engagement. So much so that a couple of years back they took a couple of their old* CLs and stripped about half of the guns off them. They replaced the gun armament with multiple torpedo tube mounts. Twenty tubes to a broadside, forty tubes in all. More torpedo firepower than any other naval vessel in history.

"Their theory was that in a fleet engagement, these ships would close with the enemy battle line at high speed, raking it with a series of massive torpedo salvos. Just one torpedo cruiser can launch enough fish in one pass to blow an entire battleship division out of the water."

"And that's why it's damned unlikely you'll find one leading the Tokyo Express," the intelligence man commented with a shake of his head. "The Imperial Navy considers the torpedo cruiser to be a strategic asset. They're all attached to the Japanese Combined Fleet, held in reserve for their general decisive fleet action of the war."

"Or at least that's what they've been doing with them." Case tossed the glass and the photograph back onto the intelligence man's desk. "Are we going to be counterpunching?"

"Tip Merrill's cruiser/destroyer force sortied from New Caledonia this afternoon, and is moving north to intercept. We figure the Japs should be ready to make their run in about two days. When they do, Merrill will be waiting for them."

"And vice versa. Thanks, Ed. Come on, Prof."

Leeland-Rhys followed Case back up onto the tender's main deck. The naval aviator was deep in silent, scowling thought. But the Englishman sensed that his presence was still wanted.

That there were still matters to be considered.

Moving back to the tender's fantail, Case leaned against the rusting steel cable railing staring out across the sound toward Guadalcanal, the larger island a pale green day ghost in the heat haze. Leeland-Rhys followed suit.

(*Author's note: The IJN light cruisers *Kitakami* and *Oi*)

"You know why they call that Iron Bottom Bay, Prof?" Case inquired abruptly.

"Because of all the ships that were sunk there, Japanese and American, during the battle for Guadalcanal."

Case nodded. "That's right. For every pound of Japanese steel down there, there's a pound of American steel rusting beside it. For every dead Jap sailor, there's one of our guys. In tonnage and in numbers it was a dead heat. We never beat 'em on skill, Prof. We just outlasted 'em. We could replace our losses faster than they could. We hung on and wore 'em down until they had to throw in the towel and fall back."

Case looked at the Englishman. "Never call a Jap no good, Prof. He might be a bastard and a son of a bitch, but he's as good a fighting man as they make."

"I've heard our lads express much the same sentiments about the Jerry. I presume you see how this is all coming together?"

Case nodded. "Yeah, it all fits now. That is a torpedo cruiser up at Rabaul. And Fleet intelligence is right on one point. The Japs wouldn't waste one of those ships on a Tokyo Express. This isn't a supply run. It's a setup. When Tip Merrill and his cruisers move into the Slot day after tomorrow, they're going to sail right into a bushwhack."

"Bush . . ."

"An ambush, Prof. They're going to be ambushed."

"Oh yes, quite. How do you think it will play out?"

"The Japs are the aces when it comes to night surface actions. It's their specialty. They've got good night optics, and, like I was talking about, they're great at torpedo work. Probably nine-tenths of our ships lost in this campaign have gone down with a Japanese fish in their belly. Some of us figure the Japs may have some kind of a super torpedo* that totally outclasses anything our navies have as far as range and hitting power goes."

Case snorted derisively and fished a pack of Camels out of his

---

(Author's note: Evan Case was correct, the infamous Japanese Type 93 "Long Lance.")

pocket. "Too bad we haven't been able to convince the brass hats back at the Bureau of Naval Ordnance of it yet. They seem to figure that if they didn't invent it, it can't exist. Smoke?"

"No thanks. I've my fixin's." Leeland-Rhys dug his tobacco pouch and briarwood out of his pocket and began the loading process. "The one advantage our forces would have in night fighting would be radar. Our ships mount sets. As yet, the Japanese don't."

"But this time around, the Japs will have radar. That hidden land-based set of theirs covering the Slot and the zone of engagement. Get the picture?"

Leeland-Rhys nodded, taking his first testing puff of his pipe. "Quite so. As our task force proceeds up the Slot, the Japanese will activate their radar and establish a plot on them, radioing the position, course, and speed of our ships to their own vessels. The Japanese task force commander will be able to utilize this data to maneuver into a position of decisive tactical advantage. By the time the shorter-range radars aboard our vessels detect the Japanese, it will be too late. The 'bushwhack' will be an accomplished fact."

"You got it, Prof. Those early mark Fubuki destroyers are all strong torpedo ships as well. They have three triple-tube mounts on their centerline. Likely that's why they were selected for this mission. Add in the twenty-tube broadside of the light cruiser, and you've got a fifty-six-round torpedo spread. You could goddamn near sink Guadalcanal with fifty-six torpedoes.

Case snapped his lighter and touched it to the end of his cigarette. "It's going to be a slaughter, and that's the whole idea. If they can knock out one of our surface action forces, they can stall our offensive in the Solomons for months. Either that, or they'll make us weaken MacArthur in New Guinea or Nimitz in the Central Pacific, bleeding off replacement ships."

"Are you going to notify your superiors concerning this theory?"

The aviator shrugged "I suppose we can kick it upstairs for what good it will do. Problem is we still don't have any solid proof of the existence of that Jap radar. Besides, radar or no, Merrill is still going to have to contest the passage of the Express. Anything else means surrendering the Slot to Japanese control."

A speculative tone crept into Case's voice. "As far as I can see, we've only got one possible edge. To make this deal work, the Japs have got to turn that damn radar on."

"Indeed." Leeland-Rhys drew on the briarwood once more. "We've already got the passive intercept receiver mounted in your aircraft, and I've got a lobe-switching unit in my kit. If your squadron metalsmiths could assist me in running up a set of one-quarter-wave Yagi antennas, it wouldn't be much of a job at all to convert your ASV set into a kind of radar direction finder. When the Japanese activate their transmitter, one should be able to get a cross-bearing, fixing the set's location and giving one the opportunity to remonstrate with its operators."

"Remon . . . ?"

"Kick their ass."

Again Leeland-Rhys tightened the last screw on the new Yagi antenna hull mount, the dicky portside unit that he'd reinstalled five times that afternoon. "Test," he yelled up at the open cockpit window, gingerly stepping back on the narrow work float.

"Testing," the muffled reply came back. "Okay . . . that's got it . . . Switching off."

A few moments later Richie Anjellico stuck his head out of the portside cockpit window. "We got that antenna short beat, sir."

"At long bloody last." Leeland-Rhys stretched his aching shoulder muscles and dropped the screwdriver back into the tool kit at his feet. "That's as good as it gets then. We shall see what we shall see . . . literally."

"Give our bobby-soxer a pat, sir. It's good luck before a mission."

The Englishman reached up and gave the Black Cat's erotic nose art a pat on one creamy thigh. "At this late date I'm willing to take any help I can get," he commented wryly. "And speaking of that, Mr. Anjellico, this job would have been impossible without your good efforts and hard labor. I'm not quite sure as to how this medals business works in your navy, but I intend to see you put up for some kind of acknowledgment."

"Forget it, sir." Anjellico grinned. "I should be the one thanking you. It's been great working with an honest-to-God scientist. I've learned a lot."

A grin of his own tugged at Leeland-Rhys's face. "I've learned a deal myself, Mr. Anjellico. Have you given any more thought about your future?"

"Yeah. I think I'm going to go for it, sir," the radioman replied. "An electronics degree for certain, and maybe a doctorate."

"Very good indeed. I think you have the ability for it. I can give you the names of some of my American colleagues who could prove useful to you when you go looking for a university. And if you ever elect to study overseas, might I suggest Cambridge. I'd like to have you in some of my classes."

"You got a deal, sir. I'll see you after the war."

The chugging growl of a diesel engine became audible, and a cargo lighter rounded the stern of the seaplane tender, angling toward the *Zazz Girl*'s moorage buoy. Commander Case could be seen standing in the bow of the low-riding craft, guiding it in.

The lighter's engine whined into neutral as it came within speaking range. "Hi, Prof, how are we doing?" the pilot inquired, snagging a hull hardpoint with a boat hook.

"We have a functional direction finder, Commander, at least for the moment. How it will hold up under operational conditions is yet to be seen. I'd like another proving flight if we could afford it."

"We can't," Case replied flatly. "We'll have to prove it in combat. The word just come down from AIRSOLS. Like the Chattanooga Choo Choo, the Tokyo Express is rolling south on track twenty-nine. Ready or not, the show's on for tonight."

"Then I suppose we just have to assume we're ready. Was there a problem with my holding over for the operation?"

"No sweat. It was a simple three-point finagle. I swapped a Nambu automatic I had to the exec of a Kiwi corvette in exchange for a bottle of scotch from her wine mess. The scotch and I then met with a guy I know at Fleet personnel over on Guadal. He'll keep your transit orders lost until we want 'em found again."

"That's good, that's quite good." Leeland-Rhys shook his head in a detached manner. "Do you want to know something funny, Commander."

"I'm always up for a good laugh, Prof."

"To put it bluntly, I find that I am totally terrified motherless about tonight and about this mission." Leeland-Rhys glanced down at his hand amazed again to find that there was still no sign of a tremor. "And yet I also find that I'd rather die than miss this particular opportunity to get myself killed. It's really . . . most peculiar."

There was compassion in Case's responding chuckle. "Not really, Prof. Around here it's pretty much par for the course. I've never been able to figure it out either."

The aviator turned and jumped down into the belly of the lighter. "Anyway, I brought back some presents from Guadalcanal." He hauled a water-soaked tarpaulin off the cargo in the lighter's belly. "The best the tender can give us are five-hundred-pound GPs and depth charges. I got the loan of these from a Marine dive-bomber outfit."

Two huge, lead-gray shapes lay chocked in place in the bottom of the boat, finned, sleek, and infinitely ugly.

"Semi-armor-piercing one-thousand-pounders," Case commented, "I figure that whatever we find out there tonight, we're going to want to kill it real good."

The long column of rakish ships was forelit by the last golden light of the setting sun. The black of their cast shadows angled off from the white of their streaming wakes as they steamed into the approaches of New Georgia Sound.

"Pretty damn things," Flight Officer Bates commented from the copilot's seat.

"They're giving Merrill the pick of the litter." Case dipped the *Zazz Girl*'s starboard wing to have a look. "Three brand-new Cleveland class light cruisers and four Fletcher DDs."

"It looks to be a fairly potent force. Enough maybe to handle the Express under any circumstances?" Leeland-Rhys inquired hopefully from his station between the pilot's seats.

Case ruefully shook his head. "In a nice, gentlemanly gunnery duel, those Cleveland CL's would murder the Japs. But tonight it's going to be like a shoot-out in a cow town saloon. The fastest on the draw wins."

He shook his head once more. "New ships mean green crews. I wish we had some of the old gang from the Asiatic Fleet down there. They knew how to fight Japs, the ones that got out alive anyway."

"Bow gunner to pilot." Edgy words sounded back over the headsets. "Aircraft at one o'clock high."

All three men in the cockpit snapped alert. After a few moments a dozen fast-moving specks appeared in the distance sweeping down the Slot, the twilight glinting on their cockpit canopies. The endmost dot closest to the PBY began to weave, banking steeply to display its unique twin-engined, double-fuselage configuration.

"Army P-38s, coming back from the last fighter sweep of the day." Case relaxed and rocked the Black Cat's wings in a pilot's reply. "Radio," he spoke into his lip microphone, "get on the horn with *Hep Gee* and *Lazy Mae*. Instruct 'em to go into a wide holding pattern around the task force and have them stand by for further orders. Nobody moves up the Slot until we get full darkness."

The aviator eased the *Zazz Girl* into a lazy bank around the ships in response to his own orders. "I've got a hunch we might have some little yellow-skinned pixies out this evening, looking to inflict FUBAR upon us cool cats."

He glanced over his shoulder. "You might as well go aft and put your feet up, Prof. Its going to be a lo-o-o-ong night."

"How soon before . . ."

"Four hours I'd figure. Just about four more hours."

In retrospect, Leeland-Rhys would find that he had lived shorter years.

———

Callahan, the First Radio, was on his fifth cigar of the night and the interior of the radio/ navigators compartment resembled a London coal fog. Leeland-Rhys would have told the crewman to, for Christ's sake, put the damn thing out, save for the fact he empathized highly with the state of the radioman's nerves.

Abruptly the radioman straightened. Pressing an earphone to the side of his head, he began to scribble onto a message blank, writing one-handed under the glowworm gleam of the radio desk's minute projector light.

"Skipper," he called over the intercom. "*Lazy Mae*'s got a contact . . . Stand by! . . . She's being bounced! . . ."

With the coming of full night, Case had sent the two other Black Cats of Detachment 3 ahead up the Slot to scout for the oncoming Japanese task force. Laden with its heavier bomb load, *Zazz Girl* had followed more slowly, moving into her old patrol ground between Santa Isabel, Choiseul, and New Georgia islands. There, they had held on station, awaiting the convergence of the two surface forces.

Leeland-Rhys put himself in position to snatch the message blank from the radioman and pass it forward into the cockpit. Case studied its content in the pinched glow of a pocket flash. "Phil, chart this. The Express is off Oka Harbor. Speed estimated at twenty-five knots, heading one-two-oh. Jake Tomlinson also reports that the Slot's crawling with Rufes west of Kolombangara. I was afraid of that."

"A Rufe is a Jap seaplane, Prof," Cyril Bates headed off the question. "A Zero fighter mounted on pontoons. Sort of our opposite number with the opposition. There's a flock of the little bastards operating out of the Shortlands."

" 'Nother signal from the *Lazy Mae*, skipper," the First Radio called. "They shook off the Rufes, but they've also lost the plot on the Express."

"They got this thing covered," Case said slowly. "With our scout Cats jinking around on the deck, dodging night fighters, we can't shadow the Jap ships on their run in. They're keeping us blind."

"Navigator to pilot," Tibbs cut in. "The last position fix we have on Task Force 39 puts them sixty-four miles south southeast of the Express. Speed twenty-five knots. Convergent courses."

"That's it. You've got around an hour, Prof. Start the music and get this ramble rockin'."

Leeland-Rhys didn't answer, he just slid back to his station at the passive intercept receiver. He had three other men seated within the sweep of his arm, but he had never felt so alone in his life. Deliberately, he cranked out the trailing antenna. Pausing for a moment to wipe the sweat droplets from the lenses of his glasses, he switched on the oscillator.

"Good hunting, sir." From his station at the A scope, Richie Anjellico gave him a thumbs-up.

It helped.

Slowly and deliberately, he began to comb the frequencies within the narrow confines of the surface search bands. At one nudge of the dial the entire circular screen fuzzed into a blur of dancing light. He had touched on the massed sweeps of the American task force, multiple search radars blasting into the night, probing for the oncoming Japanese threat.

A swift manipulation of the instruments squelched those traces, eliminating them from consideration and concern. He scanned on.

Another trace developed much fainter, wavering and intermittent; sometimes blinking out altogether. For long minutes he stalked it like a tiger might stalk through the jungle, not quite sure of the identity of his prey, not quite sure if he should make a sighting call.

"I'm getting trace spikes off the other Cats' ASVs sir? How about you?"

God forsake it! He'd wasted precious time pursuing the radar emissions of their own aircraft. *Idiot! Idiot! You've seen them before!*

"Yes, Mr. Anjellico. I'm seeing them," he replied, speaking through gritted teeth.

Maybe they were wrong all of them: himself, Case, Anjellico. Maybe there was no Japanese radar. Maybe it was all a glorious mistake, and he didn't have the lives of all those thousands of men in his hands. Please God, let it all come down to a sheepish laugh tomorrow morning.

And, then, there it was, a clean, shimmering band of green light cutting across the heart of the cathode tube.

"Got the bugger!"

"Me too!" Anjellico yelled. "I got scope ghosts! They just kicked on."

"Right on the 90 mc range! Sure as all hell that's Japanese Type 22! Commander, we've acquired the Japanese radar!"

"You've got the aircraft, Prof. Tell me what you want me to do!"

"Commence a slow wide circle to port. Mr. Tibbs, stand by to take the bearing when the signal intensity peaks. I'll call it out."

The passive intercept receiver had done its job. It was now up to the jury-rigged direction finder capacity of the ASV radar. Leeland-Rhys hunched beside Anjellico at the A scope. "Go to automatic lobe switching and pray we've put this brilliant improvisation together correctly."

Slowly, the nose of the PBY drew a compass circle in the sky. The jittering spike in the center of the radar screen shrank to a minimal, then grew toward a maximal reading once more.

"Ready . . . ready . . . there! Bearing! Mark!"

Phillip-the-Navigator caught the bearing from the gyrocompass repeater at his chart table. "Bearing three-three-two true!" He positioned a ruler, and his pencil slashed across the map. "It's either Choiseul or New Georgia."

"Right! Commander, head to the southwest with all speed. We have to establish a baseline for a cross-bearing!"

"Roger"

The *Zazz Girl* banked steeply, her engines revving to full war power. Leveling, she raced through the night, seeming to strain against the resisting air as if she, too, sensed the urgency of her mission.

Three minutes crept past.

"That should be adequate, Commander. Reduce speed and give us another wide circle to port . . . Mr. Tibbs, I'll call the make again . . . Ready! . . . Ready! . . . Mark!"

Again the pencil slashed across the chart. "Bearing three-two-five . . . We got it!" Tibbs cried jubilantly. "It's Wilson Point on New Georgia!"

Abruptly the navigator's jubilation cut off. "But wait a minute. There's nothing at Wilson Point. Nothing!"

"There's got to be" Leeland-Rhys protested. "That's where the bearings converge. The radar has got to be located at that spot!"

Outlined in the chart table light, Tibbs held up a folder. "Look for yourself, this is the Wilson Point photo file from air recon. They freshened it yesterday. There is nothing there but beach and jungle."

"Christ!"

Feverishly Leeland-Rhys scattered the photo file on the chart desk, hunting for anything that looked like a radar mast. It would have to have a clean view of the horizon, it would have to have specific degree of antenna surface, and it could not be blocked or smothered by camouflage. Unless . . . unless somehow the Japanese had stolen an incredible technological march on the Allies.

"Prof, we're running out of time!" Case called back from the cockpit. "You've got to give us something now!"

"There's one possibility left!" Frantically Leeland-Rhys consulted the chart and ran a rapid calculation. "Steer a heading of 125 degrees south-southeast, retrograde along the radar bearing! We've got to follow the Japanese emissions to their point of origin."

"You mean use the Jap radar like a blind landing beacon?"

"Exactly! The Type 22 is monopolar with a nonrotating antenna array covering a single fixed sector. When we overfly the transmitter, the signal intensity will drop. We'll have the exact location of the site no matter how they may be camouflaging it."

Case's answer was in the tilt of the deck as the *Zazz Girl* pivoted on a wingtip, coming around to her new heading. The Pratt & Whitney radials snarled angrily as their throttles were once more rammed hard against their stops. The PBY began to shudder as she accelerated into a shallow dive, nuzzling closer to her red line maximum airspeed.

"All hands! Man battle stations! Radio! Contact AIRSOLS Guadalcanal. Tell 'em the Japs *do* have a radar out here! Give 'em the cross-bearing and tell 'em we're going in to attack! Then get on with Task Force 39. Tell 'em they're being tracked by the Japanese! For Christ sakes tell 'em they're sailing into a torpedo ambush! Send it in clear and keep repeating!"

Leeland-Rhys hunkered down beside Richie Anjellico at the ASV radar. "I knew I wasn't seeing things, sir," he kept repeating jubilantly. "I knew it!"

"You were right, Mr. Anjellico." Leeland-Rhys slapped the boy on the shoulder. "Point proven. Now, you must start feeding Commander Case bearing changes as we close the range. We must steer to keep the signal strength at its peak intensity right up until we overfly the transmitter. At that instant the scope spike will drop very abruptly to zero. Call out instantly when that happens."

"Got it, sir. Do you think maybe you should take the scope?"

"No, Mr. Anjellico. You started this job. It's yours to finish."

Leeland-Rhys crawled forward between the pilots' seats. *Zazz Girl* had burned off all of her altitude in her speed run dive and was skimming only a couple of hundred feet over the straits. The wave tops rippled and shimmered below her like wrinkled silver silk, and a dark looming bulk off the bow divided the sea from the star-spattered sky.

"New Georgia dead ahead, Prof," Case said. "How the hell do you think they have this thing hidden?"

"I haven't the faintest idea, Commander. All I can hope is that when we get close enough we'll be able to see the installation well enough for bombing."

"How about them seeing us, Prof?" Cyril Bates inquired. "You figure they got us spotted?"

"That's a very good question. The Type 22, granted that's what it is, is primarily an antishipping surface search system, not an air defense radar. But as we get closer, I presume they would become aware they have callers in the neighborhood."

"Radar to pilot," Anjellico interjected, "Bring her to port, skipper. Easy . . . easy . . . back . . . Hold that bearing! On the beam! Signal strength increasing."

The shadow ranges of New Georgia loomed closer, and Wilson

Point reached out toward them like the low-riding bow of some mammoth ship.

"Still on the beam. Signal strength still increasing. Spike is peaking!"

"Not long now," Leeland-Rhys murmured. Over the sound of the engines he doubted if anyone had heard his words but himself.

A phosphorescence wavered on the surface of the sea ahead. Waves breaking across jagged coral.

"Coming up on the reefs," Case commented.

A dark blotch materialized in the surf line. Their old friend, the wrecked Japanese transport they'd touched base with on so many night patrol circuits. They wouldn't be needing it tonight. It swept past beneath their starboard wing.

"Radar to pilot! Signal strength zero! We just lost the spike, skipper. It's gone! It's gone!"

The pilots and Leeland-Rhys all looked around wildly "What the hell's going on?" Case exclaimed. "We're still a mile off the coast! There's nothing down there but water!"

Realization came crashing in on Leeland-Rhys. "It's the wreck! The Japanese have hidden their radar aboard that bloody wrecked ship!"

It made sense. It made absolute sense! They would have their clear sea horizon, the antenna could be easily concealed within the tangled ruin of the transports king posts and upperworks, and all without leaving the telltale indications of a shore-based installation.

But there were other things that could be hidden on land far more readily than a radar site.

The night blazed white as concealed searchlight batteries snapped on along the shoreline, dagger blades of illumination slashing away the Black Cat's shield of darkness.

"Uh-oh." That single anonymous statement over the intercom came only a split second before the first antiaircraft salvo exploded around the *Zazz Girl*.

It wasn't like the *daihatsu* strikes. This time it wasn't merely autocannon and machine-gun fire although the sinuous tracer whips of the lighter weapons lashed at them as well. Heavy flak batteries had been positioned to guard the precious radar, Japanese seventy-fives intended and designed to kill a plane with a single hit or even a close miss. The PBY bucked and shuddered under the concussion, shrapnel ripping through her skin and ricocheting off her frames.

Quite possibly they would have died had they not already been flying firewalled at the PBY's maximum airspeed.

Their only way out was down. Case shoved forward on the control yoke and dived yet again until the amphibian's keel almost raked the waves, sinking the *Zazz Girl* below the fire and light of the gun and searchlight batteries.

Shell bursts still tracked them. Exploding overhead, they threatened to batter the Black Cat into the sea. The black sand beach of New Georgia materialized ahead, outlined by the flash of the shore break. The transitory flicker of the antiaircraft fire revealed a looming line of trees ahead and almost upon them, trees that towered *above* the surface skimming aircraft.

Leeland-Rhys found himself making some kind of a sound that would have been a scream had his throat and diaphragm not been paralyzed with starkest horror.

Case wrenched back on the yoke, lifting the Black Cat over the timber wall like a steeplechaser clearing a hedgerow. The big plane jerked and shuddered as tree limbs splintered against her belly, then she tore through and was clear.

But for a few deadly seconds her climb had carried her into the trailing edge of the flak curtain. Bullets *thwocked* through aluminum and 25mm shells exploded within the hull, venomous bits of incandescent shrapnel hissing and slashing. The cockpit windscreens exploded and Leeland-Rhys felt glass splinters slice at his face, then a spray of something hot, wet, and sticky.

"I'm hit! Christ! Christ! I'm hit!" Bates twisted in agony, the copilot clawing at a ruined shoulder with his working hand.

"Prof, for God sakes get him out from behind the controls!" Case yelled, fighting the yoke.

"Mr. Tibbs! Mr. Anjellico! Help me!" To his eternal amazement, Leeland-Rhys found himself able to move and act with conscious thought. Reaching around, he released the Australian's seat belt, dragging the shocked and injured man out of his seat and back through the cockpit door into the radio/navigators compartment. The rangy flight officer seemed to weigh almost nothing. Richie Anjellico and Phillip-the-Navigator were assisting now, the one helping to ease Bates to the deck, the other tearing open a first-aid kit.

"Prof, get back up here! I need you!"

Leeland-Rhys turned and scrambled back to the cockpit.

The night was dark again, blessedly, mercifully dark. They were beyond the reach of the Japanese gun batteries, and the maimed PBY was climbing slowly. Climbing faster were the hills of New Georgia; an arm of the island's central range rose to starboard, blotting out the stars as the aircraft fled down the landward length of Wilson Point.

"Prof, get in the copilot's seat."

Aghast, Leeland-Rhys stared at the pilot. "Me? I don't know anything about flying a bloody airplane!"

"I'll tell you what you need to know!" Case snapped over the wind roar. "Get in the goddamn copilot's seat!"

It was no time for argument. The Englishman hunched into the seat. The slipstream slapped at him through the shattered windscreen, and everything, the seat belt, the control yoke, the headset he donned, seemed slick with congealing blood.

"Pilot to flight engineer, what kind of shape is the port engine in? . . . Pilot to flight engineer, report! . . . Franco! Talk to me, dammit!"

"Portside observer to pilot," a faint voice replied over the interphone circuit. "I'm up in the mechanic's compartment, skipper. The pylon's been hit, and the flight engineer's station is wrecked. Chief Franco's dead. But from the waist you can see the portside engine losing oil bad."

"Pilot to observer, acknowledged. Get back on your gun."

Leeland-Rhys could only see Case as a shadow play outline in the instrument glow, but in his headset he could hear the aviator swallow against a dry throat. "Prof," he said his voice level, "we've taken control surface damage, and we're losing hydraulic fluid. As they stiffen up I'm going to need your help on the yoke and rudder pedals. I'll tell you when. More important, I need someone on the manual bomb release.

"It's the white T-shaped lever next to your left knee. Arm it by rotating the T-grip ninety degrees from the horizontal to the vertical. When I give you the word, haul on it with all you've got. But not till I give you the word. Got it?"

"We're going back?" The answer was obvious, but he asked the question anyway.

"Prof, who the hell else is there?"

Obvious indeed. "Valid point."

"Coming about." The *Zazz Girl* flared and banked, doubling back on the course that had led out of hell.

"I'm not an expert at this, mind you," Leeland-Rhys commented, lifting his voice over the building wind roar, "But I've heard it mentioned that flying immediately back over a defended objective a second time is not generally considered a good idea."

"It is something to avoid if you can," Case yelled back, "But I figure we'll have a couple of things going for us. Most of the flak batteries that hosed us coming in were concealed in the tree line along the shore. They were aimed out to sea, covering the wreck out on the reef. By coming in from the landward side, the jungle will block their field of fire until we're almost out over the water. They'll only have that mile or so of clear firing arc between the coast and the reef to kill us in before we reach the target."

Case keyed the interphone again. "Pilot to gunners. On this next pass, do not fire on the searchlights. I say again, do not fire on the searchlights! That's an order!" Leeland-Rhys saw a wolfish smile gleam in the darkness. "You'll see why in a minute, Prof. Just for now those guys are *good* Japs."

The land flattened out beneath them, and they were racing across the New Georgia coastal plain. Outlined against the dimly luminescent waters of the Slot, the blunt, black tip of Wilson Point aimed them at their objective.

"Pilot to crew. Here we go again. See you on the other side."

The shadowed treetops flickered past beneath the PBY's belly as Case eased them as low as conceivable, holding off the inevitable to the last possible second. In the jungle below, keen ears would be hearing the growing thrum of the engines, and gun tubes would be swinging around, readying to unleash their barrage at the first possible second.

Forest . . . Forest . . . Forest . . . Beach! Surf! They were over water once more. And once more arc light and muzzle flame sprang up along the coast, converging on and tracking the Black Cat. Flying by a master aviator's instinct, Case dropped the *Zazz Girl* back to a bare man's height above the water, the PBY's wings slicing through the shell plumes that rose around her.

Leeland-Rhys suddenly saw the method to Case's madness concerning the searchlights. As the shore-based beams traversed, following the Black Cat out to sea, they also swung onto the hulk of the Japanese transport, illuminating it as it lay impaled on the reef, paving a silver highway through the night for the death ride of the *Zazz Girl.*

The waist gunners were firing back at the Japanese antiaircraft positions, the tunnel gunner was firing, the nose turret was firing. Case unleashed the hammering death of the Lahodney mount. Madly, the Black Cat clawed back at her enemies.

But there were gunners aboard the Japanese radar hulk as well. Men fighting for their lives against the great deadly thing that roared down on them from out of the darkness. Crouching behind their weapons' sights, they hosed death back at the ungainly silhouette outlined in the searchlight glare.

The bow turret exploded. Blood and tissue streaked back over the nose and Dwarshnik, he of the condoms, was snapped out of existence in an instant, saving the lives of his fellow crewmen by absorbing the shell that would have wrecked the cockpit.

"Arm bomb release!"

Horizontal to vertical! Leeland-Rhys chanted in his mind as he twisted the T-grip. *Horizontal to vertical! Don't pull! Don't pull! Don't pull! Not yet!*

The rusting hulk of the Japanese transport was wedged across the reef at about forty-five degrees, and they were coming at it dead amidships.

"That . . ."

Tribarrel 25s were firing from camouflaged positions at its bow and stern and from atop the bridge.

"Looks . . ."

From this angle the outspread arms of the antenna array could be seen, artfully built into the crumpled midships deckhouse.

"About . . ."

Something crashed, and the aircraft bucked wildly under a heavy impact. A second, even more titanic crash followed as the *Zazz Girl* literally bounced off the surface of the sea, somehow recovering and regaining flight. Leeland-Rhys looked away for a single fragment of a second and caught an impression of the starboard engine, the propeller windmilling and golden flame streaming back from the shredded nacelle.

"Right . . ."

Looking ahead once more, the Englishman saw the side of the Japanese hulk fill the windscreen until there was nothing to be seen but rusted steel. Little antlike figures fled madly across the decks to nowhere, and Meredith Leeland-Rhys calmly accepted his own death.

"Now!" Case screamed. "Drop 'em now!"

Startled, Leeland-Rhys felt his hand jerk in instinctive response. A ton and a half of high explosives, two standard five-hundred-pound GPs and the two giant armor-piercing blockbusters salvoed from the racks. Freed from her burden, the *Zazz Girl* gave a leap like a bullet-stricken deer, clearing the mast tips of the hulk even as her bombs ripped into its belly.

Only the encapsulation of the explosions within the hulk saved the Black Cat from being swept from the sky by her own devastation. In the copilot's side view mirror, Leeland-Rhys saw the hulk, radar station and all, lift off the reef on a cushion of spray and flame.

"Bombs gone!" he whispered.

"Prof! Get on your wheel! Help me hold her!"

Case yanked back the throttle of the blazing starboard engine, feathering its prop. The two men fought the control yoke with all of their strength, resisting the wild swerve of the unbalanced air-craft.

"Can we fly her out?" Leeland-Rhys yelled.

"No chance! She's had it! Starboard engine's shot, and the port's got no oil pressure left. Best we can do is get as far out into the Slot as we can before she comes apart. Pilot to crew! Ditching stations! Rig for emergency sea landing! Radio! Send Mayday! We're going down!"

The *Zazz Girl* staggered on, not truly flying but riding the ground effect only a few feet above the wave tops. Case and Leeland-Rhys nursed her, prolonging the agony for another minute . . . a second . . . a third.

The portside engine balked, spat sparks, and started to seize. Case slammed the throttle closed and hit the kill switches. "Get her nose up, Prof."

They hauled back on the yokes, no longer fighting the asym-metrical drag. Sluggishly, the bow lifted, and, with a grateful dying sigh, the *Zazz Girl* settled on the water.

There had been no chance to lower the wing floats, and Case kept the amphibian balanced on her keel for as long as he could as the speed bled away. Finally, a wingtip touched, and they water-looped around it, spray sluicing through the broken windscreen.

It was suddenly quiet, so very quiet. The only sound at all was the bubble of water through the punctures in the hull.

Case unstrapped and reached behind his seat, passing Leeland-Rhys a Mae West life jacket. "Come on, Prof. It's time to go."

The radio/navigators compartment was empty, at least of the liv-ing. A body lay slumped over the bullet-shattered radar chassis.

"Ah, damn it all. Damn it all to hell." Leeland-Rhys reached out and gently ran a hand over Richie Anjellico's blood-soaked hair simply because there wasn't anything else he could do.

Case's flashlight made a fast circuit of the compartment as he pulled the safety pins and snapped the switches arming the self-destruct mechanisms on the classified equipment. Lastly, he took the lead-covered codebook from its rack over the radio panel.

"We'll leave him with the *Girl*, Prof," he said quietly. "She'll take care of him."

The water was knee deep above the duckboards and rising by the time they reached the waist compartment. The remainder of the crew waited for them in the deployed life raft, the wounded Cyril Bates and the survival gear having already been loaded. Case and Leeland-Rhys rolled out of the open blister and into the rubber boat. Casting off in silence, they paddled clear of the sinking aircraft.

A few yards off they paused and waited, watching as the *Zazz Girl*'s bow sank and her tail lifted, a shadow against the stars. In a few moments more all that remained was the sheen of an avgas slick spilled upon the waves.

"She was a clapped-out old cow, wasn't she?" Cyril Bates said quietly.

"Yeah," Case replied. "It was about time the taxpayers bought us a new one."

From off to the northwest, something like heat lightning pulsed along the horizon, the sound of thunder following a few seconds later.

But then, to the southwest, a second storm replied in kind.

"Here we go, guys. Preliminary bout's over. Here comes the main event."

Star shells burst above the horizon, hot piercing sparks raining illumination on the sea battle bursting into life below, the bass drumbeat of heavy naval gunfire growing into a continuous rolling rumble.

"Were we in time?" Leeland-Rhys asked.

"Hard to say, Prof." Case shrugged and dug a crushed half pack of cigarettes out from under his life jacket, passing it around the circle of men spaced along the gunwales of the bobbing raft. "Likely we'll know who won come morning . . . by whoever it is that picks us up."

The thud and mutter of the guns continued for perhaps twenty minutes before trailing off. The flicker of muzzle flashes and star shells faded as well, leaving only a dim ruddy glow reflecting off the distant clouds as a ship burned in the night. After several long hours it, too, went out.

"Prof, hey, Prof! Come alive!"

Startled, Leeland-Rhys snapped his eyes open. Good Lord, was it conceivable that he had fallen asleep? He must have, for the sky was blue and spattered with fleecy clouds, and the sun was edging above the western horizon.

The life raft road easily atop the low swells and on the horizons the islands that flanked New Georgia Sound glowed a deep green against the sea.

Leeland-Rhys looked around at the other survivors of the *Zazz Girl* and noted that, most remarkably, every one of them was grinning.

"You want to see something real pretty?" Evan Case held out a pair of binoculars and pointed.

A column of tall gray ships was steaming down the Slot toward Guadalcanal. One of the cruisers rode low by the head with her bow distorted by a torpedo hit and a destroyer had its upperworks blackened by fire, but there were still seven.

Seven out. Seven back.

Leeland-Rhys felt his eyes sting as he handed back the binoculars. "All of this wasn't a waste then. Was it, Commander?"

"No, Prof, not a waste. And I guess that's about as good as you can do in a war."

The droning of aircraft engines echoed flatly across the waters, and two familiar high-winged shapes swept low across the Slot. The other PBYs of Detachment 3 had lingered into the day, searching for their lost sister. In response to the flare gun shell, they dipped their wings and separated, one patrol bomber climbing to mount high guard while the other lowered its tip floats to land.

The Black Cats would bring their own home.

V5

DAVID HAGBERG

DAVID HAGBERG is an ex–Air Force cryptographer who has spoken at CIA functions and has traveled extensively in Europe, the Arctic, and the Carribean. He also writes fiction under the pseudonym Sean Flannery and has published more than two dozen novels of suspense, including *White House, High Flight, Eagles Fly, Assassin,* and *Joshua's Hammer.* His writing has been nominated for numerous honors, including the American Book Award, three times for the Edgar Allan Poe Award, and three times for the American Mystery Award. He lives in Florida and has been continuously published for the past twenty-five years.

ONE

The part that bothered Sarah Winslow most wasn't the spying, it wasn't the sleeping with General Schellenberg, nor was it missing her husband back in London. It was the Allied bombs that rained down on Berlin day and night. She wanted the bombing to continue, to flatten the city to dust. But she was afraid for her life and the lives of some of her neighbors in the apartment buildings just off the Ku-damm. She had come to know and respect them even though they were Germans.

She pushed back the covers and slipped silently out of bed. It was an hour before dawn. They'd left the Cowboy Keller at three and come back here because Walther thought that making love in his mistress's tiny apartment up under the eaves would be romantic. And it was.

The bombing was far away just now, on the other side of the Tiergarten, or maybe out by Tempelhof. The general was sound asleep, one hand thrown across his forehead, the dueling scar down the side of his handsome face fluorescent in the dim night-light.

Sarah felt an overwhelming sense of guilt. She didn't think that the stench would ever wash off her. When she finally got back home everyone would smell it on her, see it in her eyes, feel it on her skin. She was tan from skiing in the mountains, well-groomed, well clothed, well fed. A major general's whore never went without. Everyone knew.

She padded nude over to the window. A letter opener lay on the small writing table. She looked at it, then back at Walther. It would be so easy to pick up the thing, walk silently back to the bed, and plunge the narrow blade into his heart. One less Nazi on earth.

But she would be arrested and shot or hung. And she would no longer send intelligence home to defeat the bloody bastards. Sometimes she asked herself which would help end the war sooner: Schellenberg's death or her spying? She didn't have the answer.

Snow lay cold and white, masking some of the ugliness of the bombed-out buildings. They'd never turned on the lights, so she'd not put up the blackout curtains. To the northeast she could see flashes as bombs exploded. But there were only a few searchlights tonight. Most of them had been destroyed or damaged beyond repair. And the electricity for them was a problem. There was no petrol to run the portable generators.

She had spent the better part of twelve months in Germany. At twenty-five she felt like an old woman. Used up. Mind-weary. Cynical. It was the constant fear that she lived with day and night. She was never able to sleep well. She woke several times a night, fearing that she was talking in her sleep. In English. She thought everyone could see the worry lines on her narrow, pretty face. But all they saw was blond hair and blue eyes.

Schellenberg stirred on the bed. "Marta?" he mumbled.

Her British MI6 code name was CECILE, but her work name was Marta Frick. She posed as an American from the Milwaukee Bund. The American-accented German was easy for her, because she'd studied to be a screen actress. A woman of many voices, a director called her. But to her German-born mother, she'd always been *kleine Liebchen,* little darling.

"I have to go to the bathroom, Walther," she replied softly. "Go back to sleep, darling."

Schellenberg turned over on his side and was soon snoring. He always slept for a couple of hours after lovemaking. It gave her time to deal with the guilt.

Serving her God and her King but not her husband. The same thought kept running in her head like a mantra.

Schellenberg was head of the RSHA VI, which was the Nazi Foreign Intelligence and Espionage Service, with offices on Berkaerstrasse here in the city.

He knew things, some of them very frightening things, especially now that the war was almost over and Hitler was becoming increasingly insane and increasingly desperate. When Walther was drunk, and they were in bed, he talked to her. Told her things. Valuable things to prove that he was an important man and to prove that he really did love and trust her. After the war was over they were going to be married, maybe go to America.

Sarah waited a full five minutes to make certain that Schellenberg was asleep before she threw a thin blanket over her narrow shoulders and left the one-room apartment. A dingy corridor ran to the back and up three stairs to the bathroom.

The house was silent. The other boarders lived in the basement, afraid of the bombs, but Sarah insisted on the top floor. Schellenberg thought she was being terribly brave. In actuality she needed the height for her radio aerial.

In the bathroom, she locked the door. She removed a wooden panel from the wall behind the claw-footed tub and pulled out the small suitcase that contained her radio. She worked quickly but efficiently.

One of her problems over the past year, and especially in the past few months, was finding replacement batteries. The last time she had stolen them from the rubble of a newly bombed-out electrical shop. The penalty for looting was immediate execution by firing squad, but so then was the penalty for spying. It was something she thought about constantly. She had almost no illusions left except that she desperately loved her husband, who was a major in the Secret Intelligence Service, and that she desperately missed home, especially at Christmas, with softly falling snow and a roaring fire on the grate, and in the spring, when the countryside came alive.

Sarah opened the suitcase, attached the headphones and telegraph key to the connectors, then opened the tiny window. She clipped the antenna lead to a bare spot on the drain gutter. The building's east–west orientation made the drain gutter a perfect long wire antenna pointing directly at England.

It took a few minutes for the valves to warm up. As she waited she listened for sounds. This was the most dangerous time for her. If someone came now, she would have no explanation for what she was doing.

With the window open, the bathroom became like an icebox. Sarah shivered and held the blanket a little closer with her free hand as she sent her recognition signal and the query that she was ready to send, were they ready to receive?

She switched the set to receive. Almost immediately she got the proper recognition signal and the go-ahead to send.

When they'd gotten back this morning she'd come up here to get ready for bed. Away from Walther for just a few minutes, she managed to encode the information she'd gotten from him. Not being able to send what she had learned last night until now had been frustrating, and she unleashed a torrent of Morse.

The scientists up at the rocket research station at Peenemünde in the Baltic Sea near the Polish border had come up with another wonder weapon. This one was very hush-hush. Even Schellenberg knew only some of the facts even though one of his jobs was to help protect the place from sabotage.

Sarah's fist was fast and very clean. Morse code was something she had taken to naturally. Only the best operators worked with her.

She did not understand some of the technical details that Walther had bragged about, but she had perfect recall. She could repeat lines of meaningless gibberish word for word if need be.

But she did understand enough to know that the Nazis were very excited about a new three-stage liquid-fueled rocket that they called A11. It could fly more than five thousand miles. Across the Atlantic Ocean to the American eastern seaboard.

The problem had been the small payload. The guidance systems had to be very heavy in order to give the rocket any accuracy, which limited how big a weapon could be delivered. Schellenberg's news was that the problem was nearly solved.

"Marta, are you in there?" Schellenberg called softly. He knocked at the door. "What are you doing?"

"I'm sitting on the pot," Sarah replied crossly. "Do you want to come in and watch?" She switched the set off and hurriedly disconnected the leads. Her heart pounded.

"You've been up here half the night. Are you sure that you're all right?"

"I think it's something I ate." She disconnected the aerial lead from the drain gutter, rolled it up, and stuffed it into a compartment in the suitcase. The telegraph key and headset fit next to it. She had to be careful not to make any noise. Her hands shook.

"Is there something I can get you, *Liebchen?*" Schellenberg asked. He knocked at the door again. "I think that you better let me in."

Sarah latched the suitcase, replaced it behind the tub, and set the panel in place. She threw off her blanket, flushed the toilet, waited a few seconds, then unlocked the door and opened it.

Schellenberg stood there, looking at her and the toilet lid. His eyes went to the open window. "My God, it's cold in here," he said.

Sarah closed the window, then ran water in the sink to wash her hands. "It's either that or the smell, Walther." She smiled at him. "Ladies do it, too, you know."

Schellenberg laughed finally and shook his head. "I didn't know where you'd gotten yourself," he said. "Come back to bed. You must be freezing."

SAME DAY

MITTELWERKE ROCKET FACTORY

HARZ MOUNTAINS

Benjamin Steinberg was a master machinist and precision parts designer, just as his father had been, and before him his father's father.

It was the only reason that a troop transport truck was waiting for him and a few other Jews at the Mount Kohnstein entrance to the vast underground complex.

Most of the twenty-three hundred men and women getting off their ten-hour shifts had to walk eight kilometers back to Nordhausen in the snow and bitter cold because Allied bombing raids had knocked out all the rail lines. Most of those workers were not deemed critical to the war effort, even though some were Aryans, so they walked while Jews rode.

Steinberg stopped at the tunnel exit and looked up at the dull gray overcast morning sky. The war was nearly over. Even isolated here most of them knew it. The two tricks were to survive until the liberation, and to do whatever it took to accelerate the Nazis' defeat.

He had managed to survive so far by being very good at what he did, and by working wholeheartedly on the new guidance system. He had become indispensable. Even the great Wernher von Braun had come in person to compliment Steinberg on his fine work.

And he was managing the second trick by spying for the Allies. All through the work week he would compile his notes in a day ledger that he and the other machinists and engineers were required to keep. The shift supervisors or key engineers would look over the ledgers on a regular basis to make certain that work was progressing as it should and to clear up problems that might be developing. Steinberg slanted his writing slightly to the left for items he thought would be of interest to the Brits. He had a terrible memory, so if he didn't do it that way, he knew that he would forget half of what he wanted to send.

On Sunday, late in his shift, he would transpose his notes into love letters to a nonexistent wife in Leipzig.

On Monday morning, when his shift was over, he made sure that he rode in the last truck and sat at the very back next to the tailgate. On the way to the workers' compound Steinberg would drop his bundle of love letters at a certain spot near a large tree one hundred meters from the highway to Göttingen.

The arrangement had been made eighteen months ago by one of the other Jewish workers, who disappeared a few weeks later on a Monday, *after* Steinberg had already made his drop. All that week Steinberg lived in fear that Frankel had been arrested by the Gestapo. Under interrogation, the poor man would tell the Nazis everything.

But nothing had come of it, and Steinberg sent his notes the same way the next week. After a while, when nothing happened, he learned to relax, as much as that was possible.

He was surviving, and he was doing his part to shorten the war. That's all he was capable of doing for now.

Steinberg hunched up his coat collar and trudged across the rubble-strewn staging area to the last of the waiting trucks. Most of the incoming shift were already inside, and most of the outgoing shift were on the way back to the camp. The few stragglers gave Steinberg and the other Jews sullen looks.

"Late as always," one of the German guards said crossly to Steinberg.

A couple of the men in the truck reached down and helped him up. He mumbled his thanks as the guard closed and latched the tailgate and signaled to the driver.

There was little or no talking on the drive back because the Germans demanded silence, and everyone was too tired to do much talking anyway. Ten-hour shifts seven days a week in the underground workshops and assembly halls, some of them unheated, sapped a person's energy.

This morning Steinberg had another reason to remain silent. He was frightened. The breakthrough that they'd been working on, the one that they'd hoped would never develop, finally came together by midweek. The lightweight A11 guidance system, which was the key to the entire program, was done. There were only three of them completed, but they were ready for immediate shipment to Peenemünde and installation in the gigantic three-stage rocket.

No one would be safe. Not the British, not the Russians, not even the Americans. New York and Washington were within reach, and the new guidance system, code-named *Gefühlstoff*, would place the payload within a three-hundred-meter radius after an eight-thousand-kilometer flight.

Steinberg didn't know what the payload would consist of, but everyone, even von Braun when he'd been up here, was respectful when they talked around the subject. Whatever it was had to weigh something in the neighborhood of 350 kilograms, and it would be superdeadly. He got that much.

It was very cold sitting by the tailgate; the canvas flaps would not stay closed. It had snowed steadily for the past three days, and the road was slippery. The truck driver was an old man conscripted just last week, and he wasn't very good.

They topped the hill and started down into the valley. The truck was traveling far too fast for the conditions. A couple of the workers at the front of the truck started banging on the back of the cab for the driver to slow down.

Near the bottom, Steinberg casually let his right hand drape over the edge of the tailgate. As they careened past the tree he tossed his bundle of letters off the side of the road.

The truck lurched sharply to the left as the driver tried to slow for the intersection. Then it fishtailed wildly to the right, sliding toward the edge of the road.

For a breathless moment Steinberg thought that they'd be okay; but the truck's rear wheels caught the edge of the steep ditch, slamming the truck around and sending it over on its side.

Steinberg felt himself being ejected from the back of the truck. He hit the side of the road hard with his left shoulder and tumbled toward the ditch. Before the pain could register, he looked up in time to see the back bumper of the truck coming right at him with the speed of one of the rockets he'd helped build.

TWO DAYS LATER
MOSQUITO FLIGHT 23R
OVER THE GERMAN BALTIC COAST

At twelve thousand feet, the De Havilland D.H. 98 Mosquito F.B. Mk VI skimmed just above a solid deck of clouds that spread in all directions to the horizon. The midmorning sun cast weird shadows in the cloud valleys and lit the tops so brightly it was like reflections off a snowfield.

"We're not going to spot a bloody thing up here," Sergeant Tony Ricco, the navigator/photographer said into his throat mike.

Lieutenant Tony Leonard agreed, but orders were orders, and this had come from the brass in London. Churchill wanted pictures. "How near are we?"

"Peenemünde should be five miles to starboard unless my arithmetic is cocked."

The mission was critical, so the "two Tonys" had been slected to fly it. They were the only choice, actually. They had the rare combination of skill and luck. In forty-seven photo recon missions over enemy territory in France, Belgium, Norway, and finally Germany, they'd been attacked numerous times. But they'd never taken so much as a single hit. Not one nick. And they always came back with their pictures.

"In for a penny, in for a pound," Leonard said, happily. He liked his job. He hauled the twin-engined broad-winged airplane hard to the right, reduced power, and shoved the wheel forward.

The all-wooden medium-duty bomber/recon aircraft responded crisply, almost like a fighter would. Capable of speeds in excess of 375 miles per hour, and with barn-door-sized control surfaces, the *Wooden Wonder*, as it was called, could outperform just about anything flying except for the new Messerschmitt and Heinkel jets. But there weren't many of them around, so running into one of them was generally just a matter of bad luck.

They plunged into the cloud deck and within a few hundred feet everything outside the cockpit turned as dark as night. Snow was thick. Leonard pulled on the carburetor heaters so that the engines would not ice up. Their rpms dropped a couple hundred revs, but they were safely cocooned for the moment, so it didn't matter how fast they flew.

The meteorologists told them that the ceilings could be as low as three hundred feet but certainly no higher than one thousand. Their best bet would have been to look for an opening in the clouds. Short of that they would either have to return home or duck below the clouds and take their chances just off the deck, where they faced the possibility of ground fire and enemy jets. In addition, flying that low did not allow their cameras to see very far. They would have to spend a lot more time searching for what they'd come to snap pictures of.

But the war was almost over. They were dancing in the streets in London. Air recon missions were becoming less hazardous every day, although conditions on the ground for Allied agents in Germany were getting increasingly tough. People were being shot on the spot or taken away to be hanged for the slightest suspicion of a whole host of crimes.

And then there were the wonder weapons. Their experimental designations began with A1, which turned into the V1 buzz bomb, A2, which turned into the V2 supersonic rocket, V3 and V4, which were special types of cannons, and finally to the latest, which was designated A11, for the V5 three-stage rocket. The Germans called them *Vergeltungswaffen*, or vengeance weapons.

Everyone was afraid of them. And that, it was said, included Churchill.

At four thousand feet, Leonard eased back on the stick. By now people on the ground would be hearing their approach. Antiaircraft gun crews would be alerted, and if there were any fighters available, the pilots would be scrambled.

"Stand by," Leonard warned.

"Right," Ricco responded. They didn't talk much during the acquisition stages of the missions. There was no reason for words. They knew their jobs, and they knew what the other would do at each critical moment.

They broke out of the overcast at eight hundred feet, but visibility was down to less than a half mile in heavy snow.

Ricco looked up from his camera eye-sight for just a second. "Shit," he said, then went back to work taking pictures.

Leonard made one pass directly over what was left of the large missile storage building, the oval earthenworks bunker where rockets were tested, and the machine shops and what was left of the research labs. There were people on the ground, scattering for cover. But there didn't seem to be any antiaircraft guns anywhere.

Then they were over a large stand of trees. There were barracks, dining halls, and administrative buildings scattered here and there. But those buildings had suffered a lot of bomb damage. Churchill's orders were to kill the scientists and engineers first, then hit the rockets and rocket factories.

Leonard hauled the Mosquito in a tight turn back the way they had come and made a second pass just east of the oval works. Still there was no ground fire, nor were any fighter aircraft rising off the runway just to the south.

But it might be a moot point, Leonard thought. In this filthy weather they might not get any worthwhile photos.

One mile south, Leonard made a hard turn to port, lining up for a pass a little farther east, where some of the remote test-firing stands had been set up over the past six months. The Germans were doing most of their rocket construction up around Nordhausen, but their static test firings were done down here in the middle of the dense woods.

A dark metal streak dropped out of the clouds ahead of them, turned on a wingtip, and headed right at their windshield at an incredible rate of closure.

Acting on pure instinct Leonard fired two short bursts from his four 20mm Hispano cannons, then broke very hard left as the Messerschmitt jet fighter turned away like a flash of lightning and disappeared back into the clouds.

The jet was very fast, but because of its speed its turning radius was well outside that of the Mosquito's. It was the only advantage Leonard figured they had. That and the clouds just one hundred feet above them. If they could make it that far. But why hadn't the German pilot fired at them?

Leonard spotted what looked like a long bed transport truck off to their right in a small clearing. He turned that way, while at the same time trying to keep an eye out for the jet.

"Looks like the jackpot," he said into his throat mike. "Stand by."

They came across the clearing. Whatever the truck hauled out here was covered by a long tarp. Its narrow, pointed shape was distinctive. And it was very big. A lot larger than the V2.

"I'm on it," Ricco said.

They were on the other side.

"Do you need another pass?" Leonard asked. The jet dropped out of the clouds a half mile off their left wing. "We've got company."

"Time to take the film home," Ricco replied, looking up. He spotted the jet. "Right now, like a chum."

Leonard turned toward the oncoming jet, and started firing his cannons in short, controlled bursts. This time the German pilot did not turn away, nor did he fire.

"He has no ammunition," Leonard said amazed. The bloody fool was trying to ram them. It meant that whatever was lying down there on the truck was important enough for the Messerschmitt pilot to give his life in a suicide crash.

Pieces of the German jet were coming off under Leonard's fire. Still the pilot did not turn away. He actually meant to ram them.

Suddenly, they were so close that Leonard could see the pilot behind his plastic canopy. He got the impression the German was just a kid.

At the last possible moment Leonard hauled back on the stick, and the Mosquito shot up into the cloud deck, the Messerschmitt missing them by less than five feet.

"Did you see the look on that kid's face?" Ricco asked.

"Yeah," Leonard said as he made a lazy turn toward the northwest, where they would cross the Danish peninsula before heading home. "I'm sure he saw the same look on my face."

TWO

Storey's Gate was one of dozens of governmental and military command installations that had been hastily moved underground during the blitz. This one was the most important, however, because it was where Winston Churchill often worked and slept.

Nearly everyone who operated in these places had done so for four years. All of them had the pale white skin that came from seldom seeing the sun.

That was in sharp contrast to the rugged outdoors look of an American Army Air Corps captain who walked just behind a leaner and older man dressed in the uniform of a U.S. Army colonel.

It was midmorning, overcast and bitterly cold. Everyone moved fast. No one wanted to linger outdoors. Just inside the unmarked entrance of a nondescript building in the middle of the block, their credentials were checked, and both men were frisked for weapons by two tough-looking Scotland Yard heavies who looked as if they ate barbed wire for breakfast.

Captain Richard Scott, Scotty to his friends, had played football for Princeton, lettering all three years he was eligible. At six-foot-two, two hundred pounds, he was much larger than the Brits he worked with, but he admitted to himself that he would not want to go up against either of the guards, even though they looked old enough to be his father.

"Just downstairs to the left, sir," one of the guards politely told Colonel David Bruce.

"Yes, thank you, I've been here before," Bruce said. He was Chief of European Operations for the Office of Strategic Services, America's answer to MI6, Britain's Secret Intelligence Service.

Scotty came across as the typical, young, brash American, while the colonel was considered by the Brits to be a proper gentleman. He was a highly respected attorney, the son of a U.S. senator, and his former wife was one of the richest women in America.

As he'd explained earlier this morning, Scotty wouldn't be allowed through the front door on a mission of this importance without a bit of muscle behind him. The British intelligence establishment was very leery of their American cousins. After all the OSS could trace its roots back only since 1941 while British spies had been at the game nearly four hundred years.

Scotty was to be the field commander on this mission, if MI6 would accept him, and the colonel was to be his headquarters controller, watching his back so that he wouldn't be hung out to dry.

They were met three stories down by a second pair of equally rugged-looking guards, who checked their credentials and frisked them a second time. Churchill was in residence. Whenever he was there the already tight security got extra serious.

Through a steel door they stepped into what might have been a floor of extremely busy offices for a major corporation, except that there were no windows to the outside, and the air smelled like a combination of stale cigars and unwashed bodies.

A youngish, very handsome man with blond hair dressed in an RAF uniform, major's insignia on his collar tabs, bounded down the hall like a rugby player, all smiles, his hand out.

"Colonel Bruce, good of you to come so quickly, sir," he said, shaking hands. He gave Scotty a careful inspection. "This is the lad you've told us about?"

Bruce nodded. "He's my number two for Special Operations. Dick Scott."

"Donald Winslow," the major said. He and Scotty shook hands. "I do hope you know what you're letting yourself in for."

Scotty was mildly irritated by the major's condescending attitude, but he'd been warned. He shook his head. "I wasn't told a thing, except that it's something important to do that needs our help in Germany."

Winslow gave Bruce a look. "Yes, it's certainly important." His eyes narrowed a little. He was like a stage actor, his expressions and gestures all over the place. "On top of that we really don't have much time, I'm afraid. Do let's get on with it, shall we?"

He led them to the end of the long corridor, past large offices teeming with men and women in uniform and in civilian clothes, all busy on telephones or at typewriters, or marking large maps and studying various documents and papers.

They went down another flight of stairs and into a similarly busy group of offices. At the end of this corridor was a large room behind tall glass partitions. One side of the room was dominated by a huge floor-to-ceiling map of England and Europe, while the center of the room was taken up by a very large contour map of the same area. Markers showing ships in the Channel and up in the Baltic, as well as military units—German and Allied—dotted the contour map.

Winslow hesitated long enough for Scott and Bruce to get a brief look, then ushered them into a much smaller, quieter room, with a conference table and a dozen chairs.

Winston Churchill was seated alone at the head of the table, his ever present cigar clamped in his mouth. He looked like an angry bulldog.

Scotty thought that if the British were trying to impress their American cousins, they were doing a good job of it this morning. He stiffened and started to salute, but then noticed that neither the colonel nor Major Winslow was saluting.

"We don't stand on formality here, Captain," Churchill growled. "Have you been briefed on the mission?"

"No, sir," Scott said. Whatever they wanted him to do had to be big; otherwise, they would not have gone to this length to get his attention. Yet the colonel had intimated that the British might not accept him.

Churchill nodded impatiently for Winslow to get on with it.

"Well, the short version is that the Germans have perfected a new rocket, one they're calling the V5. It's a three-stage monster that can fly nearly fifty miles up and five thousand miles out."

"All the way to Washington and New York," Bruce added.

"Yes," Winslow replied. "All that was holding them back was the guidance system. The old ones were too heavy and too unreliable. But we have two independent confirmations that they've solved that problem. Which leads us to where you come in. We sent a recon plane out to Peenemünde to take a few snaps. We've spotted what we're reasonably sure is one of the V5s on a flatbed truck just east of the research and development labs. It looks as if it's operational. We want you to lead a team over there to destroy the damned things."

"How many are there?" Scotty asked. This wasn't making much sense. Why him? Why an American to head the mission? Not that he minded going. Hell, he'd come over here to fight Germans. But there was more to this story than he'd been told so far.

"Only three of the guidance systems have been built and shipped so far, according to our source," Winslow said.

Scotty glanced at Bruce. "Even if three rockets made it all the way across the Atlantic and fell somewhere in Washington, they wouldn't do much damage. Not enough to end the war." He shook his head. "What do they carry? Five hundred pounds, maybe?"

Winslow looked at Churchill, then back. His face was long. "Actually a bit more than that."

"Of what?"

"Anthrax," Winslow said softly. "One of the little gems the German scientists came up with in the late thirties. It would probably be an aerosol burst of some sort. Quite effective from what I'm told."

Now it made sense. Scotty had graduated summa cum laude from Princeton with a degree in biochemistry. But he did not fit the mold of a scientist. He was more athletic than just about everybody in the field. He was not only to be the technical brains on this mission, he was going to be a part of the muscle.

If the aerosol canisters of germs were already loaded, it would be up to him to render them harmless before they blew up the rockets. There was no telling where the winds might blow the anthrax. But certainly there would be Allied and civilian casualties if they weren't careful.

"Will you do it, Captain?" Churchill asked. "Jerry will know that we're sending somebody."

Scotty looked up out of his thoughts, aware that they were watching him closely. He nodded. "Yes, sir. That's why I put on the uniform."

Churchill handed him a sealed envelope. "Take this; it might help you with our bunch."

FRIDAY AFTERNOON • BLETCHLEY PARK

Scotty arrived at the Government Code and Cipher School fifty miles northwest of London around three o'clock in a blinding snowstorm. Driving up on the wrong side of the narrow, slippery roads was a chore. But after six months in England, driving on the left seemed almost natural.

Pulling up at the gate, he was careful not to make any sudden moves as he rolled down his window. The colonel said that this was the most heavily guarded secret installation in all of England. He didn't want some guard getting twitchy on him. There was a lot of rivalry and pressure between the Brits and the Americans. Especially between the SIS and OSS.

A young kid who didn't look old enough to shave dressed in a Royal Marines uniform came out and checked Scotty's orders. "Just straight up the drive, sir. Someone'll meet you at the front door."

"Thanks," Scotty said.

"Don't stop your car on the way up," the young marine cautioned sternly. "They don't like that."

"I'll keep that in mind," Scotty said. He had a fair idea who the "they" might be. If the colonel was impressed by this place, it must be very important. Colonel Bruce didn't impress very easily.

Scotty liked England. London with its old buildings, rich traditions, and history with the royal family and all. The small towns with their quaint inns, eccentrics, and public houses. He was even getting used to warm beer. But especially he liked the people. They might be insufferable snobs half the time, but they had hung on against Hitler's army and air forces, which had overrun just about all of Europe. He was most impressed by tenacity.

Brits were stubborn. That made him feel right at home. An old spinster aunt called him the most contentious but lovely boy she could imagine.

The main operation of the school was apparently housed in an old Victorian mansion that rose like a pile of rubble from the woods as he approached. But the grounds were dotted with prefab huts, making the place look more like a refugee camp than an important part of England's war effort.

He came around the long circular driveway and stopped his lend-lease Chevy at the foot of broad stairs leading up to the house, just as a young, very attractive woman, lieutenant's bars on her shoulders, came out to greet him.

"You must be Captain Scott," she said warmly. She was small, with a fragile-looking, pretty, round face and very large dark eyes. But she moved with the strength and grace of a dancer or an athlete. "I'm happy you made it."

"If it would make you even happier, I could pretend to be Ike."

She smiled, and they shook hands. "I'm Lieutenant Miles. I'll be briefing you this afternoon."

"What do your friends call you?" Scotty asked, falling in beside her as she went back up to the house.

"Lieutenant Miles," she told him.

The place was a beehive of activity. People came and went as if they were in a footrace, but no one raised their voices. It was as if everyone was in a library, or in church. And another thing that struck Scotty was how young everyone was. Some of them looked like teenagers. Nobody he saw as he followed Lieutenant Miles back to a conference room at the rear of the mansion was much older then twenty-one or twenty-two.

At twenty-eight he felt like an old man.

They went in. Major Winslow, whom Scotty had just left back in London, was perched on the edge of a long table laden with fat file folders, maps, photographs, and what appeared to be engineering sketches and blueprints. Winslow was languidly stuffing his pipe, as if he had been here all afternoon. He looked up in irritation.

"It's about time you got here, Captain," he said. "Took your time about it, I must say."

Scotty held his temper in check. "Couldn't help but stop for a pint on the way up."

"Oh, don't let him tease you," Miles told Scotty. "He only just got here himself, all out of breath."

Scotty was taken by surprise, and he laughed. Winslow grinned as well.

"I had to pull your chain, just a little," Winslow said. "Can't quite tell about some of you Yanks, strangest damned sense of humor. But it seems as if we might be related in an offhanded way."

"Oh?" Scotty couldn't imagine what the major was talking about.

"Our grandfathers were chums. *Very* close, if you catch my drift." Winslow glanced at Miles. "There is a certain resemblance to some of the family, don't you think?"

"Get on with you," she said. "We have a lot of work to do before the weekend. Mother is expecting us to be prompt for a change."

Winslow stuck out a hand. "Call me Donald. And may I call you Richard?"

"Sure," Scotty said. He turned to Miles. "My friends call me Scotty." They shook hands.

She blushed. "Actually it's Lindsay—"

"Linds," Winslow corrected her. He waved a hand at the piles on the table. "You have two hours to digest as much of this as you can. But if you will pay attention, like a good lad, Linds and I will give you a leg up. None of this rubbish can leave here, I'm told. And you wouldn't want to stay the night."

"Fine," Scotty said. He took off his coat. "You may talk to me while I'm reading. But what about personnel?"

Winslow gave Lindsay a glance. "There'll be four of us, plus you and four of your own chaps. Who they are is up to you. But I do have a few suggestions."

"Later," Scotty said. He sat down and opened the first file folder, which contained several dozen aerial reconnaissance photographs of Peenemünde. They were keyed to a sketch map of the rocket research installation. Some of the shots had been taken at low altitudes and were very good, showing lots of detail. Others weren't so good. The images were grainy and hard to make out.

"Perhaps we should wait until you're finished," Lindsay suggested.

Scotty looked up. "No, it's okay. Really. Start your briefing. I can do both things at the same time." He set the photos aside and opened a thick file folder that detailed the missions that had already been conducted against Peenemünde.

"Well," Winslow began. "The Germans started what they call the A Program to develop a liquid-fueled rocket. That was at a research facility in Kummersdorf near Berlin. A1 never got off the ground."

"Was that the V1 buzz bomb?" Scotty asked without looking up. *South Dakota I* and *II* were the code names for two missions in which agents were placed at Peenemünde late last year. They were never heard from again.

"No," Lindsay said. "That was a different series."

"What about A2?"

"That was back in 1934, on the island of Borkum in the Baltic. Von Braun managed to get two of the things off the ground, but not much else."

When Scotty was ten his mother discovered that he had a photographic memory. The teachers at the private school he attended encouraged him to develop skill at speed reading to see just how far his memory could take him, along with the intelligence to understand what he was taking in. He was reading the material in the files at more than twenty-five hundred words per minute. Most of it was easy-to-digest intelligence and engineering details, but to anyone watching him it looked as if he were merely flipping through the pages looking for something.

He put the missions file aside and opened a third file, this one on German code words for all the research equipment and exotic chemicals used in their rocket program. *A-Stoff* was liquid oxygen, *Blaulicht* was a radar homing device for missiles, *Messina* was a radar transponder for missile guidance systems, and so on.

"A3?" Scotty asked, looking up.

"A3 was the original research model for what became A4 which was the service weapon V2. A4b was equipped with wings, which never worked, and A5 became the new research test weapon for further development of the V2 which was already in the field."

Scotty opened a second file filled with engineering materials.

"Are you getting any of this?" Winslow asked, obviously frustrated. "Or am I just wasting my time?"

Scotty looked up. "I'm getting it. What about A6?"

"Their numbering system gets a little confusing. But essentially A6 through A9 were test projects to work out various fuels and fuel systems. In the meantime, V3 and V4 turned out to have nothing to do with the A series program. They were some other vengeance weapons. One of them was a cannon, I believe. But A10 was the design for a multistage intercontinental missile that was to become V5."

Scotty looked up again. "A11 must be the combat-ready model?"

"Right," Winslow said. He glanced at the file folders now stacked in neat piles. "We'll assemble the team on Monday and push off no later than Friday morning next. But first you'll have to read this material."

"According to this, the first V5 is scheduled to be fired one week from tomorrow. Leaving next Friday will be pushing it too close," Scotty said. "We'll leave on Wednesday. Thursday A.M. at the very latest." He got up and put on his jacket. "But what are we doing this weekend? Why aren't we getting started sooner?"

"It'll take until Monday to assemble our chaps, and we assumed that it would take just as long for you."

"I can have my people ready in two hours," Scotty promised. "If

I can use the telephone, I can have them ready by tonight."

Winslow shook his head. "Telephones are out. This is too sensitive. In the meantime, I suggest that you take off your blouse, sit down, and get back to work."

Scotty glanced at the files and gave Winslow a vicious grin. "I've already read these. Are there more?"

"Listen here—"

"Trust me, Donald," Scotty said, patting the major on the arm. He turned to Lieutenant Miles. "Now, Linds, what do you have planned for the weekend that might include one incredibly lonely American boy? Far from home. Pining for company. Crying himself to sleep every night for the lack of a human touch—"

Lindsay laughed. "We were warned about you," she said.

"Yes, we were," Winslow agreed, but he, too, was chuckling.

"You're coming with me," Lindsay said. "To meet my father and mother."

"So soon?" Scotty asked. "We've barely met."

FRIDAY EVENING · MANSFIELD
SHERWOOD FOREST

There was nothing to do until Winslow could round up his team. Scotty was left with the choice of going with Lindsay or returning to his quarters in London. It was an easy choice.

Lindsay rode up with Scotty, chattering all the way about her family, about the war, and about the mission. He didn't mind. In fact it felt good to be this close to a beautiful woman. He couldn't get enough of her voice, her appealing looks, and her scent, which was soapy and warm and feminine all at once.

"My mom, Anne, is a dear, but my father the brigadier can be a bit on the stuffy side at times," she said. She immediately smiled and gave Scotty a conspiratorial look. "Don't tell him that I said anything like that, for goodness sake. He'd take both of our heads off."

"Is he actually a brigadier?"

"World War One variety, but he keeps his old contacts. They

listen to him in London. Actually he's Brigadier *Sir* Robert, so you better call him that, I suppose."

"Will they mind me showing up unannounced?"

"Heavens no," Lindsay assured him. "They're after me all the time to bring home an eligible bachelor." She suddenly thought of something and shot him a worried look. "You are, eligible, I mean?"

"Was that a proposal?"

"Goodness no. It's just that I don't want to drag a married man home with me. Dad would see right through the ruse in a second."

Scotty held up his left hand. "No ring. No missus and kiddies waiting for me back in the States."

"Good. Er, I mean—"

"I know what you mean," Scotty said. "Or at least I think I do if you're telling me the whole story. But what about siblings? Brothers, sisters?"

"One each. Kevin's the oldest. He's thirty. The Germans have him in a POW camp somewhere around Munich, I think. And my sister, Sarah—she's married to Donald—is working as a spy in Germany. She's twenty-five and has been there almost a whole year now. We're all worried about her."

Scotty had a good idea what Sarah had to be doing in order to survive for so long. "Why doesn't she come home?"

"Because she's sending back damned good intelligence," Lindsay flared.

"Sorry, I didn't mean anything. It must be tough on your parents. But at least you're safe here in England."

Lindsay gave him an odd glance, but then changed the subject. "Peenemünde might not be our biggest problem," she said.

"Are you talking about Mittlewerke?" he asked.

She nodded. "Did you actually read all those files? Donald thinks that you might be a fraud. He's checking up on you."

"I'm a speed reader," Scotty told her. "And I don't forget anything. They call it a photographic memory. It's a pain in the neck sometimes, but most of the time it comes in handy."

She was impressed. "The factory is under a mountain, so our bombers can't get at it. But that's where they're producing not only the V5's guidance system, but the rocket itself, along with the V2. We might have to get over there and see what damage we can do. That's why the mission code name is *Coalmine*."

"Getting out could be a problem," Scotty said. He'd studied the maps and the diagrams of Mittelwerke's layout and security systems. Getting into Fort Knox might be easier. But getting back out in one piece would be a couple of thousand times harder.

"The other problem is the launchers," she continued. "They're mobile. The bloody rocket can be launched from the back of a truck, or a flatbed railroad car that could be just about anywhere one day and two hundred miles away the next." She shook her pretty head. "We only got pictures of one of them near Peene-münde. But Sarah said that there were three of them operational. And our contact at Mittelwerke confirmed the number."

"Can't your Mittlewerke man gum up the process somehow?"

"He was killed last week in a truck accident, and his pickup man has disappeared," she said. She shook her head again. Her face was narrow but not angular. Her shoulders and hips were tiny, like a boy's. But her neck was long and graceful, and from what he could guess about her legs covered by trousers, they would be long and graceful, too. Like a dancer's.

It was very dark by the time they passed through Nottingham and continued on the A60 to Mansfield on the edge of Sherwood Forest, but the snow had finally tapered off. A few miles later Lindsay directed him to turn onto a narrower road that wound its way through a dense stand of trees. They came out finally on a hill that ran down into a shallow valley at the bottom of which was a manor house right out of an old British novel about the landed gentry.

"You didn't tell me that you were rich," Scotty said.

"Poor as church mice, actually," Lindsay replied, her shoulders straight. "But we do have the house and the grounds. Been in the family for three hundred years."

Scotty parked in front and followed Lindsay across the gravel drive to the massive iron-strapped oak door, where she let herself in.

A beautiful woman who was an older carbon copy of Lindsay

came across the vast entry hall, a warm smile on her face. Lindsay went to her, and they embraced.

Massive oak beams crisscrossed the tall ceiling, underneath which were stained-glass windows and huge oil paintings of what were probably the Miles ancestors. A fire was burning on the immense grate, and fabulously ornate and large oriental rugs were scattered everywhere on the stone floors.

"Mother, I'd like you to meet Captain Scott. He'll be leading our little jaunt," Lindsay said. "Scotty, this is my mother."

"I've already learned a great deal about you from my son-in-law," Mrs. Miles said. "All of it quite good." She offered her hand. She had a very slight German accent.

"And I've learned a great deal about your family, Lady Miles," Scotty said. "All of it *very* good." He brushed his lips against the back of her hand.

She smiled faintly. "Quite the chatterboxes, our children," she said. "The brigadier would like to have a few words with you, and afterward we're having just a light supper, I'm afraid. Tomorrow evening we'll dine formally."

"I didn't bring anything—"

"It's all right, Captain. You're about the same size as our son. We'll find something suitable for you."

"I'll show him the way," Lindsay said, and led Scotty across the hall and down a wide corridor.

"Your mother is as beautiful as you are," he said.

"I think you've got it the wrong way round, but thanks," Lindsay said. She stopped. "It's the door at the end." She smiled. "Remember, his bite is definitely much worse than his bark."

"Thanks," Scotty replied glumly.

THREE

The mission briefing room was in a rebuilt barn two hundred yards from the old manor house. The place wasn't nearly as grand as Winacres, Lindsay's parents' estate; it had been in rough shape when the OSS took it over three years ago, and there wasn't enough time or real need to refurbish the place to its former glory. A hundred agents were processed through here each month for missions to the Continent, and they had other things on their minds than the decor.

Scotty had placed four telephone calls to London on Sunday with the brigadier's wholehearted permission, and in response the four OSS agents he'd briefly spoken to had shown up here, no questions asked. Thinking about the weekend with Lindsay and her parents, Scotty smiled. In the first ten minutes he'd been taken under the brigadier's wing and become an instant member of the family.

His four operators were lounging in front of the small stage, their feet up on folding chairs, the air thick with smoke, when Scotty walked in. They looked up, but no one stood to attention or saluted. Everyone who went into the field was a volunteer. They were, for the most part, well educated, highly motivated, and very egotistical. That's why they had earned the nickname Cowboys early on. And each new recruit was determined to live up to the reputation of his predecessors. That meant an almost total disregard for the rules. But no one bothered the OSS because they were getting the job done.

"We're going to Germany on Wednesday or Thursday," Scotty said. "The place is called Peenemünde. It's off the Baltic coast near the Polish border, and it's where the Nazis design and test their rockets. There's too much activity going on around the place, so we'll have to go in by submarine. Someone is working on the landing sites for us. But no matter how you slice it, it could get a little dicey. They might be expecting us."

His four volunteers watched him with feigned indifference. He could have been discussing tomorrow's entertainment at the USO in London. But they were his friends, and he could tell that they were interested.

"Judging by the disreputable nature of my colleagues, I'm guessing that we're going over to blow up a rocket or two," Sgt. Douglas Ballinger said. He was tall, slender, and very dark. He was an electronics expert and probably the brightest man Scotty had ever met. Ballinger, whose nickname was NMI, because he had no middle name, wasn't shy about letting people know just how smart he was.

"That took a stroke of genius to figure out," Sgt. Stuart McKeever, Mac, said through his bushy walrus moustache. He was an explosives expert.

"We're going to destroy *three* rockets, as a matter of fact," Scotty said. "You'll get the full briefing later today. But that won't be our biggest concern. We'll have to find them first, and at some point we might have to break into their factory and destroy the guidance systems on the assembly line, or better yet kill the engineers working on them."

"Why all the fuss?" Sgt. Donald Smith asked. He was a rocket expert. His dad worked with Robert Goddard, the American rocket pioneer, and as a young man Smith, whose nickname was Kilroy because his last name was so common, helped out. "The V2 isn't causing much harm now."

Scotty nodded. "You're right. But the rocket we're after is a brand-new one. The V5. It's a three-stage monster than can make it all the way across the Atlantic."

They all sat up. He had their attention now. "How big a payload does it carry?" Smith asked.

"It's not the size that counts, its what it'll carry that has everyone worried. Anthrax."

"What's that?"

"It's a germ that could kill a lot of people if it was released over Washington or New York City."

"Hell," Lt. Vivian Leigh said. He was their combat expert. He knew nearly every weapon carried by all sides, he was brutal in hand-to-hand, and his German was nearly perfect. He was a huge man, with a perfectly bald head and large, deep-set, dangerous eyes. Under normal conditions he was as mild-mannered as they came. He was a Harvard Law School graduate and a standout football player, the only venue other than Special Forces Training School where he showed his vicious side. He could blindside you, break a couple of bones, and afterward visit you at the hospital bringing candy and even flowers. But he didn't like bugs.

"The rocket factory is not at Peenemünde," Scotty continued. "It's at a place called Mittelwerke, dug into the mountains near Nordhausen. That's a couple of hundred miles south."

"That's just dandy," Ballinger said. "Can we ask who came up with this brilliant idea?"

"Winston Churchill," Scotty replied. "Which means we'll be getting some help. Four MI6 operators, whom we'll meet this afternoon, are tagging along."

"Who'll be the field commander?" Leigh asked.

"Yours truly."

His people nodded in satisfaction. They would take orders from a Brit, but they wouldn't have liked it. This way was much better.

MONDAY AFTERNOON · BLETCHLEY PARK

Scotty and his team were driven over to the Code and Cipher School in a windowless van marked with the logo of a grocery supplier. The trip was nearly one hundred miles, and snow lay slippery on the narrow roads. The going was slow, which gave Scotty a long time to ponder what might prove to be an impossible job, the task of reaching the Mittelwerke factory and damaging it.

The solution, of course, was to break their mission into two separate parts. By submarine to Peenemünde, then by air to somewhere near Nordhausen.

He thought about hijacking a truck and perhaps some German uniforms to make the overland trip. But even if they did make it that far without being stopped, and even if they did somehow manage to damage the underground factory, they wouldn't have one chance in ten million of getting out alive.

He rode in the passenger seat and stared at the passing countryside, figuring their options. He wanted very much to return to England. Especially now that he had met Lindsay.

One of the Royal Marine guards on the gate peered into the back of the van, but he gave no outward indication that he'd seen anything other than groceries. He stepped back, raised the barrier, and let them through.

On the way up the long driveway through the woods, Scotty tried to get himself into a better mood. It was bad business beginning a mission in the dumps. But he thought it was an even worse business going into a mission from which you knew you wouldn't return.

They were directed to the kitchen pantry entrance in back, where under the cover of an overhang the five of them went inside. They'd brought their personal gear with them, but no weapons or other equipment. A man identifying himself as the charge of quarters brought them to their rooms in the west wing of the main house, where they dropped their things and went back downstairs and outside to one of the Quonset buildings.

It contained a typical briefing room, with several rows of chairs facing a slightly raised platform, at the back of which was a large map of England, the Channel, and most of Europe.

Major Winslow and Lindsay were there, along with two men who looked so pale and weak that Scotty wondered why they weren't in the hospital. Their civilian clothes hung on them as if they'd just been released from a POW camp and not had a decent meal in a year. One was blond with long hair, and the other was frizzy dark brown and short.

Winslow introduced the blond man as Sgt. Talbot St. Lo, the Saint, who was MI6's leading expert on electronics, especially pertaining to avionics and missile guidance systems. The dark-haired, slightly smaller man was Sgt. Thomass Beddows-Smythe, a hand-to-hand combat instructor with more than two dozen missions behind enemy lines since 1940. His nickname was Bedfella, and Scotty's people visibly held back sniggers.

Winslow smiled midly. "Don't let their size deceive you, gentlemen."

Scotty introduced his people, and after they'd all shaken hands he turned back to Winslow. "I thought there were four of you? Where are the others?"

"We're it," Winslow said.

It took a moment for that to sink in, and when it did, Scotty shook his head. He understood now what the weekend at Winacres had been all about. "We're not taking a woman with us."

"Oh?" Lindsay said, raising an eyebrow. "Just why might that be?"

"It's just the way it is," Scotty shot back. "The chance that we'll all get home in one piece is slim to none. And you're not coming along. I need somebody who can shoot, somebody who can speak German, and somebody who knows something about rockets or electronics."

"*Ja, denn warum nicht eine Fraülein?*" Lindsay snapped. "I'm an expert marksman, I've gone through the MI6 training course twice, both times with Thomass, and I graduated with honors last summer in biochemistry at university." She looked at him with amusement.

"If something happens to you, the team will need another biological expert."

"We'll get someone else," Scotty growled. He didn't like this at all. He didn't want the responsibility of any woman coming with them, but especially not her.

"There *is* no one else," Winslow said. "Sorry old boy, but my sister-in-law seems to be our man." He gave Scotty a look as if to say I should have warned you about her. "Shall we get sarted then? We need to be fully briefed by 2000 hours, after which we have a field drill in the woods. They've produced a mock-up of the rocket for us to practice disarming and destroying."

Scotty took out the letter that Churchill had given him at Storey's Gate. It gave him absolute authority over every aspect of the mission, including the right to commandeer or reject any piece of equipment, any plan, or any individual. The letter was signed by Churchill and by Eisenhower.

Lindsay refused to look at the letter in his hand though it was obvious she had an idea what it might be. Her shoulders were back, her tiny jaw set.

Scotty was seething inside. This wasn't what he wanted. But another part of him understood that Lindsay might be perfect for the job.

"Either I go, Captain Scott, or the mission will have to be scrubbed," she said. "We cannot afford to send only one biological expert. The risk of doing more damage than good is simply too great."

Beddows-Smythe, the MI6 combat instructor, watched with an amused expression. "Might I suggest you give the lieutenant a chance tonight on the practice range before you make a final decision?" His voice was as soft as a woman's.

Scotty considered the suggestion. It was a reasonable one, but he didn't like this kind of bickering. He glanced at them all, Lindsay included, and nodded. "Major Winslow will give the briefing, Sergeant Beddows-Smythe will conduct the training exercise, but I will be in overall command of the mission. Questions?"

There were none.

He looked pointedly at Lindsay. "No consideration will be given to your sex," he told her harshly. He thought she was beautiful.

She grinned like a vixen. "Well, that's certainly a refreshing change of attitude, Captain. Though I think that my sex, as you put it, might come in handy at the least expected moment."

THAT EVENING • BLETCHLEY PARK GROUNDS

Their afternoon briefing went without a hitch, though everyone on the team understood the near impossibility of the Mittelwerke part of the mission. But a plan had formed in Scotty's mind, which more than ever made him determined to knock Lindsay off the team.

No calls were allowed from the Park, but Major Winslow managed to rustle up a messenger to take a letter to Colonel Bruce at OSS Headquarters in London. The messenger was instructed to wait for a reply.

After a decent supper of bacon and eggs with fried potatoes and fried tomatoes and beer, they were kitted out in winter battlefield dress with white coveralls and hoods. In addition they carried the tools they would need, the blank explosives and M3 forty-five caliber submachine guns, various pistols and other weapons.

They were not going to Germany as spies, or even as saboteurs, but as commandos striking a specific set of targets. Not that the Geneva Convention held much water in Germany these days, but going over in uniform might help if they were captured alive.

"We're after destroying three missiles," Beddows-Smythe told them.

They were assembled in what was turning out to be a very strong snowstorm, just below the crest of a long, low hill. The main house was far enough away that they could not see it, nor were there any lights anywhere on the grounds. They could have been on another planet, or on the island of Usedom in the Baltic, where Peenemünde was located.

"They're bloody big things, so they'll be hard for the Jerries to hide. But the bad news is that we only know where one of them is, or was, as of several days ago. Nor does it look as if this weather will clear up in time for another reconnaissance flight."

"We'll start with the one, and go looking for the others," Winslow said. "They'll be close."

"Just right, sir," Beddows-Smythe agreed. "Since Jerry is planing on launching all three of these rockets this weekend, there'll be SS and Wehrmacht along with scientists and technicians all over the place." He held up his razor-sharp knife for emphasis. "We kill no one unless it's absolutely bloody well necessary. And if we do it, it'll be this way. Minimize the noise."

"Throat or heart?" Lindsay asked, and Scotty thought that the question was for his benefit.

Beddows-Smythe grinned at her. "The throat's the best bet, Lieutenant. With the heart stab you sometimes have to be lucky or you'll miss. It hurts, and they tend to make a terrible ruckus."

She nodded but did not look over at Scotty.

"We cannot simply blow the things up, of course, because of the payloads. So I suggest that we split up into two teams, one with Captain Scott and the other with Lieutenant Miles. It'll be their jobs to safely remove the anthrax tanks from the nose cones so that we can take them far enough away that when the rockets explode, sending burning fuel all over hell and back, the tanks will not be compromised and release the germs."

He waited for Scotty to voice an objection, but there was none. Short of coming up with another bug man, they were going to be stuck with a woman. It wasn't that Scotty thought she couldn't handle the job. He had a couple of aunts who had flown airplanes in the twenties, gone exploring in the Antarctic, and even crossed the Pacific in a small sailboat. Women were capable of just about anything. But dammit, they did not belong in combat.

"Once all three rockets are dismantled and the charges set in place, we'll set the timers for a brief delay, then hotfoot it out of there before they can guess which way we've gone."

"A lot can go wrong," Scotty said.

Beddows-Smythe nodded. "Everything, sir."

It dawned on Scotty that the sergeant did not trust or like him and his American team. The Americans had come over to England with their fancy uniforms and abundant money, sweeping the British women off their feet. He could see how Beddows-Smythe looked at Lindsay. He was in love with her. It explained a lot.

"We're not going over on a suicide mission," Scotty said. "Destroying the missiles is important, but the war will be over in a few months whether they fly or not." He shrugged. "The damned things will probably blow up on takeoff anyway. They haven't had enough time to test them. So we're going to stay as safe as possible. I want to bring everyone back."

"Right—" Beddows-Smythe smirked.

"Do you have a problem with that, Sergeant?" Scotty demanded. If he wasn't accepted as a leader right now, he might as well step aside and let Winslow do the job.

Beddows-Smythe glanced at Winslow, but then shook his head. "No, sir."

"Fine. We'll take this one step at a time. The Peenemünde operation tonight, and the Mittelwerke mission tomorrow, for which I have a couple of ideas. Unless there's a hitch, I'm pushing our departure to Wednesday, the day after tomorrow."

"We might have a problem with transportation," Winslow said.

"I'll take care of it," Scotty said. "Now, Bedfella, let's get on with it, I'm freezing my ass off. And captains don't like that."

Beddows-Smythe laughed, the tension suddenly evaporating. "No, sir, neither do sergeants."

"Or women," Lindsay added.

They spread out on Beddows-Smythe's signal and began working their way over the hill and down into the woods. The mock V5 had been set up on a long, narrow platform to simulate a truck trailer. The Royal Marines were guarding the weapon. They knew that the intruders were coming, though not exactly from what direction. Scotty and his team, however, did not know where the guards were located, nor how many there were.

Halfway down the hill Smythe held up his hand, then urgently motioned them down. They all dropped to the snow. Smythe was slightly ahead and to Scotty's left, and Lindsay was somewhere off to the right.

Effective visibility was down to about fifty feet at best. A hundred feet out everything was lost in the swirling snow.

But then Scotty spotted two men in marine uniforms, their rifles slung barrel down over their shoulders, trudging from right to left, as if on a patrol path.

Smythe looked back. He'd spotted them, too. He gave Scotty the signal for: Do you see them? When Scotty gave the affirmative, Smythe motioned for the two of them to move down the hill while the others remained where they were. Smythe would take the guard on the left, Scotty the one on the right.

Scotty slipped his knife out of its sheath low on his right leg and scrambled down the hill with Smythe until they intersected the footsteps of the guards in the snow.

Smythe gave him a nod. They rose at the same time and made the final silent rush to the patrolling marines like a pair of lions closing in for the kill.

Scotty hit his man a second before the sergeant, pulling the man's head back and simulating a throat cut.

"Bloody hell," the young marine swore under his breath.

"Sorry, son, but you're dead," Scotty said. "So kindly keep your mouth shut."

The marine grinned wryly and shook his head. "Right you are, sir. But you've already lost, haven't you?"

Smythe's marine was also down. Scotty motioned that he was returning to the others. He turned and headed up the hill in a dead run, but keeping low, all his senses alert for trouble.

The figures of his team materialized out of the blowing snow. Two Royal Marines were sitting down, Lindsay and Vivian Leigh over them.

"It was a trap," Leigh said. He nodded to Lindsay. "She spotted them."

She gave Scotty a sweet smile.

"Are they both dead?" Smythe asked.

"This one isn't," Scotty said before Lindsay could reply. He dropped down beside the young marine guard who was grinning, shoved the kid's head back with force, and brought the point of his razor-sharp knife to within an inch of the marine's right eye.

"How many other guards are there?" Scotty asked.

The marine reared back in alarm. He appealed to Smythe. "Hey, sarge, c'mon. What's with the Yank?"

"This is Germany, son, and you're the bloody SS," Smythe told him.

"First your right eye, then your left," Scotty said, pressing.

"Just the four of us."

"Where are the other rockets?"

"I don't know about any other rockets."

Scotty moved the knive closer. "Where are the other rockets?"

"Bloody hell, Sarge, tell this bloody bastard that I bloody well don't know."

Scotty withdrew the knife, got up, and helped the marine to his feet. "No harm done. This is just a drill."

"Yes, sir."

"And I don't much like your language in front of the lady," Smythe cautioned.

FOUR

It was almost dark, though Sarah Winslow couldn't detect any light in the gray overcast and swirling snow from the open bathroom window. She connected the antenna lead on the drain gutter, then hunched her blanket closer around her while she waited for the radio set to warm up. Her rendezvous time with London Station was approaching, and she didn't want to miss her schedule after cutting off her transmissions twice since New Year's Day. Both times radio-direction-finding trucks had rumbled up the street, but then had passed.

Walther had come over only once since New Year's Eve, to make love and stay the night. That was yesterday. He'd gotten up suddenly a couple hours ago and asked her to make him breakfast. He had an extremely urgent early appointment in the *Führer* bunker, and it didn't pay to be late.

He talked all the while she cooked the eggs, sausages, and spinach he'd brought over. Bragged, actually.

"The war is all but won," he told her. He laughed and slapped his hands in exuberance. "Just a few more days, now, and you'll see." He stopped and looked at her as if he were seeing her for the first time, and he smiled warmly. "Ah, *Liebchen*, if you only knew. If only I could tell you." He shook his head. "But then, you'll see soon enough. The entire world will see."

That wasn't like him, to brag so much. She didn't want to press her luck just then by asking him questions. He wasn't unusually suspicious, but there was something different about him. She couldn't put her finger on just what it was, but she was feeling an increased sense of isolation and danger.

The war was nearly over, and she wanted very much to get out of Germany right now.

She looked at her watch. It was six o'clock. She checked out the window to make sure the street was empty, then tapped out her recognition signal and got the go-ahead immediately.

She hurriedly told London what Walther had said to her just two hours ago, omitting nothing, but adding nothing either. Her job was to report facts, not to draw conclusions.

When she was finished, London Station sent the code that they had traffic for her: Was she ready to copy?

She replied in the affirmative.

EXTREMELY URGENT THAT YOU FIND OUT PRECISE LOCATIONS OF ENTRANCES AND AIR SHAFTS AS WELL AS SECURITY POSTS AT STANISLAW. BY NEXT SKED.

Stanislaw was the code name of the Mittelwerke factory near Nordhausen. But how in heaven's name London thought that she could get such information from General Schellenberg in twenty-four hours was beyond her. She was about to ask if they were joking, but then she thought better of it. London *never* joked.

She sent her will-comply signal, then added five words in a very slow, precise hand before she signed off.

I WANT OUT NOW PLEASE

London sent its acknowledgment, and she switched off.

She sat back, hunched practically into a little ball because of the cold and because she was truly and deeply more frightened than she'd ever been since arriving in Germany. She could think of little other than her husband, She knew every laugh line around his eyes, even though they'd only been married for two years before she'd been sent over. She could smell the scent of his clothes, hear his voice, and see his stupid habits, like how he put on his socks and shoes before he put on his trousers. He was forever pulling out the hems of his cuffs, but she couldn't make him stop it. Now she wished that she was there to watch him.

She reached out the window and unclipped the antenna wire as a tremendous bang hit the bathroom door. It burst inward with a crash that shook the entire house.

Sarah spun around, her heart going into her throat. The large man in a long black leather overcoat who'd broken in the door stepped aside, and Schellenberg walked in, a faint smile on his face.

His eyes went from the antenna lead in her hand to the radio and back to her face. "Good morning, Marta. Or should I call you Cecile? Which do you prefer?"

She'd always known that this could happen, though she'd been too busy or too frightened to give it much thought. But now that the shoe had actually dropped, she found that she was calm. The only problem was the L pill, the cyanide capsule that all Allied spies carried. She'd left it downstairs in the apartment.

"The general's whore, will be fine," she said, amazed at how steady her voice was.

Schellenberg's smile was a little forced. "We have a new role for you, Marta."

She saw that she had gotten to him, and her lips curled into a nasty smirk. "I faked it, Walther. Right from the beginning. You're a rotten lover."

"When it's over, you'll regret that remark."

"I regretted it every time you were on top of me grunting like a pig."

Schellenberg wanted to hit her. She could see the effort it took for him to maintain his composure, while for her it was becoming easier by the minute.

"Let's go, my dear," Schellenberg said.

"I need to get dressed first, unless you mean to freeze me to death."

"Of course. But we've already found your cipher book and your suicide pill." He shook his head. "I think that you will wish that you still had it when we're finished."

"Where are you taking me, Gestapo Headquarters?"

"No, not at all," Schellenberg said. "In fact by this afternoon you will have seen firsthand everything that London wants you to report on."

Sarah frowned. She didn't know what he meant. He could be elliptical at times.

"Mittelwerke, my dear. I'm taking you there this morning so that you can see it for yourself. And then you will send your message to London."

A cold shot of fear went directly into her heart. She shook her head. "No—"

"Oh, yes, Marta, you will cooperate with us." He smiled evilly. "You'll see."

TUESDAY EVENING • LONDON

The call from London for Scotty came a few minutes before four in the afternoon. He'd been in the training hut with the team, studying the relief map model of the Mittelwerke installation in the Harz Mountains.

There wasn't much to see except for the steep, heavily forested hills, the two entrances they knew about, and the various paved roads and narrow dirt tracks through the woods, along with the town of Nordhausen and the nearby concentration camp of the same name.

The best bet would have been to destroy the entire installation. But the workshops and assembly halls had been carved out of the living rock deep within the mountains, making the place impervious to air attacks.

And Scotty's team could not carry enough explosives to do the factory anything more than superficial damage.

The next best bet was striking at the engineers and scientists. The people who worked on the crucial bits of the rockets and guidance systems. MI6 had managed to piece together a work schedule and one critical piece of information. Most of the workers walked back and forth from the underground entrance to their quarters in the concentration camp.

But the engineers and some of the scientists, the people most important to Mittelwerke, were picked up in six trucks.

It was Scotty's intention to knock out the trucks and kill everyone aboard.

Riding down to London on the train, Scotty was looking forward to talking to Colonel Bruce. The colonel was one man over here whom he could trust implicitly. If Bruce said that the sun wouldn't rise until noon tomorrow, his people, Scotty included, would set their clocks to him, and not the Greenwich time tick.

In the letter he'd sent by messenger yesterday he'd asked Colonel Bruce's feelings about his plan for the Mittelwerke engineers. Some of the people riding in the trucks were friends of the Allies. Spies, some of them. Most of them Jews, who would be killed when their usefulness was at an end. But unless word could somehow be gotten to them to miss the trucks Wednesday night, Scotty couldn't see any other way out.

He had backed himself into a corner that he hadn't managed to get out of by the time the cabbie dropped him off at OSS Headquarters on Grosvenor Street, and he walked upstairs to the colonel's office.

It was approaching eight in the evening, but headquarters was very busy. The organization's main thrust had become focused on getting agents into Germany. But Bill Casey, who'd been brought over to head up the effort, was finding that getting his people into place in Germany was nearly impossible. There was no effective

underground in Germany as there had been in France. There were
no fields lit on schedule by farmers with lanterns or torches. There
were no safe houses. No underground railways. Nearly everyone in
Germany was so traumatized by the assassination attempt on Hitler
last summer that they had become informers. Anything real or
imagined that was out of the ordinary, no matter how tiny or in-
significant, was reported to the Gestapo.

The entire country was on the verge of imploding. It was becoming almost as dangerous for the average citizen in Germany as it
was for an Allied spy.

Colonel Bruce, his jacket on and buttoned, his tie snugged up as
usual, came around from behind his desk when Scotty was shown
in.

"Come with me," he said. He marched out of his office and down
the corridor to the rickety elevator. "Something has cropped up that
you'll have to consider."

They took the elevator to the top floor, where the colonel had
to vouch for Scotty in order to bring him into the headquarters'
communications and analysis center.

The operation took up most of the floor under the eaves. It was
the job of the young clerks, mostly women, to listen to broadcasts
of any sort coming out of Germany. In another section of the top
floor, analysts, mostly men, tried to figure out what was happening
over there. A large part of their efforts involved messages from OSS
and MI6 agents.

"One of our primary sources for your mission is a woman code-
named Cecile, who is the mistress of General Walther Schellenberg," Bruce said, leading Scotty back to the analysis division. "It
was from her that we got the first word about the three rockets at
Peenemünde, about the new guidance system, and about the payload."

"One of ours?" Scotty asked.

Bruce shook his head. "MI6. We think that she's in trouble, and
you could be walking into a trap."

Scotty's lips compressed. "Maybe we should simply bypass Mittelwerke and concentrate on knocking out the rockets before they become operational. There won't be that many more of them, and the war can only last a few more months."

"There's more to it than that. If only one guidance system is mated to one rocket, which could be hidden anywhere in Germany, we'd be in serious trouble." Bruce gave Scotty a trust-me-on-this-one look. "President Roosevelt has taken a keen interest."

Scotty thought about the problem under these new circumstances. "Even if it is a trap, we can still hit the trucks carrying the engineers."

"Some of those people are our friends."

Scotty refused to look away. "I know."

"Yet you would go ahead?"

"Hell, I don't know any other way, Colonel. Especially if they know that we're coming and expect us to hit the factory. Anyway, who's Cecile?"

"Her real name is Sarah Winslow."

It took several seconds for all the ramifications of that news to sink in. "Major Winslow's wife?"

Bruce nodded. "Lindsay Miles's sister." Bruce looked away for a moment.

This was a bad business. Scotty could see that the colonel was just as affected by it as he was. The brigadier and his wife had their only son in a German POW camp, one of their daughters captured as a spy, and yet they were willing to send their remaining daughter into harm's way.

"We realized that something was drastically wrong when she broke her schedule to tell us that she was visiting Mittelwerke with Walt. She's never called Schellenberg by that name. And then she sent the information we asked for. *All* the information. Which was utterly impossible for her to come by so quickly."

"I'm pulling Major Winslow and Lieutenant Miles off the team—"

"No," Bruce said. "Nor will they be told about this until you're in-country and only if it becomes absolutely necessary." Bruce gave him a stern look. "I'm counting on you."

Scotty didn't like it, but he nodded. "What do you want me to do?"

"Your plan for an airdrop near Nordhausen should work. We'll send you over as part of a bomb group. Your plane will stray off course for a bit, and once your team bails out, it'll catch up with the others in its group.

"You'll parachute just after dark, which will give you eleven hours total before dawn. Eight hours to reach the target, destroy it, and return to your rendezvous point, where you'll signal for a pickup. A plane will come in on your lights, pick you up, and get you down to the vicinity of Peenemünde in time for you to find someplace to hide for the day.

"That night you will find and destroy the three rockets on the ground. We believe they'll be in the vicinity of the V2 firing stands."

"What about afterward?" Scotty asked.

"There'll be a submarine waiting for you just offshore. You'll be given the signal codes."

"There'll be a lot of confusion after we hit Mittelwerke. But if we're not going after the engineers, then how do we pull it off? How do we hurt them so badly the Nazis won't recover in time to do us any damage before the war is over, and yet not risk the lives of our friends?"

There were at least fifty people busy at work up here, but none of them so much as lifted an eye toward Bruce and Scotty. People came and went at a furious pace, as if they were in a race, which in a way, Scotty thought, they were.

A large-scale map of the state of Thuringia north of the city of Erfurt was pinned to a large standup drafting table. Nordhausen was at the top of the highly detailed topographic map. The concentration camp and Mittelwerke factory were marked in red. Above the factory, about five kilometers to the north, a symbol like a parenthesis was marked across a small branch of the Aller River that flowed away from Brocken Mountain.

Bruce pointed a delicate finger at it. "A small dam. If it were to be destroyed, the resulting flood wouldn't cause terribly much damage, nor would it likely cause much loss of life. Merely an inconvenience to the Germans."

Scotty saw the idea at once. "But it will flood the underground factory."

"Indeed. I'm told that it will take five or six hours, but the underground caverns will flood, and it will take the Germans at least four months to construct a temporary dam, pump out the water, and repair the damage to the machinery." Bruce gave Scotty a rare smile. "Four months, that is, if they have nothing else to keep them occupied."

Scotty felt protective of Lindsay and even her brother-in-law, and he felt sorry about Cecile, but *Coalmine* was now, in his mind, a doable mission.

Bruce read his mind. "I'm sorry about Sarah Winslow, but it cannot be helped. I'm sure that you can see why withholding the fact she's there from her husband and sister is vital."

Scotty nodded glumly. "We'll be ready to leave in twenty hours."

"I'm counting on you," Bruce said, shaking hands.

"Business as usual, sir," Scotty replied. It had become the British national expression.

FIVE

Schellenberg was in a bad mood. His chief of ciphers, *Oberst* Hans Schmidt, told him that there was no way of telling for sure if Marta had sent an embedded code word in her message to London, warning them that this was a trap.

A special Gestapo team had come down from Berlin to interrogate her last night and again this morning, but neither her story nor her defiant attitude had changed. She was willing to cooperate. She would send whatever messages they wanted her to send. But she was certain that London would see through the ruse.

"They'll know that I'm sending with a gun pointed at my head," she told them with confidence.

Nor would she give them her real name. She wouldn't confirm or deny that her code name was Cecile. She was Marta Frick.

The Mittelwerke chief scientist and the commandant of Nordhausen shared a large hunting lodge in the hills between the factory and the concentration camp. It was where Schellenberg was staying.

His driver took him down to the camp before supper, the country road through the thick forest lovely under a fresh blanket of snow. *In happier times*, he started to think, but cut it off. There would be no happy times until this godforsaken war was over. He had seen the look of derision in Marta's eyes when she said that she'd faked her orgasms with him. She called him a grunting pig. It hurt that she had called him those names, and that she was a spy, all the more because he was sure that he was in love with her.

The guards at the front gate let him in, and they drove straight over to the commandant's office, behind which were the interrogation cells for what they called *special prisoners*, mostly Jews who were engineers or knew some science and were being selected to work in the factory.

In this case it was Marta housed there, under the horrible ministrations of the Gestapo. But she was a British spy. She'd come over here of her own free will, not as a soldier with a gun, but as a woman with her body for sale.

He went directly back to the interrogation cell block. The sergeant on duty was the only one there. The Gestapo men had gone into town a couple of hours earlier.

"I'm taking the woman with me," Schellenberg said. He took off his leather gloves and slapped them against the side of his leg. His great coat was thrown over his shoulders, his general's insignia gleaming dully in the dim light.

The sergeant jumped up and came to ramrod attention. "Sir, I was given direct orders by Captain Gestern to hold the prisoner."

Schellenberg was surprised by the sergeant's gumption. The man had to be very frightened of the Gestapo. "Do you have eyes, Sergeant? I outrank everyone here, including the camp commandant. So, unless you want to be shot for disobeying the direct order of a superior officer, bring the woman to me."

The sergeant hesitated only a fraction of a second. *"Jawohl, Herr General,"* he snapped. He grabbed some keys and hurried back to the cells, returning a minute later with a very battered Marta.

Both her eyes had been blackened, patches of hair had been pulled from her head, her scalp was oozing blood in spots, at least two of her teeth had been knocked out, and the way she held herself told him that at the very least she had cracked ribs and perhaps some internal damage. His heart sank when he saw her. But dammit, she was the dirty little spy, not he.

"What shall I tell them, *Herr General?*"

"That Six has retaken control of the prisoner," Schellenberg said. He put his coat over her shoulders and led her outside to his big Mercedes.

They headed back to the hunting lodge. Since it was likely that London Station knew that Marta was being coerced, they would have to suspect that they would be walking into a trap if they came here to sabotage the factory.

He had given that some thought. The only chance of success would be blowing up the place or killing the key personnel.

He also considered leaving that very minute for Berlin. Back in his own headquarters, he would have more control over Marta's fate than he did here. Yet something held him back.

He could not remember everything that he told her when they were in the act of lovemaking; it was very stupid of him in the first place. He'd acted like a smitten schoolboy. But whatever he'd told her was probably enough, along with the aerial photos taken last week of one of the V5s at Peenemünde and the possible links to the Jew engineer who was killed right here at about the same time, to alert the Allies to the full potential of what they were faced with. When the three rockets flew in less than seventy-two hours, all three targeted on downtown Washington, D.C., warfare would be changed forever. London Station had to know that. They also knew that aerial assaults on Mittelwerke were futile, and yet the factory had to be put of commission.

But how?

He'd pored over the engineering drawings of the installation, the reinforced entrances, the camouflaged air intake vents. In order to do the factory any serious damage, tons of explosives would have to be set in place and detonated.

He shook his head. Impossible, given the security measures in and around the place. Two hundred fifty Wehrmacht and SS troops were on guard twenty-four hours per day. No unathorized person could get in or out of the place.

Which left a strike on the personnel. But many of them were Jews. Friends of the Allies.

"Where are you taking me?" Marta asked, her voice barely audible.

"Back to Berlin tonight, or perhaps tomorrow."

"Will I be shot?"

"Yes, unless you start helping me," Schellenberg told her. He'd almost said *helping us*, but changed his choice of words. They had been lovers. Maybe she was lying, maybe she wasn't faking the whole time. He'd listened to her moans of pleasure. Maybe she did feel something for him after all.

"I'll never help you," she answered, gaining a little strength. "I'm the enemy. And in a few months Germany will lose the war." She looked out the window. "The Wehrmacht will be replaced by Allied soldiers. Right here."

Schellenberg shook his head. Not if the V5 program was successful, he thought. He just had to figure out how the Allies were planing on stopping them.

He handed Marta over to the chief of the house staff, a matronly old woman who cooed and clucked disapprovingly. Marta would be cleaned up, her injuries tended to, and if anyone asked about her, their inquiries were to be directed solely to the general.

The house was quiet at this time of the day. The commandant's three children were still in school, and his wife was probably in town, where she spent most of her time.

He drifted back to the library and poured a cognac. The engineering and architectural drawings of the factory were spread out over the leather-topped desk, along with several very-large-scale maps of the countryside immediately above and around the underground installation.

He sat down on the couch, put his feet up on the coffee table, and tried to think like an Allied commando bent on destroying Mittelwerke.

LATER THAT AFTERNOON · RAF BASE FARNHAM

It had been a rough slog all day, getting the team prepared for the switch in mission plans, making sure that they had the equipment they needed, and waiting to the last minute for Colonel Bruce to twist some arms in London and send them the go-ahead.

As it was, they were nearly an hour late arriving at RAF Farnham. The pilots' briefing had already started. Scotty sent Winslow with the rest of their team to get something to eat while he went over to the operations ready room.

A British major was conducting the evening's briefing for the pilots and copilots of the twelve Avro Lancaster heavy bombers that were scheduled to head for Berlin within the next twenty minutes. A big map of Germany was pinned to the wall at the back of the stage, with courses, speeds, and targets overlayed in red.

The team was supposed to ride over in one of the bombers, which would divert away from the squadron, as if lost, and fly south to the vicinity of Nordhausen. The *Coalminers*, as they had begun to call themselves, would make the jump, and the Lancaster would rejoin its squadron over Berlin.

It had been an imperfect plan from the beginning, one that Scotty had ranged around to improve. But it was Lindsay who had come up with the alternative late last night.

The major stopped in midsentence as Scotty walked in and went directly to the platform. Every eye in the room was on the Yank, and none of the crew seemed the least bit friendly.

"Sorry, Major, but there's been a last-minute change of plans," Scotty said.

"You're welcome to the ride, Captain, but you were not invited to this briefing," the officer said. His name tag read *Clarke*. He was short, sandy-haired, and looked as if he hadn't slept in a week. He also looked irascible. "If you'll get your arse out of here, I'll finish with my lads, and we can take off."

"Have a look at this first, sir." Scotty handed him Churchill's letter.

Clarke wanted to bite someone's head off, Scotty's first. But he took the letter, quickly scanned it, looked up in surprise, then read it again, slowly this time. When he was finished he handed it back.

"Listen up, gentlemen. There has been a change of plans after all," he said. He turned to Scotty. "You'll brief us now, Captain?" He was still mad, but he was impressed.

Scotty nodded. He went to the map, found a marker, and laid out the course across the Channel directly to Nordhausen. "My team will be in the last aircraft. We'll jump right behind the last bombs."

"If you're talking about Mittelwerke, it's been tried by your lot as well as ours," one of the pilots said. "No go."

"The bombing is a diversion. We're going in just after the mid-shift change. If you can hit some of the soldiers guarding the factory, then well and good. But my team is your primary load."

"Dropping bombs on Berlin makes more sense," another pilot said.

"Not this time," Scotty replied. "For now there is no other target in Germany with a higher priority." He turned to the major. "I suggest that you dig out your target objectives of Mittelwerke from your mission files. I'm sure there'll be photographs and way points you've already used."

Major Clarke nodded to a sergeant at the back of the room, who turned and left.

"Will there be anything else?" Clarke asked.

"No," Scotty said. He was tired, too, and a little irascible about taking Lindsay along. Very likely they were walking into a buzz saw. It was possible that they would never make their pickup point, which was nearly eight kilometers from the dam. In that case they'd be stuck in the middle of Nazi Germany with absolutely no hope of escape.

The RAF officer read some of that from Scotty's expression. "Why don't you get yourself something to eat at the officers' mess? This lot will take us a half hour to sort out."

"We can't be late. There's a lot riding on this."

"There has been all along, hasn't there?"

THAT EVENING · MITTELWERKE

"I'm sorry, *Herr General*, but this has become Gestapo business," Captain Gestern said.

They were in the soaring front stairhall of the hunting lodge. Schellenberg's left eyebrow rose. He held out his right hand. "Very well, Captain, let me see your orders."

The commandant had made himself scarce when he realized what the Gestapo wanted and what Schellenberg's position was. Gestern had only his sergeant as backup.

"My orders are verbal, sir," Gestern said. He looked Nordic, square chin, short-cropped blond hair. "Now, if you will have the prisoner brought—"

"Not good enough," Schellenberg cut in. "When you have written orders from Himmler, bring them to me."

Ordinarily the Gestapo had precedence over any German officer, no matter what rank. But the secret police was a branch of the RSHA, in which Schellenberg was head of counterespionage. Gestern was in a very tricky position, and he knew it. If he was right, Schellenberg might get his hand slapped. But if he was wrong, the ax would fall on his neck.

Gestern bowed slightly. "As you wish, *Herr General*," he said. He and his sergeant left.

"Was that wise?" Marta asked from the head of the stairs.

Schellenberg looked up at her. "You're going to help me defend this place."

"Like hell," she said. "Maybe I'll escape tonight."

"I think Captain Gestern would find that more amusing than you can imagine," Schellberg replied. He went back to the library, where he hunched over the diagrams and maps spread on the desk.

The answer was here, he was sure of it.

But where?

LATER THAT EVENING · EN ROUTE TO MITTELWERKE

Colonel Bruce was arranging the pickup. He hadn't managed to get that confirmed before Scotty boarded the Lancaster with his team.

But the rendezvous point was set. It was a narrow, sloping field northwest of Nordhausen in a valley called Unter-Harz. And the time was set for 0400. It was up to the colonel not to leave them stranded. And it was a measure of how much trust his people placed in him that the Coalminers left on what could be a one-way ride.

The Lancaster was an ugly-looking brute, with a gross weight of nearly seventy thousand pounds, powered by four 1,280-horsepower Rolls-Royce Merlin engines. It was slower and flew lower than the B-17 Flying Fortress, but all the American bombers were being used on daytime raids over the Third Reich. For all its size and muscle, however, with the addition of nine people and their gear, the cabin of the tail end Lancaster was extremely cramped.

They sat on the bare floor, their knees hunched up, in two rows, Scotty in the lead on the left and Winslow on the right. Smythe stood forward, above the empty bomb racks and bomb bay doors. He was the jumpmaster. When the time came for the drop, he would go out the bomb bay, his trajectory guided by the bomba-dier/navigator. They would follow him. Their Lancaster would come in lower than the others, at under one thousand feet. That was high enough to give the chutes time to open properly, yet low enough so that they would not drift off target on the winds aloft.

They were all thinking about the 165,000 pounds of bombs the other eleven Lancasters would be dropping right ahead of them. Scotty could imagine all kinds of disasters: landing on an unex-ploded bomb and setting it off, landing in the middle of a still burning crater, or somehow getting their signals mixed up and jumping out of the plane *before* all the bombs were dropped. A bomb fell a lot faster than a man dangling beneath a parachute. The odds of getting hit that way were miniscule, but they were odds none the less.

Just the year before a trip to Germany entailed a long swing out over the North Sea to avoid enemy fighters and radar in France and Belgium. But the American First Army had crossed the German frontier four months ago, so the direct route over Belgium was possible.

The Baltic Sea and the north German coast around Peenemünde were still socked in, and it was snowing, but meteorologists predicted that by morning the region would gradually start to clear. For now the way into Germany was moonless, leaving the landscape very dark. But there were some low-lying clouds, and what little light there was glinted like burnished silver off the snow-capped hills and frozen lakes and ponds.

Besides the two man-sized canisters filled with the TNT, detonators, and det cord they would use to blow up the dam, the team members traveled with heavy loads.

Each of them carried the American M3 forty-five-caliber submachine gun, a razor-sharp stiletto, a personal handgun, in Scotty's case a 9mm Beretta, three and a half feet of piano wire with handles fashioned into deadly garrotes, and a few pounds of Composition B explosive and several pencil fuses for taking out the rockets. In addition they carried three hundred rounds of ammunition for each weapon.

Scotty and Lindsay carried gas masks and surgical gloves for dealing with the anthrax payloads, along with compact tool kits to remove the canisters.

St. Lo and Ballinger carried small electronic multitesters and specialized tool kits to deal with the guidance systems. One of the last-minute tasks they'd agreed to take on was to try to bring back one of the electromechanical computers.

They wore standard battle dress uniforms overlaid with winter white camouflage suits. Any empty pocket was stuffed with food from C and K ration packets.

Smythe's first test of their capabilities at Bletchley Park was kitting them out with everything they would carry into the field, or at least the equivalent weights and shapes, and running the confidence course.

St. Lo, Smythe, Lindsay, and Winslow, the four weakest-appearing Coalminers, turned in the fastest times. But as Lindsay patiently explained to the vexed but impressed Americans, the Brits had a much greater motivation to do well against the Jerries than did the Americans.

The navigator in the lead Lancaster had been on two nighttime bombing runs to Mittelwerke, and one to the town of Nordhausen, so he knew the landmarks. Combined with his dead reckoning, they came in as if they were flying on a guidance beacon.

For the past fifteen minutes the tail end Lancaster had gradually reduced altitude. They could feel it in the back of the plane because of the decreased pitch of the engines and the popping in their ears.

Five minutes out the copilot, Lt. Harry Christiansen, came back to them. He had to shout to be heard over the tremendous din.

"We're nearly over the target. The bomb bay doors will open one minute out. Sergeant Smythe will give you the signal to hook up. The moment he's away, follow in his wake. You'll have just forty-five seconds to get out if you all want to be on target and not spread all over hell." He looked at them as if he thought they were insane, then he gave Smythe the thumbs-up and went back into the cockpit.

"Check your equipment, if you please," Smythe shouted.

They all checked their gear, especially their parachute straps, and then checked each other's equipment.

A large jeweled yellow light came on above the bulkhead in front of the bomb bay.

"Hook up," Smythe shouted. He hooked the carabiner clips for the rip cords of the two equipment canisters that had been positioned at the edge of the bomb bay, then his own to the steel cable that ran the length of the cabin.

Scotty and the others got to their feet and hooked their rip cords.

The bomb bay doors rumbled open, the already deafening noise rising in volume as a tremendous wind whipped through the aircraft.

They could hear the bombs detonating ahead of them as an almost continuous thunder with distant lightning pulsing in waves.

Smythe stood at the edge of the bomb bay, watching the light. When it switched to green he shoved the canisters over the edge, folded his arms over his chest, and stepped forward, dropping like a stone.

Scotty was next. A huge, cold fist of air slammed into his body as he dropped into the pitch-black night. Three seconds later his parachute opened, and he was violently pulled from 150 miles per hour to a near standstill.

Smythe's chute and the chutes of the two canisters were visible below and to the right. Scotty looked over his left shoulder, but he couldn't see anyone else. Already the Lancaster was lost in the distance as it did a climbing turn for the trip home.

Ahead, the hills were heavily pockmarked with craters. Some areas in the forest were burning, and what looked like a small convoy of trucks had been hit and lay like toys on fire, scattered on and around the highway.

He tried to get his bearings, but with bomb flashes still going off like camera flashbulbs, fire coming from distant antiaircraft guns, and the small blazes lighting up the night, it was impossible. Suddenly the land came up very fast, and he was falling through the tree branches. He tucked his elbows in and bent his knees. Then he hit and rolled with his landing, just missing the bole of a large tree.

Winslow was down about fifteen yards to Scotty's left, and two others were down a little farther in the same direction.

Scotty got out of his parachute harness and was rolling the canopy and lines into a ball when Smythe, Lindsay, and Ballinger trotted over. Winslow joined them. Something was obviously wrong.

"You two okay, then?" Smythe asked. There was some blood on his hands.

"We're okay," Scotty said. "What about you?"

"It's Talbot," Smythe replied bitterly. "His bloody parachute didn't open. He went straight in."

"It was horrible," Lindsay said. "He didn't make a sound—"

"Easy," Scotty told her. "It's rotten luck, but we can't stay here discussing the man's death. Cover his body with snow, with anything you can find, and get the team together. We're moving out in five minutes."

Smythe gave him a tight look. But then he nodded. "All right, you heard the man, let's get on with it."

SIX

Schellenberg watched from the window of Marta's bedroom as the last of the bombs fell far to the south.

It made no sense to bomb the factory. They wouldn't hit the concentration camp, and there was nothing left of any strategic value in the city. So what were they trying to accomplish? Did London Station believe the message that Marta had sent them about the air vent locations?

The commandant's family had gone down to the shelter in the basement with the house staff, while the commandant himself hurried off to the camp. It was a foolish gesture on his part, though brave, Schellenberg thought.

Marta, on the other hand, refused to leave her upstairs bedroom. "Better that I die here than in some filthy Gestapo cell in Berlin," she said.

Another futile gesture? Captain Gestern would believe that she'd remained upstairs so that she could signal the incoming bombers, which was stupid. Signal the bomb crews to do what? Of course, stupidity had never hindered the Gestapo in the past.

Keeping Marta safe was going to be increasingly difficult after tonight. But he was determined to help her—at least keep her alive until the end of the war. And then they'd see if there could be some sort of a life for them.

But he was still left with the question about the bombing raid. What were the Allies trying to do tonight?

His driver appeared in the doorway. "Captain Gestern is on his way over from the communications center."

"Has he got his orders?" Schellenberg asked.

"I don't know, *Herr General*. But I'd guess he has them."

Schellenberg nodded. "Is there any word on casualties?"

"A convoy was hit, but they were mostly Jews killed. There was no damage to the factory where most of the bombs were concentrated."

"No damage to the camp, or the town?"

"No, sir."

Schellenberg reflected on the situation. The bombing accomplished nothing, if the aim was to take out the rocket factory. But the Allies knew that this raid would be useless. Yet they had gone ahead with it. Why? They weren't stupid.

They had a plan.

"Find out if any parachutists were spotted," he told his driver. "The bombing raid may have been a diversion. And find out how many of them there are and where they landed."

"Shall I alert security?"

"Yes, by all means, Hermann," Schellenberg said. "Now hurry. I'll be downstairs in the library."

Sergeant Kolst left, and Marta laughed.

"Maybe they're already here, Walther," she said. "Maybe you're already too late."

"Perhaps you're right," Schellenberg said. He took her arm, and they went downstairs to the library, just as Captain Gestern and his partner walked in.

"We'll take the prisoner now, *Herr General*," Gestern said. He held out a Gestapo Arrest Warrant, presumably signed by the *Reichsmarshall*.

"When I've finished with her," Schellenberg said. He directed her to sit down in an easy chair by the lamp.

"Are you going to defy direct orders, *Herr General?*"

"Don't be an idiot; you can do whatever you want with her once I'm finished," Schellenberg said calmly. "But at this moment I am in the middle of a delicate intelligence operation for which I need her help."

"What help—?"

"Unless you missed the noise, there was a bombing raid on the factory this evening," Schellenberg said. "But I think it was a diversion."

Gestern was interested. "For what?"

"Security is looking for evidence that parachutists have landed. Probably from the last bomber. It did seem to come in much lower than the others."

"To try to destroy the factory?" Gestern asked disparagingly. "Well, I can tell you for a fact that they won't get very far. Security around this place is as good as anything I've ever seen." He glanced over at Marta. "If you're right, what part will she play?"

"They may be here because of the messages she sent to London."

"Here to attempt a rescue?" Gestern asked incredulously.

"Exactly. And I intend using her as bait, once we find out where they are."

"They won't get anywhere near the factory, sir."

"No, but they have a plan," Schellenberg said.

He went to the desk and shuffled through the factory blueprints and area maps. If the Allies had landed a raiding party, the answers would be right in front of him. He had to know where they landed.

THURSDAY, TWO HOURS LATER · THE DAM

Scotty held up a hand for the team to stop just below the top of the last rise before the dam. He cocked an ear to listen. Earlier he was sure he'd heard something at a distance in the woods behind them. Soldiers, almost certainly, and a lot of them. Searching for something, or someone, like hounds on the trail of a fox.

But up here there was nothing except for the soft gurgling of water. If the Germans found St. Lo's body and the hastily buried parachutes and canisters, they would instantly realize that the bombing raid was a ruse. They might come here.

He crawled up the last few feet so that he could see over the top. There was no need for binoculars. He was less than thirty yards above the tiny earthwork dam and the small lake it had created. No more than forty feet across at the top, the dam plugged a narrow gap in a rock outcropping through which the river had once splashed.

A water race, about three feet in diameter, jutted out of the hill beside the dam and disappeared underground at the base. It probably carried water downstream to a small electrical-generating station.

There were no lights on the dam, nor was there a proper road, only a narrow track through the snow to a small hut in front of which was parked a German military motorcycle and sidecar. He was directly above the hut, which, as luck would have it, was on the far side of the river. Smoke curled from the tin chimney.

Scotty slid back down to the others. "There's a guard shack twenty-five or thirty feet on the other side of the hill. One, maybe two guards at the most. I didn't see any footprints in the snow across the dam, so they're probably inside keeping warm."

"It's where I'd be," Ballinger said. He was always bitching about something.

"Smythe and I will take care of the guards. As soon as I give you the all clear, Mac and Vivian will set the charges at the base of the dam. The rest of you make a perimeter."

"Expecting company?" Winslow asked. He was very cool. He could have been talking about a stroll across Trafalgar Square.

"Somebody was making a racket behind us."

"I heard it," Lindsay said. "Do you suppose they spotted us coming down?"

"It's possible," Scotty told her. He wished that she was safely back in England, but he could not worry about that now. "If they find our chutes and pick up the trail, they'll figure out what we're up to. So we have to shake a leg."

McKeever had already unslung the two packs of explosives he'd taken from the canisters, while Leigh was unpacking the fuses they would need.

"Go," Mac said, without looking up. "We'll be ready when you are."

Smythe took out his stiletto, but Scotty took out his Beretta and screwed a silencer on the end of the barrel.

Smythe nodded, but did not sheathe his knife.

They crawled back up to the crest of the hill, then quickly made their way through the trees to a spot behind the guard shack before they started down.

The door faced the narrow track, but a window in the side of the guard hut faced the dam. Scotty motioned for Smythe to cover the door, then crept to the side of the shack and peered inside.

One German soldier, his jacket unbuttoned, his collar open, sat at a small table munching on a piece of dark bread. His rifle leaned against the table. A field telephone sat on a shelf by the door, and except for a dim lantern that hung above the table, and a tiny woodstove in the corner, the inside of the rough shack was bare.

Scotty hesitated for a moment. Something wasn't right, but he couldn't put his finger on it for several seconds. But then he saw it. There were two chairs at the small table.

Something crashed against the other side of the hut, and Smythe appeared, wrestling a very large German soldier to the ground.

Scotty broke the window with the muzzle of his silencer and fired two shots at the soldier, who'd grabbed his rifle. The man went down, but he started to bring his rifle up, his finger on the trigger. Scotty fired two more shots, one hitting the soldier in the jaw and the second his forehead just above his left eye. He was dead before he fell to the floor.

When Scotty turned back, blood was gushing from a large slit in the throat of the second guard, who was still thrashing around trying to bring his pistol to bear on his attacker. Smythe was trying to keep a hand clamped over the much larger man's mouth, while with the other shove the pistol away and still hold his bloody stiletto.

Scotty rushed over to them, put the muzzle of his pistol against the German's heart and pulled the trigger just as the man looked up at him in mute terror. His body stiffened, then went slack. He was just a kid. Probably still in his teens.

Scotty stepped back. He looked at Smythe, who was disentangling himself from the dead German. "Are you okay?"

Smythe nodded. "Thanks for the help. You?"

"He was just a kid."

"He was a German soldier who would have killed us both as was his duty," Smythe shot back sternly. "It's just rotten that he was only a baby boy, but that's one of the reasons we're here. To stop the bastards."

Scotty looked up to the crest of the hill. McKeever was watching. Scotty gave him the all clear sign, and he and Leigh came over the top and scrambled down the steep embankment to the base of the dam. Each carried large packs of explosives.

"Get the team down here," Scotty told Smythe. "We pull out in ten minutes."

"How long a delay on the fuses?" Smythe asked.

Scotty thought about it for a moment. If the Germans showed up there, they would be looking for the explosives at the base of the dam. Given enough time they would disconnect the fuses. He wasn't going to give them the time. "I want a ten-minute head start."

It was cutting it extremely close. But Smythe nodded and headed back up the hill.

THAT SAME MOMENT · MITTELWERKE

The night was made longer because nobody seemed to know what was going on except that an Allied bombing attack on the factory had failed to do any significant damage. By 1:30 A.M. an increasingly worried Schellenberg knew that the longer they waited to act, the more likely the raiding party, if one had landed, would be successful. But for the life of him he still could not think of what they meant to do. He had to know where they'd come down.

Half of the combined Nordhausen-Mittelwerke security forces was guarding the concentration camp and factory, while the other half scoured the countryside looking for parachutes. Nobody slept.

The house staff had brought food and drink to the study. Afterward, Marta had to use the bathroom. Gestern sent his sergeant to watch her, and Schellenberg did not object, though he wanted to.

There were two alternate possibilities. The bombing could have been a legitimate, though futile, attempt to destroy or at least damage the rocket factory. Or, the raid was a ruse for something completely different than a landing party of saboteurs.

Maybe they'd come to draw scarce fighter and antiaircraft resesources from somewhere else.

He called a friend at what was left of Luftwaffe Headquarters in Berlin, who informed him that he was too busy to answer every damned fool who called with stupid questions for which there were no satisfactory answers any longer. Schellenberg could hear bombs falling on the capital city over the long-distance telephone line, and the desperation in his friend's voice.

"There was an air raid on Mittelwerke tonight," Schellenberg told him.

"We know about the raid. But we didn't do anything about it because they can't hurt the factory."

"Did radar track the bombers afterward?"

"They went back to Belgium, then home across the Channel, we presume. What's your interest, Walther?"

"I think that something is going to happen down here."

"Well, if you want my advice, keep your ass covered. It won't be long now."

Sergeant Kolst appeared at the door. "You were right, *Herr General*, a raiding party did land. We found seven parachutes and one body. He broke his neck on landing."

"Good," Captain Gestern said.

"They're still looking, but just before I headed back up here, they found an equipment container and its parachute."

Schellenberg went to the desk and spread out the map. "Show me where they came down. Exactly."

Kolst studied the map to orient himself, then stabbed a blunt finger on a spot several kilometers to the north and west of the factory. In fact, not too far from the hunting lodge. Startled, Gestern looked up at Marta.

"Maybe they're coming here after all," she taunted.

"Which direction did they go?" Schellenberg asked.

"That's the bad news," Kolst said. "By the time they found where the parachutes and body were buried, the snow was heavily trampled. They had a large area to search."

"What about the factory entrances?"

"The SS are taking care of that, *Herr General*," Gestern said. "Nobody will get in that way. If they're foolish enough to try, they'll be cut down."

Gestern was right, of course. But the Allies were not stupid. They had a plan. *They were here. For what? To do what?*

Destroy the factory? Or in some way hurt its operation or personnel?

Schellenberg looked at Marta sitting in the corner, a Mona Lisa smile on her face. He turned back to the map, and suddenly he had it.

The small dam above the factory. Directly below, in the the old riverbed, were several air vent shafts. If the dam were to be destroyed, the water would flood the shafts, leading directly into the factory. It would cause a lot of damage, and possibly even completely flood the place.

He looked up. "I know what they're trying to do."

"What is it?" Gestern asked.

"I'll tell you on the way. And if I'm right, I know how to stop them."

0230 · THE DAM

Scotty waited at the top of the dam. He was becoming nervous. McKeever and Leigh were taking far too long with the explosives.

But it looked as if they were having trouble digging deeply enough into the base of the dam because the ground was frozen rock hard.

The field telephone in the guard shack had not rung. There was no way of telling if the guards were supposed to report on a schedule. But even if they were not missed, St. Lo's body and the parachutes might be found. If they also found the canisters, the Germans might put two and two together. Not all of them were stupid.

Smythe had put Ballinger, Don Smith, and Lindsay on the hill across the river in the direction they would have to go to reach the drop zone. He and Winslow had gone a hundred yards down the narrow track and set explosive charges on several large trees. If someone tried to come up, they would drop the trees across the road, slowing any sort of a mechanized attack. With luck it would give them enough time to escape into the woods.

If that did occur, their biggest problem would be leading the Germans away from the landing zone and still giving themselves enough time to get back for the pickup.

He walked back to the guard hut. Nothing could be seen down the narrow road. Only a few puffy clouds obscured the star-studded sky, but thankfully there was no moon. The night was deathly still and very cold.

Scotty started to turn when two sharp explosions echoed off the hills down the track. Almost immediately there was a third, then a fourth.

Smythe and Winslow had triggered the explosives to block the road. Someone was coming.

He ran back to the dam. Mac and Leigh had also heard the explosions. It was impossible to see exactly what they were doing, but it was clear that they were hurrying.

Lindsay stepped out from behind a tree at the crest of the ridge across the river. She was fifty feet above the dam. She motioned toward the road with two fingers in front of her eyes, indicating that she was seeing something.

She held up one finger, made a steering wheel motion with both hands, then stopped.

Scotty cocked an ear to listen. He couldn't hear a thing.

Lindsay held up five fingers, and walked them up the hill.

Five people had shown up in one car and they were heading up the road on foot.

Scotty signaled his understanding.

Smythe and Winslow should have been up here by now. What the hell was taking them so long?

McKeever signaled from the bottom of the dam that they were ready to set the fuses.

They were running out of time.

Scotty signaled them to proceed, then get up the hill to where Lindsay and the others were waiting. He turned and headed past the guard shack and down the hill.

They had ten minutes, starting now, to get the hell out of here. If the dam blew while they were on this side of the river, it'd be all over for them.

Before he got twenty yards there was the sudden crackle of small-arms fire ahead. He scrambled off the side of the track and into the woods, where he held up to try to figure out what was going on.

The shooting stopped, and Scotty worked his way farther down the hill. Four large trees blocked the path. Below them, a large Mercedes sedan with general's flags on the fenders was stopped, its door open. Two people were down in the snow beside the car and not moving.

He couldn't see anyone else. The forest was deathly still. He knew that Smythe and Winslow had to be close, but he couldn't figure out why they had gotten into a shoot-out after they had dropped the trees.

He moved from tree to tree down the hill until he was within twenty or thirty feet of the Mercedes. Still he could see no one on either side of the barrier.

"Here," Winslow whispered urgently to his left.

Winslow was crouched beneath the low-hanging boughs of a fir tree, his M3 trained on the Mercedes.

Scotty scrambled over beside him. "What the hell are you doing?

We have to get out of here. We've got less than ten minutes before the dam blows."

"Sarah is here. They've got my wife. I'm not leaving without her."

"Where's Smythe?"

"Here," Smythe said from a tree a few yards away. "I agree with the major. If we leave her here, they'll kill her."

"Go left, I'll take right," Scotty told Smythe. "Don will give us thirty seconds, then open fire on the middle of the blockade."

Without waiting for a reply, Scotty scrambled down the hill to the jumble of splintered wood stumps where the explosives had felled the trees. From his angle he could see the two downed Germans lying in the snow beside the car. One of them was a sergeant.

Something out of the corner of his eye caught his attention. A single set of footprints led away from the car straight down the hill toward the riverbed, disappearing into the dark woods. It was Winslow's wife. He'd bet anything on it. She'd taken her chance and run for it.

Her only hope would be to get across the riverbed and up the other side before the dam blew.

It was the only hope for all of them.

Winslow opened fire.

Scotty jumped up. He caught sight of two Germans, one of them with general's stars on his shoulder boards, crouching behind the barrier. He fired his M3, emptying the clip on full automatic, then ducked back to reload.

Smythe fired from the other side of the barrier.

Scotty popped back up, but both Germans were down and unmoving.

"Clear," Scotty shouted.

Winslow came running down the path. "Sarah," he shouted.

"She's gone Winslow," Scotty shouted back. "She took off downriver."

Winslow started over the downed trees, but Scotty pulled him back.

"We can't go after her now. We have to finish the mission."

"I'm not going with you—"

Smythe backhanded Winslow across the face. "You won't do your wife any good," he said sternly. "Are you hearin' me? She's survived for this long in Germany, she'll know more about escaping than we do if we're caught."

Winslow looked as if he wanted to bolt, but then some of the wildness drained from his eyes, and he shook his head. "Bloody hell. I actually saw her. She was right here."

"We've got less than five minutes to get across the dam, or we'll be stuck."

Winslow hesitated a moment longer before he turned away from the barrier and followed Scotty and Smythe back up the hill as fast as his legs could carry him.

They reached the guard shack and raced across the dam. The others at the top of the hill were frantically waving them on.

Smythe was first, but when Winslow slipped and fell, he went back. He and Scotty helped the major to his feet, and they clawed and scrambled their way up the steep slope.

At the top Scotty stopped to look back. He thought he saw a movement behind the barrier in front of the Mercedes. But then a deep-throated thump shook the ground. His eyes were dragged to the dam, which was collapsing in slow motion. Water began to stream over the crumbling top in a trickle, at first, that turned into a torrent, sending a wall of water down the dry riverbed.

He turned to Winslow, who was searching down river for as far as he could see. But there was nothing there except for a tidal wave of water moving at the speed of an express train.

0400 · THE LANDING ZONE

They'd been obliged to march single file, doubling back to cover their tracks from time to time. Even so, they made it to their rendezvous point with several minutes to spare. Increasing cloud cover made the already black night even darker. The narrow, snow-covered valley between low mountains in the Harz range was deserted.

Ballinger, McKeever, Leigh, and Smith formed a line in the middle of the field. When they heard the airplane they would switch on their flashlights to guide the pilot in.

Providing Colonel Bruce was successful in rounding up transportation for them.

"Are you certain it was your wife back there?" Scotty asked Winslow. They stood huddled at the edge of the field.

"Yes," said Winslow. He was morose, and nobody could blame him. But once they reached Peenemünde, he would have to come back on track. The team needed him.

"Then the general we shot was probably Schellenberg."

Winslow's eyes widened when he realized the significance of what Scott had said. "You knew?"

"I knew that she was at Mittelwerke. But I never dreamed they'd bring her up to the dam. Schellenberg was going to use her to stop us."

"We should have gone after her—"

"If anyone can make it out, it's her," Smythe said, trying to be reassuring.

Lindsay, who was standing with them, averted her eyes, which were glistening. Her brother was relatively safe in a POW camp. But if they caught Sarah, the Germans would shoot her as a spy.

Smythe suddenly turned toward the west. "Here comes an airplane." He shook his head. "I don't recognize the sound. It might be German."

The others in the field had heard it, too, and they turned on their flashlights and aimed them straight up.

Scotty was listening intently. He recognized the sounds of the Pratt & Whitney twin Wasps. "It's one of ours. A Dakota."

But he was hearing something else as well. Someone was behind them. In the woods. He turned in time to see a disturbed pine bough drop its snow.

"We've got company," he warned. He pulled out his silenced Beretta and motioned for everyone to get down.

Smythe and the others pulled out their weapons. He looked over his shoulder at the Americans in the middle of the field with their flashlights. "What about the bloody airplane?"

"Wait," Scotty cautioned. Something wasn't right. If the Germans had followed them, they would have made noise. Something. And there was no way that the Germans could have known about this landing site ahead of time, to set up an ambush.

The Dakota DC-3 was very low now, coming in for a landing at the far end of the valley. They had run out of time.

"Who is it?" Scotty called out in English. He had to take the chance of drawing fire before the plane landed.

A slight figure in a very large coat of some sort stumbled out of the trees. It was hard to tell who it was, but then Scotty realized that it was a woman.

"My, God! Sarah," Winslow cried. He leaped up and ran to her before they could stop him. It could have been a trap.

But he grabbed her off her feet, the greatcoat falling off her shoulders, and they kissed and held each other, as the Dakota's front skis touched down with a puff of powder snow, the mission only half over with.

SEVEN

Before Dawn • En Route to Peenemünde

The Dakota was the lap of luxury compared to the Lancaster. A British medic and two crewmen had come along to render assistance. Sarah's wounds, none of them serious, were cleaned and redressed while the crewmen handed out hot coffee laced with brandy, and cheese and bologna sandwiches.

They flew very low and fast to keep out of the range of German radar, but still the two-hundred-mile flight up to Peenemünde off the Baltic coast was made half again longer because they had to avoid towns, military bases, and major highways. At one point they were less than thirty miles west of the Berlin outskirts.

They saw plenty of military convoys, and some tank traffic heading toward the west, but no air traffic whatsoever.

Many of the roads and even some of the smaller towns were heavily damaged. Bomb craters in a corridor between Hamburg and Berlin were so numerous it was like looking down at a lunar landscape.

Another thing that struck Scotty was how dark the countryside was. There were almost no lights anywhere. Normally the sky glow of any big city such as Berlin would have been visible for miles. But the sky to the east was as pitch-black as it was in any other direction. There weren't many fires tonight.

At the start of this mission he never dreamed that Winslow's wife would show up the way she had. It was incredible. But now it was another problem he would have to deal with. The best solution would be to send her home on this airplane. But when he'd broached the subject to her, she'd completely ignored him.

She and her husband and sister had been huddled together ever since the medic had finished with her. They had a lot of catching up to do.

She was an extraordinary woman. She told them that she slipped away from Schellenberg and headed across the river not simply to escape. She knew that someone had come to blow the dam to flood the factory, and she wanted to draw Schellenberg, his driver, and the pair of Gestapo thugs to follow her, to lead them away from the dam.

After the explosion, she picked up the Coalminers' trail and followed them to the landing zone, always keeping a safe distance between her and them on the off chance that somehow Schellenberg was following her. She would provide an early warning if it came to that.

But nobody had followed, and when she heard the airplane coming in for a landing she'd made her presence known. For a few moments she thought that Scott might shoot first and ask questions later.

"I was petrified," she told them, which brought a laugh.

After everything she'd been through in the past twelve months in Germany the thought that she could be that frightened at the end was almost ludicrous.

Scotty got up and went back to them. Winslow held her in his arms, and Lindsay sat back against a bulkhead on her parachute pack, her legs stretched out in front of her. They looked up.

"We'll be over Peenemünde pretty soon. We have to start getting ready," he told them.

"I understand that you lost one of your people in the jump,"

Sarah said. Smythe had carried St. Lo's pack all the way through the operation. Sarah was kitted out with his spare uniform and jumper.

Scotty nodded. "How do you feel?"

She gave her husband a fond look. "Much better, thank you. I'm coming with you in place of Talbot to finish the job."

It was about what Scotty expected. "I don't suppose there's any use arguing with her," he said to Winslow.

"No," Sarah answered. "My husband does not make decisions for me. We make them together. I'm taking Talbot's place. We've already agreed."

"I am the team leader," Scotty shot back, even though he knew he was in a losing battle.

Sarah managed a smile. "Congratulations, Captain, you just inherited a new Coalminer. I only hope that you've secured us decent accommodations where we're headed."

Scotty couldn't help but return her warm smile. Lindsay's family was something else. "The Ritz," he told her.

0900 • MITTELWERKE

It was full daylight by the time Schellenberg reached the main road and hailed a military supply truck. A stray bullet had passed through the Mercedes' radiator and shattered the distributor cap, making the car unusable. It had been a very long, cold walk down the mountain. But there was a lot of traffic here.

"You're bleeding, *Herr General*," the young Wehrmacht driver said.

"Just a flesh wound. Has the factory flooded?"

"Yes, sir. We're taking as much equipment out as fast as possible."

"Has a command post been set up?"

"Yes, *Herr General*, at the commandant's house."

"Take me there."

A steady stream of trucks filled with personnel and equipment headed toward the prison camp, while empty trucks, like the one he rode in, headed back toward the underground factory to help salvage whatever they could.

It was a disaster, in part brought on by his own stupidity for falling in love with a British spy. He never hated anybody more than he hated Sarah Winslow at that moment.

She had caused the Reich irreparable harm. And there was more to come. He'd heard them talking when they thought he was dead. One of them was an American; he recognized the nasal East Coast accent.

"We can't go after her now. We have to finish the mission."

Incredibly enough, one of the other men was Major Winslow, Marta's husband. He had been so close to his wife that he could touch her, and yet he agreed that the mission came before saving her.

Schellenberg's fists bunched so hard his shoulder wound twinged with an extremely sharp needle of pain, and he winced involuntarily.

The driver looked over in alarm. "Sir, I think you should go to the hospital."

He wasn't going to do anyone any good if he passed out, but even now the Allied commandos might be preparing to completely destroy the factory; or worse yet, kill their key personnel.

"Take me to the commandant's house. I'll see a medic there."

Traffic was also heavy to and from the hunting lodge. Stern-faced SS guards checked everyone one hundred meters below the house and again at the front door. They snapped to attention when they saw Schellenberg's rank, but asked to see his ID nonetheless.

The living room had been set up as a temporary command post now that the regular communications and control center in Mittelwerke was flooded. A lot of radios had been set up, aerials hastily strung up in the trees outside, and maps and charts pinned to the walls.

SS Major Karl Nebel, who was in overall command of Mittelwerke-Nordhausen security, looked up from the factory blueprints that he and several engineers were poring over. His rotund figure and narrow pig eyes behind steel-framed glasses made him look like a mean-spirited small-town banker, which he had been before 1939.

"Where have you been, *Herr General?*" he demanded "I have three squads out searching for you. We thought the commandos had kidnapped you."

"I was at the dam," Schellenberg said. "How bad is it?"

"We cannot stop the flooding. It'll take at least six months, perhaps longer, to divert the river and pump out the factory." Nebel's eyes narrowed even farther. "You were up there?"

"I had a fair guess what was about to happen, so I tried to stop them. I failed."

"You should have notified me," Nebel said angrily.

"It was my decision, *Herr Major,*" Schellenberg shot back harshly. "But the raid is not over. There's more."

"I'm not the Gestapo—"

"There's more, Nebel. They might be right outside this house even as we speak."

"They've gone back to England."

"How do you know that?"

"One of my patrols spotted an airplane coming in about ten kilometers from here. By the time they could get close to the landing field, the damned thing took off. But they found evidence that at least a half dozen people, probably more, got aboard. Radar lost the plane heading west." Nebel glanced at the blueprints. "They're back in England by now, and we have this mess to clean up." He gave Schellenberg a bleak look. "And we have to determine how it happened. Someone is at fault."

"They're not in England," Schellenberg said.

"Oh?" Nebel asked, arching an eyebrow.

"They flew to Peenemünde to finish the job."

"I don't think so, *Herr General,*" Nebel said. He shook his head. "No, I think that you are quite wrong again. Even the British wouldn't be that stupid. Perhaps you have been wrong about nearly everything."

1400 • PEENEMÜNDE

Scotty lay in the snow on a rise that looked out over the thickly wooded landscape that ran all the way down to the broad mouth of the Peene River. Two German soldiers, dressed in winter whites, their rifles slung over their shoulders, worked their way up the hill from where they'd left their VW. They were still nearly a mile off, and he could see through his binoculars that they were having a hard time in the deep snow. It would be a half hour before they got up here.

The open sea was a couple miles toward the northwest. The rocket research facility was spread out for several miles along the coast.

But the soldiers approaching were more than a security patrol. Something about them, about their being so far afield, led Scotty to believe that they were searching for something specific.

He pulled back below the rise, brushing snow across his tracks, then, making sure that he stayed on the tracks he'd made coming up, hurried down to the clearing in the middle of which stood the bombed-out ruins of what once had been a nice stone farmhouse. The Coalminers were staying in the fruit cellar.

The Ritz it wasn't, but secure it had been thus far. He expected that security would be tightened because of their attack on Mittelwerke. But if the patrol on the way up was looking specifically for them, it could mean that the pilot's ruse of flying west to fool German radar had not worked. It could also mean that the launch of the three V5s had been pushed up.

Ballinger stood lookout just within the ruins of the house. He was huddled out of the raw wind in the lee of the still standing chimney.

"Anything?" he asked.

"Two Germans are coming up the hill," Scotty told him.

"Shit, we've got another four hours before dark."

"We're going to set a trap. Keep a sharp eye out." Scotty went down the rickety ladder into the fruit cellar. The light from the one oil lantern they'd found was dim. Sarah was asleep in the corner, her head on Winslow's lap. The others were cleaning their weapons, organizing the Composition B and fuses they were going to use to blow up the rockets, going over their ammunition and other supplies, or just trying to relax and get something to eat. Tonight promised to be even longer than last night. Their rendezvous with the submarine wasn't until two in the morning, twelve hours from now.

"Okay, we have a problem coming our way," Scotty said. "Two Germans are coming up the hill from the road. There's just the two of them, and they've left their car on the road."

Sarah came instantly awake and sat up. "It's Schellenberg's doing. Are you sure you killed him?"

Scotty thought back to the moment just before the dam blew. He thought that he had seen a figure darting behind the Mercedes. But he wasn't sure. "I wouldn't bet my life on it. But he was hit, I saw the blood."

"So did I," Smythe said. "What makes you think that he's here?"

"He knows that Mittelwerke wasn't the only target," Sarah said. "He knows that we know about the three rockets." She looked at her husband. "He's in love with me. If he's alive, he won't give up so easily."

"If he wasn't killed at the dam, and if he *is* here, he can only suspect that we've come after the rockets," Winslow said. "And he'd be a perfect fool if he didn't love you."

"Once those soldiers find out about this place, he'll know for sure," Smythe said.

"We're going to kill them, switch uniforms, and two of us are going to take a little tour in their car," Scotty told them. "A rocket-finding tour."

"I'm coming with," Sarah said.

"Don't be a fool," Scotty told her flatly, and she reacted as if she had been slapped. But he grinned. "Anyway, you don't look like a German soldier. And if Schellenberg is here and happens to be at one of the launch sites, he could recognize you, and the game would be up."

Scotty was right, and Sarah knew it. She nodded, but it was obvious she didn't like the decision. She was used to living on the edge, living by her wits.

"They'll be at the top of the hill shortly," Scotty said. "Smythe, Mac, and Vivian will come with me. The rest of you pack up our gear and get ready to move out. If something goes wrong, you'll know it soon enough." He took out his silenced Beretta and checked the load. He had a full magazine plus one in the chamber.

"If they spot us first, and shoot, the game, as you say, will be up," Smythe pointed out. "That kind of sound carries a long way."

"We'll let them come all the way into the house, then take them with garrotes. My pistol will be a last resort. I want as little blood as possible on their uniforms."

"Let's get on with it," Smythe said.

Ballinger was watching the crest of hill when they went up. "Nothing yet," he said.

"We'll hide in back until they get inside the front wall, then Mac and Smythe will sneak around front to get behind them, while the rest of us take them front on" Scotty said. "I want it quick and quiet."

They followed him to the rear of the house, where they spread out along the partially collapsed stone wall. From here they had a reasonably good view of the hill and excellent sight lines through to the front of the house.

Smythe spotted the top of a helmet at the crest of the hill. "Here they come."

Moments later both German soldiers appeared at the top of the hill. They spotted the partially brushed-out trail and the house at the bottom. They immediately unslung their rifles, said something to each other, and started down the slope.

It took forever for them to reach the house. But they were being cautious. As if they expected to find trouble. But if they were looking for a force of eight or nine commandos, they weren't being very smart about not first calling for reinforcements.

As they got closer, however, the mystery was solved for Scotty. He spotted the black collars of their uniforms beneath their winter whites. Twin lightning bolts gleamed. They were SS and arrogant. Nothing could happen to them. They were the masters of the master race.

One of them came up the stone step into the house. He stopped short when he spotted the trapdoor to the fruit cellar. He beckoned for his partner to come quietly.

Mac and Smythe quickly worked their way to the front of the house.

Scotty gave them to the count of ten, then handed his pistol to Ballinger. He got to his feet and raised his hands over his head.

"I give up," he shouted.

The soldiers snapped around, bringing their rifles to bear.

"Don't shoot! Don't shoot, for Christ's sake," Scotty shouted. "I'm an American."

Mac and Smythe silently came up the step and entered the house. One of the Germans started to turn around.

"Nicht scheissen," Scotty shouted. *"Bitte, nicht scheissen!"*

Mac and Smythe looped the piano wire garrotes over the Germans' necks and pulled at the same moment.

Both Germans struggled violently, but they had no chance whatsoever. Gradually their struggles weakened, and they slumped to the floor, dead, their faces purple, almost black. But there was little or no blood.

Scotty and the others came from the back. "We have to hustle now," he said. They started removing the dead soldiers' uniforms. "Get Kilroy up here. He's coming with me to look for the rockets." Don Smith was their rocket expert.

Mac went to the fruit cellar door to summon Smith.

"What do we do in the meantime?" Smythe asked.

"Get ready to move out as soon as we get back," Scotty said, taking off his winter whites and uniform. "Two teams. I'll take one, and Lindsay gets the other. That's unless Don and I don't make it back. Then Major Winslow will take my team. Move out after dark."

The others clambered out of the fruit cellar, and Don Smith peeled out of his uniform and put on one of the German uniforms. He looked scared but determined.

"If we don't get back, it'll mean that the Germans will be at an even greater state of alert. All I can say is do the best you can," Scotty said to Winslow. "But those rockets must not be allowed to fly."

"Then you'd best find out where they're set up and come back here," Lindsay said. She kissed Scotty lightly on the lips, then Smith on the cheek. "Good luck."

1530 • Peenemünde

The ride down from Mittelwerke in the spider-legged Fiesler-Storch light spotter plane was rough. The air was bumpy, and the overcast had thickened as they neared the rocket research facility. By the time they touched down Schellenberg was bone weary, his shoulder wound hurt like hell, and he was in a foul mood.

A young Wehrmacht corporal picked him up at the airstrip and drove him over to headquarters in a battered VW *Kriegswagen*. The once impressive research center was now mostly in ruins. No building was without damage, and Schellenberg gloomily estimated that 70 or 80 percent were totally beyond repair.

The mighty Third Reich was grinding to a ponderous halt, choking on the dust rising from its bombed-out towns and factories. Sending three rockets loaded with anthrax to the American capital would kill a lot of people if they reached their destination and actually detonated on target. Maybe they'd even kill the cripple Roosevelt. But would it end the war in Germany's favor? Looking around him, Schellenberg sincerely doubted it.

Then why bother? Most soldiers out of the *Führer's* direct eye were merely going through the motions. German boys were being killed, but the high-ranking officers were fleeing to Switzerland or Portugal, or, for a lucky few, even Argentina and Brazil.

But this was no longer about Germany. This situation had been made personal. Not by him, but by Sarah Winslow, the dirty little British spy who had been nothing more than a lying whore all the time. He clenched his fists again, but this time it was more than his shoulder wound that hurt.

The four-story headquarters building was situated at the end of what once had been a pleasant tree-lined lane. Research and engineering laboratories were scattered in the woods like the sprawling campus of a modern university. Now all was mostly in ruins. Where once scientists and engineers strolled along paths, the facility looked deserted.

He instructed his driver to wait for him and entered the building, where he had to show his pass to an SS sergeant, who directed him to offices down a long corridor.

Peenemünde chief scientist Wernher von Braun and chief of security SS *Oberstleutnant* Ernst Hofbauer were waiting for him in a littered conference room. Papers and diagrams were strewn everywhere, on the table, on chairs, on the floor, as if someone had been frantically searching for something.

Von Braun sat, looking moodily out a window, and he barely acknowledged Schellenberg's arrival. But Hofbauer got to his feet, an angry scowl on his narrow face.

"I understand that you are a general officer, and that you fill a vital function in State Security, but you are wasting valuable time by coming here and demanding to inspect us."

Schellenberg held his temper in check, to do otherwise would delay them even longer. "I have a car and driver at my disposal. Thank you for that, *Herr Oberstleutnant*. Now I require that you pinpoint for me the locations of the three rockets you mean to fire. I would like to inspect your security."

"As you wish, *Herr General*," Hofbauer replied. "But security may be a moot point. The rockets will be launched at midnight."

"That may be too late. The saboteurs may already be here."

"I have patrols out searching the area. So far they've found nothing."

"In any event that may be another moot point, *Herr General*," von Braun said. "The rockets will not be ready to fly *until* then." He looked away. "*If* then," he muttered.

1700 · PEENEMÜNDE

Scotty drove past the access road to launch site number three. The four SS guards on duty behind the barrier idly glanced at them, but made no motion for them to stop.

Finding the rockets had been ridiculously easy. Too easy? Scotty was becoming paranoid. No one had challenged them or asked to see their passes. It was almost as if a trap were being set for them. But that made no sense either.

Smith had found a facility map in the VW on which were marked *Spezial Sicherheit Zonen*, Special Security Zones, in red cross-hatchings. In addition to the cluster of engineering buildings around headquarters, one of the rocket assembly halls and the underground entrances to several exotic fuel storage bunkers, three areas in the woods northwest of the Central Works were so marked. They were all isolated and all within a couple hundred yards of each other, accessible by paved roads capable of handling heavy trucks.

Driving past, they were able to catch glimpses through the trees of the rockets on their launchers. None of them had been raised to the fire position yet. All of them were still protected by tarps. The casing around one of the rockets had been removed, exposing the motor. None of the V5s had been fitted with their nose cone payloads yet.

There were a lot of people around each of the rockets, most of them civilians, either engineers or technicians. A number of trucks and vans were gathered around each rocket, with wires and heavy cables snaking from what was presumably test equipment into the innards of each machine.

The Germans seemed to be working at a feverish pace. As if they were facing a fast-approaching deadline.

"How soon before they're ready to launch?" Scotty asked, following the road that led back to the main north–south transport highway.

"No way of telling," Smith said. "But it'll take them at least six hours to add the nose cones, button all the panels, and fuel the rockets. That's if nothing's wrong."

"What'd it look like to you?" Scotty glanced in the rearview mirror, half-expecting to see a truckload of SS troops speeding after them. But no one was coming.

"It didn't look like they were making repairs," Smith said. "I'd guess they were simply getting three experimental rockets ready to launch." He gave Scotty a concerned look. "In a big hurry."

"They're worried about something," Scotty said. He grinned with more confidence than he felt. "Let's get back to the others."

The main highway that ran through the facility was like an artery connecting the various research and engineering areas with the assembly halls, test beds, launchpads, and storage dumps for everything from heavy equipment to fuels. The highway also ran straight up the length of the island. The snow-covered dirt road that led to the hill behind which the Coalminers were holed up was about five kilometers away.

Coming around a curve on the main route, they encountered a small canvas truck parked beside the road. Two SS soldiers got out of the cab and walked out onto the highway and waved them to a stop.

Scotty had worried about something like this. It was just rotten luck that it happened now, when they were so close to getting out of the facility's main security perimeter.

He eased the silenced Beretta out of his jumper, felt for the safety, and switched it off as he slowed to a halt. He motioned for Smith to make no sudden moves.

The pair of security soldiers came up on either side of the car. The one on Scotty's side had not unslung his rifle, but the soldier on the other side had. Neither of them looked overly suspicious; in fact, they seemed bored. There wasn't much traffic this far out. Especially not today.

"What are you doing on this road?" the guard on Scotty's left asked.

"Checking security measures," Scotty replied in German.

The guard apparently suspected that something was wrong,

probably with Scotty's accent, because he reached for his rifle.

Scotty levered himself up against the back of the seat and fired two shots past Smith, hitting the guard in the chest. Then he turned as the guard to his left was bringing his rifle to bear and shot the man in the face at point-blank range.

Both guards were down.

"We're taking them with us," Scotty said. He went around to the passenger side of the car. The second guard opened his eyes, and Scotty shot him in the forehead.

He and Smith loaded the bodies into the backseat of their VW and scraped snow over the blood that had leaked onto the road.

"Take the truck and follow me," Scotty said.

Smith glanced at the dead Germans in the back of the VW, then trotted over to the truck and got in.

They drove out into the countryside, turning down the dirt road in the deepening gloom. Now there were four German soldiers missing. It wouldn't be long before somebody came looking for them.

The clock starts now, Scotty thought.

1730 · PEENEMÜNDE

It was almost fully dark when Schellenberg's driver pulled up at the barrier guarding the road to rocket number three. Two SS guards were on duty. They came nervously to attention as the general got out of the car and walked over to them. They saluted.

"Who has come and gone past in the last couple of hours?" Schellenberg demanded.

"Technicians, *Herr General.* They're setting up the rocket," the SS sergeant answered.

"Anyone else? Someone perhaps passing by, maybe slowing down but not stopping? Someone on foot?"

A look of recognition dawned in the sergeant's eyes. "Yes, sir. They were driving a *Kriegswagen.* Two soldiers in white. They drove past."

"Did you recognize either of them?"

"No, *Herr General,* I never saw either of them before. But there are a lot of soldiers here."

"Which way did they go?"

The sergeant motioned toward the north. "The road returns to the Central Works highway."

"How long ago?"

The sergeant shrugged. "Twenty minutes, maybe thirty."

Schellenberg jumped back in the car, his heart pounding. It was them. He knew it was the American and his commandos. They were here after all.

With Sarah.

His driver headed to the main road while Schellenberg worked it out. The Allied raiders were hiding somewhere nearby. Somehow they'd managed to get two German uniforms and a patrol car so that they could find out the locations of the three rockets.

Presumably they went back to the others to get ready for the strike, which could take place at anytime after dark.

Even with double the number of security guards it might be impossible to stop the commandos from destroying at least one of the rockets and perhaps all of them.

The fools here, Hofbauer and especially von Braun, were relying on the thick overcast, which made an air raid impossible, and on the isolation of the facility, which made a raid by land unlikely.

They had grouped the rockets all within shouting distance of each other. That was Hofbauer's idea. It made security easier, he said. And they had set them up in very small clearings that were surrounded by dense forests. There were no perimeter fences.

But then another thought struck Schellenberg. Von Braun had been eager to take the Reich's money to develop his little toys, but he had never been keen on actually firing them as weapons.

Maybe he was stalling as he had been all along. Maybe von Braun was secretly hoping that a commando raid would make it impossible to launch.

Maybe that's why the rockets were still in the stages of preparation. They had not even been fueled yet. Nor had the anthrax canisters been attached.

Oberstleutnant Hofbauer was an idiot. Von Braun was anything but.

To the left, the road ran back to the research and engineering areas of the base. To the right it led straight north to the tip of the heavily wooded island. Schellenberg pointed north. "We'll go this way."

"Pardon me, *Herr General*, but shouldn't we get help first?" the corporal asked.

Schellenberg was impatient. "There's no time," he barked. "Move!"

"Yes, sir," the corporal said, and they headed north.

Within a couple hundred meters their headlights flashed across deep ruts in the snow on the side of the road and something dark on the pavement. Schellenberg ordered the driver to pull over.

He took a flashlight from the glove compartment and walked over to the dark spots on the road. At first he thought it might be oil. But someone had taken the effort to cover the stains with snow. He scraped some of the snow away with the toe of a boot. It was dark red. Blood. And it was not completely frozen yet.

His eyes went to the ruts off the side of the road. A security patrol had been stationed here. The two commandos had driven up, shot the guards, covered the blood, and stolen the second vehicle. They had probably taken the bodies with them.

Schellenberg sprang back to the car. "They came this way, and not very long ago."

"What would you like to do, *Herr General?*"

"Follow them," Schellenberg roared. "We'll find out where they turned off."

1815 · THE FARMHOUSE

Scotty showed them the locations of the three launchpads on the map. The rockets had been grouped close together, probably for purposes of security.

"It actually makes our job easier," he told them. "We'll split into three teams instead of two. Sarah and Vivian will go with Major

Winslow. Mac and Ballinger with Smythe and Kilroy and Lieutenant Miles with me."

"What about the anthrax?" Lindsay asked.

"It hasn't been loaded aboard the rockets yet," Scotty said. "And even if it had been, we'd never get close enough to grab it. There are SS and Wehrmacht troops crawling all over the place."

"Do they know that we're here?" Smythe asked.

"I think that they might have a fair idea. From what we could see they're bustin' their humps to get the rockets ready to launch. Which is why I want to go down there, ASAP, destroy the things, and get the hell out."

"They'll come looking for us with a vengeance afterward," Winslow said. "Mightn't it be better to wait until later in the evening? Closer to our rendezvous time with the sub?" He looked at the others. "I don't fancy being chased all over this island by a lot of irate Germans."

"No," Scotty said. "If we give them enough time, they'll eventually install the anthrax containers, and we'll be in big trouble."

"I'd say blow them in any event," Smythe said.

"If it comes to that, we'll do it. But I want to avoid the issue. We go now." He turned back to the map. "We'll be on foot afterward, so it'll be up to each team to get out to the rendezvous point on the beach without being followed. That's about three miles out."

"We can slow the Jerries down if we leave a few surprises in our wake," Smythe said. "We have enough trip wire to rig some Composition B and zero-delay fuses across our path. When they come stumbling through the woods, they'll be in for a nasty surprise. Should slow them down a bit."

"Good," Scotty said.

"That sounds like the easy bit," Lindsay said. "But how in heaven's name do you propose that we destroy the rockets in the first place if we can't get close to the things?"

"We're not," Scotty said. He turned back to the map and marked a pair of small Xs in each launch area.

"Fuel trucks," Don Smith said. "We saw them parked at one of the launch sites, so we're assuming they're at the other two." He looked up. "The white trucks will contain LOX—liquid oxygen. There'll be steam coming off the sides if they're loaded. And the dark trucks will contain the fuel. Hydrazine hydrate, or maybe something even more interesting. Whatever it is, it will be highly flammable."

"The point is, the ones we saw were parked at the edge of the clearing," Scotty said. "Which means we should be able to get to them without being detected."

"The trick will be to get both trucks to blow at just about the same time," Smith explained. "If we can get the fuel and the LOX to mix, it'll make a hell of a fire. Nothing is going to survive in those clearings. Certainly not the rockets."

"Nor the people," Sarah said with a vicious smile.

Scotty looked at his watch. "It's 1815," he said. "We'll take the truck back to the base perimeter and split up there. It'll be up to each team to get to their launch site, set the booby traps, place the charges under the trucks, set the fuses, and get out."

"Time?" Winslow asked.

"Nineteen-thirty."

Everyone reacted. "That only gives us an hour and fifteen," Ballinger said. "That's cutting it a bit thin."

"Then we'd best get started now," Scotty said.

1820 · THE MAIN HIGHWAY

The corporal spotted the tracks leading off the main highway first. He slowed down. "There," he said, pointing off to the left.

"Stop the car," Schellenberg ordered. At first he couldn't see a thing. But then he saw what the corporal had spotted. A narrow dirt road led west off the highway. Clearly at least one vehicle had gone that way. Recently.

He jumped out and walked up the road and shined the beam of his flashlight on the tracks. There were more than one set. Two at least. One made by narrow tires, like those of a VW *Kriegswagen*, and the other superimposed set much larger. Perhaps a truck's.

He went back to the car. The headlights pointed north on the

main highway, which disappeared a hundred meters away around
a curve in the woods.

The Allied raiders knew where the three rockets were set up on
their launch vehicles. They had killed four German soldiers and
comandeered two vehicles. They would strike tonight.

The only thing Schellenberg didn't know was from what direction they would be coming. His map did not show this dirt road,
which had probably been used by farmers or perhaps fishermen
during the summer. For all he knew it could curve back on itself in
a large circle and approach the launch area from the south. Places
like these were often honeycombed with tracks through the countryside.

Schellenberg switched off his flashlight and climbed into the car.
"Turn off the headlights."

The corporal did as he was told. The night was suddenly pitch-
black. "What are we going to do, sir?"

"We're going to find out where this leads," Schellenberg said.
"*Gleich jetzt!*" Right now!

The corporal eased off the main road and headed west, maintaining a walking speed in first gear.

Within a few hundred meters they suddenly came out of the
woods. A long, sloping hill rose to their left. A *Kriegswagen* and a
small canvas troop truck were parked in the middle of the road two
hundred meters away.

The corporal stopped without being told. Schellenberg grabbed
the top of the windshield and pulled himself up. He studied the
two vehicles through binoculars. It was obvious from the ruts in
the snow around both vehicles that they had been turned around
with some difficulty. They faced his way. Toward the east.

He scanned the side of the hill, spotting what appeared to be a
well-used path to the top. The Allied commandos were just over
the top of the hill. Hiding. Possibly in an old fishing shack, or perhaps a farmhouse or barn.

"Return to the highway," Schellenberg said.

"It'll be difficult to turn around. The road is too narrow. We
might get stuck."

"Back up," Schellenberg ordered. "We'll wait for them on the highway."

1835 · Inside the Security Perimeter

Scotty drove the truck. Smythe and Winslow were in the cab with him, their weapons between their knees. Everyone else had climbed in the back.

He stopped twenty-five yards short of the main highway, and Winslow went the rest of the way on foot.

He came back on the run and climbed up into the cab. "No Germans. It's clear."

Scotty turned and knocked on the window to the rear of the truck. "Are you ready back there?" he shouted.

Sarah's face appeared in the glass. She gave a thumbs-up. She was eager. For her it was payback time for the hell she'd endured over the last year.

Scotty eased out onto the highway, switched on the headlights, and headed toward the launchpads. He was confused. Although there was a lot of security around the rockets, they'd not come across any patrols except for the two men on the hill and the two in the truck.

If the Germans were worried about a raid, there were no obvious signs of it. But more than one OSS mission had come to grief when they walked into what appeared to be a secure area and suddenly all hell broke loose as a trap was sprung.

He looked in his rearview mirror. There was nothing behind them.

There should have been search parties all over the island. The Germans were making a last-minute desperation play with the launch of the three rockets. And four of their people were missing. Who was in charge here?

Winslow noticed Scotty checking the mirror. "Anything?" he asked.

"We're still in the clear."

Winslow studied him. "But you're bothered."

Scotty glanced at him. "This place should be crawling with patrols."

"I agree," Smythe said.

"Not necessarily," Winslow disagreed. "For the past six months the Germans have been stripping anyone who can hold a gun from all noncombat assignments."

Scotty nodded though he wasn't satisfied with the answer. "I hope you're right. But that'd make them pretty stupid."

Winslow had to smile. "They were stupid when they drove out all their Jewish scientists in the thirties. They were stupid by not wiping us out on the beach at Dunkirk. And they were stupid by opening a second front." He shrugged.

Over a rise they came to the spot where Scotty and Smith had been stopped by the two guards in the truck. Just beyond it the highway curved to the left, and a couple hundred yards farther was the paved access road that led back to the three launchpads.

"We'll leave the truck here," Scotty said, slowing down and pulling off the road. "If a patrol should come by, the empty truck might throw them off. They might think that the two soldiers just took off."

He switched off the headlights, and they all clambered out of the truck. No one was coming either way on the highway, but they couldn't afford to linger in the open.

Scotty led them across the road and into the dense woods until they had put the highway and the truck completely out of sight.

"Smythe and his team will take rocket one, Winslow number two, and I'll take three," Scotty told them. They'd made sketch maps from the original. They looked at them under the red beams of their flashlights.

"You know what has to be done," Scotty said. "So let's get on with it, and I'll see you on the beach. Good luck."

1845 · LAUNCHPAD AREA DELTA

After the raiders had entered the woods, Schellenberg waited a full ten minutes at his vantage point at the side of the road 150 meters behind the truck. He wanted to catch them unawares. But in order to do that he would have to drive over to one of the launchpads without their seeing or hearing his car pass by.

They were on foot. The perimeter around each rocket was guarded, and they did not know that they were being followed. The advantage, if it had ever been theirs, had switched.

At least one of the commandos was smaller than the others. He hoped that it was Sarah. Although he didn't know what he would do if he came face-to-face with her again, he wanted it with everything in his soul. She had hurt him.

He ran back to the car and got in. "Take me to launchpad three as fast as you can drive."

The corporal made no move to start the car. Something was wrong with the young man. He looked frightened. "If you're worried about the Allied commandos, don't be. They went into the woods."

"No, sir, it's not that."

"What then? We're running out of time."

"Sir, I was given a direct order by *Oberstleutnant* Hofbauer to take you wherever you wanted to go, but not to let you interfere with operations."

Schellenberg was dumbfounded. He wondered if it was the same in the British, American, and Russian armies. He thought not. They couldn't have come as far as they had.

"Why is that?"

"I don't know, sir."

"Well, nine of the enemy went into the woods no more than two hundred meters from here. They mean to kill some of our soldiers and blow up our rockets. If you allow that to happen, it will mean that you are a traitor. And you know what we do with traitors in Germany."

The boy was terror-stricken. He saw no way out.

"It's your choice, Corporal. But you might consider who would be the better officer to please, and *Oberstleutnant* or a *general*."

The corporal started the car and headed down the road, his expression a study in resignation. There was no way he could win.

They passed the deserted truck, rounded the curve, and turned onto the launchpad road. A minute later they pulled up at the barrier to launchpad three. Schellenberg jumped out and darted across the road to the SS guards.

"Do you have a field telephone?" he demanded.

"Yes, *Herr General*," the sergeant answered.

"Contact Hofbauer. I need to speak to him immediately."

"Yes, sir," the man said, and he went to the back of his patrol vehicle.

Schellenberg turned to the other SS soldier, a corporal. "Put your people on alert this insant. And turn on every light that you can. This area is about to come under attack at any moment."

The soldier was flustered. "Sir, I cannot give that order. We're not in charge of security here."

"Who is?"

"*Leutnant* Rauff."

"Where is he?"

"I don't know—"

The SS sergeant held up the field telephone. "*Herr General, Oberstleutnant* Hofbauer is on the line for you."

Schellenberg walked back and grabbed the phone from the man. "This is Schellenberg. Your launchpads are about to come under attack at any moment. Get extra security out here now, and order these idiots to do as they're told."

"How can you be so sure, *Herr General?*" Hofbauer asked with maddening slowness. "Did you see the attackers with your own eyes again?"

"Yes, you fool! There are nine of them, and they're here now!"

"I see," Hofbauer said. "Let me speak to Sergeant Siefert."

Schellenberg handed the telephone to the sergeant, who listened for a few moments, then nodded. "*Jawohl, Herr Oberstleutnant*. I understand." He hung up. He gave Schellenberg a sheepish look. "*Oberstleutnant* Hofbauer is on his way out to personally take charge, *Herr General*. He asks that we wait for him."

"*Gott in Himmel*," Schellenberg said, stepping back a pace. He was in a lunatic asylum.

1910 · LAUNCHPAD THREE

The forest was quiet except in the direction of launchpad three, where someone was talking. Scotty, Lindsay, and Smith made their way from tree to tree toward the sound.

Before they had split up with the others they had synchronized their watches. It was 1910. The LOX and fuel trucks had to go up in flames in twenty minutes.

Unless something went wrong.

They saw a faint glimmer of light straight ahead. A few yards farther they heard someone laugh, and there was a faint clink of metal on metal.

Scotty stopped and raised a hand for Lindsay and Smith to hold up. The fuel trucks were straight ahead less than twenty yards through the woods. Steam misted off the white truck, which was parked only ten or fifteen feet from the fuel truck, Both faced inward, toward the V5 on its truck bed launcher.

He dropped down. "Don and I will set the charges under the trucks," he said. He took off his pack and removed the plastic explosive and an acid pencil fuse. Smith did the same thing.

"We'll strike north parallel to the highway, is that right?" Lindsay asked.

Scotty nodded. "We'll have to stay in the woods, there'll be patrols all up and down the highway. But I want to make them think that we're headed west toward the field where we came in. If we can divert some of them over there to wait for an air pickup, it'll help."

"I'll set the first booby trap to the north, which should push them west toward the highway. I'll lay the two others in that direction. Even Jerry ought to think he's got us figured out."

Scotty glanced at his watch. He crimped off all but twelve minutes of his acid fuse and shoved it into the block of explosive. It smelled like strong vinegar.

"I'll do the fuel truck," Smith said, crimping his acid fuse and arming his block of explosive. "These have to go off fairly close together."

"Let's do it," Scotty said.

They crawled toward the fuel trucks as Lindsay disappeared into the woods behind them. There were at least a half dozen technicians working on the rocket. The machine was bathed in strong lights. What few soldiers Scotty could see stood around a patrol car on the other side of the barrier.

There was something vaguely familiar about one of the figures, but the distance was too great for Scotty to tell much of anything except that he was an officer.

At the edge of the clearing they encountered a serious problem. The trucks were fifteen feet from the protection of the trees. Fifteen feet of open field in which Scotty and Smith would be exposed. Anyone looking their way would have to see them.

But all of a sudden he realized that wasn't true. The lights illuminating the rocket were so bright that by contrast the open ground between the woods and the trucks was in darkness.

"They won't see us because of the lights," Scotty told Smith.

Smith nodded his understanding.

Scotty crawled directly toward the LOX truck. Smith angled toward the truck that contained the fuel. If they were spotted, the game would be up. It would be impossible to set the charges on the trucks, then get out of there. The only other solution that Scotty had considered, though he hadn't discussed it with Smith or with the others, was to open fire on both tanker trucks in the hopes that the liquid oxygen and fuel might spill out, contact each other, and ignite.

Of course, they wouldn't get out alive in that case.

Scotty reached the LOX truck and crawled under it on his back. He stuffed the package of plastic explosive between the steel chassis frame and the support braces for the heavy tank above it.

Extremely cold air and fog rolled down around him from the sweating LOX tank.

He made sure that the acid fuse was in place, then crawled awkwardly back out from beneath the truck.

Smith came out seconds later, and the two of them crawled back to the edge of the clearing.

Smith reached the tree line first. He stood up and turned around.

Someone by the security barrier shouted, then opened fire with a pistol.

Smith stepped back, but someone else at the barrier opened fire with a submachine gun. Several shots stitched across Smith's chest, and one hit him in the forehead. He went down.

Scotty scrambled over to Smith to see if there was anything he could do, but the man was dead. A good portion of the back of his head was gone.

The Germans continued to fire indiscriminately, spraying bullets into the woods.

Scotty crawled into the forest on all fours as fast as he could move. He didn't think that he had been spotted. No one was shooting directly at him.

Twenty yards into the trees Scotty stood up. Shooting began somewhere in the distance to the south, toward one of the other launchpads.

Lindsay appeared out of the darkness, her face pale, her eyes wide. "Don?"

"Dead," Scotty answered. "Did you set the traps?"

She was shook, but she nodded. The firing behind them was decreasing. Very soon the Germans would realize that no one was shooting back, and they would be coming.

Scotty looked at his watch. It was 1927. The fuel trucks were set to explode in three minutes. "Lead the way," he told Lindsay.

She hesitated a moment longer, torn between wanting to leave and wanting to go back to see Don with her own eyes. But then she turned and headed back toward the highway, careful to avoid the trip wires she had strung between the trees at knee level.

1930 · LAUNCHPAD THREE

Schellenberg held back at the barrier. There had been shooting at the other two launchpads, but the gun battles had not lasted very long. He couldn't tell if they had been one-sided like here, but alarms jangled all along his nerves. Something was wrong.

It should not have been this easy to repel the attacks. Unless the figure at the edge of the woods they'd opened fire on was finished with his task and was trying to escape, not come in.

The security troops had fanned out across the launchpad. The technicians had fallen back and were hiding behind the rocket. The SS sergeant turned and was about to say something when there was a bang somewhere near one of the trucks.

Schellenberg instinctively stepped back as a huge plume of white smoke billowed out from the LOX truck.

There was another bang, and for a long second nothing seemed to happen. But then a fireball erupted from somewhere between and above the two fuel trucks. It grew with incredible speed, and Schellenberg realized that he was flying on a carpet of extremely hot air.

1935 · THE FOREST

Scotty heard the fuel trucks at the other two launchpads explode. He'd been concerned that the other teams had failed. He had considered going back to help, but now that all three rockets had been destroyed, the mission was accomplished. It was time to get out.

The night sky behind them was aglow with the fuel-fed fires. There were other secondary explosions and smaller fireballs rising above the trees as the gas tanks on vehicles parked on or near the launchpads cooked off.

Lindsay stopped and checked her compass. She looked up to get her bearings, then without a word set off to the right.

The highway was less than fifty yards to their left. Scotty heard someone crashing through the brush from that direction, and he frantically motioned for Lindsay to take cover.

A German soldier appeared out of the darkness. He spotted Scotty, raised what looked like a Schmeisser machine pistol, and opened fire.

Scotty fell back behind a tree but not before he was hit in the left arm just below his elbow.

Lindsay fired back with her submachine gun, hitting the German in the side, knocking him off his feet.

Scotty's arm was totally numb and useless, but there was no pain yet and not a lot of blood. He held his breath and cocked an ear to listen for someone else coming from the road.

A short, very sharp explosion came from somewhere behind them to the southwest. It was followed by three others in short succession. The booby traps were going off.

The chase had begun.

Lindsay was at his side. "My God, Scotty, you're bleeding."

"I'll live," he said. "We have to get out of here while the Germans are still stumbling around trying to figure out where we've gotten ourselves to."

EIGHT

FRIDAY 0015 • ON THE BEACH

A raw wind blew across the small cove, sending lines of nearly luminescent whitecaps marching out to open water. Steam rose in surreal wisps from the relatively warm ocean water.

Scotty leaned up against a rock, watching Lindsay and her sister Sarah work on Smythe. McKeever had been the last in, carrying the MI6 sergeant on his back. Ballinger hadn't made it, and from the looks of Smythe he wasn't going to make it either. He'd lost a lot of blood. His complexion was deathly white, and black fluid was leaking from a wound in his side.

Leigh hadn't gotten out from under his truck when it exploded, and counting Smythe, who would probably die any minute, they were down to five from the original nine plus Sarah. Winslow had received some flash burns on his face and hands when he pulled Sarah away from trying to find Leigh.

Scotty felt a sense of defeat. They had accomplished the mission, but he had lost half of his command. And he had let himself get shot. Halfway here he had fuzzed out, and Lindsay had to help him make it the rest of the way. He still felt weak.

Smythe suddenly cried out something, then was still.

Sarah got up. "Bloody hell," she said. She looked over at her husband and shook her head. "He's dead." She turned at length and headed up the beach.

Winslow got up and followed her.

After a while Scotty looked up. "I'm sorry," he said to Lindsay, who knelt on the rocks beside Smythe, holding his bloody hand in hers.

Her shoulders were hunched. She was crying. "It wasn't your fault," she said.

"I promised him that I'd get everybody home—"

"Don't be such a bloody Boy Scout," she flared. "This is the real world. People get killed."

"The young lady is correct, of course," Schellenberg said. He appeared out of the darkness holding a pistol on Sarah and Winslow. Their hands were raised over their heads.

Scotty reached for his pistol.

"I will shoot them both, husband and wife, and you will have two more deaths on your tender conscience," Schellenberg warned conversationally.

Scotty stayed his hand.

"I wonder if you feel any remorse over the German boys you killed? Especially my driver, who I sent into the woods to find out what direction you were heading. He was just a boy." Schellenberg shrugged. "But he was German, and we are the enemy."

"Yes, you are," Scotty said. "Your rockets have been destroyed, and you will lose the war. It's only a matter of months."

"We would have lost the war even if the rockets had been launched and hit their marks. The issue is what happens afterward?"

"Germany will be rebuilt—"

"To us, personally."

"Do you mean if we don't all die on this beach in a shoot-out?" Scotty asked. He glanced past Schellenberg toward the woods. But no one else was coming. The general was alone.

"Yes."

"Are you trying to make a bargain?"

Sarah slowly turned to face Schellenberg. "If the tables were reversed, I would not hesitate to kill you."

He looked at her for a long time, as if he was trying to memorize her face. His eyes strayed to Winslow. "You are married to an extraordinary woman, Major," he said softly.

Winslow turned. "Yes, I am."

Schellenberg looked at Sarah again, then lowered his pistol and started to walk away.

Sarah snatched her pistol from her jumper, but Winslow stopped her.

"The war is over," he said.

Scotty had his pistol out, but he lowered it, too. "We're taking Sergeant Smythe with us."

Sarah was shaking with rage. She watched Schellenberg's retreating figure until it was lost in the darkness, looked at her husband, then at the others. She lowered her head.

"Time to go home," Scotty said.

AFTERWORD

General Walther Schellenberg got his reward in the end. He survived the war, and at the War Crimes Trial in Nuremberg he was given a light sentence of six years in prison. He only served two before he was released.

Before that, however, at a lavish wedding ceremony at Winacres, the Miles estate in Sherwood, Richard Scott and Lindsay Miles were married. The matron of honor was Sarah Winslow, the sister of the bride, and the best man was Lt. Col. Donald Winslow, the husband of the matron of honor.

In attendance, besides Scotty's parents, who flew over from the States, were Winston Churchill and Gen. Dwight Eisenhower.

There was no press coverage.

Schellenberg never laid eyes on Sarah Winslow again.

THE EAGLE
AND THE CROSS

R. J. PINEIRO

R. J. PINEIRO is the author of several techno-thrillers, including *Ultimatum, Retribution, Breakthrough, Exposure, Shutdown,* and the millennium thrillers *01-01-00* and *Y2K*. He is a seventeen-year veteran of the computer industry and is currently at work on leading-edge microprocessors, the heart of the personal computer. He was born in Havana, Cuba, and grew up in El Salvador before coming to the United States to pursue a higher education. He holds a degree in electrical engineering from Louisiana State University, a second-degree black belt in martial arts, and is a licensed private pilot and a firearms enthusiast. He has traveled extensively through Central America, Europe, and Asia, both for his computer business as well as to research for his novels. He lives in Texas with his wife, Lory, and his son, Cameron.

LVOV, THE UKRAINE · JUNE 22, 1941

The thundering sound of heavy artillery ringing in his ears, Colonel
Aleksandrovich Nikolai Krasilov bolted out of bed and stormed out
of his tent, racing across the dusty airfield toward the communications building on the other side of the short runway. To his surprise he was the first one outside. Other pilots began to emerge
from their tents just as he tugged on the door and stepped inside.

The base's primitive communications room consisted of two ten-
year-old two-way radios and three operators, who were currently
pacing in front of their equipment. The trio turned in his direction,
fear widening their stares.

"What is going on? The artillery rounds are coming from the
west!"

"Ye . . . yes, comrade Colonel," responded the youngest of the
operators. "We're under attack . . . by the Germans."

Krasilov, a twenty-year veteran of the Red Air Force, knew better
than to jump to conclusions based on a comment from a young
enlisted man, but the fact still remained that someone had ordered
the artillery to fire, and its reverberating rumble was definitely coming from the border. "How do you know this?" he demanded.

"The radio, sir. Our bases by the border . . . the screams, sir . . .

the planes at Novovolynsk are being strafed on the ground . . . their radio just went dead!"

Krasilov inhaled deeply. "That's impossible! We have a nonaggression pact with the—"

"This is Colonel Vasili Petrosky, anyone come in, come in!"

Krasilov raced for the microphone on the table. Colonel Petrosky was in charge of the defense for the border town of Rava-Russkaja, fifty miles northwest of Lvov.

"This is Aleksandrovich, Vasili. What is your situation?"

"Flames, Aleksandr! There are flames everywhere. Our fighters are burning! Our tanks are burning! We need help immediately, or we'll be forced to retreat. The German panzers are just a few hills away! Their planes fill the sky!"

"Hold in place, Vasili. We'll contact Kiev!"

"Na pomosh, Aleksandr. Na po—"

"Vasili? Vasili?"

No response.

Krasilov pounded a fist on the table. Petrosky's cry for help was all the convincing Krasilov needed. "Get me Kiev Military District headquarters immediately!"

"Yes, sir!"

The young radio operator jumped on a chair and dialed a new frequency while Krasilov went back outside. His pilots' gaze was on him. They looked as confused as he felt. He saw fear in their eyes, but none said a word. They waited for Krasilov to speak.

After months of warnings, the inevitable—at least in Krasilov's mind—had happened. The undeniable signs that something significant was about to happen were everywhere: German planes flying reconnaissance missions over Russia for months; German ships pulling out of Soviet ports in a hurry; German embassy officials in Leningrad, Stalingrad, and Moscow burning documents and getting ready to depart. Yes, the signs were all there, but what was more incredible than the reports themselves was the Kremlin's refusal to publicly acknowledge them.

"All I know is that we're under attack," he said. "Get to your planes and wait for my order. Move!"

The pilots looked at one another. Krasilov understood their hesitancy. TASS—the official Soviet news agency—communiqués over the previous two weeks had indicated that the two nations were at peace and that war was not a possibility. In fact, many Red Air Force pilots of the Baltic, Minsk, and Kiev Military Districts had been allowed to go on leave by Moscow Military District headquarters after a recently completed night training exercise that not only left them short on fuel, but also short of sleep.

The pilots continued staring at Krasilov.

"Are you deaf? Move it! Now!"

The pilots ran to their planes.

"Sir?"

Krasilov turned. The young operator stood by the doorway.

"Yes?"

"The rifle division at Mostiska briefly came in. They were also pleading for help, sir. Then communications ceased."

"Damn! Where is Kiev?"

"I've just got them on the line, sir."

Krasilov rushed past him and snagged the microphone. "Kiev Military District, this is Colonel Aleksandrovich Krasilov of the Red Air Force in Lvov. We're under attack by German forces. Repeat. We're under attack by the Germans. Request instructions."

"You must be insane, Colonel Krasilov! Why is your message not in code?"

Krasilov narrowed his eyes at the odd response. He pressed on. "Did you hear me? I said we're under attack! German forces are wiping out our border defenses this minute! Where is General Kirponos?"

Another voice came through on the radio. *"Colonel Krasilov, this is Colonel Timoshenko. General Kirponos received orders yesterday to move his headquarters to Tarponol. They are en route. His orders were that no action must be taken against the Germans without Moscow's consent. Comrade Stalin has forbidden our artillery to open fire and our planes to fly."*

Hearing the sound of his own planes revving up, Krasilov's grip tightened around the microphone. The response was unsound. Was Stalin that far out of touch with reality? He pressed further. "It's not possible! Reports are flowing in. Our troops are being killed. Towns are in flames!"

"The order stands, Colonel! No attack must take place against the people of—" The line went dead just as a powerful explosion shook the base.

Krasilov dropped the microphone and ran outside, his stomach knotting when he spotted what must have been a hundred planes across the sky. He turned and saw the cause of the explosion. Three craft were burning at the edge of the runway from a direct hit by a German Messerschmitt fighter, which was now rolling its wings and disappearing behind the trees that bordered the airfield.

Enraged, Krasilov raced for his old Polikarpov I-16. His ground crew stood by the short, stubby plane as he climbed into the open-canopy cockpit, ignored the preflight check, flipped the master switch, set the air/fuel mixture to full rich, and threw the engine starter. The propeller turned a few times before the engine engaged with a cloud of smoke that was quickly blown away by the slip-stream.

Another explosion.

As he advanced the throttle, Krasilov spotted a German plane pulling up. Four I-16s were in flames less than a hundred yards away as two other Messerschmitts entered a dive. Krasilov could see their muzzle flashes and the resulting lines of dust peppering toward three stationary Polikarpovs on the other side of the base. The planes exploded a moment later in a sheet of fire that reached up to the sky. One of the German planes flew through it before lurching skyward.

Krasilov reached the end of the runway. One plane was in flames halfway down the runway, blocking it. Krasilov pressed the top of the rudder pedals, applied full power, and lowered flaps. The forty-five-hundred-pound plane trembled under the conflicting commands. Rpm increased to twenty-seven hundred. The tail rose, and the nose dropped to the horizon under the powerful pull. He eased back the stick, used the elevators to control the nose's attitude, and waited. Three thousand rpm. He could hear the rivets squeaking as the stress on the monocoque structure reached the outer edges of its design. Krasilov held out for a few more seconds while firmly clutching the control stick. The craft began to slide over the ground.

He lifted his feet off the pedals, and the I-16 snapped forward, pressing him against his seat. His eyes shifted back and forth between the burning craft and the airspeed indicator:

"Speed, speed!" he hissed.

Eighty knots . . . ninety.

The flames rapidly accelerated toward him.

One hundred knots.

He shifted his gaze up once more and spotted a German plane breaking through the heavy smoke rising over the burning I-16. The wing-mounted guns came alive with muzzle flashes.

Krasilov pulled back on the stick and squeezed the trigger. The slow Polikarpov left the ground. Krasilov pointed the nose directly toward the incoming German craft flying at fifty feet above ground.

Krasilov stopped firing the moment the fighter, which he now recognized as an Me 109F Franz, broke its run and pulled up. He cleared the downed craft, broke through the dark smoke, and also pulled up, but could not even attempt to catch up with the departing Me 109F. The German craft outperformed him by over a hundred knots.

It didn't matter. He was airborne with full tanks and a full load of ammunition. Besides, the Franz was not what he was interested in stopping. Krasilov's eyes were fixed on the large bombers that the German fighters were trying to protect. He pushed full power and set his craft in a fast climb.

The bombers almost within reach, Krasilov cut right to fly past them, turned again, and faced them head-on to avoid the deadly guns on top and aft of the craft. As he made his turn he noticed something behind him.

An Me 109F.

Krasilov watched his airspeed alarmingly increase past three hundred knots, almost fifteen knots above his maximum rated speed, and he was feeling it in the powerful windblast that the short windshield barely deflected, and in the savage vibrations and rocking wings. He had to slow down fast or face midair disintegration. But slowing down meant giving the Messerschmitt glued to his tail an even better chance to score.

The thundering cannons, followed by several bullets ripping through the wooden skin of his right wing, made him cut back the throttle, lower flaps, and pull up the nose. A few more rounds blasted through the left wing, and a moment later smoke and oil began to spew from the engine, but the maneuver worked. He watched in satisfaction as the German flew past him at great speed but quickly turned away from the range of Krasilov's guns.

The dense haze blinding him, Krasilov lost track of the fighter. He wasn't sure what section of the engine the German had hit, but it had at least left him with enough power to remain airborne. He pushed full throttle, and the engine responded, but only at the cost of belching even more smoke and oil.

The Russian's eyes burned not just from the smoke, but also from the anger gripping him. The Germans were just picking their targets at will and blowing them up. There was no defense. He was the only fighter that had gotten airborne. Five planes burned on the runway, and dozens were in flames on the side of the airfield. The communications building was also burning. From this high up he could see the Junkers dropping load after load of bombs on Lvov! The city was quickly being engulfed by flames.

"Not on the city, you bastards! Only civilians live in the city!" he screamed at the top of his lungs. Krasilov's wife and two daughters lived on the outskirts of Lvov.

Through tears of rage, Krasilov spotted a pair of Messerschmitt Me 110s, the heavy twin-engine fighters. They were flying in formation a thousand feet below him. Krasilov pointed his craft in that direction and idled the engine to reduce smoke and improve visibility. It worked. In a dive, his I-16 gained airspeed, but without engine power. The Me 110s were five hundred feet below and closing awfully fast. He lined up the rightmost craft in his sights and squeezed the trigger.

Nothing.

Startled, he squeezed it again.

Nothing.

The Franz must have damaged something vital to the I-I6's weapons system. The Me 110s were two hundred feet away. Krasilov could see the large white-on-black cross painted over each wing. He briefly looked into another possibility for attacking the bombers and made his decision.

Perspiration and hot engine oil rolling down his creased forehead, Krasilov aimed for the right wingtip. He had to get the entire aileron, or the bomber might survive the attack.

One of the Me 110's cannons began to move up. Someone on the plane had spotted him.

Airspeed quickly rushed above three hundred knots. The craft quavered from the windblast on all leading edges. The attitude indicator told him he had achieved an eighty-degree-angle dive, way beyond the Polikarpov's specifications. Muzzle flashes broke out of the single cannon now pointed directly at him. Sparks flew out in all directions as the Me 110's rounds struck the massive radial engine, but it was to no consequence. Krasilov maintained his dive. The wing loomed closer.

Three hundred twenty knots.

Both hands firmly gripping the control column, Krasilov saw the white-on-black cross grow larger until it filled his entire windshield. He lowered his head below the glass at the very last moment.

The impact was soul-numbing. The vibrations felt as if they were going to shake the life out of him as a hasty vision of fire engulfed him. Krasilov let go of the stick and put both hands over his face as the heat intensified. The back of his shirt was on fire, but he was still alive. He pressed his back against the flight seat to put out the flames. It worked. His back stung on contact, but it was tolerable.

The propeller was bent back over the fuselage. The nose was still in one piece, and so were the wings and tail, but the rear of his craft was ablaze. He had to land fast to avoid an explosion.

Tongues of fire pulsated from the engine. Krasilov turned it off
to prevent more fuel from reaching the front and pulled on the
fuel-dump lever on the side of the seat to minimize the chance of
an explosion during his emergency landing.

The smoke and fire subsided, enabling him to pick a spot to land,
but before he could do that, Krasilov lifted his head and searched
the skies for his victim.

A smile flickered on his face when he spotted the Me 110 with
a missing wing gyrating in a fatal spin several hundred feet away.

He focused back to his own problem. He still had to find a place
to land. The wind intensified the flames behind him. He slowly
eased back on the stick and held his breath. The craft's nose rose a
few degrees. Airspeed decreased below three hundred knots. He
tried to lower flaps, but they didn't work. He briefly tested the
rudder and ailerons. They were operational. Krasilov pulled up the
nose several more degrees.

Altitude two hundred feet. Speed two hundred knots. A field of
sunflowers extended from where he was all the way to Lvov. Krasilov glided down.

One hundred feet; one hundred fifty knots.

Still too fast for a controlled landing, but he didn't have a choice.
He was approaching Lvov at great speed. He had to slow down,
but without flaps he was forced to set the craft down at that speed
or risk running out of room or stalling. The burning buildings rapidly grew in size.

Krasilov breathed deeply, held it, and lowered the nose. The
landing gear hit hard, instantly shaking the craft. Krasilov didn't
mind the vibrations as long as he could keep the craft in control.

The gear hit a ditch. In a flash, the nose dove into the thick field
and the tail went up in the air. The craft flipped once before landing
on its side.

Krasilov smashed his head against the windshield, bounced, and
crashed his back against the flight seat. He was disoriented from
the blow. Half his body lay outside the cockpit. He opened his eyes,
and through blood he saw . . . sunflowers. The airplane lay on its
side. The left wing was gone. The right stuck straight up in the air.

He kicked his legs and pushed himself away from the wreckage. His back burned, and so did his forehead. He felt the torn flesh above his eyebrows. It was in shreds, but he had survived.

Krasilov staggered away from the wreck, tearing off a sleeve of his shirt to bandage his forehead as best he could to stop the bleeding.

Breathing deeply, he walked toward the city. The sounds of German fighters mixed with explosions. Cries hung in the air like the smell of gunpowder filling his nostrils.

Krasilov picked up his pace as he reached the rubble of the buildings on the outskirts of town.

The dive-bombers had temporarily stopped, although Krasilov didn't think they could destroy much more with another run. He couldn't see a single building intact. Most had collapsed over the streets or were about to from the intense fire.

He turned into his street minutes later, spotted a woman in the middle of the road with . . . two kids!

Krasilov's heart jumped, and he ran, desperately hoping they were his wife and daughters . . . "Zoya! Zoya!"

"Please help us, sir. Please!" Two small boys screamed as they ran up to him and hung on to his pants while the woman pulled on his hand.

"The people in this building, woman," Krasilov asked, as he pointed to a three-story building that had collapsed on itself. "Did you see anyone coming out?"

"Please, sir. Please. Help us. Help us!"

Krasilov pulled out two small dark chocolate bars from his pocket. "Here. Take this and run out of the city with your children. The Germans are coming. You must leave! Tell everyone you see to head east. You got that? Head east!"

The woman snagged the chocolate and ran away with her two kids.

Krasilov faced the ruins that had been his building. His family lived on the third floor. Krasilov walked on the sidewalk, climbed on top of the mound of rubble, and began to paw through the debris while praying that he would not find them. Perhaps they heard the noise and fled. Perhaps they managed to leave the building in time.

Time.

Tears rolled down his blackened face as he moved rock, brick, and wood aside. His muscles burned, and his head throbbed, but it did not matter. He had to know. He needed to know.

An overwhelming sense of despair suddenly filled him the moment he spotted his wife's body under a wooden panel. His two daughters were next to her. They wore their sleeping garments. Still hopeful, he knelt next to his wife, but froze when something didn't look right. His wife lay on her stomach, but her eyes stared up to the sky. Her head had been twisted at a repulsive angle.

"Zoya, no . . . no!"

Mustering savage control, Krasilov walked over to his twin daughters, Marissa and Larissa. Their bodies also faced down, but appeared intact. He turned the first one over . . . her face and chest were gone! Krasilov let her go and leaned to the side. He controlled the first convulsion, but the second reached his gorge. He couldn't even tell which of his daughters that was!

His body tensed and he purged. A third convulsion came and went, quickly followed by a fourth, this time only a dry heave.

Krasilov straightened up, breathed deeply, and walked over to his second daughter. He turned her over. It was Larissa. Her body was not maimed, but the purple hue of the flesh around her neck told Krasilov everything he needed to know.

He dropped to his knees and bellowed a scream of anger, frustration, and pain, before he burst into tears again, before he cried the desperate cry of a desperate man.

Later that morning, as German planes flew overhead and panzer divisions streaked across the Ukrainian planes, Krasilov headed east.

Hordes of Russians civilians ran past him as they fled the advancing German army. Krasilov didn't run. He wasn't afraid of the Germans. There was nothing else they could take away from him besides his life.

And that would be a blessing, he reflected.

There were dozens of airstrips between Lvov and Kiev. Krasilov headed toward them. War had come to his home. To his country.

War had taken his loved ones.

As his *Rodina* burned under Germany's crushing attack, Aleksandrovich Nikolai Krasilov concluded there was nothing left for him to do but fight.

Fight back with uncompromising resolve.

He had sworn that over three lonely graves in a sunflower field outside Lvov.

BAHRAIN, SAUDI ARABIA • NOVEMBER 25, 1942

U.S. Army Air Corps Captain Jack Towers zippered up his leather jacket and took a last, long draw from his cigarette while staring at the large merchant ships quietly steaming north, toward the port of Abadan, Iran. He slowly exhaled through his nostrils and stepped away from the edge of the hill, returning to the dirt runway, where he had landed the night before. His back still ached from sleeping on the floor, but as Jack saw it, at least he'd had a relatively quiet place where he could get a few uninterrupted hours of sleep without being disturbed by gunfire. That alone was a luxury these days.

On the way to the mess tent, Jack walked next to his plane, a Bell P-39D Aircobra he had baptized *The Impatient Virgin* after one of his wilder girlfriends during his short but busy stay at Cochran Field, Georgia, where Jack had trained side by side with Royal Air Force pilots on advanced dogfighting techniques with the Aircobras. From there Jack was transferred to Dale Mabry in Florida for additional dogfighting training. Eight months later, Jack, along with two dozen other pilots who had logged over one thousand hours, spent a week in Camp Kilmer, New Jersey, where they boarded a ship loaded with four hundred P-39Ds destined for the Red Air Force as part of President Roosevelt's Soviet-American lend-lease program.

He sighed. Little did Jack know during his year and a half of training that his first official overseas post would be teaching Soviet pilots to use their new equipment, but as it turned out, the aircraft that he had learned to master ended up being pushed aside by both the U.S. Army Air Corps and the RAF in favor of the faster and much more agile P-40 Kittihawk. The surplus P-39Ds were shipped to the Soviet Union, where their fighter aircraft technology lagged the West by a few years.

But there was another reason why Jack had been selected for this not-so-glorious duty. Jack was born under the name Jackovich Filipp Towers. His mother was a Soviet nurse his father had fallen in love with during World War I, and whom he subsequently married and brought home to Indiana.

Raised mostly by his mother, Jack spoke perfect Russian by the time he was four years old, and his mother saw to it that Jack didn't forget it by refusing to speak to him in English—something his mother did to this day.

Jack smiled as he rubbed a hand over his jacket and felt the letter—written in Russian—he'd received a few days before from his mother. He always got letters from his mother, never from his father. Jack's father was always too busy selling used cars at his used car lot—or so he claimed.

That's just as well, reflected Jack. All his old man wanted to talk about was used cars anyway. He couldn't care less about Jack's aviation career.

There had been a time, Jack remembered as he walked around two parked jeeps in front of the mess tent, when his father had had a chance to pull him closer. It was when he was about to turn seventeen. Jack had commented several times how much he would love to own a car, and in his mind he'd hoped his father would get him one. So much did Jack expect the car, that he had told his friends he was getting one. That proved to be a grave mistake, because to Jack's surprise, the old man forgot to show up for his birthday party. *I had a last-minute customer*, Jack recalled him saying when he arrived empty-handed two hours late. The carless son of the car salesman. His friends gave him a hard time about that for weeks.

Jack shrugged and exhaled as he reached the front of the tent.

Maybe that experience was the reason Jack felt as if he always got the short end of the stick in life.

He pushed the canvas flap and stepped inside the mess tent. On one side was the cafeteria line—if one could call two Arab cooks with a pot filled with eggs and another with a white soggy substance they called grits—a cafeteria line. On the opposite side were two midsize tables with six chairs each. Jack grabbed a metal plate, got some eggs and . . . grits, and walked next to one of the tables, where a pilot was already going through seconds.

"This is a warm meal, Jack. Might as well enjoy it while it lasts," said Major Kenneth Chapman, Jack's commanding officer. Chapman was also fluent in Russian. "Heard up north the Russkies are undergoing food rations."

"That's just great, sir. I can't wait." Jack sat down and filled his mouth with two spoonfuls of eggs.

Chapman pushed his plate to the side and downed a glass of water. "The latest news from the Eastern Front's that shit's just about to hit the fan in good ol' Stalingrad, pal. Better enjoy the powdered eggs while you can eat them. Most Russians are on a bread and butter diet, but heck, at least that's better than the Germans. Last I heard, those Nazi bastards are eating their own horses. Guess that's good for the assholes."

Chapman grinned, exposing the gold caps on his two front teeth.

Jack couldn't help a frown. War wasn't going exactly as he had planned it. He had visualized himself fighting Messerschmitts over the English Channel and across the French and German countryside, not in below-zero-weather eastern Russia, but orders were orders. He had to go where the Air Corps told him to. He did get to participate briefly in the battle of North Africa. Flying his *Impatient Virgin*, Jack had distinguished himself by shooting down three Italian Macchi Mc.202 single-engine fighters over Libya in the week he'd spent there.

Chapman checked his watch. "We're leaving in an hour, Jack. Our red buddies got a couple of hundred planes just sitting around waiting for us to show them how to use them. No sense in making them wait, right?"

"I guess so, sir."

"Good. Don't forget to pick up a set of long johns from the supply tent. It's gonna be one motherfucker of a winter." Chapman got up and left.

Jack slowly shook his head. His mother had told him stories of people freezing in minutes at forty below zero, and because in her days as a nurse she had seen more than her share of amputations due to frostbite, Jack received lecture after lecture on how to dress not just warm, but dress warm for a Russian winter.

There is a difference, my dear Jackovich Filipp. The Russian winter will rob you of your heat, freeze you to the bone, then cover you with so many inches of snow that your stiff body won't surface until the following spring.

The grits tasted terrible and stuck to the roof of his mouth. Jack ate them anyway and went back to the line for seconds.

STALINGRAD FRONT • DECEMBER 13, 1942

Colonel Krasilov allowed his Lavochkin La-3 fighter to reach ten thousand feet before easing the control column forward. He glanced to his right and left and nodded approvingly when spotting his seven-plane squadron adopting an arrowhead formation.

A soldier from the Soviet Fifth Armored Division had spotted a formation of German bombers possibly carrying supplies for the trapped German Sixth Army of General Paulus in the Stalingrad pocket. Krasilov's mission was simple: Search and destroy all enemy craft in the region with priority to bombers.

Upset at his government's lack of better intelligence reports, Krasilov scanned the skies and saw nothing but blue. A rare day in the Soviet winter, but Krasilov didn't mind. Hopefully temperatures would warm up to ten below so that his men could get some relief from what had been a bitter winter. On the other hand, the cold winter at that moment affected the Germans more than the Soviets. Krasilov had grown up in these regions and was used to the long, cold months—and was also well dressed for them. The Germans, on the other hand, were still wearing their summer uniforms. Paulus's army had taken Stalingrad in early September just to find that all that remained from the once-picturesque city were the charred facades of the buildings that still stood. The Soviet people, by order of the Soviet High Command in Moscow, set fire to all buildings, equipment, and anything else that could be of any use to the Germans that couldn't be hauled east in time. The Russian winter caught General Paulus and his glorious but exhausted Sixth Army hundreds of miles from home in a ghost city with fresh Soviet troops attacking from all flanks. Hitler had ordered the Sixth Army to adopt a hedgehog, or all-round, defensive position and to wait for relief. That created the Stalingrad pocket, where the Germans now slowly starved to death by an ever-decreasing channel of supplies.

Good for them, Krasilov decided. After all the atrocities that the invading troops had committed in Krasilov's motherland, he had not one ounce of pity for them. On the contrary, the Soviet pilot firmly believed that the Hitlerites had not only needed to be repelled from Russia, but also followed all the way to the heart of Berlin and exterminated.

"Germans! Three o'clock high!" came the voice from Krasilov's right wingman, Lieutenant Andrei Nikolajev.

Krasilov snapped his head to the left and spotted the formation.

"Scramble, comrades! Scramble! The Hitlerites shall not get their supplies today!"

The craft broke formation in pairs. Krasilov pushed full power. The Shvestov fourteen-cylinder radial engine puffed two clouds of black smoke before pulling the craft with monumental force. Even at a twenty-degree angle of climb Krasilov watched the airspeed indicator rush past 350 knots and climb as fast as the altimeter. He closed the gap in under a minute. Andrei remained glued to his side.

The bombers, which Krasilov now recognized as the large Heinkel He 177, opened fire from all angles, but after a few encounters with the He 177, Krasilov had learned that the Heinkels were most vulnerable underneath, where there was only one machine-gun pod. The other five were scattered on the top, front, and rear, but were ineffective against an attack from underneath.

To protect themselves from such attack, the German bombers had opted to fly in a combat-box formation. The combat box resembled a slanted flying wedge with the lead squadron in the middle. Other squadrons were stacked three hundred feet from the lead squadron's left and right. This arrangement enabled the bombers a clear field of fire for the bomber's front gunners and also allowed for coordinated cross fire of the attacking fighters. Each bomber covered the other one's bottom. The planes on each end of the formation were the most exposed, but those were usually protected by escort fighters.

Krasilov saw no escorts in sight and exhaled in relief as he approached the leftmost Heinkel. Although his La-3 plane was a remarkable improvement over the old I-16s, the craft was still not as fast and maneuverable as the Messerschmitt Me 109F or the even faster Me 109G.

The Heinkel's underside dual machine-gun pod located between the wings in the forward fuselage swung in his direction and opened fire. Krasilov broke left, away from the formation. The gun followed him.

"It's all yours, Andrei!"

Krasilov saw a few rounds exploding through his Lavochkin's wooden skin as he diverted the gunner's attention away from his wingman. The craft shuddered but remained airborne. A backward glance, and Krasilov watched Andrei unload round after round on the Heinkel's underfuselage.

The gun-pod emplacement exploded.

Andrei broke its run while Krasilov made a 360-degree turn and came back around for his pass. This time there was nothing defending the bomber. Krasilov made the turn wide enough to allow him ample time to fire. He completed the turn and aligned the Heinkel's center fuselage, using rudders and ailerons.

He squeezed the trigger. The dual cowl-mounted 20mm cannons came to life and fired at the rate of two hundred rounds per minute in synchronized fashion, through the propeller. One in every ten rounds had a phosphorus head that burned bright yellow the moment it left the muzzle. Krasilov used the tracers to guide his fire.

Pieces began to come off the middle of the bomber. Krasilov pulled back throttle to allow himself an extra second or two of firing time before he had to pull—

A bright explosion and the tail separated from the front, catching Krasilov entirely by surprise. The tail section flew down while the front fuselage shot up and to the left, blocking Krasilov's planned tight left turn.

Breaking right was out of the question. Dozens of Heinkel guns would be waiting for him in a deadly cross fire. Krasilov continued to fire and held his run.

Another explosion. The left engine went up in flames, tearing the Heinkel's wing along with it.

Krasilov rolled the wings ninety degrees and flew through the debris, fire engulfing him for a second, before turning to thick smoke followed by blue skies.

He watched in satisfaction as the wounded bomber's right engine continued to run, pulling the remnants of the Heinkel against an adjacent bomber. The two went up in a huge fireball that engulfed a third bomber.

The remaining bombers, which Krasilov had estimated at thirty, continued their trajectory toward the Stalingrad pocket.

"Messerschmitts! Five and ten o'clock!"

"Got them! Break left, Andrei! I'll handle the right!"

Krasilov swung the stick right and saw an Me 109G "Gustav" coming straight ahead. He leveled off and approached it head-on. The German opened fire. Krasilov's index finger reached the trigger and pressed it, but the game didn't last long. With a combined speed of over eight hundred knots, the two planes closed in awfully fast. A bullet crashed against Krasilov's propeller hub and bounced away. There was no smoke.

Krasilov waited until the very last second before breaking left. The German broke right and tried to execute a tight 360. Krasilov was about to do a left but instead he swung the stick back to the right, instantly pulling a few negative Gs. The restraining harness kept him from crashing against the canopy, and he completed the maneuver while the German pilot was still halfway through the turn. The Hitlerite had apparently failed to consider Krasilov's change of strategy, and was caught with his entire flank exposed. The Gustav's pilot had made a basic but fatal aerial combat mistake. Krasilov was surprised. German pilots were much more disciplined than that.

Krasilov smiled as his finger squeezed the trigger. At such close range the Messerschmitt broke apart after a three-second burst from the 20mm cannons.

As debris slowly fell from the sky, Krasilov broke left and raced after the bombers, most of which already had their payload doors fully open. The German Stalingrad pocket was less than a minute away.

The Heinkels went for a dive to increase the gap between them and the pursuing La-3s. Krasilov wished someone had informed them earlier about the incoming bombers. Maybe they could have intercepted sooner and taken out more bombers, but just like a dozen times before, all his squadron had was a ten-minute warning from field spotters.

Krasilov watched in utter disappointment as packages dropped from the bomb bays. Bright white parachutes opened a few seconds later. Krasilov pressed on. There was still a chance to prevent some of the droppings.

He approached a Heinkel from the rear at full speed and with the cannons firing. He adjusted to take out the rear gun emplacement of the closest bomber. The guns swung in his direction, but before a single round left them the tail section blew into three large pieces just as the packages began to drop. Krasilov did not let up. He maintained his run while keeping the pressure on the trigger. *C'mon, blow, dammit. Blow!*

Like a heavenly chastisement, the sixty-six-hundred-pound bomber went up into a fiery ball that also engulfed Krasilov's plane. This time, however, the fire lasted several seconds, enough to ignite the waterproof lacquer protecting the La-3's wooden skin.

He left the burning debris behind and immediately cut back power and pushed the stick forward. He had to reach land before the craft exploded, but at an altitude of over five thousand feet, he doubted he'd make it. Most of the wings and rear fuselage were already covered by flames. It was just a matter of time before the heat caused the gas tank to blow.

Krasilov leveled off the plane, turned it upside down, and pushed the nose just a dash below the horizon to get the tail out of the way. He slid the canopy open and pulled on the release mechanism of his restraining harness.

He free-fell through the open canopy and cleared the vertical fin by a couple of feet. The windblast was much more powerful than he had been told. It kept him from breathing for a few seconds. The earth, burning craft, and blue skies changed positions over and over as a peaceful feeling of isolation suddenly overtook him. Although it felt as if he was just standing still in midair, Krasilov knew he was plummeting to earth at over 150 miles per hour.

He reached for the rip cord and pulled it hard. The pilot chute came up and dragged the main canopy, which blossomed bright red, giving Krasilov the tug of a lifetime. Fortunately for him, he had managed to fly far away enough from the German pocket before bailing out. Krasilov didn't think the starving Hitlerites in Stalingrad would treat well a downed Soviet pilot who had just been shooting down supply craft—not that the Germans treated Soviet prisoners of war with any decency anyway.

He watched most bombers in the distance drop their payloads before turning back, while the remaining Messerschmitts kept the rest of his squadron busy.

Krasilov shook his head in disappointment. They needed more time to intercept, and better planes.

He silently glided over the River Volga.

KALACH AIRFIELD, TWENTY MILES WEST OF THE STALINGRAD POCKET • DECEMBER 13, 1942

For Krasilov the nightmare had returned. His wounded I-16 plummeted to earth in flames. He had no control of the air surfaces or engine. Through the flames coming from the exhausts he could see the bent propeller. His face began to burn from the intense heat.

He looked behind him and saw the Messerschmitt. The pilot was waving at him while his cannons took out the I-16's tail. Chunks of wood blew in all directions, some striking Krasilov in the back as the craft went into a reverse spin with the nose pointed at the heavens. Krasilov saw the blue sky while desperately reaching for the release handle of his restraining harness, but he could not find it. He looked to his left and watched the German pilot salute him and laugh. The bastard was laughing as Krasilov hopelessly struggled with his harness. The Messerschmitt remained there, as if hovering next to him. The pilot continued to smile. Krasilov could not unstrap his harness. The heat intensified. The heat . . .

"Colonel Krasilov? Colonel Krasilov! Wake up, sir. Wake up!"

Krasilov opened his eyes and saw Andrei's round face. He inhaled, sat up, and rubbed his eyes. He had nearly frozen from his five-mile walk in thirty below following his landing until a T-34 tank from the Second Mechanized Division picked him up and brought him to the air base, where it took him an hour to thaw and less than a minute to fall asleep.

Krasilov ran his tongue inside his mouth, which felt dry and pasty. He reached for the bottle of vodka next to the bed and took a swig. He inhaled as his throat and chest warmed up, and stared at Andrei's clean-shaven face once more.

His subordinate, a recently graduated pilot from the Red Air Force, had joined Krasilov's fighter wing six months ago and had since worked his way to the top, taking second to no one but Krasilov. In fact, Andrei had already shot down over sixty enemy fighters with a loss of only three planes, a record that only Krasilov, with over a hundred air victories, could surpass. Krasilov liked the young pilot from the Ukraine, who enjoyed women and dancing as much as he loved flying.

"What is it?" Krasilov asked, taking another sip, letting the alcohol do its magical work.

"We've got company, sir. Americans."

Krasilov bolted to his feet. *"What?"*

"Americans, sir. Actually only *one* American, but over three dozen American fighters. Three dozen, sir!"

"So soon? They weren't supposed to be here until . . ."

"They're here, sir, and the fighters are being unloaded from the cargo planes as we speak."

Krasilov put on his skin boots and heavy coat and followed Andrei outside, where five huge American cargo planes were parked on the far left side of the snow-covered runway.

As a true Bolshevik, Krasilov did not care for the Americans and their flying machines. He wanted more Lavochkin La-3s and perhaps a squadron of the newer but still scarce La-5s, but given the large need for fighters to support the Russian defense and new winter counteroffensive, Stalin had agreed to the American lend-lease program. This was one of the first shipments.

He spotted a dark-haired man wearing a black leather jacket, matching boots and gloves, and dark sunglasses. *So it is true then,* Krasilov reflected as he walked away from his bunker. *American pilots do wear sunglasses, even on an overcast day.*

Krasilov approached him, flanked by Andrei and two other pilots. The American smiled and extended his hand. Krasilov didn't take it. The smile on the American's face vanished. He removed his sunglasses and stared back at Krasilov with indifference.

"You were not supposed to have been here for another week. What gives you the right to barge into my airfield with little warning?" Krasilov asked in Russian, not expecting a response from the American.

"Is that how you welcome your allies, Colonel?" responded the American in flawless Russian. "I would hate to see what you would do to a German."

Krasilov was impressed, although he did not show it externally. The young man knew the language well.

"I shall consider you my ally when my men have been trained and your planes prove themselves in my eyes . . ."

"Captain Towers, Colonel. Jack Towers." He put the sunglasses back on.

Krasilov didn't respond right away. He simply stared at his own reflection on the American's glasses and pointed toward a single tent on the other side of the runway. "You will sleep and eat there, when there is food. When there is none, you will starve with the rest of us. There will be no special privileges for you. You will answer to me while training my men, and the moment the training is complete, you shall leave my base at once. Is that understood, Captain?"

"I will only answer to my superior officer, Major Kenneth Chapman, sir."

"Is that so, Captain. And where is this Major Chapman right now, may I ask?"

"He's training another fighter wing a hundred miles north of here."

"Like I said, Captain. You will report directly to me while on my base!" Krasilov turned and headed back for his tent. "Andrei, show him what he needs to know!"

"Yes, comrade Colonel!"

Jack frowned. This wasn't exactly the type of reception he'd had in mind, but then again, nothing had gone his way since he'd joined the damned Air Corps. Why would this be any different?

"Charming fellow, your colonel," he said to Andrei.

Andrei smiled and extended his hand. Jack shook it.

"I'm Lieutenant Andrei Nikolajev. Please forgive him, Captain Towers—"

"Jack."

"Jackovich?"

Jack laughed. "Sure, Jackovich is fine, too."

Andrei smiled, nodded, then frowned. "Don't take Colonel Krasilov too seriously today. He's pretty upset. He got shot down early this morning and spent the last seven hours getting back to the base through the snow. He's not in the best of moods."

"Well, neither am I. I've just spent the last three days traveling halfway across the world to get here."

"I understand. How long before the planes are ready?"

Jack shifted his gaze to the transports and the army of Russians dressed in white camouflage jackets unloading the P-39Ds wingless fuselages down the rear ramps. "I'll say another day at the most. Maybe less. How many pilots are available?"

"Plenty. We just need a more competitive machine than the La-3. We lose too many of them in every battle."

Jack exhaled. The P-39D Aircobras were relatively faster than the La-3s, but not as fast and maneuverable as the Messerschmitts. "How good are they?"

"Excuse me?"

"Your pilots, Andrei. How good are they?"

"We have the will to learn and the will to fight, comrade Jackovich. We are all prepared to die for the *Rodina*."

"Well, let's hope it doesn't come to that. The best pilot, in my opinion, is a live one."

The Russian gave him a puzzled look that didn't surprise Jack one bit. Chapman had warned him about the courageous—and at times suicidal—Soviet pilots. Jack wondered if perhaps that kind of spirit was what was really necessary to win a war. Maybe his cool American attitude was not what got things done, but the boldness, take-no-prisoners approach that the Russians were so famous for.

"This is a war, comrade Jackovich. Our lives are expendable. We all must fight to defend the *Rodina*."

Sure, Andrei, Jack thought as he stared into the Soviet's ice-blue eyes crowning the remnants of what appeared to have once been a boyish face. The fine lines on Andrei's forehead and around his eyes told Jack that the young Soviet pilot must have already seen more than his share of battle—probably more than Jack would ever get to see.

"Would you die for your country, Jackovich?"

Jack considered that for a moment before replying, "That's why we're here, right? Why do you ask?"

"Our perception of the American pilot is one of more show than actual fight. That's what we get told anyway. I think that's part of the reason the colonel reacted—"

Andrei's words were cut short by the high-pitched sound of an engine in full throttle very close to ground.

"Shit. I hope that's one of yours," Jack said as he scanned the skies.

"I . . . I'm not that . . . damn! It's a Gustav!"

They ran for the shelter on the far right side of the concrete runway. Jack crouched next to Andrei as the Messerschmitt zoomed over the runway.

"Damn! The Aircobras!" Jack shouted, glancing at the wingless fuselages wrapped in thick green plastic stacked next to the cargo planes.

Without firing a single round, the Messerschmitt pulled up and rolled its wing while maintaining a vertical climb. Jack saw the craft execute the corkscrew until nearly reaching a low layer of cumulus clouds some five thousand feet high.

"What's he doing?" asked Jack.

"Challenging."

"What?"

"He's challenging the best of our pilots for a one-on-one duel."

"Are you shitting me?"

Before Jack got an answer, Andrei leaped forward and raced toward Krasilov and the other pilots already gathered next to the La-3s.

"Please. Let me handle it, Colonel," Andrei said, as Jack finally reached the group.

Krasilov looked around as the Messerschmitt continued to circle overhead. "Any other volunteers?"

The rest of the pilots raised their hands. Krasilov fixed his gaze on Jack, who remained a few feet behind the group. "How about you, Captain? Would you like to show us the real capability of your craft? Up there is a good opportunity to do so."

All the eyes were on him. Jack inhaled deeply and scanned the curious looks on the Soviet faces.

"I can't, Colonel. My orders are very strict. I'm only supposed to train . . ."

Krasilov raised his right palm and waved him off. "Andrei, the German's all yours!"

Andrei raced for his craft. Krasilov stared at Jack long and hard. Jack thought he saw a smile briefly flickering across the Russian's face.

"There is an old saying in my hometown of Lvov, Captain Towers," Krasilov finally said. "Knowing and not doing are the same as not knowing at all. This is a war. Up there is the enemy. You are a pilot. It is all very plain and simple." Krasilov turned and joined the other pilots, who had circled Andrei's craft to wish him good luck.

Jack closed his eyes and frowned.

Andrei pushed the throttle handle forward and taxied the craft onto the wide concrete runway. He thought about taxiing to one end, but decided he had more than enough runway to either side of him for a short takeoff. He turned his craft into the wind, pressed the brakes, lowered flaps, and applied full throttle. The liquid-cooled Klimov bellowed dark smoke for a few seconds before slowly beginning to drag the seven-thousand-pound craft over the slippery surface.

Andrei let go of the brakes, and the La-3 shot forward at great speed. He pulled the stick when the indicated airspeed read 120 knots, and the Lavochkin fighter left the ground.

Andrei raised flaps and gear, trimmed the elevators, and turned off the auxiliary fuel pump. The La-3 cleared the trees and sprinted upward. The moment he reached the Messerschmitt, the German plane flew next to his right wing. Both pilots looked at one another for a few seconds before breaking in opposite directions.

Andrei went for another climb and reached a cumulus cloud ten seconds later. The German was nowhere in sight. The cloud engulfed him. Andrei leveled off, pulled back the throttle, lowered flaps, and began a slow and tight 360-degree turn.

Next to the runway, Jack squinted as he lost Andrei in the clouds. He anxiously waited for him to reappear at the other end, but the

Lavochkin remained hidden. He spotted the German fighter circling the area, looking for the Soviet.

Andrei inverted his craft and continued his turn while slowly descending. He did six more revolutions before the canopy broke
through the clouds. His head felt about to burst from the blood
pressure of being upside down. He remained like that for a few
more seconds as he looked up toward the ground . . . *there!* He
smiled when the German fighter came into plain view a thousand
feet below him.

The Soviet pulled the stick back, and the machine adopted an
inverted dive profile. Airspeed quickly began to gather. The
German kept the shallow turn. Three hundred knots. The German
was no more than five hundred feet away, and still did not see
Andrei . . . now he did! The Gustav also inverted and started a dive,
but Andrei already had more speed than necessary to close the gap
in five more seconds.

The Gustav's tail filled his windshield. Andrei squeezed the trigger, and the single, nose-mounted 20mm cannon began to fire. Dozens of rounds ripped through the German's rear fuselage. Three
more seconds was all Andrei had before he had to pull up to avoid
ramming the German, but that was all he needed. The empennage
broke off from the fiery punishment.

"Left, left!" He told himself aloud as he changed his evasive at
the very last second, opting for a hard left instead of a pull-up to
avoid flying into the tail. A mild two Gs pressed him against his
seat as he continued the turn at the same altitude while looking
backward and down at the falling craft.

Without a tail section, the Messerschmitt, whose engine was still
running, spun out of control along all axes for another minute before crashing next to a stream a mile east of the runway. Andrei
saw no parachute.

Jack watched the La-3 rock its wings and make two full-speed low
passes over the airfield as the pilots broke into a loud cheer. The
Lavochkin came back around, dropped its landing gear, softly

touched down, and taxied back to the side of the runway. The pilots gathered around the craft. Jack saw Krasilov staring at him as Andrei jumped out of the plane and climbed down the wingroot. The Soviet colonel shook his head, smiled, and turned around.

Jack silently cursed the Air Corps for sending him here.

KALACH AIRFIELD, TWENTY MILES WEST OF THE STALINGRAD POCKET • DECEMBER 14, 1942

Jack Towers had an audience of seven pilots, including Andrei and Krasilov. The grumpy Soviet colonel with the scarred forehead had already told Jack that he had no interest in participating in the class, but since his new La-3 would not arrive for another two weeks, he had no other choice in order to remain airborne.

Temperatures had increased to ten degrees below, creating what most Russians considered a warm winter day. The sky, however, remained heavily overcast, and a light breeze swept over the clearing.

Andrei and Jack had dragged the heavy P-39D simulator outside so that he could explain more easily to the men the basics of the Aircobra's cockpit before each test-flew his "lend-leased" craft.

There had been an instant chemistry between Jack and Andrei. The young Soviet pilot's openness and friendliness had made up for Krasilov's querulous behavior. From Andrei, Jack had learned that he was the younger of two brothers. His older brother, Boris Ivanovich, had been reported missing during the Battle of Moscow several months back. Jack saw pain in the Slav's blue eyes as he related the incident to him. Andrei's only hope was that his brother had been taken prisoner, but that hope was also a curse. Death was sometimes preferable to a German prison camp for what the Nazis considered a lower race.

Jack knew he was dealing with professional fighter pilots, most of whom had seen more aerial combat than Jack ever saw during his short posting in North Africa, and probably more than he would ever expect to encounter during the entire war.

Next to the runway, all the P-39Ds had already been assembled and their engines tested by Krasilov's mechanics, some of whom, to Jack's surprise, had been women. The craft were parked in a three-sided earth-and-wood shelter, and were spaced roughly 150 feet from each other. These precautions were to protect the aircraft from indirect hits of enemy fragmentation bombs, and also to minimize the chance of one plane's explosion igniting the craft on either side.

"All right, listen up," he began, as all eyes focused on him. "As most of you probably realize by now, the Aircobra is different from all other fighters in that it uses a tricycle-style landing gear instead of the traditional three-wheel rear landing gear scheme that all of you are used to working with. This will make your landing a bit different because right before touchdown you will have to pull the nose up and let the main gear touch down first. After that, don't force the nose gear down, simply cut back power and let it fall by itself. Everyone with me?"

Jack noticed a few of the pilots barely nodding. "All right. Next thing that is nonconventional is the engine location. As most of you have probably heard from your mechanics, the Aircobra's engine is located directly behind the pilot. That has both advantages and disadvantages. On the positive side, in addition to providing better overall balance because of its proximity to the plane's center of gravity, if the engine catches fire, the flames will be directed away from you. That's good. Also, for the most part, unless you make a basic dogfighting mistake and get caught broadside, the enemy will try to shoot you down from the rear . . . well, with the Aircobra you don't have to worry about getting your head blown off. There is a ton of aluminum and steel behind you to absorb the bullets. That is also good.

"Now, on the negative side, since the engine is on back, most of the ammo is carried in the nose. That has the effect of changing the weight ratio of the plane as the ammunition is consumed. The more you fire, the lighter the nose will get, and the more you will have to trim the elevons. It will be awkward at first, but with time it'll become second nature.

"Something that will feel strange in the beginning is the use of the 37mm nose-mounted cannon. From what Andrei has told me, the highest caliber that most of you have in your La-3s is 20mm. Well, 37mm is an entirely different beast. It will take some time to get used to its recoil, so go easy on it at first. Any questions so far?"

He got no response. Jack took it as a no and continued for another thirty minutes, covering everything from the locations of the instruments, weapon systems, radios, and throttle controls, to critical airspeeds, maximum speed, and G forces.

When he finished, he stepped away from the simulator and looked at the Soviets. "Any questions?"

All of the pilots glanced at Krasilov, who simply nodded and headed for his Aircobra. The other pilots did the same.

"Wait, Andrei. What in the hell is going on?"

"No man will dare ask a question unless Krasilov asks it first, Jackovich."

"Are you serious? You mean to tell me that those pilots would rather risk their lives and try out something they're not sure about rather than just ask?"

Andrei raised his eyebrows. "We are all professional pilots, Jackovich. To us a plane is just a plane." The Soviet pilot walked away and joined the others.

"Crazy bastards," he murmured in disbelief as he headed for the nearest burning barrel in the base. Almost an hour outside in ten below had stiffened Jack's muscles.

As he reached the barrel, Jack pulled out his gloved hands from inside his leather coat's side pockets and extended them in front of the fire. The P-39Ds' engines came alive one after the other.

Jack turned his head and watched the pilots play with the throttle controls, elevons, rudder, and ailerons, before taxiing away single file behind Krasilov.

"Crazy bastards," he murmured again, as Krasilov and the other pilots reached the runway and positioned themselves in pairs. A green rocket was fired, and the first pair rolled down the concrete runway, which was roughly two thousand yards long by about five hundred wide, and ran east–west to go along the region's prevailing wind direction. The surface was made up of octagonal concrete paving slabs about two yards across. As Andrei had explained to him earlier that morning while they dragged the simulator, hundreds of civilians had laid this surface in a vast interlocking honeycomb pattern soon after the ground had been leveled by Red Army engineers. Jack saw the advantage of such a runway when it came time to repair it by simply replacing individual slabs.

In all, the base was built with safety and practicality in mind. All ammunition and fuel was stored in underground dugouts, and all the buildings and hangars had camouflaged roofs.

"Are you going to join the crazy bastards, Captain Towers?" said a low and deep female voice behind him.

Startled, Jack spun around and stared at a tall woman dressed in an old-fashioned aviator suit—the type he'd seen in World War I pictures, with the high sheepskin boots, heavy leather helmet, scarf, and thick jacket. A pistol leaned into her slender waist as she bent to pick up another log and throw it into the barrel.

"Fire's dying out," the woman said while she pulled up her leather cap. She wore an elegant pure silk helmet underneath, which she carefully removed, folded, and tucked away in a coat pocket. She let her blond hair fall down to her shoulders, tousled it up, then regarded Jack with a mix of curiosity and amusement.

"Anything wrong, Captain?"

Jack was shocked to see an attractive Slavic women in such a harsh place. Her inquisitive hazel eyes were fixed on him.

"Ah . . . no. I'm not allowed to go along with the pilots. I'm just here to train them, Miss . . . ?"

"I'm pilot Natalya Makarova, Captain," she responded with an air of confidence that Jack was not used to seeing in a woman. Much less a woman pilot.

"You're a pilot?"

Natalya tilted her head. "Does that surprise you, Captain?" she asked with humor. The hazel eyes crinkled slightly as she grinned.

"I never thought that—"

"A woman could actually fly a fighter plane? Well, welcome to the twentieth century, Captain Towers."

Jack couldn't help but smile.

"You think it's funny I'm a pilot, Captain?" This time her tone of voice became a bit more serious.

"Oh, no, no. It's nothing like that. You'll have to forgive me, Natalya, but this is the first time that—"

"It's all right. I've seen that reaction plenty of times before. I'm used to it."

Jack extended his hand, deciding that his stay at this base might not be as bad as he had first imagined. He wondered if all of the other women pilots were this beautiful. "Well, it's a pleasure to meet you, Natalya Makarova."

Natalya pumped his hand firmly. "The pleasure is mine, Jack Towers."

"Call me Jack."

"All right."

"So, what kind of planes do you fly, Natalya?"

Natalya frowned. "What plane I would *like* to fly? Or what plane Colonel Krasilov *makes* me and the other women pilots fly?"

Before he could say a word, Natalya added, "I fly something you would never dare set a finger on, Jack." She gave him a final smile and started to walk away.

"You never told me how you knew my name."

She turned briefly. "News travel fast."

"Natalya, I . . . where are you staying . . . I'd like to get to know you better."

The smile disappeared from her face. The look in her eyes was now as cold as the Russian winter. "This is war, Jack. There isn't time for anything else. I'm having a hard time proving myself to these bunch of chauvinist pilots as it is. I don't need . . . complications, especially with an American. It was nice meeting you."

Jack exhaled in disappointment, watching her walk away and disappear behind some tents on the other side of the airstrip. Resigned to the fact that his stay here would be as bad as it had first appeared, he turned to the fire and extended his hands against it once more. These Russians were certainly different from the jovial crowd he knew from his mother's family.

He raised his gaze and saw the formation of P-39Ds in the distance.

Crazy bastards.

KALACH AIRFIELD, TWENTY MILES WEST OF THE STALINGRAD POCKET • DECEMBER 15, 1942

REF: CX/MSS/T347/67   HP3434

ZZZZZ

((HP 3434 & 3434 CR ONA GT OX YKE GU 7 & 7))

ORDERS AT ONE TWO ZERO ZERO HOURS TWELFTH FOR
THIRTEENTH. FIRSTLY, JAGDGESCHWADER 52, GRUPPE I
TO ATTACK TEN MILES NORTH OF AKSAI RIVER IN SUP-
PORT OF GERMAN TANK ATTACK IN THE KOTELNIKOVO
AREA. SECOND ALTERNATIVE EIGHTY MILES SOUTHWEST
OF STALINGRAD. GENERALLEUTNANT VON HOTHZZZZZ

AM

CR   150700/12/42

Holding the piece of paper that a Soviet radio operator had just passed to him, Jack Towers quickly jotted the Russian equivalent at the bottom, and a minute later, he entered the briefing bunker where Krasilov and his pilots had gathered to go over the day's next mission. Krasilov's mood seemed to have improved from the day before. The Soviet colonel was laughing loudly as he and Andrei slammed two empty vodka glasses on a wooden table.

Krasilov's face was streaked with oil from a heavy leak in one of the last few La-3s on the base. Krasilov, as Andrei had told him earlier that chilly morning, had gone on a two-plane hunting trip looking for Germans, but instead of taking one of the new Aircobras, the stubborn colonel had opted for a weathered La-3 instead. As it turned out, the engine began to leak oil shortly after takeoff, and Krasilov had to make an emergency landing.

As Jack got closer to the table, he could see the imprints of Krasilov's oily fingers on the empty glass. His flying helmet, also stained with oil, lay on the table next to a thick belt with a holstered pistol. The Russian colonel lifted his head.

"Ah, comrades, look. It's the impatient virgin!"

Some of the men roared with laughter. Two fell to the floor and slapped the top of their legs with mirth. Andrei slowly shook his head.

Jack reddened for a moment before sitting across from a snickering Krasilov. The smile froze on the Russian's face as Jack stared at him and slid the piece of paper across the table. The Russian's scarred forehead wrinkled as he narrowed his eyes.

"This just came in for me, Colonel."

Krasilov read on for a minute, then his face turned red. He abruptly got up, tipping his chair and stomping his large fists on the table.

"It's too late to intercept! What took this message so long to get here?"

"It went through a lot of hands to reach this side of the world, Colonel."

"Well, it's useless! The fighting starts in a half hour and it's over seventy-five miles away. We won't get there in time!"

Krasilov picked up his chair and sat back down. His face showed obvious frustration. This time it was Jack's turn to smile.

"You're overlooking one important fact, Colonel."

Krasilov briefly studied Jack. The ends of the Russian's thick eyebrows dropped a bit. "What's on your mind?"

Jack reached for the bottle of vodka, which also had Krasilov's oily imprints, took a sip, and set it down in front of him. "Even if your fighters don't get there in time to help the ground troops, you can still get there after the German planes have exhausted their fuel and ammunition . . . and simply shoot them down."

Krasilov remained silent. Everyone else in the room quieted down. For a few seconds, the only sound inside the bunker was the crack and fizzle of the stove and the constant wail of the wind outside. Then Krasilov got up slowly, glanced down at Jack once more, and scanned the room.

"Everyone to his plane! Now!"

The men rushed outside the bunker. Jack remained seated. He felt Krasilov's eyes on him. "Are you coming, Captain?"

"I'm not allowed to engage in battle, sir. My orders are strictly to—"

"You mean to tell me you get information like this and come up with this clever idea, and then you, a pilot with a plane ready to fly outside, are just going to sit and listen to the radio?"

"Colonel, I've been ordered not to—"

Krasilov exhaled. "You are a virgin after all."

Jack clenched his teeth as Krasilov walked outside. The Russian stopped by the doorway and turned around. "You wouldn't mind if I take your *Impatient Virgin*, ah, Captain? A plane without a pilot is like a woman without a husband. Perhaps she will grow to like me better than you."

Jack tried to control his anger but failed. Krasilov had crossed the line. He could take the colonel's bad attitude toward him, a sarcastic remark here and there, but not that. It was bad enough he had been sent to this godforsaken place to freeze to death, but he was not going to put up with the colonel's harassment any longer.

"The fuck I do mind, you hardheaded, egotistical bastard! You keep your damn hands off my plane! I'll fly it myself!" Jack stormed past Krasilov and headed for his plane.

Krasilov went after him. Jack picked up his pace and got to his Aircobra before Krasilov got a chance to catch up. As Jack stepped up to his plane, Krasilov extended his arms in the air.

"Listen, everyone! Listen!"

All the other pilots, including Natalya and three other women working on the engine of the La-3 Krasilov had flown earlier that morning, turned their heads.

"Today," Krasilov said in a sarcastic, half-humorous tone, "we'll be honored by having Captain Jack Towers from the United States Army Air Corps come along with us!"

"Who's gonna be his wingman, Colonel?" screamed Andrei from the cockpit of his Aircobra. "We're already teamed up in pairs."

Krasilov's smile grew wide. Jack didn't like the looks of it. "We're gonna let one of our own virgins fly with the American virgin. Natalya! You will be Captain Tower's wingman today!"

The pilots burst into a loud laugh along with Krasilov. Jack grinned and glanced at Natalya. Their gaze met. Jack winked. Natalya threw down the rag in her hands and headed over to an La-3 parked next to the one she was working on.

Jack shrugged, donned a parachute, and crawled inside the Aircobra's cockpit. He was airborne five minutes later. "Stay on my tail no matter what, Natalya," he said over the radio.

"You worry about the Germans in front of you, Jack," Natalya replied as she kept her fighter plane slightly behind and to his right. "I'll handle the rear."

TEN MILES NORTH OF THE AKSAI RIVER • DECEMBER 15, 1942

Jack Towers watched Krasilov take the lead with his wingman, Andrei. He cut back the throttle and let Krasilov get a thousand feet in front of him. Airspeed was three hundred knots, and the plane felt just right. The trimming on both throttle and elevons was as it should be, reducing to a minimum the effort Jack had to exert on the stick to maintain a level flight. He glanced backward and saw Natalya glued to his left.

"Up above, Jack!" he heard her voice crackling through his headset.

"What? Where?"

"Germans. Nine o'clock. About three thousand feet up."

Jack squinted. Even though he wore sunglasses, the glare from the early-morning sun filtering through the curved canopy glass stung his eyes. A few more seconds, and he spotted them.

"Damn! Look at them! It must be at least . . ."

"I'm counting over thirty planes, free hunters," Krasilov shouted.

"Scramble! Work in pairs! Dive-bombers are the highest priority!"

Jack slammed full throttle, jammed the stick back, and lifted the trigger-guard case. The Gs piled up on him as his craft roared higher at great speed. The altimeter dashed above nine thousand feet . . . ninety-five hundred . . . ten thousand. Airspeed quickly began to decrease. Jack lowered the nose by a few degrees and pointed it toward the rightmost Stuka formation, but he didn't get much farther in his pursuit. The escorting Gustavs broke flight in all directions. One of them made an inverted dive right turn and threatened to come around on Jack's tail. Jack broke left, rolled the plane on its side, and faced the incoming Gustav head-on while quickly verifying that Natalya was still with him. She was.

The Gustav was less than a thousand feet away and closing at great speed. Jack squeezed the trigger as he coordinated the rudder, ailerons, and elevons to keep the German aligned in his sights. The 37mm blasts started, two per second. The mighty recoil pounded against the entire fuselage, giving Jack the impression of having a second heartbeat in his chest. He noticed the airspeed indicator needle quivering with every burst. For a second he wasn't sure if it was just the vibrations from the recoil, or if the powerful guns actually had enough energy to slow down the plane momentarily. It didn't matter. His airspeed had already gone through the roof at 410 knots, way beyond the safe envelope.

The Gustav grew larger. Jack could now see the muzzle flashes from the nose-mounted cannon. There were no hits. Jack waited until the last minute before pulling up . . . and the German also pulled up!

"Jack!" he heard Natalya scream.

Instinctively, Jack swung the stick right and forward. For a brief second his entire field of view was nothing but the large cross painted on the underside of the Messerschmitt's left wing. Jack thought he was going to collide. In a blur, the Gustav's gray underside grazed his canopy as he heard the loud thump from the tail wheel striking his rudder. It was over before his mind got a chance to register it all. He had come within inches of disaster.

Jack snapped his head back as he applied both left and right rudder. The tail was not damaged, and the Messerschmitt had gone for a steep dive

"Stay with me, Natalya!"

Without giving any further thought to his near destruction, Jack pressed full power and hauled the stick back. His body was slammed down as the Gs tore at him. His vision became a narrow tunnel, but it didn't last long. The moment he reached the top of the loop, blood rushed back to his head. He continued the rear pressure until he was pointing straight down, and centered the stick. Airspeed went above 420 knots again. The craft trembled. The vibrations on the stick were getting out of control.

"Jack! We're going too fast!"

"Slow down now, Natalya, and he'll get away," he said in the most confident voice he could fake.

The Gustav continued its dive, and Jack, topping nearly 450 knots, caught up fast, but at the same time, he was dropping at a staggering rate. With sweat rolling into the corners of his eyes, Jack saw the altimeter dip below five thousand feet. The Aircobra plunged into a cloud. Jack lost the German for a second, acquiring again as he left the cloud behind.

Five hundred feet. The gap between the planes was being closed too fast. Three hundred feet . . . two hundred . . . The Gustav remained on his dive. Jack cut back power and squeezed the trigger.

The Gustav pulled up while breaking hard left. The sun flashed off the Gustav's wings as Jack tried to follow it; but outspeeding the German by a hundred knots, Jack found his craft making a wider turn than he liked. Instead of cutting back power to get some relief from the titanic centrifugal force that made his limbs feel five times his weight, Jack added throttle and instantly saw his vision reduced to a small dot—his body's warning that he was pushing maximum G. Anything more and he would either pass out . . . or the wings of the Aircobra would fold. Neither happened. Jack's gamble worked. He kept on pursuing, and as he completed the turn and leveled off, he was only three hundred feet from the German at roughly the same airspeed.

The Gustav pulled up in full throttle. Jack saw condensation pour off the wingtips as the Gs blasted over the Messerschmitt struggling for altitude. He stayed with it.

Another two turns, a throttle adjustment, and a final turn, and Jack opened fire. This time it was easier. A few short bursts, and the Gustav arched down toward the ground, leaving a trail of smoke on its path. Jack saw no parachute, and glanced back and noticed that Natalya was still with him.

"Good flying, Natalya!" he said in a more naturally confident voice.

"Good shooting, Jack."

Jack pointed his craft back toward the Stukas, who continued to fly in formation toward the Soviet tanks north of the Aksai River. He approached a Stuka from its most vulnerable spot: the rear underside. It was the rightmost plane of the rightmost formation. As two small clouds of black smoke bellowed from the exhausts and wafted away in the slipstream, Jack let go several rounds. A river of holes exploded across the Stuka's right wing before it broke apart from the fuselage. Jack cut left, dove to three thousand feet, made a 360, and as the Stuka spun down to earth, he advanced the throttle, tugged back the control stick, and aligned the next dive-bomber.

"Left, Jack. Break left!" Natalya screamed as she broke right.

Jack automatically responded to Natalya's shouts while moving his head in all directions to find . . . there! Another Gustav diving toward him. The craft caught him broadside. Natalya was trying a 360 to get the German fighter before it got Jack.

The muzzle flashes started. Jack had to figure a way to get out of the German's line of fire before he got closer. He briefly glanced at Natalya coming to his rescue at full speed, but she would be several seconds too late.

Instincts took over. As the rapidly approaching dark green Messerschmitt became hazy behind the bright flashes of its cannon's guns, Jack idled the throttle, added flaps, and dropped the gear. Airspeed quickly plummeted to two hundred knots, and two seconds later the Gustav zoomed past Jack's field of view at great speed, too fast for Jack to fire, but close enough for him to go in pursuit. The German went into a steep climb.

Gear and flaps up, full throttle, stick back, and the sun bathed his canopy as he pointed his nose at the heavens. The Gustav was pushing for altitude five hundred feet above him. Jack squinted at the glare, but it was not the sun. There was something else reflecting the bright light. Something flying very high.

Jack applied full power and slammed the stick to the right to close the gap on the departing Messerschmitt Me 109G. The Gustav went into another vertical climb while executing a left corkscrew. The palms of his hands moist inside his gloves, Jack pulled the stick back and felt his eyeballs about to burst from the Gs. His vision temporarily reddened and got cloudier while rivulets of sweat tricked down his forehead, but he did not ease on the rear pressure or power. He followed the Me 109G all the way up to eleven thousand feet before the Gustav tried to shake Jack off by executing an inverted dive to the left.

Jack momentarily eased back the throttle, pushed the stick hard over to the left, and slammed full power once more. In the corner of his eye he spotted Natalya on the La-3 getting so close to him that for a second he thought she was going to ram him, but she didn't. She executed the maneuver beautifully and stayed slightly behind and to his right.

He had the Gustav in his sights. Jack let go a short burst of the powerful 37mm nose-mounted cannon. The Aircobra shuddered with every blow as the all-aluminum structure absorbed the M4 cannon's powerful recoil once every two seconds. It took six bursts before the Gustav fell apart. Several rounds pierced through the rear fuselage, tearing off the tail and the left wing with a bright flash. The sky in front of him suddenly filled with fire. Jack pulled left and noticed Natalya breaking right. The wreckage was still too thick to fly through.

Jack scanned the skies for Natalya but couldn't find her. He half rolled the Aircobra to the left and back in the direction of the fallen Gustav. She had gone the other way and the sky was filled with . . . there she was . . . with a Gustav diving toward her!

"Natalya! Break left! Left!"

The Soviet woman did and barely missed the cannons of the Gustav as it leveled off behind her. The Messerschmitt closed for the kill. Jack saw Natalya desperately going for a steep climb and turn, but the Gustav easily imitated the maneuver and opened fire again.

"Invert and dive right, Natalya! Now!"

She did, and the Gustav followed, and he followed the Gustav. Natalya completed the dive and pulled up at less than three hundred feet above ground, with the Gustav on her tail. Jack closed the gap . . . so close that he could almost touch the Gustav's vertical fin. The dangerously low altitude at which the trio had pulled out of the dive didn't sink in until a few seconds later. Jack's concentration was so intense that he had nearly blocked everything else from his mind. Natalya's change of direction had gone from a shallow to a very intense and abrupt tight left turn. Her wingtip was less than twenty feet from the treetops. The Gustav was beginning to have a hard time keeping up, and so did Jack.

He glanced at the altimeter. Fifty feet. Natalya briefly leveled off, and so did the Gustav, but Jack already had an angle on the Messerschmitt even before the Gustav's wings became flushed with the horizon.

Another five bursts from the cannon at such close distance, and the Gustav went up in a ball of orange flames.

"Good flying, Natalya!"

"Thank you, Jack. Thanks, really."

She reduced airspeed enough to let him get by and take the lead once more. Jack pulled up and began a steep climb, when directly above him he saw something zooming across the sky at great speed. Whatever it was had come and gone in a couple of seconds.

"What in the hell was that?"

"I saw it too, Jack. Can't tell, but there were two of them."

Puzzled, Jack scanned the skies, and saw Krasilov and Andrei closing in on another Gustav. There were three other pairs in the air, each with their hands full, but they were all normal planes . . . there it went again. This time Jack got a good look at them.

"They're jet aircraft!"

"What?"

"Jets, Natalya. Airplanes without propellers using jet propulsion technology! Sweet Jesus!"

The pair of fighters dashed past a group of scattered clouds and closed in on Krasilov and Andrei.

"Watch out, Colonel! You've got two on your tail!"

Jack noticed Krasilov breaking hard left as the two jets made a quick pass from behind.

"I'm hit! I'm hit!" Jack heard Andrei scream over the radio.

"Andrei, this is Jack. Can you make it to the base?"

"I'm not sure, Jackovich. I still got some power but the smoke . . . I can't see through it."

"I'll tell you what. Don't pull back throttles. We're only ten minutes away. I'll come up on your right side and take you all the way home. Once over the field you can cut back power and glide your way in. The Aircobras float beautifully."

"Thanks, Jackovich."

At four thousand feet, Jack saw Andrei's plane, followed by a river of smoke a mile ahead of him. He was about to add throttle when something zoomed past him. It was the second jet, and it was headed directly for Andrei. A moment later the Russian's plane caught fire.

"Turn the plane over and drop, Andrei!" Jack heard Krasilov scream over the radio as he watched Andrei's craft in a steep climb. The fighter inverted, and the nose dropped a few degrees. Jack held his breath, waiting for Andrei to leave the burning craft, but no one dropped.

"Get out of there, dammit!" screamed Jack.

"I can't . . . the canopy! The bullets bent it! It's jammed . . . it won't give . . . the flames! My back is on fire! My legs!"

Jack watched as Andrei's cockpit filled with smoke first, then with fire. The Aircobra went into a dive, but to Jack's utter surprise, it was not an uncontrollable dive.

"I'm burning! I'm burning! . . . Stick left! Rudder left . . . stick forward!"

Jack was speechless. He could see clearly the inside of the cockpit filled with flames and Andrei's blazing figure talking himself into the last few maneuvers. In his agony, the young Russian had kept his hand pressed on the radio transmit button.

Jack saw the target, a slower Me 110 twin-engine fighter. Andrei's plane, now totally ablaze, dashed across the sky like a comet and approached the Me 110 at great speed. The Messerschmitt tried to break left, but not soon enough. With a final cry of despair, Jack heard Andrei curse the Germans as both planes exploded in a spectacular ball of flames and debris.

Jack saw the two jets depart the area. He didn't even attempt to pursue. Krasilov was in trouble. With all the commotion with the jets, a Gustav had managed to sneak behind the Soviet colonel.

"Hang in there, Colonel. I'm on my way!" screamed Jack as he set the craft in a vertical dive and closed in on the Messerschmitt.

The negative Gs pushing him up against the Aircobra's restraining harness, Jack lined up the Gustav and fired a short burst from the wings' 12.7mm guns. Nothing. He closed in a bit more. Krasilov pulled up and rose to the sky like an elevator. The German did likewise, and Jack and Natalya followed along.

"Take the shot, Captain! Get this Hitlerite bastard off my tail!"

"Trying, Colonel. I'm fucking trying. On my mark break hard right. Hard right. Got that?"

"Got it."

"Three . . . two . . ." Jack broke hard right and cut back throttle. "One . . . now!" Jack was now flying parallel to them.

Krasilov broke right. Jack swung the stick left and caught the German broadside. The pilot realized he'd been tricked just as Jack opened fire with the 37mm cannon at less than fifty feet. The Gustav came apart. Jack and Natalya flew through the flames and emerged on the other side.

The trio climbed to five thousand feet and were soon joined by three more pairs. Behind, they left the still-blazing wreckage of the Me 110 and Andrei's Aircobra, along with five destroyed Gustavs and three Stukas. The remaining Stukas were already out of sight and out of reach. Everyone had barely enough fuel to make it back to base. Not only had they lost Andrei, but they had not been able to stop the bulk of the Stuka force from reaching the Soviet front lines.

KALACH AIRFIELD, TWENTY MILES WEST OF THE STALINGRAD POCKET • DECEMBER 15, 1942

Jack taxied his airplane into the three-sided shelter, turned it around, idled the engine, and cut back the air/fuel mixture. The propeller stopped. He powered down the magnetos and the master switch, unstrapped his upper and lower safety harness, removed his parachute, pulled the canopy open, and climbed outside.

He walked over to Natalya's La-3. She was climbing down with her parachute still on her back.

"Your parachute," he said, pointing to her back.

She nodded, unstrapped it, and threw it inside the cockpit. "What a terrible thing, Jack," she said, jumping on the frozen ground. He noticed the lines down her cheeks. She had been crying. "I was very close to his older brother."

"The one missing in action?"

"Yes. Now Andrei . . ." Natalya lowered her gaze and slowly walked away. Jack was about to follow her, but decided against it. She needed her privacy.

That afternoon, Jack walked inside the briefing bunker and saw a lonely Krasilov behind a half-drunk bottle of vodka. Jack noticed the pad and pencil next to two crumpled sheets on the side of the table.

"Mind if I join you, Colonel?"

Krasilov pointed at a chair across the table. Jack took it while Krasilov slid the bottle over to his side. Jack took a sip, letting the liquid warm his mouth and throat before swallowing it. He took a second sip and eased back on the chair.

"I'm very sorry about Andrei, Colonel. I understand he was a close friend."

Krasilov's bloodshot eyes stared directly at him. "He was a good friend, Captain. He has a mother and three sisters living in Moscow. His older brother went missing some time back. Now I'm left with the burden of writing to them, but as you can see, the words are not there. That poor woman has now lost *two* sons."

Jack exhaled and took another sip. His chest felt warm. He slid the bottle back to Krasilov, who took a long swig, swallowed it, and took an even longer second. The Russian set the bottle down.

"Andrei was a fine warrior, Captain Towers."

"Call me Jack, Colonel."

Krasilov grinned slightly. "I go by Aleksandr. Now, listen, Jackovich . . . about today. What you did . . ."

"You would have done the same for me."

"Probably not before today."

Jack shrugged.

"You fly well, Jackovich. The American Air Corps has good pilots and good machines."

"Thanks."

"The . . . *Impatient Virgin* . . . why?"

Jack smiled. "Named it after a girl I met while in flying school. She was pretty wild, as you can imagine."

"Hmm," Krasilov retorted as he drank more vodka. "Might as well enjoy it while you're young. Before life hardens your heart."

Jack narrowed his eyes as Krasilov lowered his gaze and fixed it on the bottom of the bottle.

"The war will be over soon, Aleksandr. After that we shall all be able to get on with our lives."

Krasilov leveled his gaze with Jack and breathed deeply. "Maybe that's something you can do, Jackovich, since there is no war in your motherland, but here there won't be much left for us after the war."

"But surely you must have a family, Aleksandr. A wife maybe, or a brother or sister?"

Jack saw pained expressions brushing over Krasilov's face. The Russian took another swig, set the bottle down, and began to speak, slowly and moderately. Although the context of his words was appalling, his tone never changed. When he finished, he took another swig.

"I'm deeply sorry about your wife and daughters, Aleksandr. I had no idea."

"It happened a long time ago. It's all right now. You have a cigarette, Jackovich?"

Still a bit stunned from the revelation, Jack reached for his pack of American cigarettes and handed them to Krasilov, along with a lighter. The Russian briefly inspected the colorful design of the package before pulling out a cigarette.

"Chesterfields? What does that mean?"

"I have no idea."

Krasilov lighted up and took a draw. He narrowed his eyes, exhaled, and took another draw.

"Something wrong?" Jack asked.

Krasilov stared at the cigarette, tore off the filter, took another long draw, and closed his eyes. "Now, *this* is a cigarette."

Jack stared at the filter on the table before looking back at the burly Russian. "By the way, Aleksandr, you've got yourself one hell of a pilot in Natalya. She is very good behind the stick."

Krasilov exhaled. "But she's a woman. I need someone I can depend on as my partner up there, not some shrinking violet that might come apart during a critical situation."

"Well, I'll have to say that she is *exactly* the type of wingman I would like to have. Someone who would stick to me in all weather. Today she did just that, Aleksandr. You should give her a chance." Jack got up. "I'll leave you to your privacy, my friend. Again, I'm truly sorry about Andrei, and about your family."

Krasilov nodded. Jack walked outside. The morning clouds had broken, and the sun now warmed the airstrip. Jack inhaled deeply. The air was cold, but he could breathe it without much trouble. The thermometer outside the bunker read five below zero.

Pulling up the lapels of his jacket, Jack glanced at the fighters parked along the side of the runway behind the three-sided shelters. He stopped and smiled, spotting Natalya standing with a bucket under the engine of the La-3 she had flown that morning. Jack walked in her direction. Her back was to him.

"You're going to be an ace one of these days, Natalya Makarova."

Startled, Natalya spun around, spilling the contents of the bucket by her feet.

"Jack! Look what you made me do! You scared me!"

Jack smiled. Natalya was indeed naturally pretty. The dazzling hazel eyes inspected him. Jack thought he could look into her soul through them. His physical attraction for her went beyond anything he'd felt before. Jack wasn't sure if it was because she was so pretty, or if it was because she was so different from any other woman he'd ever known. Natalya was a woman of substance, and she also seemed to love flying as much as Jack did. He decided that was a very hard combination to find.

She lowered her gaze and picked up the bucket. "Here, now you'll have to help me."

"Help you do what?"

"Just hold the bucket right under . . . here."

Jack picked up the heavy cast-iron bucket and placed it exactly where Natalya told him, beneath the La-3's radiator drainage plug.

Natalya pulled the plug and let the steamy-hot water pour into the bucket. "Steady, Jack."

"Easy for you to say. You're not the one holding it."

"Hmm hmm, I guess I'm gonna have to get one of my Russian comrades with real muscles to—"

"Just keep pouring."

Natalya grinned. "There. You can set it down now."

"What's this for?" he asked as he straightened his back and rubbed his shoulders.

"You're about to find out, Jack." Natalya tousled her hair and leaned forward. "See that other bucket next to the landing gear?"

"Yeah, what about it?"

"It's filled with snow. Bring it over and pour some hot water into it until it gets warm."

Smiling at her ingenuity, Jack did so. Inside the large bucket was a small pint-sized pot. Jack used it to pour water on Natalya's head as she leaned over.

She pulled out a bar of soap and worked up a lather as Jack poured a little more water over her head. After a few moments, he poured some more to rinse it off.

Natalya stood up, pulled her hair back, and wrapped it with a towel. "Thanks, Jack."

He smiled. "Thank *you*, Natalya."

EIGHTY MILES SOUTHWEST OF THE STALINGRAD POCKET • DECEMBER 16, 1942

Firmly clutching a weathered machine gun he had taken from a fallen German soldier weeks ago, Aris Broz moved swiftly and quietly on a dry ravine that bordered the road where he was certain German panzers would soon be crossing through.

His sheepskin-covered boots sank deep in the snowbank as he struggled to keep his balance and move forward for another ten feet before stopping to listen. His trained ears searched for noises other than the howl of the wind sweeping through the trees, yet they detected nothing.

He continued.

Trained in the classic hit-and-run Partisan tactics by his father, who was posthumously named a hero of the Soviet Union for taking out an entire squadron of Germans before turning the gun on himself to avoid being captured alive, and by his uncle, the famous Yugoslav Josip Broz, known by his comrades in arms as Tito, the thirty-year-old Aris considered himself a Partisan in the true sense of the word. He was not Russian by birth. He was Yugoslav, although no one could tell by his accent—something that was useful during recruiting trips. And, of course, he was a Broz. Tito himself had sent Aris to these regions with orders to recruit fresh troops among the men and women of the western Ukraine and eastern Russia, and train them in the art of guerrilla warfare to fight the Germans in the region.

Most of the recruits were peasants, people who had lost everything to the Germans, including loved ones. They were people who
had nothing to lose and an uncompromising will to fight to the
death. Aris had seen fifteen- and sixteen-year-old girls turned into
women overnight after Germans had raped them, and they had
subsequently joined Aris's Partisan force with a desire to learn to
fight back that even Aris himself found extreme. Those were his
soldiers, his guerrillas, his Partisans. Missions ranged from minor
ambushes of German motorcyclists carrying messages to and from
the front, to the destruction of bridges, roads, railroads, and anything else that disrupted the flow of supplies to the German forces.

To accomplish these tasks Aris would spread his warriors in small
groups of six or seven on the outside. His logic was simple: If the
mission backfired, the loss of soldiers and equipment could be easily
replaced in a week's time. It also allowed him to strike multiple
targets in synchronized fashion to give the enemy the impression
of being attacked by a much larger force.

Sometimes, when a mission called for a large number of Partisans, Aris would be careful enough to divide the large group into
small subgroups, or packs, each with its own independent escape
route.

For Aris and his guerrillas, stealth and surprise meant survival.
Capture meant torture, mutilation, and hanging. That was the grim
fate of captured Partisans. In addition to the risk of his soldiers
being captured, the Germans had recently added another dimension to the Partisan war. They had set a strict set of guidelines that
defined how many innocent peasants—women and children included—were to be executed on the spot for a particular type of
Partisan crime. The loss of one German soldier usually meant the
hanging of ten or more civilians picked at random off the streets of
cities or villages. The new German directive was, of course, created
with the hope that it would force the Partisans to slow down or
even stop their attacks, but in the few months since its implemen-
tation the opposite had happened. More and more peasants had
approached Aris with the wish to be trained to fight the Germans.

Yes, the Germans would butcher captured Partisans, but the opposite held true. Aris had seen many German soldiers putting pistols to their heads when surrounded by Partisans, and that suited Aris just fine.

His Partisans were many in numbers, but none of them were with Aris on that chilly and humid morning as he continued uphill for another hundred meters before checking for enemy tanks once more. This time he heard them coming. With a grin on his face, the Yugoslav guerrilla leader set the machine gun next to a tree and removed a sack hanging from his back. There was a handful of explosives in there. Not enough to destroy a tank, but simply destroying a tank wasn't his mission that day. Aris had chosen something much more dangerous than that and had opted to do it alone. The risk was too high, and besides, he moved better alone. He knew the forest—every square inch of it. He knew where the hideouts were, sources of food, shelter . . . and weapons. Aris always had weapons hidden everywhere, and all his soldiers knew of their locations. It was a contingency that had saved a number of his guerrillas' lives in the past.

Aris cautiously walked up the side of the ravine and reached the edge of the frozen road. His heavy gloves made his work cumbersome, but he had no choice. At forty below, his fingers would have crystallized and fallen off after a few minutes of exposure.

First, he strapped a grenade to the trunk of a large tree that leaned in the direction of the road. He attached a thin wire to the safety pin and ran it across the narrow road to the other side, where he secured it around another tree. He walked back across the road and slid an explosive pack between the grenade and the tree. He lifted his head and looked down the road. The tanks were getting closer. Any moment now the lead tank would clear the turn in the road.

Quickly, Aris removed two bottles filled with gasoline. He poured half of the contents of the first on the booby-trapped tree, then ran a river of gas toward the middle of the road, where he emptied the second bottle.

Aris quickly stepped around the large puddle of gas and ran to the side. He slid down to the ravine and sprinted away from the trap until he estimated he was a few hundred yards from it. Then he stopped, climbed up to the side of the road, and waited.

He didn't have to wait for long. Bellowing clouds of blue smoke from its harsh engine exhausts, the first panzer tank came sweeping down the road, closely followed by several soldiers on foot, while others clung to the sides of the armored turret. The smoke swirled over the soldiers' heads and soon joined the smoke from two other tanks, along with several open trucks carrying loads of soldiers. Aris could clearly see the rows of steel-helmeted heads behind the truck.

He held his breath the moment the tank got near the wire . . .

The bright explosion had the desired effect. The tree plummeted over the lead tank, rolled in front of it, and caught on fire. The river of gas turned into a river of fire that ended under the tank. In seconds, the entire underside was in flames, along with the burning tree blocking the road.

The driver and the gunner pushed open the hatch and quickly crawled outside. Two of the soldiers hanging on to the sides caught fire. Aris could hear their guttural screams drifting across the frozen woodland while other soldiers threw snow and blankets over them.

Aris smiled broadly and slid back down to the bottom of the ravine. His father and his uncle would have been proud of him.

As he left the screaming Germans behind, Aris heard something overhead. The forest was too thick to make out what it was. The sound definitely was not that of a plane, but of something else.

Aris's smiled washed away the moment a German plane dropped from the sky and cleared the way for the panzer column with its cannons. He was both furious and also surprised. He had never seen a plane like that. Not only did the craft lack propellers, but it had the firepower to slice a panzer in half.

It didn't matter. For Aris, a plane was a plane, and it was coming back down again. Aris pulled up his machine gun and aimed it at the incoming . . . the craft rushed past his field of view at such speed that Aris didn't have time to let go a single shot. What kind of fighter was that? Did the Germans finally come up with some of the revolutionary weapons that their propaganda officials claimed they had for so long? Aris was not a pilot, but he could guess the type of damage a craft like that could have on the Allied air force.

He slid down the ravine and raced back toward his camp. The word would be passed around. If the German propellerless craft were hidden somewhere in the region, Aris had no doubt his Partisans would find them, and destroy them.

THE SKIES EIGHTY MILES SOUTHWEST OF THE STALINGRAD POCKET • DECEMBER 16, 1942

"Stay with me, Natalya!" screamed Jack as he set his craft in a vertical dive. The Me 109G Gustavs were still in formation several hundred feet below surrounding the Stukas.

Information on the German attack had come sooner this time around, giving Krasilov's free hunters plenty of time to prepare. There were a total of five pairs in the air from Krasilov's fighter wing alone, including Jack and Natalya.

The Gustavs scrambled while the Stukas remained in formation. Jack picked a Gustav and closed in. The Aircobra trembled as Jack pushed it beyond four hundred knots. The wail of the engine rang in his ears as the soul-numbing vibrations made it harder for him to get the right angle. The Gustav went for a vertical climb and turn. Jack pulled back throttle momentarily and swung the stick back. The Gs blasted on his shoulders. His vision reddened, and his palms were sweaty, but he remained on the Gustav's tail. At five thousand feet the Messerschmitt went for a dive. Jack almost pulled back throttle to avoid ramming it, but decided against it. *Reduce throttle now and you'll never catch him, Jack,* he told himself as he floated his plane right up to the Gustav's tail and opened fire with the 37mm cannon.

The tail blew up in pieces, and the craft went into a flat spin. Jack broke right. Natalya followed him. He spotted another Me 109G to his left and swung the control stick in that direction. The wickedly tight turn pressed him against the seat with such might that Jack could barely keep his hand on the throttle control valve.

The Gustav's tail was a few hundred feet straight ahead.

"All yours, Natalya!"

"Wh . . . what?"

"Go, go! It's your kill!" Jack pulled back throttle just a dash to let her take the lead. The Gustav went for a dive. Natalya waved as she dashed past him, inverted her plane, and dove straight down on the Gustav. Jack had a hard time following the maneuver, but he remained on her tail. The Gustav went for a turn and climb. Natalya remained locked on its tail but was not firing yet. She got closer. Jack understood. She wanted to take the Messerschmitt in one burst.

She did, and the Gustav's nose was covered with smoke. Natalya broke left and so did Jack. She searched for another target and found it: a Gustav on Krasilov's tail.

"Break left, Colonel! Left!"

Krasilov and his wingman turned in opposite directions, but the Gustav stayed with the Russian colonel, who turned, dove, and abruptly executed a loop-the-loop.

Natalya inched her way toward the Gustav until she was less than fifty feet away. As she opened fire, Jack spotted something in the corner of his right eye. It came and went in a flash, and for a brief second Jack also heard a thundering machine gun. When he looked down at Natalya's plane, he noticed that smoke spewed out of the front. He shifted his gaze to the sky and saw the German jet again. *Bastard!*

"Get out of there, Natalya!" he screamed as he saw the nose of her craft catch fire. "Jesus! Get out of there! Jump, dammit. Jump!"

They were flying at three thousand feet. Natalya inverted her plane and lowered the nose. Jack held his breath and saw her drop as the jet came back around, this time in Jack's direction.

As her bright red parachute opened, Jack went for a vertical climb to seven thousand feet. The German zoomed past him. Jack undid his restraining harness and turned his plane in its direction, but by the time he had done that, the jet had already completed a 270-degree turn and was approaching from his right. Jack veered the Aircobra to the right until he saw the jet head-on.

Jack's craft shook violently. He ducked under the windshield and continued to press the trigger of the 37mm nose cannon. The glass windshield shattered, and he was showered with it. The firing lasted but two seconds before Jack saw the grayish underside of the German jet dart over him. He sat up and put on his goggles. The windblast from the propeller nearly jerked his head back, and the frigid air numbed his face.

Jack looked for the German jet. He tilted his wings both ways, but the jet was out of sight. He looked down and saw Natalya reaching the woods. He exhaled in relief.

The sky was still filled with planes. "Aleksandr! Aleksandr!"

"Jackovich, I saw what happened."

"She's fine. She made it down."

"Jackovich! Behind you! Break right! Break—"

Krasilov's words were cut short by roaring cannons. Jack ducked again. The rear windshield, rated to sustain a direct hit from a 20mm cannon, was successful in deflecting the first few rounds before it collapsed, taking the overhead glass along. Once more Jack was bathed in crushed glass. The German scurried past him on his right side.

"Son of a bitch!" Jack cursed over the radio. The German had left him with a convertible Aircobra. *His Aircobra.* His *Impatient Virgin.*

Jack saw the jet returning for another pass. This time he had a plan. He put his craft in a shallow dive while pushing full throttle. Airspeed darted past four hundred knots. He let the German get on his tail.

Jack peeked behind him and saw the German approach at great speed. He waited.

"Break left, Jackovich! Break left!" Krasilov's voice crackled through his headset. Jack ignored his Russian friend and remained in a leveled flight. He waited just a little longer . . . *now!*

In the same swift move, Jack pulled back throttle and lowered flaps and landing gear. His airspeed plummeted by almost two hundred knots in under ten seconds. He crashed against the control panel, bounced, and slammed his back against his flight seat. A moment later the German plane's belly scrapped his tail as it pulled up to avoid a midair collision.

Partially disoriented from the blow, Jack tried to turn the nose in the direction of the departing jet, but the rudder wouldn't respond. He threw the stick to the left and forced the nose in its direction with ailerons, but instead, he wound up inverting the plane. For a second, the nose temporarily turned in the German's direction. Jack pressed the trigger and managed to fire a few rounds before the stick slipped away. He was not wearing his restraining harness and the canopy had been blown off. Jack dropped out the Aircobra.

In a flash, the powerful windblast crushed his chest as the craft remained inverted above him. The plane and earth switched positions while Jack, disoriented, struggled to find his rip cord. He slapped his right hand on his back but could not find it. *It has to be back there somewhere, Jack. Reach, reach, dammit!*

The peaceful sound of the wind whistling in his ears, Jack plummeted toward earth at a speed of 150 knots. His right hand was so far behind his back that he thought it was going to snap.

There!

Jack found it and pulled hard.

The canopy opened a few seconds later with a hard tug. He was roughly a thousand feet up and saw his Aircobra slowly arching toward the ground. It disappeared behind the trees, and the orange ball that followed foretold the end of his *Impatient Virgin*.

He tried to search for Natalya's canopy and spotted it about a mile to the north. He steered his parachute in that direction.

EIGHTY MILES SOUTHWEST OF THE STALINGRAD
POCKET • DECEMBER 16, 1942

Jack untangled himself from the silk parachute and pulled it down. He buried it in the snow and quickly began to feel the effect of the thirty-below weather. To both Krasilov's and Natalya's disapproval, he had not worn the heavier—and therefore bulkier—coat that was standard for all Soviet aviators, but had chosen his standard-issue USAAC leather jacket, which was good for keeping him warm in freezing temperatures, but not in the extreme cold of the Russian winter.

Snow clinging to the sides of his face, Jack began to move quickly to stay warm and headed in the direction where he had seen Natalya go down, but didn't get far. He spotted three figures roughly fifty feet ahead.

Instinctively, Jack dropped to the ground and reached for his handgun, a Colt .45, flipped the safety, and cocked it. The steel helmets protruding over the line of bushes told Jack all he needed to know. They were Germans, and they were probably looking for him.

He remained still as their guttural sounds filled the air. Jack didn't speak a word of German, so he had no idea what was being said, and besides, the German language was so rough that it was even hard for him to tell if the soldiers were shouting or simply talking to one another.

The soldiers got closer. His initial assessment had been accurate. There were three Germans and, to his relief, no dogs. The trio walked fifteen feet to his right. Jack had to move quickly or risk losing his limberness to the cold weather, which stung him hard. His arms and legs were shockingly cold. His hands were stiffening and his fingers losing sensation. A few more minutes and he probably would not be able to move them.

He took a chance. The Germans were thirty or so feet behind him now and their backs were to him. He got to his feet and took a few steps forward.

Snap!

A weathered branch under a thin layer of snow had given under his weight. The guttural voices intensified.

Jack broke into a run, the Colt firmly gripped in his right hand. He was about to reach a cluster of trees . . .

One, two, three bullets grazed past him and exploded in a cloud of bark as they struck a pine tree to his right. Their zooming sound rang in his ears long after they had lodged themselves in the tree.

Jack cut left and kept on running for another hundred feet as the noise behind him grew louder. The trees to both sides of him turned into a solid wall as his boots kicked the snow . . . the snow!

Only then he realized that no matter how fast he tried to get away, the Germans would merely follow his tracks. Sooner or later they would catch up with him.

Jack continued to run, but this time he searched for a break in the snow-covered woods. Perhaps . . . a frozen ravine!

That was it. With three more shots cracking through the frigid air, Jack raced past the frozen underbrush that led to a ten-foot-wide ravine. He could see water flowing under the ice, and there was no way for him to tell how thick the layer was, but he had to take a chance. The Germans were closing in on him.

He jumped over the ice and tried to run over it, but instead he slipped and fell facefirst. The blow stung and momentarily disoriented him. He felt a warm trickle of blood running down his forehead. For a few seconds everything appeared blurry.

Jack struggled to his feet and, instead of running, lunged forward and slid down on his belly for a few dozen feet until his momentum stopped. He stumped his feet against the ice to push himself to the opposite side of the ravine, and managed to reach a branch. He pulled himself up and was about to step on the snow by the edge, but stopped in time. Instead, Jack held on to a higher branch and swung his shivering body a few feet away, landed on his back, and rolled behind a tree as the Germans reached the ravine.

He looked for his Colt . . . his Colt! The last time he had it was when he fell . . .

"Amerikaine? Amerikaine! Hello, *Amerikaine!"*

Jack saw the German raise his Colt .45 in the air. Jack had his name engraved on the handle.

"Captain . . . Jack Towers? I have your weapon, Captain Towers! Come out with your hands above your head, and no harm will come to you! Resist, and you will be shot!" said one of the Germans in a heavily accented English.

In spite of the appalling cold, Jack wiggled his body into the snow, taking time to cover his legs and back. His arms were numb, and so were his legs. His fingers were swollen. The cold had made it into his body and was quickly stripping him of his life-supporting heat. If his temperature dropped any lower, Jack feared he would lose consciousness.

"Very well, then. Have it your way, Captain Towers!"

The Germans split three ways. Two went back to the opposite side of the ravine while the third entered the forest twenty feet from where Jack hid. Slowly, Jack reached down to his boot and gripped his numbed fingers around the black handle of a ten-inch steel blade. The pain from his fingers as he forced them to clutch the handle hurt more than the wound on his forehead from falling on the ravine.

He narrowed his eyes as the German, wearing a bulky white coat that dropped to his knees, turned in his direction. The muzzle of the machine gun held by the tall and thin soldier was pointed in his direction. Jack didn't move. He remained pressed against the ground as the German scanned the forest in front of him with the weapon before taking two more steps in Jack's direction. The cold was beginning to cloud his judgment. For a second he forgot the threat and simply stared in envy at the German's thick coat. He quickly forced his mind back and prayed that the snow over his legs and back was thick enough to disguise his presence. It appeared that way, because the soldier, after taking two more steps, turned his back to Jack.

The soldier now less than six feet away from him, Jack hesitated about attacking. Would his achingly cold body move swiftly enough to reach the German before he turned around? Jack wasn't sure, but he was certain of one thing: If he didn't move soon, he was going to freeze to death. He had to make his muscles work to get his circulation flowing.

The German remained still. The weapon pointed away from Jack.

Jack breathed the cold air once, exhaled, and breathed it again as he inched his legs forward to see how they would respond. They moved. Jack inhaled once more, recoiled, and lunged.

The German must have heard him, because halfway through his

attack, the soldier began to turn around, but it was too late. Jack kept the blade aimed for the neck and drove it in hard. Both men landed by the edge of the frozen ravine. The blade had only gone halfway inside the soldier's neck.

Their eyes locked. Jack jammed his numb right hand on the soldier's mouth as he fiercely palm-struck the knife's handle. The blade cut deeper into the German's throat until the handle met the soldier's windpipe. Jack knew that his palm should be hurting from the blow against the handle, but it didn't. Although he could still move his hands, he had lost sensation below the wrists.

The German went limp. Jack stood up and dragged him away from the ravine. His lips were trembling, and his cheeks twitched out of control. Hypothermia was slowly setting in. Jack needed protection quickly before he froze, before the cold seeped deeper into his core.

He leaned the dead German against a tree and pulled out his knife. The jagged edge cut a wider track on its way out, jetting blood over Jack's legs. He ignored it, set the bloody knife on the side, and undid the straps of the soldier's heavy woolen jacket. He removed it and quickly put it on. Next he slung the machine gun and . . .

"Hans? Hans?"

Jack's head snapped left. The other two Germans were back on the ravine. Jack got caught in plain view kneeling in the snow. One of the Germans looked straight at Jack and waved for a moment before realizing what had happened, and leveled the machine gun in his direction.

Leaving his knife behind, Jack jumped away as the slow rattle of the German's machine gun thundered in the woods and was followed by fierce explosions of snow. He got to his feet and reached a thick cluster of trees. The firing subsided. His back crashed hard against the trunk of a tree, and breathing heavily, he clutched the machine gun and glanced over his left shoulder. Gunfire erupted once more, shaving off the bark of the tree.

Son of a bitch!

His face was bleeding from the flying bark. Trying to control his quivering hands, he dropped to the ground, rolled away, and blindly opened fire in the Germans' general direction. It had the desired effect. Both Germans ran for cover, giving Jack enough time to reach a fallen log.

On his belly, Jack spread both legs, set the muzzle over the log, and waited. And waited. Minutes went by. Jack kept the gun trained on the trees protecting the soldiers. His face felt so cold, he couldn't feel it.

The German's jacket wasn't helping much either. Enough heat had escaped his body before he put on the jacket to keep him from getting warm again. Jack understood what that meant: He had lost the ability to warm himself back up. He had to get to a source of heat fast. His body was falling deeper into hypothermia.

One of the Germans ran to an adjacent tree. Jack tried to fire, but his index finger didn't respond fast enough. He missed the soldier by a few feet.

The second soldier now ran. Jack fired and missed again. He tried to shift the gun toward the new German hideout, but his arms wouldn't respond; his body wouldn't respond. He was convulsing.

One of the Germans came into plain view. Jack tried to fire but couldn't. He pressed his lips together and forced his index finger against the trigger, but it wouldn't move. It was frozen stiff!

Jack found it harder and harder to breathe now. Every gulp of air that entered his lungs felt like a hard, cold hammer squashing his chest and forcing the last remnants of heat out of his exhausted body. His vision became foggy, cloudy. The shadowy figures loomed in front of him.

Jack heard laughter mixed with the dreaded guttural words he couldn't understand, but this time he decided they were screaming, and in the middle of all the shouting he picked up the only word that his ears recognized: Hans, Hans! Jack had killed their comrade in arms. He knew the Germans would not be merciful.

His thoughts became fuzzy, irrational. His ears picked up several shots, and he tried to brace himself, but his arms only moved part of the way. His body was too rigid. Jack didn't feel any impact, and he couldn't feel most of his body. He could be bleeding to death at that moment and not even know it. He tried to find the shadows of the Germans, but they were gone. They had shot him and left him to bleed to death.

A shadow came up over him and began to lift him to his feet. Were the Germans dragging him away? Why not just let him die in the freezing woods?

Jack tried to open his mouth to say that he didn't care anymore, but his body was past the brink of exhaustion and would not respond to his commands. A sense of desolation took him over as he felt life slowly escaping him.

Slowly, very slowly, Jack surrendered himself to the Russian winter. Then all went dark.

"Is he alive?" Natalya asked while Aris Broz dragged Jack's body toward a pair of horses next to the ravine. Natalya rode on one with a heavy blanket thrown over her shoulders.

"Barely," he responded, hoisting Jack over the horse's mount, which was made of thick blankets. "I don't think he is going to make it."

Natalya looked at the craggy Partisan who had rescued her from a German patrol less than thirty minutes ago. "How far do we have to go?"

"It all depends. The nearest place where he could get any type of medical attention is over two hours away. I can tell you for certain he's not going to last that long."

"Dammit, Jack," Natalya cursed as she lowered her gaze to Jack's hunched-over figure. "I told you to wear warmer clothing!" She exhaled and looked back at Aris. "Where is the closest place that's protected from the elements?"

"The caves, but again. There is no medical . . ."

"How far away is that?"

"Just minutes away."

"Let's go!"

EIGHTY MILES SOUTHWEST OF THE STALINGRAD
POCKET • DECEMBER 16, 1942

With the help of three Partisans, Natalya Makarova quickly dragged
Jack's freezing body inside one of several huts built against the side
of a rocky hill.

"Get me some vodka!" she screamed as she set Jack down over
some blankets next to a gas lantern.

Aris ran outside, leaving the door open. A gush of cold air entered the hut. Natalya cursed out loud and rushed to close it.

Jack was still unconscious and extremely cold. She removed both
his jackets, his boots and pants, and began massaging his stiff legs
and arms, trying to get some blood to his purplish feet and hands.

Aris came in and closed the door behind him. He handed Natalya
a dark bottle. She removed the cork, took a sniff and brought it to
Jack's lips.

"Drink it, Jack."

She got no response. She put a few drops on his lips and saw his
tongue move.

"He needs immediate medical attention. A fire would probably
help him, but I'm afraid it's out of the question. There are too many
German patrols around," said Aris, feeling Jack's pulse. "There is,
however, another option to get heat into his body fast, but that's
really up to you, Natalya."

Aris turned and left the room. Natalya knew what she needed
to do if she was to save his life. Jack's body was so cold that his
core was not able to produce enough heat on its own to bring his
body temperature back up. Jack needed another heat source to ra-
diate warmth back into his body.

Natalya quickly removed the rest of his clothes. Jack braced himself and shivered. She covered his body with blankets before removing her clothes. First the wet boots, thick aviator pants and
jacket, followed by her undergarments. The nipples on her breasts
shriveled the moment she snapped off her brassiere.

Natalya maneuvered her pale, thin body under the blankets and
pressed Jack against her. Her body tensed the moment his cold

chest came in contact with her breasts, but she forced herself to remain like that. The skin of her stomach was against his; his face buried in her neck as she breathed heavily over his face to smother him with warmth. She parted his cold thighs and wedged her right leg in between his while rubbing her arms up and down his back. Heat radiated from her onto him.

Minutes went by. Natalya didn't stop. She continued to rub her entire self against him, until slowly, very slowly, Jack began to respond. His body became soft, still cold, but soft, relaxed. His breathing steadied. She could now feel his heartbeat pounding against her chest. She felt his arms pulling her tighter against him. She was his heat source. His body needed more of her to survive.

Time went by. Natalya saw Jack open his eyes, inhale deeply, and close them again. He was obviously drifting in and out of consciousness. Their body temperatures became one. She felt his fingers move on her back, and his toes against her legs.

Jack felt as if he was dreaming. The harsh cold wind had been replaced by a rhythmic warm breeze that caressed his neck. There was heat around him, and it felt good, cozy, intimate. He opened his eyes and realized where he was, and was instantly comforted by a familiar pair of hazel eyes a few inches away. He tried to speak, but she put a finger to his mouth.

"Shh . . . rest, my dear Jack. Rest."

Jack stared at Natalya's eyes as they reflected the flickering light of the gas lantern, which cast a yellow glow on her white Slavic face. The high cheekbones, full lips, and small chin looked majestic in the twilight of the room. Her powerful embrace was the most intimate Jack had ever felt. He never thought he could feel such complete union with a woman, and yet there was no sex involved, just the thrust of her lifesaving heat into him.

Slowly, all faded away. The face, the yellowish light, the eyes. Jack Towers quietly surrendered himself to the warm and soothing comfort of Natalya's nearness.

KALACH AIRFIELD, TWENTY MILES WEST OF THE STALINGRAD
POCKET • DECEMBER 16, 1942

Krasilov jumped out of his plane and raced for the communications bunker. The German jet craft was no match for their Aircobras or La-3s. The Soviets had not been able to stop the advancing Hitler-ites. The jet had taken two of his planes while the Gustavs took care of three more. Krasilov himself had been pursued by two Gus-tavs once, but had managed to escape their cannons by remaining close to a third Gustav.

How ironic, Krasilov thought. He had actually used one Gustav to shield himself from two others. The tactic worked beautifully. The pursuing Messerschmitts did not fire a single shot while he kept his Aircobra glued to the side of his German shield. But in spite of all that, the day had been a defeat for his free hunters. More than half his pilots didn't come back. The Germans had effectively pre-vented Krasilov's squadron from reaching the front lines.

Without air support, the Sixty-second Army of General Vasily Chuikov had no choice but to retreat. General von Hoth's panzers were now only forty miles from Stalingrad. If a corridor was estab-lished, he knew that Paulus's 250,000 soldiers would get enough supplies to keep the city through the rest of the winter.

Krasilov inhaled the relatively warm air inside the communica-tions bunker. They needed additional planes if they were to provide any type of air support. More planes and also a way to get rid of the annoying jets, although Jack had found a way that seemed to work . . . *Jackovich.*

Krasilov frowned. He also needed to make two more calls. One to the U.S. Army Air Corps advisor in the Kremlin, and a second to Major Chapman, who was currently training another air regi-ment one hundred miles north of Stalingrad.

Captain Jack Towers had been shot down. Krasilov knew the Americans would not react well to that. Jack's training role had been clear from the start. Krasilov felt responsible.

EIGHTY MILES SOUTHWEST OF THE STALINGRAD
POCKET • DECEMBER 16, 1942

That evening Jack Towers sat next to the fire outside the hut where he had slept most of the day. As Natalya had explained to him, German patrols were no longer in the area, making it safe to start a small fire. His body was rested, and to Natalya's amazement, he had survived without the need for an amputation. His fingers and toes were all pinkish. Jack had indeed been lucky. His mother had warned him about the Russian winter. Jack now understood her fears.

Jack took another draw from the strongest cigarette he had ever smoked in his life. At first, Aris and Natalya had smiled when he nearly turned green while smoking one earlier that afternoon, but as the day went on, he'd grown accustomed to the locally made unfiltered cigarettes.

"You're going to be all right, Jack," said Natalya, sitting next to him and smiling.

"Thanks, Natalya. I mean it."

She looked away and frowned.

"Hey, hey. What's the matter?"

Natalya didn't respond. She simply gazed down at her boots. Jack gently pulled up her chin. She was in tears.

"Look, Natalya. I'm really sorry you had to do that. I just want you to know that . . ."

"You were wonderful, Jack. You didn't take advantage. That's what makes it so hard . . ."

Now Jack was really confused. "I don't understand then, Natalya. What . . ."

"I promised myself I wouldn't fall for another pilot, Jack. Don't you see the kind of life we live? I lost a loved one once. I'm afraid to get close again!"

Her face disappeared in her hands. Jack put an arm around her and pulled her close. There wasn't much he could say. Natalya's fears were well-founded.

"Look, Natalya. The way I see it is that you must live life today, now, because there might not be a tomorrow. You're absolutely right. What we do up there is dangerous. Don't kid yourself about it. It's right damned dangerous, but someone's gotta do it, and for some reason that I still don't understand, you and I are among the lucky ones who get to do it. That's our fate. Our destiny. And fate will happen regardless of what you do today. So live for the day, Natalya. Worry about the future after the war is over."

Natalya lifted her head and kissed him on the cheek. "Thank you, Jack Towers. You are a decent man."

She got up.

"Where are you going?"

"To get some coffee."

Jack nodded and turned his head toward the fire. Natalya was a fine woman, Jack decided. A fine woman . . . and a fine pilot. Jack had a totally different opinion of Russian pilots. Unlike American and British pilots, who got to go home after a certain number of missions, the Soviets—and also the Germans for that matter—continued to fly until they either were shot down and permanently disabled, or killed. There was no minimum number of missions or a fixed-length tour of duty. Here you fought until it was over or you died, whichever came first.

"How are you feeling, Jackovich?"

Jack turned his head and stared at the thin—borderline emaciated—Aris. The Yugoslav held a bottle in his hands. He offered Jack a sip, but Jack kindly declined. Aris sat next to him.

"It's going to be another cold night, comrade Jackovich."

Jack nodded.

"That was a good job you did with the knife on the Nazi pig."

Jack frowned as he remembered the quick but brief battle. "Can't say that I'm very proud of it. I did it because I had no other choice."

Aris smiled. "You have a lot to learn about the Hitlerites. They are not humans, you know? They are . . . I don't know . . . animals? Beasts?"

"I'll just call them the enemy, if you don't mind."

Aris took a long swig from his bottle, rolled it inside his mouth for a few seconds, and swallowed it. "Whatever you say, comrade

Jackovich. Oh, Natalya told us how you and she got shot down. I saw the jet, too, you know."

Jack narrowed his eyes. "Oh, really?"

"Yes. It has no propellers, and it's very fast."

"Tell me what you know, Aris. It could be important."

In a tone that lacked emotion, the Yugoslav told him about his encounter with the panzers. He described how he saw two German soldiers burn to death, and how upset he had been when the jet blew away the roadblock.

"That's a very hot plane, Aris."

"Yes, and my people are trying to find it."

"I've seen two so far. I wonder how many more there are."

"One of our contacts thinks he saw one landing at a German field around seventy miles southwest of the Stalingrad pocket."

Jack's eyes narrowed. "Hmm . . . how far away is that from here, Aris?"

"About a day's walk northeast. Less, if we drive, but that could be dangerous. This is no-man's-land. There is no telling what we'd find on the roads."

"Could you take me there?"

"Take you where, Jack?" said Natalya from behind. She sat next to Jack with a cup of coffee in her hands. She pressed her shoulder against his. He smiled.

"Aris here tells me he thinks he knows where there might be one of those German jets."

Jack stared into her eyes. He didn't have to say anything else. Her eyes blinked understanding.

"You are crazy, Jack Towers. You are absolutely crazy."

KALACH AIRFIELD, TWENTY MILES WEST OF THE STALINGRAD POCKET • DECEMBER 16, 1942

Krasilov stood by the side of the runway as the Aircobra came to a stop, turned around, and headed for the bomb shelters. He walked up to the craft as the propeller stopped and the pilot pushed the cockpit open.

The pilot, a tall heavy man with broad shoulders and a square face, climbed down the side of the plane. He removed his helmet and scanned the base. Krasilov approached him.

"Major Chapman?"

"That's right, I'm Major Kenneth Chapman. You must be Colonel Krasilov."

"Yes, Major."

"Well, Colonel, I gotta tell you. I wasn't pleased to hear that you've used one of my bilingual trainers to fly in your sorties."

Krasilov did what he could to contain his temper. He simply stared back at Chapman for a few seconds. "We all make our mistakes, Major. And we all learn to live with them."

"What in the hell happened? You were running short on pilots?"

"Something like that."

"What do you mean? The Kremlin's not sending you enough men to fly the machines we're giving you?"

"I must make do with what I have at my disposal, Major. Unlike your country, we don't have unlimited resources available to us at a moment's notice. We have to fight back and use whatever is available at the time. Jack Towers was available, and I used him. You may include that statement in your report of the incident."

The two pilots stared at one another for a few seconds.

Chapman exhaled. "Do you have a place where I can get a drink, Colonel? I nearly froze my ass off tonight trying to get here."

Krasilov nodded. "This way, Major."

SEVENTY-FIVE MILES SOUTHWEST OF THE STALINGRAD
POCKET • DECEMBER 17, 1942

Jack and Natalya followed Aris and a dozen other Partisans as they made their way northeast. The sun had already broken through the horizon, casting enough light inside the murky woods for Jack to get a better feel for where he was.

Following Aris's advice on proper breathing in forty-below weather to avoid excessive heat loss, Jack kept a scarf around his mouth and nose, forcing himself to breathe slowly. Under no conditions was he to open his mouth unless he had to talk to someone, and even that was kept to a minimum to keep warm and also to maintain their stealthiness.

The group walked single file, with ten or so feet in between, preventing an enemy grenade from hurting more than one or two of them. It would also allow them to have ample time to seek cover if someone in the group spotted a German patrol.

The road narrowed as it began to wind its way up the side of a hill. Jack struggled with his balance. His aviator boots lacked the necessary traction for a smooth ascent. As the path turned ninety degrees, Jack slipped, landed on his back, and began to slide down the hill.

Flapping his limbs to find anything to hold on to, he crashed against a tree, stopping. He looked up and noticed the Partisans looking at him with grim faces. Jack understood the reason for the silent reprimand: Aris believed there were German patrols nearby. Jack's noise could have easily given away their position. He shrugged, struggled back up to his feet, and continued moving up-hill under the watchful eyes of the guerrillas.

Only after reaching the edge of the bluff did Jack realize how high they were. From where he stood he could see several miles of white, desolate countryside extending beyond the jagged edge of the frozen rimrock.

As they approached the summit, Aris, who was the lead, abruptly raised his hand. The caravan stopped, and the Yugoslav dropped to the ground and crawled forward to take a glimpse at the other side of the hill.

The group remained still. Jack heard a shouting or screaming of some sort.

Slowly, the team crawled up and took a spot at the edge of the hill. Jack lay down next to Natalya and shoved aside enough snow to get a clear view of a small village below. It took Jack but a few seconds to realize what was happening.

Like most villages in the region, the people there were probably Partisan sympathizers. Jack saw one truck and a dozen German soldiers gathered at the center of the village, where the villagers, whom Jack estimated at around thirty, were all kept in a tight group to the side.

One of the Germans, who by now Jack had guessed as their leader, took an old woman to the side and pushed her onto her knees. He then screamed in Russian for the Partisan collaborators to step forward.

None did, but most of the women in the village began to scream, cry, and plead with the Germans. That had no effect. The German officer unholstered his pistol, pressed it against the old woman's head, and fired.

"Jesus! What in the hell—"

Natalya squeezed his hand, hissing, "Keep it down, Jack."

"But that son of a bitch just—"

"This goes on every day, Jackovich," said Aris as he knelt next to Jack and put a hand over his shoulder.

"Are you going to let them get away with that?"

Aris smiled. Jack saw the Yugoslav's eyes burning, but the smile remained. "Justice will prevail, Jackovich. Partisan justice."

Aris then signaled his men to follow him. Jack and Natalya were about to get up, but Aris motioned them to remain put.

"We can't afford for either one of you to get hurt," said the Partisan leader. "You are air warriors. We belong to the land battle."

Jack wanted to go along anyway, but Natalya pulled him down. "We might be more burden than help, Jack. They have trained together. Let them do what they do—"

Jack heard something, like the muffled cry of a woman, but it did not originate from the village. His head turned toward a road just below them, snaking its way down to the village in the valley. Jack crawled back until he was out of sight of anyone in the village, raised to a crouch, and, weapon in hand, began to move down the side of the hill.

"Jack? What are you doing?"

"Shh . . ." Jack motioned Natalya to follow him.

She looked down at the village, back to Jack, then reluctantly crawled toward him.

"What is going on?"

"Trust me. Come."

This time Jack was careful when making his way toward the road below. He had seen Aris and the other Partisans using the land to their advantage by selecting their next foot or handhold before moving, and avoiding hesitation in midstride. The terrain was slippery, but as Jack quickly realized, as long as he remained in slow but constant motion, he could make reasonable and controlled progress. After the first hundred yards his confidence built up to the point that he started coaching Natalya. His breathing also slowly became one with his moves. He inhaled prior to moving, held his breath during transition, and slowly exhaled as he reached his next rest point.

The sound—a sound of struggle—got louder as Jack approached the frozen, unpaved road, but with trees in the way, he still could not get a clear view. The slope changed to almost forty-five degrees, forcing Jack to change his strategy. He opted to slide on his back, always using his arms and legs to hold on to roots and branches to control his descent, until he reached the edge of the trees, where the thick underbrush prevented him from seeing what Jack felt certain he would see. The struggle was indeed with a woman. It was a muffled moan while men laughed. He looked up hill and watched Natalya catching up with him and kneeling by his side.

Jack parted the foliage enough to see two German soldiers on the open bed of a truck, parked just around the corner from the village. One soldier had a girl, who couldn't have been much older than fifteen or sixteen, pinned against the flatbed while the second, the trousers of his uniform down to his knees, forced himself into her from the top. The first soldier held her arms and kept a piece of cloth over her mouth as the girl's head snapped back with every thrust.

"Fucking bastards," Jack hissed, glancing over to Natalya. There were tears in her eyes, which Jack promptly brushed away.

He holstered his pistol and grabbed the double-edge knife. "Cover me, Natalya, but don't fire."

"But, Aris . . . he said not to . . ."

Natalya's eyes were leveled with his. Jack put a hand over hers.

"It's gonna be all right. Trust me. Now cover me," he whispered.

Natalya pulled out her pistol as Jack moved down the hill until he reached a spot directly above the German kneeling down holding the girl steady. With the fingers of his right hand curled around the handle, Jack jumped over the side and landed on the German, with the knife directly in front of him. The blade entered the base of the neck at an angle, the sound of bones and cartilage snapping as he crashed against the soldier and pushed him to the side. His limp body rolled away.

The second German jerked in surprise. He was still inside the girl. He jumped off and reached for his pants, but his fumbling hands never made it past his knees. Jack lunged, slitting his throat. The soldier whipped both hands up as blood jetted from his neck. He tried to scream but couldn't, finally dropping to his knees while staring at Jack, at the bloody knife in his hand, before collapsing.

The girl was in obvious shock. She had not moved during the entire incident. Misted by the blood of his victims, Jack pulled up her heavy pants and waved Natalya over. She climbed into the rear of the truck and got to the girl's side while Jack walked up the road to see if someone had heard him.

A hair-raising scream made Jack rush toward the village, hidden around the corner, his eyes narrowing in anger at the sight.

The German officer had taken another woman from the group. This one looked fairly young. The officer had ripped off her dress and tore down her undergarments. Her chest was exposed. From behind, the German pressed a pistol to her head as she braced herself, shivering. Jack exhaled. If the German didn't kill her, then the Russian winter would.

More shouts came from the villagers, whom the soldiers were now shoving back with the butts of their rifles.

"Partisans! Enemies of the Reich! Come forward and spare the life of this woman!" the officer screamed to the mob of crazed villagers.

"Butchers! Butchers!" came the unanimous response.

A gunshot splattered across the frozen tundra.

The girl stood alone, screaming while hugging herself. The

German officer lay on the ground, his face smeared with blood. The soldiers appeared momentarily confused.

Jack unholstered his Colt, flipped the safety, and lurched around the corner while the Germans raced for cover behind their truck. Half of them never made it. They fell victims to Aris's sharpshooters. The others made it to the rear of the truck and began to exchange fire with Aris's men.

Jack approached the Germans from behind. He knelt, cocked his weapon, and fired. The first German jumped up in shock as his hands tried to reach behind his back, where Jack's bullet had entered. Before he fell to the ground, Jack already had a second German lined up in his sights, firing twice, the reports deafening. The German crashed against the side of the truck.

The other three Germans swung their machine guns in his direction. Jack jumped behind a tree as bark and snow exploded all around him, but it didn't last long. As he placed both hands over his face to protect himself from wooden chips stinging him, fire ceased.

Slowly, warily, Jack got up and looked around the tree trunk. Aris stood over the bodies of the Germans. Jack picked up his gun and walked in his direction. He noticed that two of the Germans— their chests covered with blood—were moving their heads from side to side. Aris shoved the muzzle of his weapon inside the mouth of one of the Germans and fired once. The German jerked for a second, then remained still. The Yugoslav did the same to the second fallen German. Jack felt no compassion for the soldiers, who on closer inspection appeared to be not older than twenty years.

An hour later, with all the corpses buried under the snow behind the village and the trucks driven into the woods and covered with branches, the villagers brought out loaves of bread and bottles of vodka for Aris and his rescuing band.

The men ate outside in front of the fire, while the women, Natalya included, tended the assaulted girls. Aris took a long look at Jack.

"Animals, Jackovich. Animals."

Jack stared back at his bearded friend. The Yugoslav stuffed a large chunk of bread in his mouth and washed it down with a gulp of vodka. Jack's view of the Germans had definitely taken a turn for the worse during the day's events. He no longer saw them as the mere enemy, in the classic sense, but more like common criminals.

"Jesus. What kind of war is this anyway?" he muttered, extending his hands toward the fire.

Aris took another swig of vodka and passed the bottle to Jack, who took a sip.

"Their plans have been clear from the start, comrade Jackovich. The Hitlerites seek the total destruction of this country. They have no regard for Slavic lives and take them without a second thought. See that boy over there?"

Jack spotted a kid, probably fourteen, biting into a large piece of bread he held with both hands.

"Yeah. What about him?"

"He saw his entire family get executed as he returned from the forest with a pile of firewood. The Germans raped his mother and two older sisters before hanging them. And the worst part of it was that they weren't Partisan collaborators. They were simply picked at random and executed."

Jack narrowed his eyes. "Why?"

"To create terror. The Germans have created this law that for every German killed by Partisans, ten innocent peasants will hang. The rule, of course, is aimed at trying to force the people to do what the Germans themselves have not been able to do: stop us."

Jack couldn't think of anything to say to that. Aris continued after he grabbed the bottle from Jack and took the last swallow.

"We see that as an act of desperation. The Germans are resorting to reckless measures to try to bring the situation under control, and it's not working. That frustration, of course, drives them into committing more and more atrocious acts of violence, but it will all end soon."

Jack stared at the fire. "How can you tell for sure? I mean, there are still, what? More than two million German soldiers in Russia. I call that far from being over."

Aris smiled. "And there will be two million dead Germans when this is all over, comrade. Justice will prevail. The German High Command will regret the day they decided to attack Russia. Soon, the thought of Soviet reprisal will haunt every living German. It will be their nightmare."

Jack didn't know how to respond to such harsh words, so well-spoken, and coming from a man who had just shot each of the fallen Germans in the head once to make sure there were no survivors.

"Justice will prevail, Jackovich. Justice will . . ."

Suddenly, a young boy came running to Aris's side, leaned down, and murmured something into the Yugoslav's ear. Aris lowered his gaze and exhaled before his expression turned stone cold.

"What was that all about, Aris?"

The Yugoslav guerrilla looked at Jack. "Come. I want you to see for yourself the agony that our people must endure." Aris got up and started walking toward one of the shacks at the edge of the village. Puzzled, Jack followed him. So far he'd seen plenty of despicable acts of cold murder. His skin shivered at the thought of anything worse.

Jack walked a few steps behind Aris. The leader of the Partisan band reached the shack—a round, fragile-looking structure made of stone, clay, and straw. It had an opening at the top, where he could see a trail of smoke from the burning stove, probably also used as a heater.

Aris pulled the canvas flap hanging at the entrance and held it open to let Jack in. Through the yellowish light, Jack saw a man in his early twenties lying in bed. Two older women sat by his bedside as a child held his hand.

Aris turned to Jack and whispered in his ear. "We were about to engage in a joint ambush of a German detachment of soldiers two weeks ago. He was a commando from another group of guerrillas. As we planned our attack in this village, he and three others were in an adjacent shack readying the weapons. It appears that a grenade slipped from one of the commandos' hands and went off by his feet, lightly injuring the others, but mangling his right leg.

"Because we knew the Hitlerites were coming, we all fled and left him in the care of the villagers. We hoped that maybe the Germans would bandage the wound, but they didn't. Instead, they tortured him for information, and when he refused, instead of just killing him, the bastards rubbed horse manure over the open wound and left. The villagers tried to clean the leg as best they could. I got a report on his condition every few days, and from what I heard it seemed that his leg had stopped bleeding and was healing fine. I saw him an hour ago, and he claimed to be feeling better, but that boy just whispered in my ear that he saw his leg without the bandage, and it looked blue and smelled like rotten cheese."

Jack nodded solemnly. Aris approached the young commando.

"Hello, Ivanovich."

The women and the child moved to the side of the room.

"Hello, Aris."

"You don't mind if I take a look at that leg, do you?"

A half smile appeared on Ivanovich's face. "Wh . . . why? It's all right. I already told you it's healed. I might even walk back with you tomorrow."

Aris's expression became harsh. "The leg, Ivanovich. Let me see it."

The young man turned his head to the side as Aris lifted the cover. Aris removed the cloth wrapped around most of the leg. Jack took one look and closed his eyes. The child had been right. The leg was blue with gangrene from the foot all the way up past the knee.

"Call the others," Aris said to the child, who promptly ran outside. "That leg has to go, Ivanovich."

If Jack could ever describe what fear looked like, it was definitely what he saw in that young man's eyes. His lips quivered, and his face contorted with anguish.

"No, Aris, please. No. Look, I can move the foot and the toes and . . ."

"I'm sorry, kid. It's either that or you'll be dead in a week. That gangrene is going to eat you alive, and you know it. It has to be done."

Three other Partisans arrived. One carried a black case. Aris opened it and removed a green bottle, two small rags, a thick piece of leather, and . . . and a hacksaw!

Jack felt sick and stopped breathing, turning around the moment the Partisans held down the trembling commando while the women and child ran outside in tears.

"Comrade Jackovich? Jackovich, please help us!"

Jack felt light-headed. He inhaled deeply and exhaled. He breathed in once more and turned around.

"Hold his leg!"

Hold his leg? You have to be fucking kidding me, he thought, but Aris's face looked as serious as the life-and-death decision the Yugoslav had made for the young commando.

Jack gripped the decomposed foot in his hands, lifted it up, and wedged it in his armpit while pressing his arm against his side to hold it taut. Then he used both hands to force the knee against the bed while fighting the nausea induced by the rotten smell that assaulted his nostrils.

Jack's gaze met with the young Yugoslav's for a brief moment. His pleading eyes reached Jack's soul, but what could he do? The damage had already been done by the Germans. The manure had created an infection that could have been stopped had Ivanovich been given some type of antibiotic, but just a rudimentary cleaning of the leg had not been enough to avoid infection.

Jack felt his sense of compassion about to burst the moment Ivanovich lifted his head and stared at his leg one last time before one of the Partisans pressed the young man's face down against the bed with a rag saturated in vodka while jamming the piece of leather in between his teeth.

Aris soaked the serrated blade with vodka and brought it to the fire. Jack watched the blade burn for several seconds before looking down at Ivanovich's chest rapidly swelling and deflating as the young man mentally prepared himself for the amputation.

The blade cooled. Aris brought the saw down next to the leg and used his other hand to feel the skin on Ivanovich's thigh, seemingly looking for the safest place to make the cut without robbing the young man of a healthy section of his leg. His finger stopped feeling on a spot roughly six inches above the knee, almost two inches from the last section of decayed skin.

Aris lifted his head and scanned the room. "Keep him steady! He must not move no matter what happens, or he might bleed to death!"

"I'd rather die, Comrade Aris!" Ivanovich screamed as he managed to free one hand and remove the piece of leather from his mouth. "Please, just shoot me. Please!"

"Quiet! Everyone quiet!"

"What is the use of living if I can't—"

"Keep that leather in his mouth! What's the matter with you, men? Can't hold one man down?"

The Partisans brought him under control once more as Aris pressed the disinfected blade over the selected section of flesh. The American pilot clenched his teeth, pressed the leg down and against his side hard, and closed his eyes.

The scream came, followed by sudden jerks and by a warm spray that showered Jack's face. Jack kept his eyes shut while the liquid trickling down his face and neck was accompanied by the revolting noise of rupturing skin, cartilage, and bones pounding against his eardrums.

Natalya ran outside when she heard the bloodcurdling shriek. Then she heard another one, and one more. She ran to the back of the village and saw two women crying into each other's shoulders in front of a shack. One held a child in her arms.

"Hold him steady! Steady!" came Aris's voice from inside.

More screams followed. It was the sound of a man in agony. She ran inside, froze in horror at the sight, and raced back out, staggering across the village, falling to her knees in the snow, hands covering her mouth. She tried to control her convulsions, but couldn't. Her body tensed, and her throat and mouth filled with bile.

The horrifying screams ringing in her ears, Natalya vomited until she was left with nothing but dry heaves. She breathed in and out for seconds. The screams had stopped. They had been replaced by a light moan.

She turned her head to the entrance and saw Jack and Aris carrying something wrapped in a bloodstained sheet. Jack's face had been splattered with blood. The American pilot looked different. It was in his eyes. He looked . . . older? Natalya wasn't sure.

She followed them to the rear of the village, where they had buried the Germans earlier. She helped them bury the amputated leg.

"Will he make it, Aris?" Natalya asked.

"Hard to tell, Natalya. I cauterized the arteries and disinfected the wound as much as I could. The rest is out of our hands."

Aris looked at Jack, who remained quiet, staring at the snow.

"Justice will prevail, comrade Jackovich."

Jack closed his eyes as pure white snow now covered everything, the dead Germans, the slain villagers, the infected leg . . . the sins of war.

SEVENTY MILES SOUTHWEST OF THE STALINGRAD POCKET • DECEMBER 17, 1942

Jack Towers lifted his gaze and saw the crystalline, star-filled sky. The majestic view was in sharp contrast with the desolation and suffering below it. This was Jack's first war, and the romance had long been lost. The glorified posters of fighter squadrons flying into the sunset seemed like a masquerade on a voracious wolf with an insatiable appetite for young men. There was nothing to be gained by war—Jack was now certain of that. Not for the soldiers who fought it, anyway.

An end to a brutal war was the reason Jack pushed himself harder up the hill even after marching for eight straight hours with minimum rest. The war had to end. The German killing machine had to be stopped.

Jack reached the top of the hill and crawled next to Aris. The

Yugoslav scanned the airfield with the set of binoculars he'd stolen from the German truck earlier that morning. He passed them to Jack, who slowly searched the edge of the forest outlining the German airstrip. He carefully looked at every plane, then continued to the next when he spotted its propeller. The unpaved airstrip was roughly two thousand feet long by seventy wide. The Germans had done a fairly good job of keeping it clear of snow, and the surface appeared reasonably flat. There were tents to both sides of the airfield.

"You're sure about this place, Aris?" Jack asked as he finished searching one side and saw nothing but six Gustavs and two of the larger Me 110s.

"Our contacts tell us this is where they saw one landing yesterday afternoon. Maybe they moved it to another airfield."

"Maybe . . . then again, maybe not."

Jack smiled and passed the binoculars to Aris and pointed to a spot directly behind a tent halfway down the airfield.

Aris pressed the binoculars against his eyes. "Is that it? The one without the propeller in the nose?"

"Yep. That's the one, Aris," Jack responded, taking the binoculars back from the Partisan guerrilla and studying the plane once more. It was dark, but there were enough lights by the edge of the clearing for Jack to see the streamlined outline of the German jet clearly. It looked like something out of a science fiction magazine, but it wasn't. The plane was for real, and Jack had already witnessed what it was capable of doing.

"Are you sure you want to do this, Jack?" Natalya asked as she leaned down next to him. He passed the binoculars back to Aris, who used them to scan the rest of the field.

"I have to. There is no other way." He stared into her pleading hazel eyes and put a hand over her cheek. "Look, I know what I'm doing. I can handle it. Trust me."

Without waiting for a response, Jack got the binoculars back from Aris and stared at the German jet once again. An officer came out from the tent right next to it. Jack put down the binoculars and looked at Aris. "Let's do it."

Firmly gripping his double-edged hunting knife, Aris approached the base from the east side—the side where they had spotted the jet. Jack, also clutching a knife, remained a few feet behind him. Their weapons were slung across their backs.

Natalya was not with them. She had reluctantly agreed to head back to the nearest Soviet air base the moment she got the signal that Jack's plan had worked. Aris had placed two Partisans on either side of the runway. The rest were with Natalya at the top of the small hill.

Hit-and-run, Jackovich. Stealth and surprise are your main weapons, he recalled Aris telling him ten minutes before. Jack felt much more comfortable in the woods now. He felt he blended well within its protective cover. He moved only when Aris moved, and stopped when he stopped. He used the same foot- and handholds as the Yugoslav guerrilla, and managed consistently to pace himself so that he could sustain his body's oxygen needs by slowly breathing through his nostrils.

He was about to take another step when Aris abruptly stopped. The bearded Yugoslav didn't have to say or point to anything. Jack nodded the moment he spotted the German sentries some fifty feet ahead. It wasn't very hard to notice them, Jack decided. Even in the murky woods. The soldiers were smoking.

Smoking while on guard?

Jack tilted his head. Given the forty-below temperatures, he couldn't blame them for doing that, although if it had been him, he would have chosen hot coffee—or anything else that wouldn't give away his position.

Aris pointed at Jack with his index finger and made a circle in the air with his hand. Jack nodded. The two men split. Aris's tactic was both simple and clever: attack from an unexpected angle and surprise the enemy from the place it would least expect an assault to come.

Jack made a wide semicircle to the right of the guards, while Aris made one to the left. Now Jack had to be extra careful. He didn't have Aris to guide him through the forest. He was on his own, and well aware that one false step could blow everything. The Germans were too close. Jack developed a new rhythm. He moved only when the gusts of wind swept through the trees, stopped the moment the breeze died down, and moved forward once more with the next gust. After a few minutes the rhythm was perfected to the point that Jack could almost anticipate when the breeze would come again, and how long it would last. That allowed him a few extra seconds of motion by moving just before the wind started and continuing a second or two after it died down. The feeling of control was exhilarating.

The sounds of branches and leaves moving in response to the cold Siberian wind, Jack struggled toward his objective foot after agonizing foot, reaching it five minutes later fifty feet on the other side of the guards, so close to the edge of the clearing that Jack could see the tail of the jet about forty feet away. Aris was already waiting for him.

The Partisan leader pointed to the sentry on the left. Jack nodded and moved forward as quietly as his heavy garments allowed him. Once more, he mimicked Aris's every move, advancing and stopping when he did until slowly closing the gap to twenty feet. The guards continued to smoke while their weapons hung loosely from their shoulders.

The constant whirl of the wind through the trees masking their sounds, Jack and Aris dropped to a crouch and quietly—

The guards turned in their direction and began to walk. Jack froze. Aris had to drag him down to hide behind a thick pine.

The guards stopped. Jack looked at Aris, who brought a finger to his lips. Jack nodded and remained still. He didn't even breathe.

The guards, holding their weapons in front of them, moved closer until they were directly on the other side of the tree. Aris motioned Jack to go around at the count of three.

Aris's extended his index finger. Jack recoiled. The Yugoslav extended his middle finger. Jack leaned his body forward. *Now!*

Jack shot around the tree and caught the German broadside. The knife went in through the side of the neck at an angle. Jack drove it up with all his might, nearly lifting the soldier off his feet. By the time the German dropped, Aris was already wiping his own blade clean of his victim's blood. He smiled at Jack, who felt sick.

It was one thing to pull a trigger and watch the enemy go down in a smoking plane. It was a different story to watch them roll on the ground gasping for air with a severed windpipe.

He shifted his gaze toward the clearing and saw the long cylindrical turbines hanging beneath the wings of the German jet.

"It's all yours, comrade Jackovich."

Jack carefully walked by the tail while Aris, left hand clutching his knife and right hand on the handle of his machine gun, warily surveyed the deserted airfield. Most pilots were inside their—

Another German approached the jet.

Aris stopped Jack from squeezing the trigger of his machine gun. Instead the Partisan grabbed his knife by the blade and waited until the officer was almost out of sight of the clearing.

The German stopped next to the wing and froze. He had recognized them, but before he had a chance to turn around and yell for help, Jack watched the glistening shape of Aris's knife streak across the chilly air and embed itself in the German's chest. The soldier dropped to his knees, but not before he let go a loud shriek, which Aris quickly stopped by jamming a hand over the German's mouth while he finished him off.

"Go, Jackovich! Do what you must! Hurry!"

Jack climbed on the wing and walked up next to the cockpit. He opened the canopy, crawled inside and closed it, locking it from the inside.

He spotted three Germans racing across the field. Jack pulled off his heavy gloves and scanned the cockpit. The basic instrumentation was as it should be. The artificial horizon to the left, next to the airspeed indicator and above the slip/turn indicator. On the right side were the directional gyro, clock, and dual engine gauges. The jet's controls were standard stick and rudder with a built-in trigger and radio buttons on the upper section of the control stick. The landing gear lever was to his right above the small elevator trim wheel.

His head snapped up the moment he heard gunfire, quickly followed by a loud scream. Jack glanced to his right and watched Aris's body tossed by the enemy gunfire.

Jack turned around and watched Aris dragging himself into the forest, but the Yugoslav guerrilla didn't get far. Another burst across his back killed him.

Gunfire erupted from both sides of the hill as the Partisans began their coordinated attack to draw fire away from Jack.

Natalya knew something had gone wrong the moment she'd heard a scream and gunfire, but no sign of jet engines.

"Stay down!" one of the Partisans shouted moments before a loud explosion caused three of Aris's men ten feet behind her to arch back and fall faceup. The remaining two opened fire on the squad of Germans coming from their rear. Natalya reached the fallen guerrillas, but in a moment she realized there was nothing she could do for them. Their chests had been ripped open with shrapnel. Somehow, the Germans had flanked them.

She pulled out her pistol and was about to get to her feet when the remaining two Partisans flew over her head riddled with bullets. She was trapped between the airfield and the advancing squad of Germans. As steel helmets loomed behind a line of bushes twenty feet away, Natalya rushed down hill toward the clearing. She was well aware of the fate fighting Soviet women faced at the hands of the Germans.

Jack saw five soldiers less than fifty feet in front of the plane, but for some reason no one would open fire. Three were busy returning fire from the hills. The others simply stared at the jet.

Jack threw what he guessed were the electronic switches to power the avionics. He was right. The cockpit came alive, giving him readings on fuel, oil, and turbine temperatures.

He pressed the dual set of buttons above the engines' gauges, and the turbines began to make a high-pitched sound. Jack let go and the turbines died down.

He pressed them again until the turbines engaged. The jet briefly jerked forward. Jack pushed the dual throttle controls forward, but they didn't move. Puzzled, he pulled them back some and the craft lurched forward.

"Shit! This thing works backward!"

The Germans took a few steps back as the jet inched forward. One of them leveled his machine gun at him, but before he could let go a single shot, Jack lifted the trigger guard casing and fired for three seconds. Actually he had wanted only to fire for one second, but the powerful recoil almost stopped the craft's momentum. Jack crashed against the control panel, bounced, and slammed his back against the seat while his finger remained on the trigger.

"Jesus!"

Half-startled, Jack leaned forward, and all he could see was a pile of human refuse where the five Germans had been. In disbelief at the kind of power stored in the nose cannons, Jack pulled back the throttle handles and the Messerschmitt lurched out of its hideout and onto the frozen runway. He quickly reduced throttle, deciding that it would take some time to get used to the volatile engine response.

The airstrip blared with sirens. Pilots ran for their craft as Jack slowly added more throttle. Two of them tried to climb onto the wings of the jet, but with additional power he left them behind and quickly taxied to the end of the runway and turned the jet around. The craft's tail almost touched the trees. Jack needed every single inch of runway available to him.

Now this is when the real test begins, Jack, he told himself. He had no idea what the takeoff speed for this jet was, or the stall speed. Furthermore, Jack had no idea what was the takeoff run. He had already estimated the runway was two thousand feet long. Did such short runway require him to perform a special takeoff technique? Jack decided he would try a modified version of his Aircobra's short takeoff maneuver, and searched for the flaps' handle. *Flaps? Flaps? Where?*

He spotted a vertical lever with three different settings. He lowered it to the first, and watched in satisfaction as the hydraulically driven flaps lowered. Suddenly, a spotlight blinded him. It came from his left.

Jack pressed left rudder and let go another burst the moment the nose lined up with the source of light. The light blew up in a bright flash. He recentered the nose and began to pull . . .

Jack briefly glanced at the Me 262's built-in rearview mirror and saw Natalya running in his direction.

Natalya! What are you doing?

She reached the tail of the plane. Jack turned his head toward the runway and saw a truck loaded with soldiers bustling toward him. He lined it up using rudder and throttle while stepping on the brakes, and let go another burst. The guns were impressive. The truck stopped dead in its tracks, flipped, and went up in a ball of flames. Once more, Jack lined up the craft with the runway.

Natalya made it up the wing and began to bang on the canopy.

Jack unlocked it and she pulled it up.

"Are you crazy! You want to get us both killed?" he screamed. "You were supposed to have gone with—"

"They're coming, Jack! The Germans!"

"Wh . . . what are you . . ."

"They got the Partisans . . . oh dear! It was a massacre! They're right behind—"

He pulled her by the collar and sat her between him and the stick over his left leg. He closed and locked the canopy as more machine-gun fire erupted from the front.

"Get out of the way!" He pushed her head farther to the left as several bullets ricocheted off the bulletproof glass. Jack pressed the brake pedals, pushed full right rudder, and added throttle. The Me 262 pivoted clockwise at great speed. Jack pressed the trigger.

The whole world seemed to catch fire around him as the Messerschmitt showered everything in sight with 30mm rounds.

Jack lifted his finger off the trigger. Gunfire ceased. He lined up the nose with the runway once more and, while pressing on the brakes, pulled back the dual throttle handles.

"Hold on, Natalya!" Jack placed his face over her shoulder to get a better view of the runway. The jet trembled as Jack gave the throttle handles a final pull. Full throttle. The engine whirl became deafening.

The craft plunged forward the moment he released the brakes. He felt Natalya's body crushing him against the seat from the powerful acceleration. Jack tried to get a glimpse of the airspeed indicator, but Natalya's head was in the way.

"Read out the airspeed!"

"Seventy knots . . . eighty . . . Jack! There's a tank blocking the runway. Slow down!"

Jack shifted his gaze directly ahead and saw a panzer rolling onto the center of the runway.

"Just read the airspeed!"

The tank and a number of Germans were roughly one thousand feet ahead. The massive turret turned in his direction. Jack lined up the tank and squeezed the trigger. The thundering cannons shook the entire craft.

"Airspeed!"

"Ninety knots . . . one hundred . . ."

The soldiers were cut to pieces by the guns, and the tank caught fire but it remained there, blocking the way. He estimated no more than seven hundred feet away.

"One hundred ten knots!"

Jack pulled back on the stick, but the craft didn't climb. He decided they were too heavy and were not accelerating fast enough. He needed a way to reduce drag . . . the landing gear!

"One hundred twenty knots . . . Jack, the tank!"

Jack let go another burst. The tank exploded, but he could not see if it was out of the way or not. "Speed's down to one hundred ten knots . . . fifteen . . ."

The tank's turret was gone while the bottom half burned, but Jack decided that enough of it was still there to spoil his takeoff run. Using guns, however, was out of the question. The brutal recoil would only slow him down even further.

"One hundred twenty knots."

The scorching wreckage rapidly grew in size. In the corner of his eye, Jack noticed the muzzle flashes of Germans on the side of the runway emptying their machine guns on them.

With bullets bouncing off the glass, he reached for the landing gear lever and pulled it up as he eased back the stick. The jet trembled but left the ground. The landing gear lifted and locked in place.

"One hundred thirty knots!"

Flames filled his windshield. Jack pulled on the stick hard, and the Messerschmitt bolted up a few feet. The bottom of the fuselage scraped the wreckage, but he'd cleared it.

"Ninety knots, Jack! We're gonna stall!"

The stall buzzer went off. Jack lowered the nose and regained some airspeed, but the craft dropped a few feet. A cloud of sparks engulfed them the moment the jet's belly bounced off the runway before coming back up. Jack lowered the nose even more, keeping the plane just a couple of feet over the runway.

"One hundred forty . . . fifty . . . sixty."

Jack waited. He couldn't afford another stall. A wall of trees rapidly approached. He was running short of runway.

"One hundred seventy . . . eighty! The trees, Jack!"

A dark green wall nearly engulfing him, Jack pulled back on the stick and the jet sprang upward at a steep angle. He waited for the impact of branches against the underside, but it never came. He had somehow cleared the forest. The stars were the only thing visible through the armored glass—the stars and the tiny cracks left by the rounds that had struck the sides of the bubble-shaped canopy. Jack quietly thanked the engineers at Messerschmitt for making the canopy bulletproof. There were over a dozen cracks in all.

As he watched the altimeter reach five hundred feet, Jack eased the stick forward and reduced throttle, but the plane continued to climb. He reduced throttle once more, and the plane leveled off at a thousand feet. He trimmed the elevators and relaxed the pressure on the stick.

The craft now felt very smooth. Only the quiet whirl of the turbines told him they were airborne. There was no trembling, no engine-induced vibrations, no turning propeller or black smoke coming out of the exhausts. The jet was indeed a work of art. The elevator trim worked perfectly. He briefly let go his hand off the stick, and the artificial horizon confirmed his suspicion. The craft remained perfectly leveled.

Natalya rested her head against his shoulder as Jack briefly closed his eyes. "You're crazy, Jack Towers. Absolutely crazy."

"We're not out of the woods yet, Natalya. We got to land this thing somewhere."

She turned her head and smiled. "Leave that to me."

KALACH AIRFIELD, TWENTY MILES WEST OF THE STALINGRAD
POCKET • DECEMBER 17, 1942

Krasilov and Chapman sat inside the briefing bunker and read the official report of the attempted surprise bombing of the German airfield that intelligence claimed housed two jets.

The Red Air Force colonel pounded his fists on the table and stared into Chapman's bloodshot eyes. Neither of them had slept much in the past twenty-four hours.

"Damn! The bastards have probably moved them to another field by now. We lost our chance to blow them to hell!"

Chapman sat back on the wooden chair and quietly studied Krasilov through the smoke of the cigarette hanging off the side of his mouth. "We'll find the jets again, Colonel."

"Yes, but every extra day that those infernal craft remain in the battlefield costs the lives of my people, not yours."

Chapman stared into Krasilov's weathered eyes. "Really, Colonel? Your people only."

Krasilov frowned. "Sorry. For a moment I . . ."

"Look, you have been under a lot of stress. Why don't you take a break for a few hours and get some sleep."

"I can't. I need to prepare the reports of today's sorties for Moscow, and plan tomorrow's sorties."

"You're burning out, Colonel, and you know it. You better take it easy."

Krasilov leaned forward and put both elbows on the table. "I'm burning out, Major? Well, I've got news for you. My *country* is burning, major. *My country*. Do you understand that? Those Hitlerite bastards have taken everything from me. My wife and daughters; my home; everything, except for my will to fight. If Russia loses, Major, you'll go back home and perhaps prepare for an invasion of the mainland, but we, Major, lose everything, our home, our dignity, our lives, our traditions, everything. The Nazis have sworn to tear this nation into small pieces and use the people as slaves. So if I'm burning out, Major, then I'll just burn out." Krasilov reached for the bottle of vodka next to him, took a swig, and handed it to Chapman, who turned it down.

Krasilov abruptly stood. "Sound the alarm! Sound the alarm!" He raced outside. Chapman followed him.

"Hear it, Major?"

"That's a jet engine, Colonel. Looks like the bastards have decided to pay us a visit after hours!"

"Why can't we just contact them and tell them it's us?"

"Because, Jack, all radios are off. Radio silence is essential to the night bombers."

Jack frowned and reduced throttle even further. He couldn't see much. Below, the ground was pitch-black. There was not a single ground reference he could use to guide his craft. On top of that, without a moon, there was no horizon to tell Jack if his wings were leveled. He had to depend fully on the craft's artificial horizon— something he was not particularly used to doing. The Aircobra was a day fighter. Jack had flown at night before, but only when he had no other choice.

"Where is the damned runway?"

"You'll have to drop below one hundred feet to see the approach lights. We set them very low so enemy fighters can't spot the airfield at night unless they know to fly this low. Something very unlikely."

"Below a hundred? At night? I'll say that's *very* unlikely, Natalya. If the altimeter isn't properly calibrated, we're gonna run right into the ground!"

"Do it, Jack!"

Jack exhaled and dropped the nose by a few degrees while shifting his gaze between the darkness below him and the altimeter's needle. One hundred feet.

"There. Now all I got to do is sneeze and we're dead. What's next?"

"We look for the lights. They should be around here. Blue over green, Jack. Look for them."

Jack felt the wings tilting to the right. Instinctively, he inched the stick a bit to the left to compensate.

"Jack! What are you doing?"

Jack shifted his gaze to the artificial horizon and noticed he was flying at a twenty degree angle of bank. He had allowed spatial disorientation to take over his judgment. Spatial disorientation came in when the brain, confused from lack of visual inputs, decided on its own which way was up and forced that false reference on the pilot. The only way to fight back was by forcing his brain to accept the artificial horizon as the real reference.

Feeling the nausea induced by spatial disorientation, Jack clenched his teeth and eased the stick back until the artificial horizon told him his wings were leveled again. It felt awkward, but he did it anyway. His instincts were lying to him.

"Sorry, I had vertigo."

"There, Jack. See them? See the lights?"

Jack squinted and spotted the bluish lights in the distance, but since it was night, it was hard to judge distance—at least for him.

"How far away is that?"

"About three thousand feet away. I know where I am now, Jack. Turn left for about thirty seconds, and then right to one-seven-zero. The nose should be lined up with the runway."

"How do you—"

"We do this every night, Jack."

Jack eased back throttles and inched the stick to the left.

Krasilov was about to order the searchlights on, but decided against it. It had been over two minutes since he first heard the jet engines, and he could still hear them, but they had faded away some.

"Alarms off! Turn off all the lights, including the approach lights!" he shouted. The siren died down, and the only sounds left were that of the jets in the distance and the wind swirling across the concrete runway.

"What are you doing?" asked Chapman.

"Trust me, Major. The bastards won't be able to find us. Besides, I don't feel like losing more fighters to those damn German jets."

"There, Jack! See them?"

Jack completed the right turn, narrowed his eyes, and saw the dim bluish lights a few thousand feet ahead. The lights suddenly went off.

"What happened to them? Damn!"

"They turned them off, Jack. Krasilov thinks we're the enemy."

"Lower flaps, Natalya!"

She reached for the lever on her side, and pulled it down to the second setting.

"I did this once without lights, Jack. At least we got to see the general location."

"Great," he said while squinting to see anything. "Airspeed?"

"One hundred fifty knots."

Jack Towers decided that if the jet took off at around 140 knots and stalled close to ninety, an acceptable approach speed should be somewhere in the middle. He cut back power and lowered the landing gear.

"One hundred forty . . . thirty-five . . ."

Krasilov was puzzled. The jet engines became louder, but still did not appear to sound as high-pitched as they did during his two encounters with the German fighter.

"Look, Colonel! There it is!" shouted Chapman.

Krasilov pulled out his gun, and so did most of the pilots on the field, Chapman included. Krasilov leveled it at the incoming craft, but stopped the moment the landing lights flooded the concrete runway.

"Hold your fire! Hold your fire!"

"What are you doing, Colonel? The bastard—"

"Is trying to land, Major! The German is trying to land!"

The runway quickly came up to meet him. Things were getting out of hand. Because of his unfamiliarity with the craft, Jack realized he was fighting the controls. For every adjustment in power and stick, he found himself readjusting in the opposite direction. He simply couldn't get the right response from the German fighter. Always too much or too little.

"One hundred twenty knots, Jack . . . fifteen . . . ten . . ."

Jack added just a dash of power to maintain one hundred ten knots.

"One hundred twenty knots, Jack."

"Dammit! This plane!" Frustrated, Jack reduced power again and eased the stick back, trying to descend and slow down at the same time.

"One hundred ten knots. Holding at one-ten."

Jack exhaled, but the brief surge of confidence was washed away by a gust of crosswind that brushed the craft to the side of the runway. Jack swung the stick in the opposite direction.

Krasilov felt something was wrong. Either the craft was damaged or the pilot was an incompetent. The craft drifted over the side, back over the runway, over to the other side, and finally back on the wide runway.

Someone panicked and opened fire.

Jack momentarily lost control of the stick as three rounds bounced off the armored canopy.

"Damn. Someone's firing at us!"

His left wing got dangerously close to the trees by the side of the runway.

"Right rudder, Jack! Quick!"

Jack pressed the right pedal and eased the stick to the right, bringing the craft back over the concrete.

"Hold your fucking fire!" Krasilov ran toward the young pilot who had his pistol leveled at the German fighter, and pushed his hand up in the air. "You idiot! All of you hold your fire! Now!"

Krasilov grabbed the weapon from the pilot and shoved him to the side. He shifted his gaze back to the craft.

Jack had consumed half the runway's length and still had not landed. He tried to cut back power, but instead of pushing the throttle controls, he automatically pulled them back. He realized his mistake the second after the jets kicked in full power and pushed the craft back up.

"The other way, Jack. It's the other way! Airspeed one hundred sixty . . . seventy . . . eighty . . ."

Jack was about to reduce throttles but it was to no avail. The end of the runway was too close.

"You idiots!" shouted Krasilov. "You have scared him off! The next man that opens fire will have to deal with me!"

He shifted his gaze back toward the plane slowly floating, seemingly out of control, over the runway.

Jack pulled up, climbed to one hundred feet, made a 180-degree turn, and came back around for another pass.

He kept the stick dead centered while decreasing power steadily. Once again, the runway came up to meet him. Jack felt the light crosswind that was the cause of his drifting over the runway on his first pass. This time around he had a better feel for the finesse required to control the craft during the last phase of the landing approach. He decided to change landing tactics, and eased the stick to the right to fly into the wind while applying left rudder. The conflicting commands tilted the jet's wings a mild fifteen degrees, but with the payoff of keeping the nose aligned with the runway.

This time instead of overcorrecting, Jack's hands over the throttle handles and stick barely moved. The adjustments were minimal. He felt in control.

The right gear touched down first. Jack centered the stick, and the left wheel bounced against the concrete runway once before it settled. The tail dropped as Natalya read seventy knots indicated airspeed.

Krasilov, Chapman and the other pilots ran behind the German jet, which managed to stop at the end of the runway, turned around, and came to a full stop next to the fighter shelters.

Krasilov was the first to reach it. He jumped on the wing with his pistol in his right hand, and was about to bang on the canopy for the pilot to push it open when he froze.

Jack and Natalya waved at him from inside the cockpit.

Krasilov remained silent for a few seconds before bursting into laughter.

KALACH AIRFIELD, TWENTY MILES WEST OF THE STALINGRAD POCKET • DECEMBER 18, 1942

Jack was exhausted. The debriefing with Krasilov and Chapman had gone well, but had lasted a couple of hours longer than Jack would have liked. He went over everything from the time he got shot down to the moment they landed. Everything.

Both Krasilov and Chapman took extensive notes, particularly of Jack's description of the strong points and weaknesses of the German jet. Even before he had completed giving them his impressions of the powerful fighter, Chapman had already made the decision of getting the plane flown to England, where it would be thoroughly inspected by a joint USAAC and RAF team. Jack had been assigned as the pilot, and he was to leave at dawn. Refueling stops were already being set up along a route worked out by both Krasilov and Chapman.

"Well, so much for my little tour of the Eastern Front," he murmured as he reached his tent behind the fighter shelters by the edge of the trees. Things were moving too fast for Jack. Much had happened in the four short days since his arrival there, and now he was being requested to leave for England.

He opened the canvas flap and quickly closed it to keep some of the heat still trapped inside the tent from last night's fire. Each tent had a small woodburning stove and ventilation pipe.

He walked to the stove in back, reached for a few logs, piled them up, soaked them with kerosene, and threw in a match. He remained kneeling in front of the fire for a few seconds while his face thawed. Jack removed his gloves and cap, and began to unbutton his coat when a gust of wind nearly put the fire out. Convinced that he had closed the canvas flap, Jack turned around.

"Hello, Jack."

"Natalya. What are you—"

"I heard you were leaving tomorrow to fly the German plane to England. I came by to wish you luck, and also to say thanks. What are your plans after England?"

"Sit down, please. And close that flap, please."

The Soviet pilot snapped the canvas shut and removed her furry hat. Her hair hung loose over her ears.

"I'm not sure what's going happen to me after I deliver the plane. Chapman mentioned something about training another group of pilots. There are three shipments of Aircobras on the way."

She lowered her gaze. Jack knelt down next to her and lifted her chin. "I'm going to miss you, too, Natalya Makarova."

She tried to move his hand away, but he softly cupped her face. "Look at me, Natalya. I want you to look at me."

Slowly, she raised her gaze until it melted with his. Jack smiled. "I knew it."

"Please stop, Jack. You know there can never be anything between—"

"Says who? Our governments? The hell with them. Something has happened to me in the past few days, Natalya. I've never felt this way about anybody else. I—"

"Please don't say it, Jack . . . please?" She got up to leave without waiting for a response.

"Natalya. I might not see you for some time."

She stopped. "I can't, Jack."

"You can't or you won't?"

"Jack, please. You won't understand."

"Try me, Natalya. Is it differences in cultures? Religion maybe? What? Tell me, please."

She slowly turned around. Tears rolled down her cheeks. "His name is Boris Nikolajev. He was a pilot with another air wing and was reported shot down eight months ago during the Battle of Moscow. We were married the same day that he was sent to defend Moscow, Jack. We never even had a honeymoon. After several months, I decided to get on with my life, and then you came along and . . ."

"And?"

"A letter arrived from Moscow while we were gone. It said that he was found in a liberated POW camp west of Moscow. It was a miracle, Jack. He and a dozen others were the only survivors out of hundreds of prisoners taken there. He was promptly taken to a hospital, where he is right now struggling to recover from the sub-human conditions in which the Nazis kept him for all those months."

Jack was confused. "Boris *Nikolajev?* Is he . . ."

"Yes, Jack. Boris is Andrei's brother. He needs me. Please under-stand."

Jack closed his eyes and searched for the words, but there weren't any. He lifted his gaze and stared into the hazel eyes that had somehow taken possession of his feelings. Now those same eyes told him that it could never be. They had been promised to some-one else long before he'd gotten here.

Natalya leaned down and kissed him on the lips.

"Good-bye, Jack Towers. You'll always have a special place in my heart. Thank you for giving me my life."

Jack softly pulled her face close to his and inhaled deeply. "Thank you for giving me mine," he responded as he tried to bring her lips next to his. Natalya gently pulled away.

"Please, Jack. Please understand. I can't . . ."

Jack lowered his gaze. She turned around and reached the en-trance flap.

"Natalya . . . that day in the hut after we got shot down, when you . . . did you feel what I . . ."

"I will treasure that day for as long as I live, Jack. Good-bye."

A gust of cold wind blew inside the tent as she left. Jack felt the bitter air cut through his soul.

HONOR

RALPH PETERS

RALPH PETERS is a writer and a retired U.S. Army officer. He is the author of eleven critically acclaimed novels, an influential book of strategy, as well as many essays and articles on conflict, culture, and military reform. During his military career, he served in Germany for a total of ten years. In addition to writing the introduction to recent Modern Library editions of Clausewitz and Sun Tzu, he translates German classics as a hobby.

Herr Oberstleutnant im Generalstab Draus *Freiherr* von Borchert pissed in a ditch. The autumn twilight captured the high fields and surrounded the groves, leaving Borchert alone on the darkening road. As if he were a battle's sole survivor.

He scanned, warily, from left to right.

The plateau above the Rhine lay hushed, as if a fearful world were holding its breath. The shadows stretching from the horizon gave the landscape an illusion of endless depth. Borchert might have been back in Russia, where everything had been endless. Everything but victory.

He finished his business, closed his ragged trousers, and stepped back onto the farm road. The fields were as bare as the Jews stripped down in the marketplaces of White Russia. As naked, and almost as pale. Glancing about one last time, Borchert nodded to himself, satisfied that he had not been observed. Even now, after all that had happened, it would not have done for some cackling farmwife to see an officer of good family relieving himself by the roadside.

Walking northward, he scratched at the rash beneath his tattered uniform. He had left the camp, but the camp had not left him.

The road was narrow, with a grassy ridge at its center. The packed earth of the ruts lay half a leg lower than the surrounding fields. Borchert strode along, bullying himself. Trying to ignore the soreness of his feet. Thin as cloth, the leather of his boots had cracked open, and the ball of his right foot had worn through the sole. The cardboard that filled in the gap had been torn from an American ration box. It did little to protect him from stones and nothing to keep out the wet. He had replaced the cardboard twice since leaving the camp and had enough scraps in a pocket to close the hole a few more times.

Borchert had never imagined that he would descend to hoarding trash, or that his uniform and boots one day would look like a vagabond's rags. So much had been lost, so much more taken away. He had come within seconds of pulling a better pair of boots from the corpse of a comrade who died in the camp, but, fingers inches away, he had restrained himself. To take those boots would have gone against his code of honor, and that code was all that had sustained him. That, and the thought of his wife. So he hesitated.

Other hands grabbed the boots. The man who got them grinned in Borchert's face. And the American guards taunted them both from the victor's side of the wire.

The Americans had no sense of honor, no inherent dignity, though they were better by half than the Russians. Now they ruled. Borchert had seen the effects of defeat on his fellow prisoners, their last pride vanquished by the triumphant, ever-present smirks of their captors. Men who had been good soldiers groveled and cowered. They begged. Demeaning themselves. For nothing. The Americans lacked elementary human sympathy, as well as proper respect for officers. They did not shoot their prisoners. But they did not mind starving them slowly.

In the weeks after the surrender, the prisoner-of-war camp outside of Bad Kreuznach had filled with a hundred thousand men. Then more arrived. In the unseasonable cold, under late snow and whipping rain, they had no shelter or sanitation, and what little water they received was foul. The prisoners went for days without food while the Americans only shook their heads, strutting about with their carbines and clipboards. Men who had survived the war died needlessly. Cringing against one another for a hint of warmth.

Borchert had joined a delegation of officers protesting these violations of the Geneva Convention and the fundamental laws of war. The American captain who met with them stammered excuses for his military's behavior, claiming that the supply system was overwhelmed by the German collapse and that the available food had to go first to the local civilians, who were starving. But when a German brigadier general, a proper man with good decorations, pointed out that, surely, captured officers must be fed without delay, the American dropped all pretense of civility. In mongrel English that annoyed the educated ear, the captain said, "You sonsofbitches are just getting what you deserve."

Men lived in holes scraped from the earth and woke drenched by a downpour. Sickened prisoners, too weak to support themselves, fell into the latrine trenches at night and drowned in filth, their final cries ignored. Later on, toward the end of the summer, conditions had improved. The starvation paused, though every mouth craved more than it received. But the camp never approached a level of appropriate decency, and the Americans humiliated the officers among the prisoners through sheer neglect. There was only the sameness, the lack of news, the denial of the right to send or receive letters, the endless indignities, and the slow corruption of the body.

It had occurred to Borchert during his days in the camp that dullness might be the chief characteristic of Hell. As a prisoner, he had to struggle against despair, which he had never had to do during the war. In war, you were too busy for despair. But in the drab impotence of the camp, his spirits had threatened to quit him. The world seemed pared down to nothing, and even the thought of his wife sometimes failed to lift his mood. He feared he would die amid the squalor, the last of his direct line, and he submitted without protest to being sprayed down along with the other prisoners as a preventative measure against typhus. You tasted and smelled the chemicals for days, clinging to you like the odor of death. The way his Russian mistress had clung to him, begging to be taken along when the Germans were leaving, not in love with him but only terrified for her life. He rarely thought of her anymore, and never willingly. She had been an educated woman, a beauty after the Slavic fashion. And she had made the mistake of believing that beauty and education would save her.

Nothing in this life could save a man or woman except strength. And sometimes even strength was not enough.

The camp had shamed him. As nothing in his life had ever shamed him. Nonetheless, when the interrogators combed through the prisoners, looking for officers with experience fighting the Russians and promising special treatment in return for information, Borchert had kept his knowledge to himself. Others tumbled over themselves to please their captors, hoping to extricate themselves from the camp. But not him, not a von Borchert.

He never lost his honor. He had been tested, but had not failed. In time, his own release had come about as a matter of justice. Even a matter of honor, you might say.

Borchert breathed deeply, savoring the fresh night air and his freedom. Scouring the camp out of his lungs. The smell of shit had filled his nose for almost half a year. It was cold along the high track, and his overcoat had gone missing in the first days of captivity, along with his iron cross and his father's watch. The latter two items had been stripped as he slept—by a fellow prisoner. So he was cold now, in his ragged tunic, but Borchert embraced the chill. Reveling in the good German air.

The night seemed so pure when he drank it in that he had a sudden vision of his wife, his Margarethe, on skis. He saw her smile, white as the long runs plunging down between the evergreens, her good skin pinked by exertion and the winter's bite. In memory's photograph, she wore her red sweater. That would have been in Switzerland, the last time they went, before the border closed and the days of generous leaves for officers ended forever.

Now his leave would be permanent. Unless the Americans fought the Russians. Then they would find that they needed the Germans, that they needed officers with experience, men of courage and honor. Borchert had thought the matter through: He would only serve if Germany were allowed its own units. He would *not* serve, under any circumstances, under the immediate command of an American or British officer. And certainly not under a French-man. That would have been like eating out of a camp latrine.

Suddenly, he thought of von Tellheim. Unwillingly. Von Tellheim, who had betrayed his class. Who deserved what he got.

Borchert pushed the thought of his old comrade off into the darkness.

It felt very cold now.

Why wouldn't von Tellheim let him alone? The man had brought everything upon himself. Every bit of it. It would be impossible for anyone to blame Borchert. He had behaved with honor throughout the whole affair.

Borchert folded his arms across his tunic and pushed his weary legs to a quick march. Warming himself to the extent he could. He had known greater cold than this, far greater, but his body had forgotten its experience. And he had been ill intermittently in the camp. Not so ill as others, but sick enough to emerge a weakened man. Now his legs felt withered beneath him. Pared down. As his life had been pared down. He recalled the hard, white cold of the steppes and the wind cutting through his greatcoat like a thousand razors, and he told himself this German autumn was nothing. But his body would not be persuaded.

The flesh forgot. Perhaps wisely.

His feet ached to slow their pace, but Borchert ordered himself to go faster still. The right foot was the bad one, the one that had begun to freeze when they had to fight their way out of the Russian trap on foot. You could not give up, that was the thing. In Russia, men simply gave up. And they died. In the morning, you found them covered in white and stiff as stones. You dared not give up, not ever.

But he understood it now, the delicious appeal of quitting. He understood it so well it frightened him.

He thought again of his wife, his beacon. With the unique red-blond hair that ran through her family. A von Sassen girl was always unmistakable. Margarethe had left their estate in Pomerania the autumn before, grasping the cautious hints in his letters. He had needed to write very carefully. The Stauffenberg affair, a disgraceful mess, had put everyone on their guard, and letters were scrutinized by the authorities for any hint of defeatism. Even the letters of officers. *Especially* the letters from officers. Thank God, he thought, he had managed his transfer before that pathetic business blew up.

They had all known the Russians were coming. He had known it at least since the summer before, in White Russia, and now he suspected that he had known it even longer, at least since von Paulus lost his nerve. It was the blockheads like von Stauffenberg who were slow to grasp that the war was lost. Then, when they did grasp what was happening, they went into a panic, with the Red Army threatening their family holdings. Oh, none of them had turned when the going was good. And when they did turn, they had proven ineffectual.

Borchert grimaced as he marched through the darkness. He had known the family, and that alone might have incriminated him, had he not been so careful. The von Stauffenbergs thought themselves so fine. But the truth was they didn't have a pot to piss in. And the fool couldn't manage to place a briefcase where it needed to go. That sort gave all the old families a bad name.

None of them had conspired when the going was good. And Borchert would not turn just because the going grew difficult. And the business had struck him from the first as stupidly dangerous. He had rebuffed the first—and last—overture made to him. Honor and good sense had gone hand in hand.

It had been enough for him to save his wife. Heeding his warnings, she had made the journey westward long before the Russians arrived, taking refuge with her sister in Cologne. Now the Russians were on the land that had belonged to his blood since an ancestor was ennobled by the Swedes, by Gustavus Adolphus himself, for service in the wars against the Poles. In the camp, he had mourned the loss of the land as he might have mourned a father. Perhaps even more deeply, since his father had died leading his regiment at Gumbinnen, in the opening days of the first war, and Borchert had been too young to feel the loss.

Yes, the estates were gone, perhaps forever. Unless the Amis drove the Russians out. But whether or not the land came back to him, Borchert was determined to survive and rise again. His line had known reverses before. And plenty of deaths. Nor was this the first time that the Russians had come. And the family had always endured. Outfacing even the occasional disgrace. Such as the minor scandal his wife's younger sister had created precisely a decade before.

A baron's daughter, the little fool had married a Rhineland Catholic from the middle class. Borchert did not like Rhinelanders, in any case. They were calculating and sly and hardly German. With the taint of French blood. But to marry a businessman and a Catholic, even a wealthy one, was unforgivable among the landed families who retained the old virtues. Waltraud might as well have married a Jew.

Better to be poor than stained. Of course, some good had come even of that matter in the end. With her own husband off commanding an artillery battery, Waltraud had welcomed Margarethe into her villa in an outlying district of Cologne uninteresting to the Allied bombers.

Margarethe's last letter had reached him in March, when the heavens were falling. Waltraud had been notified that her husband had been killed near Geilenkirchen, a Sunday drive from home. Ever theatrical, the young woman hanged herself, leaving Margarethe alone.

He had not allowed himself to think of the things that might have happened to his wife when the enemy arrived. He forced himself to imagine her as healthy, unsullied, and smiling with her good white teeth. Waiting for him. He knew that the Americans had been the first to reach Cologne, and they did not have a reputation as rapists. That was something in their favor, however little. He could not bear to think of his wife dishonored.

She would have killed herself over such a disgrace.

They had been a perfect match, he and Margarethe, both wellborn, with interests in common, from riding to music, though their childlessness had been a disappointment. But Margarethe was barely thirty, and he was only thirty-seven, after all. There was still time. He only needed for her to be safe a little while longer, just as long as it took a man to walk from Kreuznach to Cologne. Then they would begin to rebuild their world, their own world, excluding all the tawdriness, the shabbiness, of life outside their walls. Refusing the defeat that stretched around them. Even if the land was gone, the blood remained. Margarethe was strong and brave. Together, they would regain their lost world, all of it that mattered. Children *might* come, there might be an entirely new beginning . . .

He smelled the smoke before he saw the house. Woodsmoke, wandering through the night like a lost patrol. Cresting a swell in the wintering fields, he saw the bulk of a house and barn in black shadows. The courtyard's walls shone pale against the edge of a forest. The windows of the house had been shuttered, but cracks of light shone through.

His empty stomach filled with acid.

Borchert had mastered hunger to the degree a sane man could. He knew its varieties, the bite of the empty belly early in the day, and the hollow ache that replaced it as the hours passed. The sudden, useless rages, the urge to hurt and tear. And the growing physical weakness, the temptation to give up. He knew the thoughts that made a man ashamed, that threatened any sense of honor he might possess. The night thoughts. And the sunlit thoughts, as well.

He *knew* hunger. And the resentment it spawned. With the overfed Americans lounging beyond the wire, or patrolling lazily among the prisoners, always smirking, their weapons slack in their hands or slung over a shoulder. The Americans would never have survived on the steppes. Or during the awful days in the swamps of White Russia, before he and his staff had been rescued and brought west for one final effort. Only their uniforms made the Amis seem like soldiers at all. It was a disgrace to have been defeated by such men. With their abundant cigarettes, making a sport of flicking the butts through the wire. Immeasurably bitter, he recalled the amusement of his recent captors as the prisoners scrambled for the shreds of tobacco. The Americans could eat in front of a starving man, cold-eyed.

Borchert despised the Americans, but he had never hated them, and he could not understand why they hated him.

Making his footsore way down the slope toward the farm, Borchert smelled manure, warm and sweet and unlike human waste. The woodsmoke thickened, teasing him with visions of a hearth and a warm supper.

There was no dog. That was a bad sign. A farmyard always had a dog. Did it mean the dog had been eaten? Had the Allies starved these people, too? He knew the French had moved into the area behind the Americans. The French were capable of anything. A nation of whores. He had heard that the English had relieved the Americans in Cologne. That, at least, gave cause for hope. Their better officers were gentlemen. He had gotten to know some of them quite well before the war, on visits to his wife's cousins in Surrey. Good horsemen, most of them.

He made his way through the archway that led into the farmyard, watchful for a silent, lowering dog. Even in the dark, the place looked untended. Almost Slavic.

Borchert struggled to push back unworthy thoughts. Perhaps the poor conditions meant the man of the house had not returned from the war? Perhaps a wife had been left alone to tend the farm? Women were easier to persuade, and more generous, than men. Most of the time. Women would feed you. Even the enemy's women. Black bread and sour milk. Widows fed you and wept, remembering their own. At times, they wanted something in return.

He heard low voices within the house. He *thought* he heard them. His hearing was far from perfect now, and he would never hear music clearly again. Sometimes his ears tricked him. He imagined things. In the night, he heard the screams of dying men. And begging voices.

He knocked on the door. Firmly. Three times.

The voices fell silent.

Finally, footsteps came toward the door. They were heavy enough even for his ruined hearing: a man.

The farmer opened the door partway. Cautiously. Firelight burnished his left cheek. He had a peasant's features and the thickness of an old company sergeant. His right sleeve was pinned up at the shoulder, where an arm should have begun.

The man looked Borchert over. And his features shed their hint of fear, passing to burnished spite. Then on to venom.

He did not give Borchert a chance to speak.

"Go to hell," he said. "I've got nothing for you. Or for any other shit-boy officer."

The farmer slammed the door the way a gunner slaps shut a breech during a barrage.

Borchert passed back under the archway and turned, again, onto the farm road.

Scratching furiously at the raw skin under his sleeve, he burned with shame and outrage. The time had not been so long ago when such a man would not have dared to speak to him that way. To him. A lieutenant colonel. Or to any officer. Or to any von Borchert. Had one of the tenants spoken in such a tone, his grandfather would have taken a whip to the man. As he had whipped the leftist vermin off his land when they dared to bother his villagers with their nonsense after the first war. Oh, yes, they had thought that everything had changed, the little, grasping men. But they had found out. As Liebknecht and Luxemburg had found out. Face-down in a Berlin canal. His uncle in the *Freikorps* had described it cheerfully. And that was how it would be again, Borchert was convinced. The world would come to its senses. The common man needed an orderly regime. Proper men would take charge and provide that order.

Hitler and his pack had been common men, that was the problem. Yes, the great Führer. A shabby little Austrian nobody. That was at the root of the disaster: commonness. Men with no sense of honor. Creatures of the lower middle class. And worse. Scufflers. Touts. Adored by their own kind for their strutting theatricality, all barking and blaring. And kitsch. Bad taste had nearly destroyed the world. His own kind had been fools to go along.

He smiled bitterly. Yes. But it had been easy enough to go along.

Limping now, Borchert walked along the long, long road through the cold. He was ablaze with indignation, his hunger almost forgotten. When next he came to a farmyard where no dog howled, he slipped quietly into the barn and filled his pockets with animal feed. Even in the dark, he could tell by the feel that the grain was low in quality and cut with straw. He knew the world of stables and barns, as a landed gentleman was obliged to know it, and he could move so that no animal took alarm.

He hurried into the woods with his harvest. When he came to a stream, he lit a fire with a pack of American matches he had taken up from the floor as he waited for his release papers. Even their matches were weak and cheaply made, and the fire was hard to start. Borchert picked out the straw, then cooked the feed in a tin cup for as long as he could stand to wait, boiling it soft to spare his loosened teeth. After he gagged down the mush, he took out a scrap of paper and a pencil. He wrote down the approximate location and estimated what he had taken. He would have to return, of course, to pay the farmer. As soon as possible. As soon as he had recovered a bit. Even if it was only a few pfennigs. He was a German officer, a von Borchert.

His bowels began to rebel at the slop in his belly.

It all had begun so well. In Poland. He had been *Hauptmann* von Borchert then, leading a company of infantry, as his forefathers had done in the good years and the bad, at Kunersdorf and Leuthen, Jena and La Belle Alliance, Königsgrätz and Sedan. He remembered how troubled by secret fears of failure he had been, since he had not yet seen combat. He had been sent to Spain too late, when the battles had already given way to executions, and he had worried to himself as he led his men from the order of Silesia into the ripe, unkempt Polish fields . . . oh, the harvest had come, the harvest had come, indeed. He had been relieved to find himself calm of voice, though his heart had thundered within him at first sight of the enemy. He had given clear, crisp orders to nervous men in field gray as the sun caught the tips of the Polish lances across the valley. He positioned his machine guns personally.

He had rather admired the Poles. At least their cavalry. They had dash, for all the good it did them. As he watched them unfold into long lines and trot forward through the sun-washed fields, he had told himself, "*That* is how it should be. War should be that way. An affair for gentlemen. Not this grinding of machines."

His men had been well trained. Although there were only two old veteran noncoms in their ranks, no one opened fire prematurely. Very much the officer, Borchert watched the Poles through his field glasses as his men lay in wait on the swell of foreign ground. He recalled the rumble of the hooves, how it grew until you felt it in your knees, and the gleam of the sun on the leather and the hot, wet coats of the horses, the glint of the medals on a white-haired officer's chest, his mustache ends willowing in Borchert's lenses.

Where he stood that day, the world had assumed a wonderful stillness, reduced to buzzing flies, lazy with the advanced season, and the occasional clinking of a soldier's kit. A clarion call, then another, punctuated the cavalry's advance, and the horses took the meandering streambed that divided the low valley. After crossing, they quickly dressed their ranks and shifted to a canter. Borchert did not need his field glasses anymore.

The officers rode beautiful horses. He always remembered the horses.

He could feel his enemy's senses straining toward him, just as he could feel the earth shaking under the thousands of hooves. Perhaps soldiering truly was in his blood, for he knew what they were thinking: *Let the Germans hold their fire just a little longer. Just a little while longer.*

Borchert called out the engagement range. The lieutenants and sergeants repeated it along the line.

He raised his hand.

The Polish bugles cried again. Angry now. The first of the long, rippling lines of riders lowered their lances.

Just a little longer.

He understood it all. The timing. The yearning. The huge, peculiar longing to kill that had nothing to do with hatred.

It was a deeper, richer thing than hatred.

His rhythms were theirs. As if it all had been arranged. As if all things were in harmony.

The Polish commander tried to spare his horses as long as possible, to marshal their strength for the uphill charge into the German positions. But he waited too long. As Borchert had known he would.

The Poles looked fine and brave, and he longed to kill them.

Just as the first line of horsemen broke into a gallop, shouting a hurrah, Borchert dropped his hand, and barked, "Fire."

The world changed irrevocably.

The Poles came on furiously. But horses tumbled, spraying blood, shrieking and throwing their riders over their necks as they crashed to the earth. The machine guns cut them down with an efficiency that made Borchert wince. For just an instant, a child's fear overtook him. As if he had done something horribly wrong that would be found out. Something unforgivable. Then the fear was gone, and he was shouting, and he could not hold still for the elation bursting out of his skin. He strutted along the line, almost running, screaming at a machine-gun crew whose weapon had jammed.

"Kill them, damn you. Cut them all down!"

The earth shuddered. Other companies of Borchert's regiment had come into line while the Poles were advancing, and cross fire tossed men and beasts into the air, hurling them sideways, exploding their flesh. Artillery rounds, crisp observed fire, found the rear lines of horsemen just as they reached the stream.

No book he had ever read, no story he had been told, had prepared Borchert for the beauty and exhilaration of slaughtering his fellow man.

The Poles were valiant. But backward. Unimaginative. Suicidal. They pressed on, a handful of horsemen coming so close it seemed a perverse miracle. One lancer, facing his death with an expression of rage, hurled his shaft into the German line in the instant before a dozen rifles brought him down and turned his horse into a writhing fountain of blood.

His men did not stop firing when the Polish remnants turned and stumbled back toward their own shrinking world. Borchert would not let them stop. And he cursed the unseen artillerymen when no more splashes of earth and fire, of dust and smoke, pursued the retreating enemy.

He only came to his senses when the company's senior sergeant, the *Spiess*, a veteran of the Western Front, put his face close to Borchert's, and said, "They're out of range, *Herr Hauptmann*. They're out of range now. It's a waste."

Reluctantly, he gave the order to cease fire.

Then Borchert did the other things a leader must after an engagement, but he did them mechanically. All he wanted to do was to stare out across the valley. At the confused, meandering horses' streaming gore. At the wounded and crippled men trying to limp away. The dead horses were visible, for the most part, their bulk pressing the grass flat, but the dead and badly wounded men had disappeared into the yellow fields.

Nothing in his life had ever given him such a feeling of accomplishment, and he wondered if anything would ever make him feel so alive again.

He felt sorry for the horses, though.

Borchert woke just after dawn, shivering and itching, with his guts still quaking from his attempt to feed himself. He rubbed his face with his hand, feeling the shabbiness of whiskers, then slapped his flesh and got to his feet. Dancing absurdly to chase the cold. As men had done in Russia, even when a campfire was allowed.

No, it was not so cold as that. A field surgeon had described it as "paralytic madness," the way some men simply gave in to the Russian cold. This was warm as August in comparison.

His body would not listen. It shivered.

He would have liked a cup of coffee. He could not remember the last time he had held a cup of real coffee in his hands. It was a torment to think about it.

He followed the road into a grove. Sluggishly awake. In the morning stillness, he could hear motor vehicles down through the trees, on the good road along the river. His chosen path was little more than a forester's trail now, following the edge of the high ground. But he did not want to go down into the valley until it was absolutely necessary. The soldiers would be in the valley, in all the towns, and the French might not honor his American parole. They might send him to another camp. He did not know if he could bear that. Not with his wife only a few days' walk away.

He would have to go down at Koblenz, of course, to cross the Mosel where it joined the Rhine. There was only a military bridge now, he had been warned, and it would be guarded by the French at one end and the British at the other. They were fickle about letting Germans cross, even those with valid documents. But Borchert had no choice. The river lay between him and Margarethe. Still, he did not want to test the authority of his American papers before it was absolutely essential.

And what if they sent him back to the same camp? He knew that some of his former comrades would not understand what he had done. They would not recognize the dictate of honor in his actions. They might even try to kill him. Although it was all von Tellheim's fault, from first to last. He had sensed weakness in von Tellheim the first time they had met, years before, on the road to Smolensk. But he had not recognized the power of that weakness, or the danger it posed.

Now he knew.

But he could not go back to the camp.

And if any of them pursued him later on, after they all had been released? In a misguided quest for vengeance? Borchert snorted. Let them. He would have the law on his side then, and not the law of the camp.

Von Tellheim was the only one to blame. They would have to see that.

He walked through a swamp of fallen leaves, smelling their wet rot. Then he smelled something else, and it stopped him cold.

Meat. Cooking.

He began to move again, with his pace quickening on its own.

The road made a bend, and Borchert stopped, startled. Confronted by the ruins of a castle. A long-shattered bit of history, a reminder of other defeats.

Burned by the armies of Louis XIV? By Turenne himself? Or broken earlier, perhaps? During the Thirty Years War? Or earlier still?

So many defeats. And still the strong endured.

He saw her then, the little, round witch of a woman. Laughing silently at him as she stirred a battered pot over a fire. Even from a distance, he could see that her big chunk of face was mole-scarred and mannish. Cropped gray hair spiked from beneath a knit cap. She did not seem dressed so much as layered over with an accumulation of rags.

A huge gray cat lay flopped at her feet by the fire.

He had to restrain an urge to wrest her food from her.

She laughed again, but no longer silently.

"Come out of the woods, they do. Look, Manko. Like bugs out of the walls."

Borchert crossed the open space between them. Watched by the cat.

He stopped half a dozen paces from her fire. Unable to move his eyes from the hand that stirred the contents of the pot.

"I'll pay you," he said. "For food. For something to eat. I'll come back and pay you. My wife's in—"

She laughed out loud. As though he were the funniest thing in the world.

"Got a cigarette?" She gestured toward the pockets of his tunic. "Any cigarettes in there?"

He shook his head.

"I'm an officer," he said, shamed by the pleading tone of his voice, "I'll come back and pay you. I'll—"

" 'An officer!' " She nudged the cat with her foot. She wore soldier's boots. They were in better condition than Borchert's. And too large for her by several sizes. "Hear that, Manko? He's an officer! We're safe now, aren't we, boy? He'll defend us, sure."

Her tone was not respectful.

"My boys weren't officers," she continued. "No, sir. But off they went. Wherever the officers told them. And now they're dead. And my husband. The old idiot. The ass. Out drilling with the *Volksturm*. Everything for the Führer!" She raised her right arm in a mock salute. "Old cretins. Senile, all of them. And little boys. You know what the Russians did to them?" She cackled, almost howling. "No worse than they did to my daughter, anyway. God knows where she is." A demonic smile passed over her face. "Maybe she's with an officer? If the Russians are done with her? Would an officer take up with a woman after the Russians finished with her?"

The woman was mad.

"All the way from Liegnitz, I've come. All that way," she went on. "Every step. Leave the dead behind, I say. Just leave 'em. All of 'em. Leave 'em for the crows."

From Liegnitz? If she wasn't completely mad, if any of it were true, the woman had crossed three-quarters of Germany. And the Rhine. But it was impossible for someone like her to cross the Rhine. The Allies would never have let her cross one of their military bridges. Not without papers.

The smell of the food made him feel as mad as the woman on the other side of the fire. He wanted to plunge his hand into the churning brown broth, grab what he could, and run.

He thought he truly would go mad from the burning in his belly. It seemed to him that he had never before been so hungry. But he knew that was not true. Hunger was like the cold: new every time.

"You . . . came all the way from Silesia?" he asked. Trying to pacify her, to please her. "To here?"

She roared. "I'm not done yet! I'm going farther. To Paris! I'm going to be a dancer in the *Folies*. Lift up my skirts and get me a handsome Frenchman." She nudged the cat again, and it stretched, yawning. "Right, Manko?"

"I'm sorry about your losses, madame."

She grunted. "Why? It's over for them. They're better off."

"The Russians are barbarians."

She looked at him. Cannily. Not half so mad of expression now. "*Are* they? *Are* they now? Unlike the high-and-mighty German

Volk, then?" She made a face as if she had tasted gall. "Why should I blame the Russians? What have they done?"

He was baffled. "You said . . . your daughter . . . your husband . . ."

"If I was a Russian, I would have done the same thing. What business of ours was it to go off invading Russia? Or anybody else? We had work enough on the farm. A hard enough life it was. But not such a bad one." She reached down and stroked the cat. "Plenty of fat mice, right, Manko? We didn't need any Russian mice. Now they're all over the place, those little Russians. Just like mice. Eating everything up." She looked up into Borchert's eyes, and he saw that hers were of stunning cornflower blue. "My youngest boy wrote me from Russia, my Franzerl. He said it was the poorest place he'd ever seen. What did we want in a place like that, I ask you? Why couldn't we let them alone and eat our own soup?"

Of course, it was no good speaking of glory or strategy to a madwoman. But her eyes demanded an answer. With their immaculate, inhuman purity.

Perhaps she once had possesed her sliver of loveliness. A village beauty. And now she was nothing but lumps and rags. It happened commonly in the lower classes. A few short years with a bountiful girl, then a lifetime with a hag.

"We asked for it," she said, in a low, harsh voice. "And we got it. *Sieg Heil!*" She lifted her hand, wearily, and cackled again, forgetting the spoon in the pot. "Weren't my boys proud as could be, with their short pants and armbands and all that marching up and down? That's how it started, that's how they twisted them up." She wrinkled her mouth at her memories. "I said to my husband right off, I said, 'You watch out for that one, that Hitler. He's a wormy little turd, not a man.' But would he listen? Not if the beer was free, not my Fritz." She shook her head. "Nothing but turds and fancy boys, all of them. Dirty buggers, and not a decent, healthy man among 'em. With officers by the thousands to lick their boots." Suddenly, she smiled. "Well, they're all in Hell now, and good riddance. To Hell with 'em all. And to Hell with the Fatherland, too. Just give me my soup."

Unbidden, the old fears of dangerous speech rose in Borchert, a reflex from the years when many things could not be uttered. Involuntarily, he said:

"That's treason."

The old woman looked at him. Staring with her mad, blue eyes.

Finally, she wrinkled her mouth, and said, "I knew it was all up when they came for the Jews. What country can get on without its Jews? You think the Lord didn't put the Jews here for a reason?" She smiled at him. "Land in the shit and blame the Jews. And now we're in it up to our necks, and who do we have left to shovel us out?"

Borchert refused to think about such matters. He had had nothing to do with the handling of the Jews. Nothing at all. In Russia, when his unit was tasked for personnel to help round up the yids, he had sent only enlisted men, not officers. The Jews had not been his business, but preserving the honor of his subordinate officers had been, and he had behaved with due propriety. Anyway, everyone knew something had to be done about the Jews. Perhaps not anything so excessive. Deportation, perhaps. Deportation might have been a perfectly sound solution.

Borchert had avoided the entire issue, refusing even to listen to the rumors, although he had felt an unavoidable, human satisfaction when he learned that old Engelmann and his brood had been rounded up. But that was only to be expected. Engelmann had made enemies. Margarethe had written from their estate, telling Borchert that the local Party officials had made it clear that all debts owed by those of pure German blood to Jewish moneylenders and bankers were erased, as were all Jewish liens on Aryan property, although a small contribution to the local Party coffers would be welcome as a sign of gratitude and confirmation. All Borchert knew was that he would never again have to face the indignity of going to the old Jew, with his throbbing pink tongue, to ask for an extension on the payments for the property he had mortgaged. No, the fact was that Germany was well rid of the Jews.

After all, a man didn't have to be an anti-Semite to find the Jews a pestering lot. And those in Berlin had been even worse than those

back home. With their cultural pretensions and their social osten-
tation. Burrowing like rodents into the best positions in the universities and elsewhere. Always laying claim to a higher position
and making a great show of their abilities. Grasping. Even turning
up at a man's tailor. It was laughable. What nobility could you
derive from owning a department store? Or an underwear factory?
Hadn't the Jews brought it on themselves, in the end?

At night, in the Russian towns and villages, he had heard the
firing squads. But his men had not been involved, except when
matters became urgent. And he had always demanded a written
order from a superior before he would send a single soldier to that
sort of duty. Some of the men had rather relished it, of course. But
others were demoralized by the tasks they had to perform. Really,
he had done his best to avoid the matter. Better for the unit that
way.

Sometimes, you saw them. The bodies. Still unburied, as you
marched on. At other times you could not avoid running into a
pack of Jews being driven along the streets toward a pit or, perhaps,
a rail siding. Clutching their paltry belongings. With terror in their
eyes, or simply bewilderment. The old men always looked stunned.
With their shabby gabardines and their steel-rimmed glasses askew.
Their hands pawed the air, as if to soil it.

He recalled the old Jew with the overloaded suitcase. A shriveled
creature with a stained beard, the Jew had lagged behind a pack of
yids herded along by local turncoats. Dragging a big suitcase
through the dust, obviously incapable of managing the burden, the
old man had a useless, stinking look. The Russian *Hilfstruppen* driving the filthy bunch of them to the siding kicked at the old man,
cursing him, telling him to get along, but the yid would not leave
his suitcase behind. Then the German captain in charge of the detail, an SS man, strutted back to see what the delay was about.
Barking. What was the problem? What was holding them up, damn
it? The Russian volunteers went timid as mice at the SS man's
approach. They stepped back, letting the officer see the old man
and the suitcase. "Break it open," the officer ordered. "He's probably

got a fortune in there. That's all these bloodsuckers care about."
The *Hilfstruppen* tore the suitcase from the old man's clutches, and
the Jew wailed. Then he tried to fight them for it, but landed in
the dust with his jaw smashed. The Russian volunteers emptied the
suitcase onto the road: nothing but books. The old Jew threw himself on top of the volumes, gathering as many as he could to his
breast, until the exasperated officer shot him and walked away.

"I don't know anything about the Jews," Borchert told the old
woman. "They're not my affair. I swear I'll come back and pay you,
if you'll give me something to eat."

"Sit down, *Herr Offizier*," the woman told him. Smiling queerly.
"Sit down and eat your fill. There's more than enough. We don't
have to feed the Jews anymore. So there's lots for everybody." She
grinned. "Right, Manko?"

Scratching idly at his thigh, Borchert sat down on a stone block
long since fallen from the castle wall. The sky had lightened to gray,
but would not color. He sensed rain coming.

From behind her skirts, the old woman drew a clamor of tin
plates and cutlery. The sight of the plates, filthy though they were,
punched up the hunger in his stomach again. He wanted to grab,
to cram food into his mouth.

"None for the Jews, lots for the *Herr Offizier*," the woman sang.
She dished two clumps of gray meat onto a battered plate and held
it out to him.

He did not, could not, wait for anything. Picking the meat up in
both hands, he gnawed at it with his unsteady teeth, burning his
fingers, his lips, his tongue. When it grew too hot to bear in his
mouth, he swallowed the meat unchewed, scalding his insides. Eating with his eyes closed. Dripping juice over his chin. It was the
most generous portion of meat he had been served in a year. At
last, he opened his eyes in wonder at the ineradicable goodness of
the earth.

Across from him, the woman ate with the slowness of the aged,
glancing over at him as she fed morsels to the cat.

Borchert cleaned the bones and sucked the last flavor from them.

He was out of breath from the effort he had put into eating.

His stomach felt wonderfully warm. Almost full. He licked a bone one last time.

"I think," he said generously, "that was the best rabbit I've ever had."

That set the old woman going again. Howling with unreserved glee. When she finally calmed again, she told him:

"That wasn't rabbit. That's rat. Manko catches them in the ruins."

It had been miserable going through the Ardennes. The tanks pushed ahead, leaving the forest tracks a sodden mess, and higher headquarters was never content with the progress the infantry made. Borchert felt as if a whip had been applied to his back, and every other officer in the regiment felt the same way. There was too big a gap between the *Panzer* spearhead and the rest of the invading force, and the gap seemed to grow by the hour. The infantry slogged on, and the horse-drawn artillery bogged down in the narrow river valleys, with the engineers played out after getting everyone across the Meuse. The tanks were already at Sedan, and the infantry was still in the woods. Then the tanks passed Arras, and the infantry had barely reached Sedan. All the glory went to the *Panzertruppen* in those days.

As always, the infantry did most of the actual fighting. Not that the French put up much resistance. Small units fought, but their parent units failed. After the long stalemate of the last war, the French commanders were bewildered by the speed of their own collapse. The sharpest encounter involving Borchert's regiment had been fought against troops holding the far bank of a canal. The French were surprisingly dogged, unwilling to surrender even when German forces outflanked them on the right and the left. Borchert almost admired them as the shells wrenched apart the grove where they had dug themselves in.

Then, suddenly, a white rag went up across the canal. Borchert was the first officer of his regiment to enter the French position, where the fallen far outnumbered the able. The French battalion commander was dead, and the major who had taken his place, arm limp and bloody at his side, fought back tears.

A German officer never would have behaved so weakly. Officers did not weep.

"You fought well," Borchert had told the man, speaking the polite French that had been whipped into him by a succession of governesses and tutors. "You did all that could be done. There's no shame in it."

At that, the French major's tears exploded. But they were tears of rage, not of sorrow. "*I* never would have surrendered to you," he said, almost spitting. His face was swollen with anger and blood. "We were *ordered* to surrender. By cowards . . . cowards . . ."

After that, the sun had stayed with the regiment, and the marches were long and dusty, but mostly peaceful. Each village had its own soul. Sometimes, the houses and shops were shuttered and silent as the Germans marched by. Elsewhere, the French showed themselves submissively—curious and already anxious to please their new masters. The summer had come early and full, and the best roads led between lines of shade trees, with green fields stretching off toward church spires. In Lothringen, lindens scented the air. It hardly seemed like war at all.

The regiment's officers were furious when they heard that the British forces surrounded at Dunkirk had escaped, though the English had shamed themselves by leaving the French behind on the beach. *Oberst* von Elmerdingen listened quietly, glass of wine in hand. Then, when the junior officers had all had their say, he simply told them, "That's what we get for putting our faith in tanks instead of in our feet. I wish you a good night, gentlemen."

But if Borchert's regiment did not get to Dunkirk, they did get to Paris. The French wept when the Germans marched in. The French always seemed to be crying. Borchert found it distasteful. Had they fought harder, they might have spared themselves the tears. Really, the French were weak, a played-out people.

But the women were fine. In their own shameless way. He had been elevated to a staff position, in Paris, of the sort for which he had been trained before the war. Margarethe was able to visit, and

Borchert took her to hear Mistinguett and Chevalier. And when his wife was not on hand, Borchert spent his spare evenings in an elegant bordello where any sort of French patriotic nonsense stopped at the front door. He had even grown quite fond of one of the girls. Emma, a slender blonde from the countryside near Rouen, shameless to the point of inspiration. They had enjoyed their time together. The little slut had the gift of making a man laugh and want her furiously at the same time. And she understood, intuitively, the things he liked, and never mocked him. Those had been lovely times.

Until the silly fool greeted him publicly, a block from the Opera, while Borchert was strolling the boulevards with a pair of fellow officers. The whore sent him a little wave, followed by a *"Bonjour, monsieur."*

Borchert slashed her across the face—twice—with the riding crop he had carried in those days. What on earth had the idiotic tart been thinking? He left her on the pavement, bleeding and shivering between two friends—doubtless whores themselves. He did not bother to look back.

At the next corner, one of his companions observed, approvingly, "They have to learn. They really have to learn . . ."

A few days later, Borchert remarked, idly, to an acquaintance serving in a specialized department that the woman appeared to have Jewish blood. He never knew what happened to her, of course. It wasn't any of his business. But whatever might have come her way had been fully deserved.

He despised the French.

Borchert received his promotion to major shortly thereafter. He was bored with Paris and with the dullness the war had taken on. Through the good offices of friends in Berlin, he received command of an infantry battalion, a position that rightfully should have gone to a lieutenant colonel. But the army was expanding again, and properly bred officers already were in short supply.

His battalion was waiting for him in Poland, not far from Soviet Russia's new border with the German *Reich*.

It was in the glorious days of the advance, with the Red Army broken and surrendering in the hundreds of thousands. Just short of Smolensk, a sniper fired from a village, killing one of Borchert's lieutenants. The boy had not been of good family. Still, he was a German officer. Borchert ordered his men to surround the settlement. Then they went from house to house, searching for the sniper.

They never found him. So Borchert gave the order to burn the place to the ground.

His men had just gotten to work when an officer arrived from the staff of Borchert's new regiment. Von Tellheim had been only a captain then, but he had not been shy about confronting his superiors.

"What do you think you're doing?" he demanded of Borchert.

"I don't 'think' I'm doing anything. I'm burning out the rats and lice. As you see."

Von Tellheim stared at him for a moment. As arrogantly as if their ranks had been reversed. "You have no right to do such a thing."

"No right? A sniper killed Lieutenant Kantner. Firing from the village."

"And your response is to burn the place down? God in Heaven, man, that's exactly what the Russians want! The fanatics want us to take reprisals. To turn the population against us."

"Well, then," Borchert said, "I intend to give them what they want. If you don't approve, *Herr Hauptmann*, I suggest you take it up with the regimental commander."

And von Tellheim had done just that. The colonel backed Borchert, of course. Warning von Tellheim never to question the authority of a commander in the field again.

And the Germans found far more imaginative ways to turn the population against them than merely burning villages. Even so, to the very end, many of those who had endured the Soviet yoke preferred the Germans as the lesser of two evils. It amused Borch-

ert, who considered himself a student of the human condition. And
the local inhabitants were always glad to help with the disposition
of the Jews.

Borchert did not believe in unnecessary cruelty, of course. Personally, he did not find the least appeal in burning villages and the
like. But war required a certain sternness, and a man could not
indulge his own emotions. Especially when fighting an uncivilized
people. You had to demonstrate your strength. Every day.

Von Tellheim turned out to be a dutiful, capable officer, if overly
excitable, and a truce arose between the two of them. Over the
summer and into the early autumn, they even learned to banter
with one another. Drunk with victory. After all, the von Tellheims
were a fine, old family, though the captain's father had married a
middle-class girl, a Lessing. Most likely to get the family debts paid
down.

The snow came early and hard, and neither Moscow nor Leningrad had fallen, and the plains seemed more endless than ever,
with the great rivers freezing over beyond them. Even then, in that
first winter, Borchert had begun to doubt the wisdom of the campaign in the east. Unable to draw winter equipment, his men's feet
froze in their hobnailed boots. Lacking winter overcoats, soldiers
fell to the frost and to pneumonia. Frostbite struck the tall, lean
men hardest, and Borchert might have succumbed himself, had he
not been able to have his own kit sent out from a military tailor in
Berlin. It was hard watching the men suffer, though. And the snow
brought the Russians back to life.

They swept through the darkness, in mad, barbarian attacks
against the German trenches. Driven on by their commissars. Perhaps, even by patriotism. Neither side had enough of anything but
bullets, so prisoners became an immediate liability. And both sides
stopped taking prisoners.

It was not war as Borchert would have liked it. But the Russians
had brought it upon themselves. Through their savagery. And their
obstinate unwillingness to surrender.

Moscow did not fall.

Leningrad did not fall.

The machine guns froze up.

And the men behind the guns froze, too.

When the spring returned, there were seas of mud at first. Then the earth dried and the offensive swept forward again, toward the Volga, toward the Caucasus. Again, Russian prisoners were taken by the hundreds of thousands, the cheapest commodity on earth. German arrows swept across the map.

Borchert got his iron cross.

But something was gone. The edge of confidence that carried you forward when you were already tired out, or sick, or low on ammunition seemed ever so slightly dulled. The battles were more intense than those of the year before and, on paper, the triumphs seemed even greater. The division to which Borchert's regiment belonged was assigned to the Sixth Army, which had closed on Stalingrad. But Borchert was ordered back to Berlin, to the Army High Command's staff. He was not sorry to go.

He flew out on the same plane as von Tellheim, who had been wounded in the legs by Russian shell fragments.

Borchert marched northward under a steady autumn drizzle. In the murky, dissolving afternoon, mud oozed through the gap in his sole. His feet had gone from pain to numbness, and he was afraid to remove his boots and look at the flesh. Then, daydreaming about the past—almost hallucinating—he stumbled on the wreckage left by a skirmish where two farm roads crossed. Any damaged Allied equipment had long since been cleared away, but a litter of German vehicles and upended guns lined the roadside, where they had been pushed to clear the way. It appeared they had been taken by surprise, perhaps while retreating. In the cab of a shattered truck, a corpse hunched over the steering wheel. Picked over by animals until the remaining meat grew too foul even for scavengers, a face half skull and half leather lolled beneath a helmet. On the flapping door of another vehicle, someone had scratched, "Kilroy was here."

By the time he reached the high ground above Koblenz, Borchert was soaked through. Even if he had been able to summon the courage to remove his boots, he had no cardboard left with which to fill the gap in his sole. There was still sufficient daylight for him to cross the small, ravaged city and present his papers to the guards on the bridge. But he stopped, unable to go another step. Not because he was tired, though he was weary enough. Because he was afraid.

He told himself that it wouldn't do to approach the guards in the rain, since the poor weather would have put them in a bad mood. And he did not want to draw out his precious parole in the rain and have the papers ruined. And he really was worn-out. But the truth of the matter was simply that he was afraid.

If the guards at the bridge turned him back, what would he do? Where could he go?

He had to reach Margarethe. Nothing else mattered now. And he was afraid of the thousand mistakes and misunderstandings that might stop him.

He took shelter in a ruined house above the city. It was impossible to start a fire. The world was too wet. So he huddled in a corner, where a remaining bit of upper floor kept the rain off him. The only good thing was that the wetness of his clothing calmed the itching that had spread all over his body.

The house had been destroyed long before, likely by an errant bomb from one of the Allied planes attempting to destroy one bridge or another. The giveaway was the lack of personal effects. The ruin had been picked over countless times, until there was nothing left of the least utility or identity.

The rain strengthened. Hammering the bit of flooring that drooped above his head. Leaking through in spots.

Thunder exploded. Borchert flattened himself, an automatic response. Then, ashamed, he gathered himself together again and settled back into his corner. Wet. Cold. Weary. And already hungry again, despite the grim breakfast that had come his way.

It sounded like bombs. The thunder. The rain that had begun to pound.

All nature had gone over to the attack.

It sounded like bombs.

Always the bombs.

At night.

His first sight of Berlin after a year and a half shocked him. The Allied air raids had become earnest and routine. The beautiful city, with its gardens and grandeur, looked like a mouth with half its teeth knocked out.

More and more of the important work moved underground, into bunkers. The staff officers were well trained, and experienced now, and their work went smoothly. But it seemed to Borchert as though there was an unreality to their actions, as though all the endless staff work was a pretense. After von Paulus betrayed the Fatherland and surrendered his army, the atmosphere grew worse. Nothing was the same after that. Even though the next summer brought a last smattering of victories, and no one spoke of the possibility of defeat, a secret despair permeated the Army High Command like a gas.

And the bombing continued. Hamburg. Frankfurt. Hannover. Mannheim. Bremen. Every corner of the Ruhr. Hanau. Stuttgart. Nuremberg. Munich. Kiel. Cologne. One city suffered after the other. Borchert could not believe the barbarity of it. The Allies had no moral justification for what they were doing. It wasn't only factories and docks that went up in flames, but treasure-houses of history. Churches. Palaces. Countless homes. German civilians perished by the thousands. The brutality of it all stunned him, and made him glad that Margarethe was safe on their estate.

And the bombing continued. The *Luftwaffe* did what it could, bringing down American and British bombers by the hundreds. But the Allies seemed to have an endless supply of planes. Goering began to speak of wonder weapons, but the army had never trusted him and didn't believe him now. It was difficult enough producing tanks.

The folly hadn't been fighting the Russians, of course. That was inevitable, although the initial offensive might have been better timed. As Borchert saw it, the folly lay in Germany's inability to avoid a war with the Americans. With their factories and assembly lines that were proving more than a substitute for courage.

The Allies seemed to have as many bombers as the Russians had infantrymen.

The Führer's rages became legendary. Officers who once had flocked around him avoided him when they could. And the generals lied.

The poisonous thought had arisen in the Army High Command that the war in the east might fail, but no one believed—not yet—that the Russians would ever set foot on German soil. There would have to be a peace settlement. To give the *Reich* a chance to catch its breath, to consolidate its gains.

To give Germany a chance.

Borchert was promoted to lieutenant colonel and offered a brigade back on the Eastern Front, in Army Group Center. At the beginning of the war, the position would have gone to a one-star general, later to a full colonel. Now it was his, if he wanted it. But *General-major* von Klenstein, an old family acquaintance, let Borchert know, without needing to use words, that he could remain in Berlin if he preferred. Without so much as lifting an eyebrow, von Klenstein communicated his belief that it was all futile now.

The old man was a defeatist. And not the only one.

Borchert took the command, although his appetite for glory was less than it had been a few short years before. After all, it was his duty to serve where he was needed. The von Borcherts had never shrunk from their obligations to the Fatherland. And there might be a colonelcy, or better, at the end of it.

Despite the debacle that overtook them all the next summer, in White Russia, taking command of the brigade proved a wise decision. Von Klenstein and several others with whom Borchert had worked in Berlin were implicated in the von Stauffenberg affair. Von Klenstein shot himself to save his family, while two other officers from Borchert's department were hanged. By then, Borchert had been evacuated from the Eastern Front, along with dozens of other commanders and staffs. By the autumn of 1944, he was in the Taunus Mountains, just east of the Rhine—almost directly across the river from the ruin in which he found himself now. He had been tasked, though still a lieutenant colonel, to serve as the number two for a new division being raised for service against the Americans and the British, who had reached the Siegfried Line.

The overage men, teenage boys, and weak-limbed support troops sent to fill the *Volksgrenadier* division had appalled him at first. But Borchert never lacked a sense of duty. And he had gotten to see the Ardennes again, this time in winter.

The rain pounded down, and Borchert could not sleep. He shivered in the ruined house in his ruined country, telling himself his courage would return in the morning.

The morning came cold and gray, but the rain had stopped. The earth smelled heavily of autumn, and sounds carried. Borchert could hear heavy trucks down along the river road, their engines turning over steadily as they moved in convoy. The city drowsed under a gray blanket.

His soldier's instincts saved him. He heard them sneaking up on him and just had time to pick up a fallen board and swing it against the lead boy. The pack wielded primitive clubs and stones, but Borchert was swift and unsparing. He went for their heads and dropped three of the children amid the rubble before the rest drew back. They would have killed him for what little was in his pockets, he recognized that much by the feral look of them. Moving quickly, he got back to the road, chased by stones and curses worse than those of dying soldiers.

When he had gained enough distance to relax his pace, something collapsed inside of him. This is what Germany had come to, after all that had been sacrificed: wild children murdering their elders. He wanted to sit down by the roadside and rest his head in his hands.

Instead, Borchert gave himself orders to march down into the streets of the city. More than anything else, he would have liked a dry pair of stockings. Even more than food. His feet felt tender and shriveled, and the chill climbed up his legs to his groin.

Women worked in the ruins, shifting rubble in wheelbarrows. Picking up broken bricks with their hands. German women. Working like slaves.

It got worse as he approached the confluence of the rivers. Closing on the bridgehead, entire blocks had been flattened, one after the other. Where doorways stood, women shifting as prostitutes waited for their morning customers. And the customers came: black men in French uniforms. African troops. Borchert watched one of them disappear into a hallway with a young girl who should have been in school.

The French were doing this to humiliate Germany. It was clear. It wasn't necessary to occupy German cities with their black barbarians. Even in the camps, Borchert had heard gruesome stories of the behavior of the French colonial troops in the south, in Baden. Now they were here.

At least Cologne would be free of them. The British were in Cologne. Perhaps Margarethe had been able to contact her cousins in England?

The prostitutes, thick as lice, did not even look at him. Their attentions were all on the French soldiers. Then, turning a corner, Borchert smelled coffee—real coffee—brewing in a cellar. He almost broke down and wept.

But it was unthinkable for a German officer to shed tears in public, and he mastered himself.

The river was running high with the autumn rains, high and gray. A convoy of American-made jeeps and trucks, with British markings, snaked over the temporary bridge. On the near bank, by a guard post, a line of German civilians stood quietly, waiting their turn to cross.

Borchert got in line.

The old woman ahead of him carried just-roasted potatoes in her bag, he could smell them. Her midday meal, no doubt. Borchert pictured fire-blackened potatoes, broken apart, salted, and buttered. It made his gut ache.

He almost opened his mouth to ask if she would sell him a portion on trust. But there were too many people about—a half dozen more had already joined the line behind him—and he was afraid he would shame himself.

The smell would not let him be.

The convoy cleared the bridge, and the crowd pressed forward. Two Africans in uniform stepped from the guard shelter, and a

clamoring began. Taking their good time, even arrogant, the Africans, a junior noncom and a private, inspected papers. Sometimes
they laughed. And they turned one old man away, giggling like
children as they watched him limp off.

Borchert would have liked to shoot them down.

What had Germany done to deserve this?

A young woman with a child of six or seven excited the attentions of the guards. They held up the line, toying with her. Finally,
she went into the shack with the noncom, leaving her little girl in
the care of the old woman who was next in line. After a few
minutes, the NCO emerged without the woman, and the private
went inside. In less than five minutes, the private came back out,
trailed by the woman. The expression on her face was set, and she
didn't look back at anyone, only took her child by the forearm and
dragged her out onto the bridge. Only then did the child begin to
cry.

When Borchert's turn came, the soldiers played with his papers
and spoke in a jabbering language. Smiling their huge grins.

"It's a parole authorizing me to travel," Borchert told them in
French. "From the Americans. It must be honored by all Allied
forces."

The noncom ignored him and, for a moment, Borchert feared
the man would toss the papers into the river. Instead, he handed
back the sheets and said, in an accent Borchert could barely understand, "Cigarettes? Money? What presents did you bring us,
monsieur?"

"I have nothing," Borchert told the man. "The pass authorizes me
to go to Cologne. I'm entitled to cross this bridge . . ."

"No presents, no bridge, *monsieur,*" the NCO said. He and his
companion giggled again.

Borchert stepped forward. But the private unshouldered his
weapon, and the giggling stopped.

A jeep pulled up, with a French officer in the passenger's seat.
Another African sat behind the wheel. The guards came to attention and saluted. It appeared the jeep would simply pass by, but
the officer ordered it to halt. He stepped out and walked over to

Borchert. The Frenchman was a colonel, and his right arm hung limply in the sleeve of his uniform.

The colonel looked oddly familiar. But, then, there was a sameness to the French.

"What's going on here?" he asked the noncom.

"He wants to cross," the NCO answered, in a voice made simple. "Does he have papers?"

The NCO shrugged. "Not in French."

"Pardonez-moi, monsieur le colonel," Borchert said, in the most respectful voice he could muster. He held out his papers. "I've been paroled by the Americans. To go home to my wife. The papers are in order."

The French officer looked at him hard. After a moment, he said, "We'd all like to go home to our wives." But he took the papers.

After scanning the sheets, the colonel wrinkled up the side of his mouth, as if in disgust.

"Let him pass," he told the guards.

Borchert stepped forward to thank him, one officer to another, but the Frenchman had already turned back toward his jeep.

"Move along," the noncom told Borchert, as if it were all a matter of routine.

British soldiers manned the far end of the bridge. They let the civilians go by without interference, but stopped Borchert.

" 'Ere now, you there," a corporal called him over. He and his men wore berets with red-and-white brushes fixed upright. *"Papieren? Versteh?"* he added, in a dreadful accent.

Borchert handed over his papers.

A sandy-haired private with bad skin and bad teeth said, "Ask 'im if those black buggers give 'im one up the arse before they let 'im come over. And ask 'im if 'e liked it."

"Versteh English?" the corporal asked Borchert.

"Nein," Borchert lied. Wary of the further insults his comprehension might bring.

"About bloody time 'e learned it," the sandy-haired private said.

"Ain't that right, Corporal Jones? Time they all bloody-well learned it."

"Oh, piss off, Alf," the corporal said. "You can see the poor bastard's all in." He handed the papers back to Borchert, telling him, *"In Ordnung."*

"Danke," Borchert said.

But as Borchert stepped away, the corporal called after him.

"Halt!"

Borchert's heart pounded. He saw Margarethe as clearly as ever he had seen her in the flesh, a vision almost religious in its intensity. And he feared what was coming. With his fate—their fate—at the mercy of this lowest of noncoms, a man who wasn't fit to shine a German officer's boots.

He was about to protest that his papers were in perfect order, when he saw the corporal was holding out a pack of cigarettes, offering him one.

" 'Ere, you sorry bugger. 'Ave one for the road."

Borchert took the cigarette. *"Danke. Vielen Dank."*

As he walked away for the second time, Borchert heard the corporal say, "You look at a poor, sodding bloke like that one, and you can't 'elp wondering 'ow the Jerries gave us such a time of it. Makes a body wonder, don't it, Alf?"

Borchert did not light the cigarette until he was on the high ground again, beyond the last houses and out of sight. Then he stopped and struck a match with an unsteady hand.

It was a good cigarette, with real tobacco. He had not tasted anything as good since the previous December, in the Ardennes, in the snow, when he had taken a packet of American cigarettes called Lucky Strikes from a captured vehicle.

The Americans had cost him his promotion to colonel. But they had paid for it.

Borchert walked along a gray road, under a gray sky, with bald fields right and left. In the high ridges of the Ardennes, the snow had been packed to ice on the trails, tamped down by thousands of boots, but in the forest it might come up to a man's waist. Snow had an odd effect on inexperienced soldiers, as nearly all of the men and boys in his division had been. When they sank down in it, they imagined it would protect them, as if it were a wall of earth. He had seen men try to hide from bullets by crouching down behind a snowdrift. When they first were hit, their blood was as crimson as a red silk scarf. Then it soaked in, sometimes pink at the edges of the pools, but finally brown. Almost the color of shit. As though everything within a man was foul.

Crows sat on a gate and watched him pass: a man smoking as if a fire burned inside him. Borchert drew on the cigarette one last time and burned his lips. Still, he hated to let it go. And, yes, there was a fire inside him. It flared anew whenever he thought of that last great attempt, the winter surprise the Allies didn't expect.

He scratched his groin and remembered.

His division, green though it was, had been given a position of honor. At the cutting edge of the attack. Ahead of the tanks this time. The intelligence reports had promised that the first troops they would hit would be the broken men of the American Twenty-eighth Infantry Division. The unit had been torn apart in the autumn fighting and had been shifted to a quiet sector for rehabilitation. Borchert's own reconnaissance section, led by a veteran of the Eastern Front, confirmed that, for once, the intelligence reports were correct: The Americans before them wore the Twenty-eighth Division's red-bucket patch on their sleeves, and they were spread thinly across a huge sector. Punching through them, especially with surprise on the German side, would be only a matter of hours, if not of minutes.

Things began to go wrong the day before the attack was set to begin. The tank troops positioned to exploit the attack's initial success moved up too far too early. It was hard for Borchert to believe that the Americans across the valley had not heard them. And the tanks cut the communications wire strung along the roads and trails. Rations failed to arrive, and an inspecting colonel from the high command told Borchert that the roads were clogged with military traffic for eighty to a hundred kilometers behind the front lines. Before the skies closed in, American aircraft flew over the jump-off positions. Despite all the camouflage efforts, the pilots had to have seen some of the activity on the ground. The German troops were green and meandered past their assigned positions, their young leaders unable to read maps or lacking maps entirely.

Still, Borchert was accustomed to such confusion. Everything behind the lines always seemed a mess, he knew that much. It was only as you approached the edge of battle that things began to make sense. The rear of an attack always looked so chaotic a civilian would have mistaken it for a defeat. And the Americans were few, and tired of the war. Borchert felt confident. He would see Brussels again. Perhaps even Ostende and the sea.

The infantry moved out in darkness, then the artillery began to pound. The first reports were encouraging. Despite everything, the Americans appeared to have been surprised, indeed. Their positions were surrounded and quickly overrun. Pockets of resistance held out, but their destruction was only a matter of time. All that mattered now was opening the roads.

A crucial point of resistance lay at a crossroads hamlet on a forested bluff. Given the thickness of the surrounding trees, the angle of the slope and the depth of the snow, it was impossible for vehicles to bypass the settlement. The hamlet had to be taken swiftly and the roads opened so the tanks could pass through and strike deep before the Americans could organize their defenses.

The morning passed into afternoon, and the hamlet still was not in German hands. The first inquiries came down from corps, then from army level. Was the road open? Could the *Panzer* formations move through? What on earth was the problem?

Borchert went forward himself to crack the whip. He arrived as the early winter dusk began to thicken. A fellow lieutenant colonel should have been on the scene to meet him, but the man had gone missing. A major, recently transferred from an antiaircraft-artillery unit to the needy infantry, was in charge. He began to salute before Borchert slapped his arm down.

"What's holding you up? Why isn't there any artillery? Why don't I hear any artillery, for God's sake?"

"The land line's broken. We're fixing it."

"Send a runner, you ass."

"I did, *Herr Oberstleutnant*. The artillery say we don't have priority of fires."

"This is the division's main attack, man."

"We're trying, *Herr Oberstleutnant*. We—"

Borchert had heard enough. He relieved the man on the spot. With the threat of a court-martial. Taking charge personally, he sent a written order to the division's artillery regiment, organized a second team to trace the communications wire and find the break, then went forward to get the troops moving again. If the artillery hit while they were attacking, too bad. The crossroads had to be opened. Immediately.

With the hamlet no more than a cluster of masonry farmhouses glimpsed through black tree trunks, Borchert found the surrounding snows littered with his infantrymen. Lying there as random as casualties. But they were healthy enough, these old men and boys, former *Luftwaffe* ground crewmen, and even sailors without ships— all magically transformed into infantrymen by the stroke of a pen. Most of the sergeants were better suited to be air-raid wardens than to lead infantry assaults.

"Get up," Borchert shouted. "Move forward. This is nothing. You. Sergeant. Get your men moving or, by God, I'll shoot you myself."

He worked his way along the line, fighting with the snow that did its best to slow him or topple him over. Pressing the men forward, he saw that, as soon as they took fire from the hamlet, they went to ground again. The best of them fired their rifles at the buildings. But even those lacked the will to drive home an attack.

It was an hour before the artillery struck. Then the shells fell behind the houses. Borchert stormed back to the headquarters that had been established in a hollow. The only good news was that the field telephone was working again.

Borchert corrected the artillery fire himself. Soon, the shells were crashing down on the roofs of the buildings and into their courtyards. Borchert pressed the gunners to keep firing, to eliminate any resistance. He knew how difficult it was to blast defenders out of well-built dwellings. But the Americans were tired, and few. A barrage should be sufficient to teach them their lesson.

When the artillery officer on the other end of the line insisted he had to shift fires, by order of the corps commander, Borchert went back up to the line of troops. With the darkness compressed under a thick, low sky, the high ground was illuminated only by a pair of fires in the hamlet. Desultory rifle cracks punched the night.

It was cold.

The infantrymen had begun to huddle together, for warmth, drawing back instead of going forward. Borchert tried, again, to drive them into the attack, but the most he got out of them was a fifty-meter advance, leaving a distance of over a hundred meters between the nearest cluster of German troops and the outbuildings.

He had never seen anything like this: German troops unwilling to attack. There were two battalions, the better part of a regiment, spread over the slopes, and they had taken no more than a few dozen casualties.

Legs exhausted from a day spent fighting through snowdrifts, Borchert went back to the field headquarters and called the division commander to ask for fresh troops—and better ones, if possible. Before he could state his case, the division commander lashed out at him, demanding to know what in Heaven or Hell could be holding up the German advance. Doubtless, the man had taken his own whippings from his superiors, but Borchert could only feel resentful. He had put everything he had into trying to move old men and boys to attack. If the mission was so vital, why hadn't they been given at least one seasoned infantry regiment? Or even a single battalion of veteran troops?

At last, weary of shouting, the division commander agreed to commit the division's last infantry regiment.

But the troops arrived piecemeal, confused by the darkness. By the time Borchert could organize an assault, the sky had begun to pale again. The fires in the hamlet had burned themselves out, and the buildings looked empty and still. Perhaps the Americans had withdrawn during the night?

Borchert got elements of two fresh battalions moving through the gray-flannel light. The forward companies reached a point hardly fifty meters from the houses, and Borchert thought, *Yes, by God, the Americans are gone.*

A machine gun opened up.

Gray overcoats tumbled backward, or twisted and danced and dropped. In seconds, the entire attack had burrowed into the snow. Borchert personally directed machine gun fire toward the sources of the American bursts, but the Americans only shifted and opened up again as soon as the Germans tried to move, whether forward or backward.

Borchert called for more artillery. Additional batteries joined the barrage, and some of the shells fell short, among the German troops. Men tried to run, only to be blown into the air, sailing through the trees like kites swept away by a storm.

When the artillery fire lifted, Borchert sent forward the fresh regiment's last battalion, which was missing a company that had gotten lost during the night march. Some of the new men had watched the earlier attack. They told their recently arrived comrades what had happened, and their attack was tentative, at best. This time, the American machine gun opened up at a greater range, surprising the attackers again.

Even with the casualties they had suffered, Borchert knew he had well over a thousand able-bodied men in the ravines and draws surrounding the hamlet. And how many men did the Americans have? How many had they had to begin with? A company?

Borchert heard rumbling. Familiar, heavy, earth-shaking rumbling.

Fifteen minutes later, in the milky light, a huge whitewashed tank came up the road. With another just behind it. And another.

As soon as it had a direct shot at the hamlet, the lead tank paused in the middle of the road. The following tanks in the forward platoon deployed where the woods were thinnest.

An officer in a black uniform jumped from one of the tanks and eventually found his way over to Borchert.

The tanker was a colonel. He started out cursing and never really stopped. Borchert had to use every bit of his self-control not to strike the man. No German officer, no veteran, no von Borchert deserved such insults. It was a gross violation of the officer's code of honor.

All right, Borchert thought. *You do it, you sonofabitch. Open the road for yourself.*

"Do you think you can at least get these shit-boys of yours to follow my tanks?" the *Panzer* officer asked.

The black-clad colonel went back to his tank. Moments later, the armored vehicles fired a salvo and began to grind forward. One tank slid sidewards into a ditch, and its track broke, writhing like a snake and slashing through the snow into the earth. But the others closed toward the village.

The Americans did not fire back now. Perhaps they saw the futility of it at last. Perhaps they had slipped off the moment they saw the tanks.

The tanks blasted walls away. Beams spared by the artillery cracked as masonry collapsed. Dust and smoke rose from the hamlet.

Borchert did not need to drive the infantrymen now. A substantial number of them rose up on their own and followed the tanks. Then the lead tank penetrated the cluster of buildings.

Fire burst on the side of the tank, and the American machine gun opened up again, from an oblique position, cutting through the advancing infantrymen. But, this time, one of the tanks, then another, used their main guns to blast in the building where the American weapons crew had positioned itself.

But the lead tank was burning. Then it shook with an internal explosion. None of the crew emerged.

The division commander appeared by Borchert's side. Borchert winced even before the cursing could begin.

But the commander was a changed man. In place of the fury of the night before, there was only weariness, almost resignation.

"I've come to tell you," he said, "that I've been relieved." The elder man smiled wryly. "The division is yours now, *Herr Oberstleutnant*. Perhaps you'll be more successful."

Borchert looked up through the snow, blackened in oblong

patches by the hot waste of muzzles or by bodies, wounded and dead. The tanks were grinding on, blasting into the buildings at point-blank range. But the infantry had frozen again.

A white rag on a stick began to wave from a smoking window.

The smile on the face of Borchert's former commander grew even tarter. "Ah," he said. "You're in luck. A lucky officer is a treasure. To be prized." Then he walked off.

Borchert hurried toward the hamlet. By the time he could make his way through the snow and the litter of casualties, enough of his men had recovered their self-possession to take the American surrender.

The *Panzer* colonel was directing, personally, the removal of the burned tank that blocked the road to the west. He wrinkled his mouth at Borchert, looked at his watch, and said, "We're almost thirty hours behind schedule. Thanks to you. *Herr Oberstleutnant.*" Then the path was clear, and the colonel remounted his tank. Standing in his hatch, he pulled on a headset and began to speak into it. The tank moved, followed by others, and the stench of exhaust thickened the cold air.

Borchert's men had gathered the Americans in a courtyard. Only five of the prisoners could stand upright. A dozen more were too badly wounded to keep their feet. Their breath steamed.

At first, Borchert was taken aback. He had expected to see the remnants of a company, at least, with American bodies littered about.

The senior American was a sergeant, with his arm in an improvised sling.

For once, Borchert found himself at a loss for words.

The American watched him approach. Unshaven and cold-eyed, the sergeant's skin looked swarthy underneath the grime of battle.

An Italian, perhaps. Maybe even a Jew.

Still bewildered by the fewness of the Americans, Borchert summoned his English and said, "You . . . were wise to surrender. Your efforts were futile, you know. You—"

"Stick it up your ass, Adolf," the sergeant told him. "We just ran out of fucking ammo."

Borchert had never seen such hatred in a man's eyes. The red patch on the sergeant's sleeve looked like a bucket of blood.

Remembering his position, Borchert pivoted, doing a perfect about-face. Returning to his own language, he approached a lieutenant standing nearby, the only other German officer present.

"Shoot them," Borchert said.

A look of astonishment passed over the lieutenant's face.

"I told you to shoot them, damn you."

The lieutenant began to stammer. "*Herr Oberstleutnant* . . . they've surrendered . . . they . . ."

Borchert tore a submachine gun from the grip of the nearest soldier. He turned it on the Americans who were still standing, cutting them down before a single one of them could react. He emptied the magazine into their bodies.

Tossing the weapon back to the soldier, Borchert told the lieutenant. "Make sure they're dead. All of them. Or I'll have you hanged."

Dreaming of his wife and the future, Borchert crossed the Ahr. In the lowering hills to the north, he had a stroke of luck. After a night spent shivering in the loft of a barn, he saw an old woman with an empty sack leaving the farmhouse across the courtyard. She looked around to make certain she was unobserved, then slipped into the woods.

Borchert knew what that meant. He had learned it first in White Russia, then in the miserable expanses that led toward the Volga. The peasants always hid what food they had, careful to appear half-starved to all combatant parties.

He waited until the woman reappeared with the sack filled and slung over her shoulder. Once she was back inside her house with the bolt shot, he slipped off and circled toward the spot where he had seen her enter the trees. The old woman had grown a bit careless, perhaps because of the peace, and Borchert found a well-worn path. A Russian peasant would have gone a different route to his or her cache each time to avoid leaving a trail.

Nor had she covered up her digging very well. Where she had

closed the hole, churned, wet, matted leaves showed darker than the surrounding copper froth. After a brief look over his shoulder, Borchert began to dig with his bare hands.

Potatoes. He filled his pockets with them, but he wanted more. Despite the chill, he stripped off his undershirt, doing his best to avoid the sight of his scratched-open flesh, and made a sack of the yellowed rag. Hastily, he filled in the dirt and kicked fresh leaves over the spot.

He forced himself onward for half an hour before permitting himself a cooking fire. He did his best to note the location of the farm from which he had borrowed. Still, it would not have done to be discovered. In time, he would make amends. For now, he did not choose to explain himself to anyone.

And to whom did he owe an explanation? For anything? After all he had done for these people? While they sat safely at home, gorging themselves? They were cowards. All of them. Like those sluggish old men in the snow in the Ardennes, who would not get up and do their duty. When, Borchert asked himself, had he ever done anything but his duty?

He didn't need to explain himself to some old farmer's hag. No more than he had to explain himself to the men in the camp after the Americans took von Tellheim away.

Borchert tried to eat one of the potatoes before it was cooked through, but his teeth were too loose in his gums. So he sat, aching, and let the potatoes roast. Finally, he broke the hot skins apart and made a mush in his palm, devouring the white paste until he was sated.

As he pushed on north, Borchert had to travel along paved roads. The British drove past but never stopped to question him. Finally, he gave up on his efforts to move by stealth and went down to the good road along the Rhine. In the gray river, the cabins of sunken barges broke the current and, here and there, a bow or stern protruded from the water. All of the old bridges were in ruins, replaced, for now, by military pontoons.

When he reached Bonn, it was a shock to find the little city almost intact. A dreary university town, it must not have seemed important enough to bomb. So something was left. Of the old Germany. Something remained. Something, however slight, on which to build.

In the market square, the Red Cross had set up a soup kitchen. Borchert joined a line hundreds long.

His feet had gone numb again. But it wasn't far now. Only a fair day's walk to the other side of Cologne, where Margarethe would be waiting. Where she had to be waiting. With her red-blond hair, that von Sassen hair, and her white teeth. And a sense of self-worth and honor that matched his own.

Then, drinking from the can of soup handed to him, an awful thought pierced him. He had not thought about any practical details. What if Margarethe had nothing to eat herself? How would he provide for both of them? In Cologne, where he knew no one? Where the Rhinelanders were little better than Jews themselves? He had not thought beyond their reunion, unless it was to dream of a distant future into which they had made a successful leap. What if a hungry man returned to his wife and found her hungry, too? How would he bear that? How would he bear his inability to provide for her?

He left Bonn a frightened man.

Just short of Cologne, a jeep with two Americans passed him by. He had grown accustomed to seeing only British soldiers, and the sight of the Americans launched him into a fit of panic. He almost threw himself into the ditch by the roadside. Afraid they had changed their minds about his parole, afraid these Americans had come to take him back to the camp.

The notion was absurd, of course. The Americans drove on, oblivious of his existence. A liaison officer and his driver, most likely. Enjoying the chance to lord it over a conquered people.

Borchert never regretted killing the Americans who had surrendered in the Ardennes. They had earned their fate, and the sergeant's insolence had sealed it. Prisoners had to surrender more than their weapons. Still, the incident had not turned out well. The lieutenant who had been so reluctant to follow orders turned out

to have been a mere eighteen years of age—and the son of an in-
dustrialist, the sort of imitation Jew who always survived and always had influence. Within a month, Borchert had found himself
relieved of his command, rather than promoted, and condemned
to the task of defending a town along the Rhine that had no bridge
and no strategic value. Unless you counted the vineyards. It was a
mockery, an insult. And that was where he had surrendered to the
Americans. Surrendering the pathetic old men and children he
commanded—less than a hundred of them, all drafted into the
Volksturm from the local area—and ignoring the last orders he had
been given: *Fight to the last man. Heil Hitler!*

The men had made it clear that they would not fight and that
they did not want their homes destroyed. The local Party officials
disappeared in the night. Borchert dressed in his best uniform, with
all his decorations, and went out into the raw, late-March weather
to meet the American armored column approaching along the Nier-
stein road. But the Americans were not interested in a formal surrender. A sergeant took his Luger for a souvenir. Dismissively, the
man told Borchert just to wait by the roadside with his men until
the military police came along. So he sat in the cold for the better
part of a day, at the edge of a muddy vineyard, watching an endless
parade of war machinery go past. His own "soldiers" slipped away
and went home. Then the military police came by at last, in well-
pressed uniforms. And that was the end of his war.

But the camp had been worse than the war. A humiliation.
Nonetheless, he had never compromised his honor. Not in the ways
that mattered. When the difficulties arose with von Tellheim, it had
been his duty to do what had to be done. Other officers, men of
higher rank, should have acted. But all of them had turned into
sheep. Or into collaborators. And cowards.

Von Tellheim had broken every code of honor imaginable. Organizing a ring of thieves the way he did. The American medical
services had been overwhelmed by the squalor of the camp and the
ill health of the inmates, so they had begun to use medically qualified prisoners as trusties, first in the tents that served as the camp's
clinic, then, as the skills of the prisoners became evident, even in

the medical system that served the Americans. That was where von Tellheim had seen his opportunity.

The Americans had marvelous new drugs, capable of curing serious illnesses virtually overnight. But these were in short supply—or so the Americans said—and they rarely were expended on German patients. Von Tellheim, who had no medical attachments of any kind, nonetheless managed to convince the prisoners who served the Americans as orderlies and medical assistants that it was their duty to smuggle out the wonderful new American drugs in order to save their fellow prisoners. Von Tellheim set himself up as the arbiter of fates, and it soon became evident that he always had been a traitor to his class, perhaps even a traitor to his country. He ignored matters of rank, insisting that the war was over and they all were equal now—as if he had become a Bolshevik or, perhaps, had always been one in secret—and he gave no more priority to a sick colonel than to a sick private. He even encouraged the lowest-ranking men to address him by his first name, telling them that all the army's nonsense was finished. It was unthinkable.

But the issue of theft was worse, by far, than von Tellheim's social boorishness. German officers did not steal, not even from their enemies. Officers did not consort to bribery and corruption, cloaking themselves in claims of nobility and service. Officers had to set an example as model prisoners. How else would they retain their authority in the peace that lay before them?

Inevitably, the Americans discovered that they were being robbed. Major quantities of drugs could not be accounted for. So they began their interrogations.

Borchert had already decided to tell the truth even before the Americans called him in. He didn't know all of the details, of course, since he had resisted taking any part in the affair, but he knew von Tellheim was at the center of it. A Communist, obviously. A fifth columnist. An infiltrator. How else had the man survived the siege of Berlin and made his way to the West? The sleight of hand with the medicines was obviously no more than a way to win over the lower ranks, to seduce them with Leftist ideas.

He even recalled von Tellheim saying, "If Germany's ever going to pull itself up from the shit again, it won't be thanks to the generals and colonels."

Who but a Communist would talk like that?

And the Americans had become quite interested in Communism since the war's end. They took von Tellheim away immediately. Rumor had it that, after a brief interrogation, the Americans had driven him over the hill to Kirchheimbolanden, where they shot him and buried his corpse in the forest. Rumor also had it that Borchert had been the one who had talked to the Americans.

As a reward for his assistance, the Americans released him with a parole. Borchert took it, since he saw nothing dishonorable in his actions. Or course, those with no sense of honor of their own might not understand why he had informed on von Tellheim, so taking advantage of the release was only sensible. If Germany were to be rebuilt, it would be men like him, not traitors like von Tellheim, who would do it. He, and men like him, *had* to survive. And several of his fellow prisoners had already hinted at threats.

All that was behind him now.

Whatever had or had not happened to von Tellheim did not weigh on Borchert's conscience. Von Tellheim had made his own fate. Borchert had merely upheld the honor of the German officers' corps.

Cologne was a wasteland. The center of the city had been flattened. The devastation was grimmer than anything Borchert had seen, far worse than Berlin the autumn before or even the condition of Frankfurt when last he had passed through. For entire city blocks, not a single wall had been left standing, and the ruins stank of decay and collapsed sewers. Almost half a year after the war's end, not all of the streets had been cleared of rubble. The cathedral's walls remained standing, massive and scorched, but the roof had collapsed and the great windows had been blown to nothing. A treasure of German civilization had been destroyed. Doubtless, the Allies excused the bombing of the cathedral because it stood next to the main train station. But Borchert suspected the destruction had been done on purpose. To punish Germany.

The human beings at work in the rubble looked as beaten down as Russian prisoners. Most worked in silence. Old men wandered about, as if the disappearance of lifelong landmarks had made them lose their way forever. The warren of the old city's streets had become a new labyrinth, one of open air, that confused its former inhabitants.

Once, when Borchert asked his way, a woman in a head scarf answered, "What does it matter where your Graulillienstrasse is? One street's as good as another now."

But Borchert found his way as the afternoon withered. By dark, he was almost there, suddenly cast among streets of pleasant villas, scarred by war only to the extent that their shade trees had been cut down for winter fuel. Children played outdoor games, and cooking smells drifted through the gardens. It seemed miraculous.

Yet, his pace slowed as one street passed into another and the darkness came down. What if she wasn't there? What if a single bomb had fallen here, and that bomb . . . ? What if she had gone off looking for him?

He still had three potatoes in his pocket. They were all his willpower had let him save.

At the last corner, he turned around and began to walk in circles on his ruined feet. Afraid. It seemed to him now that all he wanted in life, all he had ever wanted, was a decent, honorable life with Margarethe. His Gretchen of the red-blond hair.

Yes, his Gretchen. Goethe's good girl. Imbued with the sacrificial power of Woman. In the camp, he had thought, bitterly, of other lines from *Faust*: "He'll eat dust, and like it."

Staub soll er fressen, und mit Lust.

He had eaten dust. But he had not liked it.

Now he only wanted a chance to begin again. With Margarethe. A chance to build their world anew.

She had always understood him. The bloodlines told. Some things could not be taught, only inherited. It seemed to him now that he had never been fighting for some abstract, idealized Fatherland, or even for a real Fatherland of earth, blood, and borders. Margarethe was his Fatherland, his essence, his purpose.

She was all that mattered.

He found himself standing under a weak streetlamp, a few blocks from the villa where Margarethe had to be waiting for him. Unable to move another step.

A mother and daughter hurried across the street, bundled against the cold and coming home late. The little girl pointed at Borchert, and asked, "Mama! Who's that? Why is that man standing in front of our house?"

The mother looked over, first with a hint of panic in her eyes, then with a dismissive expression.

"That's the *Sensenmann*," she told her daughter in a harried voice. "He carries off bad little girls and never brings them back."

The little girl drew close to her mother, pushing away from Borchert, until the two of them disappeared behind a gate.

Struggling to gather his courage, he walked until midnight struck in a parish steeple. And, somehow, he found himself in front of the house at last.

It looked completely unscarred. A single, faint light glowed deep in the interior. As if he were expected.

He ordered himself to go forward.

The bell didn't work—at least he heard nothing when he tried it—so he knocked. But no one answered.

He tested the door.

It was open.

Borchert let himself into the house, gathering his bearings for a moment before he began to step, quietly, toward the light. He had not been inside the house since a last visit to Margarethe's sister and her husband before the war, a visit he had made only to please his wife. But he remembered the feel of the place now, how the rooms were arranged. The light came from the kitchen, toward the rear of the house. Just beyond that, there was a small maid's apartment, as he recalled. And here, along the hallway, the dining room was to the right, just there, and the library to the left, past the formal sitting room The hall was gloomy, but, toward the end of the passage, there was enough light for him to mark the normalcy of its condition: Paintings still hung on the walls. The furniture remained in place.

It made him want to weep. For the beautiful commonness of it all. But officers did not cry.

The first thing he saw in the kitchen, just beyond the lamp, was a quarter loaf of bread, lying on a breadboard with a knife. A covered butter dish stood beside it.

Then Borchert heard the sounds. He jumped at the first noise, an abjectly human murmur. Coming from the maid's room. Next, he heard the bed.

The maid was up to something. Entertaining visitors. In Margarethe's absence.

He marched into the maid's room.

A lamp burned in that room, too. On the nightstand. A British officer's uniform had been arranged, neatly, over a chair.

Then he saw Margarethe. With her unmistakable red-blond hair. And her pale skin.

The Englishman turned about with a look of annoyance. "Do you mind, old boy? I mean, really. You might wait your turn."

Margarethe said nothing.

Somehow, Borchert pulled the door shut again and made his way as far as the kitchen table. He dropped down in a chair. And sat. Unable even to lift a hand to scratch his ravaged skin. Refusing to hear. Refusing to think.

Refusing.

After perhaps an hour, he heard other sorts of noises. Despite himself. Low, intimate voices, and the rustle of clothing.

The Englishman came out, correcting the line of his mustache.

"Sorry if I was cross, old boy. You understand, of course." The officer tugged his jacket straight under his leather belt. "Anyway, you'll find old Margie's worth the wait."

The officer left, and Borchert closed his eyes. Shocked by the wet, salt taste on his lips, he realized he was crying.

After an eternity or two, he heard lighter footsteps. He opened his eyes and, through a wet blur, saw Margarethe, hair awry, wrapped in a velvet robe.

"Our honor . . . *my* honor . . ." Borchert whispered.

His wife looked at him for a moment, then lit a cigarette. "You can't eat honor," she said.

Borchert didn't close his eyes again. He stared at the floor. He had not known that a man could feel so empty, or so alone. Even in Russia, he had never felt so alone. Not even in the camp. What was left for him? What was left of his world?

His wife put her hand on his shoulder, and the gray morning light came in.